The Empire of Bones

A Novel

Hilary Rhodes

Also by this author

THE LION AND THE ROSE
Book 1: William Rising
Book 2: The Gathering Storm

THE AETHELING'S BRIDE
Book 1: The Outlander King
Book 2: The Conqueror's Bane

THE TRINITY CROWN
CRUCESIGNATI
THE WIVES
WORMWOOD

THE EMPIRE OF BONES

The Empire of Bones: a novel. Copyright © 2024 by Hilary M. Rhodes.
All rights reserved. No part of this publication may be reproduced, transmitted, stored, or retrieved without permission of the author.

Display text is set in Cloudy Aurora Serif, LHFEncore Distressed,
Cinzel SemiBold, and Perpetua Titling MT.
Body text is set in Bembo.
Book and cover design by Hilary M. Rhodes.

BISAC Categories: FIC 009000 | Fiction – Fantasy – General
FIC 009100 | Fiction – Fantasy – Action and Adventure
FIC 009200 | Fiction – Fantasy – Epic

For Sam, of course

Dramatis Personae

The Three Faiths

Vashemites, worshipers of one god (the Lord, Odunai)

Tridevarians, worshipers of three gods (the Lord, the Lady, and the Prince, called Vata Korol, Mata Koroleva, and the Korolynich in the Ruthynian Tserkovian tradition; also known as the Divine Family);

Wahini, worshipers of one god (the Lord-Queen, Ur-Malika).

The Meronite Empire and the Eternal City of Merone

Coriolane Aureus IX, His Imperial Majesty the Divine Emperor of Merone;

Gheslyn Aurea, first wife of Coriolane, senior Empress of Merone;

Vestalia Aurea, second wife of Coriolane, junior Empress of Merone.

The Immortals, the imperial military's most feared and elite warriors;

Ionius Servus Eternus, a senior Immortal general;

Spartekaius Servus Eternus, an Immortal general of many centuries ago, infamous as the only member of the order to ever rebel against his emperor, consequently destroyed;

Marcus Servus, an Immortal cadet in training.

The Corporalists, the imperial order of necromancers;

Grand Magister Saturnus, grandmaster of the Corporalists.

THE THAUMATURGES, the imperial order of sorcerers;
GRAND MAGISTER KRONUS, grandmaster of the Thaumaturges.

THE HOLY ORDERS MILITANT, the military order of the True Tridevarian Church;
MELLIUS SANCTUS SIXTUS, His Holiness the Archpriest of Merone.

BELSEPHORUS, a court eunuch in the Eternal Palace;
ROMOLA, a slave girl in the Eternal Palace.

The Venerated Republic of Qart-Hadesht

ZADIA BET AMARASHA UR-NAMASQA, matriarch of the ur-Namasqa family, holder of their seat in the High House of the Adirim;
KHALDUN BEN YUSIR ITABU ONWA'KYEME UR-NAMASQ, Zadia's husband;
NOORA BET FATIMA UR-ABAJAHDA UR-NAMASQA, Zadia's wife;
ALIYAH BET ZADIA UR-NAMASQA, Zadia and Khaldun's daughter and heiress;
ALJAFAR BEN ZADIA UR-NAMASQ, Zadia and Khaldun's son;
JAYAHI UR-VORROSQ, soldier in service to the ur-Namasqas.

SAFIYA BET REBIYAT UR-TASVASHTA, matriarch of the ur-Tasvashta family, holder of their seat in the High House of the Adirim;
GHASSAN, JAHIFAR, MARISHAH, Safiya's husbands and wife;
ELEMAI BET SAFIYA UR-TASVASHTA, Safiya's eldest daughter and heiress;
MANIZAR, TAFELIN, LEILA, Safiya's son and younger daughters.

MASSASOUM BEN IMRA UR-BEIRESHT, chairman of the High House of the Adirim;
MIRAZHEL BET IMRA UR-BEIRESHTA, his sister.

The Adirim, also known as the Council of the Mighty; ancestral governing body of the Qartic Republic, consisting of two chambers and 300 representatives, now subordinate to Meronite rule;

The High House, the upper chamber of the Adirim; seats held by 150 noble families;

The Low House, the lower chamber of the Adirim; seats held by 150 elected citizens;

Daeda, ancient Qartic queen of legend, said to be a mistress of magic;

Gaius Tullius Grassus, Meronite Governor-General of Qart-Hadesht;

Vadoush, a servant.

The Holy City of Yerussala

Tselmun ben Dayoud, Vashemite magician-king of legend, ruler of ancient Yerussala;

Khasmedeus, a jinnyeh bound in service to Tselmun;

Arghan the Undying, a legendary ifrit.

The Imperial Province of Ruthynia and the City of Korolgrod

Julian Janovynich Kozharyev (Yulian ben Yanov), a young Vashemite;

Gavriel ben Avraham Coheyn, student at the University of Korolgrod and friend of Julian;

Gerasim Balovoynich Zogorov, Meronite Governor-General of Ruthynia;

The Konsilium, ruling council of Ruthynia;

Kozheks, talented horsemen and feared warriors, often dominated by the Ruthynians;

Tserkovians, Ruthynian denomination of Tridevarianism, formally broke away from Merone some time ago; often called Dvadevarians (and heretics) by Meronites.

Other Parts and Persons of the World

BRYTHANICA, IBELUS, FRANKETERRUM, TEUTYNA, northern Meronite provinces;
THE BODENI, indigenous people of Brythanica, resisters of Meronite occupation.

IFRIQIYIN, southern continent, home of the Republic of Qart-Hadesht, the Ambraz Empire, the Sun Kingdom of Gezeren, the Chieftaincy of Numeria, the Principality of Kush, and others;.

AMBRAZ EMPIRE, one of the greatest Ifriqiyini kingdoms, cultured and wealthy, known for its Great Library, Three Mahqasas, and community of scholars;
AMBRAZAKTI, capital city of the Ambraz Empire;
MUSUM BEN MANSA, king of the Ambraz Empire.

GEZEREN, once the legendary Sun Kingdom, now a tightly controlled Meronite province;
QAHIRAH, capital city of Gezeren.

MAD AR-HAHRAT, the sea that bounds Ifriqiyin, the Lanuvian peninsula, and the holy land of Yerussala; known by Meronites as the Madherian Sea;
NUMERIA, jungle kingdom to the south of the Sand Sea, rumored to be the place where King Tselmun's court fled into exile after the First Conquest of Yerussala;
THE SAND SEA, great desert in northern Ifriqiyin.

RABIYAH, spiritual birthplace of Wahinism, centered on the city of Makeyah;
THE HIEROPHANT, founder and prophet of Wahinism.

The Spice Road, the principal overland trading route between Merone and Qin;

Sardarkhand, ancient city on the Spice Road, west of Qin.

The Sultanate of Parsivat, known for the great cities of Firzepoli and Bhagarayat, home of the famous House of Wisdom.

Ahyuns, nomadic horsemen of the Qiné steppes;

The Thearchate of Qin, vast eastern kingdom and chief rival of the Meronite Empire;

Hang'i, the Jade City, capital of Qin;

Hang Zhai, Their Celestial Majesty, the current Thearch.

The Thousand Kingdoms of Indush, other large and wealthy eastern lands lying along the Spice Road; now numbering in actuality about four.

Prologue

It was no longer in question, Aliyah reflected as she huddled miserably at the bottom of the pit and waited to die, that in the end, things had gone terribly wrong. Not that she intended them to, not that anyone ever did, but that made no difference. And of the many, *many* ways in which she was fated to snuff it since this entire venture first began, death-by-pit was not the worst option. There was hanging, or burning, or drawing and quartering, or just the emperor's tried-and-true favorites: throwing you into the Colosseum or handing you over to the Corporalists, who would swiftly make you regret that you were not, in fact, dead (but when you were, the real trouble started). Of course, that was very likely to be the case for this too, which was by no means designed for merciful expediency. The pit was six fathoms straight down, walls smooth except for the bloody scratches of desperate fingernails (were her own soon to join them? It seemed unpleasantly likely), and there was no way out. The muddy ground was scarred with rancid rainwater, rotted food, and far less speakable things, and she was fairly certain that the eerie white shapes piled to every side were the remains of her unfortunate predecessors. As a matter of curiosity, she wondered what *those* poor bastards had done to get tossed in here. Led a failed rebellion, or fallen behind on their taxes, or just looked at the emperor the wrong way? Any or all were equally possible.

Aliyah shifted her weight, pulling her filthy rags closer and debating whether to bother saving her strength, or just suck it up, say her prayers, and get it over with. The duration of her sojourn down here otherwise depended on how much His Imperial Majesty wanted her to suffer (a lot, but there were plenty of gradations on that scale), and whether this was a prelude to a violent death in the Colosseum. She wasn't sure, but she doubted it. After all, she had caused enough spectacle, and the last thing Coriolane wanted was for her to go out in a blaze of glory, a blameless martyr, or even to get inconveniently spared at the pivotal instant by a thumbs-up from the crowd. Not that he would actually *honor* it, or at least not for long. But the play of it, the perception, still made a difference. Even after four hundred years of a despotically and unrepentantly murderous career, the thing that worried the antiquarian bastard the most was his public relations. Naturally.

This is your own fault, you know. Aliyah scrubbed her dirty eyes, stared at the empty place on her finger where the Ring had been, and was forced to admit that there was unlikely to be any ruler, even one less tyrannical than the Divine Emperor, who would let her live. While there were others who piled the kindling and lit the flame, this was the result of her own choices. She didn't deny that, and so she couldn't claim that she was being unfairly executed, much as she might personally object. She wasn't happy about dying, and she was deeply upset at what she was leaving behind, but she was at peace with it, as much as she could be. And even if not, what was the point? She wasn't getting out of here. The time for miracles, if it had existed at all, was over.

She tilted her head back and looked at the sky, what little of it she could make out. The moon was waning and the stars were barely visible beneath the scrim of clouds, thin as yet but promising to thicken. Come to think of it, some rain might be nice. It was high summer in Merone, and even at midnight, the air was hot and wet as overboiled soup, wringing sodden-sticky sweat even from her Qartic blood. Dawn would bring fierce sunlight and gawking onlookers to throw rocks and eggs, piss and shit, shouts and swears and slanders, and at that, Aliyah finally understood the simple and brutal brilliance of Coriolane's strategy. The public wasn't going to save her with some heart-touching eleventh-hour intervention. Oh no. Instead, they were going to be complicit in her destruction, feel like it was their idea and they were nobly carrying out condign vengeance on the rebel witch of Qart-Hadesht – the oldest of enemies, the one thing around which the Meronite society could always righteously unite. Even those who might nurse a traitorous whisper of sympathy for her cause would be swept up in the mob, whatever dark magic came over a crowd when they had a convenient scapegoat at hand and the means of doing violence. They would see that she was nothing but a scrawny, filthy, barely-grown girl, and the spell would break. To Coriolane's advantage, of course, and without his influence seeming to appear on it at all. Clearly you did not rule for four centuries, even with all the military might and thaumaturgic trickery that could be mustered, without learning how to be a master manipulator in the bargain.

Put like that, Aliyah thought, her impending demise didn't sound half so easy. Trapped here for days or at an unlucky stretch, weeks — dying agonizingly of thirst and tossed rocks, heat and hunger, an exotic menagerie for crowds of jeering Meronites. Her jailers had not fettered her, which was even worse. It created the illusion of desperate hope, that she could still try to get out, and if she continued to sit here and passively await the end, she only had herself to blame. And when she died, she might be repurposed in a far more ghoulish and sinister way. If so —

"Khasmedeus?" Aliyah's voice was thin, chafed with dryness and cracked with fear. It was useless. She didn't have the Ring, and there was no way for the jinnyeh to hear — even if it had any inclination to help, which was unlikely. It was crude, lewd, sly, gossipy, untrustworthy, arrogant, and deceitful, and those were only its finer qualities. But if nothing else, she had surprised it, and she thought — stupidly — that it meant something. But everyone who ever said that she was in over her head was right. She was just a witless child playing with awesome and ancient powers far beyond her understanding, and it was ending in the only way it could. The thought of Khasmedeus in Coriolane's control was one to chill the soul even in this infernal hellhole, but perhaps it would not be as simple as the emperor putting on the Ring and bidding its servant to come. After all, it had destroyed all but two people who ever tried to wield it. Tselmun ben Dayoud, almighty sorcerer-king of history and legend, and her. Aliyah bet Zadia ur-Namasqa, the fool.

It very much has *destroyed you,* Aliyah reminded herself. *And for that matter, did so to Tselmun too, just slower.* Khasmedeus delighted in relating the myriad ways it had tricked Tselmun, wiggled out of his commands, caused the great king to look silly in front of his seven hundred wives and five thousand concubines (who in damnation *needed* seven hundred wives and five thousand concubines?) and of course, the crowning moment of its career, when it physically hurled Tselmun away like a shot-putter and ruled in his place for forty days and forty nights, impersonating him most successfully until Tselmun returned and took revenge on the traitorous jinnyeh (Khasmedeus tended to leave that part out). Such magic always burned up its wielder like a candle to the wick. *Everyone except for Coriolane Aureus the Ninth. It's not* fair.

Aliyah let out a barking laugh, then caught herself, pressing her knuckles to her mouth as it fractured into a sob. Of course it wasn't fair, nothing about this whole situation was fair, and it was a bit bloody late to start thinking of it in such terms. Besides, it was far and away her fault too. She had failed Elemai and their people, betrayed Julian and his, and that was just the start. But something prodded her out of her stupor, made her groan and grunt and stagger to her feet. She was at the bottom of a hole in all imaginable ways, she had no real prospect of surviving, and yet a spark seared her, the sheer stubbornness that had gotten her this far in the first place. It wasn't smart, but she made no claims to that. Aljafar was the scholar, and she always teased her brother about it. She was never going to see him or the rest of their family again. Some of them for sure, but she could not think about that just now.

Once she was upright, Aliyah needed to steady herself, head reeling and starvation gnawing at her belly; the Castel Sanctangel was not known for bountifully feeding its prisoners, much less its traitors. Her dark brown skin was grey with ash and dust, and her shorn head was bare, flecked with rough stubble. The dirty shift was her only clothing, she had no Ring or jinnyeh or anything else, and if she *was* somehow to get out of the pit, her troubles were only beginning. There was no purpose, there was no one left, there was nothing that she alone could do, and nothing but an even slower and more gruesome death to repay her for trying. That was beyond dispute.

And *yet*.

The clouds were closing over the moon in earnest, and a faint chill of rain laced the muggy air. Aliyah lifted her face and opened her parched mouth, waiting eagerly for a drop. It was coming. The storm, the deluge. It was now. It was here. It was her. And for all that it felt like nothing, the very end of the earth, that wasn't quite true. There *was* one thing left, one final desperate gambit, and even worse, her mortal enemy was the one to give it to her. But still: beggars, choosers. She was a beggar, yes. But she was going to choose, and in that moment, she did.

"I am not going to die like this," Aliyah said aloud, and started to climb.

PART ONE

BLOODMOON

CHAPTER 1

ALIYAH

Of course, she hadn't always been at the bottom of a pit.

Once upon a time, unbelievable as it seemed, Aliyah's life was entirely unremarkable. She had no traumatizing childhood or crushing deprivation, no poverty or violence, no murdered family members or martial training – really, nothing that prepared her for the role of an upstart idealist politico-magical vigilante. Indeed, of all the people the Ring could have picked for the job, it seemed deeply puzzling to settle on her. Then again, it was rarely the case that some virtuous crusader rose out of nowhere to depose the evil rulers so nothing bad ever happened again, the end. Even if you did briefly succeed at removing the injustice, the system would spring back and smack you in the face. It was simply too inherent to human nature, once you got your hands on the levers of power and realized they were pretty fun to pull. Nobody was good enough to resist that temptation, even if the griots prudently ended the story before the heroes turned into the mad kings for the next generation of protagonists to duly defeat. They just weren't.

As such, the old fairytales never satisfied Aliyah, even as a little girl. She always ruined Abba's bedtime stories by complaining about their unrealistic nature, until Aljafar whined and hit her and Abba had to pull them apart. Yet if there was any logic to the decision at all, that cynical pragmatism could be why the Ring had offered itself to her. Khasmedeus was bound to it, yes, and the jinnyeh had, to say the least, its own agenda. But as for *her,* unwitting heiress to the greatest magic ever known, which led her to the pit and the world's order to the brink of its end –

That story started not so long ago, but now it felt like a lifetime. It started like this.

★★★★

"Aliyah," her mother said, not for the first time. "Pay *attention.*"

"I *am* paying attention, Amma." This was only partly a lie, since Aliyah *was* trying to listen. In her defense, the study was very hot and the books were very boring, and despite her best efforts, it was difficult to feign interest in the mind-numbing vagaries of taxation and trade, the percentage of agricultural yield or which qahin wanted more funds for his madrasah or which trade guilds were having a dispute. Besides, it was pointless, an elaborate puppet show with no practical application. What did it matter what the old charters said, or how it was supposed to work before? Everyone knew the Divine Emperor controlled everything.

Under her mother's gaze, however, Aliyah straightened her spine and attempted to look studious. "I am listening," she said meekly. "See?"

Zadia bet Amarasha ur-Namasqa looked unconvinced. "What was I just talking about?"

"Er…" Aliyah racked her brains. "The aquifer systems?"

Zadia sighed, with the disappointed expression she often tended to wear when gazing upon her eldest child. "You're bright, habibta, at least if you apply yourself. But you're lazy, and getting lazier. I don't understand why you won't take this seriously."

"I'm sorry, Amma." Aliyah looked at her hands. "I just don't see why Aljafar couldn't do this. He's the one who actually *likes* it."

"You are the firstborn daughter." Zadia's expression turned even sterner. She was a tall and imposing woman, her ink-black hair twisted in jeweled coils and heavy golden earrings dangling to her shoulders, catching on the gauzy fabric of her veil. "It is your responsibility."

"Yes, Amma," Aliyah murmured, looking at the papyri, codices, scrolls, tablets, quills, styluses, inkpots, and other scholarly detritus that heaped the table. Ever since she turned eighteen, her mother had started to prepare her in earnest to inherit the Batu Namasqa's seat on the Council of the Mighty, as if Zadia might keel over the very next morning and cause a constitutional crisis, and endless lectures were hardly conducive to cozy maternal bonding. Especially when Zadia looked at her like this, communicating regret and discontent without even saying a word, and as she always did at these moments, Aliyah resolved to try harder. For what it was worth, she meant it. It just never tended to *last* very long, and all at once, she blurted out, "I don't understand."

Zadia cocked her head, looking even more like a hawk than usual. Deceptively mildly, she said, "Don't understand what, habibta?"

"Why I have to learn this." Aliyah swept a hand at the desk. "Our family is barely important enough to have a hereditary seat as it is, so I'm sure the Adirim would keep functioning without us. Besides, why do *any* of us do this? We're deep in denial, like we still can't accept that everything has been run from Merone for centuries and this is all just stage dressing. None of the decisions you make are binding or relevant. If the Divine Emperor says otherwise – "

At that, Zadia slammed shut her heavy book, making Aliyah jump out of her skin. "If that is how you feel about your heritage, your birthright, and your motherland, you may be excused from this lesson and instead think on what a disappointment you are to me and the sum total of our ancestors. Your father could use help in the kitchen. Go."

Aliyah opened her mouth. Nothing came out.

"*Go.*"

Because Zadia's voice could have cracked stone, and she knew she had gone too far, Aliyah nodded, shame-faced, and slid off her stool. She bowed to her mother and hurried out of the study and into the riwaq cloisters; they opened into the charbagh garden at the center of the house, green and lush with verdant shade. Aliyah eyed it covetously, thinking of crawling in and never coming out, but hiding would reflect even more poorly on her. So, back stiff, she kept walking.

As promised, she found her father in the kitchen, supervising the preparations for supper. The place was full of steam, shouts, and delicious smells, sunlight daggering through the lattices, and Aliyah's mouth watered. She was tempted to steal a honeycomb or a maamoul, but just then, her father turned and saw her. "What are you doing here, habibta? I thought you were in lessons until sardiq."

"Amma… decided to let me go early." He would get an earful to the contrary later, no doubt, but Aliyah didn't feel like rehashing it again. "What's cooking? It smells good."

Khaldun ben Yusir ur-Namasq raised a wry eyebrow. "You two fought again, didn't you?"

"We…" Aliyah felt her cheeks burn again, fraying her short-lived resolve to hold her tongue. "She doesn't *listen*, Abba. She never does. It's always the same lecture, and she doesn't think anything is important except keeping up appearances. It's like if she pretends hard enough, she can think the Adirim have actual power, and not just whatever this – "

Her father cast a glance around, then took her arm and towed her out into the garden, to a stone bench almost hidden among the greenery. Insects buzzed in the sunlit foliage, and the fountain cast rippling, liquid echoes, balming Aliyah's black mood somewhat but failing to leaven it entirely. She twisted her abaya in her hands, staring angrily into the thickets, as Khaldun seated himself next to her. "So, habibta. Do you plan to tell me what is vexing you?"

"I don't know." Aliyah kept glowering. "I just don't understand why she wants me to keep pretending like she does, all the time."

"Be gentle to your mother," Khaldun advised. "She is under the sort of pressure that it is difficult for you and Alja to imagine. What do you think the alternative is, to surrender entirely? Yes, it is difficult for you, my obstinate little realist, to understand why we carry out an action with no practical purpose. But that is not why we do it, and besides, that is not the only reason she is so insistent. There is, at last, going to be a pilgrimage to Yerussala, and she wants you to be part of it."

Aliyah started to say something else, then shut her mouth. At last she managed, "Yerussala has been reopened? Finally?"

"Yes. More than that, she intends for you to manage our interests on this trip. No matter what you think, this is not empty and meaningless theater, and it is not irrelevant to make sure we are prepared for anything. Especially the practice of how to rule ourselves. There are… whispers."

Aliyah looked sharply at her father. *"Whispers?"*

"Yes," Khaldun said again. "Of what sort, or what end, I do not know. But the Adirim believe that there is an opportunity at hand."

Yet again, Aliyah was unsure how to respond. It felt impossible that, for all their stubborn pretense of upholding their ancient customs and sovereign independence, the Venerated Republic of Qart-Hadesht could ever break free from the clutches of the Meronite Empire. And not just the Meronites, but the emperor himself, personally. Aliyah's grandmother's grandmother's grandmother was not yet born when Coriolane Aureus IX came to the throne, and for her father to suggest, however obliquely, that he could be *vulnerable* – it was as absurd as hinting that the sun might suddenly cut loose from the sky and crash into the sea. Even those who hated the Divine Emperor had to admit there was a certain reassuring predictability in four centuries of iron-fisted stability, enforced by the swords of the Immortals and the sorcery of the Corporalists and Thaumaturges. Pay your taxes and send your sons to serve in the legions, and there would be no trouble. Usually.

"Yerussala," Aliyah said instead. "What are we doing there?"

"It's complicated." Khaldun scratched his thick black beard, looking slightly awed. He was from Numeria, which lay below the Sand Sea in southern Ifriqiyin and guarded the source of the mighty Iteru River, and the prospect of a visit to the Holy City was one, Aliyah knew, that her father took seriously. King Tselmun's priests, magicians, courtiers, and concubines were said to have fled to Numeria when the First Yerussalan Kingdom was conquered by the ancient Meronites, and the place was fairly stewing in the legends of it. "But this is the first time the city has been opened in ten years, and so half the world is planning to travel there as soon as they can. There are rumors that they will even allow annual pilgrimages on the holy days again, though I suspect that will only be for Tridevarians. In any event, the Adirim could soon have a number of new opportunities. Your mother thinks it's time to prove yourself."

Aliyah took that in. She was obviously excited by the prospect, even as she bristled at the idea that her mother couldn't have just told her about it. As Khaldun said, the Holy City had been strictly off-limits to outsiders for almost a decade, and perhaps the emperor had decided to let off steam; it never paid to get the religious zealots *too* mad at you, especially in unison. Most of its Tridevarian artifacts, ceremonies, and temples had been taken to Merone anyway, but there was no replacing the hallowed ground itself. Besides, it was a two-month journey to Yerussala, at least if they were going overland, and that was a long, hot, dangerous, bumpy road. "I assume I wouldn't be traveling alone?"

"Oh, no. The Adirim are organizing a High House delegation. On which, as noted, you would serve as our family's representative."

Aliyah blinked. "Not Amma?"

"She has important business here at home, and you are the heiress of the Batu Namasqa. It's time you were trusted to handle these things."

"Does she, though?" Aliyah tried to keep the bitterness out of her voice, but it bled through nonetheless. "Trust me?"

"She does," Khaldun said firmly. "But this *is* your duty, habibta. However it displeases you, it remains to be done. It would be better for us all if you did so willingly."

"Yes, Abba." Her father's gentle but undeniable reprimand instantly abashed her more than any of her mother's brusque remarks. "I'm sorry. I'll do better. I'll pay attention to all of it, I swear."

"Good girl." He leaned over and kissed her hair. "Run along."

Sensing that she was excused, Aliyah bowed, rose, and departed, heading to the villa's small mahqasa. She liked to climb to the very top of its minaret and look out at Qart-Hadesht, set like a jewel between the Sand Sea to one side and the Mad ar-Hahrat to the other. The city had been built and rebuilt too many times to count, a cascading boneyard of history, and it was one of the oldest in Ifriqiyin. It reclined magisterially within the triple-thick mudbrick walls that guarded it on all sides, pierced by six gates that opened onto long thoroughfares converging on the great bazaar. The skyline rose in domes of glass and gold and bronze, spires of clay and stone, iwans of faience and qallalin, geometric girih tiles, mahqasas and muqarnas, palisades and palaces, souks and sahns – all surrounded by lavish paradise gardens nursed by water that was channeled all the way from the Atalantine Mountains, fed into aquifers, and distributed by an ingenious system of underground viaducts. Indeed in almost all respects, Qart-Hadesht looked the same as it had for thousands of years, and even the largest change, if you had not known it before, was difficult to spot. The great Temple had once been the home of the Adirim – the Council of the Mighty of three hundred seats, the High House of the nobles and the Low House of the commoners – and the heart of the city's proud republican rule. Now it flew the Meronite imperial eagle and housed the Governor-General, the provincial official who ruled this febrile part of the world in the Divine Emperor's name. In the seven years since the last one was appointed, Aliyah had never seen the man in the flesh. Perhaps he thought *nativeness* was catching.

She continued to sit there, bathed in the late-afternoon sun that baked the city like a kiln, until there was a shout from below. "Aliyah! Are you up there again? Come down, it's suppertime!"

"Yes, Amma Noora." With a sigh, Aliyah dislodged herself and clattered to the ground. Waiting at the bottom was her other mother, plump and pretty and looking as stern as it was possible for her to do. Before she could say anything else, Aliyah interrupted, "See. I'm here."

"You are going to get yourself into trouble, my child." Noora clucked her tongue and shook her head. "You know that old spire wasn't meant for climbing. Nor am I certain of what the Hierophant, blessings on his memory, would think of using a minaret as a gymnasium, but – "

Aliyah was fairly sure the question had never come up, but the Hierophant had opinions on a dizzying range of subjects, so she could be mistaken. Either way, best to keep her mouth shut and let Noora shoo her into the dining hall. It was mostly open to the air, with plush divans set around a long table and rings of candles suspended from the ceiling. Sometimes there was a musician or a griot or a reading from the Kitab to entertain the ur-Namasqas as they ate, but tonight, as she entered at the vanguard of Noora's determined whisking, Aliyah saw only her father and her little brother, Aljafar. She took her place on her own divan, waiting until Zadia swept in and everyone hurried to their feet. Zadia surveyed her children with a gimlet stare, then administered a swift, businesslike kiss to each spouse. "Well," she said, seating herself between Khaldun and Noora. "Aliyah, would you say our prayers?"

Aliyah inclined her head and asked Ur-Malika's blessings on their health, family, and meal, hoping it met with her mother's approval. The servants began to bring the food, and for several minutes, there was only the clatter of dishes, goblets, salvers, and spoons. Then Zadia said curtly, "So, Aliyah. Your father has told you about Yerussala."

"I... yes." Aliyah felt tongue-tied. "That I am supposed to go."

"I want to go to Yerussala too." Aljafar sounded aggrieved. "Or at least to Ambrazakti. Why does Aliyah get to go, but I don't?"

"Silence." Zadia cast her son a quelling look. "Your sister is the heiress, you know that. As for Ambrazakti, perhaps. If the rainy season is not bad, and there is a suitable escort."

Aljafar looked sullen. He was fifteen, three years younger than Aliyah, and had recently taken to complaining about how he was not allowed the same privileges as her. Qart-Hadesht was a curiosity among its Wahini peers for the strength of its matriarchal culture, and Aljafar was keenly aware that in other and less enlightened places, he might have been the favored child. He had also hoped for some time to travel to the Ambraz Empire, another of the southern Ifriqiyin principalities, which was fabulously wealthy in both gold and learning; King Musum had built one of the grandest libraries in the world. Indeed, it was possibly only the parched and burning expanse of the Sand Sea that kept Coriolane Aureus from marching in and attempting to seize the lot. Either that or he had learned the chief lesson of ambitious tyrants everywhere, which was that there was always a moment where you opened your maw to gulp down just one more morsel, and it all came unhinged and devoured you instead. In the four hundred years of his rule, the Meronite Empire's borders had remained almost unchanged, neither expanding nor dwindling, neither mounting new aggressions nor countenancing old rebellions. Mere mortals could call themselves kings and even emperors, if they so pretended. There would only ever be one Divine.

"So," Zadia said, ignoring Aljafar's muttered protestations. "You are aware, of course, of the great importance of this, and the necessity of representing our interests to the best of your ability. As your father has also informed you, I will not be accompanying you, so it is vital that I am able to trust you to act as I would. Can I do that, Aliyah?"

Their eyes were on her. There was, as always, only one choice.

"Yes, Amma," Aliyah promised. "You can."

CHAPTER 2

ALIYAH

The next several weeks were consumed with preparations. There were trunks to pack, camels to buy, documents to obtain, cash to secure, interpreters and men of business to hire, and meetings to hold with the others who were traveling to the much-awaited reopening of the Holy City. Theories abounded as to why it might be. Most people seemed to think it was a cheap and easy gesture of goodwill to shore up Coriolane's bona fides as the *Divine Emperor* and defuse the discontent that had recently bubbled up again. The Vashemites and Tserkovians were being particularly noisy in Ruthynia, a few bands of rebels had sprung up on both sides but would never work together due to hating each other even more, and offering this shiny trinket would, in theory, keep everyone too distracted and disunited to seriously plot a mutiny. Still, the fact that he was doing it at all was a surprise. Merone's usual response to dissent was to mercilessly crush it, not meekly hand out bribes and treats, and Khaldun was not alone in wondering if it portended a genuine crack in imperial power, a taste of honey rather than vinegar in order to mask a more serious weakness. Others felt that this was just the next manipulation, a strategic and temporary loosening of the leash just to make the crackdown even more impactful. After all, Coriolane had not ruled for four hundred years *solely* by brute force and terror. There had to be some politics to it too.

"You must be vigilant, habibta," Zadia informed Aliyah that evening. "And listen, and learn. Whatever the emperor's motive is, you must come to know it. Do you recall your lessons?"

"Yes, Amma." It was a fair question, perhaps, but Aliyah was still nettled. She already had to serve as family emissary, Adirim-in-waiting, political spy, social facilitator, business manager, camel wrangler, and general dogsbody, and now she *also* had to find out why a wily old despot had decided to open the gates again? There was no point in scrutinizing Coriolane's actions closely, or expecting them to obey anything except the ruthless and impersonal logic that animated all forces of nature. A sea raged, a storm howled, a fire devoured, a river flooded. If it destroyed any nearby humans, that was, in some sense, their own fault. They were the ones who had chosen to live there.

"I do hope you are ready for this." Zadia's expression did not, it had to be said, particularly radiate confidence. "Remember, you should confide in and seek counsel from Elemai ur-Tasvashta. She and her household will be responsible for assuring your safety and escort."

Aliyah muffled a groan. Ever since the two families met for negotiations and finalized an agreement to travel to Yerussala together, her mother had not stopped singing the praises of *Elemai,* heiress of the Batu Tasvashta and clearly the exact sort of daughter that Zadia always wanted. Elemai could converse fluently in six languages, play the cithara and zymbeline, give erudite lectures on politics, philosophy, and history, and had achieved hafiza status with the Kitab at the age of eleven. She was also beautiful, of just-enough-higher rank to make a match considerably ambitious but not entirely out of the question, and conspicuously unmarried, right when the family had put it about that they were looking for her first spouse. Aliyah would be a fool not to assume that this was the chief factor in her mother's eagerness to attach her to the ur-Tasvashta contingent, and her repeated advice to turn to Elemai for any problems that arose in the course of the adventure. It was nakedly transactional; first spouses were usually taken for political and dynastic reasons, whereupon any of the subsequent three could be more personal matches. Zadia herself had married Khaldun first and then Noora, and Aliyah, who had always been closest to her father, kept wondering if Zadia saw him the same as she saw their daughter: a useful tool, a job to do, a duty and necessity, undoubtedly important but not truly loved. Even worse, perhaps her mother thought Aliyah could not maintain the Batu Namasqa honor on her own, and had to settle for subsuming them into the Batu Tasvashta. At least that way, her *grand*children would not constantly and diversely disappoint her.

"Habibta?" her mother repeated. "Did you hear me?"

"Yes, Amma." Sometimes, Aliyah thought she had never said anything else. "Of course."

Zadia sniffed, but could not take exception. Then she glanced at the water clock, to ensure that the sun was officially below the horizon, and rose to her feet. "It is time for sardiq. Come."

The two of them left the solarium and hurried to the mahqasa, where they were among the last to arrive; the rest of the household was gathered, including the servants. Prayer was generally an egalitarian occasion, and Aliyah picked a spot near her father, kneeling on the rug. He shot her a sympathetic look, and she did her best to give him a reassuring smile. She had told him that she could do this, and she did not mean to be so suddenly made a liar.

The qahin raised his hands, the prayer began, and as she went through the familiar motions of the rakat, trying to summon the proper sense of devotion, Aliyah nonetheless found her attention wandering. They would leave before the full moon, if all was ready, when the summer heat had subsided enough to make the desert crossing possible. They would then spend the winter in Yerussala and return to Qart-Hadesht next spring, in time for the emperor's long-awaited state visit. It would be the first time Aliyah had been away from home so long, and even though she was excited, there was a prick of apprehension as well. There was just so much that could go wrong.

The final days of preparation slipped by in a frenzied haze. It had been first bruited that they should go by sea, which was by far the fastest route, but after reflection, the plan was discarded for reasons of safety. Every pirate in the world was swarming to the Mad ar-Hahrat to prey on the new field of pickings; they had personally witnessed a few of those ambushes directly off the coast, and it dulled the appetite for a sea voyage, regardless of the fact that it could put them in the Holy City in a few weeks instead of a few months. The Meronite navy was an additional obstacle, as it treated the Mad ar-Hahrat as the empire's personal lake and was eager to harass anyone who dared to enter its waters without a clear and extensive record of permit and taxation. As well, several qahins felt that an easy journey of luxury and convenience went against the grain of a humbly devout pilgrimage. So, an overland voyage it was. Slower but safer, or at least that was the hope.

And then at once, it was time. Servants darted past with an endless succession of things, and Aliyah stood with her family in the courtyard, sunrise just flushing the eastern horizon. The stars were still out, they had just come from a dardiq prayer imploring her success, and the wind was cool enough to make her glad of her shawl and headscarf. The camels snorted and spat at tether, restless and eager to be off, and the company of guild-soldiers that Zadia had hired to protect her — after all, it would not do to be *entirely* reliant on ur-Tasvashta charity — waited a few paces off, watchful and unsmiling, black turbans neatly tied and hands resting on the hilts of saifs. The ur-Namasqa villa was mantled in shadow except for the bright pinpricks of oil lamps, earthbound stars peering from filigreed windows, lining the riwaq and transforming it into a strange dark gateway between past and present and future, the final instant before the transformation. She thought it must mean something important, momentous. If only she had known.

"*Malikallulah qa-salaam*, my daughter." Zadia bent with her usual irreproachable dignity to kiss Aliyah's head. "The hope and honor of this family goes with you. Do well in Yerussala, and your destiny and ours will be secured. We will pray for you and await your safe return."

"Thank you, Mother." Aliyah was surprised to feel a pang in her chest: a child's instinctive hesitance to part from a parent, the final impulse to cling. "I won't let you down."

Zadia looked as if she was about to offer one last caution, reprimand, or word of advice, then sighed deeply and accepted that she had done all she could. She stepped aside, Noora took her place, and Aliyah hugged her, hungry for the affection that Noora offered so freely and Zadia rarely did. "I love you, Ammi Noo. I will make you proud."

"Silly goose." Noora's voice was tight. "You always have. I love you too. We all do. Never forget that."

Aliyah's throat was too thick to answer, so she let Noora kiss her a final time, before passing to the last of her parents. Khaldun ur-Namasq looked at his daughter for a long moment. Then he opened his mouth as if to speak, failed, and hugged her hard enough to crush the breath from her, a suspicious wetness on the scratch of his bearded cheek. *"Malikallulah,"* he whispered. "Be brave."

One considerably less emotional farewell with Aljafar later – as far as teenage siblings were concerned, this was an entirely welcome opportunity to get out of each other's hair – Aliyah was handed up into her saddle, and the drivers shouted and beat their crops, spurring the train into motion. They would be on the high desert before mardiq, thus to commence the journey to Yerussala: east for six hundred leagues to Gezeren, the Iteru river delta, and the Rabiyan peninsula, then turning north along the Mad ar-Hahrat coast. Yerussala sat a hundred and fifty leagues onward from Gezeren, in remote and mountainous desert that crawled with heavily armed and ever-vigilant Meronite legions. The traveling party had taken care to obtain every official paper that anyone had ever heard of, but there was always the possibility of trouble.

The sun was coming up, thin and flinty in the enamel-blue sky, when Aliyah and her escort reached the mahqasa at the eastern gate and the ur-Tasvashtas waiting in the shadow of its minaret. Their delegation was twice the size, containing not only Elemai but ladies, relatives, retainers, servants, soldiers, scholars, qahins, and Ur-Malika only knew who else. Clearly the Batu Tasvashta saw this as the opportunity to make a big splash that it was, and as her relatively puny party rode nearer, Aliyah ordered herself not to start off by apologizing. She had no doubt that her inferiority would make itself known often enough – unless Elemai had also been issued with strict orders to woo her, but that seemed unlikely. Half the High House families were likely to put forth a candidate for her hand, and while Aliyah had snagged the prize position thanks to her mother's machinations, there would be no keeping it without hard work. But Aliyah did not have a clue how to present herself, and anything she could think of seemed ridiculous.

"Aliyah bet Zadia!" As they hewed into hailing range, Elemai raised a glittering hand. She wore a fashionable wisp of gauze over her face and a golden stud in her nose, onyx and carnelian gemstones spilling from her ears and laced around her throat. Despite the early hour, she looked the expected degree of totally radiant, her thick black hair plaited intricately and her skin glowing like a dewy flower. Naturally, it was the perfect shade of bronze; Aliyah, who had her father's Numerian coloring instead of her mother's lighter complexion, was often deemed too dark to be a true beauty. When she was younger, Zadia had made her bathe in milk and apply special tinctures and creams, but none of it ever helped. All it did was remind her of another way in which she disappointed her mother, and the memory made her bristle with shame and resentment. Why had Zadia married a Numerian, then, if there was the awful possibility of her children looking like him?

"Malikalullah qa-salaam," Aliyah said politely, touching her heart, as she drew level. "It is good to see you well, Elemai bet Safiya. I wish to convey again my thanks, and my family's thanks, that you and yours have agreed to journey with us to the Holy City."

"Of course." Elemai inclined her head, all patrician grace and poise. Next to her, Aliyah felt frumpy and overdressed, even if her sturdy wrappings looked far more suitable for the desert. "You must ride near me, my dear, so we may speak. I have heard so much about you."

Aliyah managed to keep her smile in place as she nodded deferentially and goaded her camel alongside Elemai's. After one final prayer from the assorted qahins, someone signaled the watchmen on the ramparts, and the heavy chains rattled up, hauling the gates open. Then the whole unwieldy procession lumbered into motion, passing out from the vast shadow of Qart-Hadesht's ancient walls, said to be first laid by the same jinnyeh whom King Tselmun ordered to build his great Yerussalan Temple. (Though in the Qartic histories, it was Queen Daeda who mastered them and raised the world's greatest city from the barren desert, even if the Meronites tried to insist that she was nothing but a useless lovelorn damsel.) As her camel emerged from the cool dimness and into the white-hot light, Aliyah did her best not to look back. There was only this, now. The future.

As soon as they were out of the city, the wilderness closed in fast. At first there was a path along the damp tidal sands of the Mad ar-Hahrat littoral, where the footing was firmer and the brisk briny wind made for more pleasant going. Yet once they traveled for a few hours, Qart-Hadesht shimmering out of sight like the mythic City of Brass, the coast crumbled into a morass of broken stones and steep cliffs, and they turned inland to the molten crucible of the Sand Sea. But the Bahjoun guides were intimately familiar with this dangerous territory, and led them through a maze of ridges and ravines, gulfs and gulches. At noon, in the highest heat, they took shelter in a wadi, a deep desert cleft where the red stone was sculpted into fanciful columns like frozen silk and dancing dust, sunlight illuminating the cavern like another world. Aliyah dismounted gingerly, wincing; she did not ride often, and her thighs were chafed and cramping. But since she was not about to look like a weakling in front of Princess Perfect, she kept her mouth shut.

They said mardiq, ate bread and figs, and rested until the sun receded from the top of the wadi. Then they filled their waterskins from the cool spring and rode out through a narrow defile that opened into a rocky path, wandering to and fro until it reached the high ground and the endless hinterlands of sand. Out here, you could see forever: nothing but undulating dunes, summits, and valleys, the feathery tracks that warned of the passing of a viper or scorpion, and the unflinching immensity of the horizon. As long as the Mad ar-Hahrat was on their left, to the north, they were continuing east, though the sea was barely visible, nothing but a hazy blue fracture. To their right, south, lay the endless fathoms of the Sand Sea, then cultured, gold-glittering Ambraz, her father's thick-jungled homeland of Numeria, and the tattooed barbarians of Kush. Before them, albeit another four weeks off, sat storied Gezeren, once the land of the sister-marrying, sun-worshiping firawns, though the old dynasties had been overthrown long ago and another imperial Governor-General now ruled from the great ziggurat of Khufre. The traveling party had thus brought plenty of money for bribes. Papers or no papers, filthy lucre was the one thing that could reliably turn the cumbersome wheels of Meronite bureaucracy.

They rode through the night, while the air was cooler, the sand was firmer, and the waxing moon provided ample light. Near dawn they stopped again, said dardiq, slept for a few hours, and woke in a cool foggy morning. Then they hoisted themselves onto their camels again, pinned fresh cloths over their faces because the old ones were already driven through with sand, and set off.

That, in its simple and primal essence, was the rhythm that occupied the next several days, and despite the constant throbbing in her legs and backside, Aliyah got used to it, more or less. By the end of the week, she even speculated on whether she felt up to a more formal approach. Elemai, of course, endured the rigors of the journey with perfect composure, never discomfited by cramped tents, hot sun, gritty food, and poor sleep, and while she spent most of her time flirting with the handsome guild-captain, Jayahi ur-Vorrosq, she looked at Aliyah significantly often enough to make it plain that she was expecting some sort of solicitation, or at least attention. Aliyah — inarticulate, inadequate, prickly, stubborn, self-doubting Aliyah — still had no idea what she could do to attract the interest of this literal goddess, and every time she looked at Elemai, her stomach twisted with something half jealousy and something... not. This was all a setup, surely. A cruel test to prove that she was not worthy of being her mother's heiress, and never would be.

Nonetheless, dynastic honor and her own contrarian nature could not countenance the idea of throwing up her hands and surrendering, so there was nothing for it. That evening, when they were preparing to set out again, Aliyah did her best to scrub her face, comb her windblown hair — even when she tied her headscarf tightly, it tangled something awful — and otherwise look pretty, winsome, and like the heiress of a noble house to which another noble house might wish to bind itself in blessed matrimony. Then she glanced around, saw Elemai about to get on her camel, and hurried over, elbowing Captain ur-Vorrosq out of the way. "Saeda, may I — uh — assist?"

Elemai gave her an amused look, pointing out that she had managed a week of climbing onto bad-tempered ungulates without Aliyah's help, and would therefore surely succeed in it again. But either she found this rank romantic incompetence somewhat charming or she decided to throw a drowning woman a line, because she let Aliyah make a step of her hands, cupping Elemai's elegant morocco-booted foot and hoisting her into the high-horned saddle. "Thank you, habibta," she said, settling her skirts and reaching for the reins, as her camel grated, groaned, and rose from its kneeling position, turning its head to give Aliyah an evil look. "That was very kind of you."

Likely she didn't mean it to come off quite so patronizing, but Aliyah could feel her cheeks burn. It was almost enough to make her bury herself in the sand and never be seen again, though she managed not to. Instead she inclined her neck stiffly, stood in silence as Captain ur-Vorrosq, Elemai, and the camel looked puzzled, and then ran off like a thief in the bazaar. Unbelievable.

If nothing else, brooding on her failures kept Aliyah distracted for the next segment of the journey, as they jounced and jolted across the maghreb and reached the tributaries of the Iteru, the broad floodplains and braided estuaries thick with the most fertile soil in the world, the black gold that birthed Gezeren and all its legends. It was well known that the Divine Emperor had first formed the Corporalists by enslaving Gezereni necromancers, the psychopomps who guided their people into the dark rivers of the underworld. With his usual sinister ingenuity, Coriolane had put their talents to different use, and the *Book of Daybreak* was still their founding text. For that reason, and its vital importance as the empire's principal breadbasket and producer of wheat to feed the hungry Eternal City, he kept Gezeren on a much tighter leash than other imperial provinces, and the travelers began to encounter legions and guardposts every few miles, all officious, obnoxious, and demanding to see papers and permits (and money). As they trundled closer to Qahirah, the route became increasingly crowded with hajjis from across Ifriqiyin: Wahini, mostly, but also Old Rite Tridevarians, Coptaric Tserkovians and Ge'ez Vashemites, and even a few Daevics from Kush. All of them were bound for the same place, the shining beacon of the Holy City, and Aliyah entertained an especially paranoid supposition that Coriolane was deliberately herding them together for ease of elimination. It would not be the first, or five hundredth, bloody massacre in Yerussala's history.

They reached Qahirah on the day of the new moon, a better-than-expected time, then promptly wound up on the far end of an infuriatingly slow-moving queue to actually enter the city. At least it gave Aliyah plenty of time to look around – which she tried to do discreetly, so as not to resemble a gaping country bumpkin. The great Ziggurat of Khufre dominated the skyline; like the Qartic Temple of the Adirim, it had once been the jewel of its own people's crown and now served to emphasize the imposition of the Empire's irresistible might. Qahirah was a motley patchwork that reflected its many masters through history: the colored domes, iwans, and minarets of the Bhagrad caliphs; the cold white Meronite columns, pantheons, and forums; the crammed hovels and covered medinas of the Gezereni commoners; the hanging gardens, hippodromes, and other creature comforts of the ruling class, from the Governor-General to the local nobles who corruptly profited off the foreign occupiers. The city was built in five great rings, with the ziggurat at the center; the poorest districts were at the outer edges, the richest at the inner. Under the caliphs it had been Wahin, but now, like the rest of the empire, it was officially True Tridevarian. That, however, was – usually – only lightly enforced. The Archpriest of Merone might grumble that the emperor was being too merciful to heathens, but the fastest way to get your conquered subjects to rebel against you was to deprive them of their fathers' gods.

The air was thick and hot and hazy blue, they had been traveling hard for over a month, and as they shuffled forward cubit by interminable cubit, Aliyah struggled not to fall asleep in her saddle. The line of supplicants wound back and forth under Qahirah's mighty walls, lit by torches and echoing with the babel of a hundred languages: Qartic, Semyic, Hellenic, Lanuvian, Gezereni, Ge'ez, Kush, Numerian, Ambraz, Franketerrish, Teutyn, Ibelusian, Iscarian, Ruthynian, Kozhek, Vashemysh, Parsiva, Dacian, Zagorian, Indush, Indaric, Qiné, and more. Qahirah was an ancestral crossroad of the world, where people from every corner of the map passed through. Folk went to Yerussala to pray, and to Merone to pay homage, but Qahirah was where they went to bargain, buy, sell, scheme, trade, tax, fight, and fuck. Just to name a few.

They finally reached the head of the line, Elemai bartered in fluent Lanuvian with the hard-faced Meronite captain who wore that familiar expression as if he yearned to crush the lot of them beneath his hobnailed boot, and were at long last allowed to enter after paying an extortionate toll of ten bezints, leading the camel train in single file through the narrow, curving streets. They had sent a man to secure lodgings in the Third Circle, in a hostelry often used by Qartic traders, and Aliyah's head kept drooping, only to jerk her awake again as it fell. She craved a proper bath and bed, not just the rough bucket and bunk of the caravanserais they had stayed in along the way (at least when they were fortunate enough to find them and not simply pitching camp on the high desert). Besides, perhaps spending time in close quarters would give her a chance to try again with Elemai. After the camel incident, she had kept her distance in mortification, but time was fast running out to make a good impression (or at least… *an* impression), and as they would be joining other Qartic hajjis on the last leg to Yerussala, it was bound to include several more prospective suitors. Aliyah had had weeks on the road with no competition, and yet she had squandered it. It would be better if her mother's criticism was unjustified, but it was true.

After a minor eternity, the travelers reached the hostelry, stabled the camels and found their rooms, and were allowed to bathe in the hammam. This, of course, proved a further pitfall when the women took their turn and Aliyah was obliged to share the great stone tub with a naked, warmly wet, and obnoxiously-even-more beautiful Elemai. She kept her eyes militantly downward, and wondered only later, once they were all dressed and dried, if she should have been more forward. Not that she knew how to do that without hideously embarrassing herself yet again, but Qartic youths were not necessarily expected to be virgins at marriage; indeed, too much stiff reserve and pious inexperience was prudish and off-putting. Aliyah, however, was, and that presented yet another obstacle in the increasingly doomed-looking process. She felt exhausted with the weight of her anxiety and how little it felt as if she could control any of it. If she could, if she was just given the *chance* –

Aliyah bet Zadia would later have cause to bitterly rue what she wished for, but not tonight. Tonight she ate a proper meal, prayed sardiq, and crawled into bed. As she lay there, she thought she heard something moving in the darkness outside, circling the hostelry with slow and patient vigilance. It was just her imagination that it sounded like a strange unnatural slap of rotted flesh, and she had no reason to recall the whispers of the Corporalists' darkest powers, what exactly they were rumored to do to the most unfortunate Remade who never saw the light of day again. Of course they were here. Of course they were close.

It took her a long time to go to sleep.

CHAPTER 3

IONIUS

IONIUS REGAINED CONSCIOUSNESS ONLY SLOWLY, SLOWER than usual, and with a dull cottony taste in his mouth, a sharp pounding in his temples. He lay still, waiting to ensure that everything had healed as it was supposed to; no need for that delayed waking to serve as a harbinger of other problems. It was only when he was satisfied that he was indeed no longer injured that he began to scrutinize his surroundings more closely. Splintered wood under his cheek, straw in his mouth, and rhythmic bumping that jarred his bones and made him suspect, as he likewise got a strong whiff of horse, that he had been thrown in the back of a cart. There wasn't enough light to be morning, and to judge from these fucking ruts, they weren't on one of the main roads, which had to be kept in top trim at all times to speed the passage of the imperial legions and messengers. Some squalid rural lane, likely. These local malfeasants were always the same. Doubtless they were congratulating their own success and getting drunk on cheap votke, having struck a noble blow for liberation. Well, they'd see about that.

Some time passed. It was difficult for Ionius to be certain of how much, but it was no more than an hour. Then the cart rumbled to a halt, Ionius went limp, and torchlight scalded his eyes. "Get up, bootlicker," its owner ordered, in bastard Lanuvian. "Time to rise and shine."

"Please don't hurt me." Ionius struggled to stand up, tripped over his feet, and fell headlong out of the cart and into the mud, provoking a gale of raucous laughter from the group. There were a dozen of them: young men clad in kosovorots, leggings, boots, and fur cloaks, swords and daggers strapped at their waists and longbows slung on their backs. Not peasant farmers, since their cloth was too good and their weapons too fine, and serfs usually had better things to do than sit around and cook up hare-brained plots for doomed rebellions. Merchants' sons and university students, most likely, and perhaps a boyar heir to serve as highborn patron and all-purpose financier. Indeed the leader of the group looked likely to fit the bill. He was tall and thickset, not a boy who had ever gone hungry, eyes alight with the zeal of righteous violence, and Ionius shuffled toward him, throwing his arms around the boy's knees. "Please. I'm just a humble tax collector. I don't – "

"We know what you are, scum." The leader aimed a vicious kick at Ionius's ribs. "You're the worst of the worst, the *strigoi* who goes from village to village sucking dry the common folk, to fill the Divine Emperor's greedy coffers. Don't even have enough shame to repent?"

"Please," Ionius repeated plaintively, once he stopped coughing. "I'm just trying to do my job. I don't have anything to do with politics. My wife, my children – "

"We don't care about your *wife,* you stupid fucking coward. When have the Meronites ever cared about our womenfolk, our mothers and daughters, our sweethearts and sisters? Do you think if we sent you back to the Eternal Palace in many small pieces, and promised to do the same to any other imperial leech who set foot in sovereign Iscaria, that Coriolane would get the message?"

No. Difficult as it was, Ionius kept his face straight and his expression scared. Indeed, it was more likely that these idiots would be the ones to end up in pieces, and very soon. Iscaria barely qualified as their glorious homeland anyway: a disputed and rather useless stretch of land between eastern Merone and western Ruthynia, with barren soil, hard winters, steep mountains, and ugly peasants. Nonetheless, it belonged to the Divine Emperor like the rest of the provinces, and had to be defended as ferociously as the Eternal City itself. But Vata Korol, at what cost?

"Well?" the leader repeated. "Do you value your fingers, leech? Or your cock? We're not picky which one we cut off first."

"Please." Ionius coughed a final time and drew himself up. "What happened to my takings? Just give them back and you'll have no trouble from me, I swear. I won't tell the legions about this, or – or anyone. You're good men, I'm sure. Kind. Godly. Let me go, and – "

"Your stolen money? It's here." The one with the air of the underappreciated sidekick held up a sack, heavy with coins. "We'll use it to fund the rebellion against your imperial kennel-master, dog. Thank you for the donation to the cause of freedom."

As a matter of speculation, Ionius wondered what this band of boastful imbeciles imagined that to actually entail. Gods forbid it be truly helping the poor folk they claimed to care about, or anything else useful. They would keep it for themselves and come up with a grandiose excuse as to why it was best – or rather, they would have. As it was, this was only an academic question, and Ionius glanced around, still convinced there had to be more of them. Only a dozen, was that *it?* Did they really think they would overthrow the Divine Emperor with twelve piss-drunk wastrels who felt that kidnapping a tax collector and spouting off some deeply unoriginal threats was the height of revolutionary genius? The least they could do was make it *interesting.* But since Ionius was not the first Meronite official to be seized and extorted in this neck of the woods, and there were plenty of small-time local larcenists overall who had to be made into a firm example, they had gotten him. He almost (if not quite) felt sorry for them.

"Very well," Ionius said meekly. "Take the money! Just let me go."

"I don't think so." The leader unsheathed his dagger and swaggered forward. "We have to send a message. Which hand do you like the least? We'll start with that one."

"No. No, please. How can this be fair? One man against twelve?"

"You also never care about *numbers* or *fairness* when the legions slaughter us, pig." Since this one spoke better Lanuvian, he was definitely a university student, and from the furious look in his eye, might even have real cause to resent the occupiers. Maybe he had lost a father, or a brother, or several brothers, or otherwise seen the up-close effects of how the Pax Meronorum was kept, but that wasn't for Ionius to know or care. Either way, he was forced to conclude that this was in fact all of them. One man against twelve *was* hardly fair, but not why they thought.

"Fine." All at once, Ionius dropped the groveling and rose to his feet, fast enough to startle them. He spoke now in fluent, rapid-fire Ruthynian, and saw the first uneasy realization dawn on their faces. "Let me put it in terms you treasonous maggots can understand. I don't know if this is all the turds you could scrape out of the nearby chamber pots, but if it *was* your intention to get the Divine Emperor's attention, congratulations. You have gotten it, and I don't think you'll find it to your satisfaction. You." He pointed at the leader. "What's your name?"

The boy's mouth hung open. He didn't answer, too startled by this unhappy turn of events. At last he stammered, "I don't see why I should – why? What's *your* name?"

"Ionius Servus Eternus." Ionius cracked a thin, feral smile. "I'm not actually a tax collector."

More alarmed glances were exchanged. Several of them reached for weapons, and others stared at him, finally realizing that under the standard-issue imperial livery, he didn't look anything like a soft, paunchy bureaucrat. Ionius was only of average height, but he was very solid, broad-shouldered, twisted of lean and rangy muscle, and moved with a predatory, pantherine grace. He took his time about sizing them up, until he gestured at the leader again. "I asked you a question, boy."

"Oleg. Oleg Pavelynich Vozharen." The leader looked at his friends for help, but they were frozen. Heroes to a man. "I don't – "

"Vozharen?" Ionius cocked his head. "I know that name. Your father is one of the sizeable landowners, isn't he? He faithfully pays those taxes that you and your cretinous comrades are trying so hard to steal from me, just like a good vassal. Does Pavel Vozharen know what you get up to in your off-hours? Or is he playing both sides, acting as a loyal subject while discreetly authorizing his witless offspring to run around like a common brigand? Do you have a sister, Oleg Pavelynich? A mother? You were so concerned for Ruthynian women."

Oleg blanched. "Stay away," he ordered, drawing his sword, and there was a scrape of steel as the other rebels (well, a few of them) finally did the same. "I don't know who you are, but you will pay for this – "

Ionius laughed. He couldn't help it. It was ridiculous, predictably pathetic, the same thing that always happened, every single fucking time. "Go on," he said generously. "Indulge me. Who do you think I am?"

"I don't know." Oleg slashed with his sword, looking panicky, even though Ionius hadn't moved. "Some Meronite devil. A legionnaire, or one of those damn necromancers. You pretended to be a hapless tax man, you tricked us into snatching you, you – "

"I think you'll find you did the snatching all on your own, boy." Ionius threw a quick look over his shoulder, to be sure nobody was sneaking up behind. "The knock on my head was real, and it's made me angry. I'll send someone to speak with your father soon, and for that matter, the entire university. What is it, the School of Sheep-Fucking?"

Another angry murmur. One of the bravest finally advanced, eyes afire and weapon manfully brandished. "Hush your lying tongue, or that'll be the thing we – "

"Oh, shut up." Taunting them was losing its appeal, he didn't think there was any more useful information to extract, and his head *did* hurt. "You really have no idea, do you? You have no clue what you're up against. Come now, my brothers. Let me show you."

With that, Ionius reached down and clapped both hands against his thighs, gritting his teeth and focusing the formidable magnitude of his will. It always hurt like the devil to do this, even after so long, but he had come to enjoy the pain. It was like a holy madness, divine fire, as the enspelled metal in his bones burst free of his flesh and formed into two long and glitteringly lethal knives. Ionius crossed his arms, then uncrossed them, flinging the blades too fast to be seen. There was a hiss, a slash, and a thump. Then the nearest rebel made a confused noise, raised a hand to his neck, and fell forward so completely that it was almost comical. He was dead before he hit the ground.

Ionius, however, did not take the time to admire his handiwork. The rest of the rebels were yelling in absolute cacophony, half of them running for their lives and the other half possessed of a mad courage that had nothing to lose – he could give them *some* credit for discovering it eventually, but no need to get carried away. Altogether, there was no difference in anyone's fate, a perverse egalitarianism that a bunch of self-appointed champions of the common man should appreciate, but Ionius very much doubted that they did. Instead he flicked a wrist, and the blades wrenched out of the dead man's neck and flew back into his grip. This time he hurled them in opposite directions, skewering one rebel in the eye and the other in the gut, then clenched his hands into fists. Put them together, gathered his strength, and *ripped*.

There was a split second as if the entire world sucked in its breath, or had it driven out. Then all at once, the quiet grey predawn turned into a harrowing scarlet storm.

Ionius had done this too many times to count, but the effect was still breathtaking. One moment, there were men around him — nine living, three dead. *Whole* men, flesh and bone and blood and muscle in the customary configurations. Then it was utter chaos, as every single bit of metal on or in their bodies took its instant and explosive leave. The iron in their blood, the copper in their teeth, the steel in their swords and arrows, the pewter in their brooches and buckles, the silver kopyks and gold rubleks in their purses — it all rushed toward Ionius as fast as it could, like a hound galloping to its master. When the shortest way to reach him was straight through the rebels' bodies, it did so, drilling their torsos and smashing their skulls, slicing them with their own blades and bursting their veins. They screamed, or tried to scream, but their throats were already torn to shreds. For a final moment they remained upright. Then in unison, they collapsed.

When the lot of them stopped twitching, which didn't take long, Ionius lowered his hands, breathing hard. An ache burned in his own bones; channeling that much was as exhausting as if he had killed them with his bare hands in a more ordinary way, and it felt like an athlete overworking disused muscles, fortunate to avoid a sprain. That was what he got for staying in the Eternal Palace so long, training recruits and dancing attendance on court politics. A senior general of the Immortals was not made for that soft eunuch work. He was made for this.

Ionius contemplatively wiped a gobbet of spleen off his cheek, which fell with a bloody smack. Then he strolled to the mutilated corpse of Oleg Pavelynich Vozharen, which lay face-up, staring sightlessly at the dawn sky with eyes burst half out of their sockets. His guts had likewise erupted from his belly, and his own sword had slashed his hamstrings. Arrowheads were embedded deep in his torso, bristling under the surface of his chest like caltrops, and Ionius studied it dispassionately, committing it to memory. Then he leaned down, tore a piece from Oleg's kosovorot, and used it to wipe the blood off his face and hands. "Wrong choice, Oleg Pavelynich," he said softly, letting his native Kozhek accent emerge only now, when nobody was alive to hear it. "I was your comrade once, perhaps. But now I am your master."

With that, Ionius turned away and prowled through the rest of the corpses until he found his knives. He pulled them from their respective unfortunates and pressed them to his thighs, feeling the bright sting as they once more dissolved into his bones. Then he straightened up, muffling a wince; all of this continued to be more difficult than usual, and he didn't like it. Vata Korol, he had to get out more. Coriolane was usually inclined to keep his favorite general close, but the recent spate of revolutionary fervor demanded a response.

Leaving the desecrated bodies where they lay — they would soon be scavenged by wolves and ravens, but hopefully not before any other aspiring rebels saw them and learned the lesson — Ionius started to walk, setting a brisk pace. The sun was not quite up, the world was grey and colorless and filled with chilly mist, and clad in only his tax-collector disguise with its light tunic and cloak, it nipped sharply at his skin. Yet another symptom of spending too much time in the palace, away from the field, and therefore something that was soundly good for him.

He did his best to retrace the route they must have taken from Tseyabilsk, following what, truly, barely qualified as a road. He could have stolen the cart-horse, but it was such an old nag that he could make better time on foot anyway. Besides, Ionius appreciated the chance to take in the morning, the silence and solitude. The bare black trees were as stark and elegant as Qiné calligraphy, and the thin skin of ice on streams and pools caught a burnished rosy-golden glow from the eastern sky. The birds were just stirring, but aside from them, the only sound was his footsteps. He liked it best this way, with no other folk (aside from the dead) for miles. It was clearer. Calmer. Bracing.

The bells of the tiny wooden church were just ringing First Hour when Ionius descended into Tseyabilsk (Tšebeližhke, in native spelling, but Iscarian, Kozhek, and all other regional dialects were not permitted to be read, written, printed, published, or taught – only Ruthynian). It was scarcely big enough to be called a village: just the church, a few narrow muddy alleys of thatched cottages, the communal pasture, a market square, and the Meronite customs-house, which was the one piece of civic architecture you could always count on finding in even the most recondite backwater. It was there that Ionius had enacted his little deception, posing as the tax collector long enough to attract the attention of Oleg and his minions, and he saluted it sarcastically as he passed. He had to admit, he hoped that Pavel Vozharen or another local boyar *was* up to no good, whether in cahoots with their now-deceased sons or otherwise. If not, this would just be disappointing.

Ionius shed his blood-stained tunic in a back alley, then pulled on a kosovorot and leggings, rendering him indistinguishable from the townsfolk. The feeling of Ruthynian clothes was briefly disorienting, summoning up a memory too old for conscious articulation, and he grimaced, shaking it away. Then he straightened up and set off to the market square, with some notion of buying a sweet roll for breakfast. He wasn't especially concerned about the alarm being raised. None of the dead rebels were likely to have lived here; Oleg was from the Vozharen estate to the east, and the rest probably hailed from the university in Rosganyet, ten miles down the road. Like all bored and restless young men, they must have come here to slum it, to imagine some theoretically purer or less morally taxing world, fucking village girls and drinking village beer and coming up with grand ideas for revolution. Playing at being noble peasants, salt-of-the-earth everymen, then heading back to sleep in soft beds in warm halls, while the university matrons washed their clothes and cooked their food. With that breed of opposition, Coriolane would easily rule for another four hundred years.

Ionius had almost reached the baker's stall when the church bells sounded again, and despite himself, he hesitated. It was very rare that he could attend Tserkovian services, and while it was the furthest thing from guilt or regret, he still sometimes felt the need to order his conscience and clear his mind. So he jogged across the muddy square and pulled open the door, ducking in just as the presbyter began to intone the morning trisagion. The tiny, dim sanctuary was lit by smoky candles, but even in this poor armpit of a village, they had scraped up some gold and jewels to bedizen the weathered wooden diptych of Vata Korol and Mata Koroleva that hung over the altar, with serene painted eyes and gilted haloes. The Korolynich was there too, standing with his parents, but did not have his own panel or any particular prominence, which would have been an outrage for any hardcore True Tridevarian who happened to be passing by. The question of the precise theological status and ontological importance of the Prince had caused countless intellectual schisms and bloody wars, and led to the acrimonious split into western Tridevarian and eastern Tserkovian rites; the *Dvadevarians,* as the western scholastics scornfully called them, essentially and heretically only believed in two gods, rather than three. This, of course, could not be countenanced.

Ionius murmured the prayers, blessed himself, drank the okovita, and looked at Mata Koroleva, who wore Her usual expression of serene repose. The ikon was darkened and blurred by countless hands and lips, but even if this was one of the high holy days when the congregants were invited to come forward and venerate Her, Ionius would have held back. Instead he merely looked at Her, and half-hoped that She did not see him in return. *It is Ivan Slavaynich, Mata,* he told Her, barely daring to do so even in his own head. *Do not forget about me.*

Soon after, the service was over, the congregation offered kisses and blessings to each other, and Ionius hurried out before anyone could think of attempting such nonsense with him. It was full daylight by now, the market filling with townsfolk, friends and neighbors. For a moment he lingered, taking in the cadence of spoken Ruthynian and Iscarian and the warmth of the sun, the scent of fresh babka and kalach, and hoped that these people would not also rebel against the Divine Emperor, so he would not have to destroy them. One or two cast a dark look at the customs-house, or made the sign of the horns behind their back, but even if they did know about the twelve dead men, it was difficult to say if they would care. So, then. Ionius had done them a favor, really.

He left Tseyabilsk before Second Hour, boarding the river ferry and traveling downstream to Rosganyet (or Rašagoyentívan), where he stopped at the Meronite inquisitor general's office and gave orders to arrest Pavel Vozharen and the university proctor, induce them to speak by whatever methods were necessary, and convey any information with great dispatch to the Eternal City. If this brought up the names of anyone else who could benefit from such tender treatment, the inquisitors were likewise to ensure that they received it. Did he make himself clear?

He did, my lord, clear as anything, and with that, Ionius was ready to return to Merone. From here, it was two days of riding to the western Ruthynian port of Severolgrod, from whence he would set sail on the inland Pontos Sea, journeying south via the Bosphor Strait. The chroniclers often called it the riskiest stretch of water in the world, as it spanned two short miles between Merone's second city, Coriolanople, on the western bank, and the Parsivati metropolis of Firzepoli on the east. As such, the empire and the sultanate had constantly and furiously attempted to annex the other half until they finally wore themselves out. One of Coriolane's exasperated predecessors issued a charter promising to respect Firzepoli's boundaries in exchange for no more assaults on Coriolanople, and the peace had held, more or less, for five hundred years. Still, Ionius wondered if there was more mischief afoot. It would not be wise, if so. The Two Sisters, as the twin cities were called (or the Two Whores, by the uncharitable), fought like any siblings, scratched faces and pulled pigtails, but still traded and intermarried and bound themselves together, and a strike at one would perforce imperil the other.

They traversed the Bosphor without incident, the great golden dome of the Hagia Merona shining from Coriolanople and the Blue Mahqasa from Firzepoli, then entered the Madherian Sea, which took them to the Lanuvian peninsula, the Tibir estuary, and the heart of the world. Ionius arrived ten days after leaving Severolgrod, then leaned back and breathed it in. Ruthynia might tug on his ancestral heartstrings, but Merone was different. Merone was singular. Merone was all.

There had been cities in the past, and there would be cities in the future, but there would never again be anywhere like the Eternal City. In pagan times it had been sacred to seven gods, and it sprawled on seven hills in its crown of soaring white walls, its white columns, colonnades, turrets, and towers, its white promenades and plazas quarried from the rarest northern marble, so pure that it glowed like fresh-fallen snow even in the height of summer. The Eternal Palace occupied pride of place on Palatorian Hill, and the huddled masses were all equally subordinate, whether the richest villa or the poorest tenement. Everyone came here eventually, for one reason or another. You could find shops and grocers, churches and mahqasas, shuls and sattvas, schools and societies, bars and brothels, libraries and markets from everywhere in the world, run by those who knew how fortunate they were to be part of this monolithic melting pot. It was Coriolane Aureus IX's centuries of enlightened despotism, his pragmatic and far-sighted tolerance alternated with short sharp shocks so the commoners never forgot their rightful place in the cosmogony of history, that had forged this supreme mecca of culture, this culminating synecdoche of the human experience. If a man was tired of Merone, he was tired of life. Even if Ionius had resolved to be out in the field more often, there was nothing like this place: its crackling energy, its messy striving, its proper gratitude to everything that made it what it was. A family had to live in the city for three generations, leaving for no more than a year, before it could apply for citizenship. Everywhere might be Merone, but only the loyal few were *Meronites*.

Ionius was met at the Imperial Docks by a battalion of Immortals, crisply saluted, mounted on a white horse, and escorted up the Avenue of the Heroes, past the Circus Maximus and Coriolane's Column; his statue stood atop it in yet more larger-than-life marble, laurel-crowned and toga-clad in full classical style. Then they left the common districts and entered the wealthier neighborhoods, which existed principally to house the staggering number of bureaucrats it took to make the empire run. It might have been first established, and still importantly maintained, by the might of the legions and the mastery of the magicians, but without its paperwork, it was nothing. It was only when they passed out of these precincts when they finally cantered into the immense courtyard of the Eternal Palace. Ionius was handed down with much subservience, and was about to seek out his quarters when an eunuch rushed up. "General Ionius, how good to see you. What a blessing that your travels were safe.

I am sorry to permit no time to refresh yourself, but His Imperial Majesty instructed for you to be brought to him as soon as you returned."

"Now?" It was useless; when Coriolane Aureus ordered, the world obeyed. Ionius added at once, "I am His Majesty's servant."

The eunuch – this one was called Belsephorus, Ionius thought, though in his opinion they were largely interchangeable – led him into the great hall, arched with high windows and decorated with intricate mosaics. The floor was quartz, jasper, and turquoise, the walls inset with chalcedony and carnelian, silver and sardonyx, etched in complex patterns and arcane scriptomancy: enchanted engravings that invoked the prosperity and long life of Great Merone and all who assumed the awesome responsibility of governing her. The soaring domes were cerulean and amaranthine, inlaid with constellations in gold and silver, shining like a thousand suns. The alcoves had once been lined with statues of Coriolane's predecessors, but now held images only of the emperor himself. Even if they were long dead, an inconvenient mortal foible to which he never personally planned to succumb, he had grown increasingly tetchy at any reminder that anyone had ever ruled here but him. Even the provincial warlords from when Merone was nothing more than the humble fishing village of Lanuvium had to be effaced; they had played their part in bringing the world to its apogee, and for that they should be thanked, but there was no past, present, or future but him.

With Ionius in tow, the eunuch dodged through screens, opened doors and marched down corridors, thus to reach the vast private garden at the center of the palace, where only a dozen people or so were ever allowed to set foot. Belsephorus stepped back and gestured at the gate. "His Imperial Majesty is there, General. Do note, he had a restless night."

Out of the half-man's sight, Ionius raised an eyebrow, hearing the warning. Coriolane was a martyr to insomnia, and it made him short-tempered and curmudgeonly. But Ionius had known the Divine Emperor for a long time and was familiar with managing him, so he rapped on the gate and called, "You sent for me, my lord?"

A distracted voice answered, bidding him enter, so Ionius pushed the gate open and stepped into the botanical wonderland: flowers, plants, shrubs, trees, herbs, medicines, and poisons from across the emperor's dominions, tended solely by the emperor's hand, as no caretaker could clip or weed in here on pain of death. Coriolane had always loved to garden, claiming it did good his heart and settled his head from the burden of his responsibilities, and that was where Ionius found the most powerful man in the world: on his knees in a bed of fresh-turned earth, wearing a large sun hat and rooting in thick green verdure. To judge from his disgruntled muttering, he was searching for a certain specialty trowel that he could not presently find for the life of him, and Ionius cleared his throat. "Your Majesty? You wanted to see me?"

Coriolane jumped, dropped a clump of soil, and looked around accusingly, before realizing who it was. "Ah, yes." He rocked onto his heels and got stiffly to his feet; Ionius refrained from offering a hand, as the emperor did not care to be perceived as weak even in the safety of his edenic cloisters. "General Ionius. Good of you to come so swiftly."

"Of course, Majesty." Ionius inclined his head. "It is a blessing to see you looking well."

Coriolane snorted, but brushed himself off and led the way to his favorite bench, where they could sit and contemplate an enormous jacaranda tree with clouds of luscious purple blossoms. Indeed, the Divine Emperor looked the same as ever: a fit, vigorous man seemingly in late middle age, a few stately wisps of silver in his crisp sandy-blond hair, with a nobly-profiled face that looked good minted on coins and carved in busts and could be instantly identified by any person anywhere in the world, regardless of how far they lived from Merone. He was still wearing his sleep-robe and slippers, as if he had indeed passed a restless night and wandered out here early, and folded his hands in his lap. Ionius, knowing not to speak before the emperor did, waited in silence, until Coriolane cleared his throat. "Well, then. How was your hunting trip?"

"It was less productive than hoped, Majesty, but that might be for the best." Thus permitted, Ionius recounted his three months in Ruthynia and Iscaria, of which Tseyabilsk was the final stop. "I don't think this talk of rebellion is more than the usual grumbling, my lord," he finished. "None of those I killed were any real threat to you."

"That, nonetheless, is why we prune them. Like a well-tended garden." Coriolane indicated their surroundings – green, peaceful, quiet, the epitome of order and comfort. "This place is only perfect because I keep it in constant trim, guiding and correcting, cutting off diseased shoots before they can imperil the rest. It is like the empire."

"Yes, my lord." To say the least, Ionius had heard this metaphor before, but it never paid to appear impatient. "I am glad to be of service."

"I know." Coriolane patted his shoulder with something almost like paternal affection, but Ionius, who had no memory of his own father, could not be sure. "You have done well, General. In the meantime, there are other tasks. It pains me, but I have come to the end of my patience with the Bodeni. The order has been given for them to be removed."

"Removed, my liege?"

"Brythanica has been more trouble than it is worth for some time." Coriolane pursed his lips. A tiny, rainy, irrelevant island in the back of beyond, mostly used as a convenient hellhole to exile disgraced imperial officials, it had been subject to intense Tridevarian conversion attempts for many decades, but the indigenes clung stubbornly to their paganism and their fierce resistance of Meronite occupation. Brown-skinned, face-painted savages in furs and feathers, who worshiped their ancestors and the trees and were rumored to practice human sacrifice – there was no question that Coriolane had showed far more mercy than they deserved, since even barbaric Brythanica was part of the empire and therefore subject to the empire's privileges. But this? Ionius was no naïve pacifist or irritating apologist for infidels, but it seemed extreme, out of proportion to Coriolane's usual careful accommodation of native faiths and strategic allowance of local politics, to a point. Unless he had misunderstood, but he had known the emperor too long to think so.

"Are you quite sure, Majesty?" Ionius asked, as deferentially as he could. "At this delicate moment, especially if you have reopened the Holy City as proof of your godliness – "

"I am the *Divine* Emperor, Servus. I am godly by definition." The pointed use of Ionius's cognomen was proof that in this instance, Coriolane had no desire to humor even the pretension of counsel to the contrary. "Besides, nobody will blame me for killing the Bodeni. Indeed, they will applaud it. Mellius has nagged me to take stronger methods for a while, and he will be delighted to hear that his holy warriors finally have full rein to do as they please. As for the other provinces, should they even hear what is afoot in soggy remote Brythanica, they won't care, or they will agree that those troublesome fools must deserve it, or they will take a second look at what small-time insurrectionists, what cancers in the body politic, they have been harboring, and take firmer methods on their own. Besides, the Bodeni *are* heathens. We can all agree on that."

"Absolutely, Majesty." Ionius glanced at the emperor, reminded that for all his genteel masquerade of a humble gardener, he was older than any other man, an ancient being of unfathomable depths. Whichever mystic rituals or black magics were worked on Coriolane to keep him perpetually young, his life stretched far beyond mortal years and impervious to ending in any usual fashion, was the most well-guarded secret in existence; even Ionius had no idea. "Wait – my lord, are you asking *me* to be in charge of this – "

"You? No, no, no." Coriolane chuckled at the look on his face. "You are far too valuable to waste on a distasteful business in a distant place. No, I plan to keep you closer to home, until these Ruthynian irruptions are likewise put down. Pathetic as they might be, they could grow much worse if we fail to deal with them. But I *will* need you to review your battalions and select the best candidates for the Brythanic job. This does not mean the bravest, or the wisest, or the most skilled at arms. Indeed, it is a useful opportunity to weed out the chaff. Select only those who will follow all orders and ask no questions. Is that clear?"

"Of course, my lord. It will be done. Anything else? It was a long journey from Severolgrod, and I came to attend you as soon as I arrived."

"You are weary, General?"

"Nothing that could not be overcome, if Your Highest and Holiest Majesty was to give the order." Ionius lifted the offered hand to his lips and devotedly kissed the golden signet ring. "It remains my joy and honor to serve the master of the world."

"And mine to be served." Coriolane turned away, once more absorbed in the contemplation of his garden. "Go, Ionius. Get some rest. You are likely to need it."

Ionius Servus Eternus rose to his feet. He bowed. He went.

CHAPTER 4

ALIYAH

Qahirah woke early. It was still well before sunrise when the muyzins began their ululation, urging the faithful from bed for dardiq prayer, customarily held to be the holiest of the day and the most complimentary of an individual's religious fiber. In the time of the Bhagrads, the call would have sounded over the entire city, the Sand Sea, and the Iteru delta, but now it was strictly confined to the Wahin Circle and could be punished if it too often disturbed the sleep of Tridevarians. Aliyah, eyes gritty and head dark with unsettling dreams, was likewise deeply resistant to getting up, but now she was awake, and there was always a certain amount of peer pressure to say dardiq when other people could see. So she rolled out, dressed, and muddled to the sahn with the rest, doing her best not to yawn her face off. They performed the prayer as morning suffused the world with cool light, and then went back to bed or shuffled off for breakfast and business. Aliyah was tempted to opt for the former, but she could see Elemai across the way, and there was no delaying it. Hoping she did not look as distracted and disheveled as she felt, she approached. "Good morning, Elemai bet Safiya. May Ur-Malika bless you today."

"And you." Elemai smiled cordially, so either she did not hold a grudge for Aliyah's bizarre behavior on the road or she was too well-mannered to let on. "Did you sleep well?"

"Decently, saeda," Aliyah lied, squashing another yawn. This qualified as the most successful conversation she had yet had with her prospective fiancée, and she didn't want to ruin it with insane fabulations of half-rotted things stalking the hostelry by night. "Is – is there any way in which I may be of service to you, in our time here or otherwise?"

Elemai considered, then raised a hand. "It's time we spoke more privately, don't you think? Come with me."

Abjectly grateful that someone else was taking control of the situation, Aliyah nodded and hurried after her. Elemai led them through a side gate, out of the hostelry and down to a low stone wall, where they could sit and watch the sun rise over the endless strew of Qahirah, turning muddy brown to shining gold and spilling from one circle to the next like an overturned vat of olive oil. The apex of the ziggurat's ancient steps were just catching the sun, the lower levels still swathed in shadow, as Elemai settled on the wall and beckoned Aliyah to sit down next to her – which after a moment, she did. The silence turned fraught, expectant, until Elemai cleared her throat. "If it helps, I know the task you have been given. You needn't look ready to swallow your tongue."

"Oh. Ah. Yes. I apologize for my clumsiness, saeda. I didn't – "

"Never mind." Elemai waved that off. "You are here to court me, and I am therefore here to be courted. So we should get on with it, don't you think? About me – let's see. I am twenty-five, my parents are Safiya, Ghassan, Marishah, and Jahifar, and I was born in winter, the Centaur's ninth house of the stars. I have two sisters and a brother. I enjoy reading, riding, writing, music, wine, men, women, philosophy, art, poetry, and adventure. As a girl, I greatly aspired to be a qayna who owned a tavern, wrote songs, had magical escapades with jinnyeh, and dallied with caliphs and princesses in disguise, but it seems that I am destined to be a politician instead. I am a hafiza not only of the Kitab but also Shahrzad's tales. Somewhat quaintly, I prefer to marry only once, so my first spouse should be my last spouse. I recognize that this places more pressure on you, but I am open to negotiation."

At this, Elemai paused for breath, leaving Aliyah mildly stunned. Half of her was intrigued by Elemai's frank and unsentimental approach, placing herself on the auction block like a piece of horseflesh, and the other half wanted to insist that this was far too cynical a way to arrange a marriage, even if romance had nothing to do with it. Elemai was right: it was a transaction, a business deal between families. The prospective spouses did have a say in the matter, and it would not be forced if they were plainly unsuited to each other, but they were expected, within reasonable bounds, to make it work. Yet if Elemai was lukewarm about the possibility of further spouses, that meant her marriage would be not just for politics but for love, and that was well beyond anything Aliyah felt capable of offering, as even the first one was in doubt. At last, as Elemai continued to look at her, Aliyah managed, "Negotiation, saeda?"

"Call me Elemai. We're speaking as equals, aren't we?" Elemai shrugged. "Certainly if we were to be wed. As to that, if you wanted to have other partners or find a man to give you natural children, you could take a mut'ah or morganatic spouse with my blessing. Even if I prefer monogamy for myself, I would not necessarily expect it from you."

"I am – not very knowledgeable about these things, saeda. I mean, Elemai. I could not say."

"I suppose there's no hurry." Elemai put her head to the side, studying Aliyah intently. "It's cruel to ask this of you, I think."

"It is my task, sae – Elemai. I am honored to be given it."

"Yes." Elemai's voice was dry. "You seem very honored."

Ominously aware that she might yet again be blowing it, Aliyah racked her brains. "So in Qahirah – is there any way I can assist? There must be business to conduct, people to meet – "

"There is all that, to be sure." Elemai paused significantly, glanced around to be quite sure that they were alone, and lowered her voice. "But it is not the main purpose of our visit, whether here or to Yerussala. Has your mother not told you?"

"Not told me – what?"

"Ah." Elemai surveyed her with the slightly pitying expression of someone whose Adirim-member mother told *them* everything. "She has not. Well, in the spirit of transparency, it falls to me. In short, there are rumors that Coriolane Aureus is not reopening the Holy City merely to gain goodwill, defuse rebellion, or what else. Information has been passed by well-placed sources in Merone that something is happening to him.

The emperor is genuinely weakened. Ailing. It might be, and they do not exclude the possibility, *Inshamalikah,* that he is finally dying."

Aliyah opened her mouth, sat like a fly-catching plant, then shut it. It sounded so fantastic that her first instinct was to assume that Elemai was pulling her leg, or telling a joke to see if she would laugh. When Aliyah stared at her in expectation of the punchline, and it failed to appear, she realized that Elemai might actually believe it. But – *what?*

"That…" Aliyah managed at last. "That can't be real."

Elemai raised an eyebrow. "Needless to say, we did not think so either, when we first heard. Nor do we rule out the likelihood of a cruel trick, a deliberate lie to make us think there is a chance for real freedom and leap for it, so Coriolane has the perfect excuse to crush us once and for all. But from what we've confirmed from our other spies, there *is* something unusual going on. If this is true, if Ur-Malika knows what black magic has kept Coriolane alive all this time is finally starting to fade, then… well. I needn't spell it out."

Indeed. Aliyah struggled for something to say, but she was too flattened by the idea of the Divine Emperor just being … *gone.* Could that be what her father was hinting, in their conversation in the garden? Opaque and offhand, not daring to say it directly, or did even he not know for sure? Just guessing, stabs in the dark, because who on earth would think that the sky could fall down?

"Thank you for telling me," Aliyah said. "Who else knows this?"

"Only a very small circle in the High House. A dozen at most, including your mother and mine. There is unanimous agreement that it is far too dangerous to inform the Low House, let alone the public, because it could spark wild theories and reckless uprisings. And if it looked as if we started a malicious rumor to undermine him – "

Aliyah nodded again. Even in the distant past when someone aside from Coriolane Aureus IX was the emperor, the fractious Meronite society was always united by its hatred for the Venerated Republic of Qart-Hadesht, its oldest and bitterest enemy. Perhaps they had never gotten over that embarrassing business with the elephants and the Apellines, or perhaps the republic's stubbornly continued existence reminded the Meronites uncomfortably of when they had it too, and overthrew it in favor of absolute autocracy. Either way, Elemai was correct that they could not break the news under any circumstances, or even give away that they had heard. But nor could such a monumental opportunity be ignored, and if it was possibly, remotely the case –

"That's why Amma wanted to be sure I knew how the Qartic government worked," Aliyah said, half to herself. "Because if there *was* no longer an emperor, we would have a real chance. To finally throw off the imperial yoke once and for all, and be properly free."

"Aye." Elemai wrapped her arms around her knees, looking pensive. "So there you have it. We need to find out if it is even halfway true, and if so, what we plan to do. As of now, there are two factions within the Adirim who know about it. The first thinks it's surely not true, and even if it is, we must prioritize our own independence, rather than bothering to forge alliances with anyone else. The second thinks that emperor or no emperor, we stand no chance if we don't join forces with other Wahini, other Ifriqiyini, anyone anywhere who has suffered at the Meronites' hands and might fight with us. Our mothers are both in the latter camp, but they are badly outnumbered. Massasoum ur-Beiresht, the Chairman, is against any rebellion at all, so – "

"So they want us to be the unofficial Qartic ambassadors to Qahirah," Aliyah summarized, feeling somewhat ill. "And Yerussala. And anywhere else we can find new friends who might make powerful allies and prevail on the Chairman to change his mind. It must also be why your mother is willing to consider me as your spouse. It's a useful way to present the Batu Tasvashta and Batu Namasqa as a united front, bravely leading the struggle. That's why my mother stayed, and sent me instead. Just in case Coriolane actually does die while we're gone, and the moment has to be seized."

"I expect so." Elemai bit her lip. "It's better to know, at least?"

Aliyah wasn't sure if it was or not, but there was no use in dwelling on it. Instead she said, "So if Coriolane is reopening the Holy City because of this, it's… what? A blatant attempt to curry favor with his Tridevarian gods and make the immortality magic work again? A strategic distraction until he sorts out the problem? Who could possibly be in the position to pass this kind of terrible secret to his enemies?"

"We're looking into it, but our hopes are not high. It goes without saying that they were *very* careful. But there were enough intimate details to make us think it's someone physically close to him. Perhaps a concubine, though the whole harem would be executed if they were caught. Yet the wildest theory of all, which we have nonetheless not been able to disprove, is that it was in fact one of the empresses."

If the news that Coriolane might actually be dying was shocking, this was somehow even more so. Empress Gheslyn and Empress Vestalia were deeply enigmatic figures: dutifully appearing at Coriolane's side on formal occasions, rarely speaking in public or expressing an opinion, but sometimes credited with encouraging him to grant clemency or deal gently. They had also been the queen consorts for as long as everyone could remember, but they had visibly, if slowly, grown older; while they clearly had some of whatever preservation enchantment was laid upon the emperor, it was not as strong or long-lasting. All anyone knew was that Gheslyn was the first, and Vestalia came later. Official Tridevarian doctrine held that a man should marry only one wife and remain faithful to her as long as they both should live, but Coriolane was the Divine Emperor, there was no way for anyone to challenge him, and sleeping with just one person for eternity must be far too boring to countenance. Perhaps Coriolane and Gheslyn both decided to bring in Vestalia to spice things up, though of course everyone thought the empresses must hate each other and viciously compete for his favor. Whenever they did make an appearance, citizens were encouraged to laud them as fashion icons, ideal personifications of Meronite culture, or inspirational role models, and praise their supposedly apolitical, ceremonial, and impartial role in supporting Coriolane. Perhaps Aliyah was just too Qartic, but it never made sense to her. Why praise a woman for doing nothing but bowing to her husband, as if that was any kind of civic or moral virtue?

"One of the *empresses?*" Aliyah said at last. "Why would they ever jeopardize their own husband, their own position? Surely not."

"Intimate enmity can be the most lethal, you know," Elemai pointed out. "Nobody knows how it is with the three of them behind closed doors, and there are other potential reasons for the women to want Coriolane out of power or forced to a final reckoning. When was the last time you heard about a Meronite prince or princess, or any heir at all? He's rumored to have killed all his children, born and unborn, so there would never be anyone else for the people to rally around, no one but him. If it was combined with other resentments, then yes. I could see a way for that to fester into treason."

"My mother did not tell me this. If you learn more, will you?"

"So far as I am able," Elemai promised. "Come, let's get back."

With that, they returned to the hostelry, ate and washed, and set out on the day's business. Their first port of call was the home of a wealthy Qahiran merchant, the sort of person to have connections both high and low and who might be induced to feel them out for financial resources, useful knowledge, political sentiments, or other contributions to a hypothetical rebellion (not that anyone was so clumsy as to say the word aloud). They sat in his solarium, sipped tea, and conversed with utmost gentility, as Aliyah watched Elemai closely to see how she did it. Never bringing it up directly, Elemai nonetheless expertly maneuvered the subject to the negligence of Meronite rule, the questions around Coriolane's motives for reopening the Holy City, and whether Qahirah, for so long the cultured capital of the Bhagrad caliphs and classical Wahinism, was not greatly degraded by being chained and drained as just another Tridevarian imperial province. By the time they departed, Aliyah was both awed and intimidated, feeling that she had learned more in a few hours than all of her mother's lessons. "So?" she said quietly. "Do you think he would help us?"

"Hard to say." Elemai adjusted her veil against the hot wind as their camels clopped slowly through the crowded souk. "At the end of the day, his decision is liable to come down entirely to what makes him the most money. If there's a violent and protracted war and his trade suffers, he will support whoever can end it the fastest. But if the transfer of power can be achieved quickly and bloodlessly, he might support an independent Gezeren and proclaim himself a patriot. If nothing else, he has no fondness for the endless and burdensome Meronite taxes."

Whatever the end of Meronite rule might look like — a concept so foreign that she still found it hard to think about — Aliyah doubted it would be quick *or* bloodless. Even if her imagination was stirred by the idea of fomenting a covert resistance, that old pragmatism was too deeply embedded in her. Even if Gezeren installed a new ruler with the right background and the right religion, they would want money and men just as before, the same exactions and the same manipulations. Would it be more holy, more acceptable? Or only more of the same?

They spent the week in Qahirah, conducting visits and attending gatherings with other pilgrims, forming a large enough group to ride north in safety. Because there were so many travelers on the road to Yerussala and most for the first time ever, bandits and highwaymen were enjoying a bumper crop just like the Mad ar-Hahrat pirates, and there were alarming stories of hajjis being robbed, raped, beaten, murdered, or otherwise molested and left for dead. "Where are the Meronite legions?" a plump middle-aged Ge'ez man complained, at one of these socials. "If we must be subject to the empire's governance and the empire's taxes, the least they could do is protect us!"

Elemai said nothing, but Aliyah saw her raise an eyebrow, clearly remarking that perhaps Coriolane was letting the miscreants run free precisely to make them more grateful for the Meronite military whenever it deigned to reappear. Or he had not thought about it at all and simply felt that his soldiers had better things to do than chasing down a few scabrous outlaws – might be keeping them close to home, in order to stop any enterprising rival from scenting blood. *Was* he dying? Aliyah kept returning to the question, picking it like a broken seam. Why, after all this time, would the magic suddenly fail? It just seemed wrong.

They left the city after sardiq on Khamsday, which they attended in the storied Ur-Azalam Mahqasa with its soaring friezes and white-gold domes, eternal flames burning in great bronze salvers and colorful geometric tiles on the walls. As Khamsday – Quintday, to Meronites – was the holiest day of the week and thus an auspicious moment to start the journey to Yerussala, the rugs were full of prostrating pilgrims, many of whom likewise egressed to waiting camels and mounted up to ride in the coolness of the rising moon. Once they were finally out of the city and cantering across the dunes, the dark sand painted in pearly shadows, Aliyah allowed herself, just for a moment, to think that she had not ruined everything and might even be doing well. Elemai seemed to have accepted her as a confidante, and not be totally repulsed by the idea of her as a spouse, which was progress. If the ur-Tasvashtas wanted Aliyah not for herself but as an important piece to seal the loyalty of her mother – that was something. At least it meant she was trusted to do that much.

While the worst of summer had dissipated, the heat was still fierce as they crossed through Rabiyah and turned onto the northern hajji way; the southern route to the city of Makeyah, where the exiled Hierophant had settled with his followers and began to preach the revelation of Wahinism, was just passing out of season. The landscape spanned the gamut from whitewashed cottages and cultivated terraces of wheat, olives, and grapes, to brown weeds so dry and tough that even the camels struggled to eat them, to towering red cliffs where vanished civilizations had carved whole cities from the rock, to the hide tents and colorful carpets of the Bahjoun nomads. It put her in mind of the legendary traveler Ben Betute ur-Tanji, who claimed to have circumnavigated the entire known world, reached as far west as Ibelus and as far south as the tip of Ifriqiyin, ventured into Coriolanople and Firzepoli and Sardakhand and Indush before winding up in the Jade City of Hang'i. As an old man, he finally returned home to western Marokh and wrote the *Rihla* for those hoping to follow in his adventurous footsteps. As a girl, Aliyah had pored over the book intensely, dreaming of seeing all those far-off places and meeting those foreign people. She was still a long way from matching the great explorer, but at least it was a start. By now, Yerussala was fewer than fifty leagues away, and there were hopes of reaching it before half-moon, if everything continued to go well. There was a vicious haboob that forced them to lie low, and they were almost attacked by marauders near Petrakh, but the guild-soldiers dispatched them in short order.

At last, just when Aliyah could take no more of this endless desert purgatory, they trundled around a final headland, beheld the sun dazzling on the Mad ar-Hahrat like a sheet of hammered gold, and reached the foot of the Sacred Stair. The steps switched up the face of a sheer cliff, cut vertiginously into the rock, and were barely broad enough for three to walk abreast. This formidable natural defense had deterred a number of hostile armies over the centuries, since Yerussala sat at the very top, on a high plateau that abutted the dusty mountains and was surrounded by stakes, fences, vineyards, terraces, groves, gorse, rocks, and ravines. That was even before you reached the walls mounted with catapults, crossbows, vats of boiling oil, and in a pinch, a local lad with a slingshot and rocks. There were Corporalists up there as well, but you never knew where. Not least since by the time you found them, you were dead.

The Sacred Stair was guarded by a heavily fortified gatehouse and a detachment of brusque Meronite legionnaires who allowed only a few groups at a time to start the climb; any overcrowding on the steep and exposed route could easily be fatal. The delays were further compounded by the most devout pilgrims who insisted on bowing and prostrating at every step, chanting prayers and burning incense. Finally, however, the legion commander lost patience and bellowed that anyone still dawdling by sundown would be subject to hefty fines, imprisonment, and other undesirable outcomes, which produced plenty of black looks and muttering about Meronite impiety but did induce the holy slowpokes to get a shift on. Elemai spurred her camel forward, exchanged a few words and the glint of gold with the commander, and when the gates rattled open again, the ur-Tasvashtas and ur-Namasqas were called to the front.

The afternoon was late and the shadows lengthening, and even when pressed against the rock, the drop was enough to make Aliyah's head spin. She tried not to look down, trusting in the camel's surefootedness as they climbed higher, the gatehouse and the Meronites and the pilgrims falling out of sight, out of sound and mind, until there was nothing but the rustling palms and the sighing wind. The air was thin and parched as bone, the sun spilling into the western sea, and Aliyah loosened her headscarf in hopes of drying the sweat from her hair. She could see the coastline unspooling for miles as it wandered north to Hellenica and Kyprion – crags and inlets and bays, harbors and shores – but not any sign of Yerussala. Perhaps it was like faith, which felt fitting for the Holy City. Continuing on into the dark, unable to see it or know for certain that it was there, and only trusting that it would be. Waiting.

At last, they surmounted one last ledge, passed along the towering walls, and waited while the ancient battle-scarred wood of the Golden Gate was winched open with booms and clatters. Even for someone of Aliyah's fairly indifferent religious sensibilities, it was a solemn moment, and she bowed her head, murmuring malikallulah, as others did the same. Then the gate swung away into the Holy City, and after two months on the road — weary, grimy, thirsty, and desperate to sit on anything apart from a camel — the hajjis passed inside.

At once, Aliyah looked in every direction, trying to soak in the historic atmosphere and spiritual significance, but it was dark, and aside from the lamps that burned here and there, casting shadows on shuttered windows or barred doors, she couldn't see much. She did have a sense that it was much more compact and covered than the sprawling open-air mazes of Qart-Hadesht and Qahirah, hidden under its walls and hills and roofs. Not that any defense, physical or otherwise, ever protected it for long. Franketerrish and Teutyn Tridevarian armies had repeatedly sacked it and massacred its inhabitants in the course of countless attempts to take it from the Bhagrads, some of which had even briefly succeeded (at least until the Meronites returned in force and took it from *them*). The Vashemites wanted everyone to remember that it was originally their land, stolen from the Dayoudic dynasty and its last and greatest king, Tselmun, but they often ended up as collateral damage for the other two. According to them, this was where the holiest shrines of Odunai were first built and worshiped by his chosen people. According to the Tridevarians, it was where the Lord took human form, walked the streets, married the Lady and sired the Prince. According to the Wahini, they were both wrong; the Lord had never incarnated in flesh and was not a *Lord* distinct or separate from a Lady. Hence Ur-Malika, the Lord-Queen, both male and female in eternal essence. And yet for all this endless bloody squabbling, it no longer mattered. The only divinity here was the Divine Emperor. The only law was Merone.

At last, the party reached the caravanserai in the Wahin Quarter where most of the Qartic travelers were staying, where they dismounted, offloaded the baggage, and stayed awake for a special sardiq prayer, which took twice as long as usual due to the ceremony and exaltation. Afterward, Aliyah retreated to the dormer she shared with four other women, toppled atop the bed, and fell asleep.

In the morning, after rest, breakfast, and a bath had her feeling somewhat more human, it was time to take the measure of Yerussala —

which Aliyah decided to do alone, with only Captain ur-Vorrosq along for protection. (After all, he did work for her, and should be reminded to stop flirting with Elemai.) But the result was, almost heretically, a disappointment. The tales of Yerussala in King Tselmun's day told of a splendid wonderland of gardens and temples, soaring shadowglass spires where spellsingers wove marvelous enchantments and alchemists worked miraculous transubstantiations, where jinnyeh and angels lived alongside men and every alley was rife with wonders both magical and mundane; where the air scented of cinnamon and cardamom, spice and saffron; where even the commoners wore gold and jewels; where animals spoke in the tongues of men and the power and wisdom of the great king held it all together. Aliyah was familiar with the idea of poetic license, had not expected to actually stumble on a talking tiger or wandering seraphim, and was well aware that even if half of it had been true, it was a very long time ago. But even her stubbornly, eternally practical heart could not fail to feel that this was not at all up to scratch.

In truth, the legendary Yerussala resembled a tired, squalid frontier town, its streets hazy, silent, and heaped with mud, shit, and broken stone and wood. Goats and chickens were stabled in the remnants of deserted houses; the hovels had either crumbled to pieces or burned to the ground and never rebuilt. Perhaps it was just the effect of being shut off from the world for ten years, but the vaunted Holy City looked old and ordinary, straining at the seams even when pilgrims had only just begun to arrive. If it did once boast the delights of Tselmun, those had been washed away forever in the blood of thousands and thousands of innocents. After the various sacks, the Meronites had carried off all the Tridevarian artifacts and buildings to be re-erected in the Eternal City, and left the Vashemite and Wahini holy places largely in rubble. As she paced down the dirty streets, past beggars huddled in dark corners and dull-eyed merchants under ragged awnings, Aliyah felt an emotion about which she was not at all uncertain or conflicted. Anger. It was *anger*.

"Do you want to go back, saeda?" Captain ur-Vorrosq asked, once she made the circuit of the bazaar. "There will be more to do later."

Aliyah didn't answer, gazing around the market as if expecting it to crumble like a piece of scenery and finally reveal the real Yerussala.

Surely this could not be it. Coriolane would not allow his subjects to come and see for themselves how poorly the Holy City had been stewarded. It would be flint to tinder, even in those generally reluctant to challenge Meronite rule, and if so —

"Princess," a croaking voice said. *Malikallulah qa-salaam,* Princess."

Aliyah jumped out of her skin and spun around, looking for both the speaker and who they were addressing — quite obviously, it was not her. But she saw nobody except for a tiny, wizened old man with strangely shining golden eyes, peering from beneath his tattered turban. He spoke an archaic but mostly understandable dialect of Semyic, which all Wahini had to learn regardless of their national origin; it was the holy language of the Kitab and the Hierophant. Seeing that he had her attention, he thudded down a bag of extremely suspect brassware and undid the cords, displaying the goods in what he clearly felt was an irresistible fashion. "For you."

Right. Another local entrepreneur eager to fleece the massive inrush of tourists. Since they had not had any new customers for a decade, it was hard to blame them, but Aliyah couldn't think of a reason to buy a terrible pot, even for zakat. She shook her head, summoning up her Semyic. "No thank you. Good day, uncle."

Undeterred, the brass merchant pranced closer. "Oh no, Princess. This is for you. I have been waiting. We have all been waiting. See?"

With that, he thrust a wrinkled hand into the depths of his sack, rooted around, and finally emerged with a ring. Made of tarnished brass or gold, set with a cracked black stone that was etched with some sort of six-pointed star, it was even more unprepossessing than the rest, and he thrust it at her aggressively enough that Aliyah ducked and looked for Captain ur-Vorrosq. But he was distracted across the way, she did not want to act as if she could not handle one persistent old geezer by herself, and tried to push his hand away. "Thank you, but I still — "

"Take it, Princess." His voice was low and unexpectedly urgent. "Please. For everyone."

At that, he glanced shiftily over his shoulder, as if someone or some*thing* was lurking in the dusty shadows. Aliyah was utterly lost as to why he kept calling her *princess,* though perhaps it was an old-fashioned honorific that was still in Yerussalan use. But he stuffed the ring into her hand, plucked a dirhem from her purse, and tied his bag shut, hoisted it up, and scuttled off. She wasn't sure if she had just been robbed blind by a notorious thief, the ring looked like rubbish and she was about to chuck it aside, but something stopped her just enough to snort and thrust it into her pocket. Then she strode over to Captain ur-Vorrosq and glared at him. "Some bodyguard *you* are."

He looked puzzled. "What's wrong, saeda?"

"That old man." Aliyah waved indignantly in the direction the ancient weasel had run. "Steals from me in broad daylight and – "

"I'm sorry, saeda, but what old man?"

"Him. The one who was just here. Didn't you – ?"

When ur-Vorrosq's face remained blank, Aliyah shook her head, muttered that it was nothing, and got back to the matter at hand. She seriously doubted that anyone here had an inclination to get involved in Qartic politics in any capacity, when they were too busy fighting to stay alive every day, but they would be staying here over the winter and there would be plenty of time to find out. The idea of bunking down interminably in the cold months, in this shut-down, worn-out, bloodless corpse of a city with vultures crawling over it and ripping out its remaining flesh, was patently unappealing, but perhaps it would have hidden depths. Either way, it was not as if she had a choice.

Electing not to look any more insane than she already did, Aliyah kept her mouth shut, returned to the caravanserai, and after supper and sardiq, slipped out to the courtyard. Then she sat down under a juniper tree, dug in her pocket, and took out the ring.

At close range, it was even more unimpressive: ancient, battered, and dirty, the golden band worn wafer-thin and the crack in the black stone filled with grime. Even though she examined it intensely, trying to discern even one reason a crazy old brass merchant would have given it to her, Aliyah could think of nothing. But perhaps if she cleaned it up a bit, it would be worth a few dirhems, and she collected a bit of cloth from her scarf, gripped the ring, and in one moment, started to rub.

In the next, the world exploded.

CHAPTER
5
JULIAN

The hour was late and getting later, the mood had been bad to start with and was only turning worse, and it was plain from the aggrieved looks the innkeeper kept throwing their way that he wanted them out of his establishment posthaste, though there could be any number of reasons for that. Because they were a group of angry young men; because they were Vashemites; because hushed talk and hissed dispute boded trouble by its very nature; or just because he was tired and wanted to close up and go home. Curfew had recently been tightened, and citizens were expected to be off the streets by Apodeirnon, but taverns could operate until an hour later. At least, usually. The authorities were well aware of the particular role of drinking establishments in fomenting the discontent of people like Julian and his friends, and Vashemites out late in Korolgrod were all but asking for trouble. But just now, they had no choice.

"This was the sixth attack in half as many months," Saul ben Sebberut said, after checking one more time to make sure the spell was holding. "All the same pattern, all the same targets. A group of self-declared Ruthynian patriots, dead to a man with their guts ripped out and their corpses desecrated. The ones outside Tseyabilsk were the last I heard of, but there might be more happening at this very moment. We're damned lucky it wasn't us, but if we keep this up, it *will* be."

All things considered, this was a sensible utterance, but it was met with a chorus of protests, and Gavriel ben Avraham was the first to get in a word edgewise. "Maybe so, but all those dead rebels were Ruthynian or Iscarian Tserkovians, and they're not our friends to start with. If this madman isn't killing Vashemites – which would make him one of the few fucking people who doesn't – why is this a reason for *us* to stop?"

This caused an even louder round of recriminations, straining the enchantment until Julian threw a wary look over his shoulder, certain that someone was overhearing. Seeing as he was the one who had pilfered the privacy spell from a house in Alchemists' Row and would be the chief object of blame if it failed, he was especially vested in its success. If only they had a better meeting place than a public tavern, but they didn't. Gavriel was the only one at the University of Korolgrod – several others, including Julian, had been rejected on the grounds that there were too many Vashemites enrolled already – and he shared cramped student quarters with four goye. The others lived in the ghetto or poor shtetls outside town, where they had too many family members close at hand or other risks of discovery. So they were here, crowded in a corner and looking exactly like the stereotype of the shifty, plotting Vashemite that Tridevarians most dreaded. But if Gavriel was right –

"Gavriel is not right," Yehudim ben Natanel said firmly. "Just because whoever's killing the Tserkovian rebels hasn't gotten around to Vashemites yet, it doesn't mean they won't. Besides, you know perfectly well that the regular authorities seize any excuse to crack down on us, even if mysterious murderers don't. That said – "

Gavriel and his cohort objected to that in turn, and Julian took another sip of beer, settling in for the long haul. He was personally more inclined to Gavriel's side than Saul's, but he was still a relative newcomer, didn't have much clout, and was torn between the reckless desire to continue their rebel activities and the prudent impulse to lie low until the heat died down. Either way, Gavriel was correct that the cause of Ruthynian independence had long been fatally riven along religious and ethnic lines: the Tserkovian majority, of which the Kozhek horsemen were a small but significant part, were indifferent to the Vashemites at best and actively homicidal at worst. And despite both of them being

Tserkovians, the Ruthynians likewise hated the Kozheks, viewing them as shit-smeared rustics who did not properly appreciate the glory and valor of Ruthynian culture, and constantly attacked and undermined the Kozheks' attempts to break away from the Ruthynian world and its constant mourning for its overthrown tsars, swept away in the Meronite conquest six centuries ago. For them, any glorious new homeland therefore meant a strictly Ruthynian Tserkovian homeland, where Kozheks were assimilated and Vashemites were cast out. But the first step for a would-be freedom fighter of any stripe was actually getting shut of Meronite rule, which was going as well as ever. Viz., stacks of mutilated corpses in the woods.

"Excuse me," Julian said, during a brief lull in the argument, and gestured an apology as both Saul and Gavriel glared at him. "Do we have any idea of who actually *did* this?"

"No," Saul said darkly, "but we can guess. It had to be one of those Immortal monsters."

A collective shudder traveled the table, hands making signs against evil. The Immortals were the most feared of the Divine Emperor's military forces, consummate soldiers rumored to share in the same unnaturally long life as their master and to be able to destroy an entire enemy regiment single-handedly, which in this case looked like firm factual certainty. They could conjure knives from their bones, choke a man's breath, stop his heart and tear open his veins, without ever laying a finger on him. Yet for all that, they too were slaves, given the cognomen *Servus Eternus* – *Eternal Slave* – and said to have a piece of steel in their throat that could cut it at one word from a Corporalist, if they ever took such a mad notion as to go rogue or act against their orders. Not that it ever happened, or ever would (Spartekaius being the one and only exception). The Immortals became *Immortal* because they had no doubts, no second thoughts, not a whisper of defiance. They existed to enact Coriolane Aureus IX's vengeance, and nothing more.

"We really don't want to tangle with an Immortal," Gavriel's friend Timofey said, looking suddenly less assured of his appetite to continue the righteous struggle than he had been five minutes previously. "Are we sure that they're only going after Tserkovians?"

"We know nothing." Saul gave a grim little shrug. "Most of the attacks were in the west, so maybe it was easier to get there from Merone, there are more rebels in Iscaria because they're used to fighting the emperor over it, or they didn't want to bring it to Korolgrod. Murdering a few provincials is one thing, but a spate of high-profile deaths in the capital city would be quite another."

There was a grudging murmur of acknowledgment, even among Gavriel's partisans, at the truth of that. Every imperial province had its own fraught relationship with the seat of power in the Eternal City, though the Ruthynian Tserkovians had managed to make out better than some; the Governor-General was a Ruthynian, not a Meronite, and the boyars were well used to reaping money and influence off the great imperial machine. That added an additional wrinkle to any attempt to break free, in that it could crash the entire economy. Highfalutin moral concepts of self-determination, national independence, and restorative justice were all well and good, but they tended to swiftly wilt before the simple ability to put food on the table.

"We need to think carefully," Gavriel insisted. "If we take flight at our shadow, we'll squander everything. I'm not saying we should march down Ulitsa Velikaya with a drum-and-trumpet band, but we shouldn't do the goyes' work for them. If you don't agree – "

He glanced around pugnaciously in expectation of a challenger, but while Saul and a few others remained unconvinced, they didn't contradict him. At last Saul said, "Why don't we take it cautiously? Wait and see if there are more murders among the Tserkovian rebels, or hard evidence that an Immortal is deliberately targeting them. If nothing else, we can make sure we know who, or *what,* we're dealing with."

Gavriel grunted. "As long as this *wise delay* doesn't turn into an indefinite postponement. I think it's better to seize the initiative. If we could just make old Zogorov finally *suffer* – "

Everyone made the usual disgusted noises at the mention of the Governor-General – who, despite being ancestrally Ruthynian, was an odious Meronite toady to the point where even some of the boyars were open to the idea of deposing him, no matter how much money they made. But before they could pursue the fascinating question of what

Gerasim Balovoynich Zogorov might deserve and/or should be inflicted with, the innkeeper tapped Saul on the shoulder with a very unfriendly look. "Time to leave, Vash. Taproom's closing. Pay up and get out."

Saul hesitated, both out of fear that the man might have broken the spell and heard their seditious conversation — they were speaking Vashemysh, which most Tserkovians didn't understand, but there were always unexpectedly lurking ears — and the age-old reflex of a Vashemite suddenly approached by a hostile stranger. When the innkeeper didn't summon the torch-and-pitchfork mob, but just stood there with his hand out, Saul dug in his belt and removed several rubleks. "Here," he said, switching to Ruthynian. "For your trouble. We'll be on our way."

The innkeeper bit the gold to check — he was plainly familiar with the idea that Vashemites were miserly, tight-fisted cheats who would pass counterfeit coin if one's vigilance ever slacked — but could not protest. The young men got up and spilled onto the dark streets, heading in different directions but walking in twos and threes for safety. Julian tagged along with Yehudim, since they lived on the same side of the ghetto, but when Yehudim bid him good night and turned off, Julian had several more blocks to go. He kept to the shadows, moving quickly and quietly, a skill in which he had gained considerable experience since taking up with a band of rebels. Korolgrod was a sprawling stone-and-soot city of golden-domed churches and sharp-gabled roofs that climbed gentle hills, crissed and crossed the Vena and Voyna rivers, and ambled among parks and trees, garnished with flowers in summer and icicles in winter. Right now, in autumn, the chill was sharp enough for Julian to see his breath. But it wasn't much farther, so —

"You there! Halt!"

— of course, of course, of fucking *course* it would be the one damn time that the night watch spotted him. Cursing violently under his breath, Julian skidded to a halt and tried his best to look humble and unthreatening. He had removed his kharmulke, as most Vashemites did when traveling outside the ghetto, and since he otherwise dressed and looked Ruthynian, it was possible that he could get away with a warning. The two watchmen, clad in scuffed armor and wearing truncheons and shortswords, looked equally tired of staying out to round up curfew-breakers, but there was no way to predict how it would go. Either they would be bored, impatient, and in haste to wave him on, or they would make an example of him. It was always the same calculus of potential violence, but the equation never solved to the same answer twice, and Julian felt his heart speed up. Doing his best to affect a charming smile, he said, "Good evening, officers. Anything wrong?"

They eyed him, sullen and suspicious. "Name?"

"Julian Janovynich Kozharyev." He did his best to scrub any trace of Vashemysh from his accent, and *Yulian ben Yanov* was a dead giveaway. "I'm just on my way home."

"It's past Apodeirnon. You know that's the hour of curfew, yes?"

The late-evening prayer was a solely Tserkovian measure of time, and a Vashemite had no inherent way of knowing when it was, but pointing that out would be counterproductive. "Yes, sir. Of course. I just lost track of how late it was, but I'll be sure not to do it again."

"Where are you coming from?" The watchman stepped forward, sniffing ostentatiously at Julian's breath. "Have you been drinking, boy?"

"Just some. With supper. Nothing more, honest. Like I said, I'm headed straight home."

"And where's *home?*"

Julian hesitated. "Just up there."

The watchmen exchanged skeptical looks; this was one of the major streets leading into the ghetto, which they therefore patrolled at twice the frequency of its Tserkovian neighbors. As they took their sweet time about studying him, just to make it plain that they weren't buying this feeble charade and could cause trouble if they so decided, Julian fought down the usual simmering anger. Just then, he almost envied the Tserkovian rebels (or at least the un-murdered ones) for their simple agenda: get rid of the Meronites, set up home rule for their religion and people, profit. Yes, there would be hard feelings about the loss of the imperial golden goose, and the boyars wouldn't be happy; that was why the independence movement, such as it was, had yet to catch on outside the young and idealistic (and therefore penniless). But simply getting rid of the Meronites wouldn't solve the Vashemites' problems, and would just replace the old familiar devil with a new and lesser-known one. The

Meronites had not created the Tserkovian hatred of Vashemites, which was egged on by Ruthynians and Kozheks alike, and it would not vanish when or if they finally left. Indeed, the empire's official policy of religious tolerance theoretically protected the Vashemites from the violent pogroms routinely carried out in the old days, and if that was gone –

"Where are you coming from?" the first officer repeated. "You didn't answer me. *Boy.*"

"Yaroslav's tavern, on Ulitsa Semyenenka." It was a goy establishment, so that alone wasn't proof of his duplicity. Julian did his best to think of some Tserkovian sign or phrase he could offer, thus to casually prove his religious credentials, but he was afraid of doing it wrong and blowing his cover. "Can I be on my way now, please?"

They still looked as if they were thinking about it, but just then – both welcome and deeply not – a familiar voice split the air. "Yulya! Yulya, is that you? What are you doing here?"

Julian and the officers spun around – just in time to see his older brother emerge from a nearby door and hurry over, looking both anxious and angry. Isyk ben Yanov had recently landed a job as a clerk for a wealthy goy merchant, for which he was repeatedly reminded to be profusely grateful, and while he still had to live close to the ghetto, it was just far enough from the clearly-Vashemite part that he could likewise scrape past with not being identified. He reached Julian, made apologetic noises at the watchmen, and after a few kopyks changed hands, they finally consented to wave the Kozharyevs on their way. Isyk took Julian by the arm, and they marched down the street at a sedate pace. Then as soon as they had rounded the corner, Isyk whirled on him. "Yulya, what in Hashem are you thinking? Are you still running around with – *them?*"

Julian winced. "It's not what it looks like."

"Oh?" Isyk fixed him with a withering fraternal glare. "Then what *does* it look like?"

"I just..." Fuck. "Syka, I swear, it won't happen again."

Isyk treated this utterance with the thoroughgoing contempt it deserved, since it was in fact extremely likely to happen again and both brothers were well aware of it. "You've got to be careful. Haven't you heard that someone's murdering Ruthynian rebels?"

"Only Tserkovians, though," Julian said feebly. "At least, so far."

"That does *not* help." Isyk stamped forward and drove a finger into Julian's chest. "I won't ask how you know, since I won't like the answer, but you've got to find something to do. Of course it isn't fair that they didn't let you into university, after you had the best marks in school. But all that pent-up cleverness is *getting you into trouble."*

Julian started to answer, then stopped. He still felt that rejection keenly, to the point where he had contemplated making an application to the House of Wisdom in Bhagarayat or the School of Knowledge in Hang'i; both were serried ancient universities in cosmopolitan cities that would accept a Vashemite student without the endless muttering and obstacles that dogged him at home in Ruthynia. But the Sultanate of Parsivat and the Thearchate of Qin were very far away, he had nothing to make such a long and dangerous journey possible, and his mother would kill him before he could ask permission to go. So if he was stuck in Korolgrod, bumping around with nothing to do and no chance of a proper education, was it any *surprise* that this felt like the only choice? Isyk had been fortunate to get his job, but sitting in a cold warehouse and tallying up numbers until he went blind, patronizingly informed that he was good with money because he was a greedy Vashemite, was hardly Julian's idea of a scintillating future. There was a long pause as he and his older brother continued glowering at each other. Then Isyk dropped his hand and turned away, shaking his head. "You should get married. Oksyna has a younger sister."

Julian shuddered. He liked his new sister-in-law, Isyk's wife of six months, well enough, but the idea of being bundled into the khuppah with a smaller version of her was horrifying for any number of reasons. "You know I can't do that."

"Then – I don't know – move to Ibelus." Isyk raked a hand through his hair. "Vashemites are legally protected under the Concord, and they allow all sorts of questionable behavior."

"Thanks," Julian said acidly. *"Questionable behavior,* that's me. Do you really think Mata would let me go to Ibelus?"

"I think Mata would prefer not to see you dead." Isyk's voice was cold and flat, but there was a real, raw fear in it, and it sent a chill down

Julian's back. "Which the odds are good you will be, if you carry on like this. And since there will be no more fending off the shadchan if you keep sitting around Mata and Vata's house and doing stupid things whenever you aren't, I advise you to have a nice long think about this. Unless the bloody long-lost Ring of Tselmun suddenly turns up, which it won't, and the Vashemites regain our old kingdom on the spot, which we can't, we aren't getting some patriotic new homeland. It's a nice idea, but it's fiction. Fantasy. We have to live in the here and now and watch out for the real danger. Did you know the Konsilium is thinking about making us apply for a registration permit if we want to leave Korolgrod? Some of them thought we should need it just to leave the ghetto, but that was shut down. No saying, though, that it won't come back. That's what you and your idealists should try to stop, since Coriolane certainly won't. He doesn't care, especially about Vashemites, as long as there isn't open warfare and blood running in the streets."

There was, yet again, no way to dispute this. Pro forma Meronite religious tolerance might stop Vashemites from being slaughtered in their beds, but a Tridevarian emperor, Defender of the True Faith, had no interest in their civil rights, and if a pliant Governor-General and his puppet council wanted to persecute a few heretics, so much the better. To Julian's thinking, it was the perfect demonstration of the fact that they weren't safe either with the Meronites or without them, so why not just take the chance? But he knew Isyk didn't agree, and it was hard to blame him. It was so tangled and twisted, and while Julian was very proud of his people and his faith, he preferred to dress like a Ruthynian and go by the Ruthynian version of his name – both to avoid harassment and pretend that he really fit in, that these were his folk, that he could have a future in the place where he was born and raised. He understood why Isyk had given up on the big picture and thought the right thing to do was to make the best version of the small world in front of them, but the halakhic admonition always echoed in his head. *You are not obliged to complete the work, but nor are you at liberty to abandon it.*

"Look," Julian said, trying to break the impasse. "It's late, those bastards would love to arrest two Vashemites and not just one, and we should get home. Thanks for your... help."

Isyk eyed him banefully, sensing a decided lack of gratitude, but said nothing more. Instead he jerked his head in terse farewell, and the two Kozharyevs parted ways, Isyk turning back to the small flat he shared with Oksyna and Julian continuing to the family home, which stood at the corner of the Street of Gold and the Street of Weavers. Like its neighbors, it was a tall, narrow, half-timbered townhouse with a steep slate roof and mezuzim on the doorposts, and Julian's bedroom was on the third floor. This presented a logistical challenge insofar as his parents were unaware that he was not, at the moment, inside it. If he was to make it without being caught red-handed, inventive methods were required, and he slipped around the side, surveyed the none-too-sturdy drainpipe, and took a running start, clutching with all his might and shinning up. He almost plunged into the midden heap, which would be a fittingly shitty end to the evening, but it wasn't the first time (his climbing skills were also useful when it came to stealing from alchemists), and when he reached his window, he shifted his weight, pried it open, and somersaulted inside, landing with a muffled, muddy thump.

He lay flat for several moments, to be certain he had not woken anyone, then got to his feet. Undressed, washed, said a prayer, shut the window, and climbed into bed. But even then, Julian could not get to sleep. He knew he was on very thin ice, not least due to the run-in with Isyk; any more and his brother would inform their parents, particularly their mother, and anyone not healthily terrified of Mirym Kozharyeva was a far braver man than Julian. But what else could he do? He couldn't get married, the university wasn't going to let him in, and the Konsilium was enacting yet more stupid laws simply for the purpose of gleefully harassing Vashemites. As such, the rumored registration permit wasn't entirely a surprise, but it made Julian feel even more like a rat in a trap. Perhaps if he truly lost his mind, he could go to the Eternal City and sit for the entrance exams at the Imperial Academy of Merone. It was required to admit a set quota of students from every province, even Vashemites, and it might throw off the scent of his rebel activities – who, in that case, would willingly put themselves in the lion's den? But for that same reason, it also came with an extremely high likelihood of dying, and he wasn't that desperate. Not yet, anyway.

For the next week or so, Julian did his best to act as if nothing was wrong. This was easier than it would have been, since it was almost Tor Atornatu, the holiest day in the freshly minted Vashemite new year, and the ghetto was hurrying to prepare. Then came the solemn Day of Atonement itself, with fasting and prayers and hours-long service in shul, the sonorous ceremonial cadences of Old High Yerussalan rising and falling in rhythmic time, and Julian stood between his father and mother, his younger sisters Adina and Lyova on their other side. As the rebbitek offered a lengthy exegesis on a certain Vashach passage about sin and forgiveness, Julian wryly reflected that even if he was a rebel, at least he wasn't a Tridevarian. All their priests taught them was constant fear and blind obedience; expressing doubt or independent thought was tantamount to heresy. Vashemites, on the other hand, could ask all the questions they pleased, to come to grips with the tradition and learn and debate and disagree, and no matter what else could justly be said, he did not feel that anyone could accuse him of turning his back on what his people had taught him. In a sense, Vashemites were always outlaws, always needing to find their own way of surviving and singing about it later. No, the Ring of Tselmun was not going to reappear, and nor was it likely that Julian would uncover the long-lost formula to make Rebbitek Yudah's mighty clay golem, but he had to try.

Afterward, at the great sundown supper to break the holy fast and celebrate their renewed freedom from sin, Julian had just found a place at the long table when his mother appeared out of nowhere and eyed his plate with concern. Blithely ignoring his protests, she reached for the nearest bowl and spooned up an extra portion, then sat next to him. After they all intoned a final blessing and began to eat, she said, "Yulya, you haven't been getting into trouble again, have you?"

Julian did his best not to choke on his mouthful of kugel. When he swallowed, eyes watering, he said, "What makes you think that?"

"Don't be clever." Mirym gave her younger son a piercing look. "I was speaking to Oksyna, and she said Isyk is worried about you. She didn't want to say why that was, but eventually she did. He found you on the streets late, was it? Detained by the night watch?"

Ah, yes. Foiled again by his mother's unparalleled and mystical ability to know everything about everyone, especially her children, and especially when those children were fondly and futilely hoping that she wouldn't. At last Julian said, "I'm fine, Ma. Really."

"Hmm." Mirym eyed him skeptically. "It isn't fair about the university, but no use feeling sorry for yourself. If you aren't going to ask Syka to find you a job, it's more than time you were married. I've arranged for the matchmaker to come to the house and speak with you, and she has several candidates in mind. There's the Roshensteyn girl, Rebeka, remember her? Weren't you two good friends in yeshirim?"

"Mata – " Julian's mouth fell open in horror. Yes, he had been schoolfriends with Rebeka Roshensteyn, but not for the reasons she thought. He was twenty-three, certainly old enough to have a wife and household, and while his mother could be smothering, she was a firm believer in her children standing on their own feet and making their own life. She wasn't wrong to want the same for him, but the idea made Julian feel like he was about to throw up. "Are you sure we need to – "

"Don't worry, I know what's best for you." Mirym patted his hand. "You are a restless young man, anyone can see it. Of course we need to make some changes. And you will enjoy having a wife."

It was remarkable, Julian thought numbly, how profoundly incorrect she was in that regard, especially when she wasn't often wrong about other things. Yes, Isyk had warned him that the shadchan was lurking in his uncomfortably close future, but – stupidly – Julian assumed there would be more time. Not that there was any particular reason for that, as his mother was brutally efficient at everything and leaped into action to hammer a problem into bits as soon as she spotted it. Perhaps he *should* ask if he could move to Ibelus, but the words got stuck in his throat. If he did, he would have to explain why he wanted to go, and it just seemed too difficult and frightening to countenance. Isyk knew, and had loyally kept the secret, but his brother could otherwise have told anyone at all. At last Julian said, "Does Vata think this is a – "

"Your father agrees with me, of course," Mirym said, with the serene certainty of a woman whose husband *also* knew what was best for him. "He has paid for the first session already."

Fuck. Fuck, fuck, fuck, fuck, fuck, *fuck*. Julian stared down at his plate; even after a night and day of fasting, he was suddenly deprived of appetite. However, since he couldn't get away with not eating under the vigilant gaze of his mother, he nibbled a few bites and did his best to look as if he was enjoying it. He didn't remember the rest of supper, and spent a largely sleepless night. Then when dawn did not bring any better ideas, Julian decided to hell with it. He got up, dressed, and set off into the streets, which were veiled in a filmy mist off the Voyna. He sat at a coffeehouse until the hour was more decent, then got up, walked into the university district as if he belonged there, and searched the narrow side streets until he found Gavriel's door. He hoped that Gavriel himself would answer, and not one of the goy roommates, but he knocked.

It took a while, as students were not known for springing out of bed with the lark in any age of the world, but at last the door bumped open and a tousled, squinting Gavriel peered out with a suspicious look on his face. Upon seeing Julian, it relaxed somewhat, thus to be replaced with puzzlement. "Yulya? What are you doing here? It's so early."

"Yes, I know. Can I come in? We need to talk."

Not waiting for an answer, Julian shouldered inside and up the stairs to Gavriel's drafty attic bedroom. It was heaped with books, papers, and quills; he had gotten a place in the Faculty of Law thanks to a wealthy and well-connected uncle and a quiet agreement for said uncle to pay his tuition at twice the usual rate. In other words, it wasn't impossible for a Vashemite to get into the university, but only for a *rich* Vashemite, which the Tridevarians also despised. Forcing down his jealousy about that and several other things, Julian perched on the chair and said without preliminary, "My parents called the shadchan."

"Ah." Something passed over Gavriel's face: oblique, hard to read. He could count on his studies and the establishment of a career as a way to put off marriage, but it likewise could not be postponed forever. "Are you going along with it?"

"I don't have a choice." Julian stared miserably at the fogged window, the birds hopping along the roof. "Unless you – unless we – "

"Unless we what?"

"Unless we…" Fuck it. In for a shekel, in for a shtem. "I don't know. Ran away together."

"Ah," Gavriel said again, even more noncommittally. There was a long pause. Then he said as gently as he could, "Yulya, you know I like you very much, and I've enjoyed our time together. But I'm not about to abandon my place at the university, or my family, just for you."

"So what? All that insistence on the revolution, fighting on no matter what, and the first time it might cost you the minimum of personal sacrifice, you say no? I joined because of you, I got into this trouble because of you, and now what? You're leaving me out to dry?"

Gavriel shifted uncomfortably, glancing at the walls. Julian wasn't making an effort to keep his voice down, and as they knew from doing other activities in here, sound carried. "Yulya – "

"Don't *Yulya* me, you prick." Julian clenched his fists. "If I was just a nice distraction and you have no intention of following through, be so brave as to say so. If you're going to keep fucking wide-eyed young men and talking about glorious uprisings, so you can build a devoted following like you're the melekh mashiach – fuck you! *Fuck* you!"

"Come on." Gavriel got to his feet, hands outstretched, as if to contain a wild and dangerous animal. "Don't be like that. You knew this could never last for us. And you definitely don't need to come storming in at the crack of dawn like a scorned woman. If you want to collect yourself, we can talk about this. Otherwise – "

"No. You know what? Never mind. I don't need to talk about this later, or see you again. Good luck in your dreary, rules-abiding life as a dreary, rules-abiding lawyer. Not exactly the part you play in front of the others, is it? But you're just as much a coward as the rest."

With that, Julian got up, shoved out of the room, and hurtled down the stairs. Gavriel tried to shout after him, but he didn't stop to listen. The mist was pleasingly cool on his hot face, but didn't soothe it. Instead he bit his lip until he tasted blood, then raised his collar and blundered through the morning crowds without paying the slightest heed where he was going. When he next looked up, he was standing outside the Governor-General's gated mansion with its immaculate lawns, imperious turrets, and that fucking Meronite eagle all over everything, from the flapping standard on the roof to the gilded carvings on the gateposts. Just like it was before. Just like it always would be, because Gavriel ben Avraham Coheyn was a lying bag of wind and a total bastard, good luck to anyone who believed anything he said about anything – *if we could just make old Zogorov finally suffer* – which he wasn't going to do either, because he was a fucking *liar* –

At that, a mad, unthinking rage took hold of Julian from head to heel. Before he had any idea what he was doing, he leaned down and prized out a paving stone. Then he wound up and hurled it in a fury.

There was a frozen moment, as the stone flew over the fence and directly at the front window, in which Julian fully grasped what an appallingly stupid thing he had just done, and started to panic. But it was too late, and there was no way to call it back. The stone crashed into the glass and shattered it into a thousand pieces, there were shouts of outrage from the gatehouse, and the door burst open and ejected a dozen stoutly armed Meronite legionnaires, all of whom saw him at once and started to sprint. Julian did the only thing he could. He ran for it.

He did manage to lead them on a merry chase for several blocks, but there were six of them, one of him, and too many obstacles to have any hope of a stirring getaway. They finally cornered him in a back courtyard, swearing and reaching for their swords, and Julian went to his knees, hands sarcastically raised. They would kill him anyway, but let it be done to an unarmed, unresisting man, just to drive it home what heroes they were. He looked into their faces. He smirked.

The guard in front reached him first. He seized Julian by the hair, drew his knife, and jerked his head back in anticipation of cutting his throat, then stopped. He glanced at his commander, and they exchanged a few words in Lanuvian. Then the commander nodded and waved an irritated hand, the tone unmistakable. *Fine. Do it.*

Julian had a moment in which to contemplate, in the blackest of black humor, that if the Meronites and the murderous Immortal now decided to go after Vashemite rebels too, not just Tserkovians, he only had himself to blame. Then the soldier struck him over the head with the pommel of the sword, and almost gratefully, he lost consciousness.

CHAPTER

6

IONIUS

IT WAS REGRETFULLY UNAVOIDABLE THAT AFTER SPENDING several months in Ruthynia, the longest amount of time he had been there in quite a while, he would have the old dream. It was a mercy that he had almost forgotten it, that it was no longer like the early years where he sometimes had it almost every night, but its absence had not made it any less vivid. He was scared and small and helpless, a terrified five-year-old running through the chaotic hellmouth of burning cottages and screaming for his mother, but she never answered. There were only towering black shadows of soldiers like demons, hands snatching and voices cursing, a terrible pain where his vyshyvanka was slashed open and blood dripped down his back. Then he was thrown into a wagon with a few survivors – mostly women and children, vomiting and crying and stained with blood and offal and worse, but not his mother. Yet by a dark and terrible miracle, a blessing and a curse, there was his little sister, and they called out to each other. She crawled to him and curled into his side, and he tried to shelter her. *It'll be all right,* he whispered to her, knowing the words for a lie even then. *I'll look after you, Tatya.*

Of course, he did not. He was not even given the chance. He was just old enough to be a useful slave, a page boy for a rich family, but not her. When they tore Tatyana's hand from his and dragged her away, she made the most terrible sound a human throat could manage, a primal howl of agony a hundred times her size. Just as with his mother, he never knew when or where she died, only that she did. He was the only one left. He had, he was informed, been given the ultimate honor: the chance to work hard and become a true Meronite, washing away the terrified child, the prisoner of war seized from a no-account Ruthynian Kozhek village. And so he had. He had.

The dream ended as it always did: Ionius waking with a jerk, lathered in cold sweat, staring at the ceiling as the soft light of dawn flooded the window. This high up in the city, he could leave it open for a nighttime breeze without fear of perishing from the stink, though there was still a sour whiff from time to time. It took a few moments to catch his breath, reminding himself that it was for the best. He would not have become who he was now if not, and he was grateful.

Next to him, the quilts rustled as the handsome dark-haired young man rolled over, sensing his turmoil or simply trained to wake at any disturbance, thus to soothe and coddle a restless noble back to sleep. He was Ibelusian, slim and elegant, one of the many catamites kept to service the imperial court's various needs, and Ionius had not bothered to ask his name, as it was of no interest to him. The young man was satisfactory in other ways; indeed, Ionius had been sufficiently worn out to fall asleep without dismissing him, which was a foolish error. No courtesan dared to steal from an Immortal, but half of them were in the pay of some intelligencer or other, and it was a sordid routine to execute those whose employers turned out to be foreign governments. Everyone in the world wanted to know what was going on in the Eternal Palace, and since important people talked freely in the throes of pleasure, it was a useful gambit. Except with Ionius, who never said anything no matter how hard they tried. And some of them very much had.

"My lord?" the young man murmured. "Are you troubled? Let me ease you."

"No." Ionius pulled back, turning his head sharply away when the catamite sat up and attempted to kiss his neck. "Your services to me are over. You may depart."

The Ibelusian shook his head, as if remarking that the rumors of General Ionius' utter uptight humorlessness, even in the most private of moments, were proving sadly true. He had been well compensated for his night's work, though doubtless he wanted to make that bit extra before departing, but when he reached down and seductively trailed his fingers along Ionius' thigh, Ionius struck his hand away. "Did you not," he said, low and lethal, "hear me earlier?"

The expression on his face had successfully cowed entire enemy armies, and one pretty boy was in no way equipped to withstand it. He muttered a mortified apology, clambered out of bed, and gathered his money, shrugging into his silk robe and making a final reverence. Then he scooted out with the air of a rabbit pursued by a hawk, though Ionius himself had not moved. It was just the effect he had on people.

When the catamite was gone, Ionius leaned against the rumpled pillows and rubbed a hand over his scratchy chin, belatedly supposing that he could have done with a final round after all, but it was too late to change his mind. Besides, he needed to ensure that no spying had happened while he was asleep, so he too rolled out of bed and proceeded around the room, inspecting it in exacting detail, until he was finally persuaded that all was just as he had left it. Good, so the whore did not have a death wish. Ionius availed himself of this intimate companionship only infrequently, and he had already slept later than his usual habit. Very well, now it was out of his system, and he could get back to business. He pulled on his tunic, tabard, and boots, then shaved and scrubbed and departed, striding down to the barracks and bellowing at the recruits to wake up and stand at attention. Their training had been left to others while he was gone, and so far as Ionius was concerned, miserably suffered as a result. This was why he hated delegating.

Four hours later, when he had whipped the remaining two dozen through an unforgiving program of calisthenics, climbing, sword-sparring, knife-wielding, channeling, and other skills, the exhausted cadets were finally permitted to guzzle water and collapse in the shade. Ionius eyed them up, making mental lists. Only the best of the best became full Immortals, and no more than six of these had a shot at passing the graduation trials. The second tier were destined for legion command and other army posts. The ones who failed in the customary fashion were returned to their previous masters, but those who not only failed, but embarrassed themselves in doing so, were in danger of being handed over to the Corporalists. What happened to them next was another matter about which Ionius did not trouble himself, but they would likely be Remade, in hopes of serving more honorably the next time around. After all, they were just too valuable. Candidates were identified as young as three, training started in earnest at seven, and this lot, ranging between sixteen and twenty-one, were already veterans of at least a decade of the toughest perdition the Meronite military could dish out. There was no chance of letting that time and effort go to waste.

From time to time, a noble family tried to get its superfluous sons into the Immortals, usually out of a mistaken conviction that it would offer glorification of their name and solve a problem in the succession of the eldest brother, but in Ionius' experience to date, every single one had failed. Noble sons, even the spares, were simply too coddled and self-aware, too unwilling to undergo the utter unmaking and stripping to bare bone, the constant hardship and deprivation. As such, Ionius had recommended that the Immortals stop accepting freeborn applicants at all, though it was occasionally convenient to let families believe that they still had the option. It was better to craft them from the ground up, to choose them from Merone's limitless supply of slaves, whether domestically born or taken as the spoils of war such as he had been. That way, they were grateful. That way, they knew *this* was their home, their family, their future, and they were incentivized to fight for it. Besides, Ionius didn't consider himself to be a *slave,* not really. He had the *Servus Eternus* cognomen, yes, and he was bound in the customary ways, but he was a general, a leader, feared across the empire, one of Coriolane's few true confidantes and the de facto commander-in-chief of the entire Immortal order. What he said, went. What servitude was that?

Ionius dismissed the recruits and left the training yard, stepping into the Eternal Palace and enjoying the way his footsteps echoed. He had some notion of dropping in on the Thaumaturges and seeing if more information had arrived from Iscaria, but he was waylaid by another of the omnipresent eunuchs and obsequied off to the emperor's private quarters. Since visiting the imperial sorcerers was always a fucking ordeal in *some* way, this was possibly for the best.

Not, however, that what awaited was very preferable. Coriolane, it transpired, was in a particularly tetchy mood; when Ionius entered the imperial study, he found the emperor still in his night robes, a sure sign that his sleep had again been poor, and his face looked pouchy and sallow. He was seated behind his desk, shuffling a morass of papers and barking at the eunuchs, secretaries, senators, bookkeepers, bureaucrats, aides, advisors, pages, and other assorted toadies who anxiously orbited like a hundred moons around a vast heavenly body. When he spotted Ionius, he jerked up a fist. "Finally, someone with brains! Come here, General, and get these wittering old women out of my sight. Or throw them into the Colosseum, I can't say I would mind!"

The crowd performed a communal cringe, since there was always the possibility that this was not a rhetorical threat, but Ionius took it on himself to briskly herd them in the direction of the door. A few of the senators attempted protests, but since all the Meronite Senate did these days was to throw dissolute banquets, orgies, and chariot races, nobody needed their contribution anyway. Once the door was closed and the chamber cleared, Ionius turned back. "What is it, Majesty?"

Coriolane stared moodily at the vast map of the world painted on the wall, the Meronite dominions colored red as a proud reminder of the fact that the sun never set on it; even as it went down in one imperial territory, it rose in another. The only other color that even came close was the green of Qin, long the sole country that could call itself an actual challenger to Merone in any way. The current Thearch, Hang Zhai, had their own great magicians and oracles, alchemists and astrologers, soldiers and spies, and while they were not *quite* as old as Coriolane, they had now ruled the Thearchate for almost two hundred years – an astonishing record of longevity in Qin, with its constant palace intrigue, upstart and coup-minded generals, ambitious and cutthroat queens and concubines, and brutal wars and peasant uprisings. Holding onto their own head for two centuries, far less the Mandate of Heaven, was a monumental accomplishment, but as Ionius spotted several documents in hanqin, he suspected that this was precisely what was vexing Coriolane the most. Cutting to the chase, he said, "What has Qin done this time, Majesty?"

"They have had the unbridled temerity to inform me – *me* – that they are raising the import tariffs on all Meronite goods entering the Thearchate via the Spice Road, by up to *thirty percent*." Coriolane jabbed an accusatory finger at the most offensive of these communiqués. "This is a blatant attempt to freeze our merchants out of Qiné markets and start a protectionist trade war with Merone, since they know I must retaliate even more harshly. Then silk, spices, tea, porcelain, jade, ink, paper, and all the other Qiné luxury goods will become prohibitively expensive or unavailable, and the people will doubtless be foolish enough to blame me. And that is not the only poison Qin offers for sale. Look."

Ionius bent over Coriolane's shoulder, casting an eye down the document: it looked like a cargo manifest, written in hanqin that took a moment to mentally transliterate. It listed a hundred and fifty barrels of an unspecified substance at a handsome price: fifty copper Qiné wen apiece. This was about five golden Meronite aurei and thus a sum to make any enterprising criminal a wealthy man, but Ionius was still confused. "Majesty, forgive me, but what is this? Barrels of – what?"

"Black powder," Coriolane said darkly. "A devil's brew, something the Qiné have used for a long time. It's a potent explosive, a chemical compound that sets off their weapons: guns and cannons, far more effective than crossbows or catapults. And now, it seems, they have struck a secret bargain to sell it to my enemies. What is this but another open attempt to destabilize me, to support those fools who defy me? And of course, the Thearchate is there to move into any power vacuum and keep pressing westward. I will not have it! I will not *have* it! And if those Ruthynian imbeciles get their hands on it – "

"I doubt that anything could make a difference for those idiots," Ionius said soothingly. "Besides, do we have any proof that the Qiné *are* selling it specifically to Ruthynian rebels?"

"Indeed." Coriolane pointed angrily at the postscript, written in Ruthynian kyrillic instead of Lanuvian orthox. "That would seem to be proof enough. Tell me what it says, General."

"Ah." Ionius squinted; the scribe's handwriting was bad and they clearly had no idea what the foreign letters meant, were just crudely copying the shapes. "It says, 'Dear friends: This is the first shipment. The second half can be collected upon receipt of full payment to our associates in Sardarkhand. We will be in the city until the Feast of the Ancestors. We hope to see you then.' "

"See!" Coriolane fumed. "Utter blasphemy, naked defiance. And they intend to buy more!"

"Was this taken from a Ruthynian messenger, Majesty?"

"It was seized during a routine customs inspection at the Tibir docks, from a man who gave it up under persuasion that he was bound for the residence of Vadim Khovanyich, a well-known community leader of the Ruthynian quarter. Of course, we sent a legionnaire to arrest him, but he must have been forewarned, because he has already fled the city. And the inquisitors were somewhat too zealous in their work, as the messenger has been left in no fit state to speak. We need a new informant, someone who can tell us what the Ruthynian rebels are planning and how deep their connections with Qiné arms dealers might go. And indeed, by the Mother's mercy, we happen to have one."

"What?" Ionius was startled. Following his orders, he had brought back no prisoners and left no one alive; had merely killed them all, cleanly and completely. "Who?"

"A fluke," Coriolane said carelessly. "An accident. Someone arrested in Korolgrod, who they thought was merely a local ragamuffin, but turned out to be a person of interest in one of the major local Vashemite agitator groups. He's been brought here, to Merone, and is currently our captive. Perhaps you might be able to get him to talk."

"Who is this – some useless drifter?" Ionius spoke rashly, before he could think better of it. This all sounded considerably flimsy and circumstantial to his meticulously drilled military brain: a no-account messenger conveniently too incapacitated by torture to talk further, the dubiously obtained name of a man who had already left the city in great haste, a badly-written message addressed to nobody, and a random prisoner categorically unlikely to be any different from the rest of the chaff scraped off the streets. "And did you say he's a *Vashemite?* That's especially pointless. Their rebels don't work with the Tserkovians, they don't trust them, so I don't see how this poor bastard could tell us anything we really need to know. Besides, the policy of – "

Ionius was brought up short by a sudden metallic pressure on his throat, something directed by a wave of Coriolane's hand, a threatening sharpness on vulnerable veins. "I beg your pardon," the Divine Emperor said, cold as a glacier. "Are you *questioning* me?"

"I…" Heart pounding, Ionius waited until the terrible choking sensation started to subside. "No, Majesty. No, of course not. Forgive me, I was intemperate. What was it you wanted of me?"

"That's better." Coriolane broke his basilisk stare, but the thrall still took a moment to fade. "The boy is allegedly a close associate of Gavriel Coheyn, one of the Korolgrodian rebels recently brought to our attention as a problem. I am aware of the complications in dealing with Vashemites, but I hardly think it fair that we treat them more gently than Tserkovians – who, even if they are deviants, are still technically Tridevarian. Besides, the Vashemites are like the Bodeni. If we kill them, people will not care, or will approve, or find a reason to justify it. And while the protection applies to their race as a whole, it surely does not to individuals who knowingly break the empire's laws. Otherwise we'd have to spare the lot of them for every crime, and that will *not* happen."

"Well reasoned, my lord. May I see that letter again?"

"Why? What for?"

"I want to ensure that I read it correctly. If we are obliged to intercept a meeting in Sardarkhand, it would be good to be certain."

"Is this not your own people's speech, General? Why would you not be certain?"

"I – " Ionius bit his tongue. He knew Coriolane was supremely uninterested in the fact that while his spoken Ruthynian was native, his reading was not. He had learned one or two letters from his family's prayerbook, but the rest was thanks to a tutor hired by his first Meronite mistress, the one who bought him as a five-year-old. She felt that it was her pious Tridevarian duty, and also wanted him to secretly read her husband's correspondence; he did business in Ruthynia, traveled there often, and she wished to be sure that his foreign clients were not cheating him (or indeed, sleeping with him). "Never mind, Majesty," Ionius said. "I am certain. And if we do seize a shipment of black powder, we can hand it over to the legions, or perhaps – "

"No." Coriolane shook his head. "I want all of it destroyed. No excuses, no delays."

"Why? If our enemies are using it, should we not do the same?"

"Why should we release that snake in our own house? If any village idiot can learn how to use a gun, that is exactly why they should never have it. I prefer that such power remains where it belongs: in the hands of those who know what a privilege it is to wield, and train carefully and continuously to do so. The Qiné can put their faith in commoner party tricks if they wish, but in the long term, who do you think will win? Some shit-smeared peasant with a flash bomb, or someone like us, with *magic*? What that infernal powder *will* do is give people ideas they cannot carry out, cause chaos and suffering, and trouble them with a burden that they have no need to bear. The weight of power, the right to rule – that is what I selflessly take on for them."

"Yes, Majesty. I understand. The powder will be destroyed. On that note, how do you want me to question the Vashemite? Is there something you think would be especially effective?"

"I leave it to your considerable ingenuity, General. As I said, it would be best not to damage him past repair, at least until we learn how much he knows. If he turns out to be useless, you may dispose of him how you please. He's in the Castel Sanctangel." Coriolane waved a hand and turned away. "Tell the guards I sent you."

Ionius nodded crisply and took his leave, descending through the Eternal Palace and into the underground tunnel that connected it to the Castel, the most feared of all the imperial prisons. It was an ancient drum tower first built in Lanuvium's day, reinforced and reconstructed and woven with defensive innovations both ordinary and otherwise, extending deep into the earth. Prisoners who went down there did not tend to come out again, and some cells had been occupied for years, but for most, their stay was never too long. The cold, the damp, the dark and filth, the rats and starvation, the disease and despair – it gave the gravediggers a steady business, hauling out corpses and dumping them in the lime pits along the Tibir. A prisoner in the Castel had no name or family, no law and no memory. Thus it always was with traitors.

Ionius reached the dungeons, informed the guards of his plan, and stepped around the corner to remove his tabard, armor, and boots, rip his tunic, and smear mud onto his face. Then he flexed his fingers, drew the metal from his wrists, and formed it into a blade, cutting his cheek and letting the blood run down his chin; it would heal swiftly, but he only needed the initial effect. Then he shaped a pair of cuffs, locked them around his wrists, and added a chain. Transformation complete, he stepped back and nodded to the soldiers. It still took a moment for them to work up the nerve, because they had to be convincing but not *too* convincing, but two of them seized him and marched him off. Torches flickered outside heavy stone cells, barred and rusted and dripping with filth, and the smell of suffering was wet and rank. There were noises from inside – muttering and moaning, screams and scratches – but he ignored them, and so did the guards. They reached the cell at the end of the block, where the guard unlocked the door and jerked it open. "In there," he ordered, shoving Ionius across the threshold. "Fucking traitor."

Ionius added an extra stumble and went to his knees in the fetid straw, dodging a final kick that, all things considered, the guard wasn't trying *too* hard to hit him with. He remained on all fours and breathed shallowly, though the occupant hadn't been in here long enough to make it really stink. The Vashemite was slumped against the wall, regarding his new cellmate with hostility, wariness, and muted curiosity. He had an unruly mop of dark hair, olive skin, and strikingly dark eyes, almost black. Fettered only on his wrists, not his ankles, so they must not think he was a threat. Vata Korol, this was useless, but fine, then. *Fine.*

"Hello," Ionius said in Ruthynian, trying to decide what character he was playing this time. Not the timid tax collector who enticed Oleg and friends into snatching him almost by sheer uselessness, but someone else, beaten but still defiant. He always enjoyed this part: conjuring a compelling illusion and a different persona, drawing out the enemy's stratagems and dulling their stings before they even knew that they were in danger. It was generally a more productive way of uncovering information than immediately tipping them off who they were talking to, and the shock at the great reveal was always viscerally satisfying. "I – I don't know what I'm doing here, but – "

The Vashemite grunted, but didn't answer. At last, however, he said, "Probably the same thing as the rest of us. Where are you from?"

"Severolgrod." Close enough, since it was where he had last been in Ruthynia, and Ionius had forgotten the name of the village where he was born. "You?"

"Korolgrod." The Vashemite tilted his head, regarding Ionius with those unsettlingly black eyes. "You're a Kozhek? I didn't know they lived around there."

Ionius was caught on the hop, both by the fact that the other man had picked up his ancestry in the course of a few words and by the realization that he had made a stupid mistake. The Kozhek horselords' ancestral territories were in western Ruthynia; their distant cousins, the Ahyuns, prowled the eastern steppes and made life difficult for the Qiné. But Severolgrod was well south of their traditional borders, they didn't often live in cities, and Ionius was careful not to hastily retract or apologize, as that would likewise be suspicious. "Ask my family, then."

The Vashemite took that in inscrutably. He looked dirty and drawn, gaunt and hungry, but not fundamentally broken, drained and empty the way the Castel prisoners all inevitably became. "I'm Julian. Janovynich."

"Ilya Sergeynich." Ionius lifted his cuffed wrists, as if to point out that a handshake was presently something of an impossibility. "I would say it was a pleasure to meet you, but…"

Julian barked a mirthless laugh. "Not really, no."

"So what did you do to get thrown in this pisspot?" Ionius edged closer, settling himself more comfortably in the dirty straw. "Dared to gaze too long at a Tridevarian in the street, or – ?"

Julian threw him a sharp look, but he must have picked up the sarcasm, because he laughed again. "Threw a rock at the Governor-General's house, in Korolgrod. But they must be hard up for inmates, if they bothered to drag me all the way to Merone. What about you?"

"Beat up a tax collector in Tseyabilsk." Ionius shrugged. "I assure you, he deserved it."

Julian raised a slightly wicked eyebrow, as if to remark that tax collectors by their very nature always deserved it, and Ionius bit back an inadvertent smile. They sat in silence, bathed in the filmy grey light, and

Ionius pondered his next move. It was clear that even shut in here, Julian was not about to openly confess to traitorous activities, which was probably wise, and Ionius could not seem too knowledgeable about his background without giving himself away. It was likewise apparent that he had to be careful; Julian had immediately caught his first slip, and Ionius could not assume that he would get away with another. It was a shame that the Vashemite was the first halfway intelligent rebel he'd met, but it did not change the game.

"You been in here long?" Ionius asked instead. "They haven't tortured you, have they?"

"Not long." Julian blew out a breath. "And no, they haven't tortured me, but that doesn't mean they won't. This is what I get for running away from home, I suppose. Unless I suddenly sprout wings or find the Ring of Tselmun, as I was reminded that I won't, I'm not – "

"Ring of Tselmun?" It sounded faintly familiar, but Ionius couldn't place it. "What's that?"

"Old Vashemite story. You know, King Tselmun – the wise, the famous, the magician-king of ancient Yerussala? And the Ring he worked his wonders with. There's a whole argument about where it might be now. If it was destroyed at Tselmun's death, stolen by the Meronites when the First Yerussalan Kingdom was overthrown, stolen by the Bhagrads when the Second Yerussalan Kingdom was *also* overthrown or in any of the many, *many* sacks afterwards, if it's still out there somewhere, if it can lead the Vashemites to the promised land. It's only a legend, though. Tselmun himself was a real person, or at least our tradition says he was, but what does anyone know for sure? There are plenty of rebbiteks who think the Ring is just a parable, a metaphor, a cautionary tale about how sitting on your arse and waiting for a miraculous deliverance will make you lose the chance you do have, and old Yerussala was only great because everyone worked for it. Not only Tselmun, and not only with magic."

"You're clever." Ionius was impressed. "Are you at the university?"

"What?" Julian shot him a funny look. "Do they ordinarily let Vashemites into the university at Severolgrod now? Because I assure you that they fucking don't in Korolgrod."

Shit. Ionius bit his tongue. "I just thought you might have come by an exception."

"My family isn't rich enough to bribe them." Julian shrugged with attempted nonchalance, but the bitterness cut like a knife. "So no."

There was another pause. Ionius needed to move this conversation toward the necessary information he had come here to find, but in the name of thoroughness, he had to be sure. "So this Ring. This great magical weapon. It definitely doesn't exist?"

"*Definitely* is a slippery concept with Vashemites." Julian leaned against the wall. "But no, I don't think so. And if it does, trust me. Nobody is ever going to see it again."

CHAPTER 7

ALIYAH

The first thing Aliyah realized was that she was screaming at the top of her lungs – which, given the situation, seemed like an eminently correct and reasonable course of action. The next thing she realized was that she was in midair and falling out of it like a rock, which only increased the screaming. Wind hissed and whipped past her face, she tumbled head over heels, she flailed and grabbed at nothing, her skirt snarled her legs and her veil choked her mouth, and all she could see was the sunset high above and the tiny toy walls and buildings of Yerussala impossibly far below. She had been launched into the thin blue yonder, she was going to fall for miles and then she was going to die, and she had absolutely no idea why. The last thing she remembered was trying to polish the ring, that useless scrap that the old merchant so insistently foisted on her, and then –

It was hard to put into words what exactly had happened next, the comprehensive break in the fabric of reality that led to her current airborne predicament. It was an explosion, or at least something like it, and then the world was gone. Even as she screamed, the wind punched her breath out like a fist, and then an *actual* fist – huge, flame-skinned, burning – seized her and jerked her toward a terraced hillside of orchards and olive groves, which would definitely kill her when she hit. But then another fist grabbed her, whirled her the right way up, and set her almost daintily on her feet, no harder than if she had jumped from a minor height. However, her legs were shaking so hard that they instantly gave out, and she crumpled into the dirt. It felt safer to keep lying there, eyes screwed shut, than to even attempt getting up.

Nonetheless, her slavishly grateful reunion with solid ground was not fated to continue for long. A savage orange glow beat against her eyes, and when she opened them a crack, she saw that the ring had landed on the index finger of her right hand. When she tugged it frantically, it didn't come off. This was bad enough. Then she looked up.

The creature – the *thing* – standing in the shadows of the vineyard, blazing so brightly that Aliyah screwed up her eyes, was beyond question not human. For one thing, it was twice as tall as a man, for another it was on fire, and for a third – well, there were other reasons, but she was still hung up on the whole *on fire* part. Its skin was the brilliant orange of a glowing coal, and its eyes were a feral demonic yellow. In face and form, it looked vaguely like a king of one of the ancient near eastern civilizations – Ur-Arakkian or Assyranian, perhaps, with an ink-black topknot and braided beard, a white loincloth, and thick etched-gold torques on its neck and wrists. It surveyed her as if she was a sand flea or something else tiny and vexing to be swiftly squashed, and when it spoke, flames roared in its throat like a furnace. *"WHO ARE YOU?"*

Aliyah just stood there with her mouth open, quaking like a leaf.

"Not very bright, clearly." The fire-creature made a scolding noise, shrank down to a more manageable size, and dimmed its blinding shine. *"Can you shut your mouth? Let's start there."*

It took a titanic effort, but Aliyah did so. She felt her jaw click, her teeth collide, catching her tongue. Comprehension seeped slowly into her brain, something she would have scoffed off five minutes ago, but which was the only logical explanation. "You – you're a *jinnyeh*."

"Yes. Did you not expect that? Most humans who rub their grubby paws on a jinnyeh vessel do plan for us to pop out, so they can get straight to the wishing-for-money-and-power-and-eternal-life part like the greedy little toerags they are. But you *didn't* know, did you?"

"N-no." Aliyah was tempted to pinch herself, but it would do no good. "I just – "

The jinnyeh cocked its head, sizing her up. "In that case," it said. "It can be argued that since you didn't know what you were doing and didn't consciously intend to summon me, I don't have to grant you any wishes. Though you *are* wearing the Ring and you don't look like Tselmun, so you have a lot of explaining to do. Sneaky little grave-robber, are you? Naughty, naughty."

"No!" Aliyah raised both hands, panicking. "I didn't steal it! I don't – there was an old man, a merchant, he gave it to me, I didn't want it. I'm not even sure where – "

Just then, the other thing the jinnyeh (the *jinnyeh* – had she hit her head and woken up in Shahrzad's tales?) had said belatedly percolated. She looked at the ring, her hand, back at the ring, then at the enormous fire-creature. "Wait. Did – did you say *Tselmun?*"

"You seem stupider than the average human." The jinnyeh's fiery skin dwindled down to something more ordinary, a warm dark brown not far off from Aliyah's own. "Yes, I did, and even for a dust-blooded mortal, I thought it would ring a bell. Ancient Yerussalan autocrat with a silly beard, a fancy crown, and a rather high opinion of himself? T-s-e-l-m-u-n. Surely you've heard of him, or at least seen him. They had quite a lot of statues. Or they did, last time."

"But," Aliyah said faintly. "Tselmun ben Dayoud? He's dead. He's been dead for – I don't know – thousands of years. Yerussala's not – well, the city's here, but the kingdom has been gone for just as long. I don't – you can't be saying that you're – that this – that you – "

"I know *that.*" The jinnyeh rolled its yellow eyes. "If Tselmun hadn't finally croaked, I would never have gotten a single eon's peace. Which makes it all the weirder that now here *you* are, little mite, and you plainly have no idea just what you have on your finger. Here, now. You don't want that awful monstrosity. Give it to me."

"I'm *trying.*" One final twist and wrench of the ring, but no grace. Instead it just dug in harder, and Aliyah winced in pain and let go. "I don't – I don't think I can."

The jinnyeh hissed, a steaming sulfuric gust that caused sparks to leap from the ground, and Aliyah flinched. She was only now regaining her senses after the terrifying whirlwind, and she realized that they had landed on one of the steep hillsides that overlooked the Holy City, its rooftops an insignificant scatter in the gathering dark. The force of the – unleashing, the uncorking, the summoning, whatever in blessed Ur-Malika's name had just happened – must have launched her out here, and if someone came along and saw *this*, there was no way to know what could happen. But that wasn't her biggest problem. She needed to get back into the city before curfew, when the gates were shut and locked until dawn, and being stuck out here with a fiery and exceedingly smart-mouthed mythological being was not a tonic to ease the nerves. How was it even *possible?* Every Wahin child knew the stories of the jinnyeh: greater than men but lesser than angels, magical, shape-shifting, and essentially immortal beings, creatures of air and fire who rode in the high winds and hot sands and menaced travelers, congregated in old ruins and abandoned places, and could be tricked into entering a bottle, a lamp, a ring, or some other enspelled object, whereupon the price of their freedom was three wishes. They featured in Shahrzad's tales in a variety of guises, from openly villainous to sacrificially heroic, but all the legends agreed on their duplicity, their weakness for human pleasures, their hot-headed and quarrelsome nature, and their general untrustworthiness. Which seemed to be true; this one had already tried to litigate her out of her wishes by arguing that because she hadn't summoned it with the intention of making them, they could not be granted. But even through the shock, Aliyah was aware of something else. Something... powerful.

"What's your name?" she said. "If you're a jinnyeh, a demon – "

The jinnyeh winced. "Those," it informed her coldly, "are not the same thing, and I will thank you not to make that mistake again. But for your reference, I am the Most Great and Glorious Khasmedeus, All-High Lord-Queen of Shedim and Devs, Archduke of Jinnyeh, High General of the Golden One, also known as Hammadai, Osmedeth, Shedonui, Aeshmeda, etcetera, *etcetera*. Indeed, to recite the full list of my names and exploits would become tedious, as it would take a very long time and your tiny brain could not comprehend the magnitude of my accomplishments, so – "

"Khasmedeus?" Aliyah blurted out, interrupting the jinnyeh before it could get into the full flow of its self-aggrandizing biography. "Isn't there a famous story about you? *King Tselmun and Khasmedeus?* He bound you and many other jinnyeh with the Ring and made you build his great Temple, and you retaliated by trying to literally throw him out of Yerussala?"

The jinnyeh blinked, genuinely startled for the first time since its manifestation. *"Also* for your information, little human," it said tartly, "I didn't just *try*. I *succeeded* in launching that two-bit tyrant oiled head over perfumed arse into the Mad ar-Hahrat, and it was a great pity for everyone that he accidentally managed to climb out. But you don't want to hear about that. At least not unless I had a suitable amount of time, say a fortnight or two, to relay the story properly and convey in exquisite and loving detail how very stupid he looked, how many crabs pinched his royal buttocks with their claws, and how deeply satisfying it was. Even the wives and concubines could not deny it was nice to get a little peace, when I was a better Tselmun than he was. So – "

"So it is you." Aliyah kept staring. "And you're not actually saying this is *Tselmun's* – "

"It would be a cold day Below before I mistook that awful thing." Khasmedeus regarded it balefully. "Stop waving it at me, you glorified monkey! You don't know what you're doing!"

"Sorry." Aliyah lowered her hand, though the unnatural warmth of the ring – the *Ring?* – flickered steadily against her finger. A germ of something, a sudden and wild idea, had put down roots and was starting to sprout, as much as she reminded herself that she needed to get rid of it or find the person the old merchant actually intended it for. There was nothing good to come of being mixed up with it, and yet – at least if this was not an increasingly unhinged and highly colorized dream – she was standing in the presence of an ancient legend come to life, an all-powerful magical creature who boasted about physically flinging *King Tselmun* into the sea, and it seemed foolish to too-hastily disavow it. "So if I have it, what does that mean? Can I – command you?"

Khasmedeus regarded her with hooded eyes. After a long pause, it said, "More or less."

"Even if you tried to claim otherwise?"

"When did I do that?"

"Just earlier. You said that if I wasn't intending to summon you, I couldn't ask for wishes." Aliyah folded her arms. "So what is it?"

"Typical. Quaking with terror one moment, demanding to know the fine details of magical contract law the next. Yes, *technically*, according to Tselmun's *enslavement* of myself and my kin, the holder of the Ring has the right to induce, invoke, compel, coerce, or otherwise make unlimited use of the Spirit of the Ring – which would, for the laggards among us, be me. That said – "

"Unlimited? So it's more than three wishes? It's – *permanent?*"

Khasmedeus eyed her mulishly. "You *are* going to be a problem."

"I'm not Tselmun. I'm not a magician, I'm Wahin. If I just – "

"Ah yes," the jinnyeh said sourly. "Don't worry, you're a Revelator! That makes everything all right, does it? Ooh, I feel *so* reassured."

"I can't get the stupid thing off, remember?" Aliyah gave it a few more yanks, just to prove it. "So I have to think. In the meantime, if you could just… bring me back to where I was before? In Yerussala, at the caravanserai?" She thought about it, then added, "Please?"

For a moment, she thought Khasmedeus was going to defy her. But it must be true that wearing the Ring gave her some innate mastery of its magic, because the jinnyeh, still looking baleful, raised its hand and snapped its fingers. A spark bloomed, a vortex burst up from the ground and engulfed Aliyah in dust, and when it cleared, she was standing at the exact spot she had been before, once more safe in the caravanserai and the city walls. She looked down, looked up, looked around, touched her face to confirm that she was present and correct, and then kept standing there, comprehensively and excusably stunned. Out of nowhere, a bolt from the blue: an incredible gift, an ancient and legendary weapon. She had been called *Princess;* someone thought she was truly special, and not just the underachieving, undistinguished daughter of a mid-ranking Adirim family from a fringe desert province. She could prove to her mother, to Elemai, to the aspiring Qartic freedom fighters, that she was not just a passive stand-in, an abstract representation of ur-Namasqa resolve – if she had the *Ring of Tselmun,* surely the ur-Tasvashtas would have to accept her suit. Obviously she had to be careful. She didn't know if this was a trick or a trap. But if it *worked –*

Aliyah stood for a final moment, looking down at her finger and the glint of gold. Then she clutched it to her chest like her firstborn child, glanced around shiftily, and went inside.

The next several days passed in a whirl. There was business to attend, meetings to hold and exchanges to make, coins to count and goods to purchase, and Aliyah could not think of the best way to take Elemai aside and share the news that their lives were changed. Elemai had said she was a hafiza of Shahrzad's tales; she must be intimately familiar with jinnyeh, but surely she would think that Aliyah was mocking her, or playing a cruel prank. Aliyah wasn't even sure that anyone apart from herself could actually *see* Khasmedeus, and was too afraid to summon it again to check. Her new piece of jewelry had gone unremarked, possibly because it still looked dirty, dingy, and hardly worth the time of day. It remained unshakably fastened to her finger.

Her chance arrived a few days later, in the form of another unsettling event. The delegation had attended sardiq at the Ur-Almasur Mahqasa, one of the holiest sites in Wahinism, and was returning to the caravanserai, climbing the steep twilit streets and breathing the vespertine scent of cedar, juniper, and palm. The guild-soldiers led the way, lanterns raised and saifs vigilantly at the ready, and it was from Captain ur-Vorrosq that Aliyah heard the muffled murmur of surprise and alarm. He held up a hand. "Stay back, saedas. Wait here."

"What's wrong?" Elemai hurried to the front, throwing the drape of her headscarf over her shoulder and rolling up her sleeves. Aliyah did the same, and could just make out a small crumpled shape in front of the gate. One of ur-Vorrosq's men unclasped his cloak and threw it over the form. At the sight, Elemai's frown deepened. "Wait, is that a – "

"Avert your eyes, saeda, please. It is not a – "

Ignoring him, Elemai stepped past, knelt down, and flipped up the cloak, setting off a wave of gasps. The gruesome spectacle thus revealed was the butchered body of the old brass merchant, his throat slashed with such viciousness that it had taken his head half off. A sticky pool of blood had congealed beneath him, almost black in the torchlight, until Aliyah looked again and realized it *was* black. His eyes were open and staring, and they were, she recognized, the same unnatural gold as Khasmedeus's.

His goods were spilled across the ground, the sack ripped open and the brassware's suspect quality not improved by being thrown everywhere. As if someone had attacked the old man, cut his throat, and rummaged through it in search of something, *something* that might be on Aliyah's finger at this very moment, and she buried it in her robes, feeling as guilty as if she herself was the murderer. She wasn't, was she? Not by her own hand, but if the old man had come looking for her – if the attacker believed she could be found here – if they came back –

"We should get inside," Aliyah said nervously. Once they were safely indoors with the gates latched, a double watch of armed men sent to scour the streets and surrounds, she waited. When Elemai stepped inside, Aliyah plucked her sleeve. "We need to talk."

Elemai looked puzzled, but led the way to her private room. She pulled the door open, bundling them inside. When it wedged into place with a weighty and reassuring thunk, Aliyah said, "Did Captain ur-Vorrosq know who it was? The man who was killed?"

"Some local merchant or other." Elemai frowned. "They thought the poor soul's name was Diyab. It's upsetting, but – "

Aliyah took that in. When the old merchant had ambushed her at the bazaar, Captain ur-Vorrosq hadn't seemed to notice him or know that he was there, but evidently death had made him as visible as any other – well, she was going to say *man,* but she was not sure. "Do you think it's safe to stay? If people are murdered on our front stoop – "

"I was thinking of renting a property for the winter, yes." Elemai pursed her lips. "It would be more comfortable, and I am not interested in whether this is a repeat occurrence. What did you want to say to me?"

"I – " Malikallulah, this was difficult. "The old man – I met him before, actually. A week ago, in the bazaar. He gave me something."

"He *gave* you something?" Elemai's gaze turned sharp. "What?"

"This." Aliyah drew her hand out and raised it in front of Elemai's face. "This ring. And that's not all. It's not an ordinary ring."

"That?" Elemai stared at it quizzically. "It looks like – "

"Junk. But it's not. It's – it's magical. More than that – this sounds insane, I know, I *know,* but you have to believe me. It's – " Aliyah took a breath. "It's *King Tselmun's* ring."

Elemai's face remained blank. Finally, slowly, she repeated, "King Tselmun's ring."

"Yes. Tselmun ben Dayoud, the magician-king – you know who he is. I don't know why the old man gave it to me, where he found it, or who attacked him, but – don't you see? If this is real, if we have a weapon like this – our mothers, the uprising, everything against Merone that we've always wanted to do but never had the ability – "

"*Shhh!*" Prattling on about long-lost magical rings suddenly returned to the here and now was one thing, but open discussion of very real and present treason was another. Elemai darted forward and clapped her hand over Aliyah's mouth. "Aliyah, you've had a shock, but – "

"No. *No,* I'm not some gullible simpleton. Look. *Look!*"

With that, convinced that Khasmedeus would not appear just to spite her, or perhaps dramatically blow the roof off, Aliyah rubbed the ring as before. For a long moment, just as she feared, nothing happened. Then a diaphanous mist started to hiss into the room, and Elemai turned in a confused circle. This, on the last revolution, brought her face-to-face with Khasmedeus the jinnyeh, barely visible except as a rakishly grinning ghost, its sharp black teeth bared and its eyes turned to feral pits of flame. "Well," it drawled. *"Hello* there, little lady."

Elemai screamed at the top of her lungs, lashed out, and stumbled back against the bedstead. Then – at least that answered the question of whether the jinnyeh was visible to other people – she looked at it, at Aliyah, back at it, and demanded, "What in the – what the *hell?!?!*"

A chaotic interlude of attempted explanation followed, mostly by Aliyah, while Khasmedeus chipped in unhelpful asides and sarcastic comments. Finally, however, Elemai grasped the essentials, continuing to look stunned and inexplicably furious. Then she regained her wits enough to level the jinnyeh with a narrow stare. "And we're supposed to just take your word for it? That this is *the* Ring of Tselmun, *you* were the spirit who performed his greatest magic, and that we, by virtue of some utter accident that Aliyah cannot explain and where the only other witness was just murdered, can use that limitless power as we please? With no consequences at *all?*"

"You two *really* aren't magicians, are you? Of course there are."

"And these consequences are?"

"Bad things, generally." The jinnyeh changed shape to a tiny man in a swimming costume, doing the backstroke in the remnants of its mist. Its voice notably squeakier and higher-pitched, it added, "Doom. Destruction. Ironically self-fulfilled prophecies in which you are given exactly what you thought you wanted, only to realize it was the agent of your downfall all along. You've read the stories about this, haven't you? Slightly less stupid human?"

"If you are referring to me," Elemai said coolly, as she and Aliyah glowered at it in unison, "yes, I am *quite* familiar with Shahrzad's tales about you and your kin, and the woe and trouble that comes to humans who rely too much on your so-called help. Hence my reservations. You have not even proven that you are *the* Khasmedeus, so – "

"Outrageous. Blasphemous calumny." The jinnyeh swelled indignantly back to its original size, waving a finger beneath Elemai's nose. "How could anyone else ever be me?"

"I don't know." Elemai folded her arms. "Convince me."

Aliyah's initial shock had transformed into entertainment at watching Elemai and Khasmedeus bicker, but something important was being forgotten here, and she cleared her throat. "This is well and good, but *I* have the Ring. I have to be the one to command him."

"Excuse me," Khasmedeus interrupted. "I am not a *him*. I am not a man *or* a woman, and never have been. I can take the shape of both or either, or nothing at all, and it matters less than a brass monkey's balls. You humans, always so miserably and bestially obsessed with what someone's got between their legs. The ways in which I refer to myself in the tongues of jinnyeh are multifarious, beautiful and changeful as the wind, but for your muddy and unprecise mortal vernacular, I do prefer *it*. If we're making any pretense of caring what *I* think."

"Sorry. Command *it*." Aliyah turned to Elemai. "Well?"

For a moment as Elemai looked startled, Aliyah experienced an ugly, unformed resentment, the undeniable realization that Elemai had assumed that just like with everything else, the Ring was now essentially hers to do with as she pleased, and Aliyah's consent and agency was – while not trifling, perhaps – nothing to fuss over, or consider it to differ from her own. There was a bristling pause, as Khasmedeus propped its chin on its hands and watched with a gleeful expression. "Ooh. Catfight? I'm putting my money on the scrawny one. Pathetic, but *scrappy.*"

"Shut up," both women snapped. Not particularly chastened, Khasmedeus stuck out its tongue and waggled its ears in an unnatural and insulting fashion, then wafted up into the corner, as if to watch the fight from the cheap seats. Turning with great dignity from its gargoyle faces, Elemai looked back at Aliyah. "I'm sorry. I did not mean to insult you. But, well. Does it not make far more sense for me to have the Ring? I did tell you that I am a hafiza of Shahrzad, and that's not the only thing. I am far more conversant with the politics, diplomacy, knowledge. And since you don't know why Diyab chose you – "

Aliyah opened her mouth, then shut it. None of what Elemai was saying was untrue, but it still stung like a whip. Yes, of course it made *sense* for Elemai to take it (if she could even physically do so, which remained up for debate). It made more *sense* for anyone else at all. But nonetheless, the old man had given it to *her*, a decision for which he had paid with his life, and she bristled at the idea of being asked to part with it the first time she revealed its existence, as if she was a child handed a dangerous weapon. At last she said, "That doesn't mean he was wrong."

"Of course not," Elemai agreed, "but if we are the only people in the world who know about this, we must take advantage of it at once. I would not, I vow, cut you out. Indeed, as my wife – "

"Ah." Aliyah let the word hang. Then she said, "In short, now that I have this, your family would in fact be eager to accept my suit? What happened to wanting to marry only once, for love?"

"Ideals are one thing," Elemai admitted. "The reality can be another. But it does not have to be totally forsworn. Often those who marry in arranged matches find that true feelings do come, in time. And if we were working together in this glorious purpose – "

Aliyah did not answer. Instead she looked down, worrying the shabby circlet of gold on her finger over and over, as if it might vanish if she took her attention away for an instant. She could not properly admit her anger, when this was exactly what she herself had first thought – that Elemai would have to accept her, that her mother could no longer see her as unworthy, that folk near and far would finally have to value her for who she was (even if the Ring was, ironically, the one thing over which she had no control and had come into by an accident). But just as Khasmedeus had said, it didn't feel like a triumph. *Ironically self-fulfilled prophecies in which you are given exactly what you thought you wanted, only to realize it was the agent of your downfall all along.* Was she truly so stupid to hear that warning and choose it nonetheless?

"So," Aliyah said at last. "You are, in fact, offering to marry me?"

"I… yes." Elemai flushed, but did not back down or pretend that this was due to anything other than what it was. Slowly, she went to one knee. "Will you honor me in the sight of Ur-Malika and the blessed Hierophant, the Adirim, and Mother Qart, and become my wife?"

Aliyah looked down at Elemai's bent head, her dark hair gleaming beneath the gauzy, gold-edged film of her veil, her beautiful face and her intent eyes. All that tangled, frustrating desire rose up in her again: to be Elemai, to marry Elemai, for people to look at her the way they looked at Elemai, for them to assume that she had power and prestige the way they assumed Elemai did. This was not how she wanted it to happen, not at all. And yet, there was no doubt that this would please her mother and clear the way for the greatest challenge to Meronite power that this world had ever seen, and put like that, there was no question. "Yes," she said, dry-mouthed. "Yes, I accept."

Khasmedeus, still in its corner, let out a whistle. "Incredibly romantic. Wow. Me, I'm just *brimming* with confidence that this will be a long and happy union that will definitely not crumble to ashes and leave you both disillusioned and miserable. Aren't you?"

Elemai glared daggers at it. "We told you to be quiet."

"Danger of having me around." Khasmedeus crossed its legs and leaned back, hands folded behind its head. "That doesn't usually happen, and I'll tell you that for free."

"I'll dismiss it," Aliyah said hurriedly. "At least until we – "

"One moment." Elemai held up a hand. "Jinnyeh," she said, addressing Khasmedeus. "If we *were* to engage your services, could you actually do what we want? If, say, we ordered you right now to fly to Merone and kill the Divine Emperor, could you do that?"

"Are you mad?" Khasmedeus made a crude comedy sound effect and affected to fall on its backside. "Of course not."

"No? Are you not the power that you pretend to be, or – "

"It's nothing to do with *my* power." The jinnyeh shrugged, but its yellow hawk-eyes were full of something between amusement and warning. "I'm the very best the ancient world had to offer, which is why Tselmun tied my life force to that cursed bit of jewelry. But do you really think Coriolane has ruled for four hundred years by being vulnerable to a single jinnyeh suddenly barging in and trying to kill him? Maybe Arghan the Undying could do it – *maybe* – but you wouldn't want to meet him either, as ifrits are a nasty bunch and that one worse than most. As for me, I'd be caught and torn apart by the Thaumaturges – or even worse, those bloody fucking *Corporalists* – the instant I set foot within ten miles of the Eternal City. If you did order me, I'd have no choice but to obey, but it would be useless. I'd be dead and dismembered, and then you'd have nothing. You *would,* however, reveal to the Divine Emperor that not only did you try to rise against him, you had access to an old and *extremely* forbidden magic in doing it. I'm sure he would take it very well and totally reasonably, and not in the mass-murder-of-all-of-Qart-Hadesht kind of way."

"Damn." Elemai frowned. "Well, then. *Can* you be useful in a rebellion? If, theoretically, such an event was to come about?"

"Ah." At last, properly, Khasmedeus smiled. It was blunt and terrifying, but it contained a crumb of genuine pleasure and even more genuine bloodthirst. "That, my lady, I certainly can."

CHAPTER 8

ROMOLA

HER DAY STARTED LONG BEFORE DAWN, AS USUAL. While the rest of the Eternal City remained deep in slumber, the stars still out and the moon only just set, Romola woke in the darkness, slipped off her pallet, and dressed, crouching by the grimy bucket and doing her best to wash. She received one clean robe and one change of water a week, on Septday, and today was Sextday, so they were both at the end of their service and there wasn't much to be done. But she tried nonetheless, combing her fingers through her long brown hair and knotting it into a braid, tying her rope belt, and slipping on her shoes. Her left foot hurt, but that was to be expected; it was twisted, lame, and had been ever since she was birthed anew, just like the deafness in that ear. Since such physical imperfections were ordinarily something the Corporalists could easily fix, the only thing she could conclude was that they had deliberately left her this way, as a sharp lesson to whoever she was first. After all, a person was never Remade for no reason.

Morning toilette, such as it was, complete, Romola left her cell and began the painful climb into the great and silent Eternal Palace. At this hour, even the most licentious courtiers had finally subsided into wine-sozzled sleep, and her only companions in the towering halls of shadow were just the occasional eunuch or chamberlain. There would soon be others, but Romola always tried to be first, to snatch a moment of solitude and feel as if she was the only one to walk or breathe in these splendid serried vaults. Besides, her imperfection was offensive to well-bred Meronite eyes, and she stayed away from them as a rule. Even ordinary slaves often felt superior to her, Remade and damaged with it, and such animosities could take sudden and dangerous form.

Her chores were numbingly familiar. There was dirty oil to drain from the lamps and new oil to fill them, floors to sweep and scrub, curtains and tapestries to steam, wilted flowers to remove and fresh ones to place, walls and mirrors to polish, and an endless litany of stains and rubbish from last night's festivities: wine, vomit, piss, shit, blood, and semen, golden plates and jeweled goblets tossed aside as negligently as any other trash, crusted with half-eaten food and crawling with insects. It always amazed Romola, no matter how many times she saw it. Not only that anyone could do this night after night, but be so cavalier about the leftovers. Sometimes, if she could find food that was still reasonably palatable, she ate it, imagining herself as a guest at those lavish parties. If she was ever caught doing so, she would be punished, even if the food was thrown out otherwise. Likewise, if she was so mad to steal one of the plates or goblets, she could smuggle it out and sell it for more money than she would ever otherwise see in her life, but even if she didn't get her hands cut off and her face branded as a thief, what would she do with money? Far more trouble than it was worth.

The eastern horizon was turning pink by the time Romola had restored her patch of the palace to its usual gleaming, perfect self. She daubed one final bit of dust from the emperor's favorite portrait, the one that showed him in all his martial, athletic splendor when he first came to the throne, and gathered the dishes to carry down to the kitchens. Her own breakfast was there too, and since there had been nothing to scrounge this morning, she walked as fast as she could. She tried not to limp too openly when there were other folk around, since she often had to ask them to repeat themselves or speak more loudly, and they took that as enough of an insult. What was a slave for, if not to hear orders the first time, the only time, and then carry them out?

She reached the kitchens, deposited the dirty dishes with the scullions, and hurried into line for her morning portion of potage, bread, and meat; the rest of the slaves were awake by now, and if you arrived too late, you risked finding none left, and would have to go hungry until the evening. It was cruel, perhaps, but at least she was assured of *having* one daily meal at minimum, and there was nowhere else in Merone that she would be any safer or better cared for than she was here. One in four residents of the Eternal City was a slave. Slaves worked the forges and foundries, plowed the fields and grew the food, dueled the gladiators and drove the chariots, harvested the vineyards and pressed the wine, cooked the meals and raised the children, cleaned the houses and warmed the beds, fought the wars and even taught the schools: the grammar teachers, lower-ranked university lecturers, and even some of the distinguished professors were, or had originally been, slaves. They could earn their freedom with spectacular displays of loyalty or service to the Empire, but usually only after forty or fifty years of work, when they were too worn out to do anything but gratefully accept a state pension and retire into obscurity. In fact, it was their only choice. The freeborn merchants' guilds, the landed gentry, the patrician and senatorial families – all of them kicked up an unholy fuss at any idea of permitting a slave into their midst, even one who had been freed and only then granted citizenship. Slaves were forbidden to congregate or socialize beyond their own estate; nobody wanted another Spartekaius. Down in the dirty, seething masses, crippled and half-deaf, Romola would be lucky to survive a week. Even if she did, her next lot would be much, *much* worse.

As such, while she was well aware of the shortcomings of her situation, she had no real wish to escape. And while it was no longer practiced nearly as much as it had been, not least since slaves were an invaluable asset and could be resold to cover an estate's debts, there was still a long Meronite tradition of putting all the household slaves to death when the paterfamilias died, or punishing the lot of them for the transgression of one. It kept them vigilant, paranoid, and eager to report on each other, unable to trust their fellows or resist their masters. Against that, why on earth would Romola try to kill herself (again) even faster?

When breakfast was over, there was no time to loiter. The palace was vast, the effort to keep it beautiful was never-ending, and Romola could be tasked by anyone at any time to do anything: carry a eunuch's scrolls, fetch a goblet of wine for a praetor, stoke a fire that had burned low in a chilly concubine's chamber, ferry a letter to the imperial riders, so on and so forth. Even more, ideally, those in need of services should not have to go to the trouble of asking aloud. The best slaves should presciently anticipate them and simply appear to take care of it. But Romola was slower than others, on account of her foot, and it often got her nasty looks and muttered remarks, the sort of visibility that was hazardous. She did her best to force it down. Otherwise the Corporalists might come for her again, and the prospect terrified her to the core.

It was past noon, the hour when she had to push aside the hunger and remind herself that supper was not until Vespers, when she stopped to catch her breath in a corridor overlooking the Castel Sanctangel, which squatted like a dark monster behind the pristine sanctity of the palace. It always gave Romola a frisson of horror to look at it, since the Castel was where the Corporalists did their work. But just as she was about to continue on her way, she spotted someone emerging from the portcullis. And not just anyone, but the most feared of all the Immortal generals: Ionius Servus Eternus, Coriolane's pet murderer, the Scourge of Sciatello. *Him.*

Romola shuddered, ordering herself to look away, but horrified fascination kept her in place. She had never known what it was about Ionius that compelled and repelled her in equal measure, though it had nothing to do with lust. Some of the girls thought him handsome, but Romola never understood it; his face was too harsh and his reputation too cruel for that, and besides, according to the whispers, he did not care for women anyway. Whatever he was doing, it was nothing to concern her. Best to turn back to her chores, forget she had seen him, and –

"Girl!"

The shout made her jump enough to knock her elbow, and she winced. For a mad moment she thought Ionius had transported himself up here, thus to berate her for staring at things that were none of her business, but it was a more familiar menace: her least favorite castellan. "You. Upstairs, now. Her Imperial Majesty is in need of your services."

"She – *what?*" The words bubbled to Romola's lips before she could stop them. Neither of the empresses had ever summoned her before, for anything. Gheslyn and Vestalia Aurea were distant stars in the heavenly firmament of the court, perfect cynosures and total ciphers. But everyone knew damn well that they were not nearly as powerless as they pretended. Gheslyn was the Arch-Chancellor of the Imperial Academy of Merone, which was supposed to be the sort of glamorous and empty sinecure suitable for a royal wife, but she had ruthlessly taken control of its curriculum, faculty, staff, students, tuition, exams, degrees, and all else. Vestalia's influence was more opaque, difficult to localize. Both of them had a sinister reputation for arranging the end of any concubine who caught their husband's eye too noticeably, but malicious gossip was common currency in a harem. Even if so, perhaps they had heeded the cautionary tale of their sisters in Qin. Ambitious courtesans could take over the court and the ruler and even the country if not sharply dealt with, and regardless of whether the entire Tridevarian religious establishment turned a blind eye to the emperor's brazen flouting of its moral teachings, the empresses might well feel differently.

"*Go,* you idiot," the castellan said impatiently. "And for the Lord's sake, be quick about it."

Romola flinched, nodded, and did her best to hurry, stumping up the never-ending stairs. The empresses lived on the top floor of the Eternal Palace, in expansive and airy apartments that she had only even seen once before. Her mind was racing with barely restrained panic, trying to pick out anything that would make the most powerful women in the world ask for her – *her,* as low in the strict hierarchy of Meronite society as it was possible to imagine. Did they think she was improperly interested in Ionius? No, it couldn't be. So *what?*

Romola was teetering on the edge of total terror by the time she reached the great doors, guarded at all hours by the Empresses' Own Legions. They eyed her coldly, but knocked and called inside. After a moment, when permission was granted, they unlatched the bars and beckoned her through. Doing her best to look ready, she stepped in.

Sunlight hit her in the face like a blade, and she struggled not to squint. The apartments boasted towering floor-to-ceiling windows that gazed over the Eternal City in all directions, a splendid panopticon that took Romola's breath away, but pausing to gape or gawk was the worst of mistakes. She kept her eyes forward and her back straight, crossing the black-and-white chequey marble floor, seamed with gold in the joins. To her right, there was a vast canopied bed, and to her left, there was a heavy carved desk and chair. The ceilings soared like a cathedral, and all the rarest and most beautiful art, sculpture, and antiquities were displayed like any other domestic knickknacks. The air was scented with lavender, which always made Romola sneeze, and she held it back. Not here.

She entered the room successfully, whereupon she was obliged to halt, drop a deep curtsy, and look around, then immediately regretted it. Because right there in the bed, reclining at her ease and entirely naked, was Empress Vestalia, the younger of the two: slim, beautiful, and pale-skinned, thick auburn hair caught up in golden circlets and a goblet of wine in hand. Reverencing automatically, unable to recall if it was a mortal insult to greet the junior empress before the senior, Romola did her utmost not to stare at the creamy swell of Vestalia's breasts, the thatch of hair between her legs. The occupant of the desk was older, matronly, stern-looking Empress Gheslyn, her dark braids well salted with silver. Thankfully clad, she spun around and said something rapidly in the direction of Romola's deaf ear. Which, therefore, Romola did not hear.

"I'm terribly sorry, Your Majesty," she stammered, praying for the floor to yawn open and swallow her. "Could you say that again?"

Gheslyn blinked, as startled as if nobody had ever, in the whole of her however-long-life, dared to ask her to repeat herself. Romola was braced for any sort of vicious reaction, but a smile spread across the older empress's lips, sharp enough to draw blood. "Oh, she *is* perfect. Nobody will ever look twice at this one. Suitably useless, indeed."

Romola opened her mouth, then shut it. Two emotions warred in her chest: first, abject relief that her failure had pleased the empress, rather than infuriating her, and second, the realization that Gheslyn and Vestalia had not asked for her specifically. Why would they? Instead, they asked for somebody *like* her: flawed, deformed, anonymous, so far beneath contempt that even noticing her existence would be an unforgivable insult to any self-respecting Meronite's sense of themselves. The castellan had therefore taken stock and selected Romola, apparently quite literally the worst the palace had to offer. Her cheeks burned still hotter.

"Come closer," Gheslyn said, speaking slowly and loudly, as if Romola might be a total simpleton. "Can you understand me now, girl?"

"Yes, Majesty."

"But not earlier? Why?"

"I am deaf in one ear, Majesty. I am not otherwise… abnormal."

"Hmm." With a sudden, cloying sweetness, Gheslyn added, "What is your name, my dear?"

"Romola, Majesty."

"Romola…?"

"Romola Servus." *Eternus* was reserved for the Immortals, and *Servus* was the customary designation for the rank-and-file unfree. Some masters allowed particularly accomplished or talented slaves to use the family cognomen, or to be formally recognized as part of their dynasty, but quite obviously, there was no such gilded lily for Romola. "I am at Your Majesty's complete disposal."

"Very good." Gheslyn kept sizing her up. "Well, Romola. I have an errand for you, and if you do well, there might be further tasks and privileges. I do want to be your friend. Women have it so difficult in this world, don't you think? We should help each other when we can."

To say the least, it seemed unlikely to Romola that Her Imperial Majesty, Empress Gheslyn Aurea of All Merone, had anything whatsoever in common with her, but it was unwise to say so. And while it was a blatant manipulation, it was nonetheless effective. Quite obviously, pleasing the empresses could lead to better food, better quarters, better treatment, even a crumb of the bounty laid so profligately before her now. "And what might that be, Majesty? The errand?"

Gheslyn raised a hand, beckoning her to wait, then disappeared into one of the several small antechambers that segued from the main room, interlocked like Qiné nesting boxes. In her absence, Romola kept her eyes on the floor, painfully conscious of Vestalia's gaze on her. She was relieved when Gheslyn returned, carrying a folded parchment sealed in numinous black wax – a concoction of the Thaumaturges that would reveal if the message had been intercepted, opened, tampered, or otherwise meddled with in any way. Before Romola had time to balk at the magnitude of whatever was being thrust into her hand, there it was, and when she glanced down, she saw elegant calligraphic flourishes of Semyic script. She could not read or write, and spoke no language but Lanuvian, but she wasn't *stupid*. She knew the Semyic abjad was used to write the main Wahini languages – Qartic, Parsiva, Indaric, Bahjoun, Rabiyan – and she could distinguish it from the sharp angles and spiky minims of Lanuvian orthox, or blocky Ruthynian kyrillic. This letter, therefore, must be meant for a speaker of one of those languages, who was therefore a dangerous outsider from Merone and possibly all of Tridevariandom. But Romola could not let this show on her face, and she nodded. "Thank you, Majesty. What am I to do?"

"Convey this to the Tibir docks," Gheslyn said, "and give it to a man named Vadoush. You will find him at the Brass Astrolabe tavern this evening, between the hours of Vespers and Compline. After that time, he shall be gone, and if you have not placed it into his possession, you have failed me, and there will be consequences. Is that clear?"

Romola froze. Going into the city alone, especially after dark, was her worst nightmare, and if there was any way to say no, she would have. But there was not, so she nodded again. "Thank you, Majesty. It is very clear. How am I to know this man Vadoush, when I arrive?"

"You will know him," Gheslyn said cryptically. "You will, of course, report to me anything he says to you. If he asks for a password, tell him to give you one first. His phrase should be, *The white orchids of Anteropolis are lovely this time of year.* Then, and only then, may you respond, *Yes, and they bloom still more strongly in the sun.*"

"Yes, Majesty. Understood. But am I to be given a messenger's token, in case the legions stop me and ask what I am doing out at – "

"*No* token," Gheslyn snapped, sudden and sharp. "There will be nothing linking you to us. If you are questioned for any reason, I expect you to lie, and lie *convincingly*. But that would entail you being detained for acting or looking suspicious in some way, and that would itself be a profound failure on your part. For who would ever notice *you?*"

"Are you sure about this, Lyn?" At that moment, Vestalia spoke for the first time. Her voice was pleasantly soft and husky, but her eyes were steel. "This one is too fragile, too dull. There must be someone else."

"We are running out of options." Gheslyn did not take her gaze from Romola's face. "And asking too many times for useless slaves will draw its own attention. Besides, I suspect you are cleverer than you are letting on. Aren't you, girl?"

Unsure how to answer, Romola settled for a nervous smile. Then Gheslyn said, "When you return, mention the orchids of Anteropolis to the eunuch Belsephorus. Do you know the one? He – should one refer to eunuchs as *he?* I've never been quite sure – will bring you back here. But as far as anyone else is concerned, *anyone at all,* this meeting never happened, and you never spoke to us. Yes?"

"Yes." Romola searched her memory, thought she knew who the empress meant, nodded again. "I will not fail you, Majesty."

With that, dismissed with her contraband letter and her racing heart, Romola had to work out how in hellfire to leave the palace without being noticed. She should reach the Brass Astrolabe well before Vespers, just to be safe, and the Tibir docks were clear on the other side of the city. That was far more than she could possibly walk with her bad foot and her poor knowledge of the Meronite streets, and just as the sharp edges of panic were whittling her nerves to a crisp, she seized upon it, darting down to the loading bays where a constant commerce of carts, coaches, chariots, wagons, sedan chairs, lectica, and other conveyances came and went at all hours of day and night, shuttling the endless human beehive and everything else it took to make the Eternal Palace run. Romola selected a vintner who had just offloaded a dozen crates of amphorae and was muttering bitterly about how the purser had cheated him, looked back and forth one last time, and sprinted to his cart, throwing herself under the crumpled canvas. She lay very still and tried not to think about how if the guards ordered an inspection, found her, and concluded that she was trying to escape, she would be executed long before the empresses could help her. And if she insisted that they were the ones who sent her, they would dispatch her for disloyalty.

After the longest and most nerve-racking wait of her entire life, Romola heard the merchant return, climb into the driver's seat, and take up the reins, cracking them over his swaybacked dray and creaking toward the gate. She was deeply grateful for his dispute with the purser, as it preoccupied him to the point that he was not thinking about anything else, and had no reason to suspect he was smuggling a slave; it would be his head too, if they were caught. Romola hardly breathed until she judged them to have been successfully waved through, and felt the wheels bump steadily on the road that led down Palatorian Hill and into the city. Not that she could relax just yet. There were several more walls and gates to pass, any one of them might cause trouble, and then —

Nonetheless, the Merciful Lady smiled upon her, because they were not stopped or harassed, and finally decanted into the main districts. Romola waited until they ground to a halt in a terrific traffic jam, beasts braying and drivers cursing, then slithered out from under the canvas, dropped into the noisome mud of the street, and barely avoided being crushed by heavy wheels. Then she stood up, brushed herself off, and made sure that the letter was still tucked in her bodice; if she lost it, she was doomed. But it was there, she was here, and she, *she* had done it.

Romola forced down the little thrill of pride; she would enjoy it when it was done, and not before. She waited for a brief clearing in the tidal flow of animals, vehicles, and people, took a whiff and smelled the briny damp of river-water, and saw the screeching seagulls perpetually circling away toward the west. So, then. That way.

The church bells had just started to ring Vespers when Romola reached the sprawling waterfront that stretched all the way to Sanctorian Hill in the north, where the Arch-Holy Basilica of True Tridevarianism rose to the heavens, and Praetorian Hill and its majestic white-columned Forum to the south, where the Meronite Senate had met for many centuries and continued to do so now, if only because bored aristocrats needed amusement and it was better to keep their plotting where the emperor could see it. The Tibir river twisted and coiled out to the Madherian Sea, and the docks were thronged with vessels from around the world. Romola recognized Qiné junks, Indush dhangris, Stavangri longships, and even one of the huge double-hulled canoes of the Te Rōrae Tapu'a, who dwelled deep in the southern oceans and were said to be the greatest seafarers ever to raise a sail. But she could not dawdle. She still did not know where the Brass Astrolabe was, and the port was too vast to search before Compline.

She started to walk, trying to gauge how long her foot would hold out. If it was the start of the day, it would be better, but she had been working for hours, and the persistent, stabbing cramp did not bode well. She could not stay here long; she had no money, she had to be back in time for her morning chores, and the thought of a night alone on the streets was grim for any number of reasons. It was times like these when Romola especially yearned to know just what her predecessor had done to be punished even beyond her own death – who she had been, where she was from, how old she was, any of it. The Corporalists could not reuse her *forever;* even with the best spells that modern necromancy had to offer, human flesh was still mortal, finite, and subject to wear and tear, and eventually it rejected any more reanimation. Romola did not know how many inhabitants of this body there had been before her, if she was at the beginning or almost the end of its duration, and she tried not to think about it. No creature had a choice in how they passed from this world, not even Remade. In that, at least, they were the same.

The sun was well gone behind the river, and the shadows were thick enough that torches, lamps, and lanterns were lit along the docklands, by the time Romola decided that she needed a better strategy. She had a letter written in a variant of Semyic, she had to find a man with a Semyic-sounding name, an astrolabe was a Wahin navigational instrument, and there must be a part of the waterfront where those ships were customarily serviced: counting-houses with currency exchange for bezints and dirhems; interpreters, clerks, and officials who knew the correct languages, taxes, and paperwork; fences, runners, bosses, and enforcers for the respective criminal syndicates; inns and taverns that served halal food, even whores brought from home to best comfort a lonely sailor with his own women and customs. So she turned down the quay where the feluccas, dhows, baghlahs, zambuks, and boums of Ifriqiyin, Rabiyah, Gezeren, Parsivat, and other lands were congregated, and soon spotted a large brass dial swinging in the wind before a low-slung establishment. She could not be certain, but this looked like her mark.

Romola put up her hood, glanced around, and stepped inside, whereupon she was deafened even more than usual by the din. A harried barmaid mouthed something she couldn't hear at all, and it occurred to her that she was unlikely to be a welcome customer when she couldn't pay for anything to eat or drink. The Wahini varied widely in their embrace of the latter; the rural and conservative Rabiyans insisted that the Hierophant had forbidden all worldly intoxicants, while the liberal and sophisticated cities such as Qart-Hadesht, Qahirah, and Bhagarayat celebrated wine, art, music, lovemaking, and poetry as the epitome of the cultured man and woman. Here in Merone, everything was available, but Romola was far more concerned with finding Vadoush.

The next problem, therefore, was how to do that before Compline, which was approaching at unnerving speed. Gheslyn claimed that Romola would just *know*, but there were many Wahini men in here and they all looked similar. At the barmaid's insistence, Romola ordered a cup of wine, which made her feel wildly licentious, and dearly hoped that Vadoush would appear in time to pay for it. What would happen if she asked for something to *eat?* No, no. That was unthinkable.

Just as enough time had passed to once more turn her nerves to shreds, she caught sight of a man sitting alone at a table in the corner, face mostly veiled by his long white ghutra. As this was a common accessory for the Brass Astrolabe's patrons, it was not what caught her eye. Instead, it was the faint but persistent glow that surrounded him. As if he sensed her studying him, he looked up, and she was considerably startled; his eyes were a deep, tawny yellow like a cat's, shining weirdly in the low light. He held her gaze for a moment, then nodded. He had never seen her before, how could he know if she was – ?

Either way, it would soon be Compline, and so it was now or never. Romola slid off the bench, picked up her wine, and made her way over. "Good evening. Do I speak to Saed Vadoush?"

"You do. Is there something else you wish to say to me?"

"No," Romola said. "You first."

He flashed that dervish smile, acknowledging her cleverness, and let it hang. Then he said, "The white orchids of Anteropolis are lovely at this time of year, don't you think?"

"Yes, indeed. And they bloom still more strongly in the sun."

Something flickered in those luminous yellow eyes, and he seemed to decide the test had been passed. He held out his hand. "Well?"

Romola hesitated a final instant, then removed the letter and passed it to him. Vadoush examined it closely, then concealed it in some unknown place about his person. In the same motion, he tossed her a silver sestertius. "For your drink. It should cover supper too."

"Th – thank you, saed. Is there anything else you need?"

"From you, child?" He seemed amused. "No. Go eat."

Romola nodded again and clambered off the stool, limping back to the bar and asking for whatever they were serving for supper. It turned out to be a delicious dish of rice, flatbread, lamb, a tangy sauce, and an earthy spice, so much better than any of the slave-meals, and she licked up every bite. When she looked back, Vadoush was gone, though she had not seen him leave; he would have had to walk straight past her. But it was not her affair. She had completed her task, had even paid for wine and a meal, and she still had to sneak back into the palace. Perhaps she should have asked him for help? Too late now.

Romola swallowed the rest of her wine – she had never drunk so much before, and it made her head buzz and her steps float – and wove through the now-thinning crowds to the exit. Outside, the night had cooled enough to be chilly, and as she looked around, she realized that she did not know which direction she had come from, which of the narrow lanes led back to the main street, or how in heaven's name she proposed to get three miles back to Palatorian Hill and then back inside the Eternal Palace. Everything looked twisted and strange in the dark, like sinister fetches or black mirrors. This was it, then. The end.

No, no, *no*. She could not give up, not when she had already surmounted all other obstacles. So she picked a direction and started to walk, but her foot shrieked with such pain that it squeezed tears from her eyes. She only got halfway down the alley before it gave out, and she collapsed on a pile of rope, breathing hard and trying to massage out the ache. That didn't work either, and as she continued to sit there, a blaze of light fell on her face and a loud male voice said something in a language she didn't understand. When she didn't answer, he switched to Lanuvian. "Hey, girlie. Hey. What are you doing here? Are you lost?"

"No." Romola lurched to her feet, stumbled and almost fell. "I'm fine. I just – "

"Come on." His teeth were white, his grin was sharklike, and she saw three or four of his friends behind him. They all whiffed of the same cheap wine she had been drinking, and all at once she understood their intent, saw herself as they must see her — easy prey. She backed up, and they moved with her. "Come on," he said again. "You can clearly use some extra coin. We can pay."

Romola thought that was even more of a lie than before, but two of them circled around to cut off her retreat, she couldn't run even if not, and in that moment, she realized there was nothing she could do. A slave girl alone at night in the gutter districts was the most powerless of all imaginable creatures, until she wondered wildly if the empresses *wanted* her to get killed and leave no loose ends — was that what they meant by *running out of options?* But that was totally mad. And it didn't matter, because something very bad was about to happen, and then —

Just then, there was a streak of motion across the alley, the torch went cartwheeling and landed in the mud, and the white-toothed man let out a scream of unadulterated terror. One instant he was looking madly over his shoulder; the next his throat was spewing blood from a slash that opened it precisely from ear to ear and sent him toppling like a broken toy. It was less than five heartbeats until the rest of the would-be rapists met equally gory ends and Romola was pressed flat against the wall, too terrified to make a sound, as the new attacker stalked closer. All she saw was the lethal glint of twin blades in the shadow's hands, and then a rough voice said, "You shouldn't be out here, girl."

She blinked dancing spots from her vision, still stunned. The blades disappeared, she didn't see where, and he bent to retrieve the half-extinguished torch. It was then that she saw his face, and knew it was who it could not be. Ionius Servus Eternus regarded her coolly, and she struggled not to quail. To him, she was instantly recognizable as a palace slave, and he could demand the exact explanation of her actions that she had been ordered not to give to anyone. He looked like he was thinking about it. Then he grabbed her arm. "I said, *you shouldn't be out here.*"

Romola let him drag her up the street. She had never been this close to him before, and it was terrifying. But he *had* saved her from a grisly fate, and she cleared her throat. "General, I — I am grateful — "

"Be quiet." His rugged profile was sharply silhouetted in what little of the moonlight could struggle down to the street. "I don't know what you were doing, running around outside the palace at this hour, but make yourself useful. Did you meet any associate of, or did you hear any talk of, a Ruthynian man named Vadim Khovanyich?"

"No." Romola was deeply grateful that she could answer honestly. "I don't have any idea."

Ionius grunted skeptically, as if she must be lying. They reached a waiting horse, and he threw her onto it. Then he sprang into the saddle and kicked it into motion, as Romola did her best not to fall off. She was certain that Ionius would not stop if so, and as they galloped up the streets, he barked, "Were you trying to escape? Get on a ship or – "

"No. No, I wasn't. I was on an errand for – for the palace."

"The palace? Who?"

She tried to swallow, but her throat was dust. "I can't tell you."

"You realize who I am, girl?" His voice was incredulous. "You have to do anything that I order you, yes? Or if you won't talk to me, I'm sure the Corporalists can – "

"No. No, please. Please. Not the Corporalists."

Ionius didn't answer, but his head turned halfway toward her, as if he understood more of that fear than she wanted. When they reached the first gate on Palatorian Hill, the soldiers sprang to attention and saluted Ionius, and did not venture any such impudence as asking about the young (or at least young-looking) woman with him; that was entirely the general's business, good evening sir, good evening to you. Romola was both unsettled and allured by the sheer easy power of it; the Immortals were slaves too, but this didn't feel like it. When they reached the Eternal Palace, Ionius dismounted, pulled her down after him, and gripped her shoulders hard enough to hurt. His voice was low and vicious. "Listen, girl. I'm not going to swoop in and save you again, do you hear me? And if you don't want me telling people about you, you'll consider whether keeping this secret is in your best interests. Eh?"

Romola quaked. He did not say just who he could tell about her, but nor did he need to. Everyone knew Ionius was Coriolane's favorite, and if he informed the emperor, there was nothing to save her. But she lifted her head and met his flinty grey eyes as steadily as she could. "Thank you, General. Good night."

He looked as if he could not believe that anyone would ever be so foolish, but he let go of her. He turned away. He gave her one last loathing stare, and departed.

CHAPTER 9

ZADIA

Ever since she was a small child, listening in rapt fascination to her mother's stirring tales of the mighty Qart-Hadesht of old, Zadia bet Amarasha ur-Namasqa had waited her whole life for the moment which – it seemed, it *seemed,* and how little she still dared to trust – might just have finally arrived. It had not been in her mother's lifetime, or her grandmother's, or any grandmother for four hundred years, and the fact that it fell on *her* dwelled constantly in the back of Zadia's mind, an abject fear of failure not just for her but every Batu Namasqa and Qartic foremother, all the way back to Queen Daeda herself. Even worse, nobody save one of Zadia's colleagues agreed that it *was* the moment, or even if so, that they should not sit back and wait for a better one at some point in the unspecified future. After this long spent as just as much empty set dressing as the Meronite Senate, the Qartic Adirim had become equally ossified, sedentary and timid, vastly reluctant to pursue real or alarming change; they *claimed* that they would set up a committee to elect a scholarly body to examine the potential possibility of advocating for more independence, but let us not be hasty. It was deliberately evasive and totally futile, and would do nothing but fritter this chance away and leave them to wait four more centuries (or worse) for another. But point that out, and *Malikallulah,* the screaming.

It was late, but as usual, Zadia was not asleep. Khaldun and Noora had retired several hours ago to the great bed they all shared, but she was still in the solarium, burning the latest of too many midnight oils. Her desk was awash in papers and parchments, quills and ink, codices and scrolls, letters and reports, maps and figures; she could hardly recall the last time she had seen the surface. She had attempted to create a rudimentary organizational system, but it inevitably fell out of order, so she gave up trying. It felt like paddling desperately to stay afloat, a swimmer frantic to escape the monstrous wave that was always cresting up behind, but in fascination as much as terror. This was the real stuff of the rebellion, a word she barely uttered even in her own head, let alone her own household. It haunted her as a tangled web of threads and throughlines, a house of cards that had to be made strong enough to bear the world. So, then. She worked.

Despite the heated accusations of her head-in-the-sand colleagues, Zadia was not naïve, or eager to rush into a reckless war that would solve nothing and only make it worse. Even if they miraculously managed to remove Coriolane himself, the vast and remorseless machinery of the empire would still exist, and be even more dangerous. Since he had never named or even appeared to have an heir, every ambitious patrician and general would tear each other apart to seize the crown, as succession had usually gone in the bad old days. It was not required to be a natural-born heir of his body, as many of the pagan emperors had anointed their preferred successor by adopting an adult man as their son, but Coriolane had made plain that he had no intention of doing that either. So Merone collapsing into pointless civil war, while it might be felt only fair by all those who suffered under its boot, would badly hurt the most vulnerable folk in the Eternal City, who were not Coriolane and had taken no part in his atrocities. Qart-Hadesht, despite the best efforts of Zadia and Safiya ur-Tasvashta, was not, in fact, ready to rule itself alone, and that was why they had argued for other associations. But for the calcified useless fuckers of the old guard, it was Mother Qart or nothing.

And so, that left Zadia here, in the impossible position of trying to plan the one thing that had never existed in all the bloody annals of history: the perfect rebellion, which would take place at an ideal time, only hurt the ones it was intended to hurt, minimize collateral damage, result in sustainable and lasting change, and not simply collapse into a mess of petty local wars and frozen conflicts as the would-be imperial heirs jostled and snapped like crows at a carrion feast. Would the rebellion be military, and if so, how to overcome the immediate and obvious disadvantages? First, most Wahini qahins and qadis generally taught that submission to any earthly ruler, no matter how terrible, was a preferable state of nature to anarchy and rebellion, and while it was therefore used by those same terrible rulers in nakedly cynical self-interest to keep the people cowed and meekly accepting of their lot, it would have to be successfully argued against and dismantled. Safiya, the Kitab hafiza, would have to be the one to deal with that, as Zadia had no stomach for the insufferably self-righteous nattering of religious men, who by nature and regardless of their creed – Tridevarian, Tserkovian, Wahini, Vashemite, Indushi, so on – all tended to hate women or at least think the order of the universe called for them to be silent and obedient. They were fortunate to have been spared the worst of that here in matriarchal Qart-Hadesht, but beyond their own walls, that meant increasingly little. And, she thought, within their own walls as well.

Besides, even if they did get the religious obstacle disposed of, the task grew no easier. Qart-Hadesht's once-great army, producer of legendary heroes like the Batu Barqa, had been reduced to a shadow of itself; all their manpower was bundled off to the Meronite legions like the rest of their provincial brethren, and might end up fighting against their own kith and kin. The remainder would be swept aside like shatranj pawns if they tried rising against even the ordinary Meronite army, and that was before the Immortals took a hand. So could they force an economic blockade, with what ships? Merone's trade mostly came by sea, so cutting off the Lanuvian peninsula and the Spice Road might be moderately efficacious, but it still controlled the overland routes to Brythanica, Ibelus, and Franketerrum. Hanibal and his elephants might have marched across the Apellines to storm the gates of Merone, but not only were they no longer in possession of the great general *or* his elephants, they had no way to isolate the empire from both land and sea. It was so huge, so amorphous and implacable, that it was like boxing at shadows, stabbing in the dark. Even if you hurt it in one place, it could repay the insult and then some.

Zadia blew out a frustrated breath and dropped the papers on the desk. Blessed Ur-Malika, it all seemed so *useless,* and yet she could not bring herself to call it quits. She still hungered too much to see it done, or even started. It was unlikely to resolve in her lifetime, but as for Aliyah and Aljafar... well. They might have a chance. If only they *understood.*

Increasingly often, Zadia wondered if her children were in a chrysalis, the result of growing up in wealth and comfort in a city-state nominally at peace, and if she should indulge that innocence more, respect it, rather than always trying to strip it away. To be sure, she loved them very much, even if she did not always like them. The chief cause of Aljafar's deficiencies was apparent, as boys of fifteen were largely intolerable for any number of reasons and a few more years should sort some of that out on its own. Aliyah, though... that was harder, and much less clear. Stubborn, pragmatic, cynical, independent, resisting being told what to do by anyone, even her own mother and country, her heritage, her matrimony. *And who else do you know who sounds like that?*

"Except I *listened* to my mother," Zadia said aloud, as if someone else was in the room and had demanded her to admit whether she butted heads with her daughter so often because she saw the inheritance of herself in Aliyah, as raw and messy and prone to cause total devastation as any inheritance of Merone. "She doesn't, and I don't know how to make her do so. To see what we're fighting for, all of it."

The night sky did not answer, nor the distant stars and waning moon. Her thoughts had started to run in circles, and she had not read more than a few words of the latest letter from Massasoum ur-Beiresht, Chairman of the High House, explaining in gracefully embellished, eruditely classical, and elegantly literary prose why the Adirim still could not formally countenance any move to throw off Meronite authority. No, not even with the rumors of Coriolane's impending demise, a secret that grew harder and harder to keep. *If* the emperor died — and if they could open negotiations with the Eternal City — but not now. Not when it was (Zadia was sick to her back teeth of the word) so *unwise.*

She threw aside the letter and got up, gathering her shawl closer and pacing to the far side of the solarium. There was the great map there, the same one they hung in all the institutions and universities, that shaped young minds' formulation of the world before they even had the words for it. Indeed, the amount of red swathing it in the triumphant mantle of Meronite power was, at first glance, overwhelming. But perhaps Zadia was convinced that rebellion was not just some supremely foolish and self-defeating endeavor because she knew that their power was far more fragile than it appeared, conjured by a complex illusion of cartography. Eastern Ruthynia was ever more out of their reach, ruled in patchworks of local warlords, Ahyun tribal khans, and — at least when the Qiné could get there — the Thearchate. The Thousand Kingdoms of Indush had not actually been a thousand for a very long time; centuries of war and conquest had reduced them to about four, but they still stood as a formidable bulwark against any other eastward expansionism. The Sand Sea was a natural barrier to pushing any further south in Ifriqiyin, and as for other corners of the world, Meronite dominance, even if legally claimed and formally asserted, was paper-thin. Icy northern Stavangr and its feared longship sea-raiders were much too far away for the empire to control at all, and they still included its name on official documents only because it would betray weakness to take it off. Away west over the Occidental Ocean, the Nezuan'hocoyotl Empire of the Sun, the Inhuascan Empire of the Sky, and all the other lands of the new continent had woven a vast net of protective enchantments to prevent the bloodthirsty and disease-ridden Tridevarian invaders from ever returning, after one brief and ill-starred period of contact several centuries ago, at the beginning of Coriolane's reign. But that was long enough for Meronites to arrive on its shores, triumphantly plant the eagle flag, and forcibly chrism the natives, and so all those lands, about which they here in the old world still knew so little, remained colored red. The emperors of Sun and Sky would have laughed themselves sick to hear it.

So, then. What of it? Of course the map lied; maps always did. Even if Merone was far more ringfenced, weakened, and overextended than the ever-industrious imperial propagandists wanted everyone to believe, that still left Qart-Hadesht and its fellows at its mercy. It was no less dangerous to be trapped in a cage with a starving lion just because the lion could not burst free and rampage elsewhere; indeed, that fixed its attention more directly and rapaciously on you. All the brutal gladiatorial contests and fights to the death that the Meronites put on as sport, just so nobody ever forgot the constant violence with which this ghoulish corpse was stitched together, were proof of that. And while Zadia had no way to make the High House change its mind, she had an feeling about this one, something unlike any of the previous times the provinces had flirted with declaring independence – at least until they saw what Coriolane did to traitors, especially the unsuccessful ones. If they didn't succeed this time, they weren't getting another chance.

She stood there for some time, lost in a troubled reverie, until the moon slipped behind the horizon, dawn was not far off, and she had a busy day of work to come – including a private meeting with Saeda Safiya at the ur-Tasvashta residence. Her ally (still as yet, her *only* ally) always had useful intelligence to share, and Zadia wanted to be at her best. They might have arranged to match their children off, at least if Aliyah was doing her part, but Zadia still keenly felt the inequality of their status. No looking any more inferior than she must.

She turned away, slipped out of the solarium, and into the dark and quiet bedchamber. She shucked her shawl and robe and draped them on the trunk – then, as she rustled in search of her sleeping shift, caught a glimpse of herself in the mirror, dim and ghostly. After only two children, she had not lost *too* much of her figure, but she still looked softer, stretched, older, as if someone had sketched a pretty maid in charcoal and then blurred the lines into a matron. Noora, who was younger than her, had offered to bear more heirs for the family if Zadia felt the need of them, but she refused. She had little patience for infants, even her own, and there was no guarantee that further offspring would be any more satisfying than their predecessors. Perhaps it made her a poor mother, as bristly and complicated and demanding as she was, and she wished that she could show her love as simply and easily as her spouses. But that was not her role. If she failed to sculpt them into good Qartic citizens and prepare Aliyah to succeed to the High House, all the love in the world could not redeem it. So it had been with her and her mother.

Zadia found her shift, shrugged it on, and unbound her hair from its braids and pins, letting it cascade thick and black, only somewhat frosted with silver, almost to her waist. She knelt to say a quick prayer, then got up and slipped into bed next to Khaldun, who stirred as she climbed in. "My love?" he murmured drowsily. "How late is it?"

"Late." The twelve-hour sandglass was last turned at midnight, but had already run through at least two of its rings. "Go back to sleep."

Khaldun yawned, reached out an arm, and settled it around her waist, nuzzling against her back and sinking again into the pillows. Zadia had to admit that it was pleasant to let him hold her like this, as Noora continued to slumber peacefully on Khaldun's other side. She would be the first to confess that she was as inherently difficult and unforthcoming with her spouses as she was with her children, and so she never expected to care for both of them as deeply as she did. Khaldun ben Yusir Itabu Onwa'kyeme had come from Numeria to wed her when she too was just eighteen; the ur-Namasqa family had fallen on a spell of bad fortune, and sorely needed the gold and jewels he brought as dowry. He had always been patient, gentle, and kind, and she duly reciprocated, but their union had not deepened into long-married love, older and seasoned, mature and patient, until relatively recently. Five years after her first wedding, Zadia espoused Noora bet Fatima ur-Abajahda for similarly pragmatic reasons; Noora was the last heiress of her venerable old Qartic family, and it gave the ur-Namasqas an improved inheritance, a greater luster, just as Amarasha always instructed her daughter to do. Zadia was fortunate that this too had blossomed into great respect and affection. *And I pleased you, Amma. Did I not? In the end?*

By the time Zadia quieted her mind enough to fall asleep, the sky was washing to faint grey at the edges, and the muyzin's call of dardiq came when it felt like she had just closed her eyes. She groaned, pulled the pillow over her head, and wondered how poorly it would reflect on her if she did not go, this once. But she was the head of the household, and it fell to her to set the example. If the others saw her lag or malinger, they might conclude it was acceptable to do the same, and that could not be countenanced. Zadia felt herself to be a firm but fair mistress; she did not beat the servants, or unduly shout at them, or garnish their wages.

But everything had its place, service, and submission in the great celestial order of things, as the Hierophant of blessed memory had preached and the Kitab had written, and she was nothing if not its dutiful servant.

She rose and dressed, followed Khaldun and Noora to the mahqasa, and tried to ignore the creaking in her knees as she sank to the rug; Malikallulah, she *was* getting old. Fortunately the qahin was brief this morning, and then they could retire to eat breakfast and drink hot black kafe, which Zadia felt necessary if she was to retain any scrap of wit for her concord with Safiya. However, Aljafar was once more going on about visiting Ambrazakti, and she ordered him to leave off; they would revisit the subject again, but *later*. Of course she could not tell her son that she did not want to send him far from home on a perilous journey when Qart-Hadesht could be plunged into a full-scale uprising by spring, but he felt that he was simply being mistreated, *Aliyah* had gotten to go to Yerussala, and sloped off in a sulk. The frustration welled up in Zadia again: she was trying to plan this entire damned rebellion for *them,* so her children could live in the world and the future she had always wanted, and yet they remained so miserably ungrateful.

"I'll talk to him," Khaldun said, low-voiced, once Aljafar had fled from the breakfast table in his fit of dudgeon. "You have to be on your way to the ur-Tasvashtas, do you not?"

"Yes." Zadia felt a sudden relief that he would, as ever, graciously step in to take care of it. While Numeria was respectful and supportive of women, and displayed no particular preference in the succession of male or female chieftains, it was not as resolutely matriarchical as Qart-Hadesht, and when Khaldun first arrived, there had been a question as to how well he would take to a match where he was expected to defer to his wife in both public and private. But he never complained, never resisted or tried to undermine her the way other foreign spouses sometimes did with Qartic women, and she felt a renewed and tender appreciation for him. Leaning down to kiss him, she added, "I'll tell you what I can. Safiya promised that there was much to say."

"I'll look forward to it." Khaldun flashed a reassuring smile. "It's about time that we hear from our wayward daughters, is it not? Did her Elemai not promise to send word from Yerussala?"

"She did. They have a special messenger, Safiya said, who can bear a letter at great speed." Zadia kissed Noora as well, then reached for her veil. "We'll see how true that is."

With that, she called for the household guards to fetch her palanquin, and stepped in, they lifted her up, and set off. The morning was warm and mellow; the Qartic winter months were the most pleasant, when the heat finally eased, the sun polished the Mad ar-Hahrat to shining sapphire, and a cool wind blew off its gentle waves, rather than the scouring gales of sand from the south. Palm trees rustled, walls and towers gleamed white, and people could stay out for most of the day. The markets were crowded, as Zadia saw when peering through the gossamer curtains, and commerce was steady and fruitful. Which was a good thing, usually, but added yet another wrinkle to her dilemma. The High House's chief objection to rebellion, aside from the obvious risk of being flattened by the Meronite legions, was due to the economy: Qart-Hadesht's largest trading partner was also the Eternal City, the twisted synergies and perverse dependences forged when a shackle was made not only of iron but of gold. One was easy to understand as an insulting symbol of slavery and statelessness, but when the other looked like a rich man's ornament, when it offered the delusion of power as easily and deceptively as the map, they all so readily put it on.

Indeed, the streets were busy enough that it took nearly an hour to cross the medina to the ur-Tasvashta villa, which sat in spitting distance of the Temple; the Governor-General could see it as soon as he woke up in the morning and looked out the window. Or more likely, the afternoon, as Gaius Tullius Grassus was the indolent spare of one of Coriolane's favorite patrician families and never bestirred himself to do anything that might generally qualify as governing. On one hand this was a good thing, as he had been posted here for seven years and few people would recognize him if they passed him in the street, but he took a handsome salary directly from the Qartic treasury and spent most of his time in the Temple – the seat of their hallowed history and heritage, sacred self-government and sovereignty – partying, drinking, feasting, and fucking his feckless way through a truly astounding succession of prostitutes. Malicious rumors held that he was too fat for his slaves to lift his sedan chair; that his limbs had turned black and rotten from some terrible venereal disease; that he had been dead for months and the High House was concealing it and embezzling his taxes. In that, at least, Zadia had to disappoint them. Grassus was (regretfully) alive, but he was so useless that he had come to embrace it; he rarely bothered to preside in any official capacity. That did, to be sure, make it easier to dream up sedition beneath his nose, but they still had to be careful. The last thing they wanted was for someone to tip him off at the critical instant, so he could take credit for foiling a plot against the Divine Emperor. Then he would be promoted or recalled to Merone, they would be dead in the water, and the next Governor-General would be a cold and vindictive warlord who kept them on a far more choking rein. Or worse.

Safiya bet Rebiyat ur-Tasvashta waited outside her villa, looking as short, plump, and cheerful as ever. She wore a rich golden-embroidered Parsivati chador, as her wife Marishah hailed from Bhagarayat and the family retained influential connections there, and this unassuming matronly presence, this small soft woman who would pinch your cheeks and pour your tea, served very well to disguise a mind like a bear trap, a ruthless political aptitude, and an iron will that put actual iron to shame. "*Qa-salaam*, my sister," she said warmly, offering the much taller Zadia a ceremonial hand to exit the palanquin. "Ur-Malika's blessings on you."

"And on you, honored saeda." Zadia inclined her head, trying not to show the insecurity that bubbled beneath the surface of her dealings with Safiya. The ur-Tasvashtas were only a few spots below the ur-Beireshtas in the rankings of the most senior and illustrious High House families, while the ur-Namasqas were much lower – still noble, yes, but closer to the Low House than the chairmanship. Zadia had lucked into this association simply by virtue of shared political sympathies, and might well luck out of it again if the winds changed, or Safiya found a more useful and better-positioned ally. No wonder Zadia wanted the betrothal of their children sealed as soon as possible.

Just then, as if reading her mind, Safiya broke into a broad smile. "It is particularly good to see you today, sister. I call you that, and soon, *Inshamalikah*, we will be in truth. I just received word from my Elemai. She made the formal marriage proposal, and your Aliyah has accepted."

"She — she what?" Zadia thought she must have misheard. It was good news, *wonderful* news, of course. "Proposed properly? So soon?"

"Indeed." Safiya beamed even more brightly. "All in all, there is a great deal to tell you, and even more to do. Which will be more difficult, planning a wedding or a war?"

Possibly both, Zadia thought tartly as she followed Safiya into the spacious, sumptuous halls, depending on who you asked. When they were ensconced in the solarium, twice the size of Zadia's and brimming with expensive luxuries from across the Spice Road, Safiya ordered the servants to bring two cups of sherbet and sipped the cold, creamy drink, as Zadia did the same. It was too sweet for her taste, and the small talk was likewise frothy and meaningless, but courtesies were courtesies. Then when the last servant had been nodded out and they were alone, Safiya set her cup aside and leaned forward, turning from effervescent hostess to hawk-eyed politician in a matter of seconds. "So," she said crisply. "If you suspect there is a reason for the swiftness of the betrothal, you would be correct. Elemai tells me that the two of them have found a... particular weapon, and there must not be any delay in confirming the steadfast unity of our great alliance and holy purpose."

"A *weapon?*" Zadia wished that she could stop merely repeating everything Safiya said, like a rather dim talking crow. "What sort of — a Yerussalan weapon, you mean?"

"Of a sort, yes." Safiya's smile did not change, enigmatic as an oracle. "As such, they plan to leave the Holy City much earlier than expected. As you know, they originally meant to stay the winter and return in spring, but now they hope to be home before the new year."

"How can they — " *None* of this made sense, to the point where Zadia almost feared Safiya had started deliberately speaking in riddles. "Even if they left Yerussala as soon as Elemai wrote to you, they could not arrive until the eleventh house of the stars, or the twelfth. If there were storms or other hazards, it would be still later, unless they risked a sea voyage through pirates, exactly as we chose not to do before. And would they not abjure our *other* interests, by leaving so suddenly?"

"You must trust, dear sister, that it is all in hand." Safiya settled more comfortably on the divan and took another sip of sherbet. "In the meantime, we have matters closer to home. If our daughters arrive soon, do you think they should be married at once? It is cruel to wed young people just before Qahyadin, what with carnal relations being prohibited in the holy month, but we must all make sacrifices. As to that, there are a few factors. Our girls originally intended to be home in spring, to prepare for the state visit. And since the emperor is coming here – "

Zadia started. Foolish as it sounded, she had almost forgotten about Coriolane's intention to visit Qart-Hadesht next year, part of his periodic official peregrinations. There was always extra-vindictive satisfaction in making the uppity Qartic republicans kiss his imperial Meronite boot, but he had not been here for some time; the cost and effort of transporting the whole court anywhere, but especially deep into the deserts of Ifriqiyin, was ruinous, and even the imperial treasury needed a few years to recover between each bout of it. Besides, Coriolane was growing especially watchful and paranoid, seeing assassins behind every potted palm, and it was surprising that he had not already canceled this excursion. Then again if he did, it would lend credence to those nasty little whispers of his weakness, and people might start asking whether they could, for the first time in four hundred years, live without him. Of course that was out of the question. And *that* meant –

"No," Zadia said, suddenly understanding all at once and in horrible clarity just what Safiya was suggesting. She felt cold to the bone, even though it was plenty warm in the room. "*No.* Saeda, have you lost your *mind?* If we cannot even move against Grassus for fear of alerting the Meronites ahead of time, what do you think this – "

"Ah, yes. Grossus." Safiya's lip twisted. "High King of the Banquet and Bedchamber, our fearless leader. But we can do it, and we *must*. Do you think we will ever have any better chance?"

"Do we have *this* chance?" Zadia was incredulous. "What on *earth* can Elemai have possibly found in Yerussala to make it remotely plausible? If we are very fortunate, Coriolane might have a genuine scare, but then he will recover from it, crush us, and so – "

"You think too small, my dear." Safiya's tone was pleasant, but notably impatient. "I already noted that this new… item is far beyond anyone's wildest dreams, and it will, I am confident, be sufficient to get the job done. Don't you see? Coriolane will be out of the Eternal City, isolated and on our turf, with only a token guard of legions and Immortals. He will be weakened – he might already be, with this mystery illness that continues to grow worse. There is no way we could ever get to him behind the walls of Merone, but *here* – "

Somewhere in her all-encompassing shock, Zadia noted dryly that the two of them had seriously talked of rebellion for over a year, and yet when the subject turned explicitly to regicide, she still could not quite believe it. It almost seemed unfair to play such a low and cunning trick, to invite a guest to their city with its honored ancient tradition of hospitality and then flatly murder him. Except this guest was the Divine Emperor, Safiya was right that they would never have a better shot at him – *if* this mysterious, marvelous, mythopoeic weapon was anything close to what she seemed to think, which remained substantially unclear – and there were certain substantial and pragmatic advantages. It would be very difficult for the news to get back to Merone immediately, it would throw the imperial delegation into chaos and make it easier to divide and eliminate them in turn, and it would instantly position Qart-Hadesht as the leader of the long-awaited rebellion, rising from the ashes to menace the Eternal City with a new Hanibal. Malcontents and freedom fighters from across all the imperial provinces would flock to their banner, which would serve Zadia and Safiya's aims of recruiting allies and the High House's aims of ensuring that Qartic interests and control remained foremost. If those coalitions could be hammered into a viable rebellion... Zadia wanted to believe. Malikallulah, she did. If only it could ever be so perfectly, blissfully simple.

"This is fascinating, saeda," she said at last. "Truly. But there is a vast obstacle to any such attempt. We would never be able to plan and carry it out on our own, and there is no chance of keeping it secret from everyone else in the Adirim. Even if we asked, Saed Massasoum would never help us, and we are not Coriolane, to force it done by fiat."

"Well," Safiya said. "What if Massasoum was no longer Chair?"

"What – you – " Zadia was horrified. "You would not *also* – "

"Malikallulah, no." Fortunately, Safiya seemed to find it funny, rather than insulting. "I do not suggest scandalously assassinating our honored fellow. But you know there is a certain amount of resentment that a man holds the top spot in the High House, especially when there is a feasible case for his removal. His sister, Mirazhel ur-Beireshta, has once more drawn the Adirim's attention to the fact that she should now, by all rights, be the Batu Beireshta heir, and her claim can be tested in a court of law. If it was proved, Massasoum would be forced to step down, and Mirazhel would take his place. She could finish his term with revised priorities, or as a goodwill gesture, cede the Chair to a new occupant. For which, of course, there would be… options."

Zadia opened her mouth, then shut it. Again, Safiya had an entirely valid point: Massasoum ur-Beiresht's elevation to de facto ruler of *Mother* Qart had ruffled feathers and led to worries that they would become ever more like Merone and its violently absolute patriarchy. Qartic noblemen could inherit the family's Adirim seat if there was no female child, the female child was permanently incapacitated, or there was a compelling reason why she was incapable of performing that lifelong duty, but there had not been a male Chair in many decades, and Massasoum had not eased any fears by announcing that there was no need for his power and preeminence to be unfairly fettered. Except a complication had recently emerged in the form of that sister, Mirazhel. If she was born a girl, she would supersede both Massasoum and their other brothers in the line of succession, but she had only been remade and recognized as a woman within the last few years. Now that the transition was complete, she had begun to politely but persistently point out that according to Qartic law, she was rightfully entitled to the seat her brother currently held. This was, in the abstract, entirely true, and it was also true that Mirazhel was far more likely to authorize an assassination attempt on the emperor – Malikallulah, madness to even *think* it – than Massasoum. If they could just find a way to get him out and install Mirazhel in his place… but even for the best reasons, it was a secretive and autocratic manipulation, a crass internal coup, everything they claimed to disdain and disclaim. It was not guaranteed success, it could poison the Adirim against them and make the victory useless, and even if so – *killing Coriolane,* the immortal, the eternal, the deathless –

Zadia was not the sort of person who thought that strategic and necessary actions should be avoided simply due to delicate moral qualms or excessive hand-wringing. Indeed, she often found that people *could* succeed if they made the choice to do so no matter what, but some feeble internal scruple or last-minute prick of conscience sadly felled it. If they were in the realm of murdering the Divine Emperor, then one piddling domestic intrigue – done to restore the natural order of the city and the primacy of its foremothers, clearly a good and justifiable reason – was almost comically insignificant. If the solution was right there, and they didn't take it because they might *feel* bad –

"I see," she said. "So that's our play? Support Mirazhel in taking her suit to court, and if she wins and deposes Massasoum, induce her to commit the full weight of the Adirim behind this attempt? Which will either succeed, or destroy our city and our children for generations to come? And may yet cause exactly that, even if it does?"

"That is the outline of it, yes." Safiya nodded serenely. "So you see, we have a great deal of diplomacy to perform at Elemai and Aliyah's wedding. Invite Mirazhel as the guest of honor, promise her whatever she needs, and make sure that this is done before spring, and Coriolane's visit. Truly, an imperial funeral will take even more planning."

A consuming chill slid down Zadia's back. "And you still will not tell me what this weapon is, that I must place such great faith in it?"

"Patience, sister." As Safiya rose to her feet and went to open the window-hangings – the solarium had grown stuffy in the course of the conversation – she accidentally scuffed up the great Parsivati carpet that lay on the floor, and Zadia caught sight of something strange beneath. Etchings in the wood filled with thick black grease-chalk, a line connected to a much larger diagram that stretched out of sight beneath the rug. She was not sure, but she thought it was some sort of star. Indeed – the obscure Lanuvian word suggested itself unexpectedly – a *pentacle*. The sort used for summoning demons, or jinnyeh, or any other infernal creature with which God's people should not meddle. What the – was *that* where Safiya's confidence came from, that they could finally dispose of a four-hundred-year-old autocrat once and for all? With *black magic?*

Zadia scrubbed her expression to studious blankness, as if she had not seen or suspected anything. "One other question, saeda," she said instead. "Coriolane is... Coriolane, but there has not been an open provocation, or any particular atrocity that we could use to justify an attack. Merone has been oddly quiet, and I don't like it. Half the battle will be convincing not just the rest of the world, but our own folk in Qart-Hadesht, that we had any right to do it, and if so – "

"Oh, that's the best part." Safiya sat down again, as unruffled as she had been by all of Zadia's objections so far. "Coriolane has finally gone off the deep end. He recently ordered the full-scale slaughter of every Bodeni in Brythanica, and battalions of legions and Immortals alike are presently moving northward in force to carry it out. Yes, the imperial bargain has often been that if we don't cause trouble, serve in the army, and pay our taxes, we are protected by the Pax Meronorum. But if he is exterminating an entire race of people, that will cause some hard feelings, don't you think?"

"He – *all* the Bodeni?" Coriolane was often cold and cruel as a rule, but because he was so obsessed with order and stability, even if only the painted stage-scenery of it, he was typically more discreet about his atrocities. Recklessly ordering complete genocide was simply not his usual brand of dictatorship, and Zadia felt a knot in her stomach: the grim realization, doubtless exactly as the Divine Emperor wanted, that if he could do it to one troublesome province on trumped-up charges, he could very easily do it to another. "How do you – ?"

"Our little birds in Merone continue to sing at night." Safiya nodded at Zadia's melted cup of sherbet. "Shall I order you another?"

"No thank you, saeda." Zadia was still floored. "Why would he run this risk? Why give his enemies such a convenient pretext? He's usually cleverer than this."

"Perhaps," Safiya suggested, "he is becoming desperate, and punishing any rumors of weakness by lashing out harder than ever. Then there is the eclipse. You know how superstitious the Meronites are; even all those centuries of stern Tridevarianism hasn't entirely beaten it out of them. They *will* see the same portent, and then – "

"What portent?"

"The eclipse." Safiya cocked her head. "Surely you heard of it? The astronomers say it will come on the last night of the Meronite year, in their month of Decembris and our tenth house of the stars. The moon will turn to blood and the stars will be blotted in the abyss — or something of the sort, they make it sound very ominous for a well-known scientific event. But in the Meronite tradition, strange heavenly occurrences have long been viewed as boding ill, heralding the death of kings or the end of eras. Coriolane might be the most powerful man who has ever lived, but even he can't stop every person across the empire — across the *world* — from seeing it with their own eyes, and drawing their own conclusions. I daresay that when our moment, *Inshamalikah*, does come to pass, they will see it as only inevitable."

Bloodmoon. Even if Zadia was versed in the knowledge of the stars, as many famous Wahini astronomers had made great advances in their study and observation, it still sent another primordial shiver down her spine. Not for the first time, she desperately admired Safiya's power and eloquence, the way she could make it seem as if the heavens themselves were merely waiting to bend to their will. And even more, that Zadia herself — careful and skeptical by nature, not given to fantasies and fairy tales — could believe. No matter what. No matter how.

"Very well, saeda," she said. "Where should we begin?"

CHAPTER
10
IONIUS

As any halfwit could have fucking guessed, Ionius got absolutely nothing else out of the Vashemite. He *had*, however, spent far more time in the noxious guts of the Castel Sanctangel than he ever cared to repeat, to the point that if he was a more suspicious man, he would almost wonder if Coriolane had done it on purpose. But in truth, the emperor had started to react in this overblown, irrational fashion more and more often: obsessively scrounging up any hint of guilt or disloyalty, any whisper of treason or subversion, even the ones he would ordinarily ignore, scoff off, or simply trust the vast safety net that loyally guarded him at every hour of day and night. It was as if he thought all that power did not work any longer, or had secretly turned against him, or any other bad habit of aging despots who were aware their time had passed and their subjects were growing restive. But that fear was for ordinary kings, fallible mortals, who knew death was coming anyway and jealous rivals might do their best to hasten it. Not for the eternal, the divine, the endless. It made no *sense*.

Aside from the pointlessness of the whole thing, there was no reason to rotate Ionius in and out of the cell unless they were supposed to be torturing him to a truly brutal degree, and while that wasn't totally useless as a strategy – if nothing else, it might frighten Julian Janovynich into remembering more information about the rebel cause – it also meant that Ionius had to constantly keep thinking up new ways to look beaten to an inch of his life. Like all Immortals, he healed very quickly, so self-inflicted injuries only took him so far, and there were only so many times that one could deliberately stab oneself in the face (or arm, or leg, or etcetera) as often as necessary. Even if it healed, it still *hurt*, and after that unnerving episode in Iscaria, when it took too long to mend from Oleg Pavelynich and company's amateur mugging, he was wary of stretching his resilience too far. He was not *that* devoted to method acting or the sob story of poor Ilya Sergeynich, and he had almost decided that to hell with it, he would just reveal his true identity and threaten to make Julian take his turn at suffering. It was what his fellows would have done, nobody could argue with a Castel prisoner deserving it, and then Ionius would be shut of this tedious, mindless, time-wasting exercise. True, he didn't have more information about Qiné-black-powder smuggling, but he was never going to find it in here, and at least then he could conduct a proper investigation. Which, in fact, he had been doing, just the other night. Go to the docks, ask about Vadim Khovanyich, and see if he could solve the problem in another way and save the emperor the embarrassment of having insisted on this losing gambit. After all, it was Ionius' job to fulfil the Divine Emperor's wishes, by whatever method that entailed, and if Coriolane himself hadn't had the right idea, Ionius couldn't let that stop him. Adapt, improvise, overcome.

Then, however. Fucking *then,* as if he didn't have enough to deal with, he stumbled onto the slave girl, skulking somewhere she definitely should not have been. It might seem innocuous, if badly misguided, but he knew it wasn't. Firstly, it should be impossible for anyone to get into or out of the Eternal Palace entirely unnoticed and unquestioned – and yet this unprepossessing female had done it, seemingly with very little trouble. Then she had either enacted a cunning masquerade of helplessness to trick him into rescuing her and making him believe she was merely lost, or she was bumbling on blind luck and therefore exposed a deeply troubling dereliction of duty among literally everyone. If the guards were this shamefully asleep, then Coriolane's hyper-scrutiny of every threat, no matter how minor, made more sense. Perhaps they had grown too complacent, too reliant on the self-evident wisdom that nobody would ever attack the Eternal City or the emperor, and were merely going through the motions, never expecting to face real danger. In a sense, it was a good thing this had happened now, and alerted Ionius to the problem. Vata Korol forbid it be in the wake of a major tragedy.

That was why, therefore, he had returned to the Castel this evening, but not to once more play-act the role of Julian Janovynich's unfortunate cellmate. After crawling around in rags and filth, it was a relief to appear as himself, clad in the full power and threat of his proper rank: the white toga, tall boots, and silver breastplate, the scarlet cloak, the golden bracers and pauldrons that were awarded only to generals who had won a dozen battles. In Ionius's opinion, any soldier who had to deck himself in useless bedazzlements to win respect was someone who could not prove himself where it counted, but he was well aware of the impression it made on others. Even and especially the Corporalists. They liked to consider themselves clever, urbane, and sophisticated, far beyond the petty failures and shortcomings of mere mortals. But they were, to a man, obsessed with the accessories of status, the appearance of power and success. They felt their art to be unfairly stigmatized, demonized and undervalued, when they did so much of the dirty work that made the imperial war machine run, and they were hungry for more recognition, more respect, more *anything*. It made them, all in all, pitiably easy to manipulate.

"Good evening, Grand Magister Saturnus." Ionius offered a cool nod to the master of the order: an unremarkable, slight, balding man who looked to be somewhere in middle age, but with all the experiments and modifications the necromancers did on themselves, was surely much older. Indeed, the Grand Magister himself had performed the necessary improvements on Ionius many years ago, as he did for all the Immortals. "You are looking… well."

"As are you, General Ionius. Very well. One of our best specimens." The Grand Magister beamed, pressing Ionius's big hand between his thin, papery fingers. "We are honored by your visit, my lord, deeply honored. What may we do for you, or His Divine Majesty?"

"It is me asking," Ionius said curtly, "not anyone else. I am looking for information on a certain individual, and I believe your organization knows something about her. A palace slave girl, with brown hair and a bad foot. She looks about twenty years old, and speaks Lanuvian. When I mentioned the Corporalists, she seemed especially terrified. Why?"

Grand Magister Saturnus looked momentarily blank, as if this description could fit so many people that it was impossible to narrow down – who, his expression asked, was *not* terrified of the Corporalists? But he recovered himself, bobbed sycophantically, and beckoned for Ionius to follow him. "This way, my lord. To my study. We keep detailed records, of course. You said she was twenty?"

"She looked about that age, yes. But it means nothing. Is she by any chance Remade?"

"Ah, that is quite possible, yes." Saturnus unhooked a torch from a bracket and led them down a dank corridor, where muffled but horrible sounds emitted from behind locked doors. They were accompanied by a faint but intensely foul odor, rot and shit and blood and all the other primal stinks of the disassembled dead body, and Ionius wrinkled his nose. He had been spared this unpleasantry before, since the Immortals were given special treatment and dedicated quarters while they recovered, waited on hand and foot by slavishly attentive apprentices. "Please forgive this disruption, my lord," Saturnus continued, unctuous and apologetic. "We try to keep the – ah – less savory aspects of our practice out of public view, but down here in the Castel – "

"Yes, I am aware." Ionius breathed through his mouth until they emerged from the hell-hall, descended a broad, shallow dish of stone steps, and came to halt before a heavy wooden door, which Saturnus unlocked with a key worn around his neck. "That is why I came here."

"Of course. You are familiar." The Grand Magister chuckled obsequiously, pushed the door open, and beckoned Ionius inside. In sharp contrast to its dark and ghoulish surroundings, the office was warm, well-lit, scented with sage, myrrh and balsam, and circled in salt, as if to keep any unquiet spirits safely at bay. Saturnus bustled to a cabinet, removed a decanter and pair of goblets, and poured them a bracing tipple of hippocras apiece, which Ionius sipped only briefly. Then Saturnus crossed to the ornate drawers, unlocked them, and ruffled in the files until he paused, then nodded. "Yes, my lord. Yes, I think this is her."

"Well?" Ionius held out his hand. "Let me see."

"I am afraid, General," Saturnus said, "that even for you, I cannot share such highly sensitive records without the express consent of His Imperial Majesty. State secrets and such, and since you *did* mention that this was done without troubling him – "

Ionius cursed. "Then can you be any help at all, corpse-fucker?"

He saw the Grand Magister bristle at the insult, then talk himself down and recover his deferential smile. The Corporalists furiously disdained any suggestion of necrophilia, which doubtless meant it happened at a more-than-incidental frequency and had to be strategically ignored. Not that Ionius cared who or what anyone put their prick into, but he had not come here to get nothing. "Well? Who is she?"

"Her name is Romola." Saturnus glanced at the papers, then fastidiously replaced them, a serene and scrupulous demiurge of his own little underworld. "She is, in fact, Remade. In this incarnation, it has been about five years. A useful body, but a troublesome one, evidently."

Well, then. So the bad foot wasn't a novice mistake by an inexperienced resurrectionist, but a deliberate punishment preserved from one ensoulment to the next, the sort usually reserved for particularly egregious offenders. *What are you hiding, girl?* It was surprising enough that a chronic troublemaker had been revived at all, and not consigned to permanent oblivion. Remaking was a delicate, difficult, and obscure process, but Ionius knew the basics. One took a corpse, the more recently expired the better, and applied a battery of spells, substances, and other secretive emulsions. Then by some equally inexplicable method, the necromancer infused it with a replacement soul, a mix of the old one it was born with and a new one artificially created by some bogglingly complex alchemical procedure. The resulting person, when returned to the land of the living, was not quite their predecessor and yet not totally divorced from them either. It was a useful way of retaining specialist skills, shoring up manpower, fixing any issues in personality or behavior, and otherwise minimizing the impact of any unfortunate accidents or unplanned deceases. As such, it was mostly reserved for high-status or important individuals, such as the Immortal cadets, but there were a great deal of common dead and not enough space to bury them all. In that case, why not pad out the ranks of slaves?

"I see," Ionius said, thinking hard. "And how many times has Romola been Remade?"

"Several, my lord." Saturnus drummed his fingers on the desk. "I am afraid I cannot share more details without His Imperial Majesty's permission. If you wished to ask him for it – "

"No need to trouble him with such a small matter, an unimportant slave." *At least, that is, until I know what she's been doing, and for who.* "If I was, theoretically, to discover some troubling information about Romola's conduct, what would happen to her?"

"It rests, again, upon His Majesty's counsel." Saturnus bowed, hand on his heart, as if Coriolane was in the room. "But if a serious issue of obedience or other core defect is identified over multiple resoulments, we make the decision to retire that body from further existences, and put it to use in other ways. Haruspicy or scapulimancy, mostly."

"And those are?"

"The trained haruspex opens the guts of the body and uses them to divine augurs, the future, and other mystic information, my lord." Perhaps it was just the light, but Saturnus looked greasier and more weaselly than ever. "It is often disdained as a charlatan's practice or an old wives' tale, but thanks to working closely with the Thaumaturges, we have refined our practice to a high degree of accuracy. It is similar with scapulimancy, which involves the cutting and casting of bones. Indeed, I recently read a fascinating treatise by an esteemed Franketerrish occultist, which suggested particular nuances in the polishing of the – "

"Enough." Mildly revolted, Ionius waved the Grand Magister into silence. "So is that what you were doing to those unfortunates I heard screaming on the way in?"

"Oh no, my lord." Saturnus wet his lips. "You see, the ones used for divination are dead by the time we begin. As for those presently in the black cells, well. They are not quite so fortunate."

Ionius grimaced. Aware that he didn't much want to hear the answer, but should attend to it nonetheless, in the name of professional thoroughness, he said, "And what do you do to them?"

"It varies." Saturnus spread his hands, as if to convey the sheer impossibility of distilling his beloved art into a brief explanation. "Just now, however, the emperor has taken a particular interest in our work. His Majesty insists that we leave no stone unturned in probing the deepest mysteries of life and death – those that, despite all our learning and that of our vaunted predecessors, we have not yet been able to completely and conclusively solve. As such, he has given sweeping orders that we are to have all the test subjects we could possibly need. Thus our extra demand for specimens, and our expanded methods of examining them. Of course, we live – " he tittered, so this was probably some stupid necromantic in-joke, *we live where others die* – "to serve Merone."

That, for the first time in this increasingly distasteful conversation, was the thing that jolted Ionius the most, but not for any of the expected reasons. Rather, it was the implications. *Coriolane is afraid of death.* What else could it mean, if he had fixated on the Corporalists, given unlimited license to increase their mandate, and was determined to smoke out everyone who had ever had an uncharitable thought about him? But as was so obvious that it beggared the necessity of pointing out, he was immortal. Eternal. Unchanged for four centuries. *Unless he isn't. And if so, is it because someone within the palace – or the Corporalists themselves – are sabotaging him? Or something else? Something we have not foreseen, and cannot stop?*

Ionius controlled his expression, so Saturnus could catch no glimpse of this alarming train of thought. "Forgive me," he said, in a voice strongly implying he meant nothing of the sort. "But are you and your order not principally responsible for maintaining the emperor's health? Are you not doing your job correctly?"

"General Ionius, believe me, we are the emperor's most devoted partisans and physicians." Saturnus wrung his hands. "But there comes a time when even the most perfect workings no longer function as originally intended, and enter a stage of gradual but irreversible entropy. It is why we cannot remake the Remade indefinitely, or render you and your fellows, despite the name, actually and forever immortal. Long-lived, of course. Remarkably resilient, likewise, with talents far beyond any ordinary plebeian. But eventually, life is no longer life. It is finite, and it ends. That, of course, is where we come in. Be assured, we can solve this minor trifle for His Majesty, and we must."

Ionius started to say something, then stopped. He had come down here for information on a wandering slave girl, and stumbled instead into the far worse realization — which Saturnus was far too careful to explicitly state aloud, but which hung between them like Damoscen's blade — that all Coriolane's usual methods of preserving his endless life were slowly but surely starting to fail. Which meant he was genuinely weakened, slipping into possibly-permanent decay and decline, genuinely more vulnerable than he had been in nearly half a millennium. *And if so? If it reaches its natural end? If even the Divine Emperor, the first man who was supposed to truly live forever, does... not?*

It was almost treasonous to think that, and Ionius shook it away. He felt almost light-headed, torn between terror and something else, barbed and shadowy. "You will," he said, "solve this."

"Beyond a doubt. It is the highest challenge in the history of our brethren, but we will surpass it." Saturnus attempted to offer what he clearly felt to be an avuncularly reassuring smile. "Failure is not an option. We have only begun to explore the potential solutions, including many rituals that even the most learned among us, including myself, have never previously attempted. When His Majesty is, ah, restored to his usual self, this knowledge will spur even greater accomplishments by our order. It will be a Meronite golden age unlike anything before."

Ionius refrained from pointing out that this was an excessively sunny spin on a very serious problem, as doubtless Saturnus had already offered this soothing explanation to any number of jittery imperial officials. *How many people know of this?* At all costs, it must not go beyond the palace, or even the emperor's presence chamber, unless it already had. *Vata Korol, why didn't he tell me? How am I supposed to keep him safe from all threats, if I don't even know what they are?*

"Thank you, Grand Magister," Ionius said. "Truly. While I respect your desire to honor His Majesty's discretion, I must take my own action. Is there anyone else it might be useful to speak with?"

"Well..." Saturnus vacillated. "I would never wish to betray the emperor..."

"Of course not. I see this as proof of your loyalty. On the other hand, if you withhold it..."

Ionius let the threat hang like a baited hook, obvious enough with no need to twist, until the Grand Magister gave in. "I have been working in close coordination with His Holiness. We are, of course, equally devoted to the preservation of our divinely ordained sovereign."

Ah. The Archpriest of Merone, the second most powerful man in the empire, the supreme spiritual father of the True Tridevarian Church, His Holiness Mellius Sanctus Sixtus. It seemed that Ionius was unearthing unexpected tangles of root clusters all over the place, and they were starting to coalesce into something uncertain but ever more unsettling. He thanked the Grand Magister for the information, promised that he would not reveal its source, and took his leave.

Early the next morning, Ionius changed into humble peasant clothes and hood and slipped out, descending from Palatorian Hill onto the Avenue of the Gods, which led across Lordsbridge to where the Arch-Holy Basilica dwelled in all its breathtaking splendor. Regardless of anyone's theological opinions on Tridevarians, it could not be denied that they did architectural glory second to none. It rose in great gravity-defying confections of stone like frozen lace, spun sugar and floating ice, and sunlight slanted through the massive cantilevered glass dome to the travertine marble floor five hundred feet below. The vast windows reflected shimmering colors, the crystal chandeliers glittered and flashed, the high altar rose like a snowcapped mountain above the humble fields of pews, and the art, the statues, the flowers, the cloth, the books, the paintings were all the very finest stuff. It was calculated to overawe all the senses, to summon an abject and reverential admiration of the artistic genius of man, the religious supremacy of the Three Gods, and the political power of Merone, and it did those things very well. Coriolane had personally financed a major renovation, celebrating the first hundred years of his reign, to ensure it did so for many generations to come.

At this hour, the basilica was almost empty, except for yawning deacons shuffling around to change the candles, sweep the floor, tend the sacramental flame, and prepare for the day of services. As Ionius stepped over the threshold of the eastern door and briefly genuflected, he thought of the tiny church in Tseyabilsk. He was not an ikonomiso, the hardline minority of Tserkovians who believed that all gaudy golden images of the Divine Family were idolatrous and should be destroyed, but he still wondered how any creature, god or otherwise, could live in this place for long. It was beautiful, cold, and hollow as a bone.

Just then, one of the deacons spotted Ionius and hurried over. "Are you here for confession, goodman? We do not offer it until after Prime, but if you wish to wait – "

"No need." Ionius shrugged down his rain-spotted hood; the morning was grey and drizzly, the winter rains would soon start in earnest, and it was chilly enough in this frigid stone wonderland that their breath misted faintly silver. "Where is His Holiness?"

"General Ionius." The deacon was aghast. "We had no chance to prepare a proper welcome. We surely did not intend to offer any – "

"Shut up," Ionius said impatiently. "I am in urgent search of your arch-holy master, and if you must wake him, I will wait, but not for long. So, then. Why don't you go and get him?"

The deacon hemmed and hawed, then decided, as most people did in this situation, that the wisest thing to do was precisely as he had been told. He turned and hurried off, and Ionius leaned against a pillar to wait. Mellius Sanctus, Sixth of That Holy Name, lived next door to the basilica, in the equally splendid Lateran Manse, and since his presence was not required until the main morning oblation, he usually left the grunt work and graveyard hours to his flunkeys. Though if he had gone into one of his periodic ascetic fits, when he wore a hair shirt, vigorously flogged himself with knotted cords, and spent all night lying facedown on cold stone, refusing all sustenance except bread and water, he might not be asleep. It was as if he occasionally looked around, realized that he resided in a palace to rival the emperor and enjoyed a vast untaxable fortune while preaching the virtues of poverty, chastity, and obedience, and had to go into a brief and violent seizure of self-abnegation to resolve the cognitive dissonance. However, it never lasted. He'd be back to silk sheets and rich banquets by the end of the month.

In about ten or fifteen minutes, the deacon returned, leading His Holiness – disheveled, still buttoning his cassock, and looking peeved. He was a tall man with short grey hair and a slightly vulturine face; previously thin enough to be nearly skeletal, his midsection was now showing the soft effects of increasing years and indulgent living. The rest of him remained bony, sly, and sharp-edged, like an aging hawk, and the gaze he turned on Ionius, albeit bloodshot, was shrewd. "Good morning, General Ionius," he declared, in that deep, resonant voice that said the liturgy so well. "What an unexpected pleasure. What may I do for you?"

"We should talk." Ionius beckoned His Holiness to follow him into the side aisle, past the burial-stones and grave-effigies of countless Meronite luminaries; if he bridled at being commanded like a common servant, Mellius Sanctus Sixtus did not show it. They paced along in silence, gazing contemplatively at the carved faces of the holy dead, until Ionius, having ensured that all the deacons were out of earshot, turned to the Archpriest. "Do you know why I am here?"

"I confess, I do not." Mellius's expression remained courteous but inscrutable. "On an errand of His Divine Majesty's, perhaps? I did not expect to see you on your own accord. When it came to religious sentiment, I had the impression that you preferred the Ruthynian rites."

"I am a Meronite," Ionius said sharply. "You will not insinuate that I am a heretic."

"My apologies." Mellius had perfected the politician's art of saying it and sounding genuine, while nonetheless ensuring that nobody would ever think he actually meant it. "I know that you are indeed Coriolane's most trusted servant. So is it because of him?"

"Yes. But he doesn't know that I am here, and I will thank you to keep it that way." With that, trying to convey the situation without editorializing – not least because he wanted to hear how the Archpriest's explanation matched with the Grand Magister's – Ionius revealed the reason for his visit. "Well?" he finished. "Do you have anything to say? Is that why Coriolane indulged your pleading to finally let the Holy Orders Militant go ahead and slaughter all the Bodeni? Thought that if he did, it might purchase him some proper currency in your prayers?"

Mellius blinked. "I beg your pardon?"

"Surely you are aware of events in Brythanica, Your Holiness?"

"Oh, my son." The Archpriest placed a consoling hand on Ionius's shoulder. "You must not be troubled. They are only pagans."

"Be that as it may, it is a dangerous escalation, and out of keeping with Coriolane's usual method of governance. If it is true that he is… weakened, it is a poor time to aggravate the provinces even further. And when I spoke to the emperor, he made it clear that you had been pushing for this action for quite some time. Why did he agree to it now?"

"You surely do not think I would dare speak for His Majesty, or attempt to divine his mind." Mellius ghosted a self-effacing shrug. "I simply informed him that we would never take Brythanica under control if the Bodeni were not dealt with. We have tried softer measures for decades, and all of it failed. And if it kills two birds with one stone – "

"What? What other bird?"

"Your pardons, my lord, but it is none of your business." Mellius spoke with an unmistakable aristocratic timbre, a sharp reminder that the Emperor and Archpriest of Merone were not obliged to disclose their secret convocations to a mere slave, Immortal or otherwise. "You flatter me if you think I could manipulate or force His Majesty into anything, but I did not. I only gave him the information. The choice was his."

Ionius chewed on that. Mellius was not answering his questions directly, talking in circles and careful circumlocutions, but that was to be expected. They stared at each other, waiting to see who would break. Then Ionius said, "Is there any insight you *can* offer, Your Holiness?"

"I am not your enemy, General." Mellius's voice remained smooth, but a faint defensiveness crackled underneath. "You do not need to stand and accuse me as if I were on trial. Trust that I am just as concerned about this alarming situation as you. Especially since in my conversations with my honored colleague Grand Magister Saturnus – yes, I know that you must have spoken to him, you needn't look so surprised – he revealed the troubling fact that as far as he and his order know, the magic used to keep His Majesty in good health should have lasted for at least another two hundred years. Which means, my lord, this attack on it, its unexplained decline, is not natural or timely. This is not the proper cessation of all living things. This is *deliberate sabotage*."

Ionius felt as if the Archpriest had swung a heavy silver ciborium into his face. It took a moment to gather himself and speak. "Sabotage? You are – you are sure?"

"I relay only what the Grand Magister said to me. It is his truthfulness you would have to question, if such necessity arose." Mellius turned away, gazing at the funerary plaque of a long-dead praetor. "If you ask who could have the ability or desire to do such an evil thing, rest assured that if I had the slightest indication, I would tell you. It is *imperative* that no harm comes to the emperor. Coriolane Aureus IX is the greatest champion the True Tridevarian Church has ever had, and if we must condone temporary distasteful measures to keep him that way, so be it. Our blessed Divine Family will forgive any offenses we are forced to commit in the name of defending our monarch, our faith, our truth. On this, there can be no question at all."

Mellius was obviously a practiced and polished politician, used to hedging his words and concealing his intentions, but he now spoke with a naked, burning fervor that could not be anything but genuine. Ionius often had some sense of when people were being deceitful with him, and – on this, at least – the Archpriest was telling the truth. Whatever he was up to with his insistence to Coriolane that they just stamp out the Bodeni once and for all, he did think it was for the good of the empire and the church, to stop whatever threat was trying to bring them down from the glittering apex of power. Ionius said, "If you believe it."

"I do." Mellius looked urgent. "You must too, my son. This is no time for doubt, timidity, or half-measures. His Majesty needs you to carry out his wishes, even those for which the reasons might not be obvious. If your conscience is troubled, come to me. I will absolve you."

Ionius uttered a noncommittal grunt. He looked at the white walls of dead men, shining monuments to eternal glory and blessed memory. One day, he too would sleep forever in the cold catacombs below, where all the Immortal generals were entombed; even if they died on a battlefield a thousand leagues from Merone, their bodies were brought home. He only hoped his last journey would come later and not sooner, which seemed ominously likely if he kept getting entangled in conspiracies of this magnitude. Nonetheless, he had to get to the bottom of this. Someone wanted to kill the Divine Emperor. Not only that, they were *killing the Divine Emperor at this very moment,* and Ionius had no idea who it might be, or how to stop them.

"I see," he said. "Thank you for this conversation and your wise insight, Your Holiness. I will take my leave."

With that, adroitly dodging the deacons inviting him to stay for the morning service, Ionius did just that, emerging into the awakening flow of the streets and letting it sweep him on his way. His head was spinning, and he was not sure of his next move. Perhaps Coriolane had not told him this because in the absence of any hard evidence for the murderer's identity, motive, or methods, everyone — even closest confidantes and most trusted allies — had to be treated as a suspect, and could not be tipped off or given a chance to try a cover-up. And if Ionius let on that he had delved into this without permission, contacted the Grand Magister and the Archpriest behind Coriolane's back and become privy to damaging details, there was no way to say what the emperor would do. Either way, it was unlikely that he would let it pass without censure, and even if it was his right, it would still hamper Ionius from carrying out his duties. Coriolane might lash out and do something he would regret. Ionius would simply, discreetly not give him the chance.

Likewise, he was unsure whether to confront Romola again until he learned what the hell she was up to, and that meant another round of interrogating the overseers, castellans, chamberlains, and everyone else. But that had to be done carefully, in a way that would not cause Romola's handlers to realize she was potentially compromised. Of course she had to have them, someone using her as an opportune pawn. She was just the symptom of the disease, not its cause, and handing her back to Grand Magister Saturnus and company would not be a cure. So, then. Who was using the slave girl, and where might *they* be found?

After an extended rumination, leaning on the ornate birdshit-speckled railing of Lordsbridge and watching the Tibir swirl past, Ionius settled on a startling yet inevitable conclusion: he had to try his luck with Julian Janovynich one more time. It was strictly practical, no more. His cellblock conversations with the Vashemite were strategically useless, but not entirely unenjoyable. Julian was clever, sarcastic, and shockingly unafraid of anything, and if he made a cutting remark about the empire or the emperor — well, Ionius had to chuckle, as a matter of keeping his cover. Other times it was out of startlement, disbelief that someone could be shut in the worst place any imperial citizen could think of, that routinely drove its victims mad, and still be able to mock it, as if its crushing, overwhelming, unending power meant nothing. Then again, as long as Ionius had personal purview over the prisoner, none of the jailers dared to come down too hard. Perhaps Julian thought that all those terrifying tales about the Castel were hot air, and it had always been this much of a pleasant vacation. He admitted frankly that there was nothing for him in Korolgrod right now, or anywhere else. He didn't *want* to be here, but he didn't know what he would be doing if he wasn't.

He is not your friend, Ionius reminded himself, *or your helpful little confidante. He is your enemy, an enemy of all Merone, and when this is over, you will go back to treating him as such.* The masquerade of comradely solidarity was likewise restricted by the fact that Ionius (or rather, Ilya) was supposed to be getting regularly tortured, and if he was too vivacious, Julian would start to suspect that all was not as it seemed. If he did not already, and that was why he was so cagey. Ionius could not deny that the intellectual exercise, the need to stay ahead of a sharp and observant adversary, to keep his stories consistent and his Ruthynian suitable for a rustic Kozhek rebel and not an educated Meronite speaking it as a second language, was thrilling. *And if he hasn't come clean, it's just as much your own fault. You've never made him.*

He growled aloud and shook his head, setting off up the hill and back to the Eternal Palace. From there, he hurried into the Castel, changed into his prisoner disguise, and had the guards chain him, drag him down the row, and throw him more convincingly into the cell than they had yet managed. He hit the dirty straw and rolled; it genuinely hurt, and he could feel it in his hard-used bones. But an Immortal never retired. An Immortal died in action, in glory or in ignominy, an eternal hero or a reviled coward. There was no other choice.

"Ilya?" Julian's voice came disembodied out of the dark. "Ilya, are you all right? I was getting worried. The bastards had fun with you for a while that time, didn't they?"

Ionius didn't answer, affecting to still be unconscious, and heard the clank of irons as Julian moved closer. His hand ghosted over Ionius' shoulder. "Ilya? Ilya Sergeynich? Fuck. Come on. Wake up. Hey. *Hey.*"

Ionius remained motionless even when Julian grabbed him and tried to roll him over. Then after several moments, he let his eyelashes flutter, a choked groan escape. "Where... where 'm..."

"Back here." Julian's voice was wry, trying to hide something that sounded suspiciously like relief. "Again. Sorry. You gave me a scare, though. I thought – "

He stopped. Then he cleared his throat and said, "Never mind. Anyway. What the hell did they do to you this time?"

"Wanted..." Ionius racked his body with an agonizing cough, reminded himself not to enjoy the way Julian reached for him again, and spat into the straw. Then he husked, "Shouldn't..."

"Shouldn't say?" Ionius could hear the skeptically raised eyebrow even without looking at Julian directly. "Really? They've spent the last few weeks doing the Almighty-knows-what to you, and you still think you should dutifully keep the empire's secrets?"

"Not... that." Ionius pushed himself onto an elbow. "Just doesn't even seem... real."

"Doesn't seem real? Why not?"

His eyes had adjusted to the dimness, so Ionius got a good look at Julian Janovynich for the first time in a week. It seemed that these days spent tensely alone in total darkness, unsure what had become of his companion and then to have him returned seemingly in pieces, were the most genuinely frightening of his incarceration to date. He looked gaunt and sallow, drained and dirty, as if without Ionius here to shield him, the guards forgot to mete out gentler treatment or basic necessities. *He sees what the Castel is now, doesn't he? You should have done it far sooner.*

Never mind that. Better late than never. This was profitable; this could be exploited. Ionius lay with his eyes half shut, breathing raggedly, too aware of Julian's presence next to him, and the unsettling revelation that he himself was what had kept this from being terrible. *And he thinks that only because he does not know what you really are, so don't go getting misty-eyed. Get on with it, Sazharyn.*

That was startling in another way, even if it was understandable that when he was down here, pretending so carefully to be Ruthynian, he would accidentally think of himself by his birth surname. *You are not him.*

You are Servus Eternus. Since he was in danger of squandering whatever limited chance had opened, Ionius hastily steered out of these treacherous waters. "They thought I knew something. About a plot."

"Plot?"

"To…" He hesitated a final moment, as if bracing himself to voice the unspeakable, and in a way, he was. "To… kill the emperor."

"What?" Julian laughed aloud, harsh and discordant against the damp stone. "Now they've really lost their minds. That's impossible."

"They didn't think so. They insisted that we – the patriots – had come up with a way to do it, that we were somehow weakening the spells that maintain his life. They seemed truly frightened. If it was all just a stupid rumor, I don't – I don't know if they would be so alarmed."

Julian made a sound halfway between abject longing and resigned despair. There was another pause. Then he said, "So did you? Know?"

"No. Of course not. I thought the same thing, it wasn't possible." Ionius coughed again. "But if it was true – can you even imagine?"

"Even if so, it wouldn't solve anything. For the Vashemites."

"What do you mean?"

"You know." Julian blew out a frustrated breath. "It's always the same. Some autocrat will come along and scapegoat us, conveniently blame us for everything that went wrong before, build the so-called new Ruthynian nation on announcing that now they have the power to throw us out for good, just like the tsars did once upon a time. You're a Kozhek, I thought you would care about that, but maybe you agree that your culture is inferior and should be wiped out. Gavriel was a fucking liar about many *other* things, but he's not wrong about that. If so – "

"Gavriel?" Ionius's ears pricked up. *The boy is allegedly a close associate of Gavriel Coheyn, one of the Korolgrodian rebels recently brought to our attention as a problem.* "Who's Gavriel?"

"A… friend of mine. Former friend." Julian's mouth twitched savagely, in a way Ionius didn't understand. "Gavriel ben Avraham. He recruited me into this whole rebel thing. He had all these big ideas about how we couldn't make any compromise with the goye, since they would always stab us in the back. Of course when it came down to it, he wasn't willing to do so much as give up his place at the university, but – "

"Didn't you say you couldn't go? As a Vashemite, I mean?"

"*I* couldn't go, no. *He* could. His uncle is rich. Mezudeh ben Khovan, but he goes by Maxim Khovanyich with the goye. He's obscenely wealthy and he's paying Gavriel's tuition double, so – "

"Maxim *Khovanyich?*" Ionius's heart started to pound. "Wait – does he know Vadim? Vadim Khovanyich? He's an… associate of mine. He lives here in the city, usually, but something happened to him, I've been trying to find out what. Is there any chance you know?"

"Maybe? Gavriel does have another uncle who lives around here, I think." Julian frowned in thought. "I'm not sure if that's Vadim, though. How do *you* know him?"

"We – my group has worked with him, but only through letters. I've never met him face to face. He claimed he could get something special for us. Qiné black powder."

"Qiné black *powder?*" Julian looked genuinely startled. "That's news to me. If any of our contacts could lay hands on anything like that, we would have known it long ago. Plenty of people would have been itching to use it. Are you sure it was Vadim? When did you hear this?"

"Recently, as I said. One of our operations went awry, our courier got caught at the docks. He was bringing a special delivery for Vadim, but Vadim must have gotten tipped off and run."

"You're a smuggler of illicit weapons? *Qiné* weapons?" Julian looked half-impressed, half-wary. "And here you claimed, when you first got thrown in here with me, that all you'd done was assault an Iscarian tax collector. You're clearly quite the criminal, Ilya Sergeynich."

"We all have hidden depths, do we not?" Ionius moved himself around to look at Julian's face. "Nobody ends up in the Castel by accident. Especially us totally innocent seditionists."

Julian snorted a reluctant laugh. "I suppose not. But this doesn't make sense. Gavriel's uncles aren't rebels, any of them, in any way. Trust me, they did not make all that money by acting against the regime's interests, and if Maxim Khovanyich ever found out what Gavriel was really up to, he'd pull his support and stop paying his fees. Which might be a good lesson for him, but – "

"We never know what any man does in secret, do we?"

"No. But if this Vadim is the same one, it's not right. It's a setup, some lie. I'd swear it."

Ionius opened his mouth to insist that Julian was mistaken, and then he stopped. After all, had Julian not just been complaining (accurately) how Vashemites were always unfairly scapegoated? And presumably if one was doing something so dangerously illegal as smuggling Qiné weaponry into the Eternal City, one would not use one's own name. Especially if there was a reputation to be lost; how had Coriolane described the suspect? *Vadim Khovanyich, a well-known community leader of the Ruthynian quarter.* That squared with what Julian said about Gavriel ben Avraham's relations, who had achieved wealth and prominence by cooperating with the Meronites but still had to contend with the long-standing prejudices against their people. Blaming a Vashemite was a useful way to conceal whoever was truly responsible, and Ionius would strongly wager that it was not, in fact, either of the Khovanyichs. Everyone "knew" that Vashemites were untrustworthy, rich Vashemites all the more so. There would be no question that Vadim was the culprit, even if he wasn't. Had he fled out of guilt, or because either way, the accusation doomed him?

"I see," Ionius said. "Look, Julian, if I don't come back – "

"What?" Julian looked at him askance, and with a flicker of real fear. "Why wouldn't you come back? You don't think they're actually going to kill you, do you? I doubt they'd even be able to manage. You've been tortured for days, and you look fine. So – "

At that, he stopped, a sharp line furrowing his brows. Glanced at Ionius again, up and down. "You look *fine*," he repeated, slower. "In fact, like you've never been hurt at all. And when you turned up in here for the first time, you already knew who I was. How?"

"What? What do you mean? How could I possibly?"

"You tell me." Julian pushed upright, eyes flaring. "You asked what I'd done to get thrown in here – *dared to gaze too long at a Tridevarian in the street?* Which wouldn't make sense unless you already *knew* I was a Vashemite. So who are you? Really."

"My name is Ilya Sergeynich, like I said. Who else would I be?"

"I don't know." Julian's narrow stare grew even narrower. "But it occurs to me that I should have done a lot more wondering. That meeting my friends and I were having back in Korolgrod – it was because someone was killing rebels in Ruthynia and Iscaria, and we were all spooked. They thought it was an Immortal. And Immortals are clever, aren't they? Specialize in how you never see them coming? Wouldn't it be funny if that was *you?*"

"What? Are you insane? Why on earth would I be down here?"

"I don't know. I'm not saying you are. I just – wonder."

"No. Of course I'm not a filthy fucking *Immortal*. You're cracking, you're turning against me, it's what they want." Ionius reached out with his chained wrists as if to remind Julian of their shared indignity, the bond of prison brotherhood. "You need to rest. Here. Let me help."

Julian was still barely mollified, but after a long moment, he sighed and dropped his gaze. "You're right. I just – sorry. It's this place. It's... getting to me. I'm trying not to let it, but it is."

"I know," Ionius soothed, letting Julian settle his disheveled dark head onto his shoulder, and felt the gusty, aching exhale that rattled through every sinew of the young Vashemite. "There you go. It's all right. We'll get through this together. Shh."

He sat there for several minutes, reaching out with a few other less-tangible skills and senses to help coax Julian into a restless, shallow doze. Then when it had deepened into a steady slumber, Ionius slipped out from under him, made sure he didn't wake, and eased out of the cell. Blessed Mata Koroleva, that was *too fucking close*. He had no idea what tipped it off, if Julian's suspicion was subliminally brewing for a while and clicked into place by unfortunate coincidence, he took a wild guess that he didn't really believe, or if Ionius himself had made a fatal mistake, but he had to be certain it never happened again. Nobody had ever pegged him as an Immortal ahead of time. But Julian Janovynich had seen it, seen *him,* and that could not be allowed. Not now, or ever again.

Still rattled, Ionius went up to his rooms, took a long bath to get the stink of the Castel off, and only then sent a message to humbly implore Coriolane for an audience at the emperor's earliest convenience. He still had not decided what, if anything, to say about the business with the

Grand Magister and Archpriest; for the time being, it should probably be nothing, though that ran the risk of being accused as a traitor if Coriolane found out in some other fashion. *He will not do that. He trusts me, he values me. He knows I would not betray him.*

Ionius whiled away the afternoon in terse and pacing abstraction, watching the Eternal City blur in the steady curtain of rain, until a messenger arrived at Vespers, bearing a reply stamped with the imperial seal. By the time he navigated the chilly stairs and echoing corridors and finally entered the garden cloisters, Ionius was damp, dripping, and startled to find Coriolane sitting on a bench and staring at the soft grey mist, rather than safely enclosed by the warmth of a hearty fire. "Majesty, what are you doing here? Surely it would be more comfortable inside."

"I appreciate a breath of fresh air." Coriolane gestured. "Sit."

Ionius hesitated, then did so, doing his best not to size up the emperor too obviously. Did he look ill, or drawn, or otherwise incapacitated? Had he lost weight, or was he jaundiced, or failing to pass water or stool? Ionius felt like a nervous mother hen, but Coriolane looked as he ever did. Perhaps the lines around his eyes were more obvious, or the shadows beneath them, but that was the recurrent product of chronic insomnia. Wasn't it?

"So," the emperor said. "What was this news?"

"About the task you set me, Majesty." Ionius touched his heart. "Uncovering the identity of the miscreant bringing black powder into our city. I have not found for certain who it was, but I *have* discovered that they are attempting to throw us off the trail. That being so – "

With that, carefully editing the controversial or clandestine parts, he informed Coriolane of the results of his investigation into Vadim Khovanyich, and his conclusion that the name was only a red herring – a clever ruse, offering no hint as to who was truly responsible. "What also bothers me, Majesty," he finished, "is that we have not found any of those first hundred and fifty barrels of black powder. If those things are at large, in Vata Korol-knows-whose-hands – "

"The Lord, General Ionius," Coriolane interrupted. "You refer to the *Lord*. You are not in your backward Dvadevarian province now, are you? No. So kindly do not speak like it."

The use of that insult made Ionius flinch, but he ignored it. "Apologies, Majesty. Of course. What I mean to say is that I do not think this is a trivial or low-level incident, as I did at first. Again, you have my humblest apologies. I should never have doubted you."

"What?" Coriolane looked at him askance. "Do you mean to say that you *did* doubt me?"

"At first I was..." Ionius trailed off. "I never doubted the seriousness of the threat, only the wisdom of using Jul – the Vashemite to investigate it. But if it has in fact borne fruit – "

"You would do well not to ever again imagine that you are qualified to think for me, slave. Has this become a habit with you – this dissent, this heresy – while you were in Ruthynia, steeping in the pagan air of your native soil? You know what an honor it is that you have become not only a Meronite, but an *Immortal*. Surely you are not confused?"

"No, Majesty. Never. But if someone is concealing their own treachery by scapegoating the Vashemites, that too could seriously – "

"I care not to listen to your misguided defense of those accursed Prince-killers," Coriolane snapped. "You are doing little to convince me, in fact, that you are still entirely clear on what your duty is, and to who. Perhaps another errand in the field will help to clarify your mind."

"What – Majesty, you said I was not to be sent to Brythanica?"

"No. Not Brythanica. Sardarkhand, where the second half of this transaction is supposed to take place, and the next set of barrels handed to our unknown buyers. Gheslyn suggested that you be the one to go. She is very worried about this threat, and trusts only you to manage it."

Ionius started to answer, then stopped. It was news to him that the senior empress believed only in his abilities, among the multiplicity of Immortals at her disposal, and he resisted the thought of being sent far from Merone again while this dangerous mystery remained outstanding. It took three months of hard travel on the Spice Road to reach Sardarkhand, at least for ordinary folk; the Thaumaturges could transport Ionius much faster. At last he said, "I mislike leaving you behind, Majesty, while that first set of barrels are still unaccounted for."

"What?" Coriolane laughed. "You think someone would light the fuse beneath my bed?"

Romola managed to leave the palace with nobody noticing. I fear that it might be easier than we suspect to bring something in. Ionius, however, did not say this aloud. "Very well. If you command me to go to Sardarkhand, Majesty, then I will go. Should I make a stop in Yerussala too? The spies are reporting some very strange stories."

"Not Yerussala," Coriolane said decisively. "There is plague there. It would not be safe."

"*Plague?*" Evidently Ionius truly had been out of it while he was running after necromancers and priests and rats. Surely not the Red Death, but possibly no better. "I had not heard that. Are we quite sure? It would not bode well, not at all. The Holy City reopens for the first time in ten years, and then a scourge of sickness?"

"The Lord wills what the Lord wills." A queer, unsettling little smile flirted with Coriolane's lips, but didn't quite arrive. "In any event, there is not much we can do, aside from shutting the gates to new pilgrims, preventing the old ones from leaving, and ensuring that this contagion does not spread. I am more concerned with finishing our business here. If the Vashemite has served his purpose, we can get rid of him, don't you think? Do it before you leave for Sardarkhand."

Ionius felt as if he had missed a step going downstairs. "You want me to kill the Vashemite?"

Coriolane looked both surprised and suspicious. "What else would I want with him?"

"He is…" Fucking hell, the emperor was right. Ionius wasn't thinking clearly, kept tripping on self-inflicted obstacles and unnecessary objections. He had rarely been rebuked so openly or even shown the need to be so, the last thing he should do was to keep digging in his heels, and yet. "It may be the case, Majesty," Ionius said, improvising wildly, "that his use is not yet done."

"Oh?" The emperor looked briefly intrigued. "Why is that?"

"Because – " It was as likely as anything, was it not? "He knows about something important. Something you could use."

"And that is?"

"That is, Majesty." It was, after all, true. "The Ring of Tselmun."

CHAPTER
11
ALIYAH

Nobody seemed to know what had happened, or how it unfurled with such terrifying speed. Aliyah and Elemai had only just begun the process of deciding how they would get home, and when they would leave; they still had business in Yerussala, but nothing that rivaled the importance of getting the Ring back to Qart-Hadesht and officially commencing their – whatever it was, rebellion or otherwise. They did not want to endure another grueling two-month journey across the desert, if a faster and more convenient magical option was available, but it seemed likely that they would be dropped headfirst into some cursed tomb in a Gezereni ziggurat if they did not instruct Khasmedeus with extreme caution. Nor could they, after all that time and effort spent in actually getting to the Holy City, explain their eagerness to just turn around and leave again. It would give rise to rumors, confusion, and other unwelcome questions, and yet there was no easy way to simply sneak out the back. They might miss something important, if they left Yerussala so far ahead of time, but both of them were burning with impatience to put the Ring to proper use, and if anyone else realized what they had – what Aliyah was walking around with every day, as if it was nothing more than a cheap trinket –

That, however, all came to a screeching halt in a few short hours, in the last day alone. They had been about to leave the caravanserai after mardiq when Captain ur-Vorrosq stopped them; according to him, there was a herald in the street who was strictly ordering everyone to stay inside. When they asked why, he admitted he did not know, but it was a legionnaire in Meronite livery, the one authority who could not be disobeyed. Likely it was just temporary, to quell the flare-ups between competing groups of pilgrims. When there were so many people crammed into such small spaces, streets, and shrines to which they all felt themselves to have the most important claim, and they also had different religions, languages, homelands, beliefs, and opinions, it gave rise to frequent tensions, shouting, skirmishes, and outright brawls. The Yerussalan Governor-General, Urbis Pontius Pallas, had threatened to confine Wahini and Vashemites to their respective city quarters if the trouble continued (Tridevarians, of course, could come and go as they pleased) and Aliyah's first thought was that this must be related to that. But it was not. Instead, it was much, *much* worse.

"Plague?" she said blankly, that evening, when the first garbled reports and rumors started to filter in. There was an entire street by the Temple Rock that had been struck by an unidentifiable disease, taking ill and deteriorating at shocking speed. They had first felt poorly at Prime this morning, and by now, the authorities were sealing off their houses, shrouding their corpses, and ordering their neighbors to quarantine until they could be sure it would spread no further. Outbreaks of some disease were unavoidable, the usual curse of travelers brought together from afar and forced to squash cheek by jowl with strangers, but they all hoped for nothing worse than fever, grippe, or cough. But none of that was this.

It had been over six hundred years since the last recorded epidemic of the Red Death, which killed half the Meronite Empire during the reign of Coriolane VI, including that unlucky emperor himself, and laid waste to much of the known world. Casualty figures were by nature inexact, piecemeal, and subject to wild speculation and revision; in Qart-Hadesht, the number was claimed to be three-quarters of the city, and even allowing for the inevitable exaggeration of historians, it was not far off. It boggled the mind to think of that much untrammeled, unceasing, unending loss: entire families, friends and neighbors, rich and poor, great and small, sparing nothing and no one. Faced with such relentless and savage destruction, struggling to reconcile it with the promised grace, benevolence, and omnipotence of the Divine Family, Tridevarians fell back on their all-purpose solution of blaming the Vashemites. They carried out massacres in Merone, pogroms in Ruthynia, sham trials and stake-burnings in Franketerrum and Ibelus, and other outbreaks of mindless violence that had no purpose aside from the desperate need to pin the horror on *someone,* so why not the Prince-killers? And indeed, when the terrible specter once more reared its blood-dripping head, the first suspects were again the Vashemites. Some prominent Franketerrish pilgrim, invoking the martial glory of his ancestors in this very place, was already vowing to lead a mob against the Vashemite Quarter and purge them all from the city before sunrise.

"No," Elemai said, lips pinched, as Captain ur-Vorrosq finished his grim report. "No, that doesn't – *this* doesn't make sense. Aside from the fact that it's obviously not the Vashemites, how can this be possible? It's been six centuries. It's not – it can't be *that,* is it?"

"We don't know what it is." Captain ur-Vorrosq wiped his grimy brow with the cloth he had untied from around his mouth and nose. "The Governor-General ordered the archivists to dig up the scrolls from the time of the Great Dying, but I doubt we'll learn the truth. It could cause a mass panic or worse, and the Meronites will brutally suppress any rumors of whatever pestilence they have allowed to take root in the heart of the Holy City. From what I heard, this disease kills too quickly to be the Red Death. There was no boiling blood-fever, or – saving your pardon, saedas – shitting, or vomiting, or black buboes. But this is very little comfort for anyone, and there is expected to be an edict closing the city by dawn. We will know more tomorrow, perhaps. *Inshamalikah.*"

At the sound of it, Aliyah flinched. While the captain dutifully attended prayers with the rest, he, like most career men of war, was not particularly observant or devout. Hearing that fervent invocation from him meant this was serious, and she and Elemai exchanged a foreboding look. When they had thanked ur-Vorrosq, told him to scrub thoroughly in the hammam and report at once if he felt poorly in any way, he bowed and showed himself out, and the two of them were alone. There was a frightened pause. Then Elemai said, "Do you think you should - ?"

"I suppose. I mean, yes." Aliyah's throat was dry, and her voice trembled. She was still not sure how it would work, but there was no choice. She took a deep breath, raised her hand, and rubbed the Ring. Possibly even prepared for whatever might happen next.

This time, there was no spectacular show, brazen attempt to scare them half to death, or other grand herald of Khasmedeus's entrance. It simply blew into existence like a billowing cloud of smoke, solidifying into the form it had taken in the vineyard after its first explosive release: black topknot and beard, white loincloth, dark skin. Even so, the fire flickering just beneath the surface cast unnatural shadows on its features, limned bright-edged around its teeth and sparkled in its yellow eyes. "Good evening," it drawled, sweeping an unnecessarily deep bow. "How do I have the pleasure of serving Your Grandiloquences tonight?"

"Hush," Elemai snapped. "None of your stupid jests, jinnyeh."

"Oh, and whose knickers are in a knot?" Khasmedeus blew a disdainful raspberry. "Anyway, enjoyable as it always is to see a pretty human woman in a huff, I'm afraid that your boring command holds no weight, sweetcheeks. It's only my vaunted mistress, the holder of the Ring, who can order me around. What was your name again, little mite? I don't think I caught it last time."

By instinct, Aliyah opened her mouth, then stopped. Elemai was openly apoplectic at being addressed as "sweetcheeks," but that was not relevant to her hesitation. For jinnyeh, names were rare and valuable currency. They could use them to discover your secrets, twist your orders, nullify your control, and otherwise make it an exceedingly hazardous business to traffic with them – which, of course, was just what they wanted. Aliyah did not know if it was only a concern for experienced magicians uttering strings of complex legally-claused commands, or if clueless amateurs would get into even more trouble from sheer ignorance. Either way, it was not a good idea to take risks.

"You can call me... Amarasha," Aliyah said, choosing her grandmother's name. Tilting her head at Elemai, she added, "Rebiyat."

The jinnyeh raised an eyebrow, as if sardonically commending her for evading that snare. "Amarasha," it repeated. "Not *quite* that, I think, but I can wait. Fine, then. What's the big fuss?"

Elemai made a sound as if once more intending to take the lead, but Aliyah gave her a very pointed look, and after a moment, unhappily, she subsided. When Aliyah finished with their tale of woe, the plague suddenly ripping through the Holy City and the trouble it posed to their plans, Khasmedeus mulled in silence, eddying in curls of smoke like a whirlpool. Then it said, "So what do you want me to do about it? Whisk you two home, free as a bird, leaving all those other poor sods to drown in their own fluids? Impressively ruthless, but thus are all humans."

"No. We just didn't think you…" Aliyah trailed off, feeling as if they should have discussed this beforehand and hammered out a plan, rather than improvising on the fly. "We didn't mean that. Of course not. But it's a plague, an act of the Almighty. What could we do?"

"What indeed." Khasmedeus grinned, even more ferally than usual. "It doesn't strike you that it seems extremely *convenient?* One fine day, the Ring of Tselmun and yours truly – " it spun in a flourishingly sarcastic circle – "is unearthed from its hiding place of however many centuries, by person or persons unknown, and conveyed to you by unexplained methods. The next day, the old fool who gave it to you drops dead, and now there's the Red Death or something worse, stalking the streets of poor beleaguered Yerussala all over again. Haven't you read the histories, the sagas, the pulp fiction, anything at all? As soon as you illicitly excavate some mysterious antiquarian treasure and claim it for yourself, the curse follows. Every time. Not to mention, and in case you've forgotten, I *knew* Tselmun. Personally. This is the exact sort of thing the old bastard would do, and often did. Even from beyond the grave, he would make sure that nobody could ever touch what belonged to him. And if they did, it would destroy not just them, but everyone."

Aliyah wanted to argue, to insist that it was mistaken and this could not possibly be their fault (*her* fault), but now that the jinnyeh had stated the theory aloud, it did take on a disturbing plausibility. The Ring might *look* unremarkable, but it contained the entire violence and vengeance of ancient sorcery, and by all accounts, Tselmun ben Dayoud had jealously guarded his power and privilege. But he also had a reputation as the good, the just, the wise king who used his magic for the benefit of his people, who created that dazzling city of beauty and harmony, the one

Aliyah had been so disappointed to find no longer existed, if it ever had. Surely he wouldn't – but he might. Enchant his terrible magic ring so no grubby mortal could lay hands on it without invoking an even greater cataclysm, because Tselmun would be long dead, and the consequences were nothing to do with him. Frighten the interloper into giving it up, returning it to its sleep, and so –

"No," Elemai said, making Aliyah jump. She stepped forward, regarding Khasmedeus flatly. "I don't think so. Because if that were true, the only way to stop it would be for us to relinquish the Ring, set you free, and do everything else that you want, leaving us helpless and at your mercy. Jinnyeh are tricksters, aren't they? Jinnyeh lie. No doubt you held a grudge against Tselmun, as any servant would, but it doesn't mean that the plague is because of him."

"Oh?" Khasmedeus raised the other eyebrow. "Or are you only saying that because if this plague *was* unleashed by the Ring being stolen, that might put some responsibility on you to stop it? And that would mean, for once, that you didn't get exactly what you wanted?"

"Excuse me." Aliyah was getting more and more irritated by the way Elemai kept referring to *we* and *us,* as if they were a singular entity and commanded Khasmedeus in perfect tandem. Yes, technically, they were in this together; yes, Elemai had formally proposed marriage and the wedding was likely to take place as soon as they returned to Qart-Hadesht. But it was plain that all her reminders were falling on deaf ears, and Elemai fully intended to continue acting as if she had the exact same rights. "For the last time, the Ring is *mine*. The decision is also mine."

Elemai started to speak, sputtering and heated, then shut her mouth hard enough to hear her teeth click. "Of course," she said. "How discourteous of me to forget. Please, saeda, what do you suggest?"

"Trouble in paradise?" Khasmedeus drawled. "And you're not even married yet. As I said. Totally not doomed, you two. You seem absolutely on the same page. So touching."

Aliyah ordered herself not to rise to the bait. Whenever they were in the jinnyeh's presence, their flaws and weaknesses were ruthlessly exposed: Elemai's authoritarian inclinations and arrogant superiority against Aliyah's inferiority complex and contrarian stubbornness. Even if

Diyab was dead and could not be asked why he had chosen her, he *had,* and she found herself becoming ever more possessive of that fact. Perhaps it was an effect of the Ring itself. If it was capable of unleashing a plague on an entire city, it could do far worse things to her. She had to be careful, had to make sure she too was not turning into a monster, but –

There was a simmering, nauseous silence. Khasmedeus looked smugly pleased at the obvious wounds of its prodding and poking, while Elemai and Aliyah stewed in unison. Then Aliyah said, "If – and I repeat, if – this plague *was* caused by the Ring, could you stop it?"

"Nope." Khasmedeus shrugged. "That was dear old Tselmun's doing, the same as when he enslaved me in the first place. You don't think it's a bit on the nose? You and your band of adorably scrappy rebels are struggling to break free of the Meronites, who enslave everybody, and you decide that the best way to do it is by using another slave, whose opinion or desire to participate you have never once *asked,* because you know full well that you can force me if you please? And there's no chance, no teeny tiny chance, that this makes you *total hypocrites?*"

Its voice was customarily barbed and bantering, ironic and irreverent, but this righteous fury was very real, and not easily denied. Elemai opened her mouth, shot a half-angry, half-guilty look at Aliyah, and shut it again. Feeling the weight of their gazes, Aliyah struggled for words as if she was sinking in quicksand. But this was what she had asked for, and she could not falter. "Do you *not* want to take down Merone? Look what they've done to Yerussala, your home, your – "

"Yerussala is not my home." Khasmedeus paused, then sank into a sitting position, its eyes lupine yellow and just as intent. "It is the place where the greatest humiliation in the history of my people was visited on me, and on us, where we became mindless accessories and brute labor for Tselmun's favorite piece of homicidal jewelry. Let me guess. You're in mourning for all those pretty stories of Yerussala of old, the beautiful magical city where everyone was happy, held hands and danced in circles and whose farts smelled like roses. Listen to me, girl. It never existed. Oh sure, it was lovely to look at. But how was Yerussala built? How is Merone built? How is any empire anywhere built? It was fed and fattened on endless blood, jinnyeh and human. It was in a state of constant war, slaughtering all the local tribes for any tiny difference in which gods they worshiped or the stories they believed. Slaves built those shining towers and bought those spellsingers' beautiful books. Slaves carried Tselmun's splendid sedan chair in the streets, slaves labored in the brutal sun and died by the score, and slaves were constantly called to his bed to serve his pleasure. How do you have seven hundred wives and five thousand concubines except if women aren't people to you, but just pretty dumb dolls to fuck and forget? Even with Queen Bialkyis, the story everyone remembers, he only wanted the tribute of her kingdom and the submission of her body. Tselmun was a *monster,* girl. Every king of that stature is nothing but. But it's their scribes who write the history, their bards who sing the praises. And over and over, humans always want the exact same thing. Why should I care about overthrowing Merone? It'll be back before you know it, calling itself something else. It's *useless.*"

Despite herself, that caught Aliyah short. She sensed that for once, the jinnyeh desperately and truly wanted her to listen, and was doing its best to make her do so. There was an undeniable ring of truth in its words, which she ignored at her peril, and it took her a long moment to think how to respond. At last she ventured, "It could be different for us. With Merone. Even if you don't care about it, even if jinnyeh can escape their oppression, we can't. So it would still – "

"What part of what I just said makes you think we can *escape the oppression?*" The jinnyeh looked exasperated. "If you use the Ring, your oppression is escaped only by continuing mine. So forgive me if I'm not raring at the bit to join yet another doomed human crusade for stupid human reasons. There's nothing you can offer me or mine, and that's not any equal bargain or grand moral high ground for your cause. You can force me to obey, yes. You have that power. Just like Tselmun did, and trust me, *he* didn't spend a single moment worrying about what his slaves thought. If I squint, you do look a bit like him. Or is it Coriolane?"

"I'm not like Coriolane." Aliyah bit it out, stung. "I can't be."

"Ah." Khasmedeus raised a wry, world-weary eyebrow. "They always say that too."

Another fractious pause. For once, Elemai wasn't rushing to speak up; she seemed to have gotten the message, and kept her mouth shut.

Aliyah and Khasmedeus eyed each other. Then Aliyah said, "You keep saying *we, us, me and mine*. Are there others? More jinnyeh?"

"We are a whole race of people, just like you." Khasmedeus looked away. "Or at least we used to be. There aren't many of us now. Centuries of being constantly enslaved, abused, brutalized, and otherwise trodden on by humans has taken its toll, and it was all made possible by the magic Tselmun invented precisely for the purpose of doing so. You'll have heard of his great grimoire, *The Key of Tselmun?* It's what every sorcerer has used as their main textbook ever since. The Meronite Thaumaturges stole it for themselves, the same way the Corporalists did with the *Book of Daybreak* and Gezereni necromancy. Are you getting it yet? You can't use jinnyeh magic without using Tselmun's magic, and Tselmun's magic now belongs to the Meronites. And what are you if you use Merone's weapons, methods, mindsets, texts and tools? That's right. A Meronite. If you touch it, there is no way to wash yourself clean of that blood."

"All right." Aliyah raised her hands. "You've made your point. If you were going to help us on more equal terms, what do you want? Is there something we can give you, or your people?"

Khasmedeus looked as startled as if the dead themselves had stood up and started speaking (then again, as a jinnyeh, maybe it could do that). "You don't mean that."

"Why not? Maybe I do."

"Other humans have said that. They'll promise me anything. When push comes to shove, they never follow through. So I don't put any stock in even more empty flatulating of – "

"But with what you just said," Aliyah persisted. "Doesn't it mean we could in fact have the same goal? If we finally got rid of Merone, we could free Qart-Hadesht, and we could also free the jinnyeh magic from the Thaumaturges. Wouldn't that be what you want, at least some of it? Break Tselmun's thrall on you that has endured for thousands of years, even beyond the grave?"

Khasmedeus opened its mouth, then shut it. For once, this creature as old as the stones, as changeful as fire, as quixotic as the wind, did not know what to say. At last, it mustered some relic of its usual scoff. *"Just get rid of Merone,* she says. Easy."

"It could be different." Aliyah met its gaze. "If we trusted each other."

"How?" Khasmedeus lifted its wrists and sardonically clanked its golden fetters. "As long as I'm bound like this, and you won't even do so much as gift me with your real – "

"It's Aliyah." Aliyah heard Elemai's sharp inhale of breath, warning her that this was a wildly reckless step to take without prior consultation, but too late. "Aliyah bet Zadia ur-Namasqa. There. Now you know it. Doesn't that make it much harder for me to coerce you?"

"It... does." Khasmedeus granted it unwillingly, as if still searching for the trick or catch. "I could tear you apart, girl. Throw your commands back in your face. And you'll risk that?"

"You said it yourself. I'm not a magician. I never heard of the *Key of Tselmun* until now. If you help us with this, I'll... I'll set you free. Destroy the Ring, whatever I have to. I swear."

Aliyah felt as if she was climbing above a plunging chasm without a rope, but she could sense that she had finally struck a nerve. She could see as well the naked longing in Khasmedeus's face: desperate to be rid of the way it had remained bound to Tselmun even for thousands of years after the great king's death, forced to serve whenever anyone else found the Ring, tried to use it, and promptly destroyed themselves and any other unfortunates in the vicinity. If it could be free, if it could break the magical bonds that held it and its proud kin in such wretched servitude... and if those were also the political bonds of Merone, the sinews that wove the empire together and gave it its power, if the jinnyeh and the Qartic people could finally both be their own masters...

"I'll hold you to that, *Aliyah*." Khasmedeus pronounced her name with exacting care, its furnace eyes never wavering. "And if you betray me, I will destroy you. Will you take that bargain?"

"I will." Aliyah stepped forward, offering the hand that bore the Ring. "You?"

Khasmedeus looked her up and down for a final moment. Then it blew out a gusty sigh that scattered sparks, stood up, and straightened its loincloth with a sullen flourish. "Oh, what the hell," it muttered. "It's not like I've got any better ideas. Fine, then. You have a deal."

After that, at last, matters finally began to move with something approaching speed. Elemai looked honestly impressed, as if some of her fears as to whether Aliyah could manage this had been assuaged, and went out to find Captain ur-Vorrosq's lieutenants and have a quiet word. When she returned, she informed Aliyah that she had made discreet arrangements to cover their exit; those who needed to know the truth would do so, and the others would be fed a story about an visit to the holy shrines in the mountains. Since there was likely to be a hasty exodus out of the city anyway, it would be difficult to keep track of all the hajjis. Despite her disappointment at leaving Yerussala early, Aliyah was eager to escape the sickness, see her family, and reveal her stunning success. "Thank you," she said to Elemai. "I'm sorry I was short, earlier. We do need to be a team."

"It's all right." Elemai looked apologetic. "I deserved it. After all, you *are* the holder of the Ring, and you did well. With Khasmedeus. I'm not sure that I would have seen the same parallels, made the same argument. It was… it was very clever."

Aliyah nodded, flustered but pleased, and they hurried to collect their things and prepare for departure. They were stealing out under cover of night, and when they climbed to the roof in their traveling robes and headscarves, she gazed at the dark warrens of Yerussala, lying in an enforced and misleading quiet. From here, it was impossible to tell if the plague was spreading, or where, or if there had been more deaths since the first violent spate this morning. A knot of guilt writhed in her gut, and she twiddled the Ring restlessly on her finger. *This isn't my fault. I didn't ask for this, I didn't order Diyab to give it to me. It's why we need to break Tselmun's spells once and for all. We must.*

In a few minutes, Aliyah spotted a strange dark shape undulating toward them, low against the skyline, which formed into – indeed – a flying carpet, just like the ones in Shahrzad's tales. She couldn't hold back a delighted, incredulous chuckle as it flowed in front of them, bobbing at knee-height. "Well," Khasmedeus said, perched atop it in the form of a large firebird, its gleaming feathers casting an eerie glow. "Hop on."

Aliyah and Elemai looked at each other, then stepped carefully on. Aliyah sat in the front, Elemai behind with her arms around Aliyah's waist, and Aliyah wondered if she was supposed to grab the tassels, though she couldn't see how to steer it. Or how they would not fall off. Or how they would manage not to be seen. After all, an actual *flying carpet,* complete with complimentary firebird, was hardly the most inconspicuous escape method ever devised.

She twisted her head around, looking questioningly at Khasmedeus, but the jinnyeh seemed utterly unconcerned with such provincial trivialities. "Hang on," it said gleefully, and shot skyward.

Aliyah did her utmost not to scream as unbecomingly as she had when launched aloft the first time, when she inadvertently released Khasmedeus from the Ring, but it was very difficult. They ripped upward so fast that the wind scoured their faces, squeezed tears from their eyes, and buffeted them so it felt as if they must fall to their deaths at any moment – but they didn't. Yerussala fell away like a stone down a well, and then they were *flying,* in a way that made Aliyah gasp with exhilaration even as her heart roared in her ears. Khasmedeus had grown larger, almost the size of a mystical roc, and propelled them along with mighty flaps of its burning wings, darting and dodging through the thin scrim of moonlit clouds. Elemai was clutching her so hard that Aliyah briefly feared she had broken a rib, but as the flight leveled out and they soared through the night like a pair of legendary heroes, Elemai let out a breathless laugh. "Malikallulah, this is – this is – "

"Marvelous." Aliyah couldn't deny it, even if there was nothing for *her* to hold onto and the sides of the carpet terminated sharply in a very, very long fall. "Khasmedeus," she shouted. "Nobody can see us, right?"

"Do you think I'm a *total* amateur?" The jinnyeh scoffed. "No."

Somewhat (if not entirely) reassured by this, Aliyah did her best to look down and appreciate the gods-eye view, though doing so for too long made her dizzy. She saw the vast black surface of the ocean, and the high desert they had battled on the way in. Now it pulled away like a rumpled cloth, until it seemed impossible that it had taken weeks to cross on camelback. Soon she spotted the red cliffs of the ancient city of Petrakh, where the bandits had tried to attack them, and the magnificent stone temple of its long-gone people. Then there came the great serrated shape of Khufre's ziggurat and the great sprawl of Qahirah, they whipped past nearly close enough to shine the nose off the statue of the ancient sphinx-goddess Ahemait, and struck out due west, the Sand Sea on their left and the Mad ar-Hahrat on their right, just as the first hint of sun crimsoned the horizon behind. The northern coast of Ifriqiyin rippled and folded, zigging and zagging, rising into stark cliffs and broad beaches, crashing waves and desolate headlands. Sometimes, Aliyah spotted the encampments of Bahjouns and other nomadic desert folk, ghostly hints of human presence that quickly vanished. As the sun rose properly, it filled the heavens with evanescent light and golden mist, towering and twisting, as the ground came and went in scurries and sketches. It was the most beautiful thing she had ever seen. She didn't want it to end.

And then – they had traveled from Yerussala to Qart-Hadesht in just one night, it seemed unthinkable, and yet those great walls rising from the whispering sands could be no other – it did. Khasmedeus swooped low over the medina, just as it was filling with the morning's first customers. Nobody seemed to notice a huge firebird, a flying carpet, and two bedraggled young women zooming over their heads, so hopefully the jinnyeh was telling the truth. The Temple rose majestically on its hill, then the roof of the ur-Tasvashta villa. Khasmedeus hit the brakes, decelerating them gently, and they whirled to a windblown halt.

It took several moments for Aliyah to feel confident in standing up; her legs had turned to jelly, and she did not want her future in-laws' first impression to be her falling flat on her face. Not, however, that she intended to bow and grovel. Elemai had argued it was best to arrive here rather than the ur-Namasqa residence, since her mother could better prepare for the delicate conversations with the Adirim, and Aliyah had agreed, but she planned to keep a sharp eye on all of them. Safiya bet Rebiyat was well known as an extremely shrewd and ruthless political operator, and Aliyah would be disappointed if her new mother-in-law did not try to take the Ring off her at once, whether in honor of their impending kinship or by insisting it was too great a burden for a young girl to bear. But it did not matter. It was, and it would remain, her own.

Elemai had just clambered off the carpet, equally woozy, when a trapdoor on the roof swung open and an elegant silver-bearded man emerged: Ghassan ur-Tasvasht, Safiya's first husband and Elemai's father.

Despite the early hour, he was fully awake and dressed, as if he had been sitting up all night and waiting for them, and on sight of Elemai, opened his arms in abject relief. "My child!"

Elemai hurried to hug him, he expressed his great joy at her safe return, and then turned to Aliyah. "Greetings, Aliyah bet Zadia," he said warmly, taking her hands in his own. "I understand that you are soon to be my daughter by marriage?"

"Yes," Aliyah said, though she was puzzled as to how he could already know that – and for that matter, how he had known exactly when to expect their triumphant entrance. After all, it was impossible for any messenger to have already made it here from Yerussala unless they had their own magic carpet, and it made no sense. Filing that away as an interesting question for later, she put on her brightest smile and bowed respectfully to Ghassan. "It will be my pleasure, saed."

Khasmedeus, who had judiciously shrunk to the size of a sparrow when Ghassan appeared, flew over to Aliyah, perched on her shoulder, and dulled its feathers to brown, plainly to avoid causing any heart attacks before proper explanations. As they followed Ghassan and Elemai, Aliyah whispered, "Why don't you dematerialize? I can call you later."

"You sure?" Khasmedeus cocked its bird head and eyed Ghassan with a skeptical expression. "Might need to suddenly shit on them."

"Shh." Aliyah gave it a reproving look. "I can manage."

Khasmedeus paused, shrugged, and muttered something that sounded ominously like "your funeral." But it took her advice, shriveling into a small puff of smoke that inhaled itself back into the Ring, and Aliyah hurried her steps. Once she stepped off the ladder and onto the balcony below, she cleared her throat, tugging Ghassan's sleeve. "I am eager to speak with you and Saeda Safiya, of course. But should we not summon my own parents? There will be much to plan with all of us."

If Ghassan hesitated, it was impossible to tell. "Of course. I will send a messenger."

Leaving Elemai to herd her into the solarium, he departed, and Aliyah could hear an excited murmur circulating through the house as the news spread. Footsteps thumped and floors creaked, and then the door flew open, bringing in Safiya ur-Tasvashta and her other two spouses, Marishah and Jahifar. They descended on Elemai with many clucks and cries of excitement and relief, kissing and congratulating her, and Aliyah watched from the corner, feeling like an interloper. But then Safiya hurried over, taking Aliyah's hands likewise. *"Malikallulah qa-salaam*, my daughter," she said warmly. "Welcome to our family. We are greatly blessed that you will wed our Elemai."

"Of course, saeda." Aliyah bobbed an awkward reverence. She looked around again, hoping that her parents would arrive soon, and struggled to look as if she belonged here, soon to marry the heiress of the house. A servant appeared with cups of steaming kafe and plates of shakshuka, bambalouni, and other breakfast food, and Aliyah, starved, dug in with vigor. She was just scraping up the last bites when the door opened again. Four people entered: her parents and a tall, elegant chosen woman with a deep green veil and a golden stud glittering in her nose. She looked vaguely familiar, but Aliyah could not think why.

"Habibta!" Her father rushed forward, holding out his arms, and she hurried to meet him, hugging him tightly. *"Inshamalikah,* you are home and safe. It is good. So good."

"Th-thank you, Abba." Aliyah sniffed. "And you."

"Indeed." Zadia bet Amarasha stepped up beside her husband, trailed by Noora, who gave Aliyah a warm smile but did not move to overshadow the matriarch. "Did you have a productive visit to Yerussala, daughter? Even if it was shorter than anticipated?"

"I… I think so, yes." Aliyah firmed her shoulders and met her mother's eyes. "Amma, I – I have done as you hoped. Elemai asked me to marry her, and I have accepted."

Something flickered in Zadia's eyes, but she nodded. "Yes, we heard. Saeda Safiya told me. And said there was something else you found in the Holy City, some sort of weapon? I confess, I am intrigued to learn what could have possibly brought you all the way back at such speed."

Aliyah hesitated, but her mother moved past the subject with her usual ruthless efficiency. "Permit me to introduce Mirazhel bet Imra ur-Beireshta, eldest daughter of the Batu Beireshta and sister of Massasoum, Chairman of the High House of the Adirim. Mirazhel, this is my daughter Aliyah, betrothed of Saeda Elemai."

"Greetings," the green-veiled woman said graciously, offering her hand, and Aliyah took it. "I am eager to make your acquaintance."

"The pleasure is mine, saeda, though I did not know to expect it." Then as something occurred to her, Aliyah frowned, and hoped she was not being unforgivably rude by pointing it out. "Wait, if you're the *eldest* daughter, how does your brother hold the Batu Beireshta seat?"

There was a crackling pause. But instead of looking mortally offended, Mirazhel, Zadia and Safiya seemed gratified. "Well, habibta," Zadia said. "That, and much more, is the subject of our discussion. Clearly, you have a great deal to share as well. I suggest you sit."

Aliyah paused. Then she sat.

"Good." Zadia looked again at Mirazhel and Safiya, and the three women drew up together. "Then we will, indeed, tell you how we intend to change the world."

CHAPTER

12

JULIAN

He was beginning to lose track of time. At first, he had been able to mark a rough count by when Ilya Sergeynich appeared and disappeared, but then Ilya vanished for what seemed very much to be for good, and Julian was alone in the bowels of the most infamous prison in the Meronite Empire, with ample time to sorely regret his unfathomable foolishness. How terrible could it be, if he just sucked it up and married Rebeka Roshensteyn? She was by far the least offensive option, and he had quite literally thrown it away. At least she knew the truth about him, remained his friend despite it, and would have been amenable to negotiating a suitable arrangement – not least because her affections also fell elsewhere, in the person of a rather terrifying yentl named Tovah. Rebeka and Julian had kept each other's secrets before and could continue to do so, it would have made his mother happy, nobody needed to know if they shared a bed as man and wife (though in the relentlessly gossipy ghetto, it might well get out regardless), and most importantly, he would not be here, chained to a dirty wall and strewn in dirty straw, staring down the barrel of a slow, wasting, and utterly insignificant death. Whether it would come from starvation, beating, torture, neglect, or being eaten alive by fleas and rats, Julian did not know, and none of it seemed good. Had he really thrown a juvenile fit of pique over Gavriel Coheyn of all unworthy persons, and so doomed himself like an idiot? To think, he had daydreamed about coming to the Eternal City and applying to the Imperial Academy. Now if he was fortunate, his corpse might be transported there after his death, for the medical students to dissect. *That or the bloody fucking Corporalists.*

It was almost bearable when Ilya was here, or at least less totally terrible. He wasn't bad company, the guards were more lenient when he was around, and if he had that rough-hewn, ruggedly masculine handsomeness that always attracted Julian more than it should – well, *that* was thoroughly irrelevant. If he once or twice entertained a fantasy of the two of them breaking out of prison together and going on the run, it was nothing but the pointless hallucination of a detainee who had no other amusement and did not expect it to ever come to pass. Besides, it was now entirely moot. Ilya was gone and after Julian briefly lost his mind and accused him of being an Immortal, perhaps he did not feel inclined to return. If, that was, the bastards hadn't already fucking tortured him to death. They hadn't, had they? He had seemed hurt, yes, but not *dying*. Something about it didn't make sense, but there was no reason it should. This was an exercise in sheer futility on any number of levels, and Julian would soon be reduced to scouring the walls for hidden messages or mysterious carvings, that self-sabotaging impulse of the human brain to force its suffering to make *sense,* regardless of whether it did. Maybe he should just give up and go insane. It might be easier.

And yet that innate and unending stubbornness, that spitefully dead-set refusal to let this very bad thing succeed in breaking him, goaded him onward, and he remained militantly, furiously, defiantly sane. To while away the endless, cold, dark hours of solitude, he made mental lists, recited prayers, or in the finest Vashemite tradition, argued angrily with the Almighty about why He had permitted this to happen. Julian tried not to think too much about home. It was almost midwinter, when the Tridevarians celebrated the old Lanuvian pagan festival they had piously rededicated in honor of the Prince and the Vashemites observed the Ten Bright Nights of Tor Ghezel, and there would be food, drink, dancing, warmth and family and festivity. The vile prison slop served in the Castel was obviously not shemyite, though that was also the least of Julian's concerns, and his chest ached when he imagined his mother's cooking, the merry spinning of the dredyl and the glow of the menorakh. Did they think he was dead? They must. As far as they knew, he had disappeared without a trace, and only Isyk would have any notion about just why he had fled. Would he share it with their parents, if the alternative was thinking their youngest son lost forever? Would they feel it was their fault, or blame Julian still more firmly for defying the ordered dictates of the law? In a sense, it was easy to be a Vashemite, regardless of where you fell on the spectrum of belief. As long as you *did* what you must, carried out the Lord's commands, you were still one of His own.

Still, though. He was wasting away inch by awful inch, and all the memorized Vashach passages in the world could not keep him sane forever. He was dozing fitfully when sudden light scalded his face and made him raise a protesting hand, clanking in its fetters. "What the $f-$"

"Silence, prisoner." The unfamiliar voice spoke Korolgrod-accented Ruthynian, which was – to say the least – unexpected. Julian blinked hard, and when he peered shrewishly through the bars, he could tell at once that *this* was an Immortal, or at least an aspiring one. The young man was not even Julian's age, tall and skinny, and was clad in plain tunic, undyed cloak, and the other trappings of a junior cadet who had not yet passed his final trials and taken on the unbreakable shackles of *Servus Eternus*. And he intended to do that by proving what a ruthless killer of traitors he was, no doubt. Bloody terrific.

"Who are you?" Julian croaked. "What do you want with – "

"Silence," the cadet repeated. He passed his torch to a flunkey and stepped inside the cell. Then he bent over Julian and performed some complicated prestidigitation that made the shackles unlock and fall off his wrists. "This is a great honor for you, Vashemite. You have been summoned by Grand Magister Kronus. Do you know who that is?"

"Kronus? What? No." As he was hauled to his feet for the first time in two months, Julian's knees buckled and he almost fell, grabbing the Immortal's shoulder to steady himself. The young man – *boy*, he still had acne on his cheeks and chin – looked as if he had been unforgivably molested, but dragged Julian out. His head swam dizzily, his limbs were afire as blood rushed to places it hadn't visited in a while, and as soon as he drew a proper breath, he regretted it. Almighty, he smelled *terrible*.

"My name is Marcus Servus," the cadet barked, once he was forcibly frog-marching Julian down the prison block, the torch-bearing flunkey dutifully trailing behind. "I was sent to fetch you by General Ionius himself. Do you know who *that* is, worm?"

Julian flinched. He didn't know what he could have possibly done to attract the attention of the most notorious monster in an empire brimful of them, but it did not sound good. "Yes."

"Good." Marcus Servus gave him an extra shove, just to be a prick. "Then you know what will become of you if you do not obey."

While Julian could think of several choice rejoinders to that, it seemed best for all concerned to keep them to himself. In a few more moments, they reached a small stone room with a drain in the floor and a rusty spigot in the wall, and Julian was obliged to strip naked and scrub down with caustic potash soap. The water was cold and brownish, piped directly from either the polluted Tibir or some back-alley aqueduct, but it was still cleaner than Julian had been in some time, and he tried not to pay attention to what was crawling and/or falling off him as he rinsed. Evidently they could not offend well-bred noses with his stink, and he likewise did his best not to think too much about what such a summons could mean. Who the fuck was Grand Magister Kronus, for a start? Someone important, plainly, and Marcus the Slave seemed to think it was a great honor, but he would, and it did not mean Julian was reprieved from his predicament overall. Had his family finally discovered where he was and offered to ransom him? They would, right? *Right?*

When the water cranked off, Marcus Servus threw a grimy towel at him, looking displeased at having to play body-servant to the criminal, and Julian rubbed dry, taking as long as possible just to annoy him. Then there were a set of – oh, joy – clean clothes, even if it was only the uniform of the palace slaves, and Julian gritted his teeth, swallowed his pride, and put it on. It was better than his lice-ridden rags, to be sure, and it did give him the chance to obtain intelligence about his situation. This couldn't be rushed. He would only have one shot, if that, at actually escaping, and any hasty move would destroy it. Not to mention, him.

Marcus, unfortunately, was alert to the risk of reconnaissance, and blindfolded Julian before they left the showers, but eyes were not the only way to see a place. He listened hard, mapping the phonic architecture of the sounds around him, as he was marched down one more corridor, there was a clank and groan as a heavy door swung open, and they began to ascend a seemingly endless staircase. Julian counted the steps in his head – two hundred and forty-three – and ignored the savage burning in his disused legs. Marcus was still his only escort, as they clearly thought (alas, accurately) that a single Immortal, even a junior one, was more than a match for an enfeebled, half-starved prisoner. Either that or this was a highly covert errand, meant to stay secret from the rest of the palace, and *that* was interesting. Secret for, or from, who?

Julian was so absorbed in pondering the fascinating implications of this that he almost forgot to pay attention to the next segment of the journey, and had to hastily jerk his attention back to the present. They reached another door, which Marcus unlocked in turn; there was a blast of damp air, raw wind, and wet stones; they must now be outside. The echoing vastness suggested that they were crossing a great expanse, some appropriately palatial courtyard or other space well suited to impressive public display. Smeared lights and shadows flickered through the blindfold, and he could hear the susurration of pacing footsteps and muttered conversation on the ramparts overhead. Whatever route they were taking, it was thoroughly surveilled. Good to know.

After several minutes, they passed through yet another door and into an entirely different place – different, indeed, from anywhere he had ever been before. Julian was unsure how to describe it, only that it *shimmered*, conjuring up the sensation of strange and unnatural ghosts, and the air itself was imbued with a potent charge, a slick metallic taste in the back of his throat. It was dizzying and tantalizing, as if a thousand butterflies were flapping around him, wings whispering against his skin and distant voices muttering in a maddening chorus. What *was* this place?

They reached another staircase and climbed into a total void of sound, the absolute blackness stripping any orientation or sense from Julian whatsoever; he tried to count these steps too, but kept forgetting, or startling back to awareness in the inexplicable conviction that he had been asleep. It was as if the seams of the world had come unstitched, and he had a sudden and unpleasant hunch about where he had ended up.

There was only one organization in Merone that blithely fucked with reality like this, and for the living, not the dead. Not the Corporalists, but even worse. The Thaumaturges.

Beside him, Marcus said something in Lanuvian, which Julian still didn't understand, but less so than when he first arrived; eavesdropping on the Castel guards had given him a rough sense of the grammar, though the vocabulary was undoubtedly deeply vulgar. It sounded deferential, which meant their interlocutor was someone who commanded the respect of Immortals (or at least their insufferable underlings). Then Marcus unknotted the blindfold, pulling it off. "Bow, prisoner," he hissed, switching back to Ruthynian. "Bow to the Grand Magister."

Julian's head still felt as if it was filled with shards of broken glass, and it took him a moment to process anything about his unveiling. Then, slowly, his spinning vision began to coalesce into images: a dim circular room with a ceiling so high that it vanished into crepuscular shadows; tall narrow windows that admitted no light and were caped with elaborate carved escutcheons; a high desk that filled much of the black-glazed floor and was positioned so the occupant of the tall chair behind it could gaze down in appropriately magisterial style. Said occupant was a small grey man of indeterminate age – sixty, perhaps, to look on him, but something in his eyes was unsettlingly ancient. He wore a long black robe and a velvet cap, and the crowded candelabras of half-burnt tapers cast an unnatural pallor over his hollow cheeks, as if all the vim and vitality had been sucked out of him and left only a shadow. He cleared his throat and fixed that antediluvian gaze on Julian. In old-fashioned but comprehensible Ruthynian, he said, "Do you understand me, boy?"

"I – " Even Julian, with his dangerous habit of impertinence to important people, knew that he had to tread carefully. "Yes, Your Excellency. Though I must beg your pardon. I am unsure who you are or anything about why I have been summoned here."

"Hmm." The ghoul steepled his fingers. "You have the honor of addressing Grand Magister Kronus, supreme leader of His Imperial Majesty's Most Solemn and Secret Order of Thaumaturgical and Theurgical Procurators and Practitioners, to give us our *proper* name." He sniffed, clearly judging everyone who failed to achieve the sacred duty of remembering it. "The two disciplines, though oft conflated, are not the same. One concerns the working of ordinary magic, and the other seeks the true knowledge of the divine, the arcane forces that shape our lives and everything around us. While it can be judged poorly by the blessed True Church, I assure you that we are not heretics. We are the humble servants of the Lord, the Lady, and the Prince, and so – "

The Grand Magister sounded like an elderly lecturer rolling through notes he had given so many times as to lose any interest in the material, or an aggrieved citizen in a court of law defending himself against unjust charges. Hoping it was not a mistake, Julian said, "Your Excellency, I am a Vashemite. You need not defend your Tridevarian values to me."

"A *Vashemite?*" Kronus's mouth pursed. "Yes. I do recall, thank you. You will know why you are here, then?"

"Unfortunately, Excellency. I still do not."

"The Ring, you fool!" Kronus snapped his fingers impatiently, as if every Vashemite was secretly an expert on kabbalistic magic. "The Ring, and the *Key,* of King Tselmun ben Dayoud! Can there be anything else? Especially when I have been informed by a reliable source that you are indeed a savant upon the subject?"

Julian's mouth fell open. He had not the faintest, foggiest inkling of what the Grand Magister suspected himself of referring to, who could have ever communicated such a misleading assessment, or anything else. It seemed like a bad joke, and he opened his mouth to say so. Then he stopped. If he spoke up like an idiot and removed all doubt as to whether he was any use to them, they would haul him back to his cell for good, or simply call the executioner now. "I… yes… the Ring of Tselmun, Excellency," he said, attempting madly to sound clever. "I have studied the lore for several years, and given some lectures at the University of Korolgrod. My knowledge is still humble, but – "

"Good, good." Kronus waved off any further exposition. If he contacted the proctor or the board of governors for a character reference, Julian was doomed, but as that was the case in a truly dizzying array of situations by now, he could not bring himself to worry about it. "You will be knowledgeable in Old High Yerussalan, then? I have studied it for many years, but it never entirely bends to my will."

"Ah – " Julian had been moderately good at it in school, since all Vashemite boys had to learn the holy language of the liturgy and the Vashach, but apart from that and the extra study he had undertaken for his tor mitzvah, he wouldn't call himself an especially talented linguist by any means. If Kronus started foisting decrepit scrolls on him and asking him to translate them on sight, his ruse was liable to fall apart in a hurry, and etc. etc. executioner. But he could *read* it, yes, which was only half the battle when it came to the myriad possible interpretations of an ancient language that had no vowels, sentence structure, or other common grammatical features, could blithely omit the verb as it pleased, was excessively plagued with enclitics, contractions, conjugations, and cases, and was quite possibly the chief reason why the Vashemites had spent all this time arguing what in damnation their sacred texts actually said. "I can offer some counsel on the subject, yes," he said, which wasn't even a lie. "What exactly does Your Excellency wish to know?"

"Many things." Kronus tapped the scarred wood of his desk, eyes still fixed unblinkingly on Julian. "Many things indeed. I have in my possession what is said to be the original *Key of Tselmun,* did you know? The grimoire the great king himself wrote with his own hand, charged with the potency of his blood and magic. There are powerful protective spells on it that likewise took me decades to break, so I am only recently able to countenance the idea of making a comprehensive study of its contents. Would you wish to aid me, Doctor – ?"

Julian stared at him. His heart performed a stabbing, swooping leap, a savage, traitorous joy. He should (and he would, in a moment) be righteously angry about the Meronites blatantly stealing the Vashemites' oldest and most treasured books and knowledge, but it was like something out of a fever dream, an opportunity which he would not be offered again if he too lived a thousand years. To wake this morning in his foul hellpit of a cell, unsure whether it was even worth it to try to stay alive, and now being offered a chance to study the actual *Key of Tselmun* itself? Assuming, of course, that Kronus wasn't just lying out his arse, but for better or worse, Julian didn't think so. "D-Doctor?"

"You lectured at the university, yes?" Kronus frowned. "Are you not a Doktorvater, or whatever it is called in Ruthynia? I misremember."

"Ah." Since it was the only chance he would ever have, at least until he was exposed as a fraud and dropped in a pit of crocodiles, Julian clutched at it. "Doctor Kozharyev," he said grandly, not above enjoying the way it echoed impressively in this mystic sanctuary. "That's me."

"Yes, I thought as much." With that, Kronus turned a withering glare on Marcus. "You dressed such an eminent personage in slaves' rags, Servus? The general should have you soundly beaten for this insolence."

Marcus looked aghast, and Julian bit a smirk. He was perfectly happy to watch the spotty young Immortal squirm, spluttering that he hadn't known, he would rectify it at once. When Kronus snapped an order in Lanuvian, Marcus gave Julian a baleful glare, then turned on his heel, and Julian felt an irrational fondness for the batty old coot. Or if not, something like gratitude. Sure, he would be responsible for Julian's gruesome death in the near future, but he had refrained from any tired accusations about evil Vashemites, offered him a scholarly opportunity for which most rebbiteks would kill their own grandmothers, seemed prepared to accept Julian as an expert and address him by the title he should have, and tender something like actual respect. It was conditional and deceitful and it would be much worse when it all went to shit, but Julian was not unaffected by the chance to finally have everything he ever wanted, even if only for a short while. It reminded him of when he had secretly tried to learn Lanuvian as a boy, even if it was the difficult foreign tongue of the imperial oppressors. It offered young Yulian ben Yanov the shining dream of a life beyond the ghetto and cold grey Korolgrod, like Gavriel's uncles and their success abroad with the goye, even if the usual caveats still applied. But then his mother found out and burned his books, declaring that no son of hers needed to know that Meronite muck, and that was the end of that. Much as he loved her, Julian wasn't sure if he had entirely forgiven her for it.

Several excruciatingly awkward moments passed, as Julian wondered if he should attempt to make small talk with the empire's top sorcerer. Deciding that he should not, he was then forced to reckon with a bucket of ice-cold water being tossed all over his giddy fantasies. It was hardly as if Kronus' studies would be put to innocent or benevolent use for the abstract benefit of scholarship and posterity. It would be a formidable and deadly weapon given only to the Thaumaturges and Corporalists and Marcus's Immortal counterparts, and used to ensure that nobody thought about rebelling against Coriolane Aureus IX ever again. Angry though he still was at Gavriel, Julian wasn't quite so overwrought as to want him crushed to death by some terrible ancient magic, and it would take out the rest of the rebels – Kozhek, Ruthynian, Tserkovian, Vashemite, and their would-be brothers in arms across all of the imperial provinces. It was unclear whether an existential threat of this magnitude would finally impel them to abandon their constant infighting and band together against the real enemy, but Julian doubted it. And then it *would* be over, for good and all. The Meronite eagle would reign supreme above desolations called peace for another thousand years.

So? What the hell do I do? If Julian openly refused to collaborate, he would be executed, and he wanted the opportunity too badly to turn it down. Perhaps he could clandestinely sabotage the work, mislead or deceive Kronus about the *Key's* texts and spells, but he could not count on getting away with it forever. Besides, it felt murkily like a betrayal of Tselmun ben Dayoud himself, which was even more confusing. The Vashemites had likewise argued forever over whether their most famous ruler was a merciless tyrant, a cruel but noble leader, an irreproachable pillar of wisdom and piety, the only real model for a Vashemite monarch, or an outdated relic of a bloody past that should not be emulated in the future. It always irked Julian when the goye assumed that his people didn't know their own history, or were too mindlessly mourning their lost homeland to think critically about its shortcomings. But it was not something they were likely to confront in the flesh any time soon, and there was a safety in that distance, a way to argue all theories without having to commit to one. No doubt Coriolane fancied himself Tselmun reborn; all emperors did. That didn't mean he was. And so –

"Here," a voice announced. "Your garb, *Doctor* Kozharyev."

"Thank you." Julian looked up and smiled brightly at Marcus, who glared at him. Resisting the urge to snap a cheery salute, he accepted the black robe and velvet skullcap identical to Kronus' and shrugged them on over the rags. *Now I look like a proper Meronite Thaumaturge, don't I? But either way, I'd best not forget what lies beneath.*

With that, Julian saw no reason not to try his luck a bit further. "If it's all the same to everyone, I'm starving. Food in the Castel leaves a great deal to be desired. And is there any chance it could be shemyite?"

"I'm not a kitchen slave," Marcus barked. "Find your own meal, you greedy Vash, or – "

"That is enough, Servus." Kronus did not speak loudly, but the chilly potency of his command echoed across the room and made Marcus snap his mouth shut. "It is not the place of slaves of any breed to speak so impudently to free men, and their social betters. Apologize to Doctor Kozharyev, then send for a meal. Shemyite, he said. Now."

There was a long and hideous pause. Julian was further unsure of what to feel here; Marcus was a total pain in the arse, yes, but seeing even an Immortal chopped ruthlessly down to size and reminded that he too was nothing more than a Meronite slave wasn't necessarily something to cheer. Even if the weapon of rank and privilege was being used to defend Julian in this instance (even if based on a lie), that did not mean he should cease to take notice of who it cut, and he cleared his throat. "I'm sure Marcus Servus did not mean to give insult," he said, even though Marcus Servus clearly very much had. "We can forego the apology. You surely have other servants, Your Excellency?"

Marcus opened his mouth, then stopped. He glowered at Julian, plainly aware that Julian had covered for him when he did not deserve it and disliking the sense of being indebted, then jerked his head. "By your leave, Grand Magister. Best of luck with your new… companion."

Kronus waved a haughty hand, and with a final menacing stare, Marcus showed himself out. Julian was unsure if the door he left by was the same one by which they had entered; the space was not very large, but it was difficult to keep a proper picture of it in his mind, or remember it when he looked away. This was surely down to absolute buttloads of magic, which likely also accounted for the whispering murmur, that sense that the air was charged with intangible force, and Julian looked at Kronus. "Well then, Excellency. What do we do next?"

"This way." Kronus led him to a tall black door behind the desk, which Julian was likewise not sure of seeing a moment before. Kronus waved his hand at the lock and it swung open, which just seemed like showing off. Beyond, a long corridor paved in white stone and hung with golden salvers of smokeless fire led deeper into the heart of – *wherever* the fuck they were. Kronus started down it, his footsteps eerily soundless, and beckoned Julian to walk beside him. "It is good to confer with a younger colleague. We are old men in ivory towers, we forget what it is to be out in the world. What did you teach in Korolgrod?"

"I… ah… a few subjects. History, literature, theology, the like." If Kronus did not seem to find it odd that a Vashemite was allegedly able to lecture at the flagship Ruthynian university, Julian was not about to remind him. "It has become difficult in recent years, Excellency. Gerasim Zogorov and the Konsilium are not fond of my people, and are making a number of laws intended to impede and disbar us from public life."

"Superstitious fools." Kronus sniffed disdainfully. "That is what comes of appointing bigoted provincials, eager to maintain their own rural ideas of privilege and prejudice, rather than upholding the unbiased and enlightened purity of the Meronite ideal. In my opinion, His Majesty has tolerated Zogorov's corruption far longer than he should. Should I suggest that he select a new Governor-General?"

Julian blinked, briefly floored by the magnitude of the influence that was now being offered to him, just like that. There was no denying that the temptation was considerable. Just one word in the right ear, and he could remove Gerasim Balovoynich, the Ruthynians' bane for dog years. It was easy to see how men became drunk with it, and that was also why he should not rush to anything. Zogorov was terrible, yes, but there was no knowing who Coriolane would install in his place, and Julian bowed his head. "I would never presume to offer His Majesty political advice. I am only a humble scholar."

Kronus looked pleased, as if Julian had passed a test. But as they reached another door and descended into the next corridor, he said, "Fear not, Doctor Kozharyev. You can speak freely in here. This place is impervious to any evil attack, any unfriendly ears. If you fear that you will endanger yourself, you must not. You are one of ours now. Safe."

Julian looked away, firmly ordering himself not to be seduced by this simple statement of *belonging,* and his incredulity that Kronus could pronounce it so calmly. Didn't it matter that he had fished Julian out of the Castel mere minutes ago and had absolutely no proof that he was who he claimed, or was that the true gift of power: to simply not care, to not *have* to care? If Julian was Doctor Kozharyev of Korolgrod, Kronus could unlock the mysteries of a magic beyond comprehension. If not, he could dispose of him and never think of it again. Solicitude cost the Grand Magister nothing to offer, and yet it was so damned hard to resist. "Thank you, Excellency, But as noted, I stay out of politics."

This was such a bald-faced lie that he was amazed the floor didn't crumble under his feet, but if he wanted to stay alive, he had to get better at dissembling. Soon they reached the end of the corridor and stepped into an enormous white-stone atrium, a vast staircase spiraling down to the floor far below. The splendid rotunda was eerily empty, but to every side of its circle, there were even more doors, all black, closed and locked, lost in shadow. They were etched with glowing golden glyphs that Julian couldn't read, but from above, he instantly recognized the shape laid into the floor in a vast glittering mosaic. It was the six-pointed star of Tselmun, said to be graven into the black stone of his magic Ring and used as a holy symbol by the Vashemites ever since, and the sight of it here in the very heart of Meronite power, proof that they had stolen his people's greatest legacy and used it to do this –

"What is it?" Kronus asked, as Julian had stopped dead. Then he glanced down, realized, and clucked his tongue. "Oh, that. It's just a symbol, isn't it? Useable by anyone who puts their mind to it. You must understand, Doctor, the Thaumaturges are not prone to the petty hatreds of lesser men, especially in the matter of the Vashemites. How could we hate your people, when everything we know is taken from you? Aside from the *Key,* it is why I am eager to have you answer our questions."

"You respect our people greatly, and yet I'm the first Vashemite you have ever properly spoken to?" Julian's voice came out slightly more scathing than he intended. "Just me, the ex-prisoner? No chance to ask *anyone* else? The great rebbiteks, the scholars, the – "

"Oh, you know." Kronus waved a hand. "You need the right *kind* of Vashemite, one who understands what we want to accomplish. You surely do, an educated man like you? We all have unenlightened customs and backwards traditions that must be put aside, and your people are no different. Snipping the foreskin off the male members of infant boys, for one. Don't you suppose it is rather barbaric?"

"We have debated the practice for hundreds of years, yes. But one might also suppose that the Tridevarians' habit of ransacking cities and countries and slaughtering those same children, along with their mothers and fathers and entire families, if they have not been born or converted to your faith, is considerably *more* barbaric, don't you think?"

Kronus shot him a very sharp look, and Julian, convinced that he had finally gone too far, braced for instant destruction. But the Grand Magister let out a short laugh, clapping him fraternally on the shoulder. "You are a Vashemite indeed, Doctor. Trained to quarrel, counterpose, and pick apart logic, to see things to which we Tridevarians have become blind. I have often thought that we could greatly benefit from adopting your approach to exegetical interpretation. What sort of fool reads a text only once and insists he knows exactly what it says and will brook no challenge ever again? Our most holy Mellius Sanctus Sixtus could benefit from a great deal *less* certainty, truly."

Despite himself, Julian chuckled. It was difficult to disagree with that, and he still could not get a fix on Kronus. The Grand Magister would say something horrendously offensive one moment and halfway progressive the next, and while the latter did not cancel out the former, it was more than what Julian was accustomed to from other Tridevarian Meronites. "Excellency, do you think I could have that meal?"

"Yes, yes. You must be starved." Kronus started down the grand staircase, Julian trailing after him. "We will also find you some new quarters, and I will ensure that any guard who played a role in your mistreatment is called to account. After all, we are not savages."

"Thank you." When they reached the foot of the stairs, Julian screwed up his nerve. "Is there any chance you could find out what happened to the other man in my cell?"

Kronus looked blank. "Other man?"

"Yes. His name was Ilya Sergeynich, he was a Kozhek from Severolgrod. He was being tortured or something, they kept taking him away and throwing him back in, and after they took him the last time, I didn't see him again. I do not make excuses for him, but I hoped – "

"I've not heard any such name." Kronus shook his head. "But there are many prisoners in the Castel. If you wish to make your own investigation, you are certainly – what in the devil?"

"What?"

"That." Kronus turned in a questing circle. "I'm terribly sorry, Doctor. I know you are eager for supper. But if you will excuse me – or come along, this is your purview, after all – "

Hungry though he very much was, Julian decided that indeed, supper could wait. They hurried across the great floor and through one of the doors. The environment changed precipitately from the vast cold splendor of the atrium to a hot, dim workroom, and Julian was visited by the sudden and unsettling conviction that they had not just moved from room to room but from place to place, and it was possible that the Thaumaturges' lair – or at least some part of it – was not actually in Merone at all. Kronus shut and barred the door, then stepped over to a table laden with instruments that hummed, whizzed, whirred, banged, and burbled. He plucked a spun-glass orb from the largest crucible and held it up to the light, frowned and started to put it down – then froze.

"What?" Julian asked, his voice echoing flatly. "What is it?"

"Perhaps it is a mistake." Kronus took a long moment to answer, still fixated like a storybook wizard with his crystal ball. "But if it is in fact so – Doctor, this would be a powerful omen indeed – "

"What can you possibly – "

"The Ring." Kronus turned around, his face lit from below by the red glow, so he resembled a demon leering from the inferno. "The very object and attainment of our labors. It has been found at last. The Ring of Tselmun is in Qart-Hadesht."

PART TWO

IMMANENCE

CHAPTER 13

ALIYAH

By the time she finally, agonizingly reached the top, arms shaking so hard that she feared to fall back down and break her neck, it was almost sunrise. The sky over Sanctorian Hill flamed ominously red, but the earth was still darkly, devouringly black, and Aliyah rolled over and lay flat, breathing raggedly. Her fingertips were stained with blood, metal shards jutting from her flesh, and even if it was the only reason she had managed to claw out, it gave her an awful shudder of horror and dismay. It had saved her life, but the idea of it lingering in her body and infecting her like poison – for obviously that was the only reason the general had put it in her – was terrifying. And when they realized that she had used it to escape...

No matter. No time, not now. At all costs, she could not be found like this, and though her legs were ragged and her knees barely held, Aliyah teetered to her feet. She did not dare to look at the black maw behind her, and there was nowhere to hide, unless she went into the cemeteries and lay down in a grave. Out here on the very periphery of the Eternal City, where the damned and the dead were physically cast out from law-abiding, living citizens, so they could leave the protection of the city walls to jeer or mourn and then once more safely enfold in its embrace – Aliyah understood the performance, the cadence of the movement, the exit and return. That, however, did nothing to help her.

Perhaps she was not the first prisoner to *ever* climb out of the pit, but she had to be one of very few. Nothing to do with the Ring, that time. Just a fluke of chance, or General Ionius trying to trick her. But now that she had decided not to die, what the *hell* did she do next?

The sun was coming up fast, thick humidity billowing from the sedentary shallows of the Tibir, and Aliyah did not have the stamina to go far. Perhaps she could find Julian, though she wasn't sure what that would do. He had been, to say the least, miffed that she kept the Vashemites' precious Ring for herself, and she couldn't be sure if he was still here or alive. She had told him to flee, and he should have heeded her. Her best option was likewise to run far from here and never look back, but where? *Where?* Qart-Hadesht was not safe, and *Noora* —

No. *No.* This was not over, and it was not even about politics, no exalted rhetoric of liberty and freedom. It was ugly and naked, bitter and uncompromising: the simple desire to give the bastards hell. And if her bones had become weapons, if that was all she had left, that was what she would use. They had brought it on themselves.

Aliyah stumbled blindly along the Tibir riverbank, as her bare feet slipped in the foul mud and were stabbed by sharp reeds, bobbing detritus, desultory rubbish, broken stones, and once, horribly, a staring and freshly-dead corpse. She gagged, then got an even riper whiff of decay from the great pit on the hillside just ahead. An enormous cloud of flies rose and fell in slow, endless buzzes, a dull and maddening drone. At once, she knew what it was. She didn't want to look, but she had to.

Groaning with the effort, Aliyah clambered from the effluence of the river and up the steep, rocky slope. The flies darted and dove at her, sensing fresh blood, and she swatted at them constantly, trying not to breathe too deeply. But no matter what, the stench of rot grew unbearable, and by the time she reached the top, fingers stained white with lime, it seemed to be embedded in the ground. For a final moment, she resisted. Yet there was no chance of coming this far and falling down in any sense of the word. It was the very least of what she owed them.

The mass graves of Merone were rarely empty, but this one was especially, grotesquely full. It was difficult to see through the hazy, undulating mass of insects, but the corpses were stacked so high that they threatened to spill over, in stages of decomposition from painfully recent to barely recognizable. They had all been picked over by scavengers, those who had to steal from the dead in order to preserve the living; anything with any scrap of value, from brooches, coins, ornaments, cloth, medallions or jewelry or even golden teeth, had been pilfered without ceremony. The reek was so nauseous that bile rose in Aliyah's throat, and it was only with difficulty that she kept it down. While poor folk died every day and were shoveled in here if their families had nothing to pay the necropolises, these unfortunates had not arrived as a result of old age, or injury, or disease, or bad water, or childbirth, or any of the usual ways to slip off the mortal coil. For despite the rot and bloat, the necrotic flesh and bone, they all shared one chilling feature: the red. The swollen veins and weeping sores, the septic scarlet that slashed like mortal wounds. But they weren't, at least not in the usual sense. It was the thing that looked like the Red Death, but wasn't. It had devoured Yerussala down to the bone, and now it was here in Merone, the heart of the world. Eating and eating, but never satiated.

A choked sound escaped Aliyah, the vomit followed, and she turned away, retching and gagging but not bringing anything up except sour dribbles. Hand clapped over her mouth, she forced herself to look properly and not turn away, scouring the dead faces for anyone who might be familiar, praying that they weren't. But this was only one of many pits, and Aliyah couldn't search them all. She had no idea what had become of everyone else, if they were brought here too or already killed. Coriolane might have kept her alive to toy with, but he had no reason to do so with her family, Mirazhel, the Adirim, Julian, Elemai, anyone else he suspected had helped or sympathized with her. Even worse, this grotesquerie was proof that Aliyah's worst fears were realized. The Divine Emperor had the Ring, and so he had unleashed its curse. By accepting it in the first place, Aliyah had inadvertently caused the plague that destroyed Yerussala, but so long as Coriolane had it, any Meronite citizen was fair game for the Ring's terrible price.

"I'm sorry," Aliyah wept, gulping and incoherent, agonized and staggered with grief. "I'm so sorry, this is all my fault. I should never have touched it or tried to use it. I didn't know, but that's not an excuse.

I'm *sorry,* I'm not good enough and I never have been, not in anything – I've failed my mother, I've failed you, and I can never atone for it – "

She almost didn't care if anyone heard her, and if so, perhaps they thought she was simply an overwrought family member – which indeed, she was. It didn't matter if she searched this pit bone by bone, or the others. In her heart, she knew her loved ones were gone. If not from earth altogether, then certainly from her. It was only what she deserved.

Almost blind with tears, Aliyah muttered a final prayer for the repose of their souls, then turned and started to stumble down the road worn into ruts by the gravediggers' wagons, fighting an overwhelming urge to lie down and wait for one of them to run her over. But if she did so, her desperate climb to freedom was all for nothing, and she was too stubborn to waste it. Besides, it would not be long until *someone* discovered that they were missing a very valuable prisoner and took steps to secure her recapture. At least that way she could go down fighting. Even if only at the very end, she wouldn't be an unforgivable disgrace.

The sun was well up over the mudlarkers' districts, the shabby huts built on silts in the Tibir shallows, when Aliyah finally reached the docks. There were enough people about, and her face was doubtless now sufficiently infamous, that she took the precaution of plucking a rough sack from a ragpickers' cart and pulling it over her head. The metal studs jutting from her fingers had vanished, she didn't want to think where, and she wondered if the Immortals truly lived like that all the time, forged into a literal weapon down to their bones and blood, so there was no situation in which they would ever be unarmed or off their guard or free from violence. She still didn't understand General Ionius in the least, but he certainly hadn't meant to help her.

Unsure if she dared to steal food, Aliyah started to walk, aimless and anonymous. Sized up the crowd, looking for telltale signs: burst blood vessels in the eyes, strange red swellings on the neck or limbs, a wound that wasn't healing. The Ring's curse was hardly picky about its victims, and there was no way to tell how long it might feel entitled to keep merrily slaughtering Meronites, but perhaps it had drunk its fill of blood for now. Or it would get worse. It would gain momentum and trajectory, burn through the Eternal City like fire in grease-paper, and she would… what? Run to the ends of the earth or far across the sea, as if her crimes would not find her there? To leave the Ring of Tselmun in Coriolane's hands, unquestioned and unchallenged?

Aliyah stopped short, fighting in equal measure against her desire to go and her obligation to stay. For better or (much, much) worse, she was the only person who had wielded the Ring and been able to carry the weight, and she was the only one with any chance of taking it back. She had already done the unforgivable, so there was a certain peace in it, the knowledge that the only way onward was through. She did not want to. She wanted to crawl away and curl up in the dark, to lick her wounds and lie down and forget the foolish time she ever thought that she could change the world. But if any of it had ever meant anything, it meant this.

"*Fuck,*" Aliyah whispered, a sentiment more heartfelt than she could possibly express. She gazed at the ships bobbing at anchor: nobody was paying attention to them, their masters arguing with longshoremen or the customs officers, their hands dozing off or gone to spend their wages on whores and wine, and it would be so easy to sneak aboard. She could bunk down in the hold, stay out of sight until they anchored in some far-off land, then come ashore and find where fate had cast her, begin to build a new life. She could see it. She could do it. She *could*.

And yet.

She gritted her teeth, summoned up what strength was left in her, and turned away. Lowered her head, pulled up her sackcloth hood, tried to look like just another shuffling beggar. If she was not leaving the city after all, then she had to find somewhere to hide. Either way, she didn't have the least notion how to break into the Eternal Palace, much less confront Coriolane and take back the Ring at all costs. But she had also made a promise to Khasmedeus, and as it was the only one she had any hope of keeping, it had taken on a renewed significance. And if so –

Aliyah was moving so quickly, eyes down, that she was barely aware of where she was going, and so she walked straight into someone coming the other way. Both of them tumbled backward, and Aliyah cringed. The other person was struggling to get up, and Aliyah, trying to be helpful without blowing her cover, stepped closer and offered a hand. It was a young woman with a long brown braid, and the instant their eyes locked, Aliyah knew she had made a terrible mistake. The silence rang as resoundingly as the bells of the Arch-Holy Basilica, and since it was too late to flee, Aliyah wondered if she had to kill the poor girl. Not that she knew how to do that either, but –

"You," the girl breathed. "It's *you.*"

"Yes," Aliyah started, more or less in Lanuvian. "Please – "

The girl shook her head and stumbled clumsily upright. But the look she turned on Aliyah was anything but. "You must get out of here," she said. "My name is Romola. Come with me."

★★★★

The colloquy at the ur-Tasvashta villa went on all day and well into the evening. They paused occasionally for food and convenience breaks, but otherwise talked until their throats were dry, their heads ached, and the terms of their partnership had begun to acquire firm future shape. When Aliyah revealed the shocking truth of her dirty little bit of jewelry, commanded Khasmedeus to show itself in full flaming majesty, and it exploded into existence on Saeda Safiya's fine Parsivati rug, the effect was everything she could have hoped. The ever-composed, ever-imperturbable Zadia ur-Namasqa jumped out of her skin, uttered a shriek, and seized her husband's arm, and Khaldun stared at Aliyah as if she had hung the moon. Noora clapped as if it was a splendid show, and Safiya looked between Elemai and Aliyah as if her daughter had made a wise choice indeed. At the next recess, she stepped up to Aliyah and took her by the hand. "Truly remarkable. And you were simply... *given* this?"

"Yes." Aliyah hesitated, still unsure of how the ur-Tasvashtas had seemed to know so much ahead of time. "If you mean that there are others aside from me better equipped to handle it – "

"Oh, I would not," Safiya protested. "Never. If Ur-Malika chose you for this honor, there is a good reason, and I would never defy the Lord-Queen's will. I only wish to offer my assistance in bearing this burden. When I was younger, I studied the matter of demonology, the Meronite grimoires and Tselmun's writings, the practice of summoning higher spirits and jinnyeh. It never quite achieved what I intended, but nor was it entirely useless. I could teach you."

"That is very kind of you, Saeda Safiya," Aliyah said politely. "And when we are kin, we shall see a great deal of each other. Perhaps then we can examine what transpires."

Safiya looked briefly and vaguely displeased, then smiled even more broadly. "So you have indeed become quite politic, my dear. That is good. You will need it, for what is to come."

Indeed, Aliyah thought dryly as they returned to the discussions, that was a resounding understatement. Both families wanted the wedding to happen as soon as possible, before the first house of the stars, which marked the lunar new year and the start of the holy month of Qahyadin. That was only eight weeks from now, and while it was clear what Aliyah chiefly brought to the match – viz., the Ring – she was not expected to present herself as the beggar at the feast. In other Wahini countries, the groom gave *mahr,* or nuptial gifts and money, to the bride, and since Elemai was the higher-status partner, the obligation was normally on the ur-Tasvashtas to pay it to the ur-Namasqas. But according to the main school of Qartic fiqah, when a marriage involved two women (two men could not wed, as it was felt to be undesirable for a new household in a matriarchical society to have no women), it was correct for them to pay it to each other, or bestow dowers of equal value.

Zadia insisted that she must consult the accounts to determine how much the ur-Namasqas could realistically spare, while Khaldun gently suggested that it was the principle of the thing and perhaps not the time for parsimonious penny-pinching. Safiya spoke graciously of how honored they were to welcome Aliyah to the family in one breath, and in the next, drove a hard bargain in insisting that the ur-Tasvashtas expected the customary precedent to be followed, and the exchange of *mahr* between the two brides to therefore be generously mutual. Elemai made an awkwardly apologetic grimace in Aliyah's direction, as if to say that nothing was more guaranteed to kill any prospect of romance than to watch their families bicker over money, but so be it.

After that argument, Khaldun, Noora, Ghassan, Jahifar, and Marishah were dismissed, leaving the mothers, daughters, and Mirazhel ur-Beireshta. The dispute was solved only when the latter stepped in to offer to pay for the whole wedding and if necessary, make a further contribution to increase Aliyah's *mahr*. Zadia looked as if she resented being patronized but was conscious of the need to graciously accept it, and cleared her throat. "Thank you very much, Saeda Mirazhel. You honor us. But we have another matter. Saeda Safiya, if you would?"

"Indeed." Safiya turned to Aliyah. "Saeda Mirazhel, as noted, is the eldest daughter of her family, but was born a son, and therefore initially subordinate to her brother Massasoum in the succession. Now that she has completed her transition to womanhood, she wishes to claim her proper rights. Your mother and I have agreed to support her suit against her brother, if he does not relinquish the Chairmanship — and we do not think he will. Do you wish to thank Saeda Mirazhel for her kind gesture by naming her the wedding guest of honor?"

"Ah… yes." Aliyah knew this was not a request, but she was still lost. "And we are deposing Saed Massasoum because — ?"

"Because," Mirazhel said wryly, "Saeda Zadia and Saeda Safiya know that I am far more sympathetic to their cause than my brother, and according to all laws and customs of Mother Qart, it *is* my proper right. Now that you have returned to us and with such a miracle as King Tselmun's Ring, we are ready to put our plan into action. You recall, of course, that the Divine Emperor intends to visit us here in spring?"

"Yes, but — "

"Therefore." Mirazhel tapped her fingers. "It is incumbent on us to prepare a proper welcome, and it is only practicable to do if it comes directly from the Chair. We have more time to plan it than your wedding, but not much. And it is, of course, complicated."

Aliyah frowned. "How so?"

"Well." Mirazhel exchanged a loaded look with Zadia and Safiya. "It is the first time that Coriolane will set foot outside the Eternal City in many years. You have heard the rumors that his health is not what it used to be. All of this provides an… opportunity."

Ah. She was, of course, still deeply naïve. "I see," Aliyah said. "You intend to kill him."

A small cringe traveled around the solarium; everyone might have implicitly known it, but still shied from speaking it aloud. "We certainly feel," Safiya said diplomatically, "that with the Ring of Tselmun in our grasp, there is a chance to push more strongly for Qart-Hadesht's freedom than we have henceforth been able to do. Even if we do not succeed in completely ending his tenure, we can induce him to agree to new measures, or revised terms of independence. And if so — "

"I don't think that would work," Aliyah objected. "Any agreement extracted by force or blackmail would be valid only as long as it took him to get back to the Eternal City and unleash the Immortals on us. Besides, Elemai already asked Khasmedeus if it could murder Coriolane, if we ordered. It couldn't, and even if Coriolane is here, he'll still have all his usual protections. And if we try to kill him and *fail* — "

Zadia gave her daughter an appraising look. "I am glad that you have thought of the pitfalls. But we have no choice but to succeed, and I would not put much stock in whatever the creature said to you before. It was Tselmun's mightiest and most terrible servant, it razed whole cities and peoples to the ground at his command, and jinnyeh are often predisposed to lie and malinger. I suspect that it could change its mind."

Aliyah started to answer, then stopped. This was the first time her mother had ever spoken to her as an equal, someone with commensurate ability to weigh the situation and make a proper decision, but something still nagged her. Finally she said, "So that is what we want? To become a new Tselmun, destroying everything and everyone in our way?"

"Of course not." Zadia sounded impatient. "We will use this power correctly, with wisdom and prudence, moderation and restraint. But blessed Ur-Malika has granted a miracle we are unlikely to ever see again. There must be no hemming and hawing, no balking at trifling moral difficulties. You know, habibta, that kings are never toppled alone. Rest assured that myself, Saeda Mirazhel, and Saeda Safiya will do our best to ensure that the consequences fall on those who deserve it. But if you will not do what must be done, this is over before it begins."

"Yes, Amma," Aliyah said. "I understand. As well, that this knowledge does not leave this room? Even to Abba and Amma Noora?"

"Your father and Noora do not know of this, no." If Zadia did intend to inform them before the very moment of the imperial assassination, it was impossible to say. "And indeed, you will not tell them, and certainly not your brother. You have been trusted with it because you are my heiress, the holder of the Ring, Elemai's bride, and Safiya's daughter-in-law, and we must work in close concert to carry it out. This is what it means to have power. It always comes with secrets, even and especially from those we care for the most. Remember that."

At last, when blue winter dusk had fallen, the meeting mercifully came to an end. Aliyah was so exhausted that she was seeing double; she had not slept since Yerussala, and everything had started to assume a shimmering, dreamlike quality. Safiya insisted that she stay here, rather than bumping across the city to the ur-Namasqa villa, and while Aliyah yearned to be home, it was only one more night. So she kissed her parents and promised to see them soon, then was shown to a bedchamber and collapsed. She was asleep before she could take her shoes off.

She slept straight through dardiq without stirring, roused briefly at mardiq and conked out again before she could rise, felt obliquely guilty but not awake enough to do so for long, and finally woke for good at sundown, as dazed and groggy as if she had been hit on the head. She lay on her back, comfortably swamped among the covers and cushions, and stared up at the colored murals of the ceiling and the fine filigree of the windows. Tried to imagine living here, being its mistress, it feeling like home. It seemed more possible than before, but still shockingly fanciful.

She lay there until the call of nature grew too urgent to ignore, and groaned, staggered out, and used the privy seat. Her throat was dry as the desert, so she guzzled down the goblet of water that someone had left for her. She was ungodly hungry, but the effort to go in search of food was insuperable, and she was still sitting on the bed when there was a knock on the door. Elemai's voice called, "Are you awake?"

Aliyah muffled another jaw-cracking yawn. "Uh. Yes. Sort of."

The latch clicked and Elemai hipped her way inside, as her hands were occupied with a fully laden supper tray. It smelled heavenly, and Aliyah let out a moan. "Malikallulah, I could marry you for that alone."

"Works out, doesn't it?" Elemai smiled wryly, setting the tray on the covers and crawling up next to Aliyah. "This was the least of what I owed you, after watching our mothers haggle like fishwives. Amma can be very… practical, but it would be understandable if you worried that all we cared for was the Ring. I hope to reassure you that it is not so."

"Thank you." Aliyah did not know if she believed it, but the fact that Elemai had been instructed to make a show of solicitude would have to suffice. She took a cup of mint tea and sipped, then helped herself to couscous, a lamb-meat pastilla, and a steaming bowl of tajine. She began to eat, trying not to wolf too unbecomingly, though the vehemence with which Elemai dug in made plain that it was her first post-hibernation meal as well. Several minutes elapsed in ruminative silence. Then Aliyah said, "Do you think any of this is possible? With – with Coriolane?"

"I don't know," Elemai admitted. "It's audacious and dangerous beyond any doubt, and we are on very thin ice. But we cannot wait for some mythical perfect moment. If we don't seize the chance, he will discover that we have the Ring, and then it will be too late. Surprise is the only advantage we have, and we must make full use of it."

"And you really don't think that he'll suspect anything? What if he is coming to Qart-Hadesht precisely to put us under tighter control, replace Grassus with somebody who will enforce Merone's imperial prerogatives?" Aliyah looked down at her hand, the lethal glint of gold. "This feels like a trap. After all this time, at this very moment, the Ring of bloody Tselmun just *happens* to reappear? What are the odds of that?"

Elemai squirmed. She briefly glanced away, then turned back and smiled brightly. "It is, as your mother said, a miracle. And I know we haven't had the best start, but we can move past it. I am truly eager to be wed and begin our life together, and I hope you feel the same."

It was Aliyah's turn to start a sentence and then realize she wasn't sure what she meant to say. The problem, the one that kept surfacing no matter how hard she tried to push it down, was that none of this felt *real*. She could ask, and Elemai would profusely assure her that of course their marriage wasn't only built on the Ring, and Aliyah would believe it no more than she did now. In a way, it would feel more authentic if it was like it had been at their engagement. It might not be romantic, but at least it was honest. And if they could not have that, what was left?

"Saeda Elemai," Aliyah began, stiff and formal. "I understand that a great deal is riding on this match – for our families, for Qart-Hadesht, for our long struggle against Merone. It is not possible to call it off, but if we could make clear that we – "

"Shh." Elemai leaned close, putting her hand on Aliyah's knee. "We can hash out the details later. Just now, we need to rest, know each other better. And for that, I have an idea."

"But – "

"Shhh," Elemai said again, as her other hand came up to cup Aliyah's cheek and turn their faces together. And before Aliyah could say another word, Elemai kissed her.

It was not the first time she had ever been kissed, but it was close. It *was* the first time she felt a swoop in her stomach, a warmth in her chest, a catch in her breath and the dawning realization that she *did* want this, Elemai, them. Aliyah had never thought about whether she would prefer to marry a man or woman; her spouses would likely include both, and when the time came, it would be dictated by the needs and priorities of the ur-Namasqas, not her private girlish whims. Besides, nobody ever asked other women in arranged marriages about their preferences or if they *wanted* to have sex with their husband, so why did it matter? Aliyah was lucky to be Qartic, insofar as she had a real say in the matter and would be the shared head of the new household, but the parents' role in selecting a suitable mate, the older generation ensuring that the younger did not give into wild fits of erotic passion or other unwise foundation for a sensible partnership, was still paramount. For all that it was often painted as a hotbed of female degeneracy by disapproving Wahini clerics from more conservative regions, Qart-Hadesht remained traditional, ordered, and tribal, focused on the proper honoring of one's family, faith, and forebearers. Base desire, in other words, did not enter into it, and was not something Aliyah had ever expected to care about. But this –

She uttered a small and involuntary noise, pressing herself closer, as Elemai's hand left her cheek and started to stroke her neck. Aliyah's relentlessly pragmatic brain knew this was an excellent way to distract her from whatever she had been about to say, but unfortunately, it was working. Her own hand slipped into the luxuriant tangle of Elemai's unbraided, unveiled hair, a considerable intimacy in its own right, and wound a silky lock around her finger. It was only when Elemai shifted her weight and wrapped her other arm around Aliyah's back, preparing to lay them in the bed, when she turned away. "Perhaps this is not – "

Elemai was breathing hard, her eyes glazed with a glassy shine. "Are you sure? After all, we are betrothed. It would be no disobedience or dishonor. Or is it that you do not want…?"

She trailed off, sounding more uncertain than Aliyah had ever heard her, and it occurred to her just then to wonder if Elemai was just as afraid, uncertain, self-doubting, and crushed by her mother's endlessly demanding expectations as Aliyah was. It was odd to be giving *Elemai* comfort or reassurance, but Aliyah raised her left hand, the one without the Ring, and curled her fingers lightly against Elemai's collarbone. *The Ring or reality,* she thought, with a sudden and poignant sting. *Power or truth. You can have one or the other, but not both.*

"I want it," Aliyah said, with a sudden unlooked-for honesty. "I do. I just don't know if now is the right time. And I still have questions, and I don't think you can answer them."

Elemai's gaze remained steady on her face. "What questions?"

"Just…" Aliyah trailed off. "How did your parents know we were coming? How did your father already know we were engaged? How did your mother have this entire plan set up and ready? I don't see how that's possible. Unless you have something you didn't tell me, or…"

There was a fraught pause. Elemai's fingers traced feather-light circles on her arm, and Aliyah swallowed hard. Elemai looked as if she was wrestling with her conscience, making a final decision. Then she rolled off, got to her feet, and beckoned to Aliyah. "Come with me."

Aliyah hesitated, then clambered off the bed and followed Elemai out into the gauzy blue coolness of the house. The rest of the ur-Tasvashtas were at sardiq and supper, and she felt a briefly guilty impulse to join them, but pushed it aside. In a few moments, Elemai reached the solarium and stepped inside; the room was dark, the candles snuffed, the red-gold glow of the sunset casting shadows that briefly seemed to stir. She lit a lamp and put it on the sideboard, then knelt at the edge of the splendid Parsivati rug, pulling up its heavy fringe. She rolled it up with an effort, sat atop it to prevent it from springing back down, and pointed at whatever she had revealed beneath. "Look."

Aliyah frowned, leaned down, almost started to suspect this was some trick, then saw it. Graven in the floorboards and filled with black grease-chalk, clearly the product of long years of hard use, there was a huge and intricately rune-inscribed pentacle. What had Safiya said? *When I was younger, I studied the matter of demonology, the Meronite grimoires and Tselmun's writings, the practice of summoning higher spirits and jinnyeh.* Clearly it was not only when she was younger, but continued right to this very moment. *It never quite achieved what I intended, but nor was it entirely useless.* That was likewise plainly a screaming understatement. On first approach, Safiya had been so gentle, so polite, so reasonable. The pentacle bore mute and unmistakable witness to the fact that she did not need to continue being so.

"I don't understand," Aliyah said, voice thin. "What does – "

"My mother has a jinnyeh slave." Elemai gazed down at the pentacle. "His name is Vadoush. I don't know how long she's had him, but it's a while. Possibly my whole life, since she first showed him to me when I was a little girl. He's a lesser order than Khasmedeus, not as powerful, more human at least to look upon, but she always drilled me to never make that mistake. He is one of the greatest secrets of our house. The Adirim would have a fit if they found out; it is illegal to summon or consort with jinnyeh, even if Queen Daeda did it first. Indeed, *especially* because Queen Daeda did it first, and look how that turned out. If Vadoush's existence or true nature was ever unmasked, it would cause… problems for my mother. To say the least."

Aliyah started to answer, then bit her tongue. She didn't understand what Elemai was doing by showing her, handing her such an excellent tool to blackmail or coerce the ur-Tasvashtas – unless that was the point, giving her back some power in this notably unequal dynamic? But how could that be so, when Elemai, Safiya's loyal heiress, would surely never wager her own mother in this dangerous game? Vadoush must indeed be the reason that Elemai's family knew everything so quickly, speeding on the wind between Yerussala and Qart-Hadesht and wherever else. But there was one other extremely important aspect of this revelation, and Aliyah struggled not to sound too accusatory. "So when were you planning to tell me that according to Qartic law, everything we're doing with Khasmedeus is technically forbidden?"

Elemai looked startled. "You truly did not know?"

"And even if I had, this was felt to be completely immaterial?"

"I don't know." Elemai's voice turned anguished. "My mother is – well, you know. You've met her. Difficult to resist, to oppose, to turn down. And for a long time, she has felt that her entire point and purpose in life is to finally bring down Coriolane Aureus the Ninth, once and for all. She might well be correct, and might also well be correct that the world would be a far better place without him. But that means she will break any rule or law she feels necessary, anything that gets in the way or impedes her goal, and… do you really think it was *coincidence,* Aliyah? That indeed, we traveled to the Holy City just in time for the Ring to return and fall into our laps?"

"I…" Aliyah faltered. "What do you know about that?"

"Never mind," Elemai said tersely. "You wonder why I showed you. Perhaps because I want you to know what you're getting yourself into. Perhaps because I feel it only fair for you to be forewarned. When I say that she will get rid of anything that stands in her way, I mean it."

"Including – ?"

"Including you." Elemai looked up at last, eyes dark and haunted. "I want to protect you, Aliyah. As your spouse, I should. But I must face the risk – we both must – that it will not be enough. So it is only fair that I give you the chance to be ready."

"Ready for what?"

Elemai smiled, half to herself, thin and pale as a waning moon. "Whatever comes next."

CHAPTER 14

Ionius

The ancient Spice Road city of Sardarkhand was as high, cold, and blue as a piece of fine Qiné porcelain, the queen of the Kyzylkum Desert that occupied the vast alpine plateau between the grassland steppes to the west and the soaring white Tien Shen to the east, the gateway to the Thearchate and beyond, in the Jade Sea, the reclusive island kingdom of Neiyan. For the average merchant, cultural enthusiast, wandering scholar, religious pilgrim, or other ambitious itinerant, it was a risky and difficult voyage of at least three months from the Eternal City, contending with unforgiving terrain, sudden blizzards, raiding Ahyuns, feuding tribes, local bandits, man-eating tigers, Indush k'shatriyae, Qiné tax collectors, and any number of other horrors just to make it here, where there was only a narrow window of time to cross the mountains before winter turned the already-treacherous route totally impassable. Yet such were the profits that plenty of folk dared it anyway. The city, the grand bazaar and the legendary bookshops, the splendid Three Mahqasas of Registan Square, the winding streets and low hovels were packed with people: traders, merchants, priests, qahins, rebbiteks, scholars, officials, shopkeepers, hucksters, prostitutes; Ahyuns with furry hats, felted yurts, and shaggy ponies; Qiné bureaucrats with long mustaches and huanfu robes; Indush ravanas with wild beards, saffron robes and bindis, and colored powders, standing on a box and declaiming a noisy sermon to a crowd of wide-eyed devotees. On one memorable occasion, one of them transformed into a snow leopard on the spot and almost caused a stampede.

And yet, Ionius was enjoying himself. For one thing, his voyage had been much easier: merely a matter of informing the Thaumaturges of his destination, entering the white atrium with its vast ring of black doors, stepping into one of them, and emerging in a back alley near Registan Square, just like that, traveling thousands of miles in the blink of an eye. He had repeatedly nagged that oleaginous weasel Kronus about whether the Immortals could use the doors more often: transporting troops to, say, Brythanica or any other misbehaving imperial province would be far more efficient if they could just walk through the damn magic door, rather than march for toilsome months in the field. But the Grand Magister insisted that the system was delicate and prone to complication, could not be repeatedly used without wearing out like any other mortal instrument, and the complex aetheric physics grew exponentially more difficult with each person and if they went wrong, would do so spectacularly. Whether this was true, or only a useful excuse to keep the Meronite military indebted and properly grateful, Ionius did not know. Though it was one of the several things he intended to discover.

He stood just a stone's throw from the Grand Bazaar, dressed like a prosperous Ruthynian merchant in heavy fur cloak and cap, woolen kosovorot, hide-wrapped leggings, and riding boots. There were plenty of his countrymen about, including tall, fair, sharp-chiseled Kozheks on horseback, Vashemite merchants in long overcoats and broad-brimmed black hats, and indigenous Chanuki, Tyva, and Sibyr tribesmen from the far north, in sealskin suits and white-furred hoods. But no matter where they hailed from, all had need of their wrappings. It was bitter midwinter, and everyone's breath billowed in silver clouds, which froze on eyelashes, noses, and any other bit of perilously exposed flesh. Ionius had to constantly keep moving, stamping his feet and clapping his hands, or he would turn into an icicle on the spot. Vata Korol, was this why the fucking smugglers had chosen this place for their secret handoff? Figure that nobody in their right mind would set foot in Sardarkhand at this time of year, or a nice explosion or two would properly warm it up?

As Ionius ducked into the dung-smoked haze of the bazaar in search of a cup of something very fucking hot, his thoughts drifted back to what *else* he intended to pry out of Grand Magister Kronus on his return. Before his departure, he had strategically arranged for it to be known that there was an eminent Vashemite expert on the Ring of Tselmun imprisoned in the Castel, and any scheming sorcerer worth his salt would send for him at once. Just to be sure, Ionius had also deputed Marcus Servus, one of the more promising of his Immortal cadets, to fetch Julian Janovynich and escort him to Kronus whether or not an actual summons was made. He had gambled that it would, because that acquisitive ferret could never resist a shiny new toy, but he could not be sure. Coriolane could have decided to step in and quash the whole thing, dispatch Julian to the headsman and have that be that. *It is not because I care for the smart-arsed traitor. He could yet be useful, that's all.*

After a search through the crowded aisles and narrow booths, colorful paper lanterns hung up for the Qiné Feast of the Ancestors – the date until which the smugglers said they would be here – Ionius located a verminous old crone selling black tea from a tarnished samovar, thrust a copper wen into her hand, and tried to drink it as fast as he could without scalding his innards. Somewhat fortified, he turned his attention to an actual plan. The Feast was in three days, and while the smugglers might get drunk and laze around past their deadline, they might also punctiliously keep it and get the hell out before anyone (such as Ionius) came looking for them. He could pose as an interested buyer, but if so, he had to concoct a convincing rationale. Why would a Ruthynian merchant want the stuff, if not for something extremely illegal?

Not to mention, there could also be clandestine Qiné operatives in the city, sniffing around for Meronites or anyone else trying to illegally get their hands on a large amount of shit that went boom, and the last thing Ionius needed was to be exposed, arrested, and dragged off to Hang'i in disgrace. It would be a diplomatic disaster for Merone; aside from the embarrassment of a senior Immortal failing at his task in such public fashion, Hang Zhai could use him as the perfect hostage to force Coriolane's hand on any number of issues, from the looming trade war to the disputed territories to anything else the Thearchate felt like getting back on the Empire. Even the infamously merciless Divine Emperor might have to ransom his favorite general, rather than simply leaving him to rot, but Ionius was well aware that either way, Coriolane would never forgive him. If he came back to the Eternal City as an ex-prisoner freed only by the gracious consent of Qin, he should just jump in the Tibir and save himself the bother of a traitor's execution.

Ionius shook his head and drained the dregs of the still-smoking tea. He thrust the cup back at the crone and jostled down the crammed aisle, past a Parsivati carpet merchant and yet another bloody ravana; he didn't know why the Indush authorities had allowed the scabrous street magicians to proliferate so uncontrollably that they plagued not only their own homeland but also the neighbors, but someone needed to take them in fucking hand. This one called out to Ionius as he passed, but he didn't stop. Someone else offering to tell his fortune or commune with his ancestors, neither of which he needed or even remembered. He didn't recall precisely how old he was by now, but it was old.

Once he was outside again, he drew a few deep breaths and tried to clear his head. He wore layers of wool and linen beneath the triple-thick kosovorot, but he could still feel the cold chewing into his bones, and it disconcerted him. Winters in Merone were damp and balmy, only occasionally chill enough to sleet, and almost never enough to snow. A rugged Kozhek horseman should barely turn a hair at this – but he *wasn't*, was he? This was only a costume, just another in his long line of masquerades, and for no good goddamn reason, it bothered him. And while he was being bothered, he wasn't thinking, and he still had not been struck with any sudden flash of insight about how he was going to complete this mission and not start the all-out war that had been brewing between Merone and Qin for ages. Why *had* Gheslyn insisted on him and only him? This seemed like an odd assignment for a general, when a cadet like Marcus could have handled it. And if so –

"Vanya," a hoarse voice called behind him. "Vanya."

At first, Ionius did not react or respond, because it had nothing to do with him. There were many Ruthynians in Sardarkhand, after all, and his birth name was dirt-common. When he had to introduce himself, he did so as Vadim Khovanyich, to see if it sparked any recognition or reaction, but no luck. Julian's friend's uncle was truly just an oblivious patsy, a useful cover, but if it got him closer to the real culprit, so be it. Indeed when the voice spoke, Ionius hoped, however irrationally, that there had been a breakthrough. He turned, but there were no other Ruthynians nearby. The pile of dirty rags, however, was staring straight at him, with eyes like cloudy emerald. Seeing she had his attention, she smiled. Again, in a lilting Vishvhanathi accent, she crooned, *"Vanya."*

Ionius froze. For a split second, an extremely unbecoming panic threatened to set in, until he realized what was going on. It was not just another fucking ravana, which was bad enough, but a woman. And not only *that,* but to judge from the poverty of her garb and the filth of her face, a dalit, the lowest of the low, unclean and untouchable, a pariah to her own people, forced out of Indush to wander in strange lands. Being some sort of mystic could not have helped, for it was a grave insult to the high brahmin caste that was born for priestly duties, as *men*. While the faith of the Thousand Gods was vibrantly polytheistic and counted many powerful and revered goddesses among its avatars, the vast majority of yogis, gurus, rishis, ravanas, pandits, and rajas were male; according to them, the strict order of the universe did not permit women to take on such roles. A female dalit ravana, then, was possibly the most transgressive thing that could be imagined. Small wonder she was here, but –

"Why do you not answer me, Vanya?" the witch breathed, still looking him dead in the eye. "Why do you not like it when I call you by the name your mother gave you, the one she whispered lovingly in your ear when she tucked you in to sleep? Why have you left your sister, little Tatya, the one you promised to protect? She died, you know. She died screaming for you to come, to save her, and she thought to the very end that you would. But you did not, Vanya. Why? *Why?*"

Ionius felt as if he had been flooded with black poison or freezing quicksilver. His mouth tasted like copper, and his heart roared in his ears. He was tempted to kick her, strike her, anything to make her shut up, but doubtless she endured these mundane miseries every day, too familiar to have any effect. Instead he stepped back and scoffingly shook his head. "I don't know what you're talking about, old woman."

She cocked her head. She was veiled in a black-grime bituminous haze from her brazier, looking halfway like Kali Durga herself. "Do you not, Vanya? Or should I call you General Ionius?"

That snapped him out of it, and brought a certain abject relief. So she was not any sort of mystic but a provable fraud, a paid spy, a plant. He surged forward, seized her by the scruff of the neck, and jerked her head back – which he regretted, insofar as it exposed him to a withering blast of halitosis. "Who sent you, witch? Who are you working for?"

She grinned, toothless and gummy, unleashing an even more foul-smelling chuckle. "Nobody, boy. Nobody but the truth. Do you think you can cover up so easily? The gods see the real skin of you, no matter how much Meronite blood you bathe in, until you tell yourself you have always been that color. You only fool yourself over and over, gouge your own eyes out, and what do you have to show for it?"

With a titanic effort, Ionius opened his fingers, dropping her back into her malodorous heap of rags. "You will be quiet, or I will – "

"Or what?" The old woman spat. "You'll kill me? Do you really think it frightens me, the worst thing you Tridevarians can imagine, one life and one death and one eternal punishment? I will enter into samsara and be reborn, I will live another life and another until I reach nirvana, and there is nothing you or all the might of Merone can do to stop that. You cannot harm me in any way that matters, boy. Try it if you dare."

Again, Ionius found his retort stillborn in his throat. He wanted to inform her that strictly speaking, he was a Tserkovian, but it might cause her to ask why, if he had abandoned his family's name, he had kept his family's gods. He stared loathingly at her, conscious of the desperate need to get out of here, but he refused to look as if he was cravenly turning tail and fleeing before such a pitiful inconsequence. Finally, he dug in his belt and threw her another wen. "There's an old crone in the bazaar selling black tea. You'll know when you see her, she's almost as ugly as you. It might keep you out of trouble. Go."

The ravana scooped up the coin with a gnarled hand and let loose a grating laugh. "Aren't you a hero, Vanya. A nice boy. You too. Run."

Ionius looked at her for a final moment, unsure whether to let her live. If she was installed as a deep-cover spy, shamming as a risible decrepit, she could compromise him, pass his identity to hostile entities, and that would cause more trouble. But even if so, he couldn't think how she had learned his birth name. Was it concealed in Grand Magister Saturnus's files, the ones Ionius himself could not see without Coriolane's permission? If so, where had *they* gotten it? The only person in Merone he had ever told was his first mistress, when she asked so sweetly. Then she said that *Ivan* was too Ruthynian, too reminiscent of his old life, and was *Ion* or indeed *Ionius* not better, more Lanuvian, more befitting of who he had become? Not that she wanted to sever him from his home. Of course not. After all, had she not had him taught to read kyrillic?

Ionius belatedly realized that he was clenching his fists hard enough to strain even his uncanny bones, and forced himself to relax; he could not allow this to rattle him so much. "Don't make me regret this," he warned the unrepentant hag. "Keep your fucking mouth shut."

With that, he marched away, emerging into the thoroughfare where people rushed to make the most of the daylight before the winter dark came and the temperature plunged still further. A thin dry wind hissed and scraped the frozen dust and the labyrinthine alleys. Aside from the city walls, which had been menaced by a dizzying array of would-be conquerors over the centuries and rebuilt only sporadically, there was nothing to stop it from howling for miles across the desolate steppes – at least until it ran into the towering white crown of the Tien Shen and turned into screaming snowstorms. Sardarkhand's isolation, altitude, and emptiness made it an ideal place for the study of the stars, and its humble clay towers had once housed some of the most famous scientists and astronomers in history, including the legendary polymath Ben Simna. Indeed, there were still plenty of them underfoot, muttering about an upcoming eclipse called the bloodmoon, which could likely be discarded with the rest of their usual rubbish. It was supposed to take place on the last night of the year, only a fortnight away, and if he was still here at that time, Ionius would have abjectly failed. Pray the Divine Family not.

And yet an afternoon spent combing the city turned up nothing. There was admittedly a language barrier; most Sardarkhandians spoke an offshoot of Qiné, different enough from the formal court register of Hang'i that Ionius could barely understand it, and while there were plenty of foreigners to ask instead, their linguistic skills were equally haphazard. He was fluent in Lanuvian, Ruthynian, Kozhek, Semyic, and Qiné, could get by in Ibelusian, Franketerrish, Teutyn, and a few words of Ahyun, and while this was often sufficient for most interactions, it was by no means sufficient for all. Besides, there remained the problem of being spotted visibly asking about a dangerous weapon, though there was a chance it would provoke the smugglers to break cover. But Ionius could not suppress the paranoid suspicion that this was all a setup twice over. After all, they had never found any trace of the first shipment of black powder, or proof that it even existed. And if Vadim Khovanyich had nothing to do with it, was even the note Coriolane so opportunely intercepted – the one that Ionius himself thought had such a coincidental and flimsy provenance – a bald-faced trick? Force Ionius to leave on a pointless wild goose chase, with the emperor exposed to – *what?*

Fuck. He stopped short. He had a bad feeling that he should never have left Merone at all, but how in the devil was he supposed to get back quickly? The Thaumaturges were scheduled to open another door, but not until after the Feast of the Ancestors, four days from now. If he lost his bloody mind and just started walking, he wouldn't arrive for another three months, and if he was being kept away so he could not interfere –

This is a trap. This is all a trap. It had been set with great care from somewhere deep in the palace – indeed, perhaps the very same person who, according to Saturnus, was enacting deliberate sabotage on Coriolane's eternal life. What had the emperor said, when he ordered Ionius to travel to Sardarkhand at once? *Gheslyn suggested that you be the one to go. She is very worried about this threat, and trusts only you to manage it.* Yet again, Ionius wondered why it must be him alone, and came to the shocking conclusion that it was precisely in order to get him out of the way. If this was treason on the highest and most intimate level – but no, surely not. Gheslyn had been the Divine Empress of All Merone, senior wife, Coriolane's loyal helpmeet and willing lieutenant, for at least three centuries. Why in the name of all that was holy would she turn on him now? And if Ionius made such an outlandish accusation with not a scrap of proof, Coriolane might agree that his pet had turned rabid and it was best to put him down. No. This couldn't – *no.*

Just then, Ionius became aware of a disturbance nearby, and whipped around, prepared for anything. But it wasn't some marauding attacker or hidden traitor. A child barely old enough to toddle, bundled roly-poly in furs, was squalling its head off, making an ungodly racket for such a tiny creature. Its cheeks were red with wind, its face screwed up in the effort of producing its shrieks, and its mittens, though tied to its coat with strings, had fallen off, leaving its hands bared to the ever-freezing air. A few adults slowed down with concerned looks, but when they tried to ask the child where its parents were, their expressions turned blank. Indeed, Ionius was convinced that the lot of them were deaf, mute, or otherwise moronic, until it suddenly struck him that the child was speaking Kozhek. The people trying to help it didn't understand what it was saying, it didn't understand them either, and they backed away with apologetic glances, certain that someone better qualified to assist would come along soon. If, indeed, they did. The sun had dwindled into a cold red line in the west, and darkness was falling fast.

Ionius stopped his ears to the howling, lowered his head, and made to continue on his way. It was nothing to do with him, he had wasted enough time, and if his terrible suspicion was true, he needed to get back to Merone as fast as possible. If it (please Vata Korol) was not, he still needed to track down the smugglers sometime this fucking century, and neither pursuit would be improved by playing nursemaid to a stranded infant. It wasn't *his* fault that its parents had neglected to look after the brat properly and let it wander off. This would be a suitable lesson for them, just as it had been when Ionius killed Oleg and friends in Tseyabilsk, and they should be grateful. Grateful.

Ionius had almost reached the end of the street when the child's wailing turned into a ragged shriek, a sound of utter misery and despair that despite himself – it was all the fucking ravana's fault, talking about Tatya like that – made him forcibly flash back to the moment they had torn her hand out of his and taken her away forever. *She died screaming for you to come, to save her, and she thought to the very end that you would. But you did not, Vanya. Why.* Why?

"Gods *damn* you," Ionius growled. *"Fine."*

He spun around, stormed back to the child, and briefly caused it to scream even louder, which seemed grimly accurate. But he forced himself to get on his knees, down on its level, and reached out, catching its flailing little paws in one hand. "Hey now," he said in Kozhek, which felt nakedly invasive and inappropriate. He spoke Ruthynian fairly regularly in his intelligence and fieldwork, and with Julian in the Castel, but Kozhek was different, scraping some raw nerve in him that he hadn't even realized was still there. "Hey now, what's wrong? Stop this noise."

The child was so astonished that one of the big people could finally understand it that it did so, almost on the spot. It stared at him with eyes like saucers, hiccupping and snorting, snot sliding down its face, and Ionius curtly buffeted it with his sleeve. To say the least, he did not often interact with small children – the youngest Immortal recruits were handled by lower-ranking officers, he didn't get them until they were twelve or thirteen – and therefore had no idea how to do so. He forced its hands back into the mittens and cinched the strings, then scooped it into his arms and stood up. "What are you doing? Who are you?"

The child's lip wobbled, and Ionius devoutly hoped it wasn't about to start screaming again. He sighed deeply and tried again, somewhat more gently. "What's your name?"

It sniffed. It kept staring at him. Finally it whispered, "Oleksandr."

"Oleksandr. Your mata calls you Sasha, yeah? Where is she? What's her name?"

Oleksandr – so it must be *he*, not *it*, though Ionius didn't give a fuck – nodded shyly. Then he grabbed the collar of Ionius's fur cloak, trying to burrow himself into it, and Ionius pried his hands off. "Mata," he demanded. "Where is she?"

Sasha shook his head. "Dunno." Tears welled again. "Want Mata."

"Yes, I know." Ionius joggled him impatiently on his hip. "What's her name?"

The little boy didn't seem to understand the question. "Mata."

Biting back a curse – truly, children were idiots – Ionius tried to think how else to get his point across. After sustained trial and error, he finally managed to learn that Mata's name was something like Katushka – probably Kateryna? – and they were separated somewhere in the vicinity of Registan Square, if Sasha's confused waving was at all accurate. But it was better than nothing, and Ionius blew out a martyred breath and started to trudge in that direction, Sasha nuzzled under his chin and clinging to him like a limpet. He was small but solid, surprisingly strong, still sniffing but intrigued enough by this big, rough stranger not to cry. At last he said, "You?"

"Me? What about me?"

"Sasha?" The little boy looked at him curiously. "Sasha too?"

"No. Not Sasha. I – " His tongue hovered over any number of his aliases, all the names he called himself, the people he pretended to be. Yet again, it was the old hag's fault, but somehow it stumbled past the lies and spoke the simple, bruising truth. "My name is Ivan. Vanya."

Sasha considered that, as they turned into the broad square before the Three Mahqasas; they were stunning enough by day, worked in blue and gold and ivory, but by night, in the wintry bone-glow of the rising moon, the sight was shockingly and ethereally beautiful. There were still a few Wahini leaving after sardiq prayer and merchants loitering in hopes of last-minute customers, and Ionius glanced around for any Kozheks who had mislaid their offspring. It took a moment, but he spotted a stout fur-wrapped young woman – a girl, really – with long yellow braids, clutching the hand of a young man likewise barely more than a boy, tall and gangly with a downy beard. They were tearfully addressing a pair of city guards, but there was yet again great confusion, as the guards only spoke Sardarkhandian Qiné and the young couple only spoke Kozhek, reducing both parties to broad gestures. At the sight, Sasha lifted his head and immediately perked up. "Mata?"

"S-Sasha?" The girl spun around so fast that she slipped on the icy cobbles and almost fell. "Blessed Mata Koroleva, *Sashenko!*"

She raced forward, snatched the little boy out of Ionius's arms, and covered him with kisses, as her husband likewise hastened over and stared at his son in joyous disbelief. "You – " He turned to Ionius, clutching his hands. "You found him? Thank you. Divine Family, thank you."

"It's fine." Ionius tried to brush him off. "Look after him better."

"I know." The young father shook his head weakly. "We have been busy here all day, and Kateryna only looked away for a moment, but he must have managed to wander off. Who are you, what is your village, your family name? Who is your hetman? We are from Chornovhitsy, we have furs, wheat, and honey to trade and varenyky to eat. Take whatever you want, anything you need. I am Oleksii Oleksandrynich Holoroborodka, and if you ever need help from me or mine – "

"I do not expect so." Uncomfortable with the torrent of gratitude, Ionius again disentangled himself. "I was born in Ruthynia, yes, but I do not live there now, not for a long time. You will not know my name or my people. As I said, mind your son better, and then – "

"You found him?" Round-faced and red-eyed, Kateryna pushed past her husband, Sasha snuggled in one arm, and threw the other around Ionius's neck, smothering him in a disgusting amount of kisses. "May the saints and the Holy Mother bless you! He – Sasha said that you are called Ivan? Vanya, Vanya, thank you. You are a very kind man."

At that, something went off in his head like an explosion, silent and deafening all at once. He ripped away from Kateryna's embrace hard enough to make her stumble, and turned his back without another word, scurrying out of Registan Square like a wounded animal. His mouth was flooded with that sickly copper taste, his legs had turned to glue, and he sank onto the cold stones of a back alley only a few yards from the magical door to Merone. He heaved and gasped, making a terrible sound, and he hated even more that he was utterly unable to stop. It was just – it was so stupid, so impossible, but all he could think was if Sasha had been *him* – if he, also a little boy, had wandered from his home and family into the dangers of the dark, but someone kind – truly kind, not Ionius, who was as far from the word as could be imagined – found him and took him back to *his* mother – if it hadn't been the monsters who seized him and his sister and tore her away – if he had grown up knowing any of it, his village, his family, his hetman – if he hadn't been a slave –

Some amount of time later, the fit started to pass, loosening its grip in drips and drabs, leaving Ionius's chest aching as badly as if someone had taken a knife and carved it open. He remained on all fours, hating himself and the foul old ravana for putting a spell on him, as that was the only reason he was so shamefully overcome. You would think *he* was the child who had never been exposed to the world. Stupid. *Stupid*.

But it didn't help, and he stayed crouched, breath billowing in the dark air, which was cold enough to sting tears from his eyes. If Sasha was still lost, it was unlikely that he would survive the night, and yet Ionius wished he had just walked the fuck away, not tried to act like a hero when he wasn't one and it made not a single difference in how he had failed Tatya for all time and could never atone. *Not that it matters. You know how lucky you are to be a Meronite. Stop sniveling, you weakling. You disgrace the Divine Emperor, the Immortals, yourself. Get up.*

It took another agonizing effort, bones creaking like the old man he was, to haul himself to his feet. He likewise needed to find shelter, but there was no chance of brooding his failures away in some flea-bitten hostel while Coriolane was in danger. Even if he had lost his mind, he had to get home now, so Ionius locked his knees and marched down to the door where he had first entered Sardarkhand, carved with a strange golden glyph. It was dark and dead, as the connection wasn't presently active, but he drew the metal from his wrists and instead of shaping it into the usual knives, finally managed to form it into a key. He had never done that before, and so it was lopsided and wobbly, but never mind. He shoved the key into the latch, twisted, and pushed it open.

Nothing. It only revealed a cold and dusty closet that led nowhere, certainly not Merone. Ionius swore, slammed his shoulder into the jamb and achieved nothing, and wondered if even the Thaumaturges were in on this plot and he would also have to kill them on his return (whenever or *if* ever that should be achieved). It did sharply illustrate the downsides of traveling by magic door – if it was shut, it was shut, and there was no way to get back in unless you were one of the fortunate few who knew how to open it. The cross-country marches were much slower and harder, but at least they didn't rely on this sorcerous bullshit.

As he paced in a circle, trying to think what else could be done, he caught sight of a hooded figure skulking in the shadows nearby. As if they were waiting, watching, or worse, and considering the gravity of what could be going on in the Eternal City right this minute, Ionius could not take the risk. He reshaped the key into the knife, flew down the alley, and hit the interloper in a bone-crunching tackle, jamming the blade beneath its chin. *"What the fuck are you –"*

"General! General, please!" The moon, now risen far enough over the spires to throw eerie glow into the street, revealed a petrified and familiar face. It was one of the palace eunuchs – the same one who met him on his return from Iscaria and took him to Coriolane, if that meant anything. But it was proof of *some* sort of duplicity, for how else could the unmanned bastard be here at the very same time, halfway across the world? Someone had sent this spy – Belsephorus, wasn't it? – after him for the Divine Family knew what treason, and they would pay for it.

"You slimy fucking – " Ionius jabbed the knife even harder into the eunuch's throat. "Pity they already took your balls, or I'd – "

"No, no. Listen, please listen." Belsephorus's breathing was as fast and shallow as a frightened rabbit, as being pinned by an enraged Immortal was the sort of situation that only the greatly talented or impossibly lucky ever survived. "You are upset, General, but you must heed my warning. There is – you might have already understood – there is a conspiracy. You have been lured to Sardarkhand for nefarious purposes, and the threat is not what you think. Back in Merone – "

A chill went through Ionius from head to heel. Part of him yearned to butcher Belsephorus like a pig, if nothing else than to relieve his frustration, but common sense grudgingly intervened. Slowly he pulled the knife away, but remained where he was. "Talk."

"There is no time. You must get away from this place." Belsephorus fluttered his hands in frantic appeal. "I was ordered to wait until you returned and then lead you into the trap, but I – I decided not to. You must trust me. I will explain later, I promise, I *promise*. Now – "

Ionius hesitated furiously. He was sick of ill-gotten mercy, but at least this validated his instinct that something was terribly wrong, and therefore he wasn't (hopefully) *quite* so much of a coward as he feared. "One wrong move, and – "

"Yes, yes." The eunuch gulped. "Understood. General Ionius, if you would be so kind…?"

Ionius snarled. *I am not kind.* Nonetheless, the point was taken, and he swung off, getting to his feet and forbearing to offer Belsephorus a hand. The eunuch clambered up and wasted a few moments fussily brushing the dirt off his cloak, then beckoned Ionius to follow.

They hurried down the alley, Ionius shadowing Belsephorus like a hungry demon. He was swiftly skeptical of how well the eunuch seemed to know an allegedly foreign and unfamiliar city, as he took several expert turnings, weaving a practiced route through the unmarked lanes and alleys. "You," Ionius ordered. "You've been here before, haven't you?"

"Sometimes I am bid to collect delicacies that can only be found in other parts of the world." Belsephorus shrugged apologetically. "And Their Imperial Majesties do not take no for an answer."

Ah. Yes. Of course Coriolane, Gheslyn, and Vestalia used the magic doors as their personal luxury shopping service. This, however, sparked a sudden recollection that Belsephorus was indeed attached to the private household of the empresses. That was why he was a eunuch in the first place, continuing a long tradition of fully castrating any man who had sustained domestic contact or daily service to the royal women, lest he ever be tempted to cuckold the Divine Father on earth; the practice had started in Coriolanople, probably borrowed from Parsivat, and then spread to Merone. Belsephorus must have been cut later than some of his peers, perpetual youths with the angelically high voices so prized in the Arch-Holy Basilica choir, because he almost looked like a man, if you squinted. It was cruel, obviously, and not something that anyone willingly chose, but that was the simple truth of all service to Great Merone, the price of its glory and grandeur. They were grateful.

In a few minutes, they turned a corner, descended into a narrow tunnel, and emerged into a small courtyard by one of the old astronomy towers. It bordered a spot in the city wall that was only partly repaired from all the assorted conquering attempts, low enough that it could be vaulted with a running start. Ionius stared at it in mild disbelief, as the wind whistled spookily through the broken stones. He supposed it wasn't *urgent*, since the flat steppes meant that Sardarkhand would see any invading army coming for weeks in advance and could rush to shore it up as needed, but the lack of vigilance personally offended him. In Merone, it was a lapse to get you flogged or hanged. What was it like to live in a place that was not eternally and endlessly at war, constantly administering cruelty to itself and everyone else? Where you could just exist with a gaping hole in your defenses, and not expect to get savaged?

"Wait here, my lord." Belsephorus nodded at the courtyard. "I will go up and fetch the folk. It was too dangerous for them in Merone."

"*What* folk?"

"I promise, General." The eunuch pulled his hood tight. "All will become clear."

Ionius misliked that more than ever, but he grunted assent, and Belsephorus scuttled off, opened the tower door, and vanished inside. The silence stretched long, as Ionius attempted to fathom what kind of malfeasants could be denned up in there. A bunch of crusading astronomers, determined to beat villains to death with their telescopes? The mental image forced a snort out of him, and he turned on his heel. The eunuch was taking his sweet bloody time about it, and the moon was high enough that the ground seemed to sparkle, catching a peculiar onyx glow. In fact… right where Ionius was standing.

He stopped dead. Knelt down and scooped up a handful of dirt – but it wasn't dirt. It was black, fine-grained, and smelled like sulfur. It had been spilled around the entire courtyard, and he was in the very middle. Because he was stupid. Because he was so fucking stupid that he saw it only when it was too late. The door to Merone wasn't the trap. *This* was the trap, and he had let the fucking eunuch lead him right into it, docile as a cow to slaughter. There was nobody here, nobody to meet. Belsephorus was lying about everything, and Ionius hadn't sensed it. He was off his guard, wrung out and raw, and now he was going to pay.

"*BASTARD!*" Ionius gathered his haunches beneath him and prepared to leap straight up into the third-story tower window – not that Belsephorus was still there, he had surely fled as far out of the oncoming blast radius as possible. But Ionius took a running start, launched, and –

The explosion caught him in midair. All the air and breath was sucked out of the world in an anticlimactic *crump,* and then it lit, spread, and blew outward, in a superheated roar that opened like a dragon's mouth and bloomed. It seized Ionius in its jaws and flung him into darkness, howling wind and blazing inferno. He slammed into the ground, felt an agonizing scream of pain that even his Immortal bones couldn't fully fend off, and understood, with uncanny and unquestioned clarity, precisely what had just happened. The entire Sardarkhand diversion had been set up for this one reason: to kill Coriolane's favorite general and make it look like not just a tragically heroic accident, nobly falling in the line of duty to protect the Eternal City from conniving Qiné anarchists, but also make it certain that Coriolane would declare open war on the Thearchate at long last. He had been itching for a reason, as Qin's power continued to grow and Hang Zhai proved just as adept at living for centuries, but the Spice Road trade and the other benefits of peace were too valuable to disrupt. But if it looked as if the Qiné themselves had broken the stalemate, first by raising the import tariffs and then assassinating the Meronites' top commander –

Did Coriolane himself do this? No, it wasn't true, it couldn't be. The Divine Emperor would never sacrifice *Ionius Servus Eternus,* regardless of how hungry he was for a new expansionist war, and his outrage about the black powder and the tariffs had been real. No, the only plausible suspect Ionius could think of – and it was still shocking, considering the magnitude of betrayal that had to be involved – was the empress Gheslyn. Whether Vestalia was also involved, he had no idea, but he had a feeling that for this plot to have any chance of succeeding, it had to be both of them. *I have searched across the damn world for the traitors, and it turns out they are both sleeping in Coriolane's bed, hiding in plain sight. If I am gone, do they intend to finish him off tonight?*

That thought, however, existed a world away from anything he could do to stop it. Burning debris hailed into him like falling stars, he had been hurt severely enough that he could not stand up, and if he waited for his Immortal resilience to kick in, he might be dead by the time it did. The tower had collapsed, bricks and stones spilling in blast-strewn pieces, and flames were burning even more vigorously in the wreckage. This must be where the barrels of black powder were hidden all along, a sleeping viper just waiting for Ionius to arrive, for Belsephorus to drop a lit fuse and run for his life. Murkily, muffled, Ionius heard alarmed shouts. If he was caught here, alive or dead –

With an agonizing effort, he rolled over; broken ribs made him lightheaded. Inch by inch, he dragged himself across the rubble and out of sight just as the first neighbors arrived, shouting for survivors. It wasn't clear if the tower had been inhabited, but if so, they too were dead or mortally wounded. So, for that matter, was he. Ionius's vision wavered and split; the world was a demonic carousel of flame and shadow, pain and blood. He kept crawling along the freezing cobbles as if out from the mouth of hell. If he couldn't get the door open, he was dead.

He didn't realize that he had found his way back until he spotted the door. The glyph was still dark and inert, but there was one thing he could try — the *only* thing. The metal was bound in his bones by the Corporalists, but they needed the magic of the Thaumaturges to do it, the same that animated the doors. And there was only one way to get it.

Doing his utmost not to think about how little he was going to enjoy this, Ionius raised his left hand, wrapped it around his right wrist, and pulled the metal from his bones. The effort of forming it into a knife almost defeated him entirely, and he gagged. He took a final moment, but it wasn't going to help. He lifted his right arm, took a better grip on the knife, and cut down into it — fast, deep, and straight to the bone.

The pain, even with the torment he was already in, was so bad that he let out a fresh rush of swearing. His fingers slipped in his own blood, and he nearly lost his grip as he carved a thin slice of his ulna, the marrow dark and fibrous in the firelight. If his Immortal healing didn't mend it, he would be crippled for the rest of his life — though if this didn't work, that would be very short indeed. So then. No choice. Nothing but this. His right arm gushing blood, Ionius staggered to his feet and pressed the bone into the keyhole. He couldn't stand up, and the world reeled. *Please*. He didn't beg, but this was begging. *Please. Please. Please.*

For a final instant, he thought it had not worked, it was all over, and he had nothing to do but lie down and die quickly, before Belsephorus or any other traitors found him. But then there was a dawning heat, a sudden glow, and under his bloodstained fingers — because somehow Vata Korol must love him after all — the latch gave. The lock clicked.

The door swung open.

Ionius fell through.

CHAPTER 15

JULIAN

The room at the top of the tower — or at least Julian thought it was a tower, but that was not necessarily conclusive — made him feel like an intrepid but doomed protagonist in a fairytale, Kaj locked in the castle of Snezhnaya Koroleva. The windows were too high to see out of, and the walls were a featureless white. The requested meal had finally appeared, and Julian tore into it as if it might disappear. But while he was grateful, he could only impatiently wait for Kronus to get back and explain what the fuck that was about. What did he *mean*, the *Ring of Tselmun* was in Qart-Hadesht? How could it have gotten there? Wouldn't it be, if anywhere, in Yerussala? How could he know it was real? Yes, presumably it was the exact sort of magical tchotchke for which the Thaumaturges kept a weather eye out, in case it turned up in a local rummage sale, but that was still a long way from explaining Kronus's instant and unnerving certainty. Either way, the Grand Magister must immediately investigate, so he dispatched Julian here with profuse apologies and orders to await further instructions, and hence he was locked in a cell again. It was nicer than the last one, but that didn't change its nature.

When he had finished eating, Julian wandered into the washroom, located a few items of gentlemen's toilette, and gratefully shaved off his filthy prison beard. He then trimmed his hair, which gave him a sudden pang. His mother had always bemoaned the fact that he and Isyk wore it in secular Ruthynian fashion, and not in traditional Vashemite sidelocks like their father. In turn, the Kozharyev brothers argued that Vata hardly left the ghetto, whereas they did nearly every day, and the traditions agreed that the highest duty was the preservation of life; all other mitzvot could be bent as necessary. And because walking around Korolgrod looking like you were straight out of shul in kharmulke and payot, tallyt and tzitzyt, was guaranteed to get you jeered at best and beaten to death at worst, it was therefore a binding religious imperative not to dress in a way that openly or deliberately drew hostile attention. After all, that was the sin of flaunting pride and piety, and equally undesirable. They were willing to ask the rebbitek. He was very likely to back them up.

At that point, Mirym sighed deeply, threw up her hands, and commended them for their excellent halakhic study, which she hoped they would put to use on Sabatday next. She still didn't like it, but she seemed to accept that they had won and didn't bring it up again, and yet now that Julian had wound up as the pet Vashemite for a lot of crazy Meronite sorcerers, he considered whether to play it up like a caricature, unjustly ripped out of his provincial life and into the goyish tribulations of the outside world. In the end, he decided against it. He was valuable because he was a Vashemite, yes, but that rested on not being too *much* of a Vashemite. To their eyes, he had to look normal and safe, tamed and acculturated. Someone who would cheerfully teach outsiders to read Old High Yerussalan and learn the most cherished secrets of their people. Who gave a fuck about his *hair,* if that was what he proposed to do next? It might even mark the hallowed milestone of getting all Vashemites everywhere to agree on something, and that it was very bad.

Grooming complete, Julian returned to the main chamber and dug in the trunk at the foot of the bed, looking for something to wear beneath his robes apart from the slave rags. There was a cassock-like garment that he eyed suspiciously, and a pair of canvas underpants, which seemed like asking for disaster. But he returned to the washroom and scrubbed them as best he could, hanging them on the window sill to dry. Just how long was Kronus going to take, anyway? Would he forget altogether that he had sent Julian here, and they would not discover his desiccated corpse for another hundred years or so? Was this all some sort of elaborate prank to test Julian's credulity, and should he have spoken up to deny it? Because how could it be the one thing which held almost as supreme status in Vashemite legend as the Ark of the Covenant itself, said to be spirited out of the Holy City and hidden in Numeria after the fall of the First Yerussalan Kingdom? It was impossible. It had to be. Come on. *Ring* of Tselmun? Ring of *Tselmun? Ring of Tselmun?!?!*

At long bloody last, Julian heard footsteps on the stairs, and jumped up. A few moments later, there was a knock and Kronus's croaky voice called, "Doctor Kozharyev? Are you decent?"

"Uh, yes, yes." He finished dressing, pulled the robe back on and donned the cap. "I'm ready."

When Julian opened the door, he beheld the Grand Magister looking exhausted but excited. "Please forgive me for depositing you here, Doctor, but I thought you could use some rest. Besides, I had to check the veracity of my readings, and I am delighted to report that they are correct."

"So – what?" Julian blinked. "It *is* the Ring?"

"To all appearances." Kronus preened. *"And* it has arrived in Qart-Hadesht. You have heard of the Venerable Republic, yes? In Ifriqiyin?"

"Yes. Is that supposed to mean something?"

"Well, of course." Kronus raised one weedy eyebrow. "The location is symbolic, to say the least. Hanibal and the elephants, the generations of wars, the great rivalry of Merone and Qart that shaped the ancient world, before we took it firmly in hand as one of the empire's chief protectorates and ended such unfruitful disorder. And yet, I have recently become privy to intelligence suggesting that this defiance, even after centuries suborned to the Divine Emperor's noble rule, has not yet burned out, or rather has been perniciously rekindled. They are plotting to attempt something on the occasion of His Majesty's state visit in spring, and with such a weapon in hand – "

Julian stared at him. He should clearly say something clever, conducive to his persona of a distinguished scholar, but he was too shocked by the fact that anyone, much less a senior Meronite official, could be implying what he thought Kronus was implying. "Are you – "

If the Ring of Tselmun *was* somehow in the picture, it made sense, but one insane revelation after another was sapping his ability to process any of them. "Are you actually suggesting that there's a Qartic assassination attempt in the works? On the emperor? How would that be *possible?*"

"Forgive me, Doctor, for not disclosing sensitive information." Kronus ghosted a shrug. "But I serve as an all-seeing spymaster for His Majesty, casting a vigilant eye across the empire for anything that could threaten his blessed rule. This, of course, is not the first such plan. There have been many, and will be more. But they were desperate, makeshift, and easily thwarted. This is different. You see the nature of our task?"

"What?" Julian was still lost. "Finding something that is even more powerful than the Ring?"

"Indeed. Or at least to translate King Tselmun's grimoire sufficiently enough to understand the particular character of his magic, and finally and properly use it. Come with me."

Julian's head was exploding with questions, but now was not the time. He followed Kronus to the bottom of the tower, whereupon they stepped into the white atrium with all the black doors, quite possibly a way to easily travel to any number of far-flung destinations. It occurred to Julian that if so, one of them was very likely to lead to Korolgrod, and perhaps he could try to get through. But how would Kronus and the others react, if he suddenly vanished? Would they assume he had done exactly that, and send a legion to recapture him, discover his deception, torch the ghetto and kill his family? It was the last thing the perpetually precarious existence of Vashemites in Ruthynia needed, would justify harsher crackdowns by Zogorov and the Konsilium, and waste whatever slender chance he had to learn about this ancient magic, something that could hold even Coriolane Aureus IX's fate in its sway – *their* magic, *their* Ring, *their* grimoire, all of which the Meronites had stolen. If Julian was going out, he would do so in a blaze of glory. *Not yet.*

They crossed the vast floor and entered another door, whereupon Julian's desire to stay instantly and shamefully became even stronger. It was the most splendid library he had ever seen: towering stacks and crowded shelves, gold-grilled balconies, stained-glass windows, polished tables and green-velveted chairs. It was illuminated by soaring streamers of sunlight and golden glow from smokeless torches. It had a welcoming hush, a thick seafoam silence, somewhere a person could sink into a sea of books and never be seen again. Julian had never wanted anything so badly as he wanted to explore it, peer at every volume and peruse every page, and he felt his resolve to get out of here take another blow. What if he didn't have to go? Could just stay forever, and learn?

Yes, and maybe you'll grow wings and marry a boy in shul, you idiot. Julian shook his head, ordering himself to stay remotely tethered to reality. As they stepped inside, he glanced around, expecting to see other Thaumaturges clustered over books like a murder of crows, but the library was empty. Indeed, the only living people Julian had seen since his prison break were Marcus and Kronus; even the meal had simply appeared outside his door without visible human agency. As they reached Kronus' worktable, piled high with books – one of them, ominously, seemed to be about the Red Death, which Julian glimpsed for only an instant before the Grand Magister picked it up and shut it – he said, "Where are your colleagues, Excellency? If you will forgive me."

"Thaumaturges are a solitary breed. Like cats." Kronus looked apologetic. "We do not often come together in deliberate conference. And you have seen that with our excellent system of doors, there is no reason to confine oneself merely to one library or place of study. Besides, what with the ongoing incident in Yerussala, a number of them have gone to make observations."

"Ongoing… incident?"

"It seems that the Ring's reappearance has led to all sorts of fascinating consequences. It is an unmissable opportunity to study Tselmun's magic at close range and improve our understanding of what we are dealing with." Kronus turned aside to put the books on a cart. Over his shoulder, he added casually, "Of course, Vashemites can be quite vicious when their control is interrupted or interfered with, and due caution is advised. One moment, Doctor. I will fetch the grimoire."

With that, he hurried away into the literary canyonlands, which was good insofar as Julian had opened his mouth in outrage and didn't trust himself to be civil in reply. He took a deep breath, clenched his fists, and reminded himself that he had signed up for this by agreeing to take part in Kronus' stupid little translation project. He would say that he couldn't believe the Thaumaturges were so dependent on Vashemite magic, writing, tools, power, city, and more, while remaining so scornful and misinformed about actual Vashemites, but unfortunately, he could. After all, when you stole something valuable, the last thing you wanted was the original owner to reappear and lodge a complaint. Besides, there was that thing where the Tridevarians, despite controlling the entire Meronite Empire, the True Church, and then some, had persuaded themselves that it was actually a tiny cabal of all-powerful evil Vashemites pulling the world's strings behind the scenes, and their "control" had to be stamped out. Anything to let themselves sleep at night.

In a few minutes Kronus returned, carrying a strange black-iron strongbox that was closed and sealed with insanely complicated catches, gears, wheels, and locks, all of which looked like the type to shoot a poison dart if you missed a single combination. Julian therefore did not attempt to touch it or even come closer as Kronus set it down with a flourish. He thought of Vashach scrolls in shul, kept in the open as a prized possession, read and shared and studied together, and wondered what the congregation back home in Korolgrod would make of this: Tselmun ben Dayoud's own original compendium of magic, shut in a menacing Meronite box where only a chosen few could look at it without risking literal death. It felt like far too solemn and sacred a thing to happen this way, like the Grand Magister had dug up the Ark of the Covenant and was prying it open with his bare hands. Clearly sensing Julian's discomfort, he glanced up. "Be assured that this is not a ritual object, Doctor. As I said, I removed all such spells. It is only a subject of scholarly study. Such superstitions must be overcome, you know."

"Of course." Julian bit his lip, muttering a silent apology to the book, as the complicated metallic exoskeleton split open. It revealed a thick grubby stack of age-browned parchment, worn and tattered and covered in spidery script that was faded in places and nearly illegible in others. At the thought that he could be looking at King Tselmun's own handwriting, a powerful chill passed through Julian from head to toe. The frozen awe lasted exactly two more seconds, until he caught sight of a second set of writing in red ink, scribbled liberally in the margins and in some cases, directly atop the text. This was not in the right-left of Old High Yerussalan, but the left-right of Lanuvian orthox. Failing entirely to conceal his shocked disapproval, Julian demanded, "Did you *write* in *the original Key of Tselmun,* then actually complain that you couldn't translate it?!"

"You needn't sound so prim." Kronus sniffed. "Recording my thoughts helps me recall what I was thinking, when I return to a text for re-reading. I assure you that my marginalia were in the interests of clarification, not obfuscation – correcting arcane grammatical usage, or making note of where his prototype spells connect to ours. That so – "

Julian reminded himself that actually saying everything he longed to say, "esteemed scholar" or otherwise, would get him chucked off the top of the maybe-tower, and after going to all this trouble to avoid it, it seemed counterproductive to do it now. Still, he couldn't hold back, pointing at a letter on the title page. "Look. That's *alef*, which is usually a weak consonant in Old High Yerussalan, but if it's indicated with niqqud, that means it's a vowel. But I can't tell for sure because you've written over it, and that could change the *entire* meaning of this word, and therefore the whole sentence and passage. I could try shorashim, the deictic method where I guess if it is a vowel and in what configuration based on surrounding consonants and context, but that's not guaranteed. Besides, half the original meaning could be in those spellings you crossed out! Of course Tselmun didn't use formal Lanuvian when he was writing in Yerussala thousands of years ago! You've tried to do this in a way that would get me smacked in yeshirim if I did it, and so – "

Kronus's lips pursed. "I must say, Doctor, if you customarily harangue your students in such overwrought fashion, you must be a rather poor lecturer. First of all, you shall need to simplify foreign jargon and unfamiliar terminology. What, for instance, is *niqqud?*"

"It's a… diacritic mark. A dot. Like that." Swallowing his rage with an effort, Julian searched the page to find a *vav* that had it, and pointed. "See there? When it's unmodified, it's transliterated as the consonant *w* or sometimes *v*. But when you put the dot to the left, it's the vowel *u*. On top, it would be *o*. That's the system of niqqud. I don't know what the equivalent term is, in Lanuvian."

"*Matres lectionis*," Kronus said, rather snippily. He was plainly still put out at being told off like a misbehaving schoolboy. "Surely even if your provincial university has not afforded you the chance to speak it, you can at least *read* it?"

That, Julian thought, was likewise unclear. He could scrape out some of it, mostly from memory, since the Konsilium had increasingly taken to issuing laws, papers, and public decrees in Lanuvian orthox alone, with little or no transliteration into Ruthynian kyrillic or Vashemysh abjad. Most Vashemites had to pay a notary or scrivener to get important documents rendered into orthox; the imperial bureaucracy haughtily rejected anything not written in its own letters. But figuring out how to explain that Yerussalan ו was Ruthynian у was (he thought) Lanuvian *u* was more difficult than Julian felt capable of presently achieving, and he was still trying not to have an apoplexy at this wanton mutilation of Tselmun's priceless manuscript. *If you'd let me learn it, Mata, just think! One day it could have saved the world!*

"One thing at a time," he said instead. "My Lanuvian is not terribly strong, admittedly, but nor is your Old High Yerussalan. I can translate it into Ruthynian, and as we are demonstrating, you *do* speak that. So surely you can manage the Lanuvian?"

"Hmph." Kronus jabbed a finger at the page. "Let's see what you can do first."

Well, then. Challenge accepted. Julian took a deep breath, rolled up his sleeves, and helped himself to paper, an inkwell, and a pen. Wondered one final time what in darkest Sheol he was doing, and got to work.

For all that it was a groundbreaking, once-in-several-lifetimes opportunity to read the deepest and most treasured etc. etc., it was not dissimilar to the time Julian, at the age of twelve, had gotten in big trouble for making fun of the ancient rebbitek who instructed the boys preparing for tor mitzvah and whose wheezy, droning monotone was guaranteed to put them straight to sleep in ten minutes, five if the lesson was directly after lunch. Julian's unflattering impersonation of one such episode had gone down very well with his classmates, but unfortunately he failed to notice the rebbitek standing right behind him. He was therefore detained for the rest of the day and well into the night due to being ordered to copy out the entire Book of Names by hand, with no cheating and no stopping. By the time he finished – hand blackened with ink and so painfully cramped that he could hardly uncurl his fingers, belly aching with hunger, eyes crossed, and mind graven as deeply as Moyshe's stone tablets with the necessity of being courteous to one's elders – one would think the mere action of picking up a pen would cause the cold sweats. Which it did, somewhat, but apparently not well enough. Because, indeed, here he *fucking* was again.

Time slid and spiraled into another endless span of intense concentration, muffled swearing, crossing out, and trying again. It did not escape Julian that he was doing all the miserable grunt work while Kronus got to putter about, look at interesting books and manuscripts, review notes, and otherwise relax at his leisure, but that was a metaphor for the whole damn empire in a nutshell. He could also state with certainty that while Tselmun had perhaps been a great king, he was absolutely bloody not a great prose stylist. The introduction alone was the densest thing Julian had ever read, maundering about the mysteries of power and the impenetrable nature of the higher realms, the inherent temperament of the jinnyeh race and the ineffable will of the Almighty. Indeed, it could give Rebbitek Goldstein a run for his money in the curing-insomnia department, but Julian couldn't skim it, or assume he knew what it said, or extrapolate from the beginning of a sentence where it would wind up by the end. His head felt thick and achy; after all, he had been a prisoner until less than twenty-four hours ago, and he still hadn't slept. He had only produced two or three pages when he gave up. "Excellency, I can't do any more. At least, not right now."

"This is all?" Kronus picked up the pitiful sheaf and riffled it with a frown. "It hardly seems reflective of what one might expect."

"I told you that Old High Yerussalan was difficult. And I'm not a machine, I'm a man. You are welcome to continue, if you think – "

"Once again, Doctor, you must school your temper. And while I do appreciate the value of a complete and chronological translation, it is not relevant to what we most need to know. I thus require you to find the parts pertaining to the enchantment and principles of the Ring. The summary will do. Otherwise – "

"*No.*" Dangerous as it was, Julian stood up. The sunlight had faded, and the only illumination in the library was the eerie gold torches, transforming the shelves into wells of shadow. "This is the original *Key*, but it's not the only one. You have the greatest library in the world, right here at your fingertips. Go find another copy and compare it for yourself, or actually study our language and lore, instead of just stealing it and expecting me to do all the work. Though to be frank, if you did not bother to learn something as basic as niqqud, I have no notion how you fancied yourself competent to read or translate anything. If you want me to continue, I will. *Later.*"

There was a crackling silence. Kronus looked almost comically startled, and it went without saying that mouthing off like that was a very bad idea. But even so, Julian held his ground. "Just for your reference," he added, "I'm not a slave. You're used to everyone in Merone being one and therefore always at your command, but I'm not. I'm a free man. If you *want* a slave scholar, you can find one at the Imperial Academy."

"Indeed," Kronus said slowly, after another very antagonistic pause. "Though slave or free, most people in your position would think it wise to speak more judiciously."

"Perhaps. But I've never been good at that."

"So I see. Your tenure at the university must have been quite… eventful." As gingerly as if he expected them to explode, Kronus put the pages down. "What do you wish, then?"

"For now, I'd like to have some proper sleep. Is there a key – a real key, not a book – that I need to get back into that room, or – ?"

"Here." Kronus produced a large golden key and handed it over. "Be warned that it only opens the door to your tower, and attempting to go wandering would be most unwise."

Unpleasantly reminded of the tale of the blue-bearded bridegroom, Julian nodded, took the key, and slipped it into his robes. He was briefly tempted to ask how he would know which door was his, but he wanted to get out before Kronus exacted vengeance for disrespect. It would have been politic to bow, but Julian didn't think he could stomach it. Instead he nodded again, touched two fingers to his brow, and left the library without another word.

The atrium was pitch-black except for the distant glow of the glyph-graven doors, far off and flickering as marshlights in a swamp, luring an unwary traveler to his doom. As well, there was an eerie murmur like whispering voices or rolling waves, as if the absent Thaumaturges were gathered just out of sight. It was so unnerving that Julian slowed his pace, fully expecting someone – or some*thing* – to burst out and demand to know what he was doing here. It prickled the back of his neck, raising gooseflesh on his arms, and he reached into his pocket, gripping the key, though it was utterly useless as an improvised weapon. If he could just –

At that moment, Julian tripped headlong over something lying in front of one of the doors, something large and squashy and *alive,* and only barely held back from screaming his lungs out. Instead he bit his tongue, did a somersault, and punched at the amorphous mass, which groaned and swore in a pained and muffled snarl. Fuck's sake, it was *human,* it was *breathing,* and unless he had totally lost his mind, it was *familiar.* He fumbled for the key, heart banging in his chest, and raised it, casting pellucid golden light. It couldn't be, it *couldn't* – but it *was.*

"*Ilya?*" Julian's voice was croaky with shock. "*Is that you?!*"

Ilya Sergeynich groaned again and raised a hand in protest, screwing his eyes up against the glow. But it was in fact him, and he looked like hell. Even after all the times he was tortured (or allegedly tortured) and thrown back into their cell, it was nothing to compare to this comprehensive buggeration. He seemed to have been half-conscious on the floor for some time, and whatever he had gone through before getting there was even worse. He was filthy and bloody, his clothes were torn into shreds, and there was a hideous gash in his right wrist, so deep that his hand was almost cut off. Julian's gorge rose, and he swallowed hard. Then he demanded, "What the *fuck* are you doing here? How did you get in? Did you – did you try to escape?"

"I… yeah." Ilya's eyes were closed, his face the color of bad milk. "Tried to escape."

"Into the Thaumaturges' fucking living room? Or wherever we are?" Julian looked around in badly suppressed panic, certain that Kronus was going to sail in and find him consorting with a criminal, but it wasn't *his* fault. This was utterly bizarre on every level. For one thing, Ilya was dressed in Ruthynian clothes, which he must have stolen in preparation for his own jailbreak, but were considerably too warm for the mild and rainy Meronite winter. Perhaps he hoped to travel somewhere else in the ordinary fashion, or he was trying to escape by one of the doors. Which… wasn't a *bad* plan, if you overlooked the eighty-six levels of insanity required to break *into* the imperial sorcerers' dread hideaway, but Julian couldn't fault anyone else for it. Stones, glass houses.

"Come on," he said instead. "We have to get you out of here."

Ilya muttered something incomprehensible and struggled feebly when Julian tried to drape his arm over his shoulders. Which seemed fairly standard for the pig-headed bastard, but he was a good fourteen stone of extremely solid dead weight, and Julian's muscles protested at the effort. "Come on," he panted again. "Help me out, you big idiot."

"No, you shouldn't…" Ilya seemed to forget what he was going to say, and he made an alarming noise when he breathed. "Just leave me."

"Bullshit." Julian manhandled him across the foyer with equal stubbornness, leaving a trail of blood on the stones. Anyone else who set foot in here would realize at once that something was very wrong, but that was another problem for later. For all he knew, it was a common feature in a lair of mad wizards. Had to be for the Corporalists, right?

With Ilya swearing weakly and Julian huffing for breath, they reached the far side of the atrium, and Julian held up the key. One of the glyphs flared brightly, and he stuffed the key into the matching door. He twisted it, and Ilya's pain-glazed eyes turned sharp. "Where did you – ?"

"Long… story." Julian heaved Ilya over the threshold and kicked the door shut. They then had to face the daunting prospect of the tower stairs, which twisted upward in a dizzying spiral that was bad enough in normal circumstances. Hauling a large, full-grown, and badly-wounded man was even more of a miserable slog, and Ilya kept grumbling and grumping, as if convinced that this was all a shambolic waste of time and he should be left to die like a dog. Julian puffed at him to shut up and finally, blessedly reached the boudoir. He attempted not to drop the invalid too hard, then sat down, still gasping. "Well. This is a disaster."

"I did not ask – you to help me. It would have been better if not."

"I just lugged your stupid arse up *far* too many stairs, I'm not going to hear it. There's a washroom just there. Let's get you cleaned up."

"Julian – " Ilya bit the name back as if he had not meant to utter it. Their eyes met, a peculiar and fraught awareness skittered down Julian's spine, and Ilya tried to raise his mangled arm, then hissed and dropped it. "Don't," he managed. "This isn't what – "

"Unfortunately for you, I'm bad at following instructions." Julian returned to Ilya's side, got him on his feet again, and into the washroom. Then Ilya sank down as if his legs had given out, and Julian, getting a proper look, let out a whistle. "What *the* fuck happened to you?"

"Conspiracy," Ilya growled, the cords of his throat standing out like steel, and Julian tried not to notice what the deep rumble of it in Ilya's chest did to his insides. "Treason. Murder. Thank you, you have done enough. I will handle it from here."

"Will you?" Julian arched a skeptical eyebrow. "Or will I step out, hear a loud thump, and come back to find you stone dead in the bathtub, because you are an idiot?"

Ilya opened his mouth, couldn't remember what he was going to say, and growled something extremely colorful in Kozhek instead. It was close enough to Ruthynian that Julian could mostly understand the imprecations called on his house, village, family, ancestors, descendants (unlikely), cows and pigs, ability to service his wife (also unlikely), and other searing maledictions on his trustworthiness, moral character, and manhood. Indeed it was so old-fashionedly rustic, like a cranky babushka cursing the local drunken layabout, that it didn't have the intended effect; Julian began to laugh. "How old are you? A hundred?"

"Shut… up." A bloom of blood bubbled and broke on Ilya's lips. His right hand was useless, so he fumbled left-handed at the ruins of his clothing, ripping the kosovorot and yanking it over his head, then following suit with the other layers. This revealed the alarming fact that his torso was perforated with bloody shrapnel, which he gritted his teeth and simply jerked out. Julian was not a doctor (also to his mother's disappointment), but he didn't think that was the usual treatment. Seeing him about to interrupt, however, Ilya repeated, *"You may go."*

Julian didn't budge. "What *happened?* A building fall on you?"

"Close – enough." Ilya's breathing was hoarse, more blood was running from his wounds, and it was really, absolutely, unquestionably the worst imaginable moment to notice that there was not a scrap of fat on him; he was sculpted like a pagan Lanuvian war god of old. His shoulders were broad, his arms heavy with muscle, and his chest and stomach were ridged in rough-cut lines, lightly furred with brown hair and striped with old scars. Julian realized his mouth was dry and he was looking too intently, turned his head away, and waited until his pulse tipped back to more sensible levels. Almighty, what did Ilya do in his spare time, when he wasn't fomenting localized political unrest and beating up tax collectors? Lift cows like gymnasium weights? *Fuck.*

There was silence, though the tension (in more ways than one) remained exquisite. Julian wet a washcloth and handed it over, and Ilya dabbed at himself with his good hand, extracting more bits of whatever had violently exploded. He grunted aside any more questions, glared at his right arm as if vexed that it hadn't yet fixed itself, and got to his feet. "Do you have a needle? Thread?"

"I don't know. Wait, are you going to sew up your own – "

It was plain, as he lurched out of the washroom, that it was exactly what the idiot intended, and when Julian dashed after him, he found Ilya on his knees in front of the trunk, rooting in search of surgical supplies. He had an oddly matter-of-fact affect about all this, but especially at the prospect of still more pain, as if it meant nothing whatsoever. Possibly it didn't, but Julian didn't want to contemplate what long and terrible experience could produce such a casual reaction. Not quite able to keep the indignation out of his voice, he said, "Who did this?"

Ilya glanced up. Almost accusatorily, he said, "Are you *worried?*"

"Of course I am! I don't know what happened to you, but it was bad! You're my friend or something like it, and I only stayed sane in that hellpit because of – of you. When you vanished, I thought you were dead! And now you turn up *half* dead, you apparently had some clever escape plan you didn't feel like sharing – not that I really blame you, if you had the chance then you had to take it, but – "

Halfway through this, Julian became aware that he was ranting in an undignified fashion, that he hadn't understood until this moment that he felt *betrayed,* and if there was ever a chance of getting out, he assumed they would take it together. But that was reading something into Ilya's feelings which definitely wasn't there, and getting verklempt over another unworthy boy would do him not the slightest good — hadn't he learned his lesson with Gavriel? Regardless of how fetching he looked with his shirt off, Ilya was a dangerous criminal, and he had no reason to stick his neck out for his cellmate of a fortnight. That was it. The end.

Meanwhile, Ilya was staring at Julian as if he had sprouted a second head. Indeed he looked so blank, unable to recognize this as human words, that Julian wondered if he had forgotten himself and started speaking in Vashemysh instead of Ruthynian. Then Ilya scoffed, fished out a needle and thread, and struggled one-handed to insert the one into the other — at which, regrettably, Julian was impelled to intervene. He might not be a physician, but blithely sewing up your own partial amputation was a recipe for a whopping case of sepsis, and he had had enough. "*Give* me that, you colossal dimwit. I don't know who could have even done that to you, but I don't think — "

"That?" Ilya tilted his head. Despite everything, there was a glint of amusement in his wintry grey eyes. "That one, I did to myself."

"Name of God! Why the *fuck* would you — "

"Unavoidable." Ilya bared his teeth: half-smile, half-grimace. "And I assure you, it was better than the alternative. Do you have any caustic solution, any alcohol?"

"To drink, or — "

"To wash. This will be better soon, or should be. It's difficult to explain. Just help me thread the fucking needle, and I should — "

Julian glared at him. Ilya glared back. The whole thing was entirely ridiculous, and yet blackly funny. He had no idea how Ilya planned to fix it with nothing more than supreme stubbornness, it was shocking that he hadn't already keeled over, and even if they couldn't get medical assistance for an escaped prisoner, this was deranged. Then Julian shook his head, muttered a few epithets that would have made his mother box his ears, and reached for the thread. "Don't you think I should — "

"No," Ilya interrupted rudely. "You can't. I'll do it."

There were any number of things Julian could have said to that, and even more he could have done, starting with stabbing Ilya directly in the stupid face with the needle and leaving him to fend for himself. But he handed it over, with a raised eyebrow silently remarking that if this caused an absolute conflagration of an infection, the bastard had no one to blame but himself. But Ilya took it, held out his ruined arm, and examined it with the air of an artisan before a block of marble, gauging where to place the chisel. Then he shoved the needle in, netting up the torn flesh and weaving it together with a total nonchalance that made his past far more plain than any exposition or explanation (not that he was likely to offer it). If a man could sit there and calmly fix his own hand back on like a mad scientist, he had been boiled in an unfathomable crucible of suffering and thought it nothing more than a nice bath. *How?* Julian was not all sure he wanted to know the answer, but still.

It was gruesome, yes, but Ilya's quick and pragmatic skill was equally mesmerizing in its crisp and impersonal competence. He could have been working on an animal, or a dismembered limb, or anything else that did not belong to him and had no bearing on his own existence. His hand was admirably steady; he did not look away or falter, punching the needle in and drawing it out in unflagging time. In another life, he would have been the one to make a fine surgeon, able to face even the worst tasks and most broken bodies. It was terrible, but transfixing.

Not for the first time, Julian considered how much easier his life would be if he was not a useless sodomite, which nonetheless was not something he intended to disavow. He was used to disappointment in that regard, anyway. And it wasn't as if he even *liked* Ilya (though liking him was not necessary for what he had in mind). Ilya was just… interesting, that was all, in a deeply sick way. None of it was smart or sensible, but Julian had never pretended to be either of those things and he was still far more likely to die spectacularly than get out of here. As such, a patently doomed but pleasurable fling was the least of what the universe owed him. If Ilya was amenable, of course, but Julian did not think the other man was indifferent to him, much as he pretended. What form it might take was another question, but it was not nothing.

He shook his head even harder, handed Ilya a pair of shears, and watched as he finished the stitches, tidily knotted the thread, and snipped it off. Then Julian got up, went to the bed, and tore off a strip of clean linen. But when Ilya gestured brusquely for it, Julian sat down, pulled Ilya's freshly reattached hand into his lap, and wrapped it up, tucking in the ends and tying it firmly in place. It was better not to think too much about it, even as his fingers brushed the underside of Ilya's wrist and he felt both of them tense. Mouth dry, he let go. "There."

"That was not necessary. I could have – "

"Yes, I'm aware." Julian rolled his eyes. "If you can sew your own fucking hand back on, I'm sure that you can also bandage it. But have you ever considered asking for help?"

This once more earned him a blank stare, so he sighed deeply and got to his feet. "Guess not. Look, I don't know how long you can stay here. I'll see if I can get some more food, but – "

"It is not your concern," Ilya interrupted (again). "I will find other lodging. You've not heard of anything befalling Coriolane, have you?"

"Tonight? Or in general?" Julian frowned. "Not that I know of, but – no, wait. *Don't* tell me that you were trying to kill the emperor again. You mentioned it in the Castel, the guards thought you were involved in something like that, but – "

"It's complicated," Ilya said again. "I need to rest a while, but then I will go. If you would permit me the use of your floor – "

"Floor? When you're beat to hell? There's a bed right there."

"I assumed – " Ilya glanced away. No doubt of it, there was a hint of color in his previously dead-white face. "That was for your use, yes?"

"Have you seen the size of it? We can share."

There was an even more audacious silence. Julian wasn't sure if he was being baldly obvious or somehow still too obtuse, and he wasn't sure if it was wise to push, but as well evidenced, he had never managed to stop while he was ahead. The two of them looked at each other again, and then Ilya got to his feet. He crawled into bed, lay down, and closed his eyes, and when Julian emerged from the washroom, he was already fast asleep. That was for the best, Julian reminded himself as he climbed in, briefly overwhelmed by the sensation of sleeping in a proper bed for the first time in weeks: the mattress was plush and deep, the pillows and comforters stuffed with down, all the luxury he could have had at any time if he was just willing to cooperate sooner. But he was too tired to contemplate moral philosophy or personal responsibility. He threw the covers over them both and instantly fell into a catatonic slumber.

His dreams were strange, vivid, infused with shapeless longing, and finally woke him with a jerk, heart pounding. But there was something large and warm next to him, his arm was draped over it, and his nose was nestled into the back of its neck. Indeed, half-asleep and languid, he nestled closer. It was the most agreeable situation he had found himself in for some time, and he murmured, reached out, and –

The covers exploded like a small volcano, waking Julian up all the way with a jolt, and for several chaotic moments, he struggled to free himself from the iron grip prisoning his arms above his head. When his vision cleared, he saw Ilya two inches away, eyes wild and an expression on his face that suggested an entire Meronite legion had just attempted grave indecencies upon his person. Julian was lucky the unsurpassable moron hadn't murdered him with a chamber pot or something else equally humiliating, but he was in no mood to give him another chance. "Almighty!" he spluttered, jerking his wrists to absolutely no effect; he would have had more success running headfirst into the Castel and trying to knock it down. "What are you doing? It's me!"

He had no idea why he expected that to make a difference, or why it would matter to Ilya. Perhaps he was the sort of violently repressed homunculus who considered it a terrible insult to show any weakness or affection, and Julian hadn't touched anything more egregious than his arm. If that was enough to doom him –

Ilya's face stayed frozen, unseeing, until all at once he blinked, and the spell was broken. He let go; he was only using his left hand, but even that had been impossible for Julian to escape, and he felt another uneasy frisson of wondering just who this strange, scarred, unnaturally strong man really was. "Sorry," Ilya said shortly. "You startled me."

"So I fucking see, you lunatic." Julian glared at him, doing his best to distract himself from the storm raging elsewhere. Ilya had freed his wrists, but remained where he was, straddled halfway atop him. As they shifted position, it became clear to both of them that whatever his other objections might be, Ilya's personal preference was not one of them. Indeed, quite the contrary. His hardness pressed heavily against Julian's thigh, his hips gave an involuntary jerk, and what little blood in Julian's head promptly vacated it again. Fine, then. He saw nothing to lose by making it very damned clear. "Well, do you want to do this, or…?"

Ilya kept staring at him like a hunting lion, eyes tawny gold in the morning light. Julian felt dizzy with wanting, the need to seize hold and drag them both down to drown, their noses brushing in the very last fractions of space before a kiss, and for a mad and weightless moment, he thought Ilya was actually going to agree. But he was too tightly wound, too desperately self-controlled, to make the final break. Instead he growled, rolled away, and sprang out of bed. "No. Not now. Or ever."

"Fine," Julian said huffily. "Your loss."

Ilya kept his back militantly turned as he picked up the intact pieces of his clothing and stomped into the washroom. Feeling like a corpse fresh-dug from the grave, Julian sighed, got up, and likewise dressed. He still hadn't figured out what to do about the *Key,* but Kronus doubtless did not approve of him wasting his precious study time in homoerotic tomfoolery, and Julian agreed that it had not been the most productive episode of his life. He would deal with his broken… heart later. Bastard.

Soon thereafter Ilya emerged, dressed and scrubbed sternly clean, and the two of them left the room, descending the tower stairs. Julian thought about reminding him again that he needed to get out before the Thaumaturges saw him, but there was no way Ilya could have forgotten, and there was an unsettling unconcern in his manner, as if he genuinely wasn't worried about them catching him. Something bit at Julian's mind, something said in extremity and then recanted. No, it couldn't be.

They reached the atrium, which was bathed in pallid light. Julian opened his mouth to order Ilya yet again to run, but a door swung open and Kronus stepped through. "Ah, there you are, Doctor. I thought – "

Just then, he caught sight of Julian's uninvited companion, and a look of startlement, disquiet, and servile obeisance flashed across his face, almost that quickly. "General Ionius. How good of you to visit us. I am afraid, however, that you were unannounced. When did you arrive?"

"Wh – " Julian spun around. *"What did you just – ?"*

Kronus looked puzzled. "I beg your pardon? I assumed the two of you were acquainted. After all, was he not the one who ordered the slave Marcus to fetch you from the – ?"

Fuck. *Fuck.* Julian had been so stupid – or rather, he hadn't. He had seen it, he had somehow and instinctively understood, and this piece of absolute *shit* had lied to his face. Realization fell into place with awful clarity – why he was in here with the Thaumaturges, how they had learned about his supposed knowledge of the Ring of Tselmun, all of it, *all of it.* The Immortal who had been murdering rebels in Ruthynia – was that Ionius too? It was, wasn't it? But even that wasn't enough of a thrill, so he decided on something even sicker: pretend to befriend Julian, wring him for information, and ensure that this intimate terror was the last thing Julian ever knew. It was a crass and cynical deception beyond anything he had ever imagined, and yet he was the one who could blame nobody but himself. After all, he knew exactly who the Immortals were, who they always had been. *My name is Marcus Servus. I was sent to fetch you by General Ionius himself.*

"You," Julian said. *"You motherfucker."*

Ilya Sergeynich – no, that was a lie, it was nonsense, *General Ionius Servus Eternus* – looked briefly wrong-footed. He raised his hands, including the one Julian had so tenderly, *idiotically* bandaged last night – he hadn't just slept in the same bed with that monster, he had nearly forgotten himself so far as to sleep with him in other ways. "Julian – "

"Shut up!" If he had the Ring, if he had the *Key*, if he had one fraction of Tselmun's power, he would use it to scour even the memory of Ionius's existence from the earth. All at once, Julian felt himself become possessed by a feverish lucidity, a simple and singular purpose: to translate the grimoire once and for all, to learn the secrets of the great king's magic, and use it to rectify this ghastly wrong, this grotesque betrayal. However needed. However necessary.

Ionius started to say something, stopped, and turned to the Grand Magister. "Excellency, you will speak with me at once. I am afraid that I must insist. It is a matter of His Majesty's personal welfare."

"Oh, you *bastard*," Julian said. Shamefully, something twisted in his chest like a knife, and he was briefly and horribly afraid that his voice was going to crack. "Burn in *hell*."

If Ionius wished to salt the wound still further, he could point out that Vashemites did not believe in the Tridevarian idea of hell as a place of fiery and eternal damnation, but at that moment, Julian devoutly hoped it was real, for the sole purpose of sending Ionius there for good. The Immortal's inhuman eyes flickered. Then he nodded coldly, crossed the floor, and took Kronus by the shoulder – politely, but clearly to restrain him if he decided to run. The Grand Magister and the general opened a door, vanished inside, and shut it. The echoes fell like a stone.

Fine, then. *Fine.* Julian's task was apparent, his objective likewise. If the unspeakable bastard thought he could trick, deceive, and manipulate in this fashion, he would discover to his detriment that two could play that game, and not the bedsport of this morning, which indeed Julian was very lucky to be prevented from consummating. The *Key of Tselmun* was at hand. The job was his. Despite his abject failure thus far, he could still escape with a landmark victory for the rebel cause. If he could do what needed to be done, and not flinch or fail.

I will destroy you, Julian thought. *You and all the Immortals, woven together with magic that is not yours, that does not belong to you, that you have unjustly stolen from the Vashemites and turned into the foul tools of your murderous empire. You wait. You just fucking wait.*

The library door was open. Waiting for him. Beyond that, the *Key*. Mind clear, rage absolute, Julian walked inside.

CHAPTER

16

ROMOLA

THE LAST DAY OF THE YEAR DAWNED CLEAR AND CRISP, an ideal setting for all the feasts, banquets, balls, parties, and other breeds of revelry; indeed, some had started several days ago and would continue for several more at least. Romola did her best to ignore the naked aristocrats and staggering senators who reeked sourly of wine, sex, and hedonism; a slave's job, after all, was to see nothing and say nothing. It always got bad around this time, the Prince's Fest and the winter holidays. The patricians enjoyed their sybaritic delights: lavish gifts, gourmet meals, glittering services in the Arch-Holy Basilica, elaborate decorations, the joy of tossing coins to the smallfolk, making themselves feel warm and generous. Then they returned to the Eternal Palace and wreaked more debauched spoilage than ever. Romola craved the coming of Twelfth Night and the obligation, however shallow, to return to normal life. She was so exhausted she could hardly stand.

There was, however, no chance of rest. Coriolane was throwing a splendid banquet tonight, as it was an especially auspicious occasion: the arrival of the year 450 A.C., four and a half centuries since his birth and the only calendar that mattered in the *mundus Meronitus*. There had been others, once upon a time. Previous emperors had marked the date *ab urbis* from the founding of the Eternal City; the Tridevarian Church kept the classical *postus princeps* system; the Wahini counted from the Hierophant's exile and did not begin their year until the spring equinox; the Vashemites had their own scale spanning from the destruction of Tselmun's Temple during the first Meronite conquest. But Romola did not know any of those numbers, and they had no meaning for her. Only the *anno Coriolani,* the only sanctioned way to think of the world, to quantify its distance from the past or its march into the future. The emperor's official birthday was in spring, the month of Maius, when the weather was better, but Ianuarii was long and grim. The people needed bread and circuses even more in winter, so they were provided.

As such, Romola and the rest of the slaves worked even harder than usual: arranging curtains and chaises, hanging fresh sprigs of holly and ivy, making sure the finest tapers were placed in the candelabrums. The kitchens had likewise been laboring for days in order to be sure that Coriolane's favorite dishes were prepared to perfection. The palace bustled like a beehive, and Romola's bad foot ached, but no weakness could be countenanced. Not when everything must be flawless.

She was daring to snatch a moment sitting down when she caught sight of someone watching her from behind the drapes. She tensed, about to jump up and pretend to be working again, when she recognized him, though he looked so different that an oblique, unintended concern made itself unexpectedly known to her. Whatever he had been doing since their last meeting, General Ionius did not seem to have enjoyed it much. He was battered and bruised, his right arm tied in a bandage – which was particularly shocking, as Immortals usually healed too quickly to need common medicine – and otherwise looked to be under heavy weather indeed, his harsh face set even more firmly in its forbidding crags. Then he caught her eye, put a finger to his lips, and beckoned.

Romola hesitated for a moment longer, then got to her feet. She ducked under the gauzy drape and joined him in the narrow aperture, the grainy winter sunlight filigreeing both of them like old lace. "Gen – General Ionius. Good morning. A blessed Year End to you."

He grunted, barely registering the pleasantry. "Romola, isn't it?"

She did not think he had forgotten, but this felt like a test, a perilous balance on an ever-more-vertiginous knife. "It is, my lord."

"Ah." Ionius turned to the window. "I have a question for you. A few, actually, but only one is important. You will recall the last time our paths crossed? When I caught you at night in the docks – the *Wahini* docks? You would never have gone there on your own, or ever thought to do so. Think carefully about your answer. *Who sent you?*"

She had been afraid of this, and still had no notion how to reply. Seeing her hesitate, his face darkened. "If you're protecting a traitor – "

"No. Please. Do you really think I would be so foolish? I just – if they discovered – "

"*They,*" Ionius repeated. "So it is more than one person, and they are powerful, someone whose vengeance you fear if your informing was discovered. If you tell the truth to me, I can protect you. And so – "

"How?" She wanted to bite her tongue off, but it was too late. "You don't look like you can even protect yourself!"

Ionius's expression turned even more thunderous, but he could not gainsay the truth. "Recent and deeply unfortunate events aside, yes. It is not something I plan to make a habit. Listen, girl. The stability of the empire and His Majesty's personal wellbeing are at stake. You are not a traitor? Then you have no reason to be afraid. Is that not so?"

It was, but Romola still hesitated. Ionius didn't *seem* like the sort to wantonly hurt a woman, just for sadistic pleasure, but she couldn't read him, and his manifestly forbidding air was anything but comforting. A slave had so little control of her own life, no say in where she went or who she served, and while she could not put the general off forever, refusing him now was some semblance of power. But if what he was saying was true and Coriolane's safety was at risk, was it even more dangerous to hold back? How could his own wives be plotting against him, if that was indeed what Gheslyn and Vestalia were doing? Romola had looked for the eunuch Belsephorus as ordered, but she couldn't find him, feared to ask for him too openly, and another summons had not yet come. As for now, surely there was more work to do. *Something.*

"My lord," she said, as Ionius continued to look expectant. "I would like to help you. I owe you a favor, after what you did with the men in the street. But if my transgression was known – if the Corporalists – "

"Yes." Those stone-grey eyes turned even sharper. "I paid them a visit. You evidently caused quite a bit of trouble in previous incarnations, girl. That is why – " he nodded at her foot – "that was left as it is. But it need not be so. If you were to do the emperor good service, he could issue an order for it to be corrected. Would you want that?"

Romola opened her mouth, then stopped. She was afraid to look at him, to show the naked longing on her face. Of course she wanted it: for everything to not be so difficult and painful, to walk and even run freely, not to have to hobble and hop and look even more useless and despised. She didn't know how her body had acquired the injury, but she didn't think it was congenital. Somebody deliberately wounded it, or her predecessor suffered a bad accident, or it was simply broken and never mended. It would be a mere moment for Coriolane to order the Corporalists to fix her foot, but for Romola, it would change her life. Everyone knew that General Ionius was his favorite. If it could be *real* –

"It is..." Her mouth was dry. "You must swear that if I tell you, you will never reveal where you learned it. Not to anyone."

He held her gaze. If he found it comical or absurd that a humble Remade slave would demand such solemn surety from an Immortal general, he didn't show it. "Very well. I swear."

"Fine. I was at the docks that night on the orders of Their Imperial Majesties, Empresses Gheslyn and Vestalia. They summoned me to their quarters and gave me a letter to deliver at the Brass Astrolabe tavern, to a man named Vadoush. I don't know where he was from, but the letter was written in a Semyic language. Qartic, maybe."

"So it was the empresses." Ionius didn't sound surprised; more as if something had been confirmed that he already suspected. "What other instructions did they give you?"

"When it was done, I was told to find the eunuch Belsephorus and give him a password. Something about the orchids of Anteropolis. It was the same one I used with – with Vadoush."

"And? Did you find the eunuch Belsephorus, and do so?"

"No. I looked, but I couldn't find him."

"I'll tell you why." Ionius leaned against the wall, his good hand twisting his cloak as if in search of something to strangle. "Because the eunuch Belsephorus was occupied in the city of Sardarkhand, putting together a trap of savage ingenuity, which very nearly served its purpose. To wit." He gestured bitterly at his injuries. "Killing me."

"What?" Romola gaped at him. Everything that he was suggesting was too monumental to contemplate – why would the empresses try to kill their own general, their husband's top military commander? Why would they enlist a eunuch in this complicated and underhanded scheme, why would they make Romola herself party to it, and were they indeed secretly conniving with Qart-Hadesht, Merone's oldest enemy, to do the Divine Family knew what? "Are you – are you *sure?*"

"Now I am," Ionius said, low and vicious. "I do not know why Their Majesties gave the order to kill me, but it was only blind luck that they did not succeed. But I must have proof before I can formally lodge such a shocking accusation. It is unclear if the empresses presently think I am dead; I have taken care, since my return, to keep a low profile. But I will appear at the banquet tonight, and their reaction will be instructive. If there was anything else you could gather in the way of evidence before then – you said they summoned you to their quarters, yes? And that you have not yet returned, but they were intending for you to do so?"

A cold stone of dread formed in the pit of Romola's stomach. "No, my lord. Please, you cannot send me back. If they caught me spying – "

"And yet," Ionius pointed out, "you are one of the few who might stand a chance. Nobody looks twice at you, and nobody would question why you were there. They already recruited your cooperation once, and might be wondering why you have dawdled in your further obligations. If Belsephorus has failed in his task of killing me, they might likewise be rather cross with him. You can tell them that you gave him the password, and you thought he passed it on. It will be him they are displeased with, not you." For the first time, Ionius cracked an extremely terrifying smile. "And I would very much like to see that traitorous weasel fry."

"If the empresses catch me in their apartments now, and then something happens to them at the banquet tonight, if there is some letter or document they thought was safely under lock and key and then it is not, they will know it was me who stole it. Besides, I can't be sure if anything I find would help you. I can't read, I can't – "

"Yet you knew the letter was written in Semyic – Qartic, even?"

"I can recognize the difference, tell scripts apart." She flushed. "I am not a simpleton. Folk always think that of me, but I am not."

"No," Ionius said, studying her closely. "No, I don't think you are."

There was another portentous silence. Romola glanced nervously into the hall, in case any of her fellows had noticed her conspiring instead of working, but just like her, they were well trained in the art of strategic blindness. Finally, Ionius spun on his heel. "Come with me."

Unsure if this was better, but relieved that he had not straightaway cut her loose to do it on her own, Romola hurried after him, making sure she was on his left side so her good ear, the right, was pointed at him. When she spoke with someone face-to-face, she could usually fill any gaps in her hearing by reading lips, but it grew harder as soon as they looked away, and she did not want to have to ask him to repeat himself. For a dangerously giddy moment, she wondered whether she could also request the Corporalists to fix her ear, or if that was a treasure they would strategically withhold in expectation of future service. If it was a choice between ear and foot, which one should she take? They would improve her life in different ways, difficult to quantify or compare against each other. Yet there was also a creeping fear that if she was not so obviously damaged, she would lose her safety in invisibility. There were plenty of bored noble sons who roamed the Eternal Palace in packs, daring each other to sleep with the ugliest or least well-favored slave they could find. Romola had gotten caught a few times, but all except once, they scoffed and let her go – not out of pity, more like aesthetic offense on their own behalf. As for the time they hadn't, it was better not to think of that.

Romola reminded herself that she was fortunate; unlike another woman, she had no risk of falling pregnant with an unwanted child. All Remade were sterile, could not conceive or sire offspring, and since she closed her eyes and went along with it, they hadn't hurt her much. But that was both why she was so grateful to Ionius for saving her from a much-worse repeat, and why the thought of being *visible* again was not an unqualified blessing. She believed that she was fully human, though of course she had nothing to compare it to. She thought and worked and ate and slept and feared and wanted like any of them; she was not mentally deficient or their intellectual inferior. It was true that she would never get older, not in the usual way. A Remade was no longer an organic creature, able to grow and change on its own accord. Instead, it was frozen forever at the age the original body had been when it died, an existing lamp emptied and filled with new oil, which burned down in turn and had to be replaced. The reanimation spell was usually designed to last ten or fifteen years each time, for maximizing usefulness while discouraging the development of excessive individualism. The soul called Romola had been awake in this body for five years. She could be halfway through her life, or she could be one of the Remade who made it twenty years, thirty, longer. She didn't want to be taken away from herself. No living creature did. But was that enough to make her *human?*

Distracted with these troubling questions, Romola realized that she had fallen behind Ionius, and had to scurry to catch up. It was a surprise that he had stopped, looking for her; most people only grew angry at her deficiencies. That was the thing about the general, frightening as he was and bloody as his legend might be. He spoke to her gruffly, tersely, threateningly, yes, but he still did so, and treated her, as if she was human. He saved her from the back-alley rapists; he vowed not to reveal where he learned her secrets; he thought she was capable of doing something that nobody else could, and it was a skill, not an accident; he had not abandoned her and indeed promised to protect her, as if her life actually mattered. She knew not to mistake this for true regard or real alliance, but it still counted for quite a lot, made her want to help him if she could, regardless of the danger. It wasn't just that he too was a slave. All the Immortals were, and plenty of them treated the Remade even worse than the freeborn did, to drive home the point that they were *better,* they were the exalted slaves who commanded and created other slaves, who even the masters feared and respected. But Spartekaius had been an Immortal too. When he led his uprising and it failed, they killed him in the slowest and most terrible way a man ever died in Merone, and that was saying a great deal. That was what came of forgetting your place.

Romola and Ionius had just started up a staircase when there was a shout. "My lord! My lord, thank the Divine Family that you are safe! I had heard – "

"Hush," Ionius snapped, whirling around. *"Quiet!"*

The young man – barely more than a boy – clad in the uniform of an Immortal cadet gazed worshipfully at his commander. However, he did lower his voice and step closer. "General, I wish to report that I did as you bid, and fetched the Vashemite from the Castel, delivering him to Grand Magister Kronus. Did you know he was a doctor? An eminent scholar of some sort? Or so he said, but I don't believe it, I think he's lying. You know that I am originally from Korolgrod, and it was why you chose me, since I speak the language? That would again be useful, if I was to travel to Ruthynia. I request formal permission to investigate."

Ionius looked nonplussed. "Investigate what?"

"Whether the Vashemite – Doctor Kozharyev, he calls himself – is truly who he insists. Just to start, I find it extremely suspect that one of his race could lecture at the university. He's not old enough to have completed his doctorate, let alone be appointed as faculty, especially when public sentiment is increasingly against it. His Excellency seems pleased with him, but now an ex-prisoner of questionable provenance has access to our most sensitive political and magical secrets. If he intends to act on them, or convey them to his insurgent friends – "

Ionius's guarded expression deepened into a ferocious scowl. He was, it seemed to Romola, briefly reluctant to answer. "Surely you do not intend to blame me for this, Marcus?"

"Of course not, my lord. If the Vashemite knows something useful, he must disclose it for the good of the empire. I only fear that he intends to act duplicitously in the meantime. If I was to find the truth, we could allow him to finish his work, and then… manage him."

"You have clearly given this a great deal of thought." Ionius's tone remained cool. "I am impressed with your initiative. But you are not a full Immortal, and therefore – "

"I could take the trials today, if you commanded. I am ready, my lord, I swear." The young cadet, Marcus, fervently drew himself up. "I would not fail you. I would never dream of it."

"You had best not." Ionius raised a cutting eyebrow. "Well, then. If you pass the trials, I shall consider sending you to Korolgrod. So it is in your interests to go and train harder, yes?"

"Of course, my lord. Thank you." Marcus bent and humbly kissed his general's bandaged hand, and Romola saw him swallowing a question about what had happened, as it was not his business. "It remains my joy and honor to serve the master of the Immortals."

"And mine to be served." Ionius jerked his head. "Now go."

When Marcus Servus had vanished down the corridor, and Ionius and Romola had resumed their ascent of the stairs, she glanced at him curiously. "Why do you not want Marcus to go to Ruthynia?"

Ionius gave her a look so searing it nearly set her hair afire, and she bit her tongue. Of course it was *also* none of her concern, but he needed her, and there had been a rough sort of honesty between them. "I'm sorry," she added. "It is not for me to know. But if it's true that there is a grave threat to the emperor's safety, and we must find out what – "

"Of course it's true." Ionius's voice dropped to a gravelly, menacing scrape. "You will trust, therefore, that I understand the situation a great deal better than you, including what must be done. And as I see it, the matter of Doctor Kozharyev is a foolish distraction with which no one should further concern themselves. Especially not me."

He sounded so certain that Romola decided against prying, as she had a very limited number of chances to obtain actual information and did not want to squander them. When they reached the top of the staircase, she realized that they were very close to the empresses' quarters, and her anxiety began to resurface. "What am I supposed to do?"

"Try the desk first," Ionius advised. "Look for letters or papers. Anything written in Semyic, especially, but if they aren't *quite* so clumsy, take what you can. There is also a hidden panel in the eastern wall, behind the statue of Juna, that they sometimes use to conceal sensitive items. To open it, press twice in the middle and once on the top."

Romola was fairly sure that she could recognize the goddess Juna, queen of the old Lanuvian pagan pantheon, but if the empresses were in residence, how in hellfire could she stroll in and open a secret door right in front of their noses? "If they see me – if they're there – "

"Say that you gave the password to Belsephorus and believed they wanted to speak with you again. I'll wait here, around the corner. Come straight back to me. You can do this."

She looked at Ionius, and he looked at her. His face was set, his mouth like granite. She tried to draw strength from it, whatever strange partnership they had temporarily entered into, not least since there was no choice. But just like Marcus, she did not want to disappoint him, and perhaps that was his genuine gift as a commander, hard as he was. She nodded again, and set out.

Her heart was hammering so hard that she could scarcely hear herself think, just as terrified as she had been on first approach, but for different reasons. She counted the steps down the corridor, eighty-three of them the distance between danger and safety, and when the guards outside the door asked her business, she told them that she had a confidential message for the empresses and they let her in. It was startling, the recognition that her nothingness was a certain twisted power. If they thought she was *someone,* or could do something on her own volition, or had the wit to lie, surely they would not have been so lazily amenable, but it never even crossed their minds. Why would any slave ever try to misbehave, when they could be swiftly destroyed? It was self-evident wisdom, the banality and ignorance of cruelty. She had to use it to her advantage.

Romola braced herself for anything, but when she stepped inside, the chamber was empty. That did not mean the empresses were not here; they could be in another room, or lurking just out of sight, or sunning on the great balcony, but there was no Vestalia in the bed or Gheslyn at the desk. It was Year End, after all, and they were unlikely to be shut up here in boring solitude, when they could enjoy the celebrations. Besides, if they were under suspicion for any reason, it would be wise to present the same glamorous, untroubled face, as if any accusations were just the tedious taradiddle of petty jealousy. But she could not waste time.

Romola crossed to the desk and scanned it for drawers, recesses, or other places where incriminating documents might be hidden. There was one, but it was locked, and she could not loiter to find a key or work out how to pick it. She went to the eastern wall instead and identified the statue of Juna easily enough, with its face the sculptor had clearly modeled on Gheslyn. Ionius said the secret panel was directly behind it. Higher up or lower to the ground? Or at eye level? Hand level?

Holding her breath so long it hurt, Romola reached out, skimming her fingers over the fine black lacquer in search of anything that felt like a catch, a bevel, a hinge. She kept looking around to make sure nobody was approaching on the side of her bad ear. Still nothing. Was this the right place? Press twice in the middle, once on the top. There.

For another moment, nothing happened. Then all of a sudden, a section of the wall sprang free, and a small alcove was revealed. A few folded and sealed parchments were stacked within, written in Lanuvian. It would be up to Ionius to decide whether any of them were useful, but if the empresses discovered their absence, it would still point to Romola as the chief suspect, especially if the guards remembered letting her in. If so, she had doomed herself, and there was only Grand Magister Saturnus and the other Corporalists waiting greedily in her future, certainly not to fix her ear or her foot or any other part of her. But she scooped up the letters, stuffed them into her robe, and forced herself to leave at the same sedate trot as before, not running. The guards didn't even glance up.

It was the world's longest eighty-three steps back to where she had left Ionius, sweating blood the whole time. She feared that he wouldn't be there, but he was, leaning against the wall and quickly straightening up at the sight of her. She removed the parchments and proffered them, and he took them. "Good girl. Did you see anyone? Speak to anyone?"

"No. The empresses weren't there. But I don't know when they'll be back. We might not have until the banquet."

"Let me worry about that. Come on."

Once they returned to the banquet hall and Ionius assured the chamberlain that she had only left her duties on his orders, Romola tried to get back to work, but her mind was racing. Without Ionius, she felt horribly exposed, just waiting for someone to storm in and drag her off. By the time they finished and were allowed to snatch a brief spell of rest before the feast began, she was pale, shaky, and wrung-out with fear, and a few of her fellows shot her worried glances. She did her best to nod and smile them away. Even among the ones she trusted, there was no hint of explanation that was safe to offer.

Romola retreated to her cell, slept fitfully and not very soothingly, changed into the clean robe that the slaves had been specially provided, and dragged herself out as the Eternal Palace began to fill with the Meronite elite. Patricians, senators, praetors, consuls, bureaucrats, governors, and their wives, mistresses, and other mistresses flowed by the multitudes, their jewels gleaming, their costumes elaborate, and their masks done as characters that Romola didn't recognize; for the Year End masques, it was customary to dress as figures from Lanuvian mythology and the Seven Gods, and while she could pick out some, most of the literary nuances or references eluded her. Though as she watched eight goddess-Junas sail past in a row, accompanied by their long-suffering husbands as various lesser deities – only Coriolane himself was allowed to dress as Juspiter and nobody would dream of stealing his thunder – it felt like particular and possibly-literally-murderous irony.

Romola took a tray of drinks and waded into the morass, performing the careful dance of sliding close enough to offer a cup without rudely interrupting, making the glitterati too conscious of the presence of a slave, or otherwise disturbing the illusion that the wine simply appeared when they thrust out a beringed hand and grasped for it. It vanished in moments, and she took the tray back, collected a platter of appetizers, and repeated the circuit. People jostled and snatched like seagulls, trying to shove food in without smearing their grease-paint, chewed with their mouths open, laughed and sprayed crumbs in Romola's face. Plenty of them were already well lubricated, and she dodged pinches, slaps, smacks, gropes. Looking at this loud, stupid, and dissolute lot of hedonists, it was very difficult to believe that they ruled the empire, or conversely very easy. For this, indeed, was the putrid essence of Merone.

She checked herself sharply – that was not a thought it did her any good to be having, even if it was true – and was distributing her fourth round of appetizers when she brushed against a man dressed as Marus, in a red-jeweled mask, white toga, and golden gladiator sandals. In case anyone might possibly neglect to recognize him as the god of war, he was wearing a longsword and longbow which did not look like replicas, and Romola felt a jolt of apprehension; if he was bringing real weapons to a masquerade, he plainly feared that the night might end in some very un-staged violence. "Ionius," she whispered. "General, is that you?"

His head whipped around, she glimpsed his stormy eyes through the slits of the mask, and felt something like relief for the first time since he left her earlier. "Yes. Are you all right?"

"For now. What are you going to do?"

He smiled grimly, oracularly cryptic. "Never mind that. Stay close to me, if you can. You'll know when matters become interesting."

This was, as usual, not reassuring, but Romola was glad to know he was here and what his costume looked like, in case she needed to find him again in a hurry. She could not linger, so she nodded to him and continued on, searching the crowd. She did not think that Juspiter-Coriolane, Juna-Gheslyn, and Venua-Vestalia, as it usually went, had made their entrance yet; it required a splendid announcement, a grand procession, and everyone turning to gaze and genuflect in a reverential hush. Should she read into it? Were they holding back, or had something happened to delay their arrival? Nobody seemed to think anything was amiss, or that the emperor might have been suddenly knifed in his privy chambers. He hadn't, had he? *Had* he?

Just as Romola was once more teetering on the edge of terror, the eunuchs sounded bronze gongs, the chattering fell silent, and attention turned to the great doors. A herald bellowed, "His Divine Majesty, Coriolane Aureus IX, Emperor of All Merone!" and finally, he arrived.

Coriolane's costumes for Year End were typically extravagant, but this one outdid them all, in order to commemorate the fourth-and-a-half-centenary of his life in style. In addition to a full mask and cloth-of-gold robe, silver-jeweled thunderbolts clutched in both hands, he wore a gigantic gilt crown and an intricate replica of the Seven Gods enthroned in splendor atop Mount Caelum, which made him almost ten feet tall. He stalked up the aisle alone, as if to emphasize his solitude and sovereignty, his singular position in Merone and the world. Nobody moved until Coriolane reached the high table and seated himself with haughty grandeur, and servants rushed forward to take away the divine diorama, which must have weighed a ton. Only then did the herald call, "Her Divine Majesty, Gheslyn Aurea, Empress of All Merone, and Her Divine Majesty, Vestalia Aurea, Empress of All Merone!"

The empresses came next, dressed as Juna and Venua just as Romola predicted, and she shrank into the shadows as they glided past. Both of them were also wearing masks, so she couldn't see their full expressions, but she detected a certain stiffness in their shoulders and a brittleness in their smiles. They waved with perfect poise as they climbed the dais and took seats on each side of their husband, who clasped their hands and raised them together, the triumvirate remaining whole for a final time. Once the adulation had subsided, Gheslyn pulled her hand out of Coriolane's rather too sharply, and the emperor turned his head to glare at her. Well, then. Things were indeed far from idyllic in the imperial marriage. Divine Family, what was going to happen tonight?

Three more splendidly costumed figures then ascended to the high table to join the spousal trio: Neptunus, god of the sea; Hadeus, god of the dead; and Solus, god of the sun. Romola was willing to bet that beneath those masks were Grand Magister Kronus, Grand Magister Saturnus, and Archpriest Mellius; along with Marus, that completed the principal septimate. There were plenty of others, godlings and godettes, demi-gods and quasi-gods, but only the Seven had full deific status. (There was a long argument over whether Lunea, moon goddess, virgin huntress, and twin sister of Solus, should be considered as half of him or as her own entity, but perhaps the Lanuvians had felt that when it came to women, a goddess of wives and a goddess of beauty was enough; no need to give them ideas.) They were seated on each side of the empresses, leaving the seventh chair vacant – presumably for Ionius, the only time a slave was permitted to eat with free citizens. Where *was* he, anyway? Romola had just seen him. He had to be here.

Coriolane raised his hand, and an anticipatory silence fell. When he had welcomed them to the feast and expressed his hope that the coming year would confer more bounteous blessings than ever, he cleared his throat. "It is my honor, therefore, to share the results of our special campaign of pacification in Brythanica. As reported by General Pompeus Servus Eternus, leader of the expedition, our legions have killed over ten thousand Bodeni heathens, burned Londinorum to the ground, and installed a new Governor-General who has, at last, both the mandate and the ability for true control. The surviving savages have been chrismed in the sacrament of the Divine Family and given Meronite names, and new schools, monasteries, convents, and churches are being built for the continued edification of their moral sensibilities and the salvation of their immortal souls. But we must not forget that this is as solemn as it is joyful. Your Holiness, would you like to say a few words?"

"Thank you, Your Majesty." Solus the sun god rose to his feet, speaking in Archpriest Mellius's deep velvety voice. "Friends, Meronites, countrymen, it is an honor to address you tonight, on the verge of such an auspicious year. The events in Brythanica, I hasten to assure you, omen well, not poorly. Of course, none of us *rejoice* at such extremes, or being obliged to take up arms against innocents. But we must remember that none of the Bodeni, from the hoariest elder to the youngest infant, were truly innocent. They repeatedly and flagrantly spurned our hand of friendship and cooperation, clung even more stubbornly to their devilish ways, and continued to perversely attack and harass our garrisons and officials, as if their distance from the Eternal City granted impunity from our laws, customs, and homage. That, alas, cannot stand. Merone has a long and admirable history of offering toleration to other faiths, but those faiths must *earn* our goodwill, to show they are willing to partake in building a more perfect civilization with us, ruled by our shining city on a hill. If they take advantage of our kindness, we must respond appropriately. As we mark four and a half centuries of our beloved Divine Emperor's life, entering a new period of his reign, we enter too into a new Merone. We are a gentle and enlightened people, but we are also a proud one, and we must not flinch from proclaiming our truth and defending our homeland. Therefore, in close counsel with His Majesty, we have decided that the year 450 brings a fundamental shift in our relations with our provinces, our people, our power. From this day on, anyone attempting to thwart us, rebel against us, or otherwise raise their hand in anger will receive the exact same treatment as the Bodeni, regardless of any ancestral privileges or prior grants of peace. I like it no more than you, but the Holy Orders Militant have given their word that they will only visit this wrath on deserving evildoers. And they are holy men, who have sworn their lives to serving the Divine Family. Who in this fallen world can we trust, if not them?"

Mellius's stirring oratory rang across the hall, and even the most inebriated partygoers leaned forward, hanging onto his every word. Romola felt cold to her bones, as the sheer horror of the Archpriest's words was cloaked in reasonable, regretful rhetoric, fluent explanations and artful invocations, the comforting insistence that the Meronites had not asked for this age of massacre and it was unjustly forced on them. And indeed, every costumed and masked head was nodding; Mellius's speech had had exactly the intended effect. Leaving his words at the dangling climax, the Archpriest gestured to Coriolane. "Your Majesty?"

"Thank you for those wise words, Mellius Sanctus. You are a great man of gods, and we are fortunate to have you as the father of the True Tridevarian Church, our most trusted spiritual advisor." Somewhat ponderously, Coriolane rose to his feet. "This fundamental reshaping of our philosophy must also include the intolerable threat to the east, which we have permitted to fester for far too long. You know that I am a devoted man of peace, that I ended the ceaseless petty wars which raged under my predecessors, and brought stability and quiet to the empire's borders for four centuries. You therefore understand with what profound grief I must announce that just as with the Bodeni, our previous approach to Qin is no longer fit for purpose. You are aware of the Thearchate's outrages in the matter of import tariffs on the Spice Road, but they have now escalated their provocations to an entirely unforgivable level. Just a few days ago in Sardarkhand, they brazenly attempted to assassinate General Ionius by means of their black powder. It was only by the grace of the Divine Family that this vindictive plot did not succeed."

With that, he flourished a hand, and with a sense of dramatic timing to rival any theatrical maestro, Ionius made his entrance from behind the curtains. As she looked at him – Marus, god of war – Romola felt even colder. Whispers cropped up like weeds, even as the emperor raised his voice and spoke over them. "Such a terrible insult cannot and will not go unanswered. I have thus directed the Meronite Senate to prepare a formal declaration of war on the Thearchate of Qin and the Thearch Hang Zhai, and will place my ring and seal to it in a public ceremony tomorrow, on the first day of the new year. I trust that all of us will do our duty and recall the splendid example of our ancestors, and – "

Just then, to everyone's astonishment, Coriolane stopped, as Ionius stepped forward and lifted his mask, revealing his cut and bruised face. "I beg pardon, Your Majesty. But I must offer one more revelation about the true identity of our enemies. It was not only Qin who tried to kill me in Sardarkhand, and not only the Thearch who is our most dangerous enemy. It is with utmost sorrow and horror that I accuse Empress Gheslyn and Empress Vestalia of high treason."

The silence was nothing short of apocalyptic. Juna and Venua sat frozen, finally made a convulsive movement as if to stand, then stopped. Into the abyss, Ionius continued in measured tones that almost – if not quite – veiled the cold rage beneath. "Their Majesties did not stop at trying to kill me. They also conspired with disloyal factions and persons in Qart-Hadesht to pass sensitive intelligence, foment rebellion, and degrade the Adirim into a grubby weapon of discord and chaos. Their last and greatest crime, however, is the one truly beyond all forgiveness. They have attempted – and failed, thank the Lord – to destroy the spells of eternal life that protect His Majesty, their blessed and beloved husband. They have tried to murder the Divine Emperor. For this alone, they must face trial, judgment, and if guilty, execution."

The aghast murmurs were now as loud as a bonfire, and it was then that Romola saw armed Immortals and legionnaires emerging from every side of the hall, striding toward the high table. Any doubt about whether this had been rehearsed with Coriolane beforehand vanished; there was no way he could not have known what Ionius meant to announce, and so set the stage for the greatest melodrama of all. At last, Gheslyn and Vestalia jerked to their feet and seemed briefly inclined to flee, but they had no chance. Realizing that a struggle would only damage their dignity and cement the conviction of guilt in the public's mind, they submitted to arrest with unshakeable hauteur, heads high and shoulders square as they were placed into fetters. The image of it – goddesses and queens in chains, led off by their own soldiers under charges of high treason – was seared into every mind. Yet as she was marched past, Gheslyn turned her head and stared directly at where Romola was standing, with such black malevolence that it felt like a curse. *You will not survive this, worm.*

Even when the empresses were gone, it took an eternity for the pandemonium to subside, or for anyone to make sense of what had just happened. It seemed impossible that they could all go back to reveling as if the entire world had not shifted beneath their feet, and Coriolane sat in even more splendid solitude, King Juspiter alone at the gods' high table, head bent and shoulders slumped as he bore the great and terrible burden of turning against even his own queens, his companions and helpmeets for centuries, for the good of his people and empire. The whispers and glances in his direction were openly sympathetic, and at last a senior senator ventured in quavering tones, "Is it true, Your Majesty? They – were conspiring with your enemies? But how – "

"It is true." Coriolane lifted his head, removing the mask and letting them see his face: carved in sorrow, but nonetheless steely, resolute, unbroken. "It is all true. It was suspected for some time, but only proved this very afternoon. Certain documents were exposed that detailed their treachery, their secret correspondence with Qartic radicals, their attempts to fatally destabilize the empire and my own person. We may never know what evil took hold in their hearts, other than to recall that they are women, and the wise and merciful Lady knew the weakness of Her sex, and that it was just to place them subordinate to men and the Lord. I trust that the Archpriest will speak on this subject in greater depth."

"Of course, Your Majesty," Mellius assured him. "But if so, it is unthinkable that your visit to Qart-Hadesht in spring should proceed. If there are serious plans to harm you – "

"No, my lord." Coriolane shook his head. "We must do the opposite. If we call it off, they will know that something is afoot. Besides, who is the Divine Emperor to cower before a few provincials? Am I to hesitate to set foot in my own dominions? No. No. I will go to Qart-Hadesht, and set my own trap. They have recently come into possession of an item of great value which I must acquire for the glory of the empire, and there is one other small personal matter which must also be attended. Even with the best preparations, it is not without danger, but I will take that risk. For Merone. For you."

A respectable cheer went up at that, the first real sign of life since the empresses' removal, and Coriolane rose to his feet. "I am humbled," he went on, "by your renewed trust in me, and our determination to carry out this grand vision together. Indeed, I now invite you to witness the portent written in the stars. My lord Neptunus? If you would?"

"Certainly, Your Majesty." The sea god, Grand Magister Kronus of the Thaumaturges, rose likewise. He clapped his hands, and every lamp and torch was snuffed, provoking another gasp from the guests. Then a ripple passed overhead that was indeed very like the rolling of mighty waves, and something began to happen to the hall's massive roof. It transformed from high-vaulted mosaics to shimmering vitreous glass, translucent and perfectly clear, so they could see the night sky stretching in a grand celestial sweep. Fat and full as a pearl, the moon hung above. They waited five minutes, ten. Then all at once, it began to *change*.

A crimson crescent clipped the disc, spreading over the lunar face, and slowly but steadily blossomed like blood in water or a spilled goblet of wine. As the spellbound guests watched in silence, the whole moon changed color, as if the stars were gripped in Marus's mighty fist. When the eclipse reached totality, burning an ominous red, they all burst into rapturous applause. Then Kronus waved a hand and the lamps sprang back to life, though the bloodmoon still shone like a wound through the transfigured roof. "Behold. This new age is a herald of Meronite struggle, yes, but also Meronite victory. Even the heavens speak to it."

The applause finally died, though people still gazed at the scarlet orb with looks of awe and apprehension. At last, they began to think again of mundane things like eating and drinking, and when Coriolane raised a hand, the servers hurried in with laden trays. Just like that, they had all traveled from one world to another, the beginning of this great epoch of war and slaughter, and Romola's dread had only increased. That was… there was something too easy about it, about all of it. Even if Coriolane *had* already suspected the empresses of conspiring against him, how had he laid hands on the exact material to seal their guilt in one afternoon, right before the most powerful and symbolic moment? Had Romola truly been responsible for it? If Gheslyn and Vestalia believed it, it made her the number-one target for all their aggrieved partisans in the palace, and logic dictated that she cleave even closer to Ionius for protection. But he could not mind her at all times, nor could she follow him about like a lost duckling, and looking at him now, she was forcibly reminded of who he really was. She had nearly forgotten, when she somehow went from being deathly afraid of him to only feeling safe when he was nearby. But he was still the infamous General Ionius Servus Eternus, who played his role to ruthless perfection. That he had done so with Coriolane's explicit arrangement and approval was unmistakable.

Romola lifted a pitcher and prepared to go about the rounds, hoping that everyone would soon be drunk enough not to notice anything; it wouldn't be long until they were stumbling with bloated stomachs into the vomitorium and forcing themselves to retch so they could keep feasting. Her robe was soaked with sweat, her bad leg aching fiercely. But when she glanced up again, she saw Ionius looking at her, and he tilted his head. As if he wanted her to come to the high table, directly in sight of them all. Blessed Lady, was he *trying* to get her killed?!

And yet if she *had* done the right thing, if it was her that brought down the empresses and they truly were traitors, was she finally to have her reward? She did her best to quickly cross the endless expanse of floor and climb the white marble stairs, the hallowed ground where no slave's foot dared to tread unless to pour and serve and scrub — well, that and Ionius, who was still watching her as she drew nearer. When she reached him, he put an arm around her waist, settling his hand heavily on her hip. "Your Majesty. This is Romola, who was of such assistance in the unfortunate matter of the empresses. I wish to keep her for myself."

Romola suppressed a shudder. She did not think Ionius really desired her any more than she desired him, which was to say not at all, and she could see what he was doing. It was the easiest and most self-explanatory way to allow her to leave her quarters and stay under his aegis, and a request the emperor would not think twice about granting; if a slave wanted another slave, why question it? But she did not care to be touched by a man again, even like this, and she did her best not to throw off Ionius's hand and run. She could feel Coriolane's eyes on her face, speculating whether she was pretty enough to take her for himself; with the royal bed now vacated of two of its three official occupants, he would be on the lookout for new concubines and other novelties to soothe the pain. Even the fact that she was Remade was not in and of itself a total disqualifier. If the emperor chose to personally confer his favor, such distinctions – while not falling away entirely – were made less relevant, something to which he could order the entire palace to become discreetly blind. It demonstrated the falsity of such constructs in the first place, as he could conjure them and out of existence like a shadowplay, but that was no comfort. *Please. Please, don't.*

There was another fractious pause. The Grand Magisters and the Archpriest studied her too; all of them, including Mellius, kept their own bed-companions, though they would deny it if asked. Along with the emperor, they were eating heartily, but Ionius had only a single cup of wine. Then Coriolane sighed and waved a hand. "If you must."

"Thank you, Majesty." Ionius's grip tightened on Romola's waist. "There is another boon I ask as well. Excellency – " this to Saturnus – "you see the girl has difficulty with her foot. In exchange for her loyal service, is there any way you could see toward fixing it?"

The Grand Magister of the Corporalists, deep in a vast slab of flaky venison pie, had to swallow and fussily wipe his mouth before answering. He started to say something, then stopped, eyes flicking between Ionius and Romola. "Ah, General. I am – not certain that is wise."

"Why not?" Ionius demanded. "Should we not reward those who faithfully serve the Empire?"

Saturnus looked at Coriolane as if hoping for help. Then the Grand Magister said, "While of course we *wish* to thank the girl, it is – ah – delicate. With the treachery of women recently manifested yet again, we must be careful about rewarding one – a slave, no less – too readily, when we would say it was only her duty. Surely she will be, er, happy enough with you for now, General. There are other favors to be offered."

"Your Majesty, I must protest. I told the girl that this would be – "

"Well, then." Coriolane shrugged. "You must recall that it is not your place to offer the services of the Corporalists, nor think that my subjects must be tempted by the vulgarities of personal gain in order to serve the empire. Besides, General, we have other important matters to speak of. You will, of course, command the invasion of Qin. Send the girl away, and we will begin our discussions."

Ionius opened his mouth, then shut it. The god of war seemed deeply startled to be called upon to fulfill his cosmic purpose, the essence of his existence, the only reason for which he was made. Romola felt the tension in him, and felt too its surrender. "Yes, Your Majesty. It remains my honor and privilege to serve the master of the world."

With that, he dropped his hand from her waist and gave her a long and unmistakable look. *Go. Leave. Now.*

Grateful and terrified all at once, Romola went.

CHAPTER 17

ALIYAH

She had only been in his company for thirty increasingly disagreeable minutes, and yet Aliyah was already convinced that Massasoum ur-Beiresht was the stupidest man alive. Even aside from the political rationale, the desire of her mother and mother-in-law to seek his deposal made firm sense; nobody could spend any time in his company and fail to reach that conclusion. He spoke well, in grandiloquent phrases and protracted paragraphs that projected an air of suave accomplishment, but you only had to think for a moment to realize that it was all nonsense. The five women – Zadia, Safiya, Aliyah, Elemai, and Massasoum's sister, Mirazhel – were obliged to pay this call, as he was still (for now) the Chairman of the High House, and custom dictated that he received a personal invitation as a guest of honor at the marriage. It was also polite to privately notify him that they planned to sue him into oblivion, which they were just getting around to announcing. The wedding was in five weeks, and Zadia and Safiya wanted to have preparations for Mirazhel's lawsuit well in hand by that time. Everything would eventually have to go through the Meronite district court technically overseen by Gaius Tullus Grassus, but the more they could present it as a fait accompli, the more likely that he would just shrug and sign off. He had never bothered to educate himself on Qartic customs, and it was a question whether he could even be located.

"Thank you, saed," Elemai said at last, as Massasoum was about to launch into yet another diatribe on why it was best, after all this time spent unjustly under the thumb of women, to give men a proper chance to rule, that the Hierophant had in fact meant this to be the case all along and with no exceptions, and Qart-Hadesht's insistence on thwarting it would lead to its total doom and destruction. "We understand your position, as you have made quite clear. As you say, most Wahini clerics do teach that women are liberated by accepting their role in society with clear and constructive limitations, and not trying to push past it. I'm sure we're all impressed with your Kitab study – though as a hafiza myself, I would argue that those passages are interpreted in multiple ways, especially since we do agree that the Lord-Queen is neither male nor female and thus one sex is not necessarily prized above another. It will be an honor to have such a knowledgeable man at our ceremony, and many qahins for you to speak with. But there is, in fact, a more compelling reason for our presence today, to which we must now turn. Your sister, Saeda Mirazhel, wishes to inform you of something rather – well, I might say ironic, considering this conversation. Saeda?"

"Thank you, Saeda Elemai." Mirazhel cleared her throat. "Massasoum," she said, "we have had this discussion before, and you will not be surprised to hear that my position has not changed. I am glad for you to have held my seat in trust for the Batu Beireshta, but it is now time for me to take it. You may vacate it peaceably – shall we say a notice period of two months, to be sure that all is in order? – or you may be subject to something nobody wishes, which is a formal court proceeding to order your removal. I have the full support of Saeda Safiya and Saeda Zadia and the entire precedent of customary Qartic law. You know my position, and you know the right thing to do. The question is only whether you shall."

Massasoum looked unpleasantly ambushed, even though he had to guess, upon spotting his sister in their company, that it was coming. He harrumphed, glared hotly at all of them, and settled more comfortably on his Qiné-silk divan. "I do not think it very hospitable to invite an honored guest to a marriage, while you yourselves are guests in his home, and then poison his tea with such a brazen and insolent demand. The world is changing. Qart-Hadesht must do things in accordance with the rest of Wahinism, with folk of good sense, with – yes – even the Empire. In the old days when we were isolated and our actions had little impact beyond ourselves, then yes, we could play at doing whatever we wanted. But now, here, we cannot. Don't you understand that the best way for Mother Qart to be respected in her dealings with the outside world, to be safe and protected, is to name a man as her emissary? Truly, who on earth would take *you* seriously?"

Mirazhel stiffened, fingers digging into the cushion of her own divan. "Is that something you know to be certain for all people and all places, Massasoum, or only what you think?"

"What does it matter?" The Chairman waved that aside. "Besides, you know I am right, even if you are loathe to admit it. Imagine walking into the Eternal Palace or the Meronite Senate, any gathering of leaders, and trying to command respect from real men, or for them to listen to what you say, or honor promises or treaties they made with you? Qart-Hadesht would be left entirely and unnecessarily vulnerable, and while you may not believe it, of course I care about and want what is best for my little brother. I do not think you would be happy in that life."

"Saeda Mirazhel is your sister," Safiya said, in the smooth and pleasant timbre that a woman's voice only had in the instant before she ripped a man's fool head off. "Law, custom, transformation, and her sworn declaration all recognize her as such, and even the High House does not have liberty to interfere in such affairs, or declare her legal claim to be null and void without proper examination. If by this you mean that you do not intend to honorably step aside – "

"No. No, I do not." Massasoum leaned forward, his face purpling. "I too have made my position very clear. Qart-Hadesht will not be served in this dangerous time by any leader who is not a man, and since Mirazhel voluntarily relinquished that designation, I do not see why I must be complicit in such dangerous vanity. Do not think that you can overawe me or force me aside. I need not remind you that political rebellion is generally forbidden in Wahini law, and surely you would not be so haram as to overrule the opinion of wise men. And besides, Saeda Aliyah – I have heard certain rumors of what you wear on your finger at this very moment, which is *also* contrary to Qartic law. Does it not whiff of hypocrisy for the lot of you to sit here and present yourselves as its valiant guardians, if that is what you intend to unleash?"

Everyone looked at Aliyah, as she felt her cheeks heat. It was useless to ask what Massasoum knew, or suspected himself of knowing; even as careful as they had been, there was no way to keep the secret forever, and it was not the first whisper that Tselmun's power was once more at large in the world. As such, she constantly feared that the red sickness would appear in Qart-Hadesht as it had in Yerussala, but thus far, it had not. It was a relief, of course, but a double-edged and sharply conditional one. There was no way of knowing if it would arrive later, if the outbreak in Yerussala had been a one-time event related to her initial possession of the Ring and would not repeat, or if the price would grow higher every day she kept hold of it. Khasmedeus warned her and she had not listened, or at least not enough to stop. What was the alternative? *Not* using it? That was absurd.

I should take lessons with Safiya. Now. The prospect did not thrill her, but Aliyah was not *so* prideful as to refuse the most logical course of action. If the ur-Tasvashta matriarch did in fact keep a secret jinnyeh servant, had studied the lore and legend and knew the intricacies of the craft, it made sense to learn what she could. Besides, it would please Safiya, which was a good thing for any mother-in-law and especially this one, and help her feel that she was indeed exerting meaningful power and influence over Aliyah's wielding of the Ring, even if not directly. Besides, she was growing ever more aware of the burden; the initial thrill of being the chosen one, the one who could never share the honor without some diminution of her own status, was swiftly draining away. It meant that she was the one to bring death on Yerussala even without meaning to, she was the one who could credibly be accused of breaking solemn Qartic law by consorting with demons, and she was the one who had to decide how to unleash the flood. It ate away at her, and she had only had it for a matter of weeks. What, then, must years or decades do?

"My business," Aliyah said, "is not the concern, Saed Massasoum. We are still discussing yours. You understand, of course, that this is a particular turning point in the history of Qart-Hadesht's relations with

Merone, and if the moment is not shaped by us, it will be shaped for us, and without our consent. That being so – "

"Oh, I do." Massasoum looked at them flatly. "And I ask Saeda Safiya and Saeda Zadia just why they have found no allies in their enterprise, reduced to such clumsy methods as weaponizing my... sister against me. Why have you become such pariahs in the Adirim, if not because your cause is utterly doomed? This is the moment when we should treat with Merone as equals and bind ourselves closer, not pull away. You have heard the rumors that the Divine Emperor has finally and formally declared war on Qin. We knew it was coming eventually, and it has. That will render the entire Spice Road trade network either out of commission, or drastically reduced. So what better than to present ourselves as a reliable partner, someone for the empire to count on in these troubled times, and negotiate for more privileges that way? We get better profits, we are spared from any horrors such as those allegedly underway in Brythanica, and everyone – "

"So," Safiya said sweetly. "You confess that you are much afraid of being devoured by the Meronite lion, but you think if you toss enough meat at it, cut from the flesh of your neighbors, it will be persuaded not to eat you too. All you can do is delay it, not stop it. It will eventually look up, realize it is still hungry, and gulp you down too. Appeasement is the weak delay of moral cowards, nothing more."

"You misunderstand, saeda." Massasoum jabbed a finger. "It is not foolish to be realistic, to admit that we have no chance of overcoming Merone by force of arms, and only someone with no experience of war could be so eager for it. Qart-Hadesht has been dwindling for centuries. Why do you think we tell and retell the tale of Hanibal, our one great triumph against Merone over a thousand years ago? Because we have no other victory to take its place, nothing else to celebrate! This is what comes when a land is ruled by women for too long. We have no history, no army, nothing to stand in true strength against the empire – which, for all its flaws, is not *weak*. So if you wish to consider how we ended up here, I suggest you start by gazing into the mirror!"

"Please enlighten me," Zadia said scathingly. "Which of your arguments is true, saed? That Qartic women are too savage and warlike, rushing to prosecute a bloody conflict we cannot hope to understand, or that we are so meek and domestic that we have let the republic waste into a dim and emasculated shadow of itself? You dare to claim we have no history — do you mean that we have no wars, or at least fewer than others? Is history only made when the world is torn apart in blood and fire? If so, I must object in the strongest terms."

"This is pointless," Massasoum huffed. "The great vexation of arguing with women is that everything is emotional, rather than logical. That being so, let me make it very plain. I will not step aside, and if you try to force me, whether by this lawsuit or otherwise, I will go to Gaius Tullus Grassus and inform him of the conspiracy to disrupt and overturn Merone. Out of respect for the Batu Namasqa and Batu Tasvashta, this is the courtesy of a warning, even as you so generously gave it to me. It will be the only one. I mislike to bring your names into it specifically, as the ringleaders of this treason, but if you test me, I will."

There was a crackling silence. Nobody could dispute the potency of that threat, or doubt Massasoum's intention to carry it out. The prospect of Grassus's wrath alone was not much to take seriously, but if he hurried it to the Eternal City, it would be far worse. Zadia and Safiya would be arrested and in all probability, executed; their houses would be stripped of noble status and damned in memory; the Adirim itself might well be dismantled and Qart-Hadesht transformed into a tightly controlled military protectorate like Gezeren. In short, if he felt his position to be jeopardized, Massasoum would turn to the derided Governor-General and invoke Meronite power to crush his own countrywomen, rather than ever meet them halfway. As such, it comprehensively shut down the conversation; there was nothing to be said in turn. The women rose to their feet, nodded with icy politeness, and took their leave.

"What a pathetic little man," Elemai said, when they had repaired to the ur-Tasvashta villa to lick their wounds. "So afraid of Merone that he'll willingly turn himself into their slave sooner than even try to go against them, and blame us for his fear. Well, without some sort of miracle, that plan is dead in the water. What next?"

"Nobody thought he would leave for asking politely." Safiya raised an eyebrow. "All he has achieved is to foreclose any peaceable resolution and prove that he too must be considered our enemy, and he will wish he did not. You and I will speak later. In the interim, my dear – ?"

Aliyah glanced up to see Safiya gazing at her expectantly, as were the other three women. She looked at the Ring, knowing full well what they wanted her to do, and tried to ignore the swoop in her stomach. Massasoum ur-Beiresht was unpleasant and misguided, yes, but he did seem to think he was doing what was best for Qart-Hadesht, he was a member of one of its oldest and most respected families, and they had sat in his house and drunk his tea, invited him to her wedding. Coriolane was one thing, but the Chairman of their own High House was another. She was not yet nineteen, and she had to make this choice? *You wanted the Ring. This is what comes of it.*

"I beg your pardon," Aliyah said, rising to her feet. "I wish to consider this privately. Saeda Safiya, is there a place I might be alone?"

"You should call me Amma Safiya, dear." The matriarch raised a hand, and a man appeared, a man with golden eyes that gleamed under his white ghutra. "Vadoush here will find you somewhere to think."

The name gave her a jolt. She was sure that she was not supposed to know the truth of him, and did her best to keep her face blank. When Vadoush led her from the solarium and into a smaller adjoining study, she cleared her throat. "You must now depart from me in all forms, all manners of seeing and sense, and make no attempt to return, listen from afar, or convey to your mistress or any other persons anything about my following actions, words, or otherwise. Is that clear?"

He gazed at her keenly, as if weighing her instructions or judging why she felt it necessary to issue them with such specificity, but must not have been able to find a loophole. "Very well, Saeda Aliyah," he said, and she smelled a whiff of sulfuric sparks. "The room is yours."

Even when he had gone and she barred the door, she waited a moment before sitting down and raising her hand. She had grown more or less used to the constant presence of the golden circlet on her finger; it still refused to yield its grasp in any circumstances. It was far weightier than its size suggested, as if the entire cosmos was contained in the simple black stone, and frankly, she suspected it might be. It had been a while since she spoke to Khasmedeus, with the flurry of wedding preparations and political intrigue, and she wondered if it noticed, if time passed in the same way for an immortal jinnyeh, or if it cared at all. She was still its master, and it her servant – no, *slave*, just as it said. If she was struggling with that fact, it had no responsibility to leaven it for her.

Aliyah took a deep breath, then rubbed the Ring and waited as the familiar smoke hissed out. This time, Khasmedeus manifested in the shape of a tall and willowy Numerian woman, with a luscious bosom and onyx-dark skin that gleamed like the cheek of night. It was clad in an extremely sheer gauze wrapper that left little to the imagination, and Aliyah felt an unwelcome heat rising in her chest. "Don't," she said, more plaintively than she would have liked. "It isn't polite."

"Polite?" Khasmedeus jiggled its bosom even more suggestively. "Come now. Who ever thought I was trying to be?"

"I've missed you too." Aliyah sighed, trying to keep her eyes off the undulating jinnyeh-breasts and unsure how its impertinence was almost comforting. Perhaps because Khasmedeus could be counted on to say exactly what it was thinking, instead of all this palaver and poesy that dissolved like spun sugar and bore no real weight. "I have a question."

"Ah. Figured." The woman scratched its backside. "Who am I supposed to kill?"

"What – how did you – "

"Please. Humans only summon me for one of, oh, three reasons. One, they need someone dead but don't want to do it themselves, two, there's someone they want to fuck and don't think their mammalian wiles are enough to accomplish it on their own, and three, they want to know if anyone has mislaid a big pile of gold and if so, can they have it. You're too boring and strait-laced to think of fucking anyone except Elemai – though you *are* thinking it, aren't you? – and for the moment, you have money. Or maybe you don't, because that dress is very sad. Either way, I'm not changing my wager that it's number one. Well?"

"Fine." No point beating around the bush. "A man named Massasoum ur-Beiresht has made himself an obstacle to our plans. It has been heavily implied to me that I should… address the issue."

"By murdering him, yes. Squat. Splat. Stone-cold dead. The one and only method of human problem-solving since time immemorial.

And this is really your idea, sweetheart? You look as enthused as if you've just been asked to give a speech about how wonderful Coriolane is. Or to loosen up. That'll be the real kicker."

"Shut *up.*" Aliyah massaged her temples. "No, it wasn't my idea, but it was strongly suggested. Unless you think of something else – "

"Why would I do that? I enjoy squashing a juicy human from time to time." Khasmedeus shrugged, causing its wrapper to tumble even further from what it hardly covered in the first place. "Fine, O Mistress, give the order. I'll bring his head back on whichever variety of silver or golden platter you prefer. Blood pops best on silver, but gold is classier."

"No, wait." Aliyah got to her feet, partly to pace and partly to get the jinnyeh's offensively gyrating nude torso out of her direct line of sight. "There has to be something else, another way to do this. For example, if I had you take the form of Gaius Tullus and sent you to speak with Masssasoum, and you ordered him to go along with our plan – "

"Couldn't you at least force me into a *mildly* compelling meat sack?" The jinnyeh sighed mournfully. "And it might work for a short while, but only until the real Gaius Tullius Crappus – sorry, Grassus – found out about it. What would you do then?"

"Could you bind his tongue?" Aliyah offered. "Put an enchantment on him so he couldn't reveal the truth? It's hardly as if he's such a charismatic or respected figure that people are seeking his opinion or counsel on anything else. Or at least not when – *would you stop that?!*"

"What?" Khasmedeus pouted. "I thought you had discovered a sudden liking for the female form and its associated – what's the word? Breasts? Bosoms? Bazongas? Boobies?"

"I'm going to kill you." Aliyah pinched the bridge of her nose. "If I ordered you to tell me the proper rite of destruction for a misbehaving jinnyeh, you'd have to, wouldn't you?"

"Fine, fine, Mistress Spoilsport." With a sound like a particularly splendid and protracted fart, Khasmedeus caused itself to be suddenly covered from head to toe in a Tridevarian nun's habit and wimple, prayerbook piously clutched in its hands. "Is this more to your liking?"

"One day soon, someone is going to stuff you into something a lot less pleasant than a ring, and I just hope I'm there to see it." Aliyah sat down again, but continued to glower at Khasmedeus. "And you haven't answered my question. Could you take on Gaius Tullus's form, make Massasoum think he spoke to him and the Governor-General ordered him to respect local law and acquiesce to his sister's rightful claim, and prevent either of them from discovering the switch?"

"Maybe." Khasmedeus inserted a corner of the wimple into its mouth and began to chew on it with pointed black teeth. At Aliyah's renewed glare, it sighed. "All right, fine. Yes, I could do that. But there's no guarantee that Massasoum will actually agree, and if he doesn't, what's your next brilliant plan? Can I smite him into goo then? Or at least a little goo? Tiniest amount of goo?"

"One thing at a time." Aliyah experienced a heartfelt desire for this interaction to be over and Khasmedeus banished from her presence. "When it's done, return to me in secret and let me know. Oh, and one other thing. Make sure that under no circumstances does Safiya ur-Tasvashta's servant Vadoush see you, follow you, learn of your actions, or otherwise interfere. What exactly is he? A minor jinnyeh, or – "

"Hinnyeh, I think. The country-bumpkin, bad-tempered, magically inferior, sadly inbred, and *far* less handsome cousin of the jinnyeh, at least according to me, and mine is the only opinion that matters. So you've finally cottoned on to what a supremely sketchy bunch your new in-laws are, have you? They ever tell you what really happened to Diyab?"

"I – *what?*" Aliyah stared at him. "The old man who gave me the Ring? What about – ?"

"Well, for one," Khasmedeus said. "He was also a hinnyeh, from the desert tribes outside Yerussala. For two, surely you don't think he just accidentally wandered into the Holy City with a priceless relic in hand, hoping to sell it for enough money to afford a nice bowl of camel stew? Nor was his decease any sort of accident. Don't you want to know who really killed him, and *why?*"

Aliyah stared at the jinnyeh. She wanted to demand that it explain itself, even as the usual litany of warnings about its mendacity and manipulation flitted through her head. At last she said, "If there's something I should know about the ur-Tasvashtas, that you could have told me earlier – why didn't you? Didn't we agree to work together?"

"Because," Khasmedeus said frankly. "I only tell my masters exactly what I am explicitly and inescapably ordered to, no more and no less. You think I'm your confidante, or your giggling girlfriend to share sleepover secrets? I'm not. You're a brave little human, and remarkably convinced of the moral necessity of a bloodless solution – at which you're wrong, though that's a question for later – but there's another thing which, in the spirit of fairness, you should know. I am not interested in keeping my slave-masters alive any longer than I must, and since you are presently that person for me, I only care about your life as much as I am – again – fully and carefully instructed to do. At which you have left a great deal of gaps, and believe me, I am *very* much on the lookout for them and how they could be exploited. Good luck with guessing!"

With that, before Aliyah could say anything, Khasmedeus winked out of existence, leaving not even a stray wisp of smoke in its wake. She felt slightly numb, both from what it said of itself and what it hinted about the ur-Tasvashtas, especially because it was too unsettlingly close to what Elemai herself had admitted. *My mother is – well, you know. You've met her. She will break any rule or law that she feels necessary, anything that gets in the way or impedes her goal, and... do you really think it was* coincidence, *Aliyah? That indeed, we traveled to the Holy City just in time for the Ring to return and fall into our laps?*

And this, Aliyah thought grimly, was the woman with whom she would soon have private lessons in magic, at least if she knew what was good for her. Not to mention, think very hard about which questions she needed to ask, and how. No doubt Khasmedeus could provide some version of the story, but she did not want to rely on it – as it cheerfully confessed, the faster she got killed, the better. It was difficult to blame it for feeling that way, or not suddenly throwing aside its bitter experiences with humans over several thousand years, just because she thought she was *special*. After all, she had easily fallen back on the threat of destroying it, even if she didn't really mean it. Why would it *not* scheme to achieve her removal first? It only made sense.

Feeling the start of a particularly unhappy headache, Aliyah got up, returned to the solarium, and informed the others that she had instructed Khasmedeus to take care of Massasoum, without specifying how. Safiya smiled at her approvingly, and Aliyah arranged to return on Thalathday for the first of their tutorials. Then she climbed into the palanquin with her mother, and the ur-Namasqa guards hoisted them up for the homeward journey through the bustling Qartic streets. As they regarded each other in the afternoon light, Zadia said, "You did well, habibta."

"I… thank you." Aliyah was startled, but pleased. Her mother's praise was sparsely parceled out in the best of times, and rarely so unqualified. "I'm glad you think so."

"Indeed." Zadia tapped her fingers. "It was a difficult situation – truly, a number of difficult situations – but you seemed more assured, more accustomed to wielding your new power. Though you shall, of course, report to me whatever Saeda Safiya teaches you?"

"She is your ally." Aliyah winced as the palanquin hit a bump, and she nearly bit her tongue off. "Do you have some reason to suspect she is not being fully truthful or forthcoming?"

Zadia weighed her words, as Aliyah wondered whether to confess her own suspicions. Then her mother said, "The ur-Tasvashtas have their goals and purposes, and while it is to our advantage to make them ours as well, there may be incidences where they do not align. Your father and Saed Ghassan are meeting tomorrow, in order to set out the final terms of the zawaj contract. Then we will know more about just what they expect from us. Aside from that, of course." She cut her eyes briefly at the Ring. "And the Chairman is not the only person who has heard the rumors of its true nature. We must manage this carefully, discreetly. At least until the situation is… changed."

"Amma…" Aliyah wasn't sure if she dared to speak it aloud. Finally she said, "Do you really think he should die?"

A muscle twitched in Zadia's jaw, as if even if both of them knew what was suggested, it was still distasteful to give it voice. At last she said, "It would be preferable if there was another way to resolve his opposition, of course. But if there was not – "

"And if there was?"

"You informed us you had the situation in hand." Zadia regarded her coolly. "We are aware of what that implies. Or do you mean to say that *you* were not forthcoming?"

"No, all right? No!" Aliyah had never spoken to her mother so unguardedly, but at last, it burst out. "Why don't you ever *listen* to me, try to understand what I say, instead of automatically thinking the worst of me? Every conversation with you is so hard because I have to plow through the endless assumptions before I can even approach the truth, and when I offer it, you don't believe me, or undercut me, or find another reason I'm not living up to your expectations, when – why do you think I agreed to go to Yerussala in the first place? To marry Elemai? To do this, be part of your grandiose plans, the plot to remove Saed Massasoum and – and *all* of it? I've done nothing *but* try to please you, every day of my life, and that's still never enough!"

Belatedly, she realized that she was shouting, and protocol dictated that she immediately subside and apologize. But Aliyah was sick of protocol, sick of holding her tongue and pushing herself down – she *had the Ring of Tselmun,* and yet all she had done was to order an all-powerful jinnyeh to crudely impersonate a minor and much-disliked Meronite bureaucrat. Theoretically that was better than a gruesome murder, but she was still just a pawn for Safiya and Zadia's ambitions, still not trusted to act on her own but instead constantly and tightly taught and tutored, controlled as directly and humiliatingly as a glove-puppet on a mummer's hand. Every time she opened her mouth, it was their words that came out – but not now, not *now*. If she couldn't make her own mother listen, what was any of this power even for?

Zadia was briefly stunned into silence. It was the first time Aliyah had ever seen her mother at a loss for words, and it wasn't as satisfying as she imagined. They continued to stare at each other. Then Zadia said, "Very well. I hear you, Aliyah. We should save this for a later moment."

Aliyah supposed this was true, was more of a concession than she expected, and at least her mother had called her by her own name, rather than a patronizing endearment. She nodded stiffly, accepting the temporary truce, and neither of them said another word until they reached the ur-Namasqa villa, climbed out, and went inside for sardiq and supper. Afterward, Aliyah thought about retiring to her room to read, but she was still too twisted, too pent-up, too angry and frustrated to have any hope of a peaceable evening. Instead she went to the charbagh, pulling her shawl up against the breeze, and sat there, staring into the greenery. The Kitab described paradise as a sort of garden, hence their prevalence in Wahini homes, but just now, it felt very far from that. She kept running over more things she wanted to say, things she should have said sooner, all of it. If she was brave, she would go and demand to say them now, but she wasn't.

At length, she glimpsed a shadow, heard footsteps, and looked up to see her father. "Good evening, habibta," he said, and it was more of a comfort in his voice than it ever was in her mother's. "I can go."

"It's... all right." Aliyah paused, then moved over on the bench, inviting him to join her. He too must have recalled their previous conversation here, when he told her about the upcoming pilgrimage to Yerussala. It struck her again that she was responsible for ruining it, she was the one who unleashed the Ring's plague on all the innocent hajjis, and tears bubbled up in her eyes, which she angrily knuckled away. She felt as frail as a seed-puff about to blow away in the wind, and that was not acceptable. Not when she needed to be perfectly, unshakably strong.

Khaldun sat down and put an arm around her, holding her close. Aliyah snuffled, burying her face against him, until he said, "So do you wish to tell me what is wrong, my dear?"

"I don't know." Aliyah knocked her head dully against his shoulder. "I just feel like I can't... I can't do anything right, but in a different way than usual. And I think Amma thinks I hate her, but I don't, I love her, I really do. It's just... hard, and I don't understand why it's happening. With the Ring, I mean. At first I felt important, special, when I was chosen. That it was a blessing. But now I think it's probably a curse."

"That is the thing about great power." Khaldun's voice was wry. "Everything that looks like gold from afar turns to dross in your hands. But we do not yet know either way. It could still be for a reason."

"I don't know." Aliyah hesitated, wondering if she should tell him what Khasmedeus had hinted about Diyab's fate. "The old man who gave it to me, he called me *princess,* but that's stupid. Being a princess isn't something anyone has control over, it's just what they're born into, and says nothing about their character. Not that it makes sense anyway, because I'm not a princess, but – "

"Aren't you?" Khaldun raised a teasing eyebrow. "Didn't I ever tell you that my family, the Onwa'kyemes, are supposedly descended from Tselmun? It's hardly special, though. Most of the Numerian clans say the same. After all, when the First Yerussalan Kingdom was conquered by the ancient Meronites, the Temple was destroyed, and Tselmun's court fled to my homeland, it included any number of wives, concubines, and children. Indeed, it would be more shocking if we could find a clan that *didn't* claim descent from Tselmun, rather than one that did."

"What?" Aliyah blinked. She thought he might have told her once, as a funny childhood story, but no more than that. "Wait – so Tselmun might actually *be* my ancestor? But that still doesn't make sense. He must have thousands of descendants, tens of thousands. Even if I did have some distant link of generations and generations past, why would it be *me* who was Diyab's princess? And besides, I'm Qartic. I don't think being born royal in the first degree makes you special, let alone an accident from thousands of years ago! Who would ever believe that?"

"A great deal of the world, alas." Khaldun sighed. "We may be untangling ourselves from the myth of monarchy for generations to come, but you are your mother's daughter in that regard. And indeed, in all regards. The two of you struggle to relate to each other because you are so alike, and when you see yourself in all your strengths and flaws, it is difficult to accept that it is indeed the truth. You wish it was something else, someone else, and it impels you to push even harder. As if you could just change it in her, you could finally change it in yourself."

"Thanks, Abba," Aliyah said dryly. "Very paternally wise of you."

"It's true, you know. I am extremely smart." He hugged the top of her head. "Aside from that, how are you feeling about the wedding? You know I am meeting Saed Ghassan tomorrow, yes? Is there anything you want me to ask about, to specially discuss or insist upon?"

"I..." Aliyah looked down at her hands. "I like Elemai," she said at last, which was true. "I hope we'll be a good match. It's just the rest of her family I'm not sure about, what they want from me or what they expect. Honestly, Saeda Safiya terrifies me."

"Ah. I thought as much." Khaldun gazed pensively into the dim garden. "She frightens me too, and your mother, and much of the

Adirim. It is always wiser to have such a person as an ally, rather than an enemy, but to live every day in their den cannot be comfortable. For what it's worth, I will insist that you and Elemai are granted a house of your own, so you may spend your first days as a married couple without the constant presence of family. Such intrusions can make it difficult, especially when it was not your choice. But you know my match with your mother was arranged, and we have come to care for each other a great deal. I wish the same for you and Elemai."

"So you do?" Aliyah felt briefly unsure whether she could speak to her father like this, as an adult and not a child. "Love Amma? And she… she loves you?"

"We do," Khaldun said firmly. "It was not instantaneous or easy, but it has come with time and effort – and patience, a great deal of it. It might not always be passionate or burning or whatever else, but such strong feelings can destroy as easily as sustain. When you can come in from the cold and be sure of warming yourself at the hearth fire, that is no small thing. Noora has helped as well, in steadying us. The triangle is the strongest shape, for when one point must thrust, the other two can brace. Noora and I know our greatest value is in being able to do so for your mother. I do not know if you and Elemai will eventually decide to take another spouse, but even if not, you must be able to trust each other. Do so, and truly, and love often comes in its time, in its way."

Aliyah contemplated that. She didn't know if she wished that she had been free to choose her own match or not; a common Qartic woman had great latitude to do so, but a heiress of the High House considerably less. It was no use imagining, because then she would be an entirely different person, and there was no way to say if it would be better or worse. And she had not lied when she confessed to liking Elemai. If only they could disentangle from the alexandrine knot, the tangles of politics and family, magic and war, and live as themselves – but that too was impossible, and not worth pining over. It was just this, now. The future.

She felt better when she went up to bed, and was mostly able to sleep, though her dreams were strange and dark. The next day, her father returned from the meeting with Ghassan to report that all had gone well, the zawaj contract had been prepared, and Aliyah would have the chance to read it before it was signed, which she did. Then the day after that was Thalathday, and it was time for Aliyah to return to the ur-Tasvashta villa for her first lesson with Safiya. She took care to dress well and apply cosmetics, to braid her hair and put on jewelry. She traveled across the city by herself, and when she arrived, was pleased with the response. "You look lovely, my dear," the matriarch said. "You're blossoming into a remarkable young woman before our eyes."

"Thank you." It might be offered for obviously ulterior motives, but if Zadia would not say so, Aliyah would take it from anyone who would. She let herself walk at Safiya's side, her equal, as they entered Safiya's private study – a place where even her spouses and children were not allowed to set foot without permission. It was high-ceilinged and airy, smelling of cinnamon and spice, grease-chalk and burned herbs, and flaming bronze salvers hung from the ceiling. When combined with the clear morning light, it seemed to illuminate the world itself. No matter what had led her here, Aliyah wanted to stay and learn, to take everything from it that she could.

Safiya shut and barred the door, then crossed to the worktable that sat beneath creaking shelves crammed with scrolls, codices, parchments, books, and manuscripts, in languages from across the world. She considered, then took down one in Old Coptaric. "This is the best primer, I think. Am I correct to assume that you have no previous experience, other than your recent acquisition?"

Aliyah was forced to admit she did not, and with that, she was tossed directly and mercilessly into the deep end. For the next three hours, all she did was pore over arcane symbols, try to draw them with paper and ink, and have Safiya brutally critique the results. She was tempted to insist that she had no intention of summoning any other jinnyeh apart from Khasmedeus, who was already bound by the Ring, and was thus unsure why she needed to know all this, but Safiya insisted that if she was using this magic, she had to strip it down to its essentials, know exactly how it slotted together like the bricks of a house or the numbers of an equation – know how to read it, create it, recombine it, and if necessary, unmake it, flay it to the bone. Aliyah couldn't argue with that logic, and it was preferable not to be a total ignoramus, but Malikallulah, at what cost?

Around noon, Safiya deigned to permit a break and lunch, and the two of them said mardiq on the floor of the workroom. As they sat in the sun and ate, Safiya said, "So tell me, my dear. When you assured us that you had the jinnyeh deal with Saed Massasoum, what was that supposed to mean? Because not only is the man still in his position, he maintains his opposition to standing aside for his sister under any circumstances. Surely you understand this is not the result?"

"What?" Aliyah was startled. "I told Khasmedeus to do it. I did."

"To do what? Exactly?"

She tried to think of any other explanation, but couldn't. Finally she confessed the truth, that she had sought a course of action that would be less damaging and prone to cause unforeseen complications, and which did not rely on bidding the jinnyeh to brazenly assassinate – for better or worse – the highest-ranking official in Qart-Hadesht aside from Gaius Tullus Grassus himself. Yet the more she tried to explain, the flimsier it sounded, and she had the sinking feeling that she had failed at the first hurdle, a test of resolve far more important than chalking complicated runes and muddling through musty old books. "I don't know why the jinnyeh would not have done it, Saeda Safiya," she finished at last. "I did ask it, and I thought that it would – "

"And that is your mistake." Safiya ate the last bite of her lunch and put the tray aside. "You think you can do this with minimal effort and sacrifice, that asking politely and avoiding bloodshed will achieve the objective, and it is preferable to the alternative. Of course the jinnyeh did not obey you. Why would it, when by your own admission, it openly confessed that the sooner you die, the better? You are not Tselmun, and you are not a magician. It will take every opportunity to defy you, because *you cannot make it do anything else*. You cannot punish it, you still promise to treat it gently, and that is your mistake. What do you think Khasmedeus *is*, my dear? Do you know anything of what Tselmun did to the jinnyeh, or who they were before he brought them down and bound them as his servants? No? No. Let this be a lesson to you, Aliyah. Will you do what is necessary, or not?"

The workroom was full of dusty sunlight and whispering secrets. She wanted to ask Safiya about Vadoush, Diyab, any number of things.

But if she did not, if she wasted their time – if she wanted to make Khasmedeus do anything except mock her, for it to *mean* something –

"Yes, saeda," Aliyah said. "Yes, I will."

"Good." Safiya rose to her feet, brushing the crumbs off her skirt. "Then for your sake, and everyone's, I hope you are ready. For indeed, we have a great deal to do."

CHAPTER 18

ELEMAI

Since its founding thousands of years ago in the distant annals of time, the greatest challenge facing Qart-Hadesht – all politics, wars, empires, rulers, and other external concerns aside – was how it could flourish in a brutal desert, where years could pass with little rain and the largest source of water, the Mad ar-Hahrat, could not be used without laborious and time-intensive desalinization. The nomadic tribes of the Sand Sea used salt pans and ancient drying processes, but that was vastly impractical for a city of almost a quarter million people, who needed to wash, drink, irrigate, cook, and clean every day and could hardly labor for hours each time in order to do so. Fortunately they did not have to, because of the aquifers and viaducts that lay deep in the foundations, criss-crossing beneath the massive city walls and delivering cool, fresh water to all households, even the poorest ones. They might have to share a communal spigot with the neighbors, but at least they had it, and as Wahinism prized cleanliness, ritual ablutions, and frequent washing, no Qartic citizen had to go without this religious mandate. It was so familiar that few ever thought about it, or where it had come from, or if it would work in the same way forever. Who worried if the sun would rise and set, the day and night come, the world go on? It always had.

And yet, as she walked with her mother in one of the huge clay tunnels, the floor overgrown with slimy weeds and high-water marks well over her head, Elemai could see the signs of something else, a decay that sent a chill down her spine. The vast underground reservoirs were kept clean and filtered by an elaborate system of pools, pipes, pumps, and purifiers, and an Adirim subcommittee was responsible, or at least usually, for its maintenance. Perhaps that was the problem. Everyone expected someone else to take the lead, and so they never did. It certainly wasn't as if the Governor-General was mucking in, sleeves rolled up, to solve the city's banal municipal infrastructure issues.

"What is this?" Elemai's voice echoed eerily as she stared at the dark water far below – indeed, considerably farther than it should be. There was a great net strung up over the mouth of the basin to prevent anything from falling in (or, she thought with a shudder, *jumping* in), but she could see the alarming degree to which the level had fallen. She racked her brains, trying to recall her lessons. "The water is piped all the way down from the Atalantine Mountains. We have to send inspectors to the high villages every winter to check the snowfall, the sluice gates, and holding tanks. If the season is bad or the drought is long, they inform us as soon as possible, so the Adirim can pass rationing orders. Yes?"

"Yes." Safiya shrugged. "But with the preoccupation of the emperor's visit, the question of whether we will or will not rebel against him, and all the rest, nobody has attended to it in quite some time. I don't believe the inspectors were sent either this season or the last, and humans have a bad habit of assuming that anything that will not instantly kill them can be safely ignored forever. Who, after all, thinks of the city sewers, when there are far more interesting dramas elsewhere?"

Elemai was briefly flummoxed. At last she said, "We're down here, aren't we?"

"We are." Safiya cracked a bladed smile. "I see no one else, do you?"

"No."

"Which means indeed, this is our matter to solve." Safiya tipped her head at the reservoir. "We may begin by exploring and eliminating the obvious hypotheses. Was the winter snow poor, or is there a mechanical breakdown along the route? Do you recall who had the aquifers built?"

"It was Queen Daeda, wasn't it?" She had not been Qart-Hadesht's first ruler, but she was still the one that mattered most in the city's long and storied history. It vastly vexed Elemai that all anyone in the outside world knew of her was as the heartsick damsel who supposedly killed herself after Aeonius left her and sailed away to found Merone (baldly contradicting the *other* story about the twins suckled by wolves, but such was the nature of mythology). Instead, Daeda had defiantly burned herself alive rather than surrender to Aeonius and his invading army; inspired by her example, the Qartic soldiers fought to the death and put the foreign besiegers on their heels. At least, that was the tale Elemai had grown up with, though she did wonder if it was as embroidered as the Meronite version. It also felt as if dying dramatically, regardless of any exalted reasons, was a good bit less useful than living, and what else could Daeda achieve, if she survived? But the other story, the less heroic and stirring version, held that Daeda hadn't actually meant to die at all. She was angrily summoning an army of jinnyeh to lead the attack against her former lover Aeonius, and she made a small, stupid, avoidable mistake, some flaw in her technique or mispronunciation of her words. As such, one of the creatures sprang free of its bonds and devoured her in an instant, and her shocked captains were forced to concoct the story of a heroic sacrifice, were blindly lucky that it worked and the Qartic defenders did not just fling down their weapons and flee. Young Elemai hadn't liked that one nearly as much, and insisted that it was just another posthumous Meronite smear, but it was difficult to reconcile with the fact that ever since, consorting with jinnyeh had been strictly prohibited in Qart-Hadesht. Why, indeed, would they risk a repeat tragedy?

It was clearly a cautionary tale about doing magic that one did not understand, or counting on it as a savior to the exclusion of one's own basic efforts, the proper study of war or the strength of ordinary defenses. However, the chroniclers often cast it as a case of womanly power gone terribly awry, with deleterious consequences for everyone. To Elemai's dismay, these unflattering interpretations were not limited to Meronites or other obvious enemies. There were plenty of Qartic male writers and influential Wahini clerics who agreed, and she strongly suspected that Massasoum ur-Beiresht had been reading them.

"Queen Daeda, yes," Safiya said, in answer to Elemai's guess. "She designed this system, worked out its architectural and engineering specifics, and ordered her jinnyeh to build it. She wanted it to function *without* magic, even if jinnyeh were bidden to lay the stones and mix the mortar – all by hand just like mortals, with no sorcerous or unnatural shortcuts. And as you see, we have an unfortunate shortage of human workers at the moment. Who, then, might mend this for us?"

Elemai could see where this was going, and wasn't sure she liked it, but there was nothing to do but get it over with. "Another jinnyeh?"

"Indeed, that might be a solution, though it would take a number of them, or one that was powerful enough for many." At last, Safiya took her eyes away from the depleted reservoir and looked accusingly at her daughter. "So tell me, Elemai, why after all my planning, my painstaking efforts to be sure it would be ours and ours alone, the Ring of Tselmun has ended up in the hands of your *fiancée?*"

Elemai winced. She had suspected this question was coming from the moment her mother invited her down here on pretense of inspecting the aquifers. It was true that she had wondered the same thing ever since Yerussala, with a bitterness that was difficult to fully disguise even (and sometimes especially) in Aliyah's presence. After all the books and manuscripts Safiya had consulted, all the hours she spent studying until her back ached, all the times she sent Vadoush to Ambrazakti to raid King Musum's Great Library for arcane scholarship, her meticulous work to cultivate the impoverished tribes who lived in the desert near the Holy City, the dusty scavengers who rummaged in forgotten tombs and might stumble upon a priceless ancient artifact – all that labor to find the Ring of Tselmun and ensure that Elemai was in prime position to claim it, and then what? Safiya's instructions to Diyab could not, or so she thought, have been more explicit. Was he just an addled old geezer who honestly mixed up the two saedas of the ur-Tasvashta and ur-Namasqa traveling party, or was it worse? A deliberate betrayal, or more?

"I don't know," Elemai said. "If you had not left orders for Diyab to be killed as soon as he found the Ring and passed it on, thus to prevent anyone from discovering your meddling hand in this so-called miracle, we might have been able to ask him."

Safiya did not look particularly repentant, not that Elemai expected it. "It is never wise to leave loose ends, and Diyab could not say what he knew. It had to look providential, coincidental, as if it simply emerged from the timeless mists and chose you as its bearer. That was the plan. But it all went wrong, Aliyah holds it instead, and we are left attempting to control her from a clumsy remove, forced to delicately suggest and insinuate. Yet the girl is unbearably headstrong and contrary. The instant she gets a whiff of anyone trying to pull her strings, she revolts."

"She is," Elemai agreed, trying not to badmouth her future wife. Nor did she want to; she found Aliyah's unyielding stubbornness, her refusal to be defined by anyone except herself, her willingness to push on the stifling strictures of her mother's expectations, to be inspiring, in a way Elemai sorely wished she was brave enough to emulate. "Isn't that good? That she cannot be influenced?"

"Influenced by others, perhaps." Safiya shook her head. "But she needs *our* influence. This has been my ambition longer than you can imagine. Why do you think I raised you to be a hafiza of Shahrzad in addition to the Kitab, taught you politics and history, magic and law and languages, social graces and talents, everything you needed to become a new Daeda? The final piece would be avenging our greatest humiliation, overturning this short-sighted rule that keeps us from consorting with jinnyeh. Daeda used them to raise Qart-Hadesht to great heights, to repel and even defeat Merone, but it was only once, and it did not last. She made a foolish mistake, and it all came crashing down. Who thought it was wise to ban us from ever trying again, rather than doing all we could to be sure that when the time came once more, there would be no mistake? That is why I dedicated myself to the task. If you had that legacy, and you *finished* the job – "

"I'm sorry," Elemai said. "Are you telling me that my entire life, you groomed me to be the new Ringbearer, and that was the sole reason behind everything you taught me? So I could be Tselmun but greater, Daeda but greater, and break our Meronite shackles once and for all?"

"Yes." Safiya looked at her straight, utterly unflinching. "I did not think it wise to tell you when you were younger, but you are a woman now, about to be married, and deserve the truth. From the moment you were born and the astrologer told me what glory lay in your stars, I knew this was your destiny. That was when I began my efforts to solve a mystery many hundreds of years old, and uncover where the Ring of Tselmun had last come to lie. Your whole life has prepared you for this moment, Elemai. And when it came, what happened? You failed me."

"I didn't, Amma," Elemai pleaded, voice cracking. "I didn't! I knew that Diyab would be waiting when we traveled to Yerussala, I knew he was supposed to find me and give me something special, but if it went wrong, if he got confused and went to Aliyah instead – if there was any way I could have stopped it or realized it wasn't going according to plan or even what it *was* – all because you wanted it to be a *miracle,* and yet not enough to tell me the *truth* – "

"Don't snivel, my dear. It isn't becoming. Don't you understand what an opportunity you have? Which I have *given* you, at great cost?"

"What? You expect me to become *Queen* Daeda the second, when we are rather famously a republic? Daeda was our greatest monarch, but she was our last monarch. Whether you believe that she died heroically or foolishly, that was also when we decided to form the Adirim, to delegate responsibility to a conclave of the people, so the death of one leader would not threaten to destroy our entire state. So yes, Mother. As you pointed out, I do know my history."

"Indeed." Safiya studied her daughter coolly. "Then you will also recall that the ancient Hellenics could select an *autokrator,* one individual who could operate with absolute power and no prior consultation with the Anteropolian ekklesia, and the old Meronite republic could elect a sole dictator to assume the full authority of the state, in order to simplify the logistics of dealing with a major crisis. They did, of course, return their mandate when the crisis had passed, but – "

"And?" Elemai let out a bone-dry laugh. "You want to overthrow the Meronite Empire, but their political philosophy could be useful? Do you want to ask the Meronite Republic how that worked out, the time they gave it to Coriolane Caesar and he *didn't* give it back?"

"Democracy is important in theory. It is the best system that the human race has yet created for governing itself in something approaching fairness, justice, and equality. But it is, we must admit, considerably flawed in practice." Safiya turned on her heel and started deeper into the tunnel, and Elemai, still numb, trailed after her. "It is slow, contradictory, plagued by contrasting opinions and clashing priorities. It only enacts half-measures and partial solutions, and it can rarely build enough power and consensus to act with true decision and resolve. Whatever it achieves in one session can be undone by the next, and often is lost in squabbling, factionalism, special interests, and selfishness. We must oppose the Meronites, yes, but we must recognize that our methods, precisely because they are stretched so thin among so many people, have become profoundly ineffective. Besides, we don't live in a democracy now, do we? It is only a pathetic puppet theater permitted on sufferance by our conquerors, overseen by a useless toady who, if he ever decided to haul himself out of the slop trough and do his job, could scupper anything we came up with. It is simply acknowledging reality. We need *one* person to lead the rebellion against Coriolane, and yes, I have spent your entire life ensuring that person would be you."

"Ah," Elemai said. "So you subscribe to the Ruthynian model of independence from Merone. The problem is not that there is an absolute ruler, the problem is that *they* are not the absolute ruler. They would restore their lost tsar in an instant, and go back to brutally lording it over the Kozheks and Vashemites. Do we truly need to do the same?"

"Don't prate puerile schoolgirl objections at me." Safiya was more impatient than ever. "There is far more at stake than you can fathom. Likewise, do you think this months-long communication with Merone, this careful passing of sensitive intelligence, simply *happened?* When I already *told* you that none of this is an accident?"

"I thought – " Truly, she had flattered herself that she knew her mother's mind and motives, and yet she was a hopeless novitiate. "We were not aware of the identity of our source within the Eternal Palace? But we are, aren't we. Or rather, *you* are."

"Indeed, and therein lies the difficulty." They came to a halt beneath a grille that opened down from the street above, and Safiya leaned on the sun-warmed bricks. "Especially when they have just been arrested for treason, even though they both wear a crown."

The significance took a moment to percolate. Then Elemai's brain caught up, and her jaw dropped. "No. The *empresses?!*"

"Yes. I do not know how their seditious activities were discovered, but such is ill fortune. Very well, there is no reason for you not to know. Gheslyn and Vestalia were the ones who told me that Coriolane's health was in decline. They told me as well that they were the ones to do it."

"*What?*" Elemai knew it was suggested, had hinted it to Aliyah, but the empresses passing information about the emperor's weakness was not identical to them being responsible for it. It had felt like a complicated manipulation or a covert warning, a secret attempt to hold the empire together in a dangerous transition, none of which automatically meant that they wanted to undertake a light spot of regicidal mariticide. "What on *earth* did Coriolane do, to make them turn on him now?"

"Simple." Safiya smiled. "It is true that the spells used to extend his immortality are not as effective as before. On its own, Coriolane's original life is no longer sufficient to renew them; it has been used too many times, gone through too many cycles, and like every other natural force, it is now spent. So if he is to maintain his existence for centuries more, it must be taken from elsewhere, in greater and greater quantities."

Elemai felt slightly nauseous. Her mother was clearly waiting for her to connect the pieces, even as a far larger and unspeakably monstrous realization unfolded. "So he's stealing it from Gheslyn and Vestalia. After three hundred years of marriage or however long, he told them that the Corporalists would no longer maintain their immortality, only his, and they were expected to graciously submit and give their lives for him. Which, to nobody's surprise except his own, they did not take well."

"Indeed." Safiya raised an eyebrow. "That is why they were so furious as to take matters into their own hands and open back-channel communications with Merone's oldest enemies in Qart-Hadesht. I do not believe in the least that the empresses want to help us gain our independence or change the political status quo, but they were angry enough to tell us about Coriolane's weakness, in hopes that we would exploit it. They are doing the same; they have been searching for all possible ways to weaken the magic used on him, whether by that living ghoul Saturnus or that mad cannibal Kronus. I believe their idea is that once he is dead, they will take over and rule together, but that is not the end of it. Why do you think Coriolane is now willing to slaughter all of Brythanica, declare indiscriminate war on Qin, and otherwise destroy the Pax Meronorum – the one gift he could justly claim to have given us? Because even taking strength from the empresses is a temporary solution. When it runs out, he will need more. And more. And more."

Elemai's knees felt weak. "So that's why he's doing this? Because the more people he kills, the more energy he funnels into his immortality spells, preserving them when his own can no longer suffice? He can keep himself alive forever, at the expense of absolutely everyone else?"

"Yes." Once again, Safiya saw no need to gild the lily or blunt the blow. "This will get worse, Elemai. It is only the beginning. Coriolane will turn the world into a ruin of fire and slaughter sooner than give up his position, his power, and his life. Once the Bodeni are dead and the Qiné and Meronites likewise – it does not matter who dies, even his own subjects, they are merely grist for the mill – who comes next? Who is safe? Qart-Hadesht, the eternal bane of Merone's existence? I think not. And you wish to tell me, still, that your tender sensibilities cannot handle using the Ring of Tselmun to *stop it?*"

"Aliyah has it. She can't give it up."

"Does she?" Safiya evaluated her with that twisted half-smile. "Or can she? I believe she is finally realizing what a burden it is, and in our lessons, I have made her ever more aware of it. But you know the magic, because I ensured it. You will use the Ring correctly, without despotism, barbarism, or madness. She has had it for months now, and she has asked for *nothing,* done nothing, not even a single frivolous wish. And it, I think, remains cleaved to her because she is not – yet – willing to give it up. If she is, it will go. So you must convince her. One way or another."

Elemai feared to even ask it, but she had to. "And then?"

"The other useful feature of the aquifer system, aside from nourishing our rose of the desert, is to allow one to move around the city undetected." Safiya indicated the place where they stood. "Were you to release a certain spirit right here, the spirit would enter the house of Massasoum ur-Beiresht, unseen by anyone, without even the need for magical connivance. Do you think that is useful for his sister's claim?"

"Come on, Mother. Why are we still pretending that you want *Mirazhel* to take over her brother's role as Chair? *You* want that seat."

"No." Safiya smiled faintly. "I do in fact want Mirazhel in it. If I was the one to assume the Chair *and* put forth my own Ring-wielding daughter as temporary dictator, it would appear, shall we say, indelicate. But this is not about my power, or the ur-Tasvashtas' legacy. You may disagree with my methods and motives all you like. If you never speak to me again once this is finally over, you would be within your rights. But there is no time for that. I am *trying to save the world.*"

Elemai stood there, mute and stunned. She wanted to argue, to insist that Safiya's remorseless manipulation was unforgivable, that her mother was as dishonest and dangerous as any of their enemies. But if what she was saying *was* true, none of it mattered. If Safiya ur-Tasvashta, for all her flaws, was the only thing standing between them and Coriolane burning down the world to save himself – if this was the choice, traditional notions of morality, right and wrong, good and evil, entered into it not at all. It was callous beyond anything Elemai wished to think her mother capable of, but if the alternative was *utter annihilation* –

"Yes, Amma," Elemai said. "I will do it. I will ask Aliyah to give me the Ring."

And then, she had to step out of the tunnels, emerge into the light of day, and *do* it.

Their nikah was now little more than a week away, and was planned to be held in the great mahqasa of the eastern gate, the same one where they had met on the way to Yerussala. It was thus hosting an increasingly frantic flutter of preparations, decorations, consultations, and tussles about which family members would be seated where. If Elemai was not obliged to scurrilously murder the Chairman of the High House on the eve of the wedding, there would also be guests from the most illustrious Adirim families, and juggling their precedents was always an exercise in potential disaster. Elemai didn't know if Aliyah was there, but it seemed like an opportune place to start, and she forced herself to set off like an ordinary person, and not as if everything she had learned was swilling in her mind like poison. It was not decorous for a well-born saeda to travel alone and on foot like a common maidservant, but Elemai did not care.

When she arrived at the mahqasa, the qahin told her that Saeda Aliyah had recently arrived with Saeda Noora, and there was some new saga about the placement of the chairs. Elemai smiled, thanked him, and hurried over to where her betrothed was also looking deeply harried, though for a different reason. At the sight of Elemai, she glanced up with a start. "I didn't know you were coming, I thought you had something to do with your mother. Is there an issue with the – "

"Not that I know of. I am sorry, could we speak? Privately?"

Aliyah blinked, looking wary (which was likely for the best). Then she turned to her mother to ask her pardons, which Noora graciously granted, and led the two of them off into a corner by the qibla. "What is it?" she asked, low-voiced. "Did something *else* go wrong?"

"Not exactly. I was just thinking… as a wedding present, a token of trust. I did promise not to press, but you've seemed so burdened of late, and… could you lend me the Ring? Briefly?"

Aliyah stared at her. "Lend you *what?*"

"Temporarily." Elemai was unsure if it was true. "Only to help."

There was a portentous pause. It undercut her earnest protestations of spousal loyalty and assistance, but her mother would kill her if she spilled the truth. Besides, it was for Aliyah's own protection, and that was no exaggeration; Elemai had tried to warn her on the night after they got back from Yerussala. For there was something her mother hadn't said aloud just now, but which Elemai sensed nonetheless: if she couldn't get Aliyah to share the Ring, even briefly, then Safiya would be within her rights (as she saw them) to order Aliyah herself to be killed. After all, she was convinced it was a mistake, Diyab was never supposed to give the Ring to anyone but Elemai, and Aliyah's unauthorized possession jeopardized Safiya's work of decades. Of course she did not *want* to. It would be a scandal even if the death looked natural, it would ruin the alliance with the ur-Namasqas and any chance of giving Coriolane a proper welcome – and yet. If it put the Ring into Elemai's hands, as Safiya intended all along, she would do it, and damn the rest.

Aliyah frowned. "Are you all right? You look terrible."

"Fine," Elemai said, bright and brittle. "You're the one I'm worried about, really."

Aliyah kept frowning. At last she said, "I know that I wasn't very gracious about the idea of letting you have it. But it — it's hard, all right? It's very hard, and I don't want to put that on you without preparation."

"I am prepared, though," Elemai blurted out, a little recklessly. "I've had the lessons, the training — like I said in Yerussala, doesn't it make far more sense to be me? And I've seen how tired you are, the way you're struggling. I could have it. Just for a little while. I think that if you *wanted* to give it to me, you could. To… share the burden more equally. We have to, right? With each other. That's what it means. Being married."

Aliyah's solemn dark eyes searched her face, as Elemai wondered bleakly if all her deceptions and desperations were laid bare. Then at last, Aliyah nodded. Clearly unsure what would happen, if the Ring would let go, she raised her hand and pulled. And just like that, it came free.

Both of them were clearly surprised by it, that the Ring could drop into Elemai's hand like any other bit of jewelry. She should feel thrilled, but instead it twisted her in half, like the physical manifestation of dread had wrapped freezing hands around her lungs and squeezed the breath out. This should be her moment of triumph, but she could think of nothing she wanted less than to put it on. Still, she forced her stiff lips into a smile. "Thank you, my dear. I look forward to letting you rest."

It wasn't until much later, when she had returned home, gone to her room and shut herself in, that Elemai finally gritted her teeth and slid it on. The gold flared with a steady warm glow, whether a signal of Khasmedeus's presence or otherwise. Elemai was not eager to commence another sparring match with the insufferable creature, so she told herself to take it one step at a time, be careful. Wasn't that the point?

She sat there until she almost made herself sick with her cowardice. Then she dragged in a breath, squared her shoulders, and got to her feet, reaching for the Ring before she could lose her nerve. Then it occurred to her that she had possibly unleashed the plague-curse for a second time — another unlawful interloper, another thief who wasn't Tselmun daring to put it on and claim its power. But surely Safiya had made preparations to enable her to do so in safety. She had to believe it, at any rate. Or else.

Elemai raised the hand that bore, at long last, the Ring of Tselmun, and faced her destiny.

She expected Khasmedeus to appear in its usual fit of vulgarity, and it did not disappoint; it burst into existence singing a very rude song that was popular in Qartic brothels, describing in lurid detail what sort of pleasure two women could give each other without the need for a man. "Just a few ideas for the wedding night," it explained, doing a whizzing loop-the-loop that caused its loincloth to flip up and its flaming bare buttocks to be indiscreetly exposed. "Thought you could use the help, as you won't have – *hold* on. What's this? You're not Aliyah."

"No." Elemai spoke as coldly and flatly as she could. "Nor will you parade such vulgar nonsense again. This is your only warning."

"Somebody's tetchy today, aren't they?" Khasmedeus whistled. "Is that why it's you now, Sweetcheeks, and not the other one? Where *is* my dear mistress? Finally killed her, threw her into a shallow grave, and claimed the Ring for yourself? Took you long enough."

"*Shut up.*" Such jests cut too close to the quick. "You forget that I am not her, and can exact true penalties for insolence. Here are the terms. First, you will address me as *Mistress,* and behave according to the highest standards of decorum whenever I summon you. Second, you will carry out my commands quietly, quickly, and without question. Third – "

"Ooh, playtime's over?" The jinnyeh affected a supercilious yawn. "Now it's time for the foot-stamping and dire threats? Never knew how good I had it? Also, your eye's twitching, did you know that? You should get it looked at. Not advisable for your head to explode at your own wedding. How's it going, by the way? Still full speed ahead, or dampened by you murdering your blushing bride? If you marry a man, I'll have to learn a whole new dirty song. So much work."

Elemai had heard enough. She raised a hand, uttered a complex command in Old Coptaric, and a whip of white fire materialized in her grasp, glowing with vicious heat. She hauled off and lashed Khasmedeus as hard as she could, enough to make it stagger; while it was down, she wound up and delivered an even more ferocious blow. "You forget that indeed, I am not Aliyah. I am *trained.* If I am nothing but an empty vessel for my mother to pour *accomplishments* into, I will not fail her now! Did you hear, demon? This is the least of what you will receive!"

She pulled her arm back again, but the jinnyeh held up its hands, its eyes fixed on her in an expression she couldn't read. It spoke in a much different voice, low and toneless, stripped of mockery. "Yes, Mistress."

"That's better." Breathing hard, Elemai let the whip drop. She ached to keep going, to unleash her wrath and her guilt and her mangled emotions somehow, but it had gotten the point, and she didn't need to start off in an unbecoming orgy of sadism. "Now. Are you listening?"

"Yes, Mistress."

"Good." She swiped an arm across her forehead, wondering why she felt no better, and possibly even worse. "We have work to do."

★★★★

THE MORNING OF THE WEDDING arrived in what felt like ominously appropriate gloom, in thick dark clouds and a chill breeze off the Mad ar-Hahrat that broke whitecaps in the bay and caused the trundling line of guests to snatch at runaway clothing. Elemai had slept very little and her nerves felt like sandpaper, even as she tried to muster the appropriate excitement and enjoyment of the traditional wedding activities. Her two little sisters, Tafelin and Leila, and her female friends had painted her hands with henna, rubbed her skin with richly scented creams, lined her eyes in kohl, and done her hair in an elaborate crown. Her dress was white, with a high collar and long sleeves, and trimmed in elaborate cascades of golden lace that fell over her wrists and trailed behind her in dreamy sweeps. Her heavy red-silk veil was almost as long, and even with Tafelin and Leila carrying her train, Elemai could only walk in small mincing steps for fear of falling flat on her face in front of Qart-Hadesht's assembled dignitaries. The only one missing, in fact, was Massasoum ur-Beiresht. He sent his last-minute regrets, as he had been taken with a sudden and severe attack of illness and could not leave his bed.

The hall was chill and airy, and wind whistled eerily in the minaret as Elemai reached the front, where the qahin waited. Her mother was also there; she met Elemai's eyes and gave her a small, approving nod. Elemai's face felt cold, her limbs like unfired clay, but she nodded back, as another hush fell and attention turned again to the great doors. They swung open, and Aliyah ur-Namasqa made her entrance.

Elemai was not, of course, undertaking this match for any reason other than naked ambition, but she was not above appreciating the rather remarkable beauty of her bride, in a way she hadn't truly seen before; Aliyah always seemed so quiet, ordinary, and plain. Today, however, she was clad in ivory, turquoise, gold, and silver that set off her dark skin to dazzling effect, her eyes were lined in gold and her lashes dusted in shimmering powder, her veil was thick scalloped lace, and she wore heavy earrings and a coiled and bejeweled choker that made her look like a Numerian queen of old. She proceeded sedately up the aisle, escorted by her parents. Zadia's face was cool and serene, while Khaldun stole quick glances at his daughter in both pride and trepidation. When they reached the ur-Tasvashtas, Zadia formally gave her permission and placed Aliyah's hand into Elemai's, and Safiya graciously accepted. Then the brides knelt before the qahin, and the ceremony began.

It was all the usual architecture of a marriage: prayers and promises, readings from the Kitab, vows and benedictions, their hands bound with a red silk scarf, rings exchanged (what with everything, Elemai could not help but find that murderously ironic). Then the qahin pronounced them wed, and Aliyah turned her face up so Elemai could bestow a brief, chaste kiss. So, then. It was done. However one was supposed to feel on this occasion, she wasn't sure that she did.

The bridal parties recessed out of the mahqasa and into the courtyard to receive the blessings and well-wishes of their guests, though this was cut short as it started to rain in earnest. It was possible, Elemai reflected, that this was her fault; refilling the aquifers had to come from somewhere, and she had given orders for her goals to be accomplished as subtly as possible. While rain on your wedding day rarely boded well by anyone's standards, she was not about to worry about superstitions more than she must. There were real troubles enough.

The feast took place at the ur-Tasvashta villa, and the newlyweds sat side by side, sharing a cup and plate; while Elemai was tempted to down several jugs of wine, she reminded herself to keep a clear head. However, this resolve was not shared by the man seated on her other side in an unavoidable position of honor, who kept beckoning the servants and shouting for more. Elemai was startled both to finally meet Gaius Tullus

Grassus in the flesh and realize he was much younger than she thought, only in his thirties; he had been assigned to Qart-Hadesht as Governor-General when he was barely older than she was now. But all his excesses had prematurely aged him; he had a double chin (more like a triple chin), his jowls hanging like a hound and his eyes bloodshot. His toga strained at his waist, and he gave off a sweaty, unwashed reek. He was therefore not the best company for that alone, but after his third cup of wine, he unfortunately decided to make conversation. "So," he said, addressing Elemai in Lanuvian; even after almost a decade, he still spoke no more than a few words of Qartic. "This is indeed customary in your parts?"

"I beg your pardon, my lord?"

"This." Grassus waved a pudgy hand at her and Aliyah. "You know it goes against the True Tridevarian Church to let two women be wed. I could have ordered to stop it on grounds of heresy, but I've decided to be tolerant of local habits. How does it work, anyway? How do you decide that you've properly fucked her and now it's consummated? Just a finger up the cunny, or is there more to it?"

"My lord." His voice was loud and slurring, and heads were turning. "Either way, it's not a subject for the supper table. Saeda Aliyah and I are honored that you joined us – aren't we, my dear? And if you wish to taste another local specialty, the next course will be a preparation of – "

"I've tasted it." Grassus waved it off. "I've tasted it all. I've been stuck in your sandy barbarian hellhole, far away from the Eternal City, for *seven fucking years,* just to please my stupid father and His Divine Majesty, and if there's something to eat, I've eaten it. Or if it's there to fuck, I've fucked it. Just out of curiosity, do your people have the custom of prima nocte? I could give your bride a proper swiving on your behalf, make sure she has a cock up her at least once, so it's good and official. Or you, Lady Elemai, if you prefer. What does it matter? You're savages! *Savages!* All this time Merone has spent at her own expense to culture and civilize you, and instead you've only dragged me down to your level, with your decadent heathen pleasures! It's your fault!"

His voice rose to the brink of a roar, a mortifyingly awkward silence had replaced the chattering and clattering of the guests, and just as Elemai was wishing that she hadn't left the Ring locked in her room, her mother appeared, carrying two goblets. "My lord Grassus," Safiya ur-Tasvashta said, flashing a smile that was nothing but teeth. "I'm glad that you are availing yourself of our excellent libations. Rare to see you in company, isn't it? No wonder you are out of practice with behaving."

Gaius Tullus glared at her, but even his abused sense of propriety must have warned him to tread carefully. "Lady Safiya," he said, chewing his tongue. "Good evening."

"Indeed." Safiya handed him one of the goblets, keeping the other for herself. "I am sure you were about to congratulate my daughter on her marriage, but let us do so, shall we?" Turning to the hall, she gestured for them to rise to their feet and lift their cups – which after the briefest of pauses, they did. "To my daughter, Saeda Elemai and her bride, my beloved daughter-in-law, Saeda Aliyah! May their years together be full of joy, great in number, blessed in family and riches, and smiled on by the Lord-Queen, Ur-Malika. This I ask in the name of our ancient heritage, our Mother Qart, and our Venerated Republic. Hail."

It was truly an outstanding brazenry to make such a toast to Grassus' face, when he had just been railing at how shamefully un-Meronite and un-Tridevarian they still remained, but it left him no way to gainsay it without looking even more churlish. His face turned aubergine and his knuckles clenched white on the goblet, but he raised it, clinked it against Safiya's, and drank. Then there were more toasts and blessings, elaborate desserts, honey-cakes drizzled in pomegranate syrup and almond cookies dusted in powdered sugar, but Elemai couldn't focus. She had only drunk a little wine, but it was buzzing in her sleep-deprived, wrung-out head. She was hungry, but couldn't eat. She felt like she was floating slightly ajar to her own body, and a strong breeze would blow her away.

She twirled through the traditional dances with her father Ghassan and her brother Manizar, and then with Aliyah, feeling like a horse on show. It was all noise and blur and color, the smiling faces of people having a far better time than she was, and it felt like it would go on literally forever. At some point Grassus excused himself with stomach cramps, and nobody was sad to see him go. The musicians began to play the favorite Qartic wedding ballads and everyone looked set to settle in for a proper all-night party, but Elemai didn't think she could stand it.

She caught Aliyah's eye, and during the next round of Bahjoun circle-dancing, they managed to slip out into the hall without anyone noticing. Whenever they did, the guests might be aggrieved at being deprived of the fun of putting the couple to bed, but that was their burden to bear.

Elemai's head was reeling by the time they reached her chambers, which had been cleaned, aired, laid with flowers and candles, and overall prepared for the wedding night. But she sank onto the covers without noticing, roughly pulling off her veil and jewelry and scrubbing away the paint on her face. "S-sorry. I'm sure this wasn't how you saw our wedding going. I've not been myself today. I don't know why."

"It's all right." Aliyah paused, then perched next to her. "Do you... want to talk about it?"

"I don't know." Elemai let out a miserable, hiccupping giggle. "It's not your fault, I assure you. You look lovely, and you've been very kind. That pig Grassus – "

"Maybe he'll burst," Aliyah said, lightly but with an unmistakable dark intent. "That would be a suitable present, don't you think?"

"Indeed." Elemai wiped her eyes with her veil, leaving a dark smear of kohl on the rich scarlet silk. "Though it's not him, really. I just..."

She trailed off, and they sat in silence, listening to the muted revelry filtering through the floor from below. Then Elemai said, "Do you – would you like it back? The Ring?"

Aliyah's shadowed head lifted with a start. "After all that? When you wanted it so badly?"

"It will not surprise you that my mother ordered me to ask you for it." Elemai blew out a gusting breath. "There is more I hope to tell you one day, but that was the essence of it. I did want it, or at least I thought I did. I was so jealous in Yerussala, when you had it and I couldn't understand why, but this week, I... I don't know. My mother tried her best to prepare me, but maybe she failed, or I failed. I've felt absolutely terrible. It makes me into someone I don't like, and don't want to be. But I don't know how to stand up to my mother. Not like you."

"What?" Aliyah let out a laugh as dry as dust. "You think I really know how to stand up to her? I'm glad it looks like it, but – "

"It does." Elemai sighed again. "I'm sorry. I don't want to give the wretched thing back to you either, but one of us needs to have it. There's nobody else we can trust with it, and if Grassus catches wind of it – we heard how badly he wants to get out and go back to Merone – "

Aliyah considered that. "All right. I'll take it again, if you're sure. And I won't tell Safiya."

"Thank you." Elemai felt genuinely faint with relief. "Truly. I wonder if Diyab did indeed know what he was doing, giving it to you."

Aliyah looked as if she was going to say something else, but didn't. Another moment elapsed in dreamlike stillness. Then she cleared her throat. "Well. It is our wedding night."

"It is," Elemai agreed. "And regardless of all else, you doubtless wish to get out of that accursed clothing. I've been roasting for hours."

Aliyah's mouth quirked in a smile, and she nodded. Then she stood up and began to matter-of-factly strip, dress and veil falling to the floor as she removed the earrings, unwound the choker, and pulled out the pins that held her long black braids. Beneath the layers of stiff and heavy finery, she was clad in a simple linen shift; her body was long, lean, and angular, devoid of Elemai's softer and more generous feminine curves. There was something comforting about her unflinching pragmatism, neither expecting nor extending fuss or sentiment. Elemai was still something of a romantic at heart, had dreamed of her one true love sweeping her off her feet in a shower of flowers and rainbows and happy endings, but when it came down to it, there was a deeply reassuring aspect in treating it like any other business. It was less frightening, with less terror that it would catch afire and consume the world. From what Safiya had said, there was more than enough of that.

When Aliyah had undressed save for the shift, she returned to the bed and crawled onto it with a determined air. "We – we can, if you want. Or we can just go to sleep."

Indeed, Elemai was unsure whether to suggest that they fuck until they couldn't see straight, or just put this entire misbegotten day to rest and try again tomorrow. There was something to be said for both, and her eyes ventured down the slender column of Aliyah's neck to the deep vee of the shift, the angles of her collarbone and the shadow of her cleavage. Elemai traced a finger along Aliyah's cheek and under her chin, thumbing her lips open and leaning close to press their foreheads together, then their mouths. It was half a kiss and half a shared breath, its undemanding sweetness a much-needed balm, and Elemai sighed again, her other hand coming up to cup Aliyah's face. It lit a fire in her that she couldn't deny, and to judge from the way Aliyah's hand moved to tangle in Elemai's hair, it did the same for her. But just as Elemai was thinking that she could push through her exhaustion a while yet, she was forced to break off by a jaw-splitting yawn. "I'm sorry," she said again, feeling utterly inadequate. "I want to. I'm just – I'm tired. I'm so tired."

Aliyah regarded her, eyes dark and liquid as a starless sea, then nodded. She did not ask for elaborations or explanations, force Elemai to justify herself or wheedle otherwise; she simply accepted it, and that was that. She rolled away, Elemai likewise pulled off the rest of her clothes and jewels, and then they got back into bed, curling up on the pillows. Even if nothing else was presently in the offing, it was still nice to lie close like this, sharing warmth and small touches, linked fingers, beneath the comforting weight of the covers. The wind continued to howl outside, rain pattering on the screens. Well, then. Even if she had held the Ring of Tselmun for only a week and discovered that was quite enough, at least she had done something. This and the rest of it.

Elemai slept like the dead, and when she next opened her eyes, the room was full of pale-washed light and the rain had stopped. There was a warm hollow beside her in the bed, and Aliyah was gone, doubtless to gamely face the jokes and teasing about her first night as a married woman. Elemai should get up and give her a hand, but she couldn't move. She lay on her back, staring at the stippled shadows on the ceiling, until at last there was a knock on the door. "Saeda Elemai?"

She groaned. "What?"

"If you are awake, saeda, your mother wishes to speak with you."

Of course she did. Elemai rubbed a hand across her face, sat up, and swung her legs over the side. Not bothering with toilette, she padded barefoot to the door. "Lead on."

She expected to be escorted to the dining hall, the solarium, the study, but to her surprise – the matriarch rarely slept past dardiq, and was known for chiding those who did – the maid led her to her mother's private rooms. When Elemai stepped in, she was astonished and disquieted to see that Safiya was indeed still in bed, looking undeniably ill. Elemai whirled on the maidservant, once more feeling like a terrible eldest daughter. "What is this? If Saeda Safiya is not well, I should have been informed immediately!"

"Leave it," Safiya said, her voice hoarse but calm. "I wish to speak to my daughter alone."

When the servants had hurried out, Elemai took a seat at her mother's bedside, reaching convulsively for her hand. All her anger had evaporated; she felt like a small child, terrified at the reminder that a beloved parent was, in fact, mortal. "Amma, what's this? Are you – ?"

"I will recover." Safiya's lips twisted in a grim smile. "If I have not perished by now, I am not going to. The same cannot be said for poor Gaius Tullus Grassus."

"He is… no. Mother. No. The Governor-General is – he's *dead?*"

"Well." Safiya shrugged. "At least he'll get to go back to Merone this way, albeit in a box. Perhaps, as ever, he should have been more specific in what he wished for."

"No. He left with cramps, that was all. How can he – what?"

Safiya said nothing. Kept looking at her. Waiting.

"Mother." Elemai felt cold to the bone. "What did you do?"

Safiya kept waiting. Arched an eyebrow. As if it was, indeed, blindingly obvious.

"You poisoned him." Elemai put her face into both hands, but the words kept spilling out. "Malikallulah, you did it in front of everyone, didn't you? At the feast, with the goblet you gave him for the toast. And not only that, you put poison in your own cup, so you too would blamelessly fall afoul of whatever sickness gripped him. Did you – did you *know?!* That it would be *safe?!*"

"I did not set out to commit suicide, no." Safiya coughed, and Elemai, unsure whether to offer water or wrap her hands around her mother's throat and squeeze, sat in mulish silence. "I trusted that my dose would be unpleasant but not fatal – and as you see, it was, so no use in getting upset. As for Grassus, there is nothing to cast suspicion on anyone, much less me. It bears every appearance that he simply gorged one last time and his guts burst. I apologize for using your wedding, but that was the only chance to get to him directly. I could not waste it."

"Are you – if this happened after the empresses were already arrested on suspicion of Qartic collaboration – Coriolane won't just come here, he'll *invade* here, and good luck to us in – "

"Very well." Safiya smiled again. "I want him angry, determined for revenge, off his guard. We must not make the mistake of thinking that he is entirely unaware of our plans. I put nothing past him. But you have the Ring, don't you? You will be ready."

Elemai looked at her mother. Warred with love and hate, fear and admiration, the desire to be everything like her and nothing at all. Understanding that Safiya had worked her entire life to make Elemai into her perfect shadow, her obedient fetch, a woman uniquely suited to take on the awesome power that had been lost since Tselmun and Daeda alike. And she had tried, she had. But it had not been enough. It might never be. More than anything, that realization was the worst.

"Yes, Amma," Elemai said. "I am."

CHAPTER 19

IONIUS

It seemed inconceivable to most people that there could be anything worse than war, but that was an opinion only held among those who never had the misfortune of trying to *plan* a war. The problem grew exponentially worse when this task fell to the greatest conglomeration of idiots known to gods or men, all of whom happened by some cruel fate to be in the room with Ionius at this very moment. This was either his deserved penance for his multitude of recent sins, or a scathing indictment of how complacent and comfortable the Meronite military brain trust had gotten after four centuries of firmly enforced peace. Battles were a constant part of maintaining an empire, skirmishes and sieges and sharp punishments of disobedient provinces, but that was very different from a full-fledged war of conquest against a powerful and well-prepared enemy, and these absolute dickheads were seizing the opportunity to demonstrate that indeed, none of them had a fucking clue. Either that or they were competing to impress Coriolane with splendid fables of how many attacks they could launch and how many casualties they could cause, and it was all Ionius could do to hold his tongue. Finally, the Divine Emperor looked at him. "Well, General?"

"Saving your pardons, Majesty, it's…" Ionius tried to find a diplomatic way to say it, then decided that sometimes, indeed, a spade must be called a spade. "Absolute steaming horseshit."

Several high officials glared at him hotly, but Coriolane seemed amused. "Go on."

"As you wish, Majesty." Ionius folded his hands behind his back and tried to avoid working at the stiffness in his bad arm. He couldn't fathom why it was still so slow to heal, as if something was siphoning off the Immortals' resilience or otherwise interfering with their abilities, and it was his fault anyway, for almost cutting his own fucking hand off. At least it hadn't taken infection, but the stitches made an ugly sight, and it was prone to sharp pains like lightning whenever he moved too quickly. The thought occurred to him that this wasn't much state for leading a triumphant invasion, and then that it might be a blessing in disguise. Alone among this pack of geniuses, he was convinced that any war with Qin had the makings of a truly catastrophic mistake, and he did not understand why Coriolane was so set on pushing it forward. He had told the emperor the truth about how Gheslyn and Vestalia tried to have him killed in Sardarkhand, but stressed that it should *not* be used to declare war on Qin, that this conflict was still just avoidable and should be deescalated. And yet, while Coriolane could often be deaf to counsel he did not wish to hear, this was different. Worse. Just how much, Ionius was not sure, but he had to talk them around before it was too late.

"May I draw Their Excellencies' attention to a few facts." Ionius strode across the study, picked up the pointer, and indicated the wall map. "This – " he tapped the green-colored east – "is the Thearchate of Qin. You will note it covers far more territory than the Eternal City and the Lanuvian peninsula, which is the extent of our direct demesne. Indeed, Qin consists of not just the core dominion of Hang'i, the Jade City, but the outer provinces, some of which are very large. While Hang Zhai is the ultimate arbiter of the law and all major decisions must receive their approval, the provinces do have a certain degree of autonomy. They are primarily run from a yamen, or regional capital – like this one, Zin'qiang, in Tiberian Province. Local administration and military matters are devolved to the yamen magistrate, and they are empowered to act as they see fit in raising levies and taxes, issuing orders of muster, and other actions in the national defense. As long as they submit the proper paperwork in triplicate to the Ministry of War, of course."

A few of the officials glanced at each other, unsure if this was a joke and if so, if they should laugh. "Is there a point to this, slave?" one of them complained. "If we required a tedious lecture about the political organization of Qin, we would bring in a scholar from the Imperial Academy. Are you advising us on how to conquer the place or not?"

"I suggest, Excellency, that one cannot begin to think about how to conquer a place until one understands its basic realities. For example, can anyone tell me the difference between a Qiné yamen magistrate and a Meronite Governor-General in one of our own frontier provinces?"

The military brass looked at each other again, this time like naughty schoolboys who hadn't done their homework. Nobody was willing to raise their hand and submit to the humiliation of being called on, so Ionius did it for them. "A Meronite Governor-General only acts on orders from the Eternal City, directly implementing His Majesty's wishes without deviance or discrepancy, and personal initiative is severely frowned upon. A Qiné magistrate has the authority to make more decisions on his own, which offers flexibility in responding to threats, allocating resources and troops, and other critical tasks in war. Again in contrast to Merone, where the only authority is vested in His Majesty and every matter of import is decided by him alone, the Thearchate has a well-developed system of state administration, divided into three branches. The Secretariat drafts recommendations for law and policy, the Chancellery reviews it and advises the Thearch, and the Bureau of State implements it. The latter is split into six ministries – Justice, Personnel, Revenue, Rites, War, and Works – and there are numerous sub-ministries. Most prominent is the Censorate, which supervises and disciplines imperial officials and controls the Bureau of Information, formerly known as the Bureau of Propaganda. That being so – "

"General Ionius, this is outrageous." One of the members began to stand up. "If I didn't know better, I would suspect you were blaming Merone for being under the rightful rule of His Divine Majesty, and intimating that Qin's system is preferable. How long must we sit here and listen to such treasonous pabulum from a – "

"Commander Gregorius, please sit down." Coriolane raised a languid hand. "General?"

"Thank you, Majesty. But as Their Excellencies see fit to remind me repeatedly, I am only a slave." Ionius's mouth twisted. "How could I distinguish between systems of governance, or question Merone's authority? My point is this. When it comes to war, a nation that has the ability to respond in many facets, through many people, has the advantage over one that does not. Even with the assistance of the Thaumaturges to speed messages over long distances, if we demand that every major action is approved by His Majesty first, we will be at a critical disadvantage. The Qiné may outmatch us not due to justness of cause or greatness of knowledge, but because they can make the decision required in the moment. Not to mention, they have science and technology that we do not. The black powder, which all present will recall, is used to power guns, cannons, even hand weapons for their rank-and-file infantrymen. I have been assured that magic is always superior to such things, and perhaps it is true. But tell me, is every ordinary Meronite legionnaire a sorcerer? Because every ordinary Qiné soldier has a gun."

"You're just inventing things now, Servus," Commander Gregorius complained, bristling at the implicit slight on his legions. "Do you think we don't have experience in launching a shock-and-awe assault on a credulous bunch of natives? Either way, the guns will not be an issue."

"The Qiné are neither credulous nor natives. They are their own proud people, and despite many centuries of effort, they have never bowed to us and are not likely to start now. And while they study magic as an academic subject, they never rely on it to the exclusion of ordinary methods. For example, if the magistrates do require the approval of a superior, their ability to communicate with the Jade City is considerable. A yamen rider can reach Hang'i, even from the farthest northern reaches of Khaganate Province, in a week. If we are in the field and far from our centers of power, in deeply unfriendly territory – I have not yet touched on the question of supply lines, and the impossibility of ensuring the safe movement of provisions and personnel over the Tien Shen, especially in winter – how exactly do we plan to address even one of these problems?"

There was an unfriendly, uneasy silence. The generals and commanders looked at each other again. Coriolane tapped his fingers on the carved arms of his chair, his expression less amused than before. "So,

General Ionius," the Divine Emperor said tartly. "If you have all these objections, what indeed *is* your strategy for the success of this war?"

"Majesty, forgive me. At the moment, considering the fragility of the cause, and the serious challenges in even a modest expedition, I cannot in good conscience recommend that we proceed."

There was a crackling silence, as the brass exchanged aghast looks. None of them had ever dreamed of openly saying no to the emperor; if he ordered something done, they must find a way to do it. Simply telling him flat out that it was not feasible was not an option; they must press forward, they could not admit failure, they could not contradict him, regardless of what mischief it caused. Ionius was skating on very thin ice, but he held Coriolane's gaze. *Please, Majesty. I want to save you too.*

"Well," Coriolane said, his voice dangerously calm. "That is not a statement I would expect to hear from a general of your stature, my lord. So after I have held the ceremony, affixed my ring and seal to the Senate's solemn declaration of war, and informed our citizens and legions of their patriotic duty, I am to – what? Say it was all a mistake, swiftly squashed?"

"You are the Divine Emperor, Majesty. Whatever you say, your people will believe. You can spin a story of the terrible treachery of the Qiné, an attempt to lure us into a trap of deliberate destruction that by your wisdom alone we managed to escape – whatever you need. We could also send a secret ambassage to Hang'i and negotiate a more permanent settlement. This does not need to become a reckless calamity. We can still turn around now. Any longer, and it will be too late."

"I beg your pardon?" Gregorius spluttered. "You think the Divine Emperor, our holy and sovereign master, is creating a *reckless calamity?*"

"I say nothing of the sort, my lord. I only point out that events can spin out of control and take on a life of their own. His Majesty is wounded by the treachery of the empresses, understandably so, and wishes to be sure that all remains of their treason is stamped out. In that case, would it not be much better to direct our retribution against Qart-Hadesht? They are a far easier target, and they *have* done us wrong."

"Qart-Hadesht is another matter," Coriolane said irritably. "We speak now of Qin, and if you do not wish to assist us in that pursuit, you may be excused. Now, and later."

"Majesty, if you wish to relieve me of command in this – "

"If you so pusillanimously fail me before the eyes of my entire military leadership, Servus, it is the least of what you deserve," Coriolane snapped. "Commander Gregorius, you seem to be a man of proper spirit and priorities. What might you suggest?"

Gregorius preened, rising to his feet and clearing his throat. "Thank you, Majesty. I wish to point out that unlike the slave's small-minded assessment of the tactical situation, we have a number of options. For example, the splendid magical doors of the Thaumaturges. Haven't we all thought for some time that we should use them more extensively in war? If we simply insert our troops in various locations around the Thearchate, they can mount a lightning attack and decapitate these yamen magistrates before they know what hit them. Our legions will be marching on the Jade City within weeks, if not days. Then there is no need for supply lines or whatever else the Immortal was rattling on about. Qin will be yours, Majesty, as it was always meant to be."

Coriolane raised an eyebrow, scribbling on his notes. "Fascinating."

"Majesty." It felt ever more like a lost cause, but Ionius had to try. "We have indeed had that idea before. Grand Magister Kronus continues to refuse, to insist that it is dangerous to transport a large number of persons at once and repeatedly. And if so – "

"Grand Magister Kronus is a perverted old has-been who will say anything to preserve his own importance," Gregorius said dismissively; the irony was heard to make a small whistling noise as it escaped him. "I'll wager that those doors work just fine for as many people as we need, and he lies about it in order to make it seem more difficult than it actually is. If he won't agree, we should find some ambitious underling and promote them in his place. Where are the other Thaumaturges, by the way? How is it that we only ever speak with that old goat?"

It occurred to Ionius just then that there *was* at least one other Thaumaturge, or pseudo-Thaumaturge, currently in residence, but the downside was that they hated him. It might be only what he deserved, but this was too important to allow petty jealousies to get in the way. It was that knowledge which caused him to bite his tongue and hold his peace for the rest of the meeting. Then he rose to his feet, hurried out of the imperial apartments, and braced himself for a return visit to none other than his dear old friend, Julian Janovynich.

It was always a particular odyssey to reach the damned place, and by the time Ionius finally stepped into the soaring white atrium at the heart of the sorcerers' tower, the black doors circling silently to every side, he was breathing hard and once more troubled by the stabbing pains in his arm. He mulled the possibility of visiting the Corporalists and seeing if Saturnus could offer some amelioration. Though if he was out of favor with Coriolane, even temporarily, that made it more difficult. What the fuck was going *on,* anyway?

"Hello?" Ionius called. "Grand Magister Kronus? It is urgent."

No answer, which he had expected. Finally, since the whole point of the visit was to move past previous unfortunate animosities, he raised his voice. "Julian! Julian Kozharyev! I know you're here!"

Once more, it splintered away without answer, and he swore under his breath. Then at last, one of the doors opened and a lean dark-haired figure stepped through, looking about as delighted to behold Ionius as he would to be served a platter of live slugs at a feast. "You," Julian bit out. "Don't you have a lot of innocent people to slaughter somewhere?"

Ionius tried to decide if he deserved that, ignored it instead, and shook his head. "Never mind. I understand that you are still upset with me, but it is not something you must – "

"Oh no. Who would think I could have any reason to be angry?" Julian's black eyes snapped with fury. Ionius had hoped that the interim might have knocked some sense into him, but plainly the opposite was true. "Here, let me spell it out for you, using small words and simple concepts. You're a fucking Meronite war criminal who lied for weeks to get me to trust you and tell you things I never would if I knew who you really were, and you took advantage of it until the very last minute. If Kronus hadn't accidentally blown your cover, you would never tell me the truth, so don't pretend otherwise. Whatever you have to say for yourself now, I don't care. Get lost."

Ionius opened his mouth very wide, realized he looked undignified, and managed to shut it. Despite himself, he was grudgingly impressed at the fact that even when Julian *did* know his true identity, he spoke with the exact same fearlessness as before. It went without saying that Ionius could order a number of unpleasant repercussions for such talk — not that he planned to do so, as he did need the stubborn git to cooperate, but personal pride could not resist. "When you found me injured, I ordered you to go away. You were the one who insisted on helping."

"Yes, my mistake." Julian took another step. "Basic human decency isn't valued in Merone, especially nowadays. And considering what I heard about your little performance at Year End, I should have let you bleed out. First you accuse the empresses of treason and then you start a war with Qin, as if you haven't caused enough trouble. So — "

"Listen to me. *Listen* to me." Ionius raked a hand across his brutally short-cropped brown hair. "All right, I lied to you, I took advantage of your trust. As for the situation with the empresses — it is complicated, it is regrettable, and I wish that it did not happen. But as for Qin, I tried to set the record straight. Mellius Sanctus and the others have coaxed Coriolane into some misguided delusion that we should declare a holy war on the Thearchate, and so — "

"No, you listen to yourself." An even more scornful smile twisted Julian's lips. "You still want to fall back on the old chestnut that the emperor is always noble and giving and good, but he has the regrettable tendency of listening too much to his evil advisors. Do you really think anything in the Meronite Empire happens by accident, or without Coriolane's personal initiative and approval? If this war is going forward, it's because he wants it. Nobody else."

Considering that he had just been lecturing the entire first rank of military leadership about this very fact, it felt hypocritical of Ionius to even try to refute it. But he was not about to back down, and he let out a huff. "You're a common Ruthynian rebel who is lucky to be alive. Forgive me if I do not take your opinions as entirely trustworthy."

"How did you end up like this, anyway?" Julian's tone was still contemptuous, but laced with genuine curiosity. "You *are* a Kozhek, aren't you? From somewhere in Ruthynia, even if not Severolgrod? It's extremely naïve to claim that we should automatically be brothers-in-arms, but Kozheks and Vashemites have both suffered a great deal from the Ruthynians, not to mention the Meronites. Yes, I know Kozheks often kill or harass Vashemites just so they get to oppress *someone,* but you yourself don't have to. So you were a prisoner of war, I'm guessing? Taken from home when you were just a child, and brutally brainwashed into believing that your captors were glorious heroes?"

"Shut up." Ionius clenched his fists, and regretted it as his bad arm spasmed. "Just because I was born elsewhere does not mean that I am not a proper Meronite. I will do my duty."

"Clearly." Julian's flat dark gaze didn't waver, studying him with an uncompromising clarity that made Ionius want to flinch as if from the blinding light of the sun. "You know *all* the excuses."

"Look, you – " Ionius blew out a breath that was aggravated beyond endurance, reminding himself that if he walked out of here with nothing, all of Merone would be at risk. "Never mind. Believe me or not, but I am trying to stop the war against Qin before it starts, and I am the only one. That may make me a traitor, but so be it. Will you listen or not?"

At last, something other than disdain flickered in Julian's face, though it rose no further than the level of muted and noncommittal curiosity. He continued to stare at Ionius for another deeply unpleasant moment. Then he jerked his head, beckoning Ionius to follow him, and led the way through the door from which he had emerged. There was a brief strange ripple, and then they were standing in a magnificent high-ceilinged library, drenched in etheric golden light and crammed to the skies with books. Indeed, Ionius was tempted to point out that it was far preferable to the dank misery of the Castel, and it would behoove Julian to show a little gratitude for this felicitous change of circumstance, but he had a feeling it would instantly backfire on him. He didn't know how the Vashemite managed to win every argument, but it was vexing.

"Fine," Julian said, fixing him with a frigid stare. "You have one minute. Talk."

Concluding it best to seize the moment, Ionius launched into an explanation that he could only hope made sense. "Therefore," he finished, "I am here to learn more about the Thaumaturges' doors, and discourage Kronus from letting them be used for war. That does not guarantee it will be called off entirely, but marching an entire invasion force three thousand miles east, having to cross Parsivati and Indush and

Ahyun territory before it even gets in sniffing distance of Qin, would be well-nigh impossible. None of those countries are inclined to just let a Meronite army pass without trouble, and it would give the Thearchate as much time to prepare its defenses as it could possibly require. So if Kronus insists that the army cannot travel from here – "

Thus far, Julian had grudgingly listened, but at that, he scoffed. "You actually think the Grand Magister will bar the way, if he receives a direct order from Coriolane? You should hear that old ghoul talk. The world is all theoretical to him, a great game of power and influence and nothing to do with reality, and he loves to prove how clever he is about moving its pieces. So he'll change the doors as necessary, and if he does – "

"You realize that I am not asking Kronus, yes?" Ionius lifted his chin and stared into Julian's eyes. "You are the only other person who currently has access to all the Thaumaturges' knowledge and magic, and is resident in the tower. If you could cut them off – "

Julian shook his head. "You think, you *really* think I can do that? When both of us are well aware that I'm not an eminent scholar from Korolgrod, I'm a luckily reprieved prisoner who's dead as soon as they figure it out? Kronus is a sclerotic ancient lunatic who hasn't set foot in the real world for decades, and that's the only reason he still believes me. You think I'll risk my neck doing magic that I barely understand, to stand in the way of the Divine Emperor's precious holy war, for *nothing?* After you already lied to me, *comprehensively?*"

"I don't – " Ionius's hands tightened on the table. "I am not here because I have so many choices. As long as Coriolane is convinced that he cannot back down without losing face, this will only get worse. If you want to resist Merone's power, how else are you going to do it? If you truly believe in what you preach, isn't this your duty?"

Julian glared at him. "Oh, so you'll try to make me feel like I have an obligation to get the Meronites out of the mess they made themselves? After four hundred years or however long that bastard has been on the throne, you finally discover that he might *not* be a good thing? *Really?*"

"Julian – " Vata Korol, why was every single conversation with him a bear trap, a slap across the face, and an uncomfortable, undeniable truth all at once? Ionius tried to think what else to say, to impress the necessity of working together, but there was no getting around the fact that he himself had already poisoned the well. He was shocked to hear Julian openly call Coriolane a bastard in the very heart of Meronite power, and he wanted to chide him to be careful, you never knew who was listening. "You shouldn't," Ionius said. "Say such things about the emperor. You disagree with him, and you have that right, but he's still a great man."

Julian cocked his head. The sheer intensity of his gaze made Ionius want to look away, but he didn't. At last, Julian blew out another sigh, this one more exhausted than angry, and slid into the chair next to Ionius, their knees briefly brushing. "Do you really, genuinely think that? He's starting a pointless war that's going to get millions of people killed for literally no reason, but that's just a symptom of the fact that he's lived for four centuries and learned absolutely *nothing*. Someone with this much experience, more than anyone else in all of history, doesn't *have* to be a petty two-bit tyrant obsessed with avenging every tiny slight he ever suffered, who has the charm and charisma of an overboiled pudding and still acts like a petulant teenage boy. The most frustrating thing about you, Ilya or Ionius or whatever your real name is, is that I *know* you know better. I can see you struggling with it, but in the end, you always come to the answer that's been beaten into you. Is it because you really believe it, or you think your whole life would fall apart if you didn't?"

"I..." To his mortification, Ionius's voice was less than steady. "I didn't have a choice! Fine, yes, I was a slave, all right? I *am* a slave! I was five years old when the Meronite legions burned and sacked my village in Ruthynia – I don't remember the name, or anything else about it, or why it was attacked – and took me here, to the Eternal City! Are you going to blame me for learning what I had to learn, doing what I had to do, in order to survive? Because if so, you can just – "

He didn't know why he was so undone, what it was about Julian Janovynich that dug under his skin and pulled out the raw and bleeding truth, and he was so prepared for a blow or a shout or anything else in his life's endless litany of violence that when Julian reached out and put a hand over his, it scared him half to death. "Listen," Julian said. "What happened to you is a crime, and you're not responsible for it. But you're not a child now. You're a grown man, you're a general of the fucking

Immortals, you've risen into a position where you *are* responsible for what you believe and do. I know you're a slave, but you can make a different choice. You can be a different person. It's not too late."

"I have no life, no home, no family but Merone. Of course I must defend it."

"Well." Julian's voice was determinedly casual, and he didn't meet Ionius's eyes. "What if, hypothetically, you did have something else?"

There was another pause that threatened to devour the world. Ionius's mouth was dry, his cock was hard, he was imagining utterly fanciful things that he could never, ever have, and he did not want to hurt himself further by remembering it. Sharply, he pulled his hand out from under Julian's. "I do not. Nor will I ever. Regardless of how I came to this place, it is still who I am, where I owe allegiance and service, and I will never forswear my oath. Let me know if you are willing to assist, or not. Either way, it is nothing to me."

"Suit yourself." Julian's voice was again remotely, remorselessly cool, the moment of – vulnerability? Trust? Something else entirely? – snuffed out as if it had never been. "But let *me* just remind you that from now on, everything you do is who you are. You're the one who must kneel before your Mata Koroleva and know that in your heart of hearts. I wish you well of it."

The invocation of the Lady rocked Ionius onto his heels. He wanted to shout at Julian, to insist that a Vashemite who didn't believe in Her had no right to speak Her name, but it made no difference; the blow had been struck, and it was all he could do to pretend he did not feel it. He desperately needed to get away before his inner (and indeed, outer) turmoil became even more apparent. He rose to his feet, nodded once, and left without another word.

All the way back to his quarters, he tried to convince himself that the errand had not been a miserable failure, and at least he put the idea of cooperation in Julian's mind, for whatever fucking good it did. Ionius should have stayed longer and tried to talk him into it more vehemently, but arguing with Julian was often a lost cause. How dare that insolent rebel suggest that Ionius could *be* someone else, just like that, when it was massively and terribly impossible? Or even worse, if it *wasn't*?

Ionius was so distracted that when he finally reached his rooms, he realized that he had forgotten about his *other* ongoing headache. Now that he had so publicly taken Romola as his own, she had therefore been sent to live with him. That meant she was *always there*, a state of affairs which the fiercely solitary and private Ionius found nigh intolerable, and he had no idea what to do with a woman constantly hanging about. He didn't want her to keep trying to clean his things, but she was obviously convinced that she must make herself useful lest he revoke his protection, and when he stormed inside and found her daring to tidy the papers on his desk, his fragile patience snapped. "Get away! I don't care if you don't have the wits to read, I never told you to touch that!"

Romola jumped and dropped her dust-cloth. She folded her hands, eyes on the floor and shoulders hunched, the usual posture of a slave expecting punishment. "Yes, my lord. I apologize, my lord."

There was a pause. She was clearly waiting for him to continue scolding her, or even strike her – not with fear, but a resigned acceptance that was even more distasteful. When he took a step forward, she inhaled sharply and bit her lip, but didn't flinch or duck. Why should she, when she knew her role as well as he knew his own, when resistance was a self-evidently idiotic thing to do? There was nothing it changed and only suffering it caused, and anyone who suggested it did indeed sound like the greatest fool on the gods' green earth. It wasn't Romola he wanted to shout at, for proving his point. She had, hadn't she? She had.

"I'm very sorry, my lord," Romola squeaked, when he remained mute and motionless. "If there is anything else you wish – "

"No." Finally snapping out of it, he went to the desk and ensured that nothing was missing, which of course it wasn't. He stayed a moment longer, looking down at it, until – completely against his will, it wasn't what he meant at all and yet – he said, "Do you remember how you came here, Romola? Who your people are? Were you born in Merone?"

She gawked at him. That, to say the least, was a non sequitur when she was still bracing herself to be lambasted. Finally she said hesitantly, "I could not say, my lord. I – you are aware that I am Remade. I have no memories of who this body was, where it came from, or anything else. Some Remade are allowed to keep that knowledge, but I was… not."

It was a simple statement of fact, but just then, Ionius wondered if *Remade* could be applied in a far broader sense than he had ever realized. It wasn't just the corpses revivified with black magic, but those who had not yet died, all the still-living souls trapped in the maw of empire and slavery. They had been gulped down en masse and turned into walking ghosts, empty shells divorced from their kin, their memory, their roots, their ability to call on their own people's gods in their own people's tongue. Just like Ionius, it was drilled into them that it was the greatest honor to reach the highest echelons of their tormentor's society, and be able to inflict that unmaking, that categorical destruction, on their brethren in turn. The process of career advancement in the imperial army always went like that. The legions recruited from frontier provinces were never integrated; they were barracked strictly in their original national and linguistic groups, discouraged from socializing across those lines and often reminded of some bloody ethnic rivalry or barbarous local practice that had existed before the Meronites benevolently swept in to put an end to it. Of course, they never thought they were oppressing anyone. Instead, they were told that they were emissaries of freedom, civilization, enlightenment; they had been given a chance to transcend the limitations of their birth. When their dusty little hometowns were impoverished and dysfunctional, often thanks to the Meronites ransacking their wealth and destroying their social structures and traditional governments, of course they wanted to be *more*. Oleksii Holoroborodka in Sardarkhand might be only a dirt-poor peasant, but at least he knew what Ionius, with all his imperial glory and Immortal power, did not, and that was the simple truth of himself. *Who are you, what is your village, your family name? Who is your hetman?*

"Thank you, Romola," Ionius said curtly. "I do not require you to do any more work today. Here, take this."

He tossed her a golden aureus, which she caught in shock; it was plainly more money that she had ever touched. "My lord – !"

"Find Marcus Servus," Ionius ordered. It should, at least for now, keep the snooping little upstart distracted; he even seemed to be thinking of going over Ionius's head and asking Kronus himself if he was not allowed to pursue his precious fucking investigation. "Have him take you down into the city. Tell him that you have my permission to buy a new dress and cloak, and a pair of proper shoes. If there's leftover money, have a treat. Whatever looks good to you, I don't care."

Romola stared at him as if he had truly lost his mind. She kept standing there, plainly afraid that he was playing an especially sadistic trick — some masters might, after all — and would snatch the coin back and beat her senseless if she did. "Go," he said gruffly. "I mean it."

At last, Romola nodded, making an awkward half-curtsy. When she had scuttled away, he struggled to understand what the fuck he was doing now and what the fuck he planned to be doing in the future, whether short or long-term. It was plain that Julian's latest salvo had rattled him far more than was comfortable, and combined with his unfortunate honesty to Coriolane that put him in the emperor's bad graces, it was a very precarious place indeed. But what was he supposed to do? Return and meekly abase himself in front of those fucking freeborn Meronite warmongers, so convinced of their superiority to a mere Kozhek slave that they would light the world on fire for nothing? If only there was someone else who knew a damn thing. Who could do *something*.

The idea came to him almost abstractly, an impossibility more than anything, or a bad joke. Then all at once, he jerked up. It was doubtful that they wanted anything to do with him, but that could not stand in the way. Not when he might understand, at last, the smallest part. *You're a grown man, you're a general of the fucking Immortals, you've risen into a position where you are responsible for what you believe and do,* Julian's voice said. *From now on, everything you do is who you are.*

Ionius left his quarters, and went down to the Castel Sanctangel.

Of course, nobody would ever dream of questioning General Ionius's right to be there or what he wanted, and they hurried to let him in and pull their forelocks. The object of his visit was not the miserable dungeon where he and Julian had first struck up their — well, whatever it was, *you're a fucking Meronite war criminal who lied for weeks to get me to trust you and tell you things I never would if I knew who you really were* — but a private cell at the far end. It was sequestered from the other inmates and furnished in relative comfort, but for its current inhabitants, it was an unconscionably mortifying squalor that made a mockery of the lap of luxury where they lived until just a few weeks ago, when Ionius opened his mouth at the Year End fete. That might be a mistake he could not take back, but as with all else, it was too late.

"Your Majesties," Ionius said, when he unlocked the door and stepped inside. "Good day. I understand that I am not the visitor you wished to see, now or ever, but we must talk."

Gheslyn and Vestalia Aurea – clad in plain dresses, devoid of jewelry or makeup, their faces looking older than he had ever seen them – glared at him in heartfelt unison, their hatred filling the air like choking smoke. "Burn in hell, you rancid Dvadevarian sodomite," Vestalia informed him. "We have nothing to say to you, after what you did to us."

"Understandable." Ionius kept a keen eye on the surroundings; he doubted that their jailers would have left any sharp objects in easy reach, but it never paid to slack his vigilance. "Though you *did* try, nearly successfully, to murder me in Sardarkhand. So it was not unwarranted."

"Of course we tried to murder you in Sardarkhand, you insufferable buffoon." Gheslyn was the one to speak this time, spitting her words like daggers. "You, our husband's loyal lapdog, sniffing around in blind determination to thwart our plans, even if you had no notion why we did any of it? Have you guessed yet, or must we inform you?"

"Indeed." Ionius leaned against the wall. "I was hoping you would."

Gheslyn and Vestalia exchanged a look, momentarily thrown. It was Vestalia who recovered first. "Ah, yes. So you can obtain a full confession and have us fitted for nooses? How foolish do you think we *are?*"

"At the moment," Ionius said, "I have no intention of telling anyone – yes, including your husband – about anything that I might learn. If it interests you, I also found myself in his disfavor today, when I told him and the rest of the military that their grand scheme for a war on Qin was massively flawed and could not be carried out. All Coriolane did was insist on it even harder, and gave that halfwit Gregorius permission to plan – I use that word in the loosest possible sense – it instead. I do not think he is in his right mind, or if he is, he is acting according to a strategy that I can neither understand or countenance. I know that you have no reason to like or trust me, but if you want to finally achieve whatever it is that you lost everything for, you must tell me *why.*"

"Even if so," Gheslyn said scornfully, "you will rush to Coriolane and spill it into his lap. Yes, I heard you insist that you would not tell him, but I do not believe it for an instant. Besides, what are we supposed to do? Tell you, then meekly wait for the executioner? I think not."

"If you…" Ionius paused. What he was about to offer was treason by any imaginable metric, especially when it was his dramatic public accusation that had placed the women in their predicament, but never mind. "If you tell me what you did, and its truth is proved, I will find a way to get you out of here. Without His Majesty's consent, if I must."

Gheslyn opened and shut her mouth. Her subsequent sneer, while still plenty sharp, was not quite as acerbic as before. "You would not."

Ionius shrugged. "Very well. You have no interest in bargaining and no interest in saving yourselves. And forgive me if I am mistaken, but I don't see hordes of others storming down here to help you. It will grieve me to see you hang, but it is your choice. Good day."

He had turned to leave when Vestalia said loathingly, "Wait. Gods damn you, slave. *Wait.*"

Careful not to smile, Ionius turned back. "Yes, Your Majesty?"

"I will flay the flesh from your body and eat your heart in the marketplace," Vestalia informed him. "You are an upjumped and mud-stained piece of provincial arse-fucking shit who thinks he can arrogantly blackmail us, but it would behoove you to know the truth of your beloved Coriolane. Sit and listen, or go to hell. That is *your* choice."

"As you wish." Ionius shrugged again, took a seat, and looked at them expectantly. "Well?"

It took a moment, as they were still praying for his spontaneous combustion to occur on the spot, but when it did not, Gheslyn twisted her hands together and began to speak. Her claims were both simple and shocking. She informed him that the two of them, herself and Vestalia, had recently received a death sentence, as the magic used to sustain their existence was abruptly cut off and repurposed to Coriolane. That, however, was only the tip of the iceberg. The genocide in Brythanica, the war with Qin, and even the sickness that still ravaged Yerussala were all part of the plan. It was clear that neither Gheslyn nor Vestalia gave the least shit about any of these atrocities; in the ordinary course of things, they would have been perfectly happy for it to continue, and it was only the direct threat to their own position that impelled them to take action against Coriolane. For all that massive, indiscriminate, mindless death was used to fuel his life, fed into his failing immortality spells. It would buy him more time, more life, at the cost of absolutely everyone else. What was their duty, if not to sacrifice themselves for the glory of the Divine Emperor and the eternity of Merone?

As such, Gheslyn informed Ionius with savage satisfaction, she and Vestalia felt it entirely permissible to do anything they must in order to remove both Coriolane and his most loyal servants, especially Ionius himself. They thus set up the Qiné black-powder plot with exacting care, covering their tracks and going through intermediaries at every step, to purchase two dozen barrels (not three hundred) from the Jade City, then selected Sardarkhand as the scene of the crime. When Ionius pointed out that they could be blamed for starting the war with Qin and this was counterproductive to stopping Coriolane from doing it, Gheslyn scoffed. "It would serve those scheming yellow weasels only as they deserve, and we needed *someone* to take the blame. May I continue?"

"Yes," Ionius said with glacial courtesy. "Please."

Gheslyn glared at him, but did so. They selected Vadim Khovanyich to take the fall for similar reasons; he was a rich Vashemite living in Merone and had influential connections in Ruthynia, so he must be up to *something*. No, he didn't have anything to do with their plot, but they didn't care if he got killed, as he was surely guilty anyway. When all was in place, the empresses forged the letter announcing a meeting in Sardarkhand at the Feast of the Ancestors with a mysterious Qiné agent, and arranged for it to fall into Coriolane's hands. They knew him well enough to be sure that he would be hellbent on taking it from there, and lo and behold, he had. In short, Ionius was completely justified in thinking the message was flimsy and coincidental, that it framed Vadim Khovanyich just because he was a Vashemite, that it was simply copying Ruthynian kyrillic without understanding it, and everything else. He felt both vindicated and more furious than ever. He had *known,* he had been *right,* yet he still walked into the trap. And if the collective idiocracy had their way, they would again, and far worse.

"I'm sorry," Ionius said, when Gheslyn finally stopped talking. Of all the awful things she had said, he didn't know why this stuck out the most, but he felt it paramount to clarify. "Are you saying that the real reason His Majesty reopened the Holy City, why he encouraged pilgrims to travel there, was to gather them together in one place for ease of – of what? Unleashing a terrible plague and killing them more efficiently?"

"Yes." Gheslyn cracked a mirthless smile. "Come now, General. You didn't really think it was about religious feeling or pious sentiment? Yerussala was the test case, even before the crusade in Brythanica. He commissioned the Thaumaturges to create a sickness that resembles the Red Death, the most efficient killer of humans in history, and ordered it to be unleashed in the packed quarters of pilgrims, where an epidemic was inevitable and would not be unexpected. It was only by wiping out enough of them at once that he could generate a sufficient burst of magic to make a real difference for his health. It did seem to work. Small wonder that he and the Archpriest now intend to spread it even further."

"No." It was reflexive, a final insistence that as horrible as this was, it could not be *that* horrible – that Mellius Sanctus Sixtus, for all his willingness to sanction atrocities in the name of True Tridevarianism, would never agree to this, or didn't know. But he did, Ionius thought. Mellius did know, and he actively approved. *Coriolane Aureus IX is the greatest champion the True Tridevarian Church has ever had, and if we must condone temporary distasteful measures to keep him that way, so be it. Our blessed Divine Family will forgive any offenses we are forced to commit in the name of defending our monarch, our faith, our truth.*

Ionius felt frozen. He could not wrap his head around it – should he indeed return to Coriolane, get back into the emperor's good graces, and attempt to influence events behind the scenes, or was the only option that of outright rebellion? But how could he do that when everyone knew the story of General Spartekaius, the first and last Immortal to take up arms against his master and who paid a terrible price? They taught him as a cautionary tale, frightened servants and children with him, made sure that nobody ever forgot the agony and idiocy of defying Merone. They made changes after that, ensured the Corporalists could swiftly kill any Immortal who ever took ideas above his station, but they never did.

Not when, as Ionius himself had beaten into any number of cadets over the years, it was their holy duty to serve without question.

Just then, something else occurred to him, and he looked at his bad arm. The knowledge all the way back in Iscaria that something was wrong with him, the inexplicably slow recuperation of his injuries in Sardarkhand. *This is why. Coriolane is draining the Immortals too.*

Gheslyn must have seen the dawning realization on his face, and her own expression flashed with bitter triumph. "So, General," she said. "Do you understand what you must do?"

No. No, he *understood* nothing, even if he finally knew the truth. The world had transformed at the drop of a hat into a terrifying void, an absence of purpose or meaning, all his certainties ripped from him and turned to dust. Whatever came next, whatever he did or did not do, it would shape the destiny of Merone forever, and he had never asked for that, wanted it to be thrust away from him, wanted this to be a terrible dream. But it was all he had left, perhaps only what he deserved, and so he chose what he must. Silently, not looking at her, he nodded.

CHAPTER 20

JULIAN

JULIAN WAS ASLEEP WHEN THE BANGING ON HIS DOOR scared him nearly out of his fucking skin, not least since he logically assumed it was some outraged Meronite agent of the law who had finally uncovered the truth and was here to pulverize him. He dove out of bed and cast around for some sort of weapon, wondered if this was a cosmic lesson about how he should have translated the *Key of Tselmun* faster and therefore been able to attempt even the most basic of spells in his own defense, and briefly and indignantly took a moment to inform the relevant parties (whoever those might be) that he had done his best and if he died now, it would definitely never get finished. Then he stole across the room with makeshift truncheon in hand, concealed himself to one side of the door, took a deep breath, and pulled it open.

A large dark figure rushed in, Julian uttered a cry to stir the loins of his Vashemite-warrior ancestors in their dusty Yerussalan tombs, and took a swing. What happened next, however, did so at great speed and most unpleasantly for him; the truncheon was ripped from his fingers, his arm was twisted behind him, and he was slammed face-first into the rug. He also couldn't breathe, as his nose and mouth were pressed flat and there was a crushing weight on top of him. He made a useless flailing motion and uttered another cry, and the crushing abruptly leavened. A familiar voice growled, "Are you insane? What are you doing?!"

Oh no. This was it, this was the last straw and then some. Slowly, massaging his wrenched hand and wondering how hard it could be to murder one of the Meronite Empire's most feared commanders in cold blood, Julian sat up. It couldn't be, and yet, oh yes, it was. *Terrific.*

"General Ionius," he said, as frigidly as could possibly be considered polite (and even then, not by much). "May I dare to enquire what you're doing in my chambers at fucking midnight?"

Ionius glared at him. "You didn't need to attack me."

"What was I supposed to do? Wait to get killed?"

"You could, for example, ask who it was," Ionius snarled, clambering to his feet and dusting himself off with an air of utmost aggrievement. "Such actions are often customary when a person receives a visitor at an unexpected hour, and can save a great deal of confusion."

"You're literally the worst." Julian, still seated haughtily upon the floor, glared up at Ionius, which really didn't make him any less imposing and indeed might have had the opposite effect. "You're lecturing me about manners, when you're the one who burst into my room? Haven't you made it *repeatedly* clear that you want nothing to do with me?"

"Oh, is that how it is?" Even now, the absolutely humongous arsehole had the audacity to look offended. "Aren't you the one who called me a fucking Meronite war criminal?"

"Because you are a fucking Meronite war criminal." Julian climbed to his feet. "It's not that difficult. Keep up."

The expression on Ionius's face, even as childish as all this was, was deeply enjoyable. "Some day your mouth is going to get you murdered, Julian Janovynich. I only pray I am there to see it."

"You and half the world," Julian said flippantly, which was possibly an overstatement of just how many people he had managed to seriously piss off in his twenty-three short years of life and indeed, possibly wasn't. "But never mind. Why are you here?"

Ionius started to answer, then stopped. He paced like a caged tiger, his heavy boots wearing grooves into the rug, and despite the late hour, he was fully dressed and armed, a chill hanging around him that made it plain he had come from some secret errand in the winter dark. His eyes flicked around the room. At last he said, "Can we speak freely?"

"In here? Theoretically. Kronus said the Thaumaturges enchanted the tower so nobody else can eavesdrop on them, but I don't know if that means he himself can still hear us."

Ionius snorted. "Good. You're developing the appropriate level of skepticism you should have for that crazy old goat. But that is likewise irrelevant. You need to come with me. Now."

"Correction, I don't need to do shit, and especially not for you. It's late, and I want to get back into that comfortable bed I was just in, before you so rudely rousted me out of it."

Ionius's gaze flickered unwillingly toward said bed – as if he was remembering from personal experience, that night they spent together in it, that it was indeed quite comfortable. Just as Julian was set to properly enjoy his discomfiture, however, Ionius seized him roughly by the arm and marched him to the trunk. "Get dressed. I mean it."

The moment teetered on the brink of something indefinable, confrontation or calamity or another thing altogether. Their faces were quite close, enough for Julian to see the whites of Ionius's eyes, the strained expression and the slightly wild air. He could think of any number of clever gibes and take pleasure in doling them out, but if it came to blows, it had just been humiliatingly proven that he couldn't hold a candle against an Immortal, and he felt a reluctant mix of spite, curiosity, and concern. He knew that he was not among friends, that Ionius was the only person in Merone who knew his true identity and hadn't (well, yet) disclosed it, and if he was indeed the culprit who had let slip to Kronus about the presence of "Doctor Kozharyev" in the dungeons and the necessity of getting him out – well, Julian hadn't solved that one. It seemed to imply that Ionius did in fact care whether he lived or died, but he was a fucking Meronite etc. etc. It meant nothing.

Deciding to save his questions for a more opportune moment, Julian got dressed, gave Ionius an extra glare just for good measure, and folded his arms. "Now what?"

"I need to know what you've been working on, all this time. Some kind of magical project, yes? And it probably has something to do with the Ring of Tselmun. Down in the library?"

"*Why?* What in the Name of God is *going on?*"

"Can you just – " Ionius seemed to realize that the irony was enough to flatten the tower, but there was nothing for it. "Can you just trust me? For now?"

"No," Julian said mulishly. "Not really. But if I'm not getting rid of you, fine. Come on."

Leaving Ionius no chance to get the last word, he marched to the door, pulled it open, and descended the tower stairs. He was too aware of the general's glowering presence, the solid and ferocious weight of him at Julian's back, and reminded himself not to mistake it for safety or refuge. They reached the atrium and the library door, then passed inside, whereupon they had to go slowly until their eyes adjusted to the all-encompassing dark. By night, the shelves were transformed into monstrous creatures, spiderwebs of shadow strung between the tables and climbing the grilles and girders of the balconies, flooding the high windows with ink-black spills of paint and filling the air like something solid. Once more, Julian could swear he heard the eerie whispering that haunted the rotunda on the night he stumbled (literally) across Ionius. As if there was a whole multitude of ghosts in here, watching and waiting, and possibly not inclined to being interrupted.

Julian shivered, telling himself to put such overheated imaginings aside, and finally came to a halt at his worktable. As he had still not seen any other person in the tower except for Kronus – his meals simply appeared without any need for human intervention – he had grown slightly careless about putting the *Key of Tselmun* away at the end of the day, but something had made him do it tonight, and it took a moment for him to work the catches and clasps of its iron cage. Before he actually sprang it open, however, he hesitated. "If I tell you about this, you're not going to hit me over the head and run away with it, are you? Not that it would do you much good, but – "

"No." Ionius was plainly at the end of his patience and then some, and the word was gritted through his teeth. "No, I will not hit you over the head and run away with it."

"Good, because now you've promised." Julian waited a beat longer, both to annoy him and to be sure the reveal was appropriately dramatic, then touched the last hasp. "Here."

Ionius looked at the pile of grimy parchment with a furrowed brow. "Is this a joke?"

"It's the *Key of Tselmun*," Julian said, feeling slightly silly even as he did. "And according to Kronus, it's the original copy, the one that Tselmun himself wrote long ago in Yerussala. It's the basis for all the Thaumaturges' magic, and yet they never bothered to translate the whole thing, straight from the source. Kronus also claims there was a nasty protection spell on it that he only recently managed to break – which, knowing Tselmun, is certainly plausible. So that's what I've been doing. I'm not a genius, but at least I can read Old High Yerussalan."

"You've been translating this? For Kronus?"

"Something like that. Actually, I was planning to kill you with it, but I *was* quite angry."

"*Kill* me?" Ionius reared back. "Why?"

"We don't have time for a discussion on all the reasons you deserve it. Look, all right, there's something else you should know, though you probably already do. The Ring of Tselmun, the one magical artifact that can perform every spell in this book, is apparently not only very real, it's been found. And as Kronus told me on the first day he pulled me out of the Castel, the Meronites also know exactly where it is. It's in Qart-Hadesht. I have no idea how or why or when, but – "

"Qart-Hadesht." A look of horror so profound that Julian himself could feel it in his bones crossed Ionius's face. "And if a person needs both the Ring and the *Key* to unleash Tselmun's power – if Coriolane has the latter and will very soon have the former – "

"Aren't you Coriolane's favorite little errand-boy? Why would that bother you? I'm surprised you aren't handing this over right now."

"It's… complicated." Ionius struggled to recover his composure. "Coriolane is just about to leave on a state visit to Qart-Hadesht, and I know for a fact that he plans to punish them. A long story, something to do with the empresses. But if he's also planning to seize the Ring – "

"That…" Anything would be a resounding understatement, but this managed to be the most resounding of all. "Well, that's not good."

"No. No, it's not. We can't let him have both, and we should not let him even have one. You should destroy this right now."

"*Destroy* it?" Julian's nostrils flared. "This is a literally priceless piece of Vashemite heritage and history, and I should set fire to it because the Meronites, yet again, want to use it to fuck everyone over? I don't think I will, thanks. And again: *why do you care?* You've spent the Almighty only knows how long *eagerly* helping in that process, and now you're swooning in terror? If you want me to cooperate, you'll explain. *Now.*"

Ionius looked as if he would prefer to leap into a flaming pit of lava. He turned away, chewed his tongue, stood in absolute silence. Then, without looking back, he explained.

The longer it went on, the longer Julian hoped, against every shred of evidence to the contrary, that Ionius had suddenly developed a sense of humor, or a desire to pull a profoundly unfunny practical joke. When he finished, Julian had no idea how to react, whether he should treat it as a world-ending apocalypse or just the next step in the absolute batshittery that the Meronites had inflicted on everyone for far too long to get worked up about. Finally he said, "You're serious."

A muscle in Ionius's jaw leaped. "Yes."

"And you're going against your beloved emperor because of this?"

"I need to stop it, yes." Ionius's voice dropped to a growl, his eyes like ice. "When he comes to his senses, Coriolane will thank me."

"Because he's so known for his mercy and generosity to those who thwart his plans." Julian had hoped, however unrealistically, that Ionius had finally seen the light, but it was clear that even if some progress had been made, it was not nearly as much as would be necessary. (Necessary for what, he avoided speculating.) "I'm sure he'll pin a medal on you and grovel at your feet for saving him from committing a world-ending genocide, small mistake, total trifle. Which if you think about it, is not all that different from what you and the rest of the imperial army do anyway, destroying anyone and anything you want in order to preserve Coriolane's personal power and position. Do you realize that to stop him, you'll have to kill him, or make sure someone else kills him? Are you prepared to let that happen, or will you have a crisis of loyalty? *I'm* prepared to let that happen, but I'm a filthy rebel. You're a general. An *Immortal* general. You know what they did to Spartekaius."

"Yes." Ionius's face was even more of a mask. "I am well aware."

"So," Julian said. "You can't go halfway. Anything you try, the most mild defiance you make, will get you called Spartekaius no matter what, and subject to his fate. I would guess that talking to me right now, telling me the truth and trying to warn me, is over the line. If the emperor has lost it to this degree, there is no way to save him, no forgiveness that will ever be offered, so forget about doing it for that reason. Didn't you say that you're not healing properly because he's taking Immortal strength for himself, he's feeding off you and his wives and everyone else who's supposed to be important to him, who's supposed to be *special*? If so, what happens to the rest of us who *aren't*? He's a mad dog who needs to be put down, the end. Can you accept that, or not?"

The muscle in Ionius's jaw jumped again. "Even if so, what happens to the empire? Coriolane has no heir, no children, no successor of any kind. If he dies and nobody is there to pick up the pieces – the empresses would try, but it is unlikely they would be any different – "

"Because he did that on purpose. He made it this way, he made that choice." Julian reached out, gripped Ionius' obnoxiously broad shoulders, and shook him. "Look at me. Look at me, listen to me. Coriolane is a monster. He was a monster long before, and just like the empresses, you're only realizing it because now you're in danger too. Maybe if you *listened* to us when we tried to warn you – but you didn't. Because as long as that monstrosity was turned on someone else, and you had memorized all the arguments about why it was right, it didn't matter to you. But now it has to. It *has* to."

Ionius ducked backward, detaching himself from Julian's imploring grip. The silence grew and towered, remote and fathomless, broken only by the bodiless whispering. Then he said, "Here is what I intend to do. I will travel with Coriolane to Qart-Hadesht and allow him to believe I have seen the error of my ways, repented of my insubordination and returned to his side. I will therefore be in position, as soon as he finds the Ring of Tselmun, to take it and hide it, and return here. Then I will give it to you, and you will… do what needs to be done."

"What? You'll give it to me? For real? The *Ring of Tselmun?*"

"Are you not the noted expert, Doctor Kozharyev of Korolgrod?" Ionius's mouth curved into the ghost of a smile. "You the one reading the *Key* word for word and letter for letter, who admitted that you were planning to use it to kill me? I cannot kill Coriolane, not by my own hand. I know that, and for better or worse, it is so. We must not rely on me to do it. But you, Julian… you're brave. Braver than I will ever be. If anyone can see this to the end, it will be you, and I will give you every chance. You have no reason to trust me. But I pledge it nonetheless."

Julian's mouth was open, though he didn't recall doing so, or if there was anything he could possibly have intended to say to that. If he was clever, he would have demanded a notarized oath, a promise in blood, a magical bond, or anything else that required Ionius to offer something more substantial than just his word. But he didn't, and there was only one thing he wanted to do. He took a few steps forward, closing the space that Ionius had opened. Reached up, took the stupid idiot's stupid face in both hands, and kissed the ever-living stupid fuck out of him.

Ionius jerked as if he had been struck by lightning. For a moment, he seemed to be on the brink of tearing away, sprinting out of the library, and all the way to Qart-Hadesht. But he didn't, and his own hands came up and curled around Julian's back as carefully if he was made of porcelain, as if one swift motion or sudden reaction could shatter them. His mouth was rough and scratchy and still faintly cold, his lips parted, and all at once, he seized hold far more insistently, lifting Julian off his feet, swinging him around, and shoving him against the nearest bookshelf. Julian wrapped both arms around his neck, clawed at him, might have cursed at him, but couldn't get enough air to do it, and didn't care. Ionius kissed him again, downright savage, as if his next move might be to bend Julian over the table and fuck him senseless right there – Julian didn't mind if he did that either, though it would be hell to explain in the morning. The world remained utterly lost, nothing but this and them, until Ionius finally pulled away, chest heaving. "I – no."

Julian was breathing too hard to even attempt a response, and he swiped the back of his hand over his wet-bruised mouth. "No?"

"Not… no." Ionius shook his head, like a horse tormented by flies. "Neither of us are thinking clearly, especially not me. I apologize."

"*You* apologize? I was the one to do it first." Julian straightened up, reaching out for Ionius again, but he darted away, once more enforcing the distance between them. "And you can't pretend you haven't wanted to do that for a while. I have eyes, you know. And other things."

"It isn't..." Ionius forgot where he was going, and had to stop and start again. "It is beside the point," he said instead. "If nothing else, I hope it proves I am sincere in what I said about ensuring your success. But it will never be anything more, Julian. Not with us, not with me."

"Because you're convinced you'll die in the course of this attempt to stop Coriolane and it's no use thinking about your future, or you don't deserve it, or – "

"It is, indeed, none of your concern." Ionius's voice was once more turning cold, as if they had not been clutched together for dear life a scant few moments previously. "Do not try me. You have my word, I will bring the Ring to you as soon as I can. I hope you will be ready."

Once more, Julian started to answer, then stopped. "Of course."

"Thank you." Ionius straightened his cloak. "Coriolane plans to set sail with the imperial fleet at the end of this week. Preparations are in the final stage. We will first put in at the northern Gezereni port of Xandropolis, where he will inspect the Meronite troops and receive reports from the garrisons in the Iteru delta. Then we will turn west along the Madherian coast to Qart-Hadesht. Our visit comes at a delicate moment regardless of the Ring, as the local Governor-General has, it seems, finally eaten himself to death. The man was useless, but if His Majesty intends to put Qart-Hadesht under the same yoke as Gezeren, it might be best to have an opening for a more competent replacement. But never mind. While I'm gone, stay here. You will be safe."

"Yes," Julian said wryly. "In the haunted tower with the insane sorcerer. Snug as a bug."

"Safer than anywhere else, at least." Ionius's head lifted, and their eyes met. "I have one other request. You need not heed it, but – "

"What is it?"

"I..." Ionius looked as if this was somehow the most wrenching thing he had ventured yet. "I suspect that as an honorary Thaumaturge, you could gain access to the Corporalists' files. I want to know what happened to someone, and they are legally entitled to keep a copy of all records pertaining to slaves, in case they need to make use of them later.

It was a long time ago, so there might be nothing at all, but I have to know. Her name is – was – Tatyana. Tatyana Slavanyna Sazharyna."

Julian blinked. "Someone... important to you, I take it?"

"Yes. She was my sister. She was even younger than me, when we were stolen from our village. I have no idea what became of her. I might wish that I never looked. But slaves are a valuable commodity. There is usually paperwork for their buying and selling, or their transfer. If I just knew what her fate was, after all this time, perhaps I could have peace."

The hollow tone of his voice suggested that he greatly doubted it, and he looked away as if to hide the grief that still lingered close to the surface, raw and jagged as an unhealed bone. Though the risk of having it literally bitten off was not inconsiderable, Julian reached up and put his hand on Ionius's cheek. "All right. I'll look for her, at least, though you know I can't promise. If that was her name, then yours must be – "

"Ivan." It came out of somewhere deep and primal, rusty and disused, and took an incredible force of will for Ionius to spit it out. "Ivan Slavaynich Sazharyn. We are, as you say, Kozheks. I do not remember the name of my birthplace, or anything else about my family. My mother was killed in that raid. My father died the winter before, of typhus. The epidemic wiped out half our village. My mother thought we were reprieved, when it only took her husband and not her children. It did not take her long, when the Meronites came, to learn the truth."

"Fuck." Julian kept his hand where it was, and could feel the tension bubbling in every inch of Ionius's – Ivan's – body. "So what should I call you? Who do you want to be?"

"I don't know." Ionius, as he still plainly was, looked away. "Perhaps one day I will, even the slightest much as you. Farewell, Julian Janovynich. I hope we see each other soon."

"Farewell, Ivan Slavaynich. I hope the same."

Ionius nodded, simple and unpretentious. Then he stepped back, took Julian's hand from his cheek, and lifted it to his mouth, kissing it as if to pay his respects to a great lord. Let it drop, looked at him once more as if he was all the light and air and breath in the world, and went.

★★★★

IN THE NEXT FEW DAYS, Julian did his best not to dwell upon his heartbreak, if that was even the right word. It seemed overblown to describe it as such, considering that it involved a man who had hated his guts and vice versa until about five minutes ago, but it was persistent and painful enough that he had a hard time categorizing it as anything else. He heard that the imperial fleet had indeed weighed anchor with great pomp and ceremony, fifty ships of it, and set out south to Gezeren, so Ionius must in fact be gone. Julian pushed at the thought like a tongue at a sore tooth, testing it and turning it, reminding himself that it should only hurt as much as expected, and no more. After all, there was no way to be sure that Ionius hadn't been instantly overwhelmed by remorse at ever daring to go against the Divine Emperor, crumbled and confessed everything, and returned to Coriolane in truth. Julian was increasingly certain that if he just had enough *time,* he could get Ionius to properly turn, but he hadn't, and that was the thing. Everything hinged on the sincerity of that conviction, and there was nothing more he could do.

Instead, as had long been his habit, he threw himself ever more into his work. He was just reaching the point where his translation of the *Key* was taking on a life of its own, where he could understand most of a passage at first (well, second or third) glance, and have a deeper sense of how Tselmun's magic actually worked. It was undoubtedly fascinating, though anyone less devoted to bogglingly obscure linguistic and archaeological details would not have agreed. Fine, though. Somebody had to do it, and against all odds, that somebody was him.

The thing that kept nagging at Julian the most, however, was different. He tried to push it aside, to consider it merely as rhetoric or too abstract to be of real concern, but he couldn't ignore the fact that a great deal of this magic was built on the slaughter, enslavement, and destruction of jinnyeh. This was by no means limited to Tselmun, since he only followed the precedent of other ancient magicians – Ur-Arakkians, Assyranians, Hatetites, Babelonians. But the justifications reappeared consistently: jinnyeh were devious, sly, untrustworthy, deceitful, a race cast out from Odunai and the angels, but not so evil as to be fully fallen to Shaitan. It was for their benefit that wise Tselmun, beloved of the Lord, son of great Dayoud, put them in a bond of eternal servitude and obliged them to build monuments to the glory of Yerussala, temples and gardens and palaces, all intended to endure for millennia. The fact that the ancient Meronites invaded and burned the place to the ground within a few years of his death was, to say the least, an anticlimax. Then the Bhagrads turned up several centuries later and did it again, and that kicked off the Franketerrish and Teutyn wars. Seen from this perspective, it did not flatter anyone, whether Vashemite, Tridevarian, or Wahin. They all claimed that Yerussala was their most holy ground, theirs and theirs alone, and therefore should be razed into cinders sooner than letting their rivals have a single sniff.

Thus, most of what was commonly described as *Tselmun's* magic was, in Julian's reading, actually *jinnyeh* magic, even if Tselmun was the one to refine and use it to the most lasting effect. And when Tselmun was a young boy, they still had an extensive society of their own, just like humans. There were Seven Jinnyeh Kings, led by the High King, known as al-Madhab or the Golden One, and each ruled a vast and legendary magical city. At the age of twelve, Tselmun had visited the City of Iron, domain of Zawba'ah the Cyclone, the four-headed king of Khamsday, the planet Venua, the color green, and the metal iron, and found it splendid beyond all description. *It appears very near to Paradise,* Tselmun wrote. *Huge green mountains rise into a crystalline blue sky, thundering waterfalls spill over towering cliffs, and atop the shoulders of the tallest promontory, which rises far above the heaving jungle, sits an enormous walled city. Seven levels climb to the palace at the top; the streets rise in concentric circles and the buildings gleam in glass and gold and iron. Ziggurats, chaityas, towers, temples, domes, and spires compete for space; the jinnyeh are like magpies, traveling the world and stealing whichever innovations they favor, so the city is built according to no one single layout or fashion or period in time. Its almighty walls stand a hundred feet high, and its gates and crenels gleam with iron, a warning to any enemy who would think of straying where he did not belong, for the touch of iron is baneful to all jinnyeh save Zawba'ah's own descendants. It is girded with ravines too deep and dark and choked with trees to see the bottom, a massive citadel that looks still and silent as a dream, yet this is no* serene retreat or peaceful refuge. The Seven Kings are ambitious, restless, and constantly eager to increase their prestige at the expense of their rivals, and the walls bear the scars of ancient bombardments.

Julian was desperate to know where this splendid place actually *was*, but Tselmun was thin (perhaps deliberately so) on the details, saying only that from Yerussala, he had ridden on a flying carpet into a whirlwind, accompanied by his father King Dayoud and their palace guard. They spent the day in the City of Iron, had a personal audience with the terrifying King Zawba'ah and his court, established diplomatic relations between the two monarchs, and swore to treat each other as friends and allies. Yet when Tselmun came of age and inherited the throne, he had not kept to this treaty. Instead, he conquered the City of Iron and its fellows, and did so with such thoroughness that by the end of his reign, none of them were left. He had achieved this with the help of one jinnyeh in particular, previously a prominent general of the High King. The cause of its defection had been some scuffle, a minor dispute, where the Golden One did not give its proper due and it wanted revenge. Tselmun *was* correct that the jinnyeh quarreled fiercely, and this traitor general — considering what he was doing with Ionius, Julian couldn't help but feel the irony was rather *too* pointed — thought little of going over to Tselmun to get one up on its ex-master. When its race was reduced to nothing, their seven kings slain or permanently imprisoned, their seven splendid cities burned to ash, their greatest magic stolen and their greatest warriors enslaved, the general — it went by several names, but the one most used, the one Julian recognized from the halakhic texts — Khasmedeus regretted it bitterly, but it was too late. *I bound it to my Ring,* Tselmun wrote with satisfaction, *and made it my own, my servant, for as long as myself and my descendants should live. The scholars will argue over the tale of King Tselmun and Khasmedeus for generations, the mastery of human over jinnyeh, and the glory that attained to us when many felt it impossible, that those without magic should always be at the mercy of those with. But it is not so. I have proved it.*

Much as Julian wanted to deny it, this bore an undeniable echo of the Meronites' favorite strategy, their insistence that they had only come to deliver the barbarians from themselves; so had Tselmun, or so he claimed, when he destroyed the jinnyeh kingdoms and overthrew their rulers, cast their people into chains, and broke their backs in service of the greater good. He did not appear to have any reservations or regrets about it even by the time he got around to writing a paean to his own efforts in the *Key,* and while the halakhic tradition made good use of questioning whether he was justified in doing so, it rarely went so far as asking outright if this totally disqualified the rest of Tselmun's accomplishments. It was easy to identify brutality and hypocrisy among one's enemies, but when it was imbricated in one's own people, one's own history, it was much harder.

The more Julian read, therefore, the less he was sure if the Ring, for all the grief and misery and death it had caused, could actually undo the latest imperial iteration that was presently embodied in the Meronites. It was tempting to think that all they needed to do was to use it *right,* to kill the *right* people for the *right* reasons, not like the foolish zealots of the past. But it was far more than Tselmun and Yerussala, or Coriolane and Merone. It was the eternal and seemingly unbreakable cycle of what humans thought and did and destroyed all the time, over and over down the centuries, in different places and for different ideologies, but always to the same dreary bloody end. Even if Julian did get his hands on the Ring, if Ionius brought it back on bended knee and offered it up for his sole and sovereign use, was it actually a good idea? Did Julian truly want to take it and become Tselmun anew? A month ago, it would have been his only dream. Now, he was far from certain.

To distract himself, he decided to make a stab at fulfilling the other part of his bargain, though he experienced a qualm at the idea of setting foot outside the tower. He hadn't left since he was first extracted from the Castel, and with Ionius's warning upmost in his mind, it might be a very, very stupid idea. But that was hardly different from the rest of his misbegotten life, Ionius was the one who had asked him to do it, and Julian was getting bored; going to the library, back to his room, then back to the library, over and over, was the extent of his daily peregrinations. He wasn't sure if he was supposed to ask Kronus for permission to leave, but he would explain later.

He chose his moment carefully, on an evening when Kronus informed him that he would be occupied all night with a special divining session; evidently the movement of the stars after the bloodmoon of Year End provided all sorts of fodder for those who read the heavens. Hopefully this included the other Thaumaturges, though Julian had still not seen hide nor hair of them. Once the Grand Magister departed, Julian waited to be sure he wasn't coming back, then sprang into action.

It took several tries, opening various doors only to discover nothing on the far side (that or deeply creepy hallways of doom where he *definitely* didn't want to go), but he finally twigged that he had to focus intensely on where he planned to go and hold it consciously in his head. He didn't know if the door that finally worked was meant to go somewhere else and he was forcibly overriding it, or if all potential paths out of here were fluid and changeable, but that was far more experimental architectural ontology than he felt like doing, and at last, he managed to get it right. He pushed it open and stepped into the courtyard of the Eternal Palace, the sky mantled in late-winter dusk and the first hint of spring gauzing the wind. It was the first time he had felt fresh air and open space for months, and tears stung his eyes. He sniffed hard, glanced around, and braced himself; he was in no hurry to return to the Castel Sanctangel for all imaginable reasons. But he had promised.

Julian crossed the sprawling cobbled courtyard, adopting the casual stroll of someone who had every right to be there, until he reached the portcullis. When the guards asked his business, he gave them a coldly superior stare. "Grand Magister Saturnus is expecting me," he said; his Lanuvian was now roughly functional, if nothing else. "His Excellency will be dismayed if I am late."

They glanced at each other, then his Thaumaturge robes, and didn't argue. Julian hurried into the underground passage, following its damp twisting and turning until he reached yet another door. This time, it took a considerable amount of banging to produce an answer, in the form of a black-robed acolyte who was literally holding a bloody bone-saw, as if to frighten off any loitering dilettantes. "May I help you, Magister…?"

"Doctor Kozharyev," Julian said, far more confidently than he felt. "Is His Excellency Saturnus here? I was hoping to speak with him."

The saw-wielding underling looked put out at being interrupted from his busy schedule of hacking apart dead (or *hopefully* dead) people, but grudgingly agreed to enquire, and Julian did his best not to speculate on what sort of nightmare he was walking into. There was a foul, gamey smell like congealed blood and bad meat, and while nobody expected a bunch of necromancers to be entirely on the up-and-up, he was dearly hoping to get this over with and hurry back to the tower, which resembled a beacon of warmth and shelter by comparison. The air was cold enough to see his breath – no sense making things too toasty when trying to slow the rate of mortal decay, after all – and he blew on his hands. Surely it would not be a sin if he used the Ring to smite *this* lot, right? Look at them. They were bloody asking for it.

At last the acolyte returned and permitted that Julian could have ten minutes, no more, as the Grand Magister was very busy and normally not inclined to grant an audience to supplicants who turned up out of the blue. But he was willing to make an exception for a colleague, and when Julian stepped into Saturnus' surprisingly cozy office, the Grand Magister smiled in a sycophantic fashion. "So there's another of you, apart from that old miser Kronus? I was beginning to wonder."

"Yes, Excellency," Julian said deferentially. In the back of his head, he noticed that several people had now commented on the peculiar lack of other Thaumaturges, and this might be something to which he should pay attention. "Thank you for receiving me."

"Where's that accent from?" Saturnus cocked his head. "Ruthynia, I venture. Korolgrod?"

"Yes, Excellency. My Lanuvian is better than before, but still not perfect. If I misunderstand or must ask you to repeat yourself, please forgive me."

"And a Vashemite as well? Curious, very curious. I was under the impression that it was increasingly difficult for your people to participate in public life."

See, Julian reminded himself, this was why his cover story would never survive any scrutiny from someone who had been out in the world for even an instant. Still, he did his best to emulate Gavriel as he said, "My uncle Maxim is very wealthy. I find that it makes matters easier."

Saturnus chuckled. "It does, at that. Sit down, sit down. I can't deny, I've very much hoped to meet you, ever since I heard about this remarkable new translator that Kronus has been hoarding for himself. Do you happen to be familiar with ancient Gezereni hieratic scripts from the Middle Kingdom? There's plenty of work I would have for you, if so."

"I'm afraid not, Excellency. Would you be able to tell me anything about a slave named Tatyana Sazharyna? Taken from a small village in Ruthynia when she was very young, and brought here to the Eternal City, along with her brother."

The Grand Magister kept smiling, but his eyes turned still, watchful. After a moment he said, "Where did you hear that name?"

"It doesn't matter." Julian shrugged. "You are aware, of course, that we are entering a rather difficult period for Merone and the world, where loyalties may be compromised. If the Thaumaturges have an interest in ensuring that certain high-ranking military figures do not succumb to… misguided temptation, you would of course understand?"

Saturnus tapped his fingers together, then smiled again, with genuine amusement. "That is cold-blooded indeed, Doctor Kozharyev – it is Doctor Kozharyev, isn't it? Do you have any reason to suspect that General Ionius's commitment is anything less than steadfast?"

"Not at the moment," Julian said smoothly, "but you might have heard whispers of an unfortunate confrontation with His Majesty and other leadership during a recent strategy meeting. It is best to ensure that such sentiments are not given a chance to grow further, and that the ability exists to sharply counter them. With Tatyana, or otherwise."

"Clever." Saturnus even sounded as if he meant it. "Though your people are familiar with secretly plotting an enemy's destruction. If you will forgive the personal enquiry, do you have family back in Korolgrod? Anyone who would particularly notice if you failed to return?"

Julian kept smiling, though he felt it curdle on his lips. *What sort of fucking question is that, you murderous old pervert? Want to see if anyone would put up a fuss if you smothered me in my sleep and hauled my corpse down here to chop to bits?* "My family, yes. Many friends and students, scholars, others. I assure you, my absence could not possibly go unremarked."

"Of course. You must not suspect any impropriety, Doctor. It's only that we always have need for such expertise as your own, and I hope to convince you to extend your stay in the Eternal City. And forgive my bluntness, but a healthy young Vashemite male *is* a prime – "

"I beg your pardon," Julian said coolly, suddenly very eager to get out of this maniac's sight (and that of any other bone saw-wielding minions). "We were speaking of Tatyana Sazharyna."

Saturnus looked disappointed at being distracted from his evidently cherished wish to turn Julian into dog food, but got up and moved to his filing cabinet. He ruffled about, considered, then finally removed a folder. "I cannot lend this to you permanently, Doctor, but if you were to borrow it for a day or two, I would know nothing of it."

"Of course. You may rely on my utmost discretion, as I hope I may rely on yours." Heart pounding so hard that he was sure the horrible necromancer could hear it, Julian took the folder and slid it into his robes. It was time to go right now, before Saturnus could ask any more questions or start sharpening his dissection scalpel, and Julian smiled as obsequiously as he could. "I am most indebted. If you need a favor from the Thaumaturges, you must not hesitate to let us know."

With that, fearing to look back lest something pale and haunted follow him out, Julian made his exit, walking as fast as he dared without running. He wasn't sure how to return to the tower, aside from retracing his steps the same way he had come, and once more made a note to find out where it was actually located. He pushed open what he hoped very much was the same door in the courtyard wall, visualized the atrium waiting at the top of the stairs, and began to climb.

It felt much more difficult to enter than it had been to leave, like he was pushing through thick glue that grew colder and harder with every step. He kept clawing onward and upward, afraid to stop, even though it felt like the labor of Heraklion. If he was permanently locked out, it was what he deserved. Yet again, if only he was not a useless sodomite and could prevent himself from the world's most ill-advised infatuation, all of this could have been avoided. But alas.

Finally, by dint of sheer stubbornness – which indeed, was how he proceeded through most of life – Julian reached the top of the stairs, pushed open the door, and stepped into the atrium, whereupon he had to pause for breath. The file was burning a hole in his robes and he was overcome with the need to take it out and look, but he didn't dare to do so, not yet. Besides, while he could just barely speak and understand Lanuvian by this point, reading orthox was a far greater labor and would take time, and he didn't want to do it where there was the slightest chance of anyone catching him. He crossed the atrium, pushed open the door that led to his room, and –

He didn't look, he didn't think, he didn't assume it would do anything else than what it had always done, and that was his mistake. One moment there was the floor beneath his feet, and then there was nothing. He fell like a rock, as if he had simply stepped out of existence and into the ravening void. He did not know if he had chosen the wrong door, if they moved around, or if it was his punishment for forcing the way out. But it didn't matter. He didn't have the breath to scream, he couldn't remember the Shema or the Kadysh or anything, and then –

And then, impossibly, something did break his fall. It punched up out of the darkness like tangled tree roots, catching him brutally across the midriff and splaying his limbs out. He dangled there, desperately trying to see if there was anything below. Then his robes disentangled from what they were snagged on, he fell a few more feet, and hit the ground with a teeth-jarring thump.

Julian lay flat on his face, comprehensively winded and too stunned to move, not entirely sure he *wasn't* dead, and likewise convinced that he would start falling again at any moment. When the world seemed, for the moment, to settle back into its accustomed physics, he struggled to sit up and so nearly brained himself on the cage that stretched to every side, which had slowed him just enough to avoid a fatal impact. He couldn't tell what it was made of. When he staggered to his feet and fumbled at it, it felt porous, spongy and grainy – not like wood, more like polished ivory. And the knobs at the end almost looked like –

His hindbrain realized it a split second before his waking mind, and he ripped his hand away. Bones. This was all made of *bones,* and to judge from the size and shape of them, not just any bones. Human bones, assembled in a vast diagram of such precise lines and angles that it must be deliberate, fulfilling a particular intention and function. As Julian kept blinking, he finally grasped the layout. He had fallen into one segment of an enormous pentacle, and its tangles were thick and twisted like underbrush in the depths of a dark forest. He could possibly clamber out through the hole he had made by falling in, but he had not the faintest idea where he had ended up. Besides, to state the blindingly obvious, anyone who built a giant magical focus out of *human fucking bones* was not someone Julian wished to meet at any time, but especially not now. He could feel the power that coruscated in this place, awake and sentient and malevolent. He had to get out.

Julian tilted his head back, surveying the elaborate ossuary, and tried to assess the best route for climbing out. The pentacle was so huge that aside from extending a hundred feet horizontally, it rose ten or twelve feet vertically, constructed of intricate layers of bones – not just the big straight ones most convenient for building, whether the ulna, radius, and humerus from the arm or the femur and tibia from the leg, but smaller ones too. Metacarpals and metatarsals built links and chains, ribcages and spines served as bridges and connectors, and skulls opened their grinning jaws to bite down on ends and serve as anchors. Julian tried not to look as he climbed, but there was no way to ignore that it was everything he touched. He beetled over the interlocked branches, spotted the edge, descended as fast as he dared, and landed on the floor. If there was any way out aside from whatever he had fallen through, he needed to find it *now*. But there was a faintly metallic scent, his foot skidded in something liquid, and when he looked down, he realized that the giant bone pentacle wasn't the only horror. It needed runes to make it work, and there were runes aplenty, carved into the floor and painted in blood. Some of it was wet and red enough to be fresh.

It was only with a fittingly legendary effort that Julian kept himself from screaming aloud. He prepared to run, imploring his lucky stars (which, frankly, seemed to be falling down on the job quite a lot these days) that there was a way out, but then he heard the scrape and creak of an opening door, not far away. He froze, then dove out of sight. If someone was coming –

Someone was indeed coming, and even in the dimness, glimpsed between twisted jungles of bones, there was no doubt as to who. It was Grand Magister Kronus, and he was pulling a cart loaded with even more of them, giving off a fresh-washed nacreous sheen as if they had just been boiled in an acid bath or other special preparatory solution. If that meant they had recently belonged to a living person and needed to be stripped and cleaned, it was unclear, but as Kronus parked his bone-wagon next to the pentacle, rolled up his sleeves, and began to work, fitting the newcomers in alongside their peers with painstaking care, there could be no doubt of who was responsible for this ghastly structure in the first place. So much for that story about divining the heavens tonight. Either it was an outright lie, or it was only part of what he intended to do. It was unthinkable to imagine how many people had already died to build this thing, but as he crouched out of sight, still not daring to move a muscle, Julian could feel the horrified certainty forming in his head. *Ionius is right. Merone is slaughtering the world to perform black magic on an unprecedented scale, to ensure once and for all that Coriolane will never die. Are these the people the Thaumaturges killed in Yerussala, by creating the new Red Death? Or even –*

Something about that bit at his brain, a reminder of what Kronus said when Julian asked where the other Thaumaturges were. The Grand Magister had claimed first that they were solitary creatures unaccustomed to gatherings, then that they were studying in other libraries, and then that they had gone to Yerussala to observe the effects of the Ring of Tselmun's curse, but if that was a lie – if it *wasn't* the Ring's curse, and the Meronites needed as many sacrificial victims as possible – Saturnus being shocked to speak to a Thaumaturge who wasn't Kronus, the haunted whispering in the hall and library, the lack of anyone else in the tower except for Kronus and Julian themselves –

There are no other Thaumaturges. Kronus killed them all, either to take their power or to use their bones to build this atrocity – possibly both. This is what will happen to me, the instant I finish translating the Key *and my living use to him is done. Time for me to be sacrificed and my bones added to the pentacle. I'm the next one to die, trapped in here with the madman. And Ionius thought I would be* safe.

His foot must have slipped, or he must have lost his balance, made some small noise, because Kronus looked up with a jerk, eyes black and fathomless. "Who's there?"

Julian backpedaled as quickly and soundlessly as he could, heart hammering in his throat. He spotted a door just a few dozen yards away, though the question of where it led was something else entirely – it did, however, seem unlikely that it could be worse than here. Just then, however, something else occurred to him, and he patted himself down, looked around, and realized in abject horror that he had lost Tatyana Sazharyna's file in the fall. He had no idea where it was, he could not climb back in and look for it, and if Kronus found it here – if he put two and two together, and realized as well that the only person who could have told Julian that name was Ionius –

There was nothing for it. No other option. Julian had to get to the library. Had to get the *Key*. Had to do anything to save himself from being locked in a cursed tower with a monster until it was too late. Which indeed, it might already be.

"Who's there?" Kronus repeated. "Anyone?"

Julian waited in utter stillness until Kronus finally shook his head and returned to his macabre work. Then he turned around, took a final step clear of the boneyard, and ran like hell.

CHAPTER 21

ZADIA

"Please permit me, Saeda Mirazhel, to be the first to congratulate you on your new position. Of course, we grieve your brother, and hope that Blessed Ur-Malika will receive him into Paradise. But this is a moment of great importance, the beginning of a new era for Qart-Hadesht and the Adirim, the High House and the Low and all our people, and we must put aside our sorrow and focus on the chance to come together in a spirit of rebirth. Among the matters that await our deliberation, one in particular stands out. The Divine Emperor and the Meronite fleet have just set sail from Gezeren and will arrive in our beloved Mother Qart in a matter of days – at a time when our Governor-General has also come to a regrettable decease. As demonstrated, brothers and sisters, by the fact that we gather in our own Temple for the first time in years, cleansed at last of Grassus's filth and corruption, we have a short time to act according to our own wishes, without interference, and in the service of not just ourselves, but our children, our future, and our matrimony. The risks are no less, but the rewards are at last in sight. I pray our new Chairwoman will be bold enough to seize the moment. Saeda Mirazhel, do you wish to inaugurally address us, and gird our hearts and souls to action?"

The silence in the great hall after Safiya ur-Tasvashta finished speaking was depthless, charged with eagerness and anxiety alike. There was no denying the significance of the moment; every Meronite eagle had been carted away with the rest of Gaius Tullus Grassus's rubbish, and the banners that hung in their place were old and dusty, as they had been taken out of storage for the first time in far longer than just the late Governor-General's undistinguished tenure. The ancestral Qartic symbol – a silver crescent moon perpendicular to a golden sun, a flag that had not been raised in the Temple since the conquest of Coriolane II swept away the old republic – shone like the heavens, and the eyes of even the most pugnacious and contrarian Low House firebrands were suspiciously wet as they gazed at it. That, Zadia thought with something that felt dangerously like hope, was half the struggle. As long as people couldn't see it, they believed it was impossible. But when it became tangible, they wanted it. More than anything.

"Thank you, Saeda Safiya, for that gracious introduction and firm call to action." For the first time as the newly confirmed Chairwoman, Mirazhel bet Imra ur-Beireshta rose to her feet. She was clad in mourning whites, as were half the High House; Massasoum's funeral had ended only a few hours ago, and most of them had come straight here, after paying perfunctory respects to the rest of the Batu Beireshta at the wake. Zadia herself was wearing head-to-toe mourning, as it seemed wise both to do so and to prominently attend the funeral, and to judge from the way Safiya's eyes brimmed with silent pathos as the qahin recited the burial prayers over Massasoum's shrouded body, he might have been her own dearest friend or beloved family member. It was indeed a perfect performance. Too overwrought would be insincere; too unemotional would be suspicious. But she had carried herself in such a way as to make it impossible to doubt that she truly mourned his loss and could not have had anything to do with it. Which, of course, she had. Zadia was unclear on whether Safiya or Elemai had arranged the actual killing, but she knew it was one of them. The rest was beside the point.

Not, of course, that she disagreed. This was what it had all been for: to get Mirazhel standing there in her brother's place, Grassus dead and out of the way, the full Adirim sitting in a joint session in their own

Temple with their own flag above them, and Coriolane's visit imminent at a moment where it truly felt unthinkable that they could fail to finish the job. Zadia could not help the swell of pride that rose in her chest, outweighing any minor moral qualms at the methods necessary to accomplish it, as Mirazhel strode to the lectern and took Safiya's place, greeted by applause from across all the benches. It was exceedingly rare for the High and Low Houses to agree on anything; the former disdained the latter as common rabble-rousers always agitating the masses into mindless violence, while the latter cursed the former as elitist collaborators who didn't give a damn about the Meronite occupation so long as it was profitable, and consistently sabotaged any attempts to overthrow the foreign infidels. When it came to Massasoum, they had a point, which was why they were especially happy to see him gone. For a dangerous moment, Zadia allowed herself to imagine that it would be easier than they thought. If the Low House was already inclined to accept this proposal, the High House could hardly do any less. Indeed if they tried to stop it one more time, they might be flayed alive.

"Honored delegates of the Council of the Mighty," Mirazhel began. "Great families of the High House, esteemed servants of the Low House. We come together, as Saeda Safiya says, at a critical moment for our sovereignty and our chance to shape our own future. As she also says, the so-called Divine Emperor will soon arrive in Qart-Hadesht, for the first time in many years. What can we expect from such a momentous occasion – and more importantly, what must we plan? He will not be pleased that the Governor-General has finally met his end, even if by no fault of our own, and with the disturbing rumors about events in Brythanica, Qin, Yerussala, and beyond, we must face the fact that Coriolane does not come to offer us friendship or peace, or anything but a sword. I know there are those of you who still feel trepidation about opposing Merone, that the costs are too great and the benefits too little. My late brother Massasoum, Ur-Malika rest his soul, was one such person, and his hesitation was, to a point, understandable. But here we stand in our own Temple, under our own emblem, with no Gaius Tullius or other Meronite stooge desecrating this holy ground – can we hold back from acknowledging what this means? Can we turn a blind eye any longer? My colleagues of the High House have, it cannot be denied, often acted to safeguard their own fortunes and positions in life, rather than the weal of all our people and the sacred rights of the Low House. My brothers, my sisters, this is not just. It must end."

That got a roof-shaking roar of approval from the Low House benches, who had not heard words like that from a Chair in all of known history, and the High House grandees looked briefly stunned. Taking advantage of the surge of approbation, Mirazhel pressed onward, raising her voice. "At such a pivotal moment, the old constraints that stop us from doing what must be done can no longer be allowed to hold us back. For thousands of years, since the death of our great Queen Daeda, we have been forbidden to consort with or study the magic of the jinnyeh race, as if that was what was truly responsible for Daeda's downfall and not the treachery of Aeonius and the Meronites. But learning it was why Daeda rose so high, built our great city into the jewel of the desert, and made us a worthy rival to Lanuvium in the first place. It has been a very long time, yes, but the wheel of history has finally turned around again, and brought us to the place where once more embracing jinnyeh magic is our only hope of finishing, at last, the struggle for which Daeda gave her life. So, then. Saeda Safiya has one other thing to say to us."

At that, Mirazhel paused, looking back to Safiya, as an enthralled silence hung over the hall. It was, Zadia had to admit, a superlative speech, striking the perfect blend of progressive populism and traditional respect for the past, honoring patriotic heroes while questioning the lessons that had always been drawn from them, challenging the audience to take up the fight one more time and finally do everything necessary to win it. Mirazhel had only been Chairwoman for five minutes and when it came to the Low House, was clearly already the most popular in the entirety of the Adirim. Indeed, she had placed them expertly on the hook, and as Safiya rose to offer the final bait, Zadia felt something both thrill and terror. This had to work. It *had* to.

"Brothers and sisters," Safiya said. "High House and Low. May I present my eldest daughter and heiress, Elemai ur-Tasvashta. By blessed fortune and dedicated work, Elemai has become the bearer of a certain ring, and not just any ring. The Ring, no less, of Tselmun ben Dayoud."

In the absolute silence, broken only by shocked whispers, Zadia's daughter-in-law rose to her feet from where she was sitting in the first rank of benches – Aliyah was there as well, watching her wife ascend the steps – and joined her mother at the lectern. Elemai held up her hand, glimmering with gold. "It is true," she said. "Behold."

With that – everything hung on this, the moment they had planned and scripted with such blood-sweating intensity, late nights and tiny details – Elemai touched the Ring and spoke a crisp command. There was another fractional instant of silence, and then fire exploded from it in a vast, billowing sheet. It burned white, then blue, then green, then red, then purple, then black, and the giant figure that took shape in its blazing heart was twenty feet tall and wielding two enormous axes, shaking the earth. *"BEHOLD,"* it boomed, in the thunderous roar of a thousand voices at once – man and woman, young and old, crying and laughing, whispering and screaming. *"I AM KHASMEDEUS, ONCE THE GREATEST GENERAL OF THE GOLDEN ONE, HIGH KING OF THE JINNYEH, AND THEN THE GREATEST SERVANT OF TSELMUN BEN DAYOUD, KING OF YERUSSALA AND MASTER OF MY PEOPLE. SEE ME AND KNOW MY POWER. BOW BEFORE ME.* **BOW**.*"*

There was a final dumbstruck instant, and then a scraping of benches and rustling of robes as the entire Adirim, prudently, did as advised. Even the wealthiest and haughtiest members of the High House got down on the ground before the awesome and terrible apparition, its flames scouring the hall, magical and monstrous, *beautiful*. Even Zadia, who had known this was going to happen and just how much Khasmedeus had been threatened, bound, and commanded to make sure it did and said exactly this and nothing else, felt a tear slide down her cheek. If only she could believe the rest of the performance. Earlier, she had seen Elemai and Aliyah conferring in the corner, just before they went into the great hall, and unless Zadia was much mistaken, Aliyah had covertly slipped the Ring to Elemai – Elemai, who was supposed to have had it all along. She had evidently taken possession of it just before the wedding, in some transaction Zadia did not know about and was therefore powerless to prevent, and she did not object to the idea that Aliyah had stood up for herself and seized it back. But it meant the girls were conspiring in some way they had neglected to share with their mothers, and even if they were married now and it was good to have trust between them, Safiya dealt poorly with being cut out of the loop on crucial information. *Should I tell her?* Zadia wondered. *Or would it make everything worse? If my daughter and not hers is still the true holder of the Ring, is it not better for my family to keep it that way?*

At that, she checked herself. In this moment where all that mattered was their unity, above and over everything else, it was mean and petty to still be thinking of personal ambitions. But she should ask Aliyah, see if she could catch her before the girls returned to their new marital home, to best understand what sort of clandestine connivance might be afoot, and to ensure it did not catch her off guard. Then she could decide whether she needed to pass it on to Safiya. But with Coriolane on his way, and the imperial visit (and therefore *Inshamalikah*, the imperial assassination) mere days away, the last thing they could afford was a self-inflicted implosion at the critical moment. If Safiya was inclined to throw a fit, she would just have to wait. No matter what.

"So, then," Elemai shouted, over the roaring inferno. "Do you understand just what power we have in our grasp, what we can finally do? Free ourselves at long last from the Meronite yoke, avenge the humiliation of ourselves and our foremothers alike, and stand as a free nation, a venerated republic, once more? As the holy month of Qahyadin begins tomorrow, is that not the most blessed time to cast off the shackles and liberate ourselves in the name of our homeland, our ancestors, our Lord-Queen? I ask you not to bow, not to kneel as we have done for far too long, but to *stand*. To *rise,* and swear with me that Coriolane shall rue the day he thought he could once more lord over us. Do you? Do you so swear, my brothers, my sisters? Say it! Say it with me!"

Zadia climbed to her feet, one among many, a tide of nodding heads and shaking hands that pressed to hearts, mouths opening to echo the oath in a thunder that swept the Temple and made the columns quake. Safiya's gaze as she looked upon her daughter was undoubtedly proud, and well it should be; Elemai had played her part perfectly. But there was also a shrewdness, a suspicion, that something had transpired over which she did not have full control, and that was less to her taste. When the shouts and stamps finally died down and Khasmedeus dematerialized, Safiya swept to the lectern and made a gesture of dismissal. "Thank you, Saeda Elemai. Thank you, brothers and sisters, for understanding our task. We ask now that you make ready. You will know when the time is right. Wait wakefully."

With that, the session was dismissed, and the gathering collapsed into a riot of murmur and gossip. Some groups included both High and Low House members, which was likewise unusual; especially under Meronite rule, inter-Adirim solidarity was rare even in ordinary circumstances. Zadia noted that she was already thinking of "Meronite rule" as a bygone era, or at least something that was no longer germane to their glorious new Qartic dawn. It was difficult to say whether the bloodmoon on Year End had had the intended effect. Safiya and Zadia had done their best to draw attention to it, to insist it spoke of the downfall of tyrants and the coming of a splendid revolution, but the thing about such portents was that they were so slippery, so eager to bend this way and that; no matter how steadfastly you tried to confine it to one narrative, it could always spill into another. There were still those who feared that it presaged a red slaughter, and with the disturbing news that continued to trickle out of Yerussala, it seemed as if they might not be wrong. And for that matter, more and more as if Elemai and Aliyah were the only ones in the world to escape the great Holy City hajj with their lives. No matter how fortunate, it looked... opportune. For now, the Adirim was swept away on the narcotic of heart-stirring patriotism and magical spectacle, but Zadia would be a fool to assume that this euphoria would last forever. Poor Massasoum, cold in his grave so soon after Grassus, a scion of one of their greatest families. If this went wrong –

Zadia shook her head and went to greet her daughter and daughter-in-law, complimenting Elemai on the excellent reveal and then turning to Aliyah. "Well done, habibta. Very well done indeed. I hope you are finding married life to your taste?"

"I – er – I think so, Amma, yes." Aliyah coughed, cheeks turning slightly pink. "We have managed. We'll see you, Abba, Amma Noora, and Alja tonight for the first tarawih of Qahyadin?"

"We will," Zadia promised. "And for iftar tomorrow, I hope?"

"I intend to host it at our villa, yes," Safiya said, before Aliyah could answer. "Elemai, may I have a word? Just briefly, please."

Elemai looked startled, but obediently followed her mother away, as Zadia tried to keep an eye on them without being obvious. She exchanged a few more words of polite conversation with her daughter and Saeda Mirazhel, but she couldn't help but notice that Safiya looked displeased, and Elemai defensive. So, then. Perhaps that earlier exchange of the Ring had not been as unnoticed as either Elemai or Zadia thought, and Safiya, never one to miss anything that might threaten her schemes, demanded a prompt explanation. Elemai appeared to be demurring, insisting this was not the place for such a discussion, though Zadia couldn't hear them to be sure. When the ur-Tasvashtas returned to the group, she said, "Is there anything wrong, saedas?"

"No. Nothing." Elemai's cheeks were flushed, but she set her jaw. "My mother only wanted to be clear on a few things, that was all. Aliyah, we should be on our way, yes?"

"Yes." Aliyah turned to Zadia. "I will see you at mahqasa, Amma. May Ur-Malika smile upon us all and guard us in this endeavor."

And that, Zadia thought as she watched the girls walk away arm-in-arm, leaving the Temple for their own palanquin, their own house, Aliyah suddenly so grown up and gone from her in what felt like overnight, and she was still not sure if it did not grieve her greatly, if it was all too soon, too *soon*. That, indeed, was the question, and yet when she got down on her knees in prayer, when she asked the Most High for an answer over and over, all she heard was silence.

****

CORIOLANE AUREUS IX, DIVINE EMPEROR OF MERONE, supreme sovereign of Qart-Hadesht since the distant days of his ancestor's conquest, arrived at the end of the week, on the Wahini holy day of Khamsday, which might be a pointed commentary on what they should hold the most sacred or merely reflected the fact that the winds and waters from Xandropolis had been favorable. Indeed, the spring weather was warm but not too hot, the sky a hammered dome of cerulean blue, the walls and towers fresh-washed in white, gold and brass polished to a perfect shine and palm trees waving in the breeze, as trumpets boomed across the Old Harbor and the fifty ships swept in: only a small part of the imperial navy's power, but more than enough to dazzle and overawe. Coriolane's flagship was a massive triple-masted octireme, running a total of sixteen hundred oars on two decks per side, and the cut, carve, and splash of its paddles in exactly synchronized time was a remarkable sight even to those who hated everything it stood for. It was escorted by septiremes and quinqueremes that bristled with Immortals and legionnaires, and quadriremes and triremes that served as supply tenders and fast-attack frigates. The Meronite eagle flew from every vessel, soaring and snapping in the sun, and Zadia wondered how long it would take the Divine Emperor to notice the lack of matching heraldry atop the Temple. It depended on how much he wanted to play the gracious lord. She *had* met him before, as a young girl, but that was a long time ago, and she forced down the unease in her stomach. They were ready.

After another extended fanfare, the glittering figure of the emperor, recognizable even from this distance, stepped from the flagship and onto a trireme, which raised its oars in salute at having the imperial personage aboard and then clipped for the shore. The Qartic dignitaries drew up and stood at attention – even if they *were* planning to kill him, that was no excuse for bad manners – and then with a final flourish and blatting of trumpets, Coriolane stepped onto the quay, where a lavish purple-velvet carpet had been unrolled so as not to sully the imperial foot with common (and foreign) wood. He processed forth under the shade of an ornate golden canopy hoisted by four slaves, reached Mirazhel where she stood at the head of the delegation, and studied her up and down. Then he extended his signet-ringed hand. "Good day... my lady?"

"Saeda Mirazhel bet Imra ur-Beireshta, Chairwoman of the High House of the Adirim, at your service, my lord." Mirazhel took his hand and pressed an exquisitely correct kiss to the ring, while Coriolane's expression soured at the fact that she had not called him *Your Divine Majesty*. "It is a very long time since we have been afforded the pleasure of receiving your honored person in your territory of Qart-Hadesht. We hope that you find your visit to be most enjoyable."

"I'm sure I shall, yes." Coriolane turned to Safiya and Zadia, and Zadia fought a shiver at the fact that indeed, he looked the same as when she traveled to the Eternal City with her mother forty years ago. She knew, of course, that he lived forever (well, until next week), but it was still startling. Yet she remembered him as far more prepossessing, tall and golden and handsome enough to cause even a loyal Qartic daughter to briefly come over starstruck. Now he was jowly, haggard, and bloodshot, had put on a notable amount of weight, and would not be overawing anybody. It was jarring, seeing the way the world groveled for a man proclaimed the greatest, the wisest, the most accomplished, the most important, and then he was... this.

As Coriolane moved up the docks, accepting the greeting and genuflecting with a bored expression, Zadia took a closer look at his immediate entourage. As expected, the empresses weren't there; the shocking news of their arrest and imprisonment in the Castel had recently reached Qart-Hadesht, but she wasn't sure whether to let on that they knew. There was a pretty young woman who must be Coriolane's new pet courtesan, taking on the duty of hostess and dripping in borrowed jewelry; senior senators and praetors and other functionaries; a few high-ranking cardinals of the True Tridevarian Church, overheating in their heavy crimson robes, and two dozen Immortals. They were led by a harshly handsome man with the hard-chiseled look of a Kozhek, who had grey eyes and a bandage on his right arm. Unless Zadia missed her guess, *that* was General Ionius Servus Eternus, Coriolane's favorite, best known for single-handedly slaughtering the entire garrison in Sciatello, a city in the south of the Lanuvian peninsula that, around a decade ago, turned briefly (and wildly unwisely) seditious. The emperor sent Ionius in there alone, against five thousand rebels, and he came back untouched, leaving five thousand corpses in his wake. Malikallulah, what was *that* monster doing here? Just as a matter of form to ensure his master's safety, or to add the Curse of Qart-Hadesht to his long list of atrocities?

Uneasy, Zadia turned away and plucked at Safiya's sleeve. "Look who Coriolane brought with him. We need to be careful."

"Indeed." Safiya studied the Immortals with a cool expression. "Well, no saying that we can't make it two for the price of one, is there?"

Zadia thought that not just advisable but necessary, since Ionius would lay waste to the city if they kept him alive after disposing of his imperial master, but it was much too dangerous to even hint at it. She gave Safiya a warning look, Safiya nodded, and the entire delegation repaired to the reception in the Temple, which was an ignominious but necessary sacrifice so soon after reclaiming it from Grassus. Because it was daylight in Qahyadin, none of the Qartics were eating or drinking, though they set out plenty of food and wine for their Meronite guests. Safiya had suggested that they poison it, but they needed more care, more misdirection, more knowledge, before they made their move. Besides, if all it took was a pinch of aconite to dispose of Coriolane, it would be done long since, and a botched attempt was worst of all.

Therefore, the conspirators continued to make their rounds, glad-handing and pressing the flesh as if nothing was wrong. Which for now, at least, it wasn't. But it was good to have an obvious justification to keep a clear head while encouraging the Meronites to imbibe, which they did with gusto. All except for General Ionius, who sipped half a cup of wine and then put it down, his gaze never wavering, cold and watchful. When the current brought them together once more, Safiya murmured, "We need to distract that one. Get him thinking about the dissolute pleasures of Qart-Hadesht, and not his duties to the emperor. I'll attend to it."

Zadia nodded, they parted again, and the next time she looked over, there was a gorgeous dancing girl in flowing silks, caressing and grinding herself against the general – who jerked away and gave this bounteous beauty a look as if she was a dead rat. That was interesting, but not very helpful, and Zadia had to think about what else to try. That bandage, now. Normally Ionius would heal too quickly for it to be an issue, but the stilted, slow way he used his right arm made plain that it was a weak spot. If only they could be sure of how to exploit it, or at least –

"So, my lady," a voice said. "Do I recall you correctly as Amarasha ur-Namasqa's little slip of a thing? I daresay that if so, you've changed a great deal, but it *has* been forty years."

Zadia briefly blanked, didn't process, and then spun around to realize that it was, in fact, the guest of honor himself. Coriolane had had several cups of wine, turning his jowls even more florid, but his eyes were alert and sharp. Mortified that she had let her vigilance slip enough for him to sneak up on her, she bowed her head and dropped an especially deep curtsy. "Your Majesty."

"Rise." Coriolane waved a languid hand. "Though I'm glad one of you recalls my proper title, after that strange woman earlier. *Is* she a woman? I confess, I am not entirely sure."

"Saeda Mirazhel is a woman and the Chair of the High House of the Adirim, yes. I am sure she intended no disrespect."

Coriolane's lips went thin, suggesting that he did not share that certainty, but he shrugged. "Indeed, I have not come to Qart-Hadesht in many years. It is understandable if you have failed in the proper rituals – my fault for letting them lapse, yes, but also the fault of the city in forgetting its master. An oversight to be remedied in multiple fashions, I hope. How is your mother?"

"My mother is dead, Your Majesty. It was several years ago."

"Oh, yes. Of course." When one was immortal, perhaps it was difficult to recall that was a thing other unfortunates did. "My sympathies. We were… friends, you know. Her and I."

"What?" Amarasha had always been such a steadfast supporter of Qartic independence, the cause she had drilled into Zadia from childhood, that it seemed impossible for her to be on anything more than the most remotely cordial terms with their imperial oppressor, and even then only insofar as political reality demanded. "I – I am afraid I do not know what you mean, Majesty."

"Is it so unthinkable?" Coriolane took another sip of wine. "She only brought you on a few visits to the Eternal City, but those were not her only ones. Your mother was a lovely woman, Lady Zadia, and far more flexible in private than her public rhetoric might suggest. I did not approve that she did it, to be sure, but it did keep things fresh, and prevent anyone from suspecting us."

"I *beg* your – " Even drunk as the emperor was, Zadia would not stand for this slander. "My mother was faithfully married to my fathers and mothers, an observant keeper of the Hierophant's commandments, a devoted servant of her people, her faith, and her country. She taught me everything I know. She could not have been – "

"My lover?" Coriolane seemed to find this funny. "Do you want me to describe her body in detail, Lady Zadia? Her intimate parts? Will that convince you?"

"I – " Zadia felt like the floor was crumbling out from beneath her. She had not drunk *that* much, and she couldn't figure out why he would choose this, of all things, to lie to her about. Of course you never knew your parents as well as you thought, had to accept there were some things you had no right to learn, but this – suggesting that Amarasha was a brazen hypocrite even as she taught her daughter to oppose the Meronites so steadfastly, the cause to which Zadia was giving her life, only to be secretly bedding the whole time with Coriolane – *Coriolane,* their most hated enemy, *Qart-Hadesht's* most hated enemy –

"Ah," Coriolane said, studying her horrified expression. "She did not tell you. It is especially ironic, then. But as my wives and concubines have always known, there are no exceptions. I did love her, in my way, but your mother was no different from all the others, or so I thought. To find out that she deceived me in this fashion for so long – well, she was clever, and I could not be certain until very recently. Now I am, and, well. My lady, if you could follow me, please?"

Too numb to react, Zadia nodded and trailed after him into a small side chamber, where Safiya, Elemai, Aliyah, Noora, and Khaldun were waiting. They had plainly been herded there by the four Immortals standing guard, including General Ionius, and as the emperor stepped inside, the general glanced up. "I believe this is all of them, my lord."

"Good, good." Coriolane let the curtain drop and beckoned Zadia to join the others; petrified with fear, she did so, scuttling to Khaldun and Noora and holding them tight. "Very well, no need to drag this out. Which of you has the Ring of Tselmun?"

A stunned, crackling silence reigned over the room. Safiya looked almost comically blank, then clasped her hands entreatingly. "Your Majesty, I don't understand what you're – "

"You may cease the worthy turn as a thespian, Lady Safiya. We are fully aware of what you found in Yerussala, and which against all good sense and pragmatic loyalty, you failed to hand over to me. Grand Magister Kronus was quite specific." Coriolane sized them up, taking his time, as the Immortals took a collective step inward, forcing them into a tighter circle. "I am also aware that you intended to use it to make an attempt on my life. Do you hear that out there? All those revelers, all those innocent people? If you struggle or make a sound or utter another lie when I ask you for the truth, every single one of them will die. So, then. Who has the Ring of Tselmun?"

Silent, panicked glances were exchanged, but nobody spoke. Safiya looked at Elemai, then straight at Aliyah, and Coriolane honed in on her. "Lady… Aliyah, was it? Do you wish to share?"

The moment hung frozen. Then Aliyah lifted her chin. "Yes. It is me. I have it."

"No," Zadia said, the words breaking out of her like a bursting dam. "Aliyah, habibta, don't. Don't. No, it's not you, it's – it's someone else. Saeda Safiya, didn't you have something to – ?"

Safiya looked at her. She didn't say a word. She was, Zadia realized just then, fully prepared to let Aliyah sacrifice herself so nobly and opportunely, the accidental Ringbearer Safiya had never wanted in the first place and who was nothing but an obstacle to her carefully laid plans. Zadia had not said anything, let Safiya continue her meddling with Elemai and the Ring and trying to take it back for the ur-Tasvashtas out of a conviction that now was not the time for minor rivalries, and Safiya had not returned the favor – indeed, *not returned it* as drastically as could be imagined. This was too soon, far too soon, they weren't ready, they hadn't prepared to make their on the first day – indeed, the first *hour* – of Coriolane's arrival, but that was their fatal mistake. He knew everything and he was striking at once, to leave them no time to do it. Zadia wrenched Khaldun's hand, trying to get free, but her husband hissed at her frantically, jerking his head at the sounds of the reception beyond. The entire Adirim and their families, anyone in the city who meant anything, were inside the Temple. If Coriolane turned the Immortals loose on them –

"Thank you for your honesty, Lady Aliyah." Coriolane gestured. "General."

Ionius Servus Eternus stepped forward. He sized Aliyah up. Then he raised his left hand and hit her hard in the stomach, knocking her to the ground. While Aliyah was still wheezing and spitting, Ionius reached around her neck, pulled out the chain on which she was wearing the Ring, and tucked it into his cloak. "I'll keep this safe, Majesty."

"Good." Coriolane beckoned to two of the Immortals. "Take the girl away. Keep her on my flagship until we depart. She will face punishment in Merone as she deserves."

They stepped forward in equally precise time, tied the unresisting Aliyah's wrists and ankles, gagged her, and half-carried, half-dragged her out, as Elemai, Zadia, Khaldun, and Noora uttered a strangled cry. Only Safiya made no sound, and Zadia turned on her in blind fury. "You *bitch* – you fucking bitch, you're just going to let them do this? You – when you could – but it was *my* daughter who was given the Ring, not yours, and you couldn't *stand* that? So Coriolane can kill us all?"

Safiya still didn't answer, gaze fixed straight ahead. But as they were all forced to their knees and Coriolane stepped aside to confer with Ionius, she breathed, "It's a fake."

"What?"

"The Ring he has now. It's not real." Safiya tipped her head at Ionius. "Yes, I was angry. Yes, I knew that Elemai failed me, and gave the Ring back to Aliyah when I had expressly ordered otherwise. So I made a copy and switched them, so Aliyah kept the fake one and I had the real one in trust. Besides, do you think I would risk having the actual Ring exposed to Coriolane before we were ready to make our move? In case something exactly like this happened?"

Zadia didn't know if Safiya had saved or doomed them, or worse. "So where," she whispered furiously, *"is the real Ring now?"*

But Safiya did not have any time to answer. Coriolane and Ionius stepped apart and moved toward them again, and Ionius pulled her to her feet. "You, Saeda Safiya bet Rebiyat ur-Tasvashta," he informed her in coldly fluent Semyic, "are under a sentence of death for high treason. It will be carried out immediately. Do you have any last words?"

"No," Elemai choked. "No, Mother. Mother, no."

"Be silent, Saeda Elemai, or you will transgress on His Majesty's mercy." Ionius cut his gaze at Coriolane, who was watching with the air of a spectator at the circus. "By rights he should put all of you to death, but he has chosen to only punish the most guilty. Well, saeda?"

"Kill me yourself if you've got the balls to do it, you sniveling coward." Safiya's eyes burned with loathing. "At least I will die having never betrayed my motherland, my kin, and my faith, just to get a pat on the head from a tyrant and a madman. Do you enjoy that, boy?"

Ionius flinched. For a moment, his icy self-control cracked down the middle, and something black and raw and violent could be glimpsed inside. "Do not speak of what you do not understand, you traitorous Qartic hag. If you do not obey, you will be forced."

Safiya hesitated. She exchanged a glance with Elemai, who still looked panic-stricken. Then she nodded with icy, queenly dignity, and went to her knees in front of Ionius, chin tipped back to meet his gaze, never flinching or turning away. The general looked at Coriolane, who nodded in turn. Then Ionius raised his hands, put them together, and made a strange ripping motion, pulling the air like it was a crumpled cloth he needed to straighten, forcing it into Safiya like an oncoming wave. Elemai started to scream, and Zadia grabbed her and pressed her daughter-in-law's face into her chest; Elemai didn't need to see it, didn't need to have her nightmares haunted by the moment that *nothingness* hit Safiya and exploded her flesh like an overripe fruit. Something terrible and intangible tore her apart from the inside, and she collapsed on her ruined face, as a slowly spreading pool of scarlet lapped from beneath her head. The whole thing had taken less than ten seconds.

Elemai made a wretched sound as if she was about to be sick, and Zadia kept holding her, even though she too was shaking from head to toe. "Don't look," she repeated numbly. "Don't look, Elemai. It's all right, it's all right, I'm here, don't – don't look."

"Majesty." Ionius stepped back from Safiya's exsanguinating corpse. "The traitor has been punished. It is sufficient."

"No." Coriolane spoke at last, his face pale and his eyes feverishly bright. "It is not. For it was not merely the ur-Tasvashtas conspiring against me, and not an ur-Tasvashta who was carrying the Ring. Lady Zadia's mother was a particular friend of mine, and this once, I will be merciful to her daughter. But we must not leave the ur-Namasqas unpunished. Which one will it be, my lady?"

"What?" Zadia, still holding Elemai, stared at him in even greater incomprehension. "Your Majesty, what are you talking about?"

"I allowed you to choose." Coriolane indicated Khaldun and Noora. "Which one? They will take your punishment in your place."

"Wh – no. Majesty, please, no. They had nothing to do with this, they were innocent, they know nothing! They never had a part to play, they didn't attend our councils, they are my loyal spouses, they – " Zadia was half-screaming. "If you loved my mother at all, if you – "

"Oh," Coriolane said. His eyes were fixed on her with something else she didn't understand, almost regretful. "I did, in fact. That's why I am making an exception, and I doubt you appreciate just how rare that is. Which one? If you do not answer, Ionius will kill them both."

"Majesty," the general said. "This is not becoming. Saeda Safiya killed Gaius Tullius Grassus and organized the plot for your destruction. Her death should suffice for justice."

"And the ur-Namasqas aided and abetted them in treason at every step." Coriolane folded his arms. "This is not a difficult matter. Well?"

"Let me," Khaldun said, hoarse-voiced. "Zadia, let me – "

"No!" she screamed at him. "No, Aliyah needs you!"

Khaldun's mouth quivered, as if to remark that if Aliyah was not already dead, the odds of her surviving the Eternal City were very low indeed. "Zadia, my love, you know it's – it may no longer be a – "

"No," Noora interrupted desperately. "I'll do it. It should be me."

"No. No!" Zadia couldn't imagine that either. "Don't you *dare* think that just because you didn't sire or birth Aliyah, you're less important! You're the mother she loves! You're the mother she talks to, the mother she trusts, the mother who didn't fail her! If you leave her with me – if I did this to her and I can't fix it – no, no, Noora, no, I can't, not the way you can! Please!"

"I grow weary of these histrionics," Coriolane snapped. "One or the other, my lady."

"No. No, you can't, please, *please*." Hating herself, Zadia let go of Elemai and crawled across the floor, prostrating herself flat in front of Coriolane. "Kill me. Please. Kill me. You should, shouldn't you? It's what you've always done before!"

His eyes gleamed. Almost as if he was proud of her acuity, the unspoken understanding that this was all they would ever have of each other. "I should, yes. But – today, at least – I won't. So if you are not settled on your choice, it will have to be both. General – "

"No," Ionius said flatly. "No, this is not just. Veronus, take Saeda Zadia away in chains, but the other two should not be harmed for sins they had no part in. Do you hear me?"

The other Immortal looked at him, then at Coriolane, unhappy to be caught between two dissenting superiors. Coriolane was equally displeased. "Captain Veronus. Do your duty."

"I'm sorry, my lord." The Immortal inclined his head to Ionius. "I must obey the emperor."

With that, he stepped forward, raised his hands, and prepared to strike. Then Noora broke free with maddened speed and threw herself at Veronus's feet, as Khaldun and Zadia screamed in unison. The full force of the captain's blow ripped through her, tearing her apart just as effectively as the general's had done to Safiya. Noora was dead by the time she hit the ground, lips still upturned in a sad smile. The silence that followed that was like the end of all things.

Zadia could hear herself screaming, howling, pounding, cursing, but it was only in her head, and she was in fact frozen, unmoving, silent, staring. Coriolane made another gesture, and Veronus tossed a sheet over Noora's body, then Safiya's. "You see," the Divine Emperor said. "I will once more be merciful and allow your families to bury them, even if they deserve to be eaten by buzzards. I will also allow a moment to collect yourselves. In the meantime, I will return to the gathering and inform the Adirim that the traitors in their midst have been exposed and disposed, and it is time to swear their allegiance to me, more fervently than ever before, if they wish to avoid the same fate. You may join us soon, Lady Zadia, Lord Khaldun, Lady Elemai. General, if you would?"

Ionius remained still for a moment longer. Then with another unreadable look, he nodded and followed the emperor out. Captain Veronus marched dutifully in his wake.

Elemai looked like she was about to faint, rocking back and forth, clutching her knees and whispering brokenly. Khaldun looked even more numb than Zadia felt. He reached for her hand, but she pulled back. She couldn't touch him, couldn't reconcile the horrible knowledge that burned in her head, not just the enormity of her mother's lies but the unspeakable reason for their existence in the first place. *Coriolane has killed all his children, born and unborn, from wives and concubines. Coriolane has no heir. Everyone knows it.*

Except he did. Except Amarasha ur-Namasqa had lied to him, and to Zadia, and her own spouses, and everyone. And this — and now —

Kill me. Please. Kill me. You should, shouldn't you? It's what you've always done before.

There was no way to live with this. No way to die with it either. Nothing except the awful, awful enormity of it, the truth.

Coriolane Aureus IX is my father, Zadia ur-Namasqa thought. *And I must bring him down.*

CHAPTER 22

ALIYAH

She hardly recalled anything after they threw her in the ship's hold, in an iron cage that sat barely a few feet above the reeking bilge and swayed nauseously with the tide. Her arms and legs were bound painfully enough to cut off her circulation and turn her extremities numb, but she bit and twisted and worked the gag until she finally managed to slide it down her chin, wet with spit. Her jaw was sore, her throat was parched, and even if she had the wherewithal to scream, it would not have done her a damn bit of good. The only people who could hear her were Meronites, Immortals and legionnaires and sailors and slaves, and none of them would lift a finger to help. Her mind was a blank, her memory a void, her heart pounding and her stomach knotted. It felt as if she opened her mouth, her entire soul might come pouring out, sick and blackened and burnt to a crisp, and it was no more than she deserved.

In her more lucid moments, Aliyah tried to decide if she had done the right thing, or it was just a stupid noble instinct of the sort that got people killed for no reason. It was the truth; she had the Ring, she was its bearer before and now, it was the only way to deflect Coriolane's fury from the others, and even as strong and clever as Elemai looked, it had not taken Aliyah long, in the few weeks of their marriage to date, to realize that it was only a hollow illusion. Perversely, it had the effect of making her feel better about herself. She had spent so long putting herself down, assuming there was no way she could ever be as good as *Elemai,* that seeing the truth of her wife's flaws made Aliyah finally realize that she too was just a person, a young woman under an inhumane amount of pressure which, despite everything, she could not carry. And in some things – including this, the godforsaken Ring of Tselmun and the trouble and woe it had brought, all for the hoary old reason of obtaining endless power – Aliyah was in fact the stronger. Elemai had lasted barely a week when chained to the devouring anchor of the Ring, and here Aliyah was after several months of carrying it: still alive, still sane, still not particularly tempted to unleash its wrath and ruin. She had seen enough to know that this ability was far from ubiquitous. And so, whatever consequences arrived, she was best equipped to take them. She had to.

It could be argued, however, that it was her refusal to unleash said wrath and ruin which had led her to the guts of Coriolane's flagship, destined for torture and death or something equally insalubrious. She should have done it, the instant it became clear that they were caught, but it was that instant of hesitation, the fact that her first instinct was *not* to wreak spectacular magical carnage, that allowed them to catch her – Coriolane himself, who was far less impressive than she expected, and the terrifying General Ionius, who she briefly thought was the emperor because he looked so much more the part. But it didn't matter, when they were one and the same anyway. Ionius had the Ring and would give it to his imperial master at the first opportunity, if he hadn't done so already. And if so, if Coriolane had full and unfettered latitude to carry out his plans… Safiya clearly knew far more than she was saying, which she hadn't shared with Zadia and Aliyah, and if she *had* done so with Elemai, Elemai likewise stayed mum. But they were terrible, that much was clear. Perhaps if Aliyah lied, or attacked them, or tried to slaughter four full-grown Immortals and the Divine Emperor in a single blow, she could have stopped it, or at least delayed it. If not…

She leaned her queasy head against the bars, listening to the lapping of fetid water, the clunk of footsteps on the deck overhead. She kept looking at the bare spot on her finger where the Ring resided until she put it on a chain, and strenuously second-guessed that decision too – if it was back on her hand, perhaps Ionius couldn't pry it away so easily? Or because the bond had been broken before and it was therefore proven that she would indeed give up the Ring if she had to, there was no longer a magical sinew tying it to her? On one hand, it was a good thing, allowing her to picture some hazy future without it and everything it had taken from her, from all of them. On the other, the odds she actually lived to see that future were vanishingly remote.

She dozed on and off, fitful and restless, never slipping under for long; she was always woken by the stink or the pain or the shouting from above. Hours passed. The sun slipped off the boards, drowning the hold in purple dusk, and she wished pointlessly that she was sitting down to iftar with her family. Were they going to feed her, or just let her waste slowly to death? It seemed unlikely that a man with Coriolane's finely honed instinct for a show would let her die out of hand, unseen and unremarked. He'd want a spectacle, probably. Maybe a fight in the Colosseum, with gladiators and lions. It was unwise to let everyone in on the exact nature of her transgression, lest it set off an undignified scramble for the Ring, but when it came to empires, truth was a deeply flexible and relative concept. All they needed to know was that she had done them wrong, was a threat to their existence, their lands and their gods. Mindless public obloquy would do the rest.

At last, Aliyah woke again, smelled an amount of smoke that meant a lot of things were on fire (such as the entire city of Qart-Hadesht, finally fulfilling the ancient Meronite orator Cato's most cherished dream), and heard more thumps and bumps of the sort that heralded a large number of people returning aboard. For a brief and useless moment, she entertained the hope that it was a rescue party, that the Meronites had been overwhelmed and the Adirim had sent someone to find her. But they were speaking Lanuvian, not Qartic, and their conversation was jovial and vindictive, the sound of victorious soldiers returning from a decisive battle. Her heart sank even further. She didn't know if the city had been left standing, or any of her family were still alive. Mercy was not one of Coriolane's noted qualities even on a good day.

The anchor chain bumped and rattled, the decks creaked, and in the rhythmic rise and fall, scrape and splash that meant four slaves had started to pull every massive oar, chained at the neck so they could not rise from their benches and could only keep time to the galley-master's shouts and drum and whip, they started to move. The Meronite octireme was the biggest watercraft Aliyah had ever seen; it seemed impossible that it could float, let alone move at a good clip, but that was what all those slaves were for. Long ago, Qart-Hadesht's navy had been the pride of the nation and an unmatchable weapon (at least until the Meronites captured their ships and copied their designs), but they used smaller trieres and hepters designed for speed and maneuverability, manned by free citizens. At least in the days when they *were* their own nation, not just a meek and humbled imperial protectorate. After this, independence had been put off by another few centuries at minimum.

Eyes hot and dry, feeling like she should cry but couldn't, Aliyah closed them and listened to the distant, steady smack of wood on water, the inexorable knowledge that they were sailing into the Mad ar-Hahrat and toward the Eternal City, and whatever fate awaited her there. Her lips were split with thirst, but there was no water except the excretions of the bilge, which she would have to be a great deal more desperate to touch. She was just wondering when that moment might arrive when she heard footsteps descending the ladder. They landed with a thump, and a lantern was raised. She made out a stern figure, a forbidding gaze, and knew who it was. Of course. It could be no other.

"General Ionius." She spoke in Qartic, unsure if he understood her. "Good... evening."

"Saeda Aliyah." He answered in crisply correct Semyic, hanging the lantern on the spar. With his other hand, he thrust a cup of water through the bars. "If you are hungry, you may inform me. We are not savages."

It was on the tip of her tongue to barb back that he could have fooled her, but this man had killed more of Merone's enemies than anyone else, and Aliyah was in no hurry to add her name to the list, though it would surely end up there before long anyway. "Excuse me, General," she said politely, holding up her tied wrists. "I cannot take it."

Ionius's gaze burned into her. Then he raised his hand and made a gesture, and Aliyah hissed in pain as something burst out of her wrists to cut the ropes. Thus freed, she accepted the cup and thought about throwing it in his face, but she was too thirsty. She seized it and gulped it down; it was brackish and lukewarm, none too clean, but she didn't care. She drank until it was gone, as he watched her with that impenetrable stare. At last he said, "Do you require food?"

Aliyah thought about refusing, or virtuously insisting that she was fasting, even though it was well after sundown. But the Qahyadin fast was supposed to provide moral and spiritual clarity, not to parade piety or threaten health, and she was unhappily light-headed. "Yes."

He reached into his cloak and thrust chunks of bread and cheese at her, which she snatched and started to gnaw. Her wrists were bleeding from whatever strange magic he had done to cut her bonds, and finally she couldn't help it. "What – what did you do? With the ropes?"

She expected him to continue to stare in silence, but to her shock, he answered. "Immortals can channel and control an affinity with metal. The Corporalists embed it in our bones, and we can draw upon it, bend it to our will and shape it into weapons. That includes the iron and other metals in your blood, girl. If I ordered, it would turn into knives and cut you apart from the inside. Count yourself fortunate that on this occasion, I only instructed it to cut the ropes."

Aliyah couldn't disguise her flinch, the bread tasting even more like sawdust in her mouth. She swallowed heavily, wishing she had saved some of the water. Then, quiet and vicious, she said, "Is that what you did to my entire family, the moment the Immortals took me away?"

If she hoped to rattle him, she was disappointed. His expression did not even flicker. "No," he said. "Saeda Safiya and your mother's wife Noora were the only ones to be punished. At least for now, as there is no telling what will transpire later. We left half the fleet behind to supervise the subjugation of Qart-Hadesht. If your family cooperates, they will be spared. If not – "

"What did you do to Amma Noora?" Aliyah didn't want to hear the answer, didn't want to confirm what she already knew was true, but it burst out nonetheless. "For that matter, she's not *my mother's wife* – she's my *mother,* and she had nothing to do with any of it! If you want to punish somebody, you should at least do it to the guilty! She was innocent! She did *nothing!*"

This time, ever so minutely, Ionius looked away. "I know," he said. "I attempted to argue to the contrary, but was… overruled."

Aliyah stared at him without answering, trying to choke down the tears in her throat, the vise around her heart, the terrible knowledge that Noora was gone and there was no way to bring her back. She was shocked that General Ionius Servus Eternus, the blood-soaked boogeyman of every imperial citizen's worst nightmares, actually agreed that Noora's fate was unjustified, as *fairness* was the last thing she would ever suspect him of caring about. She didn't understand him or the barely constrained fury burning off him, the stiffness in his jaw and how he looked deeply angry but not even quite at her – the archetypal traitor, bearer of the Ring of Tselmun and prime mover in the plot to assassinate his beloved emperor. At last, as if catching the echoes of that thought, he said, "So how do you use the Ring of Tselmun? Exactly?"

"What?" Aliyah's voice cracked. "Are you insane? Do you think I'm going to just *tell* you how to give ultimate power to *Coriolane?*"

Ionius looked at her as if she was the simpleton, not him. His voice was measured, perfectly controlled, but it simmered with a dangerous curiosity nonetheless. "So does it grant that? Ultimate power? Does it do anything the bearer wishes, within limits or otherwise?"

"I don't know. And if I did, I certainly wouldn't tell *you.*"

She wanted him to bridle, to look angry, to react at all, to treat her as someone capable of hurting him if she got the chance – in other words, an *equal*. But of course, one grubby girl from Qart-Hadesht, Ringbearer or otherwise, was not within a hundred leagues of a senior Immortal, and it was profoundly stupid to expect he would think so. He kept looking at her, almost as if there was something unspoken that he needed her to understand, and she wasn't. Then he said, "I intend to find out if it can destroy the empire's enemies, yes. Whoever they might be."

"Me and my family, I'm sure. At least according to you." Aliyah had lost her taste for any more charity or conversation, just wanted him to go away and leave her alone in the dark to bleed. "You have the Ring of Tselmun. That makes you the most powerful person in the world. Learn how to wield it, if you think you can. But don't expect me to tell you a *fucking thing.*"

Still he didn't answer. Finally he nodded, cold as ice. "Very well. So be it, Saeda Aliyah. If you change your mind and wish to save your own life, let me know."

And with that, he left.

★★★★

THE REST OF THE VOYAGE was a blur. Aliyah woke and slept, slept and woke and woke, in fitful cycles that bore no resemblance to the rest of the world, any ordinary mark of day or night. Not that it mattered, at least in terms of the Qahyadin fast, since she had to eat any food as soon as she received it. If she didn't, or tried to save it for later, there were rats and fleas and other vermin who would happily devour it first, and while she didn't quite starve, it arrived infrequently enough to make her feel that keeping her alive was not as important as barely ensuring she didn't die. Her belly gnawed constantly, her throat dry as a bone, and while she did her best to view it as necessary tribulation, it rarely worked. She was scared, sad, hungry, dirty, and alone, and that was all.

After his first visit, Ionius did not return; all further food was brought by flunkies and slaves. Sometimes they also brought water or changed out the bucket she had to use for relieving herself; sometimes they did not. None of them answered her questions or acknowledged her presence, even when Aliyah finally lost her temper and screamed obscenities. She did not exist to them, and like all Meronites, they were nothing if not good at obeying orders. She wondered if this was Ionius's doing, whether cold-blooded revenge or backwards protection, and couldn't tell that either. Maybe she had been too hasty in burning that bridge, when she was utterly bereft of allies otherwise. He had implied that if she cooperated, she might be treated with leniency, but she couldn't. Not if it meant giving Coriolane the Ring.

At last, on a warm, muggy morning that was thick with fog, grime, smoke, and fluvial mist, they arrived in Merone, proceeding up the Tibir estuary and dropping anchor at the Imperial Docks. Twenty-five ships returned, where fifty set out; they had, as Ionius informed her, left the other half in Qart-Hadesht, and since each five and seven, as the quinqueremes and septiremes were known, carried anywhere from four hundred to one thousand men, that meant close to twenty thousand Meronite soldiers on the ground. The vast majority were ordinary legionnaires, but one Immortal was the equivalent of several battalions, and there was no telling how many of *those* had been sent along. Qart-Hadesht could presumably rise up en masse and drive out the occupiers if they decided to do so, but the ruthless logic of empire never relied on raw numbers. Indeed, the colonizers always lived in fear of such an event, the colonized discovering that they had ten or twenty men for every one of their tormentors, and did everything possible to forestall it, with greater and greater extremes of cruelty. If Coriolane had swept in, killed Saeda Safiya and Noora and whoever else, demanded binding and extensive new oaths of loyalty, burned the city down, and left a heavily armed garrison to turn it into Gezeren, defiance would be thin on the ground to start with. *It's my fault. All my fault. Mine.*

Aliyah was bundled out of her bilge-brig, tied onto a donkey, and escorted up the streets under heavy guard, the scrolled cornices and shadowed carapaces of fabled buildings towering above on storied hills. The fog was too thick to make out much, but she sometimes found herself straining her neck, trying to catch a glimpse of this or that famous landmark. It felt foolish, traitorous, but if it was the last thing she was ever going to see on this earth, she might as well.

It took forever, not that there was any reason to wish it shorter, but they reached the Eternal Palace, passed through a humble postern gate, and fell under the glowering shadow, the devouring jaws of the dread hellmouth where prisoners went in and never came out. The Castel Sanctangel looked almost innocuous, like any other vast old drum-tower girded with arrow-slits and crenellated wallwalks, its upper reaches veiled in mist and the Meronite eagle banners hanging slack in the ominous, breath-held stillness. At the sight, a spear of panic went through Aliyah for the first time since her ordeal began; until then, she had been too numb to think. But she threw herself off the donkey, didn't actually fall because she was tied to the saddle, and received only a stinging backhand for her trouble. Just then, she might have even been glad to see Ionius, but he still wasn't there.

Inside, the Castel was dim, cold, and smelled like rot, misery, and gloom, and they marched her to a holding cell, where she had to strip off her clothes and change into prison rags. Someone held her down while someone else cut off her hair and shaved her head, none too gentle with the scrape of the blunt-edged razor, and rivulets of blood oozed off her skull. She bit her bruised lip until it hurt worse. She wouldn't cry or beg. She wouldn't give them the satisfaction.

When that was done, she was put into irons and escorted to a cell — which was cleaner than her dungeon on the flagship, but only barely. The guards shoved her, she stumbled inside, and the door shut with a boom, echoing like the fall of an axe. Throughout the intake procedure, nobody had spoken a word to her, explained how long she would be here (until the execution, but that involved a variety of possibilities) or anything else. She felt at her wits' end, and she could not be brave any longer. She buried her face in her knees and cried until she passed out.

It was another unformed amount of time later when she woke. She stared at the ceiling, utterly disassociated, when she spotted movement in the shadows outside. If someone was here to kill her, they should get it over with, and she hauled herself up. "Go on. I don't care."

There was a pause. She couldn't see whoever was there, but they sounded close by. Then a young man's voice said in a language she half-understood, "Are you the Qartic girl?"

"What?" It sounded vaguely similar to Semyic, with an accent and antique intonation she didn't recognize. "What are you speaking?"

"Old High Yerussalan. It's fairly similar to Semyic, they're derived from the same root. I could try Vashemysh, if that works better, but the dialect I know is more Ruthynian than Semyic. But if you are from Qart-Hadesht, I thought you might be able to – ?"

"I can understand you, yes. Sort of. Halfway." Aliyah rubbed her filthy face. Switching to Semyic, which seemed easier for him to parse, she added, "But I don't want to talk to you. I'm not going to tell you anything. Just leave me alone."

"Are you sure?" The shadows rippled, and at last, her interlocutor stepped out. But instead of providing answers, his appearance confused her even further. He was wearing rich velvet robes that confirmed her impression of status, but they were as dirty as if he too had been down here a while. Yet he didn't look like a prisoner, as he was wearing no chains and carried a strange metal box. In contrast to her expectation of some etiolated and enervated old geezer, he was young and good-looking, with thick dark hair, strikingly black eyes, a strong nose, and dimples that flashed when he smiled. "My name is Julian Janovynich Kozharyev," he said, speaking slowly enough for her to follow. "I was hoping we could talk."

"Go away."

"I mean it." Undeterred, he pulled up a stool, sat down, and dug in his robes, pulling out a piece of fresh bread. He pushed it through the bars, and she snatched it. "I know you have no reason to trust me, but if you're the girl they arrested for having the Ring of Tselmun – "

"How did you know about that?"

"Because." Julian Janovynich paused significantly. "I need to know how to do the exact same thing you and your people were planning."

"*What?*" This was obviously a trap, to get her to confess her criminal intention in no uncertain terms. "You can't think I'll believe that."

"I'm a Vashemite," Julian said. "From Korolgrod. So neither I nor *my* people have any love for Coriolane either. I assure you that I don't want to be back in the Castel either, since I was also stuck here for quite a while before getting out by luck. Unfortunately, however, that luck turned out to be not nearly as good as it looked. So if I don't want to be murdered in my sleep and have my skeleton made into a giant fucking pentacle by an insane old wizard, it is in my best interests to hide out here for now. Is – is General Ionius back?"

"What? *Ionius?*" Aliyah stared at him. Julian had tried to ask it casually and offhand, but she could hear the desperate hope that he couldn't quite restrain. "Do you – do you *like* him?!"

"What? No! No, I don't like him! He's an idiot, he's obnoxiously loyal to Merone, and if he was here, he would offer utterly boneheaded suggestions that we would have to immediately ignore. But he also – it's true, yes, but he's complicated. Or it's complicated. We have a plan. Or we *had* a plan, I don't know if it's still the case, I haven't seen him since he left for Qart-Hadesht. Maybe he went to look for me in the

Thaumaturges' tower and I should go back, but if Kronus has set some stupid booby trap and I die the instant I set foot inside – "

"You're a..." Aliyah squinted. "You're a *Thaumaturge?*"

"As far as anyone knows, yes. It's a long story."

Aliyah kept staring at him, suspicious and dangerously curious all at once. Finally she said, "How on earth is a Vashemite from Korolgrod in Merone dressed up as a Thaumaturge, hiding out in the Castel Sanctangel and talking to a Qartic prisoner about the *Ring of Tselmun?* I don't – "

"As I said. Long story." Julian's shrug didn't look as unbothered as he clearly hoped. "But to make it short, there was a girl my mother wanted me to marry, back home. I didn't want to marry her. So I left."

Aliyah blinked. She couldn't help but ponder the sudden parallels, the mirrored trajectories, that they had faced the same event and reacted in utterly opposite ways. When there was a girl *her* mother wanted her to marry, she tried her hardest to make it happen, mold herself into a politically and personally worthy partner for Elemai, her family, her homeland, bonding herself more deeply and deliberately to each one. But if this story was true, Julian had not. Instead he rejected it and ran away, only to wind up in the very same place as her. She wanted to ask if it was worth it, if he was at peace or if it didn't matter, and he didn't *seem* like the kind of assassin the emperor would send. She would think that either way, no doubt, but still.

"Why do you think I'll tell you anything about the Ring?" she said instead. "Yes, I had it for a while. No, I didn't do anything with it, though I should have. Or at least tried."

Julian regarded her narrowly. His voice was coldly disapproving as he demanded, "So you *took* the Ring for yourself? The *Ring of Tselmun?* And what, used it as a fun fashion accessory? Yet again, the goye think they can just steal what belongs to the Vashemites and – "

"No, I didn't *take* it. It was likewise complicated." Aliyah nodded at the iron box. "What's that, then? Are you carrying around your own special relic, or – "

"It's more than that." Julian husked a mirthless laugh. "It's why I need the damn Ring. This is the original *Key of Tselmun,* the king's grimoire with all his spells and secrets. I've been translating it for Kronus, or I was. He's surely noticed that it's gone by now, but I can't let him get hold of it. The bone pentacle, the sheer amount of power that he's preparing to unleash – "

"The *Key of Tselmun?*" Aliyah goggled at him. Safiya had told her about it in their lessons, how everything would be much easier if they had a copy, but the extant versions were largely incomplete or corrupted, rarer than gold and even more jealously guarded. Khasmedeus had also mentioned it in Yerussala, that it was the Thaumaturges' founding text in the same way that the Gezereni *Book of Daybreak* was for the Corporalists, and if Grand Magister Kronus owned the original, that must be true. But it was also a stomach-lurching realization that the Meronites were inches away from possessing both of Tselmun's mighty magic tools, everything they needed to unleash the kind of devastation and dominion that could never be ended. If Julian had the *Key,* Ionius had the Ring, and Julian had been bamboozled into thinking that Ionius was some sort of ally – he seemed so smart, it was difficult to see how, but if there was more to his refusal to marry the girl than just not liking her, that eagerness when he spoke about the murderous Immortal –

"I don't know where the Ring is," Aliyah said. "They took it from me when they arrested me back in Qart-Hadesht. They've probably already given it to Coriolane."

"Almighty, I hope not. But see why I can't, at any cost, let a Meronite get the grimoire?"

"But you're desperate to meet up with *General Ionius?*" At last, Aliyah couldn't hold back. "As if he won't kill you and seize the *Key!* I know he – he's handsome, but – "

"Once again, I do not *like* him. Regardless of whether he is or is not handsome, because I haven't noticed. I don't know what the fuck his moral code is, but he does have one. Do we want to hang the fate of the world on it? I don't know. But I don't think we have a choice."

Aliyah was quiet. She almost felt sorry for him, that he could be so clever and yet still so deluded. At last she said, "If you have a way to get out of here, to leave, you need to do it now. You can't give that book to the general under any circumstances, and you can't keep loitering in Merone and thinking someone else won't take it by force. Besides, I don't care if Ionius thinks he has a moral code or not. When push comes to shove, he'll still obey the emperor, even if he disagrees. He – he killed my mother. Noora. Back in Qart-Hadesht. He said that he objected, but that didn't stop him from doing it. And she was innocent. She didn't do anything. You need to listen to me. You can't let any Meronite have the *Key,* ever, and that includes him. *Especially* him. You need to *run.*"

Julian started to answer, then stopped. He didn't seem to know how to immediately counter that. At last he said, "I'm sorry about your mother. I know that doesn't make it better, but still."

"Thank you." Aliyah stared dully at the wall, not allowing herself to take in her own words, lest she break to pieces and never pull herself back together again. "Don't let it be in vain. Don't let the Meronites get the power to do it to everyone, everywhere. Run. *Run.*"

"Well," Julian said, his voice very dry. "It *is* almost Tor Shchedysh, if I haven't completely lost track of time. An appropriate moment to flee from the land of the oppressors and go into exile in the desert. But I just – I don't know if it's the right thing to do. Ionius – "

"Forget him. Please." Aliyah sat up and looked Julian in the eye. "You don't know me, you have no reason to trust me, but you want to do the right thing. I tried to do it too, and it led me here, so maybe I'm not the best person to give advice. But I would die before I ever trusted any of them, for any reason. Especially the Scourge of Sciatello. You know who he *is,* don't you?"

"Of course I know." Julian looked down. "I let him hear about it. Fine, I'll think about it. I don't know if it'll be safe for me to speak to you again, so… this is goodbye. Good luck."

"Yes." Aliyah's throat was tight. She nodded to him, as he did the same to her. Touched two fingers to his brow in silent salute, picked up the *Key,* and walked away.

Time after that once more became extremely relative, only barely remarked, hardly relevant to her continued existence. Aliyah first feared that she would be paraded through the streets as a stern lesson to traitors, but that did not come to pass either. She was fed infrequently, enough that the bones showed sharp against her skin, and left alone; she was not given a cellmate or any other company, as if they feared that any contact could contaminate an ordinary prisoner with her heresy. She made lists in her head and marks on the walls, closed her eyes and dreamed that she was home in bed with Elemai. The two of them had not gotten much chance to explore the exciting new aspects of their relationship before Qahyadin arrived and put a halt to carnal matters, but she could curl her fingers and feel the softness of Elemai's skin, the generous curve of hip and breast, the tender wetness between her legs, the squeak she uttered when Aliyah happened on a sensitive spot. Elemai herself was not unskilled in the art of giving pleasure, and could lick and nip in a way that drove Aliyah gasping to the edge – the interlocking of their legs as Elemai climbed on her, the delicious friction where they ground together, knees digging and hands clenching, riding to the brink, to small deaths and sweet release, to where nothing mattered but them, alone in the warm dark sanctuary of the quilts. But that too eventually could not be dwelled upon any longer. Not when it would never happen again.

At last, Aliyah was roused by the clanking of metal, a blare of torchlight, gruff voices and rough hands. Her presence had been ordered by His Divine Majesty, and she would be attending him at once. It was almost a relief. No more moldering; she would be dead before the day was out. She had tried to organize her mind and prepare herself, to be sure that she left this world as much in order as she could, but as the guards pulled her out, she quailed. She had marked her nineteenth year down there in the dark, and she did not want to die. Not yet.

After a curt bath and change, she was marched through the courtyard of the Eternal Palace and up into the sprawling, airy halls of the private apartments. Her legs were weak with disuse, and she stood in the appointed spot, head down, as everyone groveled in an excessively obsequious manner. Then a voice ordered, "Bow before your rightful sovereign, Qartic witch."

Aliyah glanced up a fraction, through her eyelashes, and saw that at last, Coriolane Aureus IX was in arm's reach. He looked even more bloated and unwell than he had in Qart-Hadesht, skin yellowed with jaundice, and even a heavy coating of makeup could not disguise it. Her heart gave a savage leap of hope that perhaps he was actually and actively dying, but it was foolish to think so. She searched his hands, which glittered with their usual rings of state, but she didn't see *the* Ring. Did he have it and was just keeping it strategically out of sight, or had Ionius *actually* not given it to him? If for some wild reason the general had been sincere, and she told Julian to run for his life and never look back —

No time to wonder. She had her own sins to dwell on, and Coriolane studied her with an unsettling intensity. At last he asked, "What do you have to say, girl? Is there any defense to offer?"

"No, Your Majesty," Aliyah replied politely. "I did what you think I did, and to which I freely confessed. I received the Ring of Tselmun and kept it for my own. I intended to use it in the liberation of my people and my country, against the might of Merone. This included, if I was given the chance, the intention to harm your own imperial person."

Coriolane scowled. He seemed especially frustrated at her refusal to bow, to recant or plead for mercy. "You force my hand, I'm afraid," he said, after a pungent pause. "Your lot could be a great deal better than it is, and none can fault your courage. It is the first time I have looked upon an… enemy of mine in such fashion, and I would almost wish to be lenient. But I cannot. You are, by your own admission, a thoroughgoing and unrepentant traitor, and the precedent would be disastrous. Do you know what the Meronite Empire does to traitors, Lady Aliyah?"

"Yes, Your Majesty. It would be difficult not to."

He scowled again. A thrall of silence hung over the presence-chamber, everyone waiting for the emperor's pronouncement of sentence. Yet unless she had become utterly unmoored from reality, she thought he was genuinely… hesitant. As if he wished that she had offered him a reason not to kill her, or at least an opportunity for remediation. But as they remained there, staring each other down, he sighed and raised a hand. "Very well. You have chosen your own fate. So will it be with you as it always is with those who think they can defy Merone. Your mother failed you, Lady Aliyah. If she had understood the truth, this would be a very different conversation. But she did not, and I wash my hands of it. Take her away. I will not look on her again."

The guards took hold of her. They did as they were bid.

Outside, the summer heat had begun to grip the Eternal City properly in its jaws, and the air was thick and sweaty. Aliyah was hauled along like a broken puppet, and the sunlight tormented her head. She closed her eyes and waited for it to be over, gave up hope of it being otherwise, wished only for it to be quick. That was the only mercy left.

The pit lay outside the city walls, on the north end of Sanctorian Hill, on land which was in hot demand as a graveyard due to its proximity to the Arch-Holy Basilica. Thus it was already dotted with markers and mausoleums, humps of fresh-dug and grown-over earth, crematories and cenotaphs. But the pit was beyond all those pious bowers of the humble Tridevarian dead, sleeping in the earth until the Great Awakening. It sat in unconsecrated ground, the sort saved for suicides and sinners, whose death heralded no serene entry to the afterlife but only an endless torment. Since Aliyah was Wahin, the religious implications had less impact on her, but it seemed foolish to expect she was destined for anything better. Only the dark domain of Ur-Malika's great foe, Ur-Rajim, the devilish master of those who lived unworthy lives and had to face atonement and expurgation in the hereafter. She stood on the brink. She braced. She –

"Wait!"

Her head jerked up. She looked around, still hoping it was salvation, a last-minute stay. But it wasn't. It was General Ionius, the first time she had seen him since their ill-fated interview on the flagship. He looked grimy and tired and angry, alone and on foot like a common legionnaire, and as he reached them, the soldiers snapped upright and saluted, which he ignored. "This is the Qartic girl? She has had no trial, no proper conviction. We do not understand anything we need to know, about her secrets or her people's plans. She cannot yet be consigned to death."

"Apologies, my lord." The soldier shrugged. "His Majesty's orders."

Ionius's gaze locked with Aliyah's. It was that same impossible-to-understand expression, that look that brimmed both with rage and something else. She had the sense he desperately wanted to say something to her, to demand the truth. But if he had in fact come to intervene, for whatever purpose of his own, he had done so too late. There was no stopping this, no thwarting the emperor's will in front of everyone, and she was mad to think he even wanted to. And yet.

The Immortal reached out. He closed both hands around Aliyah's wrists and squeezed, and she felt a sudden, surging pain, similar to when he used her blood to cut the ropes in the brig, but worse. She staggered, biting her lip and half-thinking he meant to start her perdition before she was even thrown into the pit. But for an instant as he took his hands away, she saw something sharp and metallic shining in her fingers. *Immortals can channel and control an affinity with metal. The Corporalists embed it in our bones, and we can draw upon it, bend it to our will and shape it into weapons.*

His eyes met hers again, silent and furious. She had no idea what he was playing at. He had not meant to give her a weapon, surely. He only meant for her to suffer. To die even more slowly, be tormented by the illusion of power or escape. And yet –

The soldiers tied ropes around her waist. The abyss yawned open. Ionius stepped away.

Aliyah bet Zadia ur-Namasqa went down into the dark.

PART THREE

IMPERIUM

CHAPTER 23

IONIUS

IONIUS HAD RETURNED FROM QART-HADESHT IN A HAZE. HE tried to pretend otherwise, to insist that he was not stripped to the bone and left with a jagged asymmetry of pieces that he had no idea how to put together again, but it was useless. Half of it had been a deception to start with, a carefully crafted cover to pretend that he was the same man as ever, when it was as if he had awoken for the first time in his life and watched it unfold with new eyes, no longer blinded with the cataracts of Meronite logic. Once Ionius would have savagely enjoyed it: the dramatic accusations, the proud ur-Namasqa matriarch falling on her face to beg, the way Safiya ur-Tasvashta's defiance was crushed in Ionius's own hands and her blood stained the tiles red, red, red. The stunned faces of the Adirim as Coriolane announced the truth of the treachery unmasked at their very heart, the one chance they had to save themselves, and how after the final instant of useless hope that it was a nightmare or a trick, the lot of them went numbly to their knees. All except Mirazhel ur-Beireshta, the new ruler they had put in place just in time to lead this coup. But when a legionnaire hit her with his spear, she went down too, spitting blood. The silence reigned like the breaking of the world.

After that, it was violent and mundane in equal measure, a well-rehearsed play that had been put on a thousand times in every part of the world where the imperial eagle flew and the faithless natives tried to tear it down. The taking of hostages from High House families, the swift execution of the most notorious Low House troublemakers and the severed heads put up on stakes, the legions sent door-to-door to drag out terrified civilians, demand how deep the treachery had gone. Was Qart-Hadesht planning to throw off its shackles (but not *shackles,* no, that was a cruel word that connoted cruelty, when the Meronites had always been so gentle and enlightened) and rise up en masse, or was this just another betrayal by the elites, dragging the poor folk into a needless war to decide who had the right to beat them down, collect their taxes, and take their children? Surely there could be no call for that, not among sensible folk who knew their duty and could trust the emperor to protect them. Indeed, it was easy for them to see him as a blameless sovereign let down by the plotting and conniving of the corrupt local powerbrokers; the Adirim were here, demonstrably and imperfectly embroiled in their everyday lives, while Coriolane was a distant figurehead in a distant palace in distant Merone. He could be protector or persecutor, hero or villain, and just now, he was both. If the Qartic citizens foreswore their evil leaders, they would be spared. If not, if they looked at the hand of mercy and spat in its face, their fate would be far worse.

It was difficult to say how this ultimatum went down. Most of the frightened people, who had no idea what transpired among their rulers at the best of times, disclaimed any knowledge of the plot, frantically affirmed their loyalty to Merone, and knelt in the dust and blood to swear it anew. But some didn't – after all, the Low House had caviled so long for freedom because there was real popular sentiment behind it – and they had to pay. Ionius was ordered to stay in the Temple with Coriolane, to personally guard the Divine Emperor from any more treachery, and they stood in silence, watching the city burn. Great gusts of black smoke billowed from the rooftops and hazed the sea, devouring the beauty and architecture of a thousand generations – the palaces, the gardens, the great bazaar, the mahqasas, the fountains, the streets. It didn't seem holy, or justified, or any of it. It was sheer and simple terror.

After a while, Coriolane turned away and made a smug comment about whether anyone truly thought the Qartic rustics could have killed him even if the Meronites had not known everything in advance, and for a wild instant, Ionius almost attacked him. He could feel the memory of it even now, the decision that had taken form in his head to actually raise a hand against his own master, *Coriolane*. He had to stop him, he had told Julian as much and did not intend to swerve from it, but the thought still terrified him. It felt impossible, suicidal, like throwing the earth out of orbit. He couldn't possibly do it – but he *could*, and he nearly had. If Captain Veronus had not stepped in at that moment, Ionius was still unsure what he might have tried.

After that – returning to the fleet and going to speak with the girl, Aliyah. She was not inclined to pay him any heed, which was not surprising but still frustrating. Of course he couldn't speak freely in the emperor's flagship, and she would never trust that an Immortal – the Scourge of Sciatello, as if Coriolane was not the one who had sent him there and given the order – could ever be on her side. Besides, he needed to understand what he held, the immensity of what he had taken from her. *You have the Ring of Tselmun. That makes you the most powerful person in the world. Learn how to wield it, if you think you can. But don't expect me to tell you a fucking thing.*

No, Ionius thought grimly. No, indeed. There was no doubting the conviction in her voice or the hatred in her face, and he had lost his taste to beat it out of her. So he kept to himself for the voyage back to Merone, and when they arrived, had to fight his foolish instinct to rush straight to the Thaumaturges' tower. Yes, he had the Ring, and yes, Julian was expecting to see both of them, but Ionius couldn't keep slipping so badly. At their last meeting, he had, forgotten himself so much, as to ask Julian to look into Tatya – *why?* She was dead, he knew that. Why trouble that ghost?

So, then, he went to his own rooms. Made sure that Romola was gone, sat down, and took out the Ring of Tselmun; he was surprised that Coriolane had not already demanded him to hand it over, but the emperor currently had so many other ways to occupy his bloodlust. The Ring itself also looked, at least on the surface, far too uninteresting to bother. For an item of such legendary power, it seemed oddly senescent, lifeless. Ionius raised his hand, braced himself, and rubbed it.

Nothing happened.

It was possible that Aliyah ur-Namasqa or another traitor had cut it off from being used by anyone except them, but the more Ionius worked it with no reaction, the more he suspected that even at the moment of her death, Safiya ur-Tasvashta had managed, one last time, to pull the wool over Merone's eyes. He didn't know what precisely she had done, but it was a posthumous fuck-you of a scale hardly doubted and much deserved. But if Ionius had been foisted with a fake and the *real* Ring was in Qart-Hadesht – if they had incinerated the city and yet left the true weapon in its grasp – either that or all the magic was drained from it, but he felt the former more likely –

Even if all his prior allegiances and certainties were swiftly unraveling, Ionius's well-drilled military brain could not accept such an unforgivable lapse. After all, they had just given even the most passive and ambivalent Qartic citizen every reason to join an actual rebellion, created a self-fulfilling prophecy of violence against Merone by dint of the violence Merone had visited on them, which entailed yet more violence to put down. He could see the endless cycle of it, what the ravana in Sardarkhand had called samsara, begetting itself over and over to the same bloody end. If someone in Qart-Hadesht found the real Ring, dug it up from wherever the fuck Safiya ur-Tasvashta had hidden it – and they had left her daughter Elemai alive, so she was now the head of the family and likely inclined to serve revenge very cold indeed – this was not the end of the rebellion, the plan to kill Coriolane, and everything else. It was just the beginning.

So what? What in hellfire do I do? If Ionius handed over the fake Ring to the emperor and it was uncovered, Coriolane would demand to know where the real one was, and could suspect Ionius of deliberately authoring the switch. Which he hadn't, not consciously, but at such a delicate moment, he could not have his conflicted loyalties explosively unmasked. Besides, even if he was determined to no longer serve the emperor as much as could be managed, it did not extricate him from everything else that still tied him to Merone, in ways large and small. He still had command of the Immortals, for one, and if he resorted openly to defiance, it would see the lot of them brutally punished and probably executed. It had once been the Eternal City's habit to cull all the household slaves at the master's death, after all, and while the Immortals were theoretically far too valuable to simply wipe out en bloc, it might also be the case that Coriolane expected to no longer need them. If he could now simply ask the Thaumaturges to unleash the deadly blood-plague on anyone who crossed him, and no longer wanted to share the limited wellspring of immortality magic with anyone apart from himself, it made them an obvious liability. And if he entertained the smallest whisper of doubt about their fidelity – as he might already with Ionius himself – then they were too powerful to remain on the board, unchecked and uncontrolled. They must go.

If it came to that, Ionius could possibly get them out of Merone and away from immediate danger, but for a supreme warrior whose only purpose in life was to destroy the empire's enemies, there was little prospect of sending them to peaceably vegetate on a farm somewhere. The chief option for the field, however, was either the slaughter of Brythanica or the invasion of Qin, which continued to accelerate under Commander Gregorius's maladapt management and would get them killed even faster. As well, none of *them* had any questions of where their loyalty lay, and would turn on Ionius instead for suggesting anything to the contrary. So, then. *What?*

The facts were plain. He needed to get back to Qart-Hadesht and search for the real Ring, but it was in an uproar, there was no chance of sneaking around behind the scenes when there were twenty thousand Meronite soldiers taking the place apart, and since everyone had seen him depart with Coriolane, it would be difficult to explain his abrupt reappearance. Then again, why should he? He was General Ionius, he could do as he pleased, there *was* one way to return swiftly, and it would allow him to ensure that Julian was still in place, awaiting the moment of action. They could not put it off, could not wait any longer, if it was not already too late. Soon, even if Coriolane *was* gone, the processes put in motion would be impossible to stop. And if Ionius thought too long of what was required, he might balk. He could not. *They* could not.

And yet, it was far from a simple prospect. He could not assume that Grand Magister Kronus would blithely grant him yet another use of the Thaumaturges' doors (especially after the debacle of Sardarkhand) without asking questions, reporting to Coriolane, or conspiring to obtain sensitive intelligence, and it was even more foolish to think that the wily old bastard was unaware of the entanglement between Ionius and Julian. He might have listened to their hushed plotting – and witnessed that kiss – at his leisure, and be saving it for the greatest impact. Ionius, who had exposed the empresses' treason at Year End in costume as Marus, knew not to underestimate the knack of a dramatic revelation, and any attempt to return to Qart-Hadesht to search for the Ring would be compromised on every level. He would be on his own in enemy territory, the Meronite garrison might prove an active liability, and he was not fond of the idea of cutting off his hand again. Getting himself killed likewise availed nothing, but if they were out of time and options…

The invitation came a few days later. He was summoned to join the emperor in the Colosseum, in Coriolane's private box, at a special event for the whole city to enjoy the spectacular punishment of the Qartic traitors. People were encouraged to bring picnics and children, pack the stands and place wagers, and Ionius, who had attended many of these bloodlettings before, knew all too well what to expect. He wondered if this included Aliyah. If so, what was he supposed to do? Leap into the ring and wrestle a lion with his bare hands? He *could,* but it would turn into an even greater imbroglio, and he was unsure if he should save her at all. What made her different? What entitled her to live? According to Meronite law, she was a traitor in no uncertain terms. But after all, the law could be such an opportune and immoral thing.

In any event, the invitation could not be refused, so he accepted. Ionius was aware that he was also expected to bring his paramour along; after so publicly claiming her at the feast, it would be odd if he didn't. But as they climbed into the wagon, Romola looking almost like a proper Meronite lady in her new dress and cloak, hair braided with pearls and an elaborate silver choker coiled around her throat, he muttered, "Be warned, girl. This will not be pleasant."

Romola looked at him sidelong but didn't answer, with the carefully unrevealing expression most slaves mastered as a survival tactic. She folded her hands neatly in her lap, and as the wagon jolted into motion, she said, "I will not embarrass you, my lord. If that is what you fear."

It wasn't, but Ionius was unsure how to explain, and he was the one who felt dread, which made no sense. They joined the convoy that thronged down Palatorian Hill, into the city and the Avenue of Justice that surrounded the vast Colosseum. It sat near the Circus Maximus used for horse and chariot racing, but its purpose was far more visceral. It hosted splendid feasts and celebrations, elaborate mock battles and mythical hunts, acrobats and circuses and conjurers. But by far its most popular and notorious attractions were the gladiatorial fights and public executions, of which there were always plenty. This one was the greatest draw of all, and a line wrapped around the huge stone amphitheater as the commoners jostled for entrance. As the wagon rolled into the private dock at the back, Ionius felt that twist in his stomach. He could only imagine what Julian would make of this, and was briefly glad they hadn't yet seen each other again. It would be hard to look into his eyes and think of some way to excuse this, or anything.

The wagon came to a halt, he stepped out and helped Romola down, and allowed her to take his arm as they proceeded inside. It was difficult to know what she thought of him, or what she felt she had to offer in return for his protection. She had made a few determinedly oblique and offhand enquiries as to whether he expected her to warm his bed, and accepted with commensurate relief when he informed her bluntly that he didn't. He preferred not to speculate on what other experiences she had had with men, and indeed her small flinches if he stood too close, the way she visibly braced and held her breath when he touched her in any way, told enough of *that* tale. Once or twice, he found himself contemplating whether to ask if she knew the names of any of the useless noble pissants who roamed around the palace in search of girls just like her. If a few of them drank too much and accidentally fell off a parapet, it could be no loss to anyone.

That fascinating question, however, would have to wait. They climbed the staircase to Coriolane's private box; Romola started to labor on the last few turns, and Ionius unobtrusively slowed his pace. The box was located halfway up the vast open-air tiers, shaded in purple drapes, cooled by fan-waving slaves, and furnished with seating for fifty, in silken divans and padded chairs. The two smaller thrones to each side of

Coriolane's sprawling dais had once been reserved for the empresses, but were now occupied by Mellius Sanctus to the right and Commander Gregorius to the left. It was an unprecedently high station for a mere legionnaire, and he gloated at Ionius, demanding to know if it chafed the mighty Immortal to see his position so usurped. Perhaps it might have before, but Ionius found it difficult to care now. He nodded shortly and took a seat, Romola sinking down next to him. When servers appeared with trays of delicacies, cups of chilled wine, and other lavish snacks, Romola looked briefly as if she hoped for some, but Ionius shook his head. "You won't want it once the show starts. Trust me."

She gave him another unreadable look, but as ever, did not utter a word to the contrary. The box continued to fill with Coriolane's usual favorites, and Ionius kept an eye out for Grand Magister Kronus, in case he dragged himself out of his books and bones to attend the show, but it did not appear so. Then last of all, Coriolane swept in as everyone hurried to their feet, accompanied by the lissome young concubine he had taken to Qart-Hadesht. According to the malicious palace gossip, she was already forgetting herself, insisting on being given the empresses' clothes and jewels and seated beside the emperor at formal functions, paid homage and curtsied as if she was the new queen and not just an upjumped whore, but looking at the slightly strained quality of her smile and the glassy fixedness of her eyes as she giggled and tempted Coriolane with a bunch of grapes, Ionius wondered if it was anything she should be faulted for. After all, she was one inadvertent offense or imperial fit of boredom away from being thrown into the arena herself. No wonder she wanted to seize this opportunity, if only it would make her safe.

Coriolane waited until the last seats were taken and the doors were shut – the Colosseum was at capacity and then some, over a hundred thousand people, every bench filled and every aisle jammed. Then he rose to his feet and made a speech, magically amplified and booming to every corner of the arena. It was the usual rote about the punishment of traitors and the force of the law, musing metaphors on how a bundle of sticks together was far stronger than just one, reminders of how the brazen Qartic terrorists tried to defraud and destroy Merone as their infidel race had done for centuries, but – thanks to the emperor's strength and power, wisdom and bravery – had not come close to succeeding. Coriolane modestly allowed that even with the best of plans and preparations, there was some amount of danger, but he had not hesitated to face it for their sakes, and lo, he returned unscathed, protected by the grace of the Divine Family and the glory of the Eternal City. Ionius was briefly afraid Mellius was about to get up and lead them in prayer, but *that*, apparently, was where it might become too much. It wasn't needed, anyway. Coriolane basked in the applause that rang out for so long that the master of ceremonies had to stand up and make officious noises, and the emperor waved indulgently like a father pestered by his children on Prince's Fest morning. Then he took his seat, raised a hand, and signaled the event to be officially underway.

A set of bronze gongs were struck, and the portcullis that opened into the enormous packed-dirt oval clanked and rattled as it was raised. Everyone leaned forward in anticipation as fifteen or twenty ragged figures stumbled out. Condemned prisoners were usually sent naked and unarmed to their fate, but evidently the magister ludi had decided that it would look more sporting, and more entertaining, if they were equipped with clothing and weapons. The convicts ranged in age from barely twelve to over sixty, all Qartic, and Ionius recognized them as the hostages taken from the High House families in the Temple. He tensed, still thinking that there must be a mistake. After all, hostages were taken for the purpose of being strategically kept alive; the threat of them coming to harm was generally more effective than actually doing so. But if Coriolane thought there was no value in preserving them at all, or was daring Qart-Hadesht to retaliate if they could, when the Meronite boot was already there to stomp even harder on their throat –

Ionius shifted in his seat, and almost got to his feet. But he couldn't do anything to stop it, and his fists contracted hard enough to send another sharp spike of pain up his damaged arm. It was certainly far better than it would be if he was an ordinary man, but it remained unhealed, another chilling reminder that he was no longer equipped to take extravagant risks with the assumption he could not be hurt. Part of him hoped, briefly and foolishly, that if he could just *talk* to Coriolane, convince him it was a bad idea to steal strength from those who dedicated their lives to serving him, that the Immortals still needed to live up to their moniker and should remain as usual, the emperor might listen. But if it had not saved his own wives, what hope for slaves?

What came next was both terrible and inevitable. The beastmasters unlocked the cages, the starved lions and tigers and bears and aurochs stampeded in, and a guttural howl of delight went up from the crowd as the panicked prisoners struggled to fend them off, to bat at them with blunted swords or flimsy spears; it was just for show, prolonging the outcome, making sure nobody died too quickly and spoiled the fun. One of the old men sacrificed himself in order to give a young girl time to run for it, a move the crowd applauded and jeered in equal measure, but she was still cornered and gored to death soon thereafter. Ionius didn't think he saw Aliyah down there, but he couldn't guarantee that he would recognize her. The screams echoed like a vicious thing, the beasts' jaws and paws stained with blood, tearing flesh and spilling intestines. Coriolane sat with an intent, greedy expression, drinking in the spectacle. Whenever the magisters and lictors glanced at him, seeing if he would call it off or instruct them to offer mercy, he didn't. Only watched.

Ionius didn't realize he was halfway out of his seat until Romola's hand clamped onto his wrist. She looked nauseated, and glad she had followed his advice to avoid the victuals, but she tilted her head at their fellows, who were giving him funny looks. "My lord. Be careful."

Right. Yes. *Careful*. That was what he should be. Listen to that, to her, and not the ringing in his ears, the demented giddiness in his head, the pure and perfect conviction that the only thing to do was to stand up and kill every person in the Colosseum, just to put a final flourish on it. Yes, Coriolane was the one who gave that loathsome speech and arranged this entire fiasco, and everyone in attendance had been raised from birth to suckle at the same poisonous teat, but the emperor was not physically forcing them to crowd in by the score, boo and jeer, take grisly delight in the carnage. They were not *as* responsible, but they *were* responsible, and just then, Ionius hated every single one of them, every Meronite everywhere, all these twisted and terrible voyeurs of violence who built their city and their empire and their world out of this. They deserved to die. All of them, from the emperor himself to the lowliest laborer who saved his meager wages to bring his children to the death-orgy and properly train them who to hate. What was the Scourge of Sciatello for, if not that?

"My lord," Romola hissed again, her fingernails digging into his arm. "Don't. Not now."

"Let go of me." Ionius jerked wildly at her grasp. "Don't tell me what to – "

"General Ionius." Coriolane, finally deigning to look away for even an instant, turned his head. "Trouble with your lovely new consort?"

"No, Majesty." Ionius's jaw felt like glass, his blood banging in his ears. "None at all."

"She does look far nicer than she did at Year End." Coriolane cocked his head, gaze turning speculative, as the concubine tensed and glared at Romola with the air of a competitor sensing a threat. "Cleans up well, doesn't she? Come closer, girl. Let me examine you again."

Romola shot Ionius a pleading look, unwilling to obey but terrified of openly defying the emperor. But there was nothing Ionius could do to stop it, and it was just then when the sheer falsity of the comforting lie he told himself – that he was a *different* slave, a *special* slave, he had greater power and prestige than those other unfortunates and should take comfort in it – was finally and entirely hammered home. The only point was that he was a slave, no questions and no qualifications. Not one of the freedmen would support him if he told Coriolane where to stick it. On the contrary, they would shout *Spartekaius* and urge him to be thrown in with the remaining Qartic prisoners; at this point, about half were still alive, the others strewn in many pieces across the dirt. The first act was coming to a close, the beastmasters herding their sated charges back to the cages, as slaves wheeled away the limbless torsos, severed heads, and heaps of guts, and threw sand and quicklime on the pools of blood. Acrobats and magicians came out to entertain the crowd in the interval, people getting up in search of food-sellers and wine-vendors and the lavatory. The weight pressed on Ionius's shoulders as if the pressure would burst him apart: the urge to agree, to stand aside, to obey, *obey*. It was his first and deepest reflex, the training of his existence, the marrow in his bones. It was what he had to do. He had to.

Ionius Servus Eternus said, "No."

"No?" Coriolane blinked, looking as blank as if he had never heard the word before. "I beg your pardon, Servus?"

"She is mine." Ionius reached out and gathered Romola roughly into his lap, trying to look as if he knew what he was doing and indeed, had done so repeatedly beforehand. "And surely you do not wish to sully your magnificence with a mere slave, especially with a lovely freeborn woman at your side already." He inclined his head to the courtesan, as it couldn't possibly hurt to appeal to her vanity. "But you granted me this boon at Year End, when both she and I did you such good service. Surely you do not mean to take it from us now?"

Coriolane's eyes narrowed, trying to parse if this was bald-faced defiance, and if so, if he should punish it. But he did not want to be distracted from the second act, which was setting up elaborate man-traps for the surviving prisoners to run as a gauntlet. Of course, they would be cut, crushed, skinned, sliced, scorched, stabbed, impaled, disemboweled, decapitated, eviscerated, or otherwise ripped apart at any mistake, and the lictors were moving among them, dividing them into teams and careful to separate anyone who desperately tried to stay together; they had been promised that the last two survivors would be given a pension and celebrated as a hero of Merone. It was unclear if this was any sort of reward or just the final insult, and with that, Ionius stood up abruptly, causing Romola to slide off. "If you will excuse us, Majesty."

"What?" Coriolane looked even more baffled. "The interval is over. The show is about to resume. Did you think you were leaving now?"

"If you will excuse us." Ionius steered Romola through the aisles of the crowded box, not especially careful as to whether he literally stepped on their well-bred toes. "I must discipline my consort in private. As I said, Majesty. You would not want her for your own."

Heads were still turning, gaping and whispering – nobody, not ever, in the entire history of the Colosseum, had walked out of the emperor's private box without leave. Ionius did not look back as he marched down the stairs, the awful baying of the crowd starting again outside the thick stone walls that enclosed the passage like a tomb. It was muted, muffled, but it kept rolling over him like a wave, forcing his head underwater to drown. He couldn't breathe, felt like he had in Sardarkhand after fleeing from the Holoborodkas, as if his knees might buckle and leave him adrift among the other broken corpses. He still could turn around, return to the box, and give them what they deserved. He had once killed five thousand men by himself, though that had taken a while. Fifty would be nothing, the blink of an eye, and the other Immortals present were not as strong as he was. How the fuck did they think they could stop him?

The bottom of the stairs came as a surprise, and he almost lost his balance. Then he leaned against the wall, breathing raggedly, as Romola eyed him in alarm and confusion. At last she ventured, "Ion... Ionius?"

It was the first time she had ever called him anything apart from *my lord,* and it rang like a curse in his ears. *Ionius,* the name his Meronite slave mistress chose for him, the one he had taken to heart and been so eager to become, deliberately effacing any remnant of his old self. Little Ivan Sazharyn was as dead as his sister Tatyana, strangled and dumped in the same shallow grave, and even worse, it was Ionius who had done the job. Killed everyone, killed himself, killed everything he touched. The only thing he knew how to do, always. Over and over.

"Don't," he said, voice grating in his chest. "Don't – call me that."

Romola looked startled and abashed. Before she could apologize, he held up a hand. "When we're – when nobody else is around – just – Ivan. Call me Ivan. Don't argue, girl. Just do as I say."

She stared at him, unsure how to take this very strange order, as he led the way back to their wagon, where the dozing driver awoke with a start. "My lord? Is there a – "

"Take us back to the palace. Now." Ionius climbed in and tossed another sestertius. "For your discretion. Is that clear?"

The driver nodded, prodded his beast to wakefulness in turn, and they rumbled away from the Colosseum, into the city streets, which were nearly empty as everyone flocked to the arena. Ionius sat in silence until they returned to the Eternal Palace, which was likewise all but deserted. At that, he had a sudden and insane idea. If metal could be ripped out of human beings and result in their destruction, the same was obviously true of buildings. This place glistened with gold, silver, steel and pewter, iron and copper. If he put all his strength into it and gave one good *pull* –

"Iv... Ivan." The name still clearly sounded wrong to Romola, and he could see her biting back the instinct to add *my lord*. But she reached out and took his arm with simple, unpretentious gentleness, and even if he did not deserve it, he let her. "Come now. Let's just... let's just rest."

He wanted to tell her that he did not, he would not, he *could* not. But the strength and the fury had drained out of him, he felt cold and dry and dead, and there was nothing he could do – he, the general, the commander, the leader – but follow. He nodded. They went in.

✯✯✯✯

IT TOOK IONIUS THE NEXT WEEK to learn that Aliyah ur-Namasqa had not perished with her fellows in the Colosseum. Instead she languished in the Castel, fate uncertain, which had been ordered expressly by Coriolane. This was unusual, though by no means evidence of mercy; the emperor had a thousand ways to put prisoners to death and liked exploring them all. In the meantime, there were even darker whispers: the blood-plague had finally overstepped its bounds in Yerussala and stolen into the poorer quarters of Merone, from whence it spread like wildfire. Streets were cordoned off, quarantine orders issued, but none of it would have the slightest effect. After all, this was no natural disease, which would be bad enough. It was the purposeful creation of the Thaumaturges, unleashed even on the Eternal City, the one place that was supposed to be untouchable, safe from every enemy – except the one that sat on the throne, crowned and serene, holy protector of the realm. If Coriolane was leeching and killing his own subjects, things must be even worse than feared. Ionius had no time. He had to act.

He didn't manage to intervene for Aliyah; she was finally dragged out of the Castel and sentenced to die in the pit, but he did catch up as they were about to throw her in. He gave her the only help he could, though doubtless she neither recognized nor appreciated it. But so be it, and that evening, Ionius sent another messenger in strict secrecy. Not that it mattered; once this got out, he was dead. Yet until the last moment came, there was something to be done, and when Marcus Servus was shown into his presence, looking extremely confused, Ionius strolled forward in his old chilling nonchalance. "Good evening, Marcus."

"Good evening, General." The boy blinked. "Did I do wrongly at training today?"

"I'm sure it was fine," Ionius said impatiently. "I have a question for you. You've always said that you wanted to serve me, and to uncover the truth of our enemies. Yes?"

"Yes. I'm ready to go to Korolgrod at once, if you – "

"You're not going to Korolgrod." Ionius turned away and took two letters from his desk, sealed with the enchanted wax that would detect and warn of any tampering. "Listen closely. You will go to the docks – not the Imperial Docks, the common ones – and board a ship bound for Xandropolis, in Gezeren. From there, proceed to Jedya, in Rabiyah. It's a major port city, and ships leave daily for the east. Take the first one you find – your best route is likely the one that calls at Malabarium in Indush and Guangzhi Province in southern Qin, at least if the monsoon is blowing in the right direction. Likewise, if there is any opportunity for magical transport that gets you there faster, take it, regardless of the cost. In Guangzhing or whichever city you should first reach Qin, present yourself to the yamen and tell him that you need transport to the Jade City and an audience with Hang Zhai as a matter of supreme urgency. Give him this first letter here. The second you must place only, and I repeat *only,* into the hand of the Thearch themself. Is that clear?"

Marcus looked stunned, but he had not made it so far in Immortal training because he was a dullard. "I – yes, my lord. I understand. Is this something relating to the war, my lord?"

"More or less. I do not need to stress, but I will, that this is an errand of the strictest secrecy. Talk to nobody, reveal yourself to no one. You are a humble trader's son, Meronite or Ruthynian, whichever you feel more comfortable in pretending. You must give it to Hang Zhai alone, do you understand? They may try to put you off, or ask you to return when the stars are more auspicious, or bog you in a mire of bureaucracy, or any other of the well-mannered delays the Qiné do so well. You must not let them. Insist on an audience and do not take no for an answer."

"Yes, my lord." Marcus frowned. *"They?* Is it more than one?"

"No. The Thearch's *they* is singular. The Qiné believe their divine ruler transcends such grubby and earthly limitations as human sex, and do not view them as male or female. If you attempt to refer to one over the other, you will be shunned in disgrace. Do *not* lose this battle just because you couldn't be culturally sensitive."

"Yes, my lord. *They.* I'll remember. I'll be on my way tonight, if it pleases you. It was just – before I go, I don't suppose there's… any way I could say farewell to Lady Romola?"

"*Lady* Romola?" Ionius could discern a faint blush in Marcus's cheeks that made him realize what was going on. Of course after spending all this time squiring her diligently around Merone and otherwise serving as her personal bodyguard, Marcus, in all of his sixteen or seventeen years, had decided that he was in love. "You really thought you could venture liberties with *my* consort?"

"No, no, no, my lord. Never." Marcus looked aghast. "You must not think that I have ever behaved in any way that was remotely inappropriate. I just – we have grown friendly, so – "

It was cruel of him to make the boy squirm so badly, but even as Marcus continued to look terrified that he might be smote out of existence on the spot, it gave Ionius the final realization of something he had suspected for a while. And that was: as much as he was eager to prove himself as a full-fledged Immortal, Marcus would in fact fail the trials. He could not pass, or if he did, it would be only by blind luck. There was no doubting his technique or his proficiency. But because he was still human enough to eagerly seek Ionius's paternal approval and form a puppy-dog crush on the pretty and vulnerable young lady who had fallen into his stewardship, that meant the fundamental making of him, the moment when such things had to be completely and forever stripped from an Immortal's inmost sinews, had gone wrong, and it could never be gotten back or done over. If so, there were two choices. Marcus could be returned to whoever owned him before he was brought to the Eternal Palace, or handed to the Corporalists. To be Remade like Romola, whether as an Immortal without any troubling conscience or something else entirely, like the ghouls that patrolled by night in Qahirah and were said to devour anyone who went outside during curfew. Another alchemical abomination, another unperson, another casualty on this endlessly blood-drenched altar. Why, then? *Why?*

"Marcus," Ionius said. He wondered at the name of the boy who was born in Korolgrod, and how Marcus had come to Merone, if anyone at all remembered. "There is one more thing I wish you to do for me, when your errand to Qin is finished."

"Anything, my lord." Marcus looked at him with shining eyes. "Anything at all."

"Leave," Ionius said simply. "Don't come back here. There is no future for you in Merone. Go back to Ruthynia if you can find your family, or if you want to. Otherwise, go anywhere in the world, do what you please, live your life far from the Eternal City and its throne. Do not bend your knee or swear your fealty to Coriolane Aureus IX, or his successors, ever again. Is that clear?"

Marcus looked absolutely floored. Before he could interject, Ionius once more spoke over him. "I do not ask it to make sense to you now, as I am sure it does not. I do not ask you to understand or agree with me. But I am your general, and this is the last order I will give to you. I leave it to your own heart to decide whether it is worth obeying."

"General Ionius, my lord..." Marcus was still flabbergasted. "Do you suggest that we should not – that we will not see each other again?"

"I don't know." For the briefest moment, as it had never done that he could recall in waking memory, Ionius felt the shadow of tears thicken his throat. "It may be so. Go now, boy. *Go.*"

When Marcus had taken his leave, Ionius stood for several moments, staring at nothing. Then he turned on his heel, went into the next room, and said, "Romola."

She looked up with a start. "My lord?"

"I am leaving." Ionius tried to say it coolly and unemotionally, but the catch in his throat made it click. "I do not know how long, or if I will ever return. I am sorry that I cannot explain, but it would put you in danger as well. You are welcome to live in my rooms as long as you wish, and call yourself my consort, so they do not dare to lay a finger on you. I thank you for the help you have been, and the... the kindness you have shown. I have poorly repaid it, but I am indebted."

Romola stared at him just as Marcus had, as if it truly mattered to anyone that Ionius Servus Eternus would finally and forever depart from their life. "My — Ivan. Is there no way you might consider taking me with you? I wouldn't be a burden, I promise."

"You are not a burden. Not there, and not here." Ionius offered the ghost of a smile. "I am sorry you have been told that for so long. If there is a chance to help Aliyah ur-Namasqa or any of the other Qartic rebels, you should take it. It may be far too late, but so be it."

Romola continued to stare at him. Then at last, she hurried forward and wrapped her arms around his waist, hugging him tightly. It was so foreign and so strange — he was never touched by anyone, aside from his brief and perfunctory trysts with the Ibelusian catamite or his fellows — that Ionius almost jerked back, but forced himself to accept it. He even slowly, stiffly hugged her in return, then stepped away. "I won't forget you. I hope you will do the same."

"No." Romola's eyes were bright. "No, I won't."

With that, Ionius was ready, come what may, to do what must be done. He took the false Ring of Tselmun, put it in his cloak, and left the Eternal Palace for what might be the last time. When he reached the atrium, he was not surprised that Julian did not come to greet him. Indeed, he had known instinctively that something had changed and Julian was gone, and while it might doom his fairly flimsy plans, it might not. He called, "Grand Magister."

It took a long moment for Kronus to appear, looking more emaciated and ghostly than ever. Creating the red plague on a regular basis and unleashing it on multiple cities could not be easy, and must require a great deal of energy, or perhaps the actual blood from Kronus's own veins and good riddance to him. The only reason Ionius was not going to kill him now was because he needed Kronus's magic for the last part of the plan. In the meantime, however —

"Good evening, Excellency," Ionius said, faultlessly polite. "Is Doctor Kozharyev here?"

"No, in fact. He is not, and I was wondering if you, with your apparent… coziness, could offer any enlightenment on why he has not only disappeared, but taken an extremely valuable item from my library. I have attempted to locate him myself, but he managed to master enough of the magical art to cover his tracks. Indeed, General, while I would never wish to make wild accusations, I do wonder why a loyal imperial servant like yourself would consort with such an inherently unsuitable person. Especially when, it seems, said loyalty has drastically waned."

"What makes you say that, Excellency?"

"Come now, my lord." The Thaumaturge spread his hands. "Your increasing reluctance to carry out your duties has not escaped my attention. And so – "

"You did not think Doctor Kozharyev was *inherently unsuitable* when you gave him access to your most secret tools and texts. If anything, you were too arrogant to believe that anyone could outsmart you in here and did not bother to take the most elementary precautions, so baseless threats about my loyalty must be matched with the truth of your incompetence. If I went to His Majesty and told him how you let this *item* be lost, do you think he would be best pleased?"

Of course, Ionius had no intention of doing any such thing, but it had, he was gratified to see, caused Kronus a visible moment of hesitance. The Grand Magister licked his papery lips, then smiled. "Your point is understood, my lord. If we both have minor failings best kept out of sight – those can be remediated, can't they?"

"Indeed." Ionius allowed himself a brief and feral grin. "I have a bargain for you. You open a door, and I go through it. In return, I give you the item of your study, and permit you to decide whether it is truly necessary to pass it on to His Majesty. Are you interested?"

A brief, greedy gleam came into Kronus's eyes. "What is this item?"

"Why." Ionius reached into his cloak and removed the Ring of Tselmun, at least to every appearance. "Would this suffice, Excellency?"

"I...." Kronus made a sudden convulsive motion, as if only barely restraining himself from snatching it. "Where did you get that, my lord?"

"I took it off the Qartic traitor during His Majesty's recent pacification of the city. He asked me to keep it safe, and I can think of no safer hands than the master of magic in all of Merone. So, then. Do you think we might be able to see our way to an accord?"

"We... we might." Kronus was almost vibrating. "And His Majesty has many cares, so many other affairs of state. It might not be necessary to burden him with another."

"Indeed." Ionius shrugged. If and when Coriolane found out about this, it would look as if Kronus had conspired to keep the Ring from him and performed some reckless experiment that destroyed its power, and if the Grand Magister was to be accidentally executed as a result, that was merely the unfortunate reality of treason. "Now, about that door?"

"Of course, my lord. Of course. Where did you intend to travel?"

"You leave that to me." Ionius dropped the ring into the Grand Magister's clammy palm. "I wish you well of your new possession."

"Indeed, indeed." Kronus scuttled to the far side of the atrium and raised his hands before the dark circle of doors. In a few moments, one of them began to glow white, and Kronus gestured to it. "Here, my lord. It will open wherever you wish it to open. If you intend to return – "

"We will see. Farewell, Grand Magister."

"Farewell, General. I am grateful. Most grateful."

"I'm sure you are." Ionius smiled, close-mouthed. "Good fortune."

With that, he stood before the door, took a deep breath, and closed his eyes. Had to draw up that which he had pushed away, ignored, thrust down. Had to admit what he wanted, and *who* he wanted. If Julian had magically covered his tracks, it seemed plain that he did not, in fact, want to be located, but that would be as it was. Ionius would do what he could, and pass once and for all from everything and everyone he had been before. It was both terrifying and thrilling – like being born again, like waking up and opening his eyes, like remembering his own name. He was far beyond anything he had ever known before, but at least it was his choice now. It was him.

The glow turned even brighter, and he thought of the last time he had passed through this place, cutting his arm and using his own blood and bone as the key. This was different, but no less frightening. He was still carving his flesh, laying himself bare, only hoping it would take him where he wanted to go, unsure what awaited. He could hope, he could trust, but it remained a mystery, even as his old self crumbled to ash and was devoured. It was time to go, and so as he never had before and might never again, he stepped into the great unknown.

CHAPTER 24

JULIAN

AMBRAZAKTI, CAPITAL CITY OF THE EPONYMOUS empire, was not the worst place in the world for a hideout. For one thing, it was warm – indeed, warm enough that Julian, born and raised in the chilly northern climes of Korolgrod, often found himself sweating like a pig. For another, it was incredibly, obscenely wealthy, in a way that hardly seemed real. Even the ordinary people wore golden earrings, jeweled rings, or kente cloth, and every street was paved, every building glittering. The city was crowned by the complex built around the Djingebey, Sankahre, and Sid Yahya Mahqasas, their madrasah schools, and the Great Library, one of the most renowned and ancient centers of learning in the world. Julian was far from the first indigent scholar to turn up dressed in rags, clutching a precious text, and begging for shelter from an oppressive government that wanted to kill them and burn their books, and there was a lively community of academics-in-exile who welcomed him to their bosom. Likewise, nobody gave a shit that he was a Vashemite. King Musum ben Mansa, the patron of this largesse and learning, was Wahin (indeed, upon his hajj to Makeyah many years ago, he spent so much gold in Qahirah that he accidentally crashed the Gezereni economy), but Ambraz policy was one of broad ecumenicism. Not even strings-attached, conditional Meronite "tolerance," but just that, truly dumbfoundingly, nobody seemed to care.

Even aside from that, to be in a place that called itself an *empire* and yet was not Merone, realizing their world was not omnipresent and all-devouring, was likewise mind-boggling. While Ambrazakti was not some fairytale land of everyone holding hands and working together for the greater good, it did not attack or annex its surrounding territories, not least because it did not need to. If you were a downtrodden citizen of a nearby region, laboring under a greedy magistrate or a bloody warlord, you went out of your way to invite the Ambraz to come in and take over. And why wouldn't you, if it gave you this?

Julian was shrewd enough to realize that no nation-state rose high without exacting calculations of self-interest, and this munificence did not come without other costs, but that was the thing. As long as human beings were forced to live in flawed reality, making complex choices and necessary sacrifices, there was no polity or ruler that would be perfect, and demanding that and that alone would only lead to tearing down all possible options and making everything worse. Ambraz's version of empire was orders of magnitude better than Merone's, but that did not mean it was innocent or undemanding. It still required its subjects to pay Ambraz taxes in Ambraz coinage, to swear fealty to Ambraz kings, to prioritize Ambraz national matters over personal or tribal ones, to speak and read enough Ambraz to understand and obey the government's proclamations, and otherwise assimilate into the civic and political culture. But if that was the trade-off for living comfortably and freely, able to worship their own gods and speak their own tongue in their own home, it was less onerous than what that social contract could otherwise be. At least if and until something better came along – and it would have to. After all, much of the agreeable present arrangement rested on the personal will of King Musum, and if he or his successors ever took it into their heads to be just as much of a merciless despot as Coriolane, there was no way to stop them; they still had all the power. Hereditary monarchy was the least effective system known to man at selecting a competent or caring head of state, and despite the golden and prosperous age of Musum's rule, he was getting old. His eldest son and heir apparent was also rumored to believe in far more severe methods of authority. Even a few years from now, Ambrazakti could be a very different place.

That, however, was still safely in the future, not a current concern. Julian had arrived here in a bit of a blur, unsure if he had done the magic correctly either to travel or conceal that travel, and dearly hoping he wouldn't suffer a sudden unscheduled discorporation. Yet his weeks of laboring over the *Key* managed to serve him that much, and here he was. The city was international enough that he didn't stand out as much as he feared, though he didn't speak a word of Ambraz and was reliant on sign language and the good nature of his interlocutors whenever he ventured into the streets. But there were some scholars who knew Ruthynian and Lanuvian, and as with Aliyah ur-Namasqa, Old High Yerussalan could (usually) be understood by a speaker of Semyic enough to get the job done. It was a messy stitched-together linguistic pastiche, but so be it.

For the most part, Julian spent his time in the cool, dim halls of the Great Library, seated at a writing bench and continuing to pore over the *Key*. For obvious reasons, he told no one what it was, and kept it with him at all times. Even if he had found refuge for the time being, the original grimoire of Tselmun ben Dayoud was a prize for which any self-respecting scholar would in fact commit murder, and Julian was ever-vigilant to the possibility. It made him rather solitary and standoffish as a result, though academics were not known for being gregariously outgoing. This was temporary, anyway. Hopefully he could stay safe long enough to finish the translation, and then he had to go back. Had to finish the job, with or without help. Even if Coriolane had the Ring like Aliyah feared, the reason she told him to run. And if Ionius –

That was where Julian had to cut off, to remind himself the choice had been made of his own free will and could not be taken back. Whatever might happen with Ionius in some alternate reality was one thing, but this, here and now, was another. Perhaps Julian had broken a solemn agreement, or it was indeed only a cynical ploy. Either way, it was irrelevant, and one kiss was nothing to moon over. If it could have been more – well. Julian was used to disappointment.

Tonight, he stayed in the library long past dark; it was open late to accommodate the insomniac bookworms who just *had* to find the proper text or theorem, and even if the wardens came around at midnight on the ostensible premise of chasing them out, it was easy to hide under a desk and wait until they were gone. Julian was finally on the brink of understanding the principles of pentacle magic, and after seeing the bone monstrosity Kronus was building, that was one of his main priorities, since permanently destroying a locus of that much power was not a matter of just taking a sledgehammer to it. There were confusing tangents on how exactly the figure worked, or how a jinnyeh, hinnyeh, shedim, dev, or other spirit could be bound in it – the six-sided Seal of Tselmun was a hexagram, of more refined functionality than the usual five-pointed pentagram – and which incantations and inscriptions served best. There were also a few types of spirits even greater than jinnyeh. Ifrit, godlike fire-beings such as Arghan the Undying, Ur-Aswad the Black, and others whose names were too powerful to write down, and marid, almighty water-elementals who commanded seas and storms and could destroy entire fleets of warships; their names were not known because nobody had survived to recount them. Of course, everything Tselmun said had to be taken with a large grain of salt, but ifrit and marid were too strong even for him to control, so he had generally gone for jinnyeh or lower. A magician of his métier, assisted by the Ring, could summon and bind spirits in up to six pentacles, but the risk increased exponentially with each one. Only the most accomplished magicians tried to run even two at once. Six was tantamount to a death wish.

Nonetheless, while this was all very interesting and might even one day tell Julian how to locate the fucking Ring, his eyes were scratchy with exhaustion, he had read the last sentence ten times while barely absorbing it, and the dryness in his throat and the gnawing in his belly reminded him that he had yet again spent the entire day (and much of the night) cooped up in here. Indeed when he stood up, the cramp in his back doubled him over like an old man, and it was with much cursing and grimacing that he rolled up the parchments, put them back in the box, and left the library, careful to avoid the wardens. Even if they accommodated the peculiarities of scholars, a place packed with magical and dangerous books was still not somewhere you wanted too many sinister strangers to wander alone at odd hours, entirely unsupervised.

Outside, the night had mellowed to a pleasant coolness, and the sky stretched from horizon to horizon in a lucent empyrean of stars, the milky band of the galaxy smeared more clearly than Julian had ever seen it before. Ambraz lay south of the Sand Sea and north of the Numerian jungles, stretching to the Occidental Ocean in the west and the mountainous highlands of Ge'ez in the east. If Julian was planning to travel back to Merone without magic, it would take him several months. Ideally, he would have the Ring *and* the *Key* and could do as he pleased, but that was a very slender wager. Not least because it outrageously presumed that things would work the way they were supposed to, which had heretofore failed as a hypothesis at every turn. That, or –

Preoccupied with his thoughts, Julian didn't look where he was going as he crossed the courtyard, and walked hard into a hooded figure coming the other way, causing them to spring apart with mutual outcries. Yet as he stooped to retrieve the fallen *Key,* something pricked at him, as the figure likewise stopped in its tracks. Just because Julian could not even flee halfway across the world and avoid literally stumbling into Ionius Servus Eternus on a dark night, as if there was some unbreakable weight of gravity that kept bringing them back together, he knew it, he *knew* it, as the voice said, "Julian? Julian – Mata Koroleva, it is – ?"

"You." Julian wanted to summon up more indignation or outrage or anything at all, but he couldn't. He sat back on his heels, glowering without surprise or heat. "If you're here to arrest or kill me or whatever, if you had a crisis of loyalty and went back to Coriolane, just get it over with. I don't want to know why or how. It'll just disappoint me."

"I'm – I'm not." Ionius coughed, sounding more reticent than Julian had ever heard him. "It's a long story, but I came in search of you on my own accord, not anyone else's, and especially not the emperor's. Is there somewhere we could speak in private?"

"What makes you think I want to talk to you?" Julian scooped up the *Key* and got to his feet. "I didn't leave for no reason. If you have the Ring, or had it and gave it to Coriolane, and *then* had the crisis – "

"It's a fake," Ionius interrupted. "The one I took in Qart-Hadesht, and bribed Kronus with. Otherwise, I would not have given it up."

"A *fake?*" Unfortunately, that startled Julian enough, and sparked to life the damnable ape-brain of his curiosity, that he knew in resignation that he was doomed. "What do you mean?"

Ionius tipped his head at their surroundings, plainly reluctant to have this delicate conversation in the open, and while there was every likelihood that this was a trap and would end with Julian being trussed up and hauled back to the Thaumaturges' tower for Kronus to slow-roast over the fire, he was by no means defenseless. He still couldn't compete with an Immortal in hand-to-hand combat, but his mastery of Tselmun's spells was no longer incidental. If something in Julian yearned to believe this miraculous reappearance was genuine, that Ionius had finally relinquished his old prejudices and *understood*... that might not be a solid foundation on which to build, but it was not nothing. After all, he was here, and he was just standing there, waiting. For Julian to say yea or nay, to lead him on or turn him back, and for it to be the way of things. It was a dangerous and alluring gift, that power. Very different from that which had shaped both of their lives so deeply, that had brought them here, and yet for all that, no less strong. No less necessary.

"Fine," Julian said. "Follow me."

Ionius did so without demur, as they crossed the courtyard and descended into the winding alleys of hovels that housed the Library's staff and scholars. They were built of straw and stucco, mud-brick and mounded clay, and Julian opened the door into his hut. It was only large enough to hold a bed, a washing pot, a firepit, and a cooking area, and as Ionius ducked in after him, Julian had a sudden stupid moment of self-consciousness, recalling how they last met in the well-appointed comfort of his tower chambers. Even if that was in the purview of a mad old murderer who would have boiled *his* bones the instant Julian let his guard slip, at least it was (however foolish it sounded) *nicer*.

Ionius, however, did not seem to notice or care. When Julian awkwardly beckoned at the bed, as there was nowhere else to sit, he did so, and Julian paused a moment before joining him. They sat side by side in the darkness, listening to the soft sounds of the night, and Julian was intensely aware of the rumpled hollow of the blankets where their fingers nearly brushed. Then he said, "Why are you here, then? And if I ask, are you actually going to tell me the truth?"

"Yes." Ionius didn't look at him, arms resting loosely on his knees; the posture appeared casual on the surface, but the tension continued to thrum through him, a chilling reminder of the violence he was capable of unleashing at any moment. "I'm sure you have many questions, and I doubt that what I have to tell you will make me look better in your eyes, but let me say it all first. Then you can chastise me as you wish."

Julian was tempted to make an impertinent remark about how the mighty Immortal general was concerned about what a lowly Vashemite scholar might think of him, but he restrained. This was a moment requiring support, not goading; there was plenty of time for that, and he had made good use of it, but this was different. "Very well," he said, moving his hand just a bit closer, in case Ionius should find himself in need of clutching it for moral support. "I'm listening."

With that, Ionius took a breath and launched himself forward like a man off a cliff. He recounted the visit to Qart-Hadesht, the revelation of the Adirim's treason, and the deaths of Safiya ur-Tasvashta, which he carried out by his own hand, and Noora ur-Namasqa, which he did not. He made no excuses for his culpability, did not pretend he had not done yet more terrible things in the service of the emperor; Qart-Hadesht was left burning, brutalized and terrified, and things would surely only get worse. But he had spoken with Aliyah ur-Namasqa, who understandably wanted nothing to do with him. It was not until they returned to Merone that he discovered the deception which Safiya or one of the others had enacted in a desperate attempt to keep ultimate power out of Coriolane's hands. Whatever Ionius had taken from Aliyah, it was not the Ring, but a fake. Wherever the real Ring might be now, and who knew of its location or anything else about it, was utterly unknown.

After that, there was more: the gruesome execution of the Qartic hostages in the Colosseum, how Ionius had lost his taste to sit through it and walked out with a girl named Romola (Julian felt an unbecoming prickle of jealousy and desire to ask just who she was, but Ionius had told him to shut up and he nobly held his tongue); the arrival of the blood-plague in Merone itself; the way he was too late to save Aliyah but tried to give her what he could in the way of a weapon; and then sending Marcus Servus on a secret mission to Qin, bribing Kronus with the fake Ring, and stepping through the door here, to Ambrazakti, whereupon they had once more been reunited. At that, his torrent of words finally failed, and he stared at his hands even more fiercely. "I'm sure you have much to comment on. Don't hurt yourself by restraining."

"I..." Julian wasn't sure how to make sense of his competing emotions. Beforehand, he had optimistically thought he could *talk* Ionius into seeing the light, if he just had a little more time, but he was realizing that he couldn't, that he could only push him to a place of finally being ready to understand and hope that he would. "I'm glad to hear you helped Aliyah, though it is ironic. She was the one who told me to run."

Ionius looked at him sharply. "What?"

At that, Julian was obliged to explain his own dungeon colloquy with the prisoner, how Aliyah insisted that Ionius wasn't trustworthy, and Julian therefore took it upon himself to abandon the Eternal City and his hideout in the Castel at his earliest convenience. That unspooled into why he left the Thaumaturges' tower in the first place, that he had found and then lost Tatyana's file, and all of it was because Kronus was building a giant bone pentacle and whatever it was being used for and *would* be used for, it could not possibly be anything good. "I'm sorry," Julian finished. "I didn't know what to think. You were gone, and I couldn't stay, and... yes, I just... sorry."

"No," Ionius said. "It was my fault. I should never have put you in that position, asked you to go to the Corporalists, any of it. I was not thinking correctly. My sister is dead, has been dead for a long time, and it was only foolishness. But if Kronus is the *only* – "

"I... think so. Yeah." Julian blew out a ragged breath. "And I'm also quite sure that he was planning to kill me, as soon as I was done with the *Key*. So either way, I did have to run."

"Fuck," Ionius muttered, mostly to himself. "I heard palace gossip calling Kronus a cannibal, but I didn't think anything of it. I thought it was just the usual jealousy, but *this* – "

"Wait." Julian's voice rose nearly an octave. *"Cannibal?!"*

"There is an old school of magic that believed you should eat the flesh of others to assume their powers." Ionius's voice was even grimmer. "Particularly those gifted in sorcery, or clairvoyance, or anything else beyond ordinary ken. If Kronus is a devotee of such a school – "

"If *that's* where he's getting the bones from — if he fucking *ate* the people and then — "

"Fuck," they chorused again, as Julian contemplated with a shudder how very close he had been to becoming a mad old wizard's literal supper. "I just want to clarify," he added firmly, "that this *doesn't* come from the *Key*. There isn't anything like that in there. Tselmun was power-hungry in other ways, but not *literally*. I know we talk about how the Thaumaturges stole all their magic from the Vashemites — well, they didn't just steal from us, but from everyone. And we don't *eat people*. We don't take Tridevarian children and sacrifice them in the Black Mass, the blood libel, all the other things they accuse us of in order to justify pogroms. I'm sure that if this ever got out, the Meronites would declare that Kronus had been corrupted by all that heretic Vashemite magic and this was something we secretly do, so we should be the ones punished instead. But aren't the Tridevarians the ones who proudly proclaim to *eat the Prince's flesh?* The bread is transfigured into his real body, the okovita is his literal blood? And we wonder where the notion of cannibalism for special powers and spiritual blessings really *came* from?"

"Hush." Ionius put his hand on Julian's arm. "I promise, I do not believe that Vashemites eat people. Perhaps we should have seen it coming. After all, in Lanuvian mythology, is *Kronus* not the father of *Juspiter*, the one who devoured his own children? It seems pointed."

"I suppose." Julian felt hot and cold at once, trying to focus on his anger, his insistence, anything except Ionius's hand seeming to consume (ha) all his light and air and being. "But even if you don't, other people will. I'm just angry that he stole our magic, our book, our legacy, and now he's going to get us blamed, *again,* for something that we don't — "

"Hush," Ionius said again, voice as tender as Julian had ever heard it. It snapped something in him, his increasingly frayed rationalizations and his insistence that it would have been fine, *fine,* if Ionius *had* betrayed him without a backward glance and that was that. He didn't want to give in, to feel the full weight of everything that threatened to break its dam and flood his mind, his heart, his stupid, stupid flesh. But it was likewise a battle he was losing, Julian leaned forward at the same time Ionius did, and their mouths collided halfway.

It was difficult to say who was more surprised, even though they had both initiated it. For a final moment they both held back, and then, desperately, blindly, starving in an altogether different way, they did not. Ionius's hands clamped like iron on Julian's wrists, hauling him closer, and Julian shoved him hard in the shoulders, knocking the great Immortal flat on his back. The bed was hardly big enough, just a clay shelf built into the wall with a thin mattress, a bolster pillow, and a brightly-woven blanket, but neither of them paid the slightest attention.

They kissed until they absolutely had to part for breath, and that only a raw, ragged half-gasp against each other's cheeks, mouths open and heaving. Then Ionius rose up like a sea monster and flipped them over, pushing Julian down beneath him, and Julian fought back just as vigorously, both of them refusing to cede control. At some point he found himself on top again, pulling Ionius's tunic open and biting his collarbone, musing at the strong clean lines of it, nipping his jaw and musing hot slow kisses down his neck and into his shoulder, the broad chiseled strength of his chest. Ionius *growled* at him, which did even worse things to Julian's rapidly vanishing self-control, snatched him and rolled him over again, and fully repaid the favor, but with far more biting. Someone should talk to him about that, but it would not be Julian. He could not remember a word in any of the languages he knew, even his own name was a hazy prospect at the moment, and when he was pinned down beneath the full and formidable force of General Ionius at war, he wondered if the bastard always fought this dirty. Small wonder he razed his enemies like ripe wheat.

There was, however, a very different sort of razing on the agenda at the moment, and Julian could not think of anything he had wanted more in his life. There was a brief interruption as Ionius got up to collect the vial of oil from the cooking stone, the rest of their clothes came off in a flurry of pulling and tearing, and then they tumbled onto the bed again, entangled and devouring. Ionius' hands gripped his hips, his knees pushed Julian's legs apart, and then Julian huffed and gasped and bucked, snatched at the coverlets and swore over and over in a mindless litany, as Ionius thrust into him and pressed him flat, possessed him, filled him to the hilt and began to move like a thunderstorm, the lightning and the rain. His mouth remained sealed to the back of Julian's neck, fusing them like the final result of alchemy, two elements blending into something new, the creation of the philosopher's stone. Ionius kept moving, the mad slick sweetness building the friction to a higher and higher peak, and Julian moved back. "Yes," he muttered. "Come on now, Ivan Slavaynich. Fuck me properly, you bastard. Do it. Yes. *Yes.*"

Ivan Slavaynich responded by doubling his intensity, if such a thing was possible, and Julian groaned, all further witticisms or helpful suggestions driven comprehensively out of his head. Their clasped hands twisted into white-knuckled knots, knees digging and muscles straining, heaving and writhing. Then there was nothing but mindless white heat, spilling through every dark and deprived sinew of him and sending him head over heels, and he lost sense of himself altogether.

He had no idea how long it was before he began to surface, became aware of the throb between his legs, their sticky skin wicked together and Ionius – Ivan's – weight atop him heavily enough to crush the breath from his lungs. Julian wriggled and made a plaintive sound, and it eased, but he continued to lie flat on his face, fucked into messy deliquescence. At last he said, half-muffled into the pillow, "Name of God."

"Mmm." Ivan slipped out and off, causing Julian to groan with the withdrawal of contact, and wedged himself in the limited space between Julian and the wall. His body was still as warm as a bonfire, damp with sweat, and they settled into an awkward spooning position, Julian's back pressed to Ivan's chest. At last Ivan said quietly, "Are you – ?"

"Fine? Yes. More than fine." Julian's hand settled on Ivan's thigh, tracing the hard cords of muscle. Almost accusingly, he said, "You've done this before."

"Did you think I lived like a monk?"

"No, I just didn't expect – with men, you know." Julian hesitated. "You're not – that is, the girl you mentioned, Romola – "

Ivan's laugh was a buzz into the back of his neck. "I assure you, Julian Janovynich. I am not in the habit of being disloyal. Nor is Romola a matter about which you need to concern yourself. Our relationship is… complicated, yes, but not in the least like this."

"Oh." Julian couldn't deny it, a small spring of relief bubbled up. "Well. That's good, I suppose."

Ivan didn't answer, but his grip tightened on Julian's waist, pulling him closer. There were any number of things that could be said, arguments to be had, but not now. Now, at last, they slept.

★★★★

TO SAY THE LEAST, JULIAN'S DREAMS were strange, passionate and heated and twisted all at once, and he woke with a start at dawn, in desperate need of a piss and a long drink of water. He attended to both, then glanced over at Ivan, still fast asleep on the bed. The first gleam of sun was cresting atop the roof and turning the fine brown hair on his chest and arms to gold, and Julian wondered what on earth they did next. As far as he knew, he was perfectly permitted to have guests, but when that guest was an ex-Meronite Immortal who defected in the dead of night by bribing a cannibalistic wizard with a fake Ring of Tselmun, it might be more than the Ambraz felt like putting up with. They had long been shielded from Meronite attacks by the Sand Sea, but it was an especial thorn in the Eternal City's foot that a Wahin Ifriqiyini black man would ever dare to proclaim himself the equal of the Tridevarian Divine Emperor. Now that Coriolane was determined to kill anyone who had ever done either himself or Merone even the slightest wrong –

That's why you need to finish your translation of the Key, *fool. Get the Ring and do what you have to, even if you won't like it much.* Julian did not want to be a new Tselmun, but nor did he want to just throw away the power when it could finally be used for something important. After all, power alone was not good or evil; it was simply a sword. What it did depended on the intentions of the wielder, and sometimes its violence was necessary. There was no way to defeat men like Kronus and Coriolane by piously wringing one's hands and simply *hoping* they would see the light. They would not stop until stopped. And if it had somehow fallen to Julian Janovynich Kozharyev to do it...

He shook his head, dipped his hands in the water basin and splashed it on his face and hair, and debated whether to climb back into bed or get dressed and ready. He didn't want to slip out before Ivan woke and leave him alone, but he had spent enough time getting well laid (*very* well laid, thanks) and there was work to do. Fortunately, he did not have to ponder for long. Even subliminally, Ivan's well-honed warrior senses became aware that someone else was in the room and moving around, and his eyes flew open. He sat bolt upright, on the brink of leaping out of bed, before remembering. "Oh," he said, low and rusty. "Yes."

"Good morning." Julian pulled his robe off the hook and shrugged it over his head. "Hope you're feeling all right with... everything?"

Ivan cleared his throat, shoulders tensing, and that quickly, with a sinking heart, Julian realized that he was Ionius again, not Ivan. Ivan had let his guard down, but in the cold light of morning, the walls had gone right back up. "About last night. I should... not have done that."

"*You* should not have done it?" Julian couldn't keep the incredulity out of his voice. "And here I was thinking it was thoroughly mutual."

"Yes, perhaps. But you should not have let me." Some of that growl edged Ionius's words again, colder and darker. "You know who I am, but you don't *know*. I may have made the choice to start anew, but it does not wipe away everything I did before. All those rebels in Ruthynia, the ones you and your friends thought were killed by an Immortal? It was true, you know. It was me. I was that Immortal."

"I... do know that. Actually." Unsure whether to move closer or step away, Julian remained where he was. "I guessed it when Kronus told me your real name, and I was briefly planning to kill you. Besides, I'm not sure you can accuse me of not knowing who you are or what you've done, when most of what *I've* done is to yell at you about it. And if you feared that you fatally besmirched my youthful innocence – take it from me, it was besmirched a long time ago. I'm an adult, and I made a choice. We both did. Nothing will take it back, I don't regret it, and now, if you'll excuse me, I have work to do in the business of actually defeating Coriolane, not just sitting around and feeling guilty. I know the Tridevarians drill it into you, but I'm not about to send you groveling to confession on your knees." Julian paused. "Though I do have other ideas for what else you could do on your knees, if you're in the market."

Caught off guard, Ionius snorted a begrudging laugh. He still didn't look entirely pleased, but some of the darkness on his face lifted. "You are a wicked creature, Julian Janovynich."

"Thank you, I try." Julian kicked his feet into the soft velvet slippers. "Anyway, as I said, I have things to do. You should lie low and not cause an international incident."

Ionius started to say something, then stopped. But he could not gainsay it, and settled back with a displeased expression. "I will not remain idle," he warned. "I will do what I must."

"Good." Julian picked up the *Key* and his Library pass. "About time, wouldn't you say?"

And with that, confident of getting in the last word – he very much enjoyed fucking Ionius, no doubt of that, but still enjoyed bickering with him and didn't want it *all* to change – he left.

It was a more or less quiet morning at his usual worktable, as if nothing was different, though it was difficult to focus on binyanim and begadkefat without his mind consistently wandering back to last night. He didn't know if that was supposed to be an ongoing thing, or just for the purpose of Ivan-Ionius getting it out of his system and heretofore dedicating himself to stiff celibacy. There had been too much raw attraction and need for Julian to consider it a realistic possibility in the long run, but Ionius was nothing if not good at lying to himself in the short and indeed also-long runs, and it might take several years, which would be frustrating to Julian's own aims of... what? What were they, exactly? Ionius would be hunted as a traitor in every Meronite territory they set foot in, he was not remotely the kind of person that Julian could bring home to his mother and prepare for a proper Vashemite wedding in shul, and any life they did have together (there he went, thinking about a *life together* like it was something you really planned on having with an ex-imperial general you had fucked a grand total of once and originally met when he lied about his identity in jail) would forever be peripheral, ephemeral, exiled and outcast. Ionius had already tried to call a halt this morning and insist that Julian was making a terrible mistake, and perhaps he was right. Maybe it was wise to amputate and cleanly cauterize this now. Better not to get any more confused.

This, Julian's head agreed, was the correct and sensible course of action, and he spent more time than he should on talking his heart into following it. Obviously he couldn't throw Ionius out without another word; that was not what either of them deserved, and they had to work together to find the Ring, return to Merone, and make an end of the Divine Emperor. But after that, a mature and reasonable conversation agreeing to go their own way... yes, that was best. Ionius was, as Julian himself had called him, a monster, and you didn't marry the monster, if it was even possible. You didn't do anything except kill it. And while Julian wouldn't do that, it was cruel to keep Ionius near other people who might. Let him go, close the door, and let that be that.

Even for all the excellent logic of this plan, it still ached, and it was in low spirits that he turned back to the *Key*. He had almost finished translating the incantation that Tselmun used to summon and bind the jinnyeh Khasmedeus, and since Khasmedeus was the one *in* the Ring, it was just possible that it could be altered sufficiently to summon the Ring itself. It would take a lot of complicated substitutions and rewrites that Julian was only half-confident of making, and if it went wrong it would definitely blow him up and/or get him sucked into a cosmic void of eldritch horrors for all eternity, but such was the risk. He was fairly sure that "don't write wildly experimental spells by yourself and try them out on an all-powerful higher being, *idiot*" was the first rule of successful magicianing, but he understood the theory. He diddled on a spare bit of parchment, altering clauses and conditions and verb tenses, adding "the Ring of Tselmun" and "the Ring" to the invocation of "the jinnyeh" and "Khasmedeus." There was no chance of a test run; he would have to read it for the first time when trying to make it work, and if it didn't...

Julian was just attempting to decide if he felt like committing suicide tonight or tomorrow when he heard a disturbance, got to his feet, and peered around the shelves. Whereupon he spotted Ionius, still dressed like a Meronite because of fucking course; why try to blend in? He was having a disagreement with the librarian attempting to eject him for not having the proper documents and also looking *incredibly* suspicious, and Julian sighed, then raised his voice to the discreet half-whisper at the outer ranks of permissible for a library. "Sorry. He's – he's with me."

Ionius haughtily bestowed the librarian with an *I-told-you-so* look, and the librarian, lucky to pick a fight with Ionius Servus Eternus and live to tell the tale, sniffed deeply and departed. When they were alone, Julian hissed, "What are you doing? You're not allowed in here."

Ionius snorted. *"You* are allowed in here, aren't you?"

"And what, you thought that automatically meant you too? For one thing, I have a permit, and for another, I turned up begging sanctuary in the first place by claiming that Merone was trying to kill me and steal my book. If you barge in here and drag me out, there *will* be an incident."

"I wasn't dragging you out." Ionius made an impatient noise, loud enough to earn a tide of death glares from the nearby tables, and Julian yanked him further into the stacks. When they were wedged in the narrow aperture by an ancient mystery-cabinet, he said, "You've been gone all day. I wanted to be sure nothing had happened."

Considering the eventful nature of their acquaintance, that was a wise precaution, and even if he had just decided that they should behave as professional colleagues and no more, Julian was… touched. "Oh, were you worried about me?"

"No." Ionius scowled at him. "And even if so, I regret it already."

Julian smirked. Better judgment or no better judgment (possibly, he feared, the latter), he was tempted to push for more information on this fascinating topic, but he had left the *Key* on his worktable, alone and unattended, and if he lost it due to being busy flirting with Ionius fucking Servus Eternus, he would kill himself and then Ionius, more or less in that order. So he led the way back, hastily assured that the parchments were not disturbed, and then in a whisper, relayed to Ionius that they might have something to try. They collected the book and hurried out, heads still turning in their wake, and Julian sighed deeply. "Fairly sure that's my ruse gone, thanks."

Ionius gave him another cold stare, which failed to intimidate Julian whatsoever, and since it was early evening and the sun had slipped behind the minarets, they walked into Ambraz in search of supper. As they navigated the narrow lanes, blazing firepits, and bright awnings, Julian couldn't help but wonder what it would be like if they met when Ionius *was* Ivan, all the time and originally and without qualifications and damages. Of course, it would be such a different world, in such different circumstances, that it was useless to speculate, but he couldn't help it. Besides, men had lived together and loved each other in every era of the world, regardless of which religious authority or political demagogue tried to stop it. The Vashemites debated if the Vashach verses about men lying with each other were meant to prohibit the relationships of men and young boys in the old Hellenic pederast custom, or with male whores, or foreigners and slaves and prisoners of war, or any other of the nuances of grammar, context, and meaning that attended all halakhic interpretation. It wasn't necessarily accepted, but it wasn't completely barred either, depending on who you asked. There were the commandments about marriage and children, which were more difficult to fulfill with a male partner, but hardly impossible. There were plenty of orphans around, if it was really so bindingly urgent. It could be done.

In sum, Julian couldn't just appear with a man on his arm and expect the whole ghetto to be sanguine about it. But sometimes he felt that if he was ever brave enough to tell his mother who he really was, he could argue her into it, reason and persuade, the same way he and Isyk had done with their hair. And there was precedent, in a way, if you squinted. If a Vashemite family did not have a son, their eldest daughter was allowed to attend yeshirim, so they might have one child able to read and study the Vashach; that was how Julian had met his friend Rebeka. Those girls who continued to dress and live as boys outside school were known as yentls, Rebeka's paramour Tovah was one such person, and even the most traditional rebbiteks generally used "he" when discussing her-him. They weren't allowed to marry or live together, hence why Rebeka was available for the shadchan, but it wasn't unthinkable that the argument could be made. And no, none of this was remotely comparable to turning up with a goy war criminal, the darling of the murderous Meronite regime, and thinking it would be accepted on any level; at least Tovah was an observant Vashemite, a member of their community, who lived by their laws and was known to their ancestors. All in all, it was foolish, but when Julian was unlikely to see his family or home again, he gave into the comforting illusion that he could have done it, if he chose. What did it matter now?

Unexpectedly, Ionius turned out to speak fluent Semyic, and they bought dinner with the least trouble Julian had had since his arrival. "You're full of surprises," he remarked, as they sat in the market square to eat, the sun going down in blood and gold among the cluttered clay spires. "Though I didn't know the Meronites let you study anything apart from war."

The instant the words were out of his mouth, he regretted it; why call that specter back, when they had such a short time without it? Ionius, however, did not seem offended. "We are not just warriors. The legions are the ordinary soldiers who only fight battles, but Immortals are much more. We can do many things. Charm and spy, manipulate and influence and pull strings. Destruction is our primary task, but not always."

Julian glanced sidelong at him. "Are you proud of it?"

"I don't know." Ivan ate another bite. "I used to be. I thought that being an Immortal was the ultimate vindication for a Kozhek slave. I was determined for nobody to ever call me less of a Meronite, and to show I could be better at it than the very best. I don't know if I can understand it in any other way, what it made me into. But I... I am proud, yes. Of knowing I could do that, and be *good* at it. As I said, I am still who I was, who I have been. I am still dangerous to you."

"I know." Julian was sorely tempted to reach out and slip their fingers together, to hold on in the fast-falling dark, and it was only with difficulty that he held back. "I can't grant absolution for your past. I can only tell you that the way forward is to *act,* to *do*. You can't just talk — well, not you, since you never talk anyway. But as you say, you're good at *doing*. That's what makes the difference. Maybe it's just because I'm a Vashemite and that's how we understand faith, but still."

Ivan's mouth curled up, though he didn't answer. He returned his attention to the hazy twilight, as Julian issued a stern mental reminder that he could be the same as Gavriel: fucking Julian when it was useful for his own purposes, then casting him aside the instant it wasn't. Either way, he couldn't say that Ivan wasn't warning him, or didn't know that Ionius was still very much a part of him and would not simply vanish overnight. They continued to eat. Then Ivan said, "At the library, you said there was something we could try. What is that? Is it going to work?"

"Well." Julian coughed. "I estimate the odds of success at no more than fifty percent, and the odds of failure as a lot more than that. It is, I must stress, *extremely* experimental. But if we're pressed for time, and we are, it's an... option."

With that, he explained the prospects of actually implementing his jerry-rigged incantation, while Ivan looked more and more skeptical. Finally he objected, "You have the entire *Key* at hand. Couldn't you search for something that does what we need, instead of this nonsense?"

"Unfortunately," Julian said. "No. The thing is, even if I read the *Key* cover to cover and translate every single word, there is never going to be anything that tells us exactly how to find or summon the Ring. Why would there be? Tselmun already *had* the Ring, he didn't need to summon it, and even if he was writing this grimoire to boast about his accomplishments and keep his best spells handy, there was never any chance that he would blithely inform some enterprising rival how to get his hands on the Ring. It was only ever supposed to belong to Tselmun, and it's plain that he didn't envision anyone inheriting it after he was dead. So even if there was a foolproof magical way for Tselmun to call the Ring to him, in case he left it in his *other* set of robes, he was never going to write it down. He alone knew it, and he died with that secret."

"Fuck." Ivan's brow furrowed. "And aside from that, Safiya ur-Tasvashta, the only person who knows where she hid the real Ring, is dead. So nor can we ask her."

"Because you killed her," Julian said, with an edge. "Yes?"

"Yes." Ivan's fingers drummed restlessly on his thigh. "There was no other choice, and the chance for a great deal more carnage, if Coriolane had his way. Besides, I doubt anything less than torture could have dragged the secret out of her, and there is no guarantee that anything she told us would be truthful. Her daughter Elemai may or may not be privy to her mother's machinations, and would stab me if I tried to ask her anything. If I had been able to save Aliyah – there could be some leverage there, as she is Elemai's spouse, but – "

"Wait, what?" It was decidedly not their most pressing concern, but Julian could not help but catch on that. "They're married? As in, *married* married? That's something they can do?"

"The Qartic Wahini allow for the marriage of two women, yes. I do not believe it is lawful for two men, however." Ivan paused, then shook his head. "Never mind. If there is nothing you can think of that might work better, I suppose we are obliged to try this."

"Not in the middle of a crowded marketplace." Julian ate the last bite of supper and got to his feet. "And for that matter, not in my hut. We'll need to find somewhere a bit more private."

He hoped that sounded stern and not coquettish, as they made their way out of the square and into the surrounding streets. The sun was fully down, though the summer evenings were long and the air was pleasantly warm and blue. The residential districts of Ambrazakti were coming to life, rich with chatter and cooking, as neighbors congregated on corners and children and dogs ran about, laughing and squealing and barking. It summoned a deep ache in Julian for the White Nights of Korolgrod, when the summer dim glowed even at midnight, and the close-knit community of the ghetto, the easy camaraderie of people who had known each other for generations. He kept thinking he had resolved himself to never going home again, and then it hit like an anvil.

It was difficult to tell if Ivan noticed this inner emotional turmoil (unlikely, as he seemed like the sort of man who didn't even notice his *own* inner emotional turmoil). Yet Julian wondered how it was possible for them to have finally actually slept together and for it to have solved nothing whatsoever. Instead, he knew the steel-wire strength of Ivan's hands and the steady rough thrusts of his hips, the heft and hardness of his cock, the planes of his chest and collarbone, the hollow of his knee and the calluses of his fingers, the urgent raw revelation of his mouth and the devouring heat of his kiss, and Julian could not do damn-all about it, at least if he was making a very belated and after-the-fact attempt at being sensible. But if he played too blithely with fire, the way he often did in the rest of his life and somehow got away with, it would hurt him in a way he just didn't want. But Almighty, at what cost? It was as unfair as taking a starving man to a banquet and only allowing him to eat a few bites. And Julian *was* starving, more than even he had ever realized. Not for sex, which had never been a problem to find, but for being *free*. To act, to speak, to live, to love, to fight, to rule, to have real control over his own destiny, his own self. And regardless of how little sense it made – or perhaps the most of all, with a slave finally realizing the same – when he was with Ivan, he felt it. And Hashem, how it *burned*.

Yet again, however, there was nothing to be done, and at last, they arrived at a sufficiently out-of-the-way spot to attempt some extremely amateur and illicit sorcerous experimentation. It lay beyond the city walls, at the edge of the savanna: a stretch of soft and flat dirt shaded by rustling acacia trees. The moon had risen high enough to provide good light, and they had also purchased a bundle of cheap tallow candles before leaving the market. If he was planning to kill himself by summoning one of the most powerful jinnyeh ever to exist, they could do worse.

He took out his notes, and aided by Ivan, who could draw the most rigorous and precise of straight lines even without a compass and ruler (there was an obvious joke to be made about how well it reflected his personality, but they were in a hurry), began to assemble the circle. The basic form was the six-pointed hexagram of the Seal of Tselmun, and the runes and glyphs were more or less straightforward, though Julian had to draw them himself since they were Old High Yerussalan and any tiny imperfections could fail at the crucial instant and leave them vulnerable to devouring. Indeed, that was the likely outcome in a truly dizzying number of scenarios, depending on how peckish Khasmedeus was feeling. The former right-hand warlord and feared general of the Jinnyeh High King, who then turned against its own people – indeed as noted, Ivan's mirror-reflection – was unlikely to be inclined to mercy for a pair of audacious human fools in the first place. Well, then. At least if they died, they didn't have to worry about never fucking again.

Julian was extremely careful not to step on his lines or smudge his runes, using a bit of water and mud to make sure they held their shape, then lit the candles. When he was finished, he reviewed the incantation yet again, as if there was anything he could have missed. Fuck, this was so stupid. It wouldn't work. Or even worse, it might.

Ivan watched him, waiting. This was it. It was all on Julian. He paused a final moment. Then he found his place, made very sure of his pronunciation, and, his voice a whisper in the dark, began to read.

CHAPTER 25

ROMOLA

The route from the docks, through the streets, and up to the Eternal Palace was one that Romola had almost – *almost* – grown used to taking. As General Ionius's consort, she could go where she wanted, when she wanted, which terrified her to such a degree that she parceled it out carefully, in small increments. She did not have to walk, which would be impossible anyway; now she had a cart and driver at her command. She also had her own bodyguard, the impeccably polite and attentive Marcus Servus, and money to buy clothes or food or anything else she pleased. Shopkeepers inclined their heads and spoke respectfully, called her *m'lady*. It was a state of affairs to which she took care never to become accustomed, and indeed, this was an excellent way to destroy it. Ionius had told her to help Aliyah ur-Namasqa if she could, but then to find her like this, in the open –

Part of Romola wondered if this was a trick, and even if not, if she truly planned to stash away the empire's most wanted prisoner like a choice find at the flea market. For an unworthy moment, she debated whether to leave the Qartic girl to her fate. Then she shook it off. If nothing else, she had given her word, and she did not mean to be made a liar so swiftly. And if she *was* caught, perhaps she could lie or put on airs. If Coriolane's new courtesan could strut around as if she was in fact the empress, it was at least possible that Romola could do the same.

Keeping their heads low and their hoods up, Romola herded Aliyah up a side alley and into the street where her cart was waiting. Marcus was not with her today; he had departed last night around the same time as the general, and Romola strongly suspected that the two absences were connected. Ionius told her only that he was leaving and did not know if he would return, and could not share details for her own safety. It was startling for him to think he owed her even that much explanation. After all, it was entirely within his rights for him to order her to quit his rooms and return to the slave quarters, or otherwise revoke the aegis of his patronage. She hoped he had not gone to his death, and that they would see each other again. But that was not her task, and she could not afford distractions. If any of this mattered, she had to make it so.

"Get in," Romola said to Aliyah, helping her into the cart and gesturing her to hide beneath the seat. Then she climbed in and turned to the driver. The patricians never offered explanations or excuses; they simply commanded. "I am ready to return to the palace. Go."

The driver shrugged, cracked his whip, and spurred the oxen into motion. They rolled up the steep and crowded streets, he shouted at pedestrians to make way, and as they flattened themselves against walls and buildings, Romola kept her gaze straight forward, the image of a noble lady untroubled with the commoners. Her heart was pounding, and she wondered what to say if the guards demanded an inspection. But as they drew rein beneath the massive shadow of the Eternal Palace's great white walls, the driver shouted up that he had Lady Romola here, and they were waved in without further question. It was *astonishing*.

Inside the courtyard, Romola waited until the flow of traffic had subsided before she looked both ways, pulled Aliyah out, and stuffed her through the nearest door. It was fortunate that Romola knew the back routes and secret passages the slaves used, and she managed to get them all the way to Ionius' rooms without being spotted. If the general had abruptly returned in the interim, it would be hell to explain, but when they tumbled inside, it was still empty. Romola shut and barred the door, then felt an explosive gasp leave her lungs. At last she said, "You can stay here, for now. But I'm not sure what to do."

Aliyah regarded her with those dark and unblinkingly intent eyes. At last she said, in slow, stilted Lanuvian, "You know who I am. Yes?"

"Yes." Romola straightened up. "Aliyah ur-Namasqa, the girl from Qart-Hadesht. As I said, my name is Romola. I was asked to help you."

"By who?"

"General Ionius. I am his... consort." No need to get into the weeds, especially when the fact remained that Aliyah *was* a foreign traitor who might not be trustworthy. "These are his rooms. Nobody should disturb us here, but I cannot be sure about later."

Aliyah's brows rose in patent surprise. "General *Ionius?* When I was put into the pit, he was there, he... did something to me. I did not – you mean – was he actually trying to *help?*"

"I think so. Yes." Romola exhaled again. "As I said, he asked me to do the same for you, if the opportunity arose. I will not ask where you have been, or how you escaped, but you should be safe here, if you wish to wash and eat. I will try to think of something."

This took a while to fully translate, since Aliyah's Lanuvian was barely better than Romola's Qartic, but at last Aliyah went to do as suggested, and Romola racked her brains. She did not have Ionius for protection if things went catastrophically awry, and the consequences would fall fully on her. Aliyah could not stay here for long, but turning her onto the streets again was a death sentence. Ionius could return tomorrow, or never again. So what? *What?*

Romola paced until her foot began to hurt, then sat down and waited tensely until Aliyah reappeared, looking slightly revivified but still hollow, haunted, hungry, and on edge. She sat across from Romola, and the two young women regarded each other in strained silence. Then Aliyah said, "Do you know how I can get into the emperor's quarters?"

"What?" Romola stared at her. "You've barely escaped some terrible fate, and you want to go *back* to Coriolane? Why?"

"The Ring." Aliyah's shoulders tensed. "He has it. I need to get it."

The Ring. It sounded glancingly familiar, and Romola could hear the implied importance of the capital letter. Still, she shook her head. "You will be killed immediately. And if anyone discovers that I helped you, or General Ionius asked me, it will spill onto us as well."

"So?" Aliyah's voice was sharp with frustration. "What am I supposed to do? Sit here and wait to get caught? You brought me to the *Eternal Palace,* so isn't it past time for quibbling about whether Coriolane is personally going to take notice?"

"I... no." An idea had begun to coalesce in the back of Romola's mind, so transparently preposterous that if the situation was any less desperate, she would worry that she had finally gone completely insane. "But what if I tried? Before, with the empresses. I was invisible. I could just walk in. And Coriolane is... not uninterested in me. At the Colosseum, he wanted a closer look – when he killed the rest of the Qartic hostages, but not you, for whatever reason it was – "

She wasn't making much sense, and it was doubtful if Aliyah understood more than half of it, but when she grasped the essential point, her jaw dropped. "What do you mean, he killed the – never mind. You actually think it's a smart idea for *you* to try to get it?!"

"Well." Romola's voice was calm, chillingly logical. "You can't do it without sending the entire place to hell. I would at least stand a chance at taking it from Coriolane without immediately raising suspicion, and buying enough time to get it back to you. Then if you snuck it out of the palace and did whatever you have to do – "

Aliyah was still thunderstruck. At last she said, "Why on earth would you risk that for me? Just because your general told you to, or – ?"

Romola shook her head. She couldn't explain the revelation she had had at Year End, the awful knowledge that Coriolane had finally and fully cast aside all restraints or shackles or anything else that would stop him from killing as many people as he could, on whatever flimsy pretense he pleased. She had heard Mellius's speech with everyone else, and she was the only one who seemed to grasp the full horror of what he was saying – or perhaps the only one willing to do so. *I am doing this because there is no hope, not for anyone, if Coriolane is not stopped. Because I am not stupid, I am not weak, and I am not a burden. Because I want to keep my promise and do my part. Because I am a Remade slave, but I am also a person, a human being. And I must stand up.*

"I can," she said, as it was the simplest way to explain it. "You can't. We both agree it must be done. Does there need to be anything else?"

"I don't think this is a – "

"I am not asking your permission." Romola rose to her feet. "If I am successful, I will bring it to you. If not – well."

With that, as Aliyah was still goggling, Romola got up and marched off into her room. She had been very conservative in her purchases, fearing to be told off, but she did have some new clothes, jewelry, and a few other accessories. She brushed her hair and scented it with attar of roses, braided it and fastened it with pearls, and shrugged on her nicest dress, draping it far lower at the neck than she would have otherwise. She lined her eyes with kohl, her lips with paint. She had never done it before and feared it would look childishly clumsy, but when she inspected the results, she was shocked to discover that she was... *pretty.* It was unclear if it went so far as *beautiful,* but she might truly draw Coriolane's eye. After that – her heart gave a nervous skip. If he forced his attentions on her, or any other assumption he would make about a woman coming to him alone, after he had expressed his interest –

Don't, Romola told herself. *Don't shy from what needs to be done.* She turned on her heel and left the room, and Aliyah gawked with flattering stupefaction. "You look lovely. But – "

"It is my business to manage," Romola said firmly. "The Ring. Tell me what it looks like. Do you think he will be wearing it, or – ?"

"I don't know." Aliyah shook her head, still stunned. "It's a plain golden band with a black stone, engraved with a six-pointed star. The jinnyeh bound to it is called Khasmedeus, and you might accidentally summon it if you rub too hard. And that would tip off Coriolane, so – "

"I'll be careful." Romola wondered what a *jinnyeh* was, but now was not the time for such questions. "Khasmedeus is a... creature? A monster? Something that will harm me, or – "

"It can't hurt the Ringbearer," Aliyah said. "Technically. But even if you do get it, it will try to outsmart you. This is too dangerous. At least it knows me. I should be the one to – "

"No," Romola said. "Stay here, and don't draw attention."

With that, she stepped past Aliyah, opened the door, and emerged into the hallway, feeling as if she herself had walked into the Colosseum arena and was being stared at by a hundred thousand eyes, the beasts gathering to every side to devour her in turn. Yet she did not slow or falter, keeping her head high and proceeding as if she did in fact have every right to be here, and as far as anyone knew, she did. Even if it was only a hollow illusion, it could be maintained as long as Romola gave the audience good reason to believe in it. If that included her, she must believe the hardest of all.

She knew where Coriolane's apartments were, of course. All the slaves did, and went there often, as routinely as the emperor's absolute comfort and satisfaction demanded. There was no task that was too demeaning, no request that was too small, at any hour of day or night. Romola hoped the courtesan was not there, or this might devolve into an undignified catfight, but even that had the potential to please the emperor; his ego would be flattered by two women jealously competing for his regard. It was startling to think about this so coldly, and to realize that while she was anxious and apprehensive and tense, she was not particularly frightened. *I can do this. I must.*

When she reached the imperial apartments, the Immortals on guard outside looked at her in surprise, clearly aware that she was supposed to be the paramour of their fearless leader. But when Romola informed them that she had come to see the emperor, they exchanged looks in the way that meant they were silently agreeing not to mention this to Ionius. They told her to wait, vanished inside, and returned shortly with the news that His Majesty would indeed receive her.

Romola thanked them, lifted her skirts, and tried to enter with the small effortless steps used by highborn ladies. She smelled something fruity and floral, felt steamy heat, and when she entered the inner chambers, found the emperor in his bath, submerged in foam and reclining in the lap of a pretty young slave, who was scraping his oiled flesh with a strigil. At the sight of her, Coriolane raised a languid, dripping hand. "Lady Romola. What a surprise."

"Forgive me, Majesty." She dropped a deep curtsy. "I would never wish to interrupt. I only hoped to make amends for the scene at the Colosseum. If we did you any insult – "

Coriolane considered her for a nerve-wracking moment, then made a curt gesture to dismiss the slave, who snatched his jars and implements and scuttled away. Then the emperor beckoned her closer, and Romola crept to the edge of the tub. "I am gratified by your initiative," Coriolane said, nodding at the nearby goblet of wine, and she picked it up and passed it over. "I was hoping to examine you, before General Ionius's unfortunate fit of temper. He has recently become rather peculiar, don't you think? I trust that you are not the reason for his unhappiness."

"I would be mortified if so, Majesty. I have done nothing but try to please him."

"Hmm." Coriolane flicked a wash of water at her, dampening her dress. "To be sure, you are very lovely. I would indeed think you are pleasing him, and also that a mere Ruthynian slave does not deserve to have such delights all to himself. Does he know you are here?"

"He is… occupied, Majesty." Romola scanned the rings on the hand holding the goblet, but none of them matched Aliyah's description. "But I did remember that Your Majesty had regard for me, and I did not wish to see that squandered."

"Of course not." Coriolane smiled; this was not suspicious to him in the least and invited no questions, because what would anyone do, having caught his attention, but want to bask in it? He leaned back in expectation, and Romola crouched down and began to wash his hair. When she finished, he said, "Mmm. Very nice. We must be careful that Adelina does not poison you, but she takes too many airs already, when she is just a whore. If you would – "

He stood up, sending another surge of water onto the floor, and Romola hastily averted her eyes from the emperor's nakedness. Awkward and tentative on the slippery stones, she went to retrieve the lush towel and held it out for Coriolane to step into. When he had dried himself, she also fetched the dressing gown and he pulled it on. "There is an advantage to having you already trained. It's almost enough to make me overlook your imperfections. That foot – what is it?"

"I was… born with it, Majesty."

"Were you?" Coriolane tipped his head, a few stray droplets running from his wet hair and streaking his cheeks like tears, if only the Divine Emperor was known to weep about anything. Then he took a sudden step closer and gripped her face, twisting her head. Against her ear he hissed, "Do you think I'm such a fool that I don't know who you really are? Not just Ionius' little cunt, but a *Remade* cunt? Are you so monumentally deluded as to set foot in here and truly think it will make me forget you are no better than a rotten corpse? A foul dead thing, existing only by the power and glory of my necromancers – an abomination, a revenant? I have no doubt that if I were to put my prick into you, it would *feel* like any other woman. But it wouldn't be, would it? You would suck my life like a succubus, and I nearly *let you?!*"

He gave her a sudden, violent shove, and Romola, already unsteady on the slick marble, lost her balance altogether, tumbling onto the floor and catching her wrist hard enough to hear it snap. She tried to crawl backward, but he kept pace, towering over her and stepping on her skirts. "That said," he went on, "I cannot deny a deep and vulgar curiosity. What it feels like to truly die, to have life leave you altogether and yet awake – not quite who you were before, but not dissimilar. The Remade fascinate me, as much as they horrify me. I have spent my life in the pursuit of never leaving it, and yet your kind do it several times. Of course it is not *life,* not really. But you walk, you speak, you eat, you sleep, you fuck – or can, at any rate. Yet it is a pretty masquerade, a hollow lie. You are a shell, a parasite. Like other distasteful measures, you *are* necessary. You fix mistakes, you sustain, you endure. But that's not the same thing as living, now is it? *Is* it? Tell me. I must know."

"I…" Any response had fled Romola's head. "Majesty, I…"

"You deceived me," Coriolane went on musingly. "Or at least you tried, gauding yourself like a common prostitute and thinking that would be sufficient to tempt me – when I am the *Divine Emperor,* the earthly manifestation of the Lord and the sacred guardian of all life in this world, and to debase myself with a dead thing would be an unforgivable blasphemy. I suppose it's all right for a slave; they're not exactly human either, don't you think? And the Ruthynians rut with their sisters and sheep, so a pretty corpse like you might be an improvement. On that note, there is something General Ionius has in his possession, something else he owes me. I desire to use it now. The Ring of Tselmun. Go fetch it from him and bring it to me, and perhaps I will spare your life for this lewd audacity on my royal person. Get up, you crippled bitch. Get up."

Romola's brain was locked, her tongue frozen, yet one thing stood out. *Coriolane doesn't have it.* He thought *Ionius* had this Ring of Tselmun, the same one Aliyah was after. Of course, it was equally unthinkable for Coriolane to lay hands on it, but if she failed him –

"I understand, Majesty." Romola's voice was choked. "But as you said, the general has recently been... peculiar. If he is not about, is there another place I could search for – "

"If the general has been careless enough to lose the *Ring of Tselmun,* his degeneration is even more advanced than I feared. Perhaps it is time to Remake him too, eh? Give him back to the Corporalists, start him over as the proper Immortal he was before. But there is someone else I wish to know about. The prisoner in the Castel, the one who told us about the Ring. I *did* order the general to be rid of him, yet he ended up in the company of Grand Magister Kronus himself. Julian Kozharyev, of Korolgrod. Do you know his treason? He is a Vashemite, it must be something."

Frantically, Romola shook her head.

"I suppose not. Who would ever entrust such matters to you?" Coriolane clicked his tongue like a reproachful schoolmaster. "But that could also work to my advantage. Kronus likes to present himself as some mystical being, transcendent beyond the needs or weaknesses of ordinary men, but he's still flesh and blood, however rotted. If the likes of you were to walk in and offer a tempting diversion from his lonely crone-work – yes, I think so. Your effort is not wasted after all."

He bent down, seized Romola by the bad wrist, and pulled her up, then dragged her to a vast mahogany door that stood alone in the far wall. "Here, girl," Coriolane said. "Step inside and ask the Grand Magister about this, why don't you? Tell him that I sent you as my personal gift. If you bring back something useful – the Ring, or Julian Kozharyev's head – I'll think about letting you live. Or you'll die, which doesn't strike me as a loss to anyone, even General Ionius. So – "

Keeping hold of her wrist with one hand, he reached out with the other and twisted the doorknob. There was a shimmer of something cold and uncanny, the air rippled, and Coriolane shoved Romola in the back, sending her stumbling over the threshold. She flung out her hands, expecting to run into a wall or fall from a great height, but she didn't. She simply stepped out into a vast white atrium that seemed impossible to be contained on the far side of the door, as if she had transited from the Eternal Palace to somewhere else entirely, crumpling the boundaries of time and space like a cheap length of cloth. The atrium was lined with a circle of black doors, engraved with burning-golden glyphs, and the air was thick and silent, weighted with sorcery. She spun around in search of the door she had just fallen through, but there was nothing.

Romola limped across the floor and tried to see if any of the doors could be budged. Yet none did, her wrist throbbed too hard to put any force into it, and she slid down the wall. *This was your idea. If you die in the depths of the Thaumaturges' lair, it is no more than what you –*

"My dear? What on earth – is something wrong?"

Romola jerked her head up, looked around wildly, and spotted the small grey man standing nearby with an expression of fatherly concern. He hastened forward and offered her a hand, which she took, allowing him to lift her to her feet. "I am Grand Magister Kronus, at your service. Are you not General Ionius's consort? How did you come to be here?"

"It is… a long story, Excellency." Every part of her felt as fragile as blown glass, but if she didn't keep her wits, she was done for. "But I was visiting with His Majesty just now, and he bid me come and offer his greetings. It was an unexpected way to arrive. I beg your pardons."

"Nonsense, nonsense." Kronus escorted her across the atrium, reached one of the doors, and waved his free hand, causing it to swing open. Beyond there was a small office crowded with books and papers, made cozy by a fire in the hearth and the smell of dust and ink. "Sit down," he said kindly. "Can I get you something to drink? You look as if you could use it."

"Yes, Excellency. Thank you."

Kronus bustled to the sideboard, poured a dram of warm spiced wine, and passed the cup over. Romola wrapped her hands around it and lifted it to her mouth, venturing a sip; it was good, sweet and strong, and made her head swim. When Kronus had taken a seat at his desk, he said, "This is fortunate. I hoped to speak to General Ionius, and you will carry a message to him. Yes?"

"About what, Excellency?"

"You see." Kronus sighed, reaching into his robes and removing a small gleaming thing – a ring with a plain band of gold and a black stone. "Upon his departure the other night, the general gave this to me as surety for an important bargain. I was, at the time, delighted to receive it. But it transpires that he was not as honest *or* as helpful as I thought. Do you know what this is, my dear?"

"The Ring of Tselmun." It came out before Romola could stop it. "How do you – ?"

"As I said." Kronus tapped his fingers together. "He gave it to me before he left. But this is *not,* in fact, the Ring of Tselmun. It is a fake, a forgery. If I had been allowed to inspect it properly, I would have realized at once, but General Ionius did not give me the chance. Which leads me to conclude that he intentionally deceived me, after Doctor Kozharyev already made off with a very valuable manuscript. I do not welcome being *twice-*cheated, my dear. Not at all. It makes even a gentle scholar such as myself feel that repayment is due. And lo, here you are!"

At that, Romola made to get up. But her limbs were suddenly muddy and uncooperative, and she could not pry herself out of the chair. The wine slipped from her fingers, and Kronus shook his head. "Try not to struggle, my dear. I don't want to make it messy. This isn't your fault, but you will make a very important contribution to the study of magic in Merone. Be proud of that."

He sat there watching her avidly, waiting until whatever drug he had put into the wine had taken effect and she was immobilized, perfectly aware of what was happening but unable to move or react in any way. Then he stood up, hoisted her out of the chair, and dragged her to another door – Romola was truly starting to loathe the godforsaken things – which opened into yet another impossible space. This one was high-ceilinged, vast and echoing, and the walls spread out so far in every direction that they were lost in shadow. But that was by no means its most notable feature. That would be the huge structure made out of strange white rods, interlocked in some immense star-like shape. It was laid in multiple levels, in thick cages of…

Once again, Romola's instincts caught up to the truth before her conscious mind, and she tried uselessly to recoil as Kronus dropped her flat. She was face-to-face with a skull, its jaws opened in merry expectation of devouring her, and it struck her just what the Grand Magister was planning to do. "Take note," he instructed. "You will join your fellows, and my fellows, and everyone else who trespassed where they did not belong, or attempted to cheat the Thaumaturge of Merone of his rightful due. Indeed, your bones are almost the last set I need to give the pentacle its full power. And when *that* happens, I shall no longer have to muck about with grimoires or jinnyeh or any other ordinary tools of the trade. Even Tselmun himself could not hold a candle to me, and then we can decide whether Coriolane is truly the most powerful man in Merone. Why should any of us – why should *I* – have to kneel to him, when I can remake the world in my own image, a better image? So I should thank you, my dear. You and General Ionius alike."

He stepped a few paces away, pulled out a strange black-bladed knife, and began to whet it, as Romola threw every scrap of will into forcing her abused body to cooperate, to move, to twitch even an inch. She had been dropped atop a trough that was clearly meant to drink her blood and channel it through a careful intaglio of runes, and there was no telling what other devilries Kronus planned to commit on her corpse. *And they think I am the walking dead, the ghoul preying on the living?* Coriolane's words still stung, but where once she might crumple under their cruelty and take them to heart, this time – for whatever reason, Ionius or Aliyah or her own fragile, ferocious self – she didn't. *I am a person. Not a monster or a revenant or a corpse. And I deserve to live.*

She couldn't move her eyes enough to close them, but she did her best to focus, drawing up whatever made her Romola, regardless of anyone or anything she had been before. *It does not matter, now. I am enough. Just like this, I am enough. I will not die like this. I will not.*

"In the interests of fairness," Kronus said, striding back to her with knife held at the ready, "I will allow you a proper moment to compose yourself, ready your mind for death. So if you wish to prepare or say any prayers privately, I would do so now."

He hauled her upright, pushing her against the bone-cage and pulling her head back by the hair, exposing the jugular vein. She could smell the sourness of his breath, see the avid desire in his eyes as he pressed the blade against her throat, and then –

The strength came from everywhere and nowhere, all at once. As Kronus readied to execute the fatal stroke, Romola snapped her head forward with the force of a battering ram, striking him in the nose with a juicy, shattering thump. He howled and reeled away, and she stumbled after him, still clumsy and impaired but free, *free*. She scrambled for the dropped knife, but he threw out his hands and an intangible force slammed into her, as he stalked forward. "You – you *dare* – "

Just then, something on the floor caught his attention, and he stopped short, staring down at it. He bent down and pawed it out from where it had been trapped: a folder, a file of some kind. He flipped through it and was about to throw it aside, then hesitated. He looked at her again, then broke into a bloody smile. "No. No, it can't be – ? Surely not. Or can it? *Can* it?"

"Stay away from me." Romola's voice was a husk. Her surge of impossible strength was already fading; there was still nowhere to run, no way to fight against a sorcerer who was cosmically powerful and on the verge of only becoming more so. "If you – "

"Well, well," Kronus said. "I have no idea how this got here – though on reflection I may have *some* idea – but it does mean that your execution is stayed. You will remain my prisoner until your brother brings me the Ring, the *real* one, and the *Key*. After which, I will use your bones, his bones, and Doctor Kozharyev's bones to finish this pentacle, so I may summon and bind ifrit and marid, spirits even greater and more terrible than anything Tselmun dared to touch. After all, if the Ring is so powerful with only *one* of them, what can I do with a pentacle strong enough to master *all* of them? And when your brother discovers this, he will do as I say. So there is some truth to that hoary old chestnut that Ruthynians bed their sisters? It's almost like a Hellenic tragedy."

"What are you – " Nothing he was saying made sense. He was a madman, he was raving, and she only wanted to get away from him. *"What are you talking about?"*

"Why. This." Kronus held up the file. "Romola — or should I call you Tatyana Sazharyna? It does make sense, when I look at it again. Don't you want to know what really happened to you? Evidently at the age of twenty, you — or rather Tatyana Sazharyna, the original owner of the body you presently inhabit — tried to run away from her Meronite masters, the prominent Grassus family. Not only that, she tried to get the other slaves to join her and raise a proper rebellion. I do recall hearing about that, a long time ago, but I never knew the identity of the slave responsible, or that it was *you*. Practically a new Spartekaius, though you aren't an Immortal — not in the usual sense, anyway. That's what happened to your body. The foot and ear were among the injuries sustained when she fought to the end and was cut down, and the Corporalists felt it useful to retain them in further incarnations, to keep you from causing more trouble. But they *did* take the risk of Remaking you, albeit without your memory, because your dear brother was who he was. General Ionius Servus Eternus — a consummate soldier, a brilliant commander, a deeply loyal servant of Merone — and yet still too prone to thinking for himself, threatening to give into that same germ of rebellion that ruined you. So they needed you alive, or at least Remade. The instant he thought to take up arms against *his* masters, there you were, the ultimate blackmail. You are, I believe, the fourth or fifth iteration of Tatyana. She eventually gets the same idea, and must be taken to the drawing board and restarted. So this was just a matter of time."

Romola stared at him. He was lying, clearly he was, she didn't know — it didn't — she couldn't be, it wasn't — it didn't, it *didn't make sense —*

Does it not? that small voice asked, more coolly pragmatic than ever. *When you looked at Ionius from the beginning, when you were terrified of him but nonetheless thought you knew him, when something always pulled you back to him? When it was never sex or romance you wanted, but something stronger, deeper, darker, a bond that could not be severed even through however many deaths? When you've always known your body must have been left this way to punish the person you were born as, for whatever great sin they committed in order to be Remade in the first place?* Kronus was right. It was sensible, straightforward, if such words could ever encompass this horror. *No. No —*

"You can't," she said, slurring as if she was drunk. She folded to her knees almost in slow motion, her face pressing against the cool stones, the metallic stickiness of old blood. "It's not going to work. This is – I don't know – I don't think – he's not going to – Ionius won't – "

"Oh." Kronus's footsteps drew closer, and his hands slipped under her arms, lifting her. A great shadow was falling over her, swallowing her whole, and she felt an unbearable regret that she had failed Aliyah and Ionius both, that there was no chance of finding the Ring and saving them from Coriolane and Kronus and all the other voracious tyrants competing to devour the world. The Grand Magister's words were a whisper, almost soothing, as she fell down and down, down and down, into darkness without end. "I think he will."

CHAPTER 26

ELEMAI

Elemai did not sleep for almost a week after the death of her mother, the disappearance of her wife, and the destruction of her city. Any one of these crises on its own would have been enough to bring the world to a screeching halt, and so all of them at once compounded and crashed on each other like the tumbling of a great tower, kicking up dust and debris until she could not see the horizon for the crushing darkness. She reacted numbly, by instinct, taking cold comfort in the fact that the correct protocol had been drilled into her bones and could be executed with little or no conscious thought, so it looked as if she knew what she was doing even when she didn't. First, she had to do her utmost to calm bruised, burned-out, battered Qart-Hadesht, one half furious that the Adirim's scheming had invited such a terrible vengeance on them and the other half furious that they weren't declaring war on Merone right this minute, the only suitable response to the outrage they had suffered. Then she had to arrange her mother's funeral; Wahini believed that the deceased should be buried as soon as possible, and the family stood in their mourning whites while the qahin intoned prayers and smoke wafted up from the scorched skyline. Elemai stood in pride of place as the newly minted matriarch, trying to pretend she didn't notice Tafelin and Leila throwing hot stares from behind their veils. Her little sisters thought she was to blame for getting their mother killed, even if Safiya ur-Tasvashta had gone out in a blaze of glory, defiant to the end. And yet, Elemai wasn't sure. Everything else was her fault. Why not this?

Once Safiya was interred, Elemai had to attend Noora ur-Namasqa's funeral, mouth clichéd condolences to Zadia and the rest of her in-laws, promise that they would do their best to discover Aliyah's fate and save her if they could, pay out damages, pacify the Meronite occupiers, and more. To think of how far they had fallen from that transcendent moment in the Temple, cheering under their own flag and carried away on the glory of their imagined liberation – well, Elemai supposed blackly, that was why historians did not write their chronicles until *after* the war was over. When it was brought face to face with the full might of the Meronite iron fist, all the good intentions and stirring spectacle had not mattered a damn. They had not only failed, they had failed *miserably,* in a way that meant they might not pick themselves up and try again for another few generations at least. Qart-Hadesht was heavily garrisoned from both sea and land, a bristling henge of warships blockading the bay and legionnaires stationed on every gate, crossroads, marketplace, mahqasa, or any other location that could flare into a trouble spot. Nor was the "pacification" by any means complete. There were raids and arrests, anyone who spoke too loudly or put a toe out of line was dragged off, and it was impossible to do so much as walk around in public without being stopped, questioned, or detained. The new Governor-General, a career Meronite hardman named Cincitus, had threatened that if order was not fully restored, public executions would soon follow.

This is my fault, Elemai thought miserably. *My sisters are right to blame me, because I could have stopped this.* If she had not shirked so terribly from the first weight of power, had not hastened to return the Ring to Aliyah and forsake the destiny for which Safiya had so carefully prepared her, this could have been avoided. She had been tried and found abjectly wanting, and now there was nothing left, among the wreckage of her mother's grand plans and their smoking city alike, but the bitter hemlock of failure. In the meetings with angry survivors, she had tried the argument that the rebellion failed precisely because it was so tentative, so provisional, desperate to test the waters and only proceed if conditions were favorable, which fatally undermined them and gave Coriolane time to learn everything in advance. Therefore, the solution was to move harder, faster, and without hesitation, but it fell on deaf ears. Nobody wanted to hear any high-flung rhetoric about freedom or grand moral lectures about the mandate for opposing Merone. They just wanted to bury their dead, grieve their losses, lick their wounds. After all, they had spent centuries under imperial rule, and when trying to pull free came with such swift and severe penalties, who in their right mind would want to do it again? Just give up, give in. It was easier.

Elemai didn't know how to answer, and she could not blame them for their anger. She was angry at Safiya too, which felt paradoxical and disloyal when her mother was dead and could not be shouted at, or there to weep on her shoulder, or begged for advice, to know what, *what* Elemai was supposed to do when she was the only one left. Zadia ur-Namasqa had collapsed in grief at the loss of her wife and daughter; Elemai would never have thought it from someone who seemed so strong, but as she knew herself, oftentimes fortitude was only skin-deep. It had not felt tactful to press for a meeting with her mother's only ally, and Mirazhel ur-Beireshta was likewise in shock; it would be difficult for any ruler not to feel transparently cursed. Besides, what was there to plan? What was there to do? More fanciful fairy tales about killing Coriolane and driving out the occupiers in a single glorious sweep? That had just come crashing down, and everyone was paying the price.

Since she was now the ur-Tasvashta matriarch, Elemai left her barely-broken-in marital home and returned to the villa, where it felt even more absurd to try to fill her mother's shoes. Ghassan was more or less bearing up, trying to be strong for his children. Jahifar and Marishah were torn; they had lived here a long time and were close to Elemai and her siblings, but as they were now widowed, it was not unthinkable that they might wish to return to their birth families, Jahifar's in Gezeren and Marishah's in Parsivat, whether temporarily or permanently. Manizar was all right, sort of, or at least acting like it, and Elemai wasn't sure whether to insult him by asking. Tafelin and Leila hated her guts. Aliyah was gone and probably dead, but the idea of contracting a new match made Elemai want to tear her own skin off.

Tonight marked the end of an especially bad day. Elemai had attended three funerals for elderly members of High House families who expired of grief upon hearing the bloodstained news from the Eternal City: the Qartic hostages had all been killed in the Colosseum for the sport of the Meronite public, in brazen defiance of the usual rules of war and as a sneering ultimatum daring them to do anything in retaliation if they thought they could. There had been a few protests, quickly stamped out by Cincitus's thugs, and Qart-Hadesht lay in a mutinous, simmering quiet, ready to explode at any spark. Elemai sat at her mother's desk — it by no means felt like hers — staring into the darkness, twisting the quill in her hands and staining her fingers with ink. She should write condolence letters, but the words wouldn't come. It was still Qahyadin for four more days, but the privations would not end just because the holy month did, and nobody felt in the least like celebrating Eid ur-Fatr. The fast had been wrecked because of the need to survive, which was scripturally permissible but still felt like a failure. All of it was. All of it.

At last, Elemai gave up and set the quill down, surprisingly gently for all that she yearned to throw it against the wall and shatter everything in reach. She did not know what else to do; she was at her wits' end. Even if she wanted to, she could not use the Ring of Tselmun, as it had been taken to Merone by General Ionius — and she *would* try her utmost to find out how immortal the Immortals actually were, if she laid eyes on that murderous brute again. Besides, even if she did have the Ring, it would only pile kindling on the inferno. Khasmedeus would gleefully poke and prod the situation into the worst possible configuration, as it was entirely upfront about the fact that its chief entertainment and revenge for its eternal enslavement was to make a wreck of its masters' plans. Elemai had thought she was being prudent and shrewd, making only three wishes like the heroes of Shahrzad's tales and not trying to overstretch herself. First, for the city's aquifers to be refilled and the water to return to bountiful levels. Second, for Massasoum ur-Beiresht to die quickly, quietly, and in a way that invited no suspicion. And third —

That, there. That must be the problem. Yet again, she had thought it wise. She had even been aware of its risk of backfiring and was careful with the wording. But the essence of it — that she be raised to her rightful place without the power of the Ring – was inescapable. Now she *was* in her rightful place without the power of the Ring, just as she asked, and everything else had gone wrong. *Ironically self-fulfilled prophecies in which you are given exactly what you thought you wanted, only to realize it was the agent of your downfall all along.* Khasmedeus had said it in so many words at the start. It was therefore difficult to claim that it *had* been deceitful or misleading, when it baldly spelled out the consequences and they took them anyway. And Elemai had made the wish from fear: fear that she would not be enough, that the Ring would be lost or stolen, that it would be forced it on her for good, that Safiya's preparations would fall to pieces and it would be her fault. If Elemai found a clever shortcut to ensure that she could still do everything that was expected of her and not need the Ring as a crutch – well, that was the thing about shortcuts –

You were afraid. You were afraid, and you failed. Everyone and everything, because magic could not give you what you were too weak to carry in the first place. Elemai got to her feet, haunted out of the study by the furious whispers in her head. If she just hurled herself out the window, would it solve anything? Even that didn't seem likely. Tafelin, who was just sixteen, would have to take over as ur-Tasvashta matriarch, unprepared and out of her depth, and that would make her hate Elemai even more. Besides, after ruining it for everyone else, it didn't seem fair that Elemai should get to simply and permanently excuse herself from the aftermath. Later, maybe. Later, she could sleep. But for now –

Elemai turned around and wandered back to the study, possessed of a dull notion to search her mother's papers and parchments, books and manuscripts, artifacts and curiosities. There must be other buried secrets, other avenues to pursue. Safiya had sent Vadoush to steal books from Ambrazakti's Great Library so often, there had to be something that –

Vadoush. Elemai stopped short. She hadn't thought of her mother's jinnyeh slave in weeks, because his bonds had broken at Safiya's death and therefore he was free to go where he pleased, wherever that was. It seemed rude in the extreme to drag him back, but he was the only person (well, spirit) who knew the extent of Safiya's plans and schemes – and it was shatteringly apparent that this category barely included Elemai, whose greatest use was as her mother's pawn and vessel, the younger body to carry into the future when Safiya succumbed to the inevitable atrophy of time. *She was supposed to die peaceably as a great old matron with her children and grandchildren around her, at the end of a long and illustrious life. Not murdered by a monster and knowing everything she did had failed.* And yet even worse than the grief and anger was the creeping sense of… relief. Not that her mother was dead, not that she wanted it, not that she didn't yearn to see Safiya every day and drown in bitter recriminations every night. But it could not be denied that part of her fundamental disorientation, the way she felt too wobbly to stand on her own, was because for the first time in her life, she was free of the constant and crushing burden of her mother's expectations and manipulations, the way Safiya had molded and sculpted her from the very beginning, pushed and prodded and often seemed to see Elemai as a political weapon more than a daughter. That her mother did love her, Elemai had never been in doubt. But that love was always wielded like a knife, to sharpen and assess and incentivize — the implicit message being that if Elemai loved her too, and of course she did, then she would try even harder, do even more. And so, she had. To this.

Elemai stood there for a final moment, then teetered suddenly into action. She went to the shelf and pulled down one of the heaviest tomes, lit a lamp and hung it up while she reviewed it, then crossed to the Parsivati rug and rolled it up to reveal the great grease-chalk pentacle. It had remained untouched since Safiya's death, the runes still intact and ready for use, and Elemai knew the arrangement of bells, books, candles, and other accessories for a bog-standard summoning. She emplaced them, stood in the assigned spot, and began to read.

It was easier than she expected. Vadoush had been bound in the ur-Tasvashta family's service for a long time, the spell was well-oiled with use, and after several moments, the handsome, ageless, golden-eyed man shimmered into existence. He looked the same as always; if there was any grief for Safiya, it was invisible. At last he said, "Saeda Elemai."

"Va… Vadoush." It seemed scandalously informal, though she had no idea what else to call him. Indeed, she did not think they had ever spoken face to face without her mother. "I am sorry for summoning you again, when I am aware that you were freed. I do not intend to keep you here any longer than I must. I do not know if that means anything to you, but you have my word."

He took that in, still inscrutable. "What is your wish, saeda?"

"Not a wish, exactly." Elemai wanted to sit down, but if she stepped out of the circle and broke its protection, it would leave Vadoush free to do the same, and for all her pretty words about reparations and repentance, clearly she was not prepared to put her money where her mouth was. At last she said, "You are the only person who knew everything about my mother's plans. If you could see a way to divulge those, if she did not bind your tongue or command your secrecy – "

"I am at your disposal, am I not?" Vadoush indicated the circle with a sardonic flourish. "You do not have to ask, or make a complicated masquerade of consent to soothe your conscience. You may command. Or do you wish to pretend you are not, in fact, your mother?"

Elemai winced. He was right, but still. After another pause she said, "Very well. What can you tell me that may be of use? Is there some spell she worked, some book she especially consulted, a tool or a trick of which I may not be aware? If I was to regain the Ring, is there anything I can do to control Khasmedeus's tendencies for mischief, or – "

Vadoush raised a hand, and Elemai subsided. He chewed it over, as if weighing what he wanted or was able to disclose. Then he said, "Lord Hammadai is a deeply damaged creature, saeda. An ancient being of nearly-godlike power who takes nothing and no one seriously, not any more, because everything It believed in was torn apart by Its betrayal of our people to the Great Destroyer, Tselmun ben Dayoud, who sacked our cities and killed our kings, cast us into chains and made us slaves. One of those kings was Lord Hammadai's original master, the High King of the Jinnyeh – the Golden One, as He was known. Lord Hammadai, the Golden One's favorite general, was different in those days: stern, serious, devoted and dutiful, full of ideas for the improvement of the jinnyeh and insistent on casting aside the old prejudices that separated us from humans. It thought we should work together to create a brave new world where all could thrive. As such, It increasingly clashed with the Golden One, whose interest was in maintaining His supreme power and therefore stoking the fears and superstitions about humans that kept our people resistant to ever joining them. At last, Lord Hammadai deserted Its post, went to King Tselmun, and offered to tell him everything It knew about the jinnyeh and our magic. Tselmun listened and learned it all. Then he betrayed Lord Hammadai, bound It in the Ring to be kept in his thrall forever, and set about his campaign of conquest and subjugation. So in the end, Lord Hammadai only traded one tyrant for another, and destroyed our entire race, Its greatest dreams, Its idealistic notions, and all else. Small wonder It now finds Its only solace in crass mockery and cheerful nihilism."

Elemai opened her mouth, then shut it. It struck her how differently the same shared history of the world could be written, depending on who you asked and how they recalled it. Human magicians blamed the "inherent" dishonesty and frivolity of the jinnyeh for the failure of their own prideful and selfish plans, while in Vadoush's telling, Khasmedeus was so crushed by trauma and the eternally unexpurgated guilt of its mistake in trusting Tselmun, in daring to dream of a better world and having it fail so terribly, that it drowned itself in shallow cynicism and silly nonsense as a survival mechanism. If nothing mattered, nothing could hurt it. Not like that, not again. No humans could be trusted or believed, so they must be tripped up and forced to reveal their duplicity sooner rather than later, because they always would. And had they, this time? Yes. Yes, they had.

"Thank you," Elemai said, finding her tongue. "That is... useful."

"Of course, Mistress. Does it surprise you to learn that we have complicated motives for our beliefs and actions that do not rest on capriciously spiting humans? Did you know that jinnyeh are called deceitful and unreliable because Tselmun wrote it about one jinnyeh, Lord Hammadai, and assumed it applied to our entire race? And that all human magicians were happy to believe it, if their remorseless binding and enslavement of us could be presumed to correct our flighty natures and demonstrate the value of stern discipline? After *Tselmun* was the deceitful and unreliable one, by betraying Lord Hammadai? Did you *also* know that your mother, regardless of her exalted beliefs and her work of decades to free the Qartic people and bring down the Divine Emperor, never once thought it necessary to ask *me* whether I wanted to be her slave or even her loyal assistant in this enterprise, and took my obedience for granted? Another slave killed her in the end, though, so my bonds were finally broken. Where is General Ionius? I owe him my gratitude."

Elemai flinched. She was tempted to summon the white-hot whip with which she chastised Khasmedeus, but resorting to mindless brutality simply because she could not stand to hear the truth would confirm Vadoush's worst beliefs about her and what she had inherited from Safiya, the good and bad alike that she could not pick apart or selectively disavow. They stood and looked at each other, neither saying a word. Then Elemai said, "My people have failed and mistreated yours for many generations. There is no disputing it, and nor will I try. There is one last thing I must ask, and then I will let you go with my sworn oath not to summon you again. If there is any possibility that the Ring can be retrieved from Merone, so Coriolane cannot abuse it, then how?"

Vadoush considered that. Then he let out a short, unamused laugh. "It so happens, Mistress, it's your lucky day. The Ring of Tselmun is not in Merone, and the Divine Emperor does not have it. As one of her last commands, your mother bade me create a replica, a crude copy, and switch it with the real one. She did not trust that you would not give it away or lose it again, to Aliyah or another unworthy interloper, after you were so swift to relinquish it in the first place. So what General Ionius took was that one. The copy. You're welcome."

Elemai clenched her fists, fighting down the helpless rage that once more bubbled up. Yes, it was a shockingly good twist of fate that Coriolane didn't have the Ring, but since it was borne from Safiya's final gesture of distrust in her, it stung like a slap. "So, then. If the Ring is not in Merone – if you hid it on my mother's behest – *where is it?*"

"Unfortunately, Mistress." Vadoush shrugged. "She did not leave any explicit command as to whether I should reveal that information to anyone. She did not expect to die, of course, and assumed she would have time to decide what to do next. But that is the fragility of humans, the curse of mortality that cuts plans short. And the incantation she used to compel my compliance and my silence is one you cannot easily countermand. Even if I wanted to tell you, I could not."

"What?" Elemai scowled. "I am my mother's heiress. Everything she – " she was about to say *owned,* then changed her mind – "managed is now mine. Can you not make an exception?"

"I am unsure if you understand how *slavery* works. Especially for jinnyeh." Vadoush's voice was cooler than ever. "I physically cannot speak of it. The compulsion did not break with her death, and attempting to overcome it might destroy me. If you are a more talented magician than your mother, perhaps you can find a way to unstitch it, to supersede it, to work the contract and clauses until a loophole is opened. But I do not believe you are. Does it make sense, do you grasp what it means, that I do not have free will? That it has been stripped from me by conscious decision and careful intention, and cannot be returned simply because it is inconvenient for you? I shall give you a final piece of advice which you may or may not merit, and tell you to speak instead to Zadia ur-Namasqa. You may learn any number of matters to your interest."

"Zadia? Does she know about this? Either way, she's in mourning, I could not – "

"So you extend tender consideration of her personal feelings to her, but not me?" Vadoush's eyes gleamed gold, cold and bright as fresh-minted aurei. "Perhaps, Elemai bet Safiya ur-Tasvashta, it is time to stop making pathetic excuses about what you *cannot* do, and discover once and for all if you *can*. Now, you said you had only one question, and you have more than exceeded it. Dismiss me or destroy me, whatever pleases you, and then see if you can finally step out of your mother's shadow. In case you haven't noticed, she is dead. She can neither approve nor judge. So if you can, girl, stand up. Stand up and do something for yourself. See if you even know *how*."

Yet again, Elemai wanted to answer that, and yet again, there was nothing to be said. Instead she nodded, as crisply as she could manage. "Thank you. For your service, and your honesty. I will dismiss you now, and I will not summon you again. But before I do – "

She screwed up her courage and before she could think better of it, stepped out of the circle. The candles snuffed and the runes went dark, breaking the bindings on both herself and Vadoush. His eyes went wide in surprise, as she struggled not to back away. Both of them knew this meant he finally had full license to hurt her, to summon a horde of locusts or flay her flesh from bone, anything that was her and her mother's rightful due for the wrongs they had done him. To be sure, he looked as if he was thinking about it. Then he nodded and spun away in a flare of sparks. "Farewell, daughter of Safiya. May our paths never cross again."

When he was gone, Elemai didn't feel better, not exactly, but she did feel more decisive, clear-eyed, less paralyzed by useless grief and guilt. It was midnight, and therefore an unsociable hour for visiting, but it was not something that would wait for daylight, and she was afraid that if she gave up and went to bed, she would once more be frozen in the morning. So she changed into sturdy dark clothes, was briefly flummoxed over the problem of how to travel across Qart-Hadesht without being caught by Cincitus's thugs, and then realized that her mother had given the answer to this at least, in exactly as many words. *The other useful feature of the aquifer system, aside from nourishing our rose of the desert, is to allow one to move around the city undetected.*

"Thank you, Amma," Elemai muttered. "I will do my best."

With that, she left the villa, slipped to the street-grille, and pulled it open: swinging her legs over the edge, pushing off, and bracing for the drop into the tunnels below. She landed awkwardly, straightening up and peering at the ancient stone arches that opened into the darkness like caverns and cathedrals. Thanks to the rains summoned by her first wish, the water was much higher than before, rushing through the pipes like the arteries of a great heart, and Elemai fought the fear that it was about to burst loose and sweep her away, drown her for good and all. In places the water spilled from the cisterns and rose to her knees, then her waist. There was just enough light from overhead that it was never fully dark, but she heard the slow, heavy tramp of armed footsteps and the murmur of low-voiced conversation in Lanuvian, and held still until the patrol passed. Then she kept moving, sopping wet and starting to shiver. It could not be much further.

At last, she had almost reached the ur-Namasqa villa, but it lay on the far side of a fully flooded sump, the bricks dark with water that left barely an inch between it and the ceiling. There was no way to gauge how far the flooding extended, whether there were air pockets or an alternate way around. That was not even to mention the possibility of hidden obstructions, broken stones, fallen debris, or other hazards, and if she dove in and tried to swim through, the odds were not high that she would emerge on the far side. She did not have to. She could turn back.

Elemai stood there for what felt like forever, sizing it up. She scouted out to either side and found the passages there were even smaller and also flooded; there was no possibility of going that way. If she was not home by dawn, her family might think she had been kidnapped by the Meronites in the dark of night, and if Cincitus discovered she was gone, there was no knowing what could happen. But Vadoush had told her to speak to Zadia, and there was no way to do it in daylight; any sight of ur-Namasqa and ur-Tasvashta together would result in harsh punishment for both. She had done enough harm, and she could not risk them again. Only herself. Venture into the dark alone, or give in. Make a choice, once and for all, and live with the consequences.

Gritting her teeth, Elemai put one foot down into the sump, feeling for the floor and trying to see how deep the floodwaters ran. It was chest-deep and cold enough to make her recoil, but she refused to step out again. Now there was nothing but to throw the dice and wager her life, and while she had happily splashed in the Mad ar-Hahrat as a little girl, she was a daughter of the desert, her blood of sand and sun, and she was not confident in her ability to swim for very long in a cramped and dark underground space. Indeed, the panic began to well in her stomach and close around her lungs, and she tried desperately to loosen it. Come now, Elemai. Don't be a coward. *Come on.*

She took three quick breaths and then a deep one, plunged her head under, and began to kick for all she was worth. Her groping fingers quested over slimy moss and crumbled bricks, and she did her utmost not to think about what would happen if the sump suddenly narrowed and she was stuck. When her lungs began to burn, she kicked up, surfaced very carefully, and managed to gulp some squashed, damp air, then dove again. The walls closed in, and the roof slanted down far enough that there was no chance of a second breath. Don't think about that, or anything. Like how it was your wish that filled the aquifers, when this might have been much easier. Just swim. *Swim.*

Just when her chest was strained to bursting and she could no longer hold back the primal instinct to open her mouth and desperately breathe, her head broke the surface, she stumbled out onto an apron of slippery bricks, and lay flat, wheezing. The relief was so giddily euphoric that she laughed aloud and kissed a slimy knot of black weed, then grimaced and wiped her mouth, crawling on all fours up to the grille. After she listened to be sure that all her hard work would not be undone at the pivotal moment, she pried it loose and spilled onto the street. Then she got up, shook herself like a wet dog, staggered the final few yards to the ur-Namasqa villa, and knocked on the gate.

Aside from it being the dead of night, the place was in mourning, under heavy guard, and not expecting visitors, and it took a long time to summon a response. The groggy servant was startled to see the newly minted ur-Tasvashta matriarch looking like the lowliest of street rats, and expressed hesitation about rousing Saeda Zadia from bed, she having finally been persuaded to get some rest. Elemai offered her sympathies, but she really did have to insist.

At the end of this, the servant finally departed, and a few minutes later, wrapped in a shawl and her long hair hanging loose, Zadia ur-Namasqa appeared like a wraith. At the sight of her daughter-in-law in such watery dishabille, her eyes went wide. "Elemai? Are you – ?"

"I'm all right. I apologize for the hour, and waking you." Elemai rose to her feet. "Is it safe to speak in your solarium? Will the Meronites hear us, by one method or another?"

Zadia jerked her head, and Elemai followed her upstairs to the study. At least it did not look as if there were any of Cincitus' spies hiding under the rug, and Zadia touched a small golden orb that started to emanate a faint shimmer of sound. Then she sat down and said, "I apologize for forcing you to call on me in this way. I have... not been myself."

"I know." Elemai stared at her hands. "I did not want to trouble you either, but this is necessary. I have told you before, but I am terribly sorry for Noora's death. She did not deserve it."

Zadia's jaw clenched. "No. No, she did not, and it made a deserving mockery of all my deliberately short-sighted pretenses that we could manage this in a bloodlessly perfect fashion, that the only ones to suffer would be the ones who earned it. I knew it was foolish, but I convinced myself otherwise. And then to find out that this was in fact *all* a monstrous lie, since my devotion to the rebel cause was instigated in me by my mother, and *she* – "

Zadia cut herself off, bitterness tangible, as Elemai waited to see if she would continue. Then she said, "Thank you for your kindness, when General Ionius – you know. I thought I should bear witness, but – "

"No." Zadia shook her head. "Whatever your struggles with your mother, you do not want to watch her die like that. Nor is a peaceful death a grant of a peaceful memory. My own mother died in bed at an advanced age, a respected matriarch with her family at her side, and yet everything she told me, everything I believed in – it was a lie. A *lie*."

"Amarasha ur-Namasqa? She was a great leader of the Adirim, and of our people. I would not believe she could be anything other than – "

"Nor could I." Zadia's lips went white. "Yet it turns out that not only was she a liar, she was a hypocrite in the worst way. You see, I spent my life believing that my father was Fayzal ur-Namasq, the man I called Abba and loved as such, and he me. There was never any reason to think otherwise, nor would it ever have crossed my mind. But as I learned only after both he and my mother are dead and therefore unavailable to ask, Fayzal was not my father, at least in body. Nor was it my mother's second husband, Mahmet, or a Qartic noble or even commoner. Instead – "

"What do you mean? Are you suggesting your mother was dishonest in her marriage vows, or took a secret lover – if it was not any of those, then who can your father possibly *be?*"

Zadia remained still an instant more, then spoke. "Coriolane," she said simply. "Coriolane Aureus IX is my father. I did not realize until the visit, when he boasted that he and my mother had been longtime lovers, even while Amarasha continued her public defiance of Merone and preached the cause of Qartic freedom. I was the result of that union, and he too only realized for certain when we were face to face. The rest – if it was why he did not kill Aliyah on the spot, and why he spared me when I begged to be slain in Noora's place – I do not understand."

She said all this so matter-of-factly that for a moment, Elemai didn't realize what it meant. Then she felt as if she might fall out of the chair, or that Zadia had gone fully mad, or was clutching onto the most fragmentary and fallacious of explanations as a salve. "Saeda…" Elemai started, then shook her head. "Coriolane has no children, no heirs of any kind. Everyone knows that. Whatever he hinted, whatever he made you think, this is a lie. Your mother would never – "

"In this, at least, he was not lying." Zadia rubbed the dark circles under her eyes. "And the reason he has no children is because he killed them all, not that they were never conceived or born. If my mother returned to Qart-Hadesht before she knew she was with child, and I was born into the safety of wedlock… Coriolane would be easily able to recognize and kill any offspring of Gheslyn or Vestalia or his concubines, but if I was out of reach, out of sight, and even my own mother might not have been certain that I was not, in fact, her husband's seed…"

"Saeda, this is – this cannot be – you are imagining things, in your grief. Even if your mother was one of Coriolane's lovers, there is no proof that you are his – his *daughter*. He wanted you to think it as a mind-game, or that he had been merciful in sparing you, but – "

"Believe me," Zadia said, grim as winter. "I want Abba – Fayzal – to be my father. I don't want any blood or bond with *Coriolane*. I don't want to believe that my mother ever touched him, or that she let her people – *our* people – see her as a champion of liberty and principled opponent of his rule, while she was making regular trips to the Eternal City to fuck him and secretly bore his child. I grew up at her knee hearing tales of Qart-Hadesht's glory days, the need to swear myself to the struggle in body and soul – there was never any question that I must continue the fight, and *this* – "

Elemai opened her mouth, then shut it. At last she said, "It is not the same, but I understand the feeling that my mother was never entirely honest with me. I too wish that I could ask her to explain, but I cannot, and neither can you. But if – and I stress *if* – you *are* Coriolane's daughter, do you understand what this means? You, or Aliyah if she lives, or Aljafar if she does not, are the *heir to the entire Meronite Empire*. Unrecognized, of course, but still."

By the stunned look on Zadia's face, Elemai could tell it had not, in fact, occurred to her. "No," she said. "No, I do not want it. The empire would not become any less awful and oppressive as an institution if I was suddenly in charge of it, and I do not wish to lend it legitimacy, to think that I can be bought off and convinced to stop opposing it if I was to personally benefit from it. And Aljafar – no. He is already too convinced of his own importance and that I am doing him ill, the last thing he needs is to think he is the long-lost heir to the Eternal City itself. Besides, Aliyah is *my* daughter, Aliyah is better than me and you, the only one who could bear the Ring of Tselmun and remain herself. If she is Coriolane's granddaughter, the only descendant to attain her majority because he killed all his children save for me – I would not want that for her. I do not think it would be just. But nor do I have the right to reject it for her out of hand. And you are wrong about one thing, Elemai. Aliyah's heir, should she no longer live, is not Aljafar. Her heir is you."

Elemai should have something to say to that, but she didn't. Yes, by the laws of matrimony, the heir of a deceased spouse was the surviving one; in the absence of living children, she would be entitled to Aliyah's inheritances, titles and monies and appurtenances – and if it was true that it included a claim to the throne of Merone, she was not so noble as to immediately cast it aside. Just then, she could not help but picture herself as the Divine Empress, enthroned in splendor and controlling the vast power of the empire – but in the *right* way, for *good,* to return justice and peace and freedom to all those Merone had stripped it from in the first place. Surely if the system did so well at taking it away, it had to work the same in reverse? Her mother's shade could gaze proudly from the afterlife and see that Elemai had not been too weak to hold ultimate power. It wouldn't be as it had been with the Ring. It could be *right*.

And yet, even as she allowed herself to indulge in the fantastical dream, Elemai knew in her bones that it would not be. The only person who had a true right to decide if she wanted this great and terrible destiny was Aliyah, and until it could be known once and for all if she was indeed alive, the point was moot. Besides, it was tempting for anyone to think that if such awesome power and responsibility was abruptly thrust onto them, they would obviously do the right thing and not abuse it, stay who they were, and not be crushed beyond recognition. Yet Elemai had already faced that test, and she also knew that she had failed. She *couldn't* bear it, not even to please her mother, and continuing to try even when Safiya was dead and gone was the greatest lunacy of all. *So if you can, girl, stand up. Stand up and do something for yourself. See if you even know* how.

"I see," Elemai said at last. "I cannot deny that I want it. But it is Aliyah's choice, not mine, and either way, we must know the truth. Do you have siblings, saeda? Brothers or sisters who might have some point of comparison, or family knowledge, or – ?"

"My brothers were conscripted into the Meronite legions, long ago." Zadia's eyes were still distant. "But they were the spitting image of Fayzal, there was no doubt of their paternity, and my mother was most upset when it happened, as if perhaps she had previously received certain secret assurances that they would be spared. They were sent to the Franketerrish provinces, and did not return. My sister, Hanifah, married a Daevic man from Kush and my mother disowned her. I have not seen her in many years, but she was Mahmet's daughter, and they were close. So it is only me who was – is – Coriolane's. Doubtless my mother felt that one secret imperial bastard was enough of a cuckoo in the nest, or she broke off their affair, or he grew tired of her, or – I don't know. I don't *know*. She's dead, she lied to me for my entire life, and I cannot ask her why. Whatever her intentions, why she dared for her eldest daughter and heiress to be me, we will never know." She blew out a breath. "Never mind. Why did you come here, Elemai?"

What with this string of shocking revelations, Elemai's reason for daring the hair-raising midnight journey had been briefly forgotten, but now she explained what Vadoush had told her. Zadia listened until she was through, then nodded tersely. "Yes," she said. "Your mother said, just before her death, that the Ring which General Ionius took from Aliyah was a fake. I did not know what to think, but – "

"So what? Do we try to find it, or – "

"I think," Zadia said, "it is best, for now, to leave it where it lies. If – Coriolane – does not have it, there is no good in finding it and allowing him to remedy that mistake. But we need to get to Merone and save Aliyah. I will not fail her again, not when too many of our mothers have done ill by their daughters. I did not hear that she was killed in the Colosseum with the others, so – "

Elemai wanted to hope, but even entertaining the thought felt like a terrible risk. "Even if Aliyah is alive, does Coriolane know that she is his granddaughter, and would it impel him to mercy if he did? It seems quite the opposite. After all, he has killed all his progeny, and she is of legal age, the bearer of the Ring of Tselmun, the ringleader of a failed Qartic rebellion – would not she, out of everyone, be too dangerous to even consider being kept alive?"

"Perhaps," Zadia said. "In which case, there is nothing we can do, we are already too late, and she has been rotting in the Castel Sanctangel or a pauper's grave for weeks. But we both know that Aliyah is stronger than we have ever properly credited her – than *I* have ever properly credited her – and it may be that she strikes Coriolane in a way he did not expect. He has never laid eyes on his own descendants, and for a man as vain as he is – well. It may not be quite what he expected."

"Merone." Elemai looked at her mother-in-law. "I will go with you, of course. But I can't think how to leave the city, especially now that I dismissed Vadoush. Besides, we are already stained with shame, closely watched, and could never escape on our own. So – how?"

"As to that." At last, Zadia smiled. It was thin and cold and sad and fragile, but it was still a beacon of hope and a declaration of war all at once. "I have an idea."

CHAPTER

27

ALIYAH

OMOLA DID NOT COME BACK. ALIYAH WAS UNSURE whether to expect her, if this was a trap, if something (well, something *else*) had gone wrong, or if General Ionius' consort had clearly rushed off to inform the Immortals exactly where to find the fugitive. If so, they could barge in and drag her back to the pit at any moment, but it felt counterproductive, after Romola smuggled her into the Eternal Palace and put herself to the trouble of finding the Ring in Aliyah's place. Hopefully they had properly understood each other; the language barrier had been circumvented but not surmounted, and perhaps Aliyah had missed some crucial detail. But as the hours dragged on and on, the simplest explanation appeared by far the most likely. Romola had tried to get the Ring back and failed, Coriolane killed her or threw her into the Castel, and that was that. And if Aliyah was waiting to be caught by the general himself –

She did think he wanted to help you, Aliyah reminded herself, for whatever good it did. Indeed, Romola had insisted that this was on the general's orders, and it was hard to square why Ionius put the Immortal metal into her if he didn't want her to do – *something,* but what? If a slave was caught trying to filch the emperor's prized new possession, Coriolane would send *someone* to search here, right?

Either way, it was not something Aliyah could do anything about, she felt an all-consuming somatic exhaustion, and she could hardly stand up with its weight. She did not dare to sleep in General Ionius's bed for any number of reasons, so she went back into Romola's chamber, hoping her hostess would not mind. If Romola was the general's mistress, it was odd that they did not sleep together, but plenty of men wanted a woman around only when they felt like it. Either way, it was not her concern. Aliyah crawled into bed and fell asleep before she could close her eyes.

She slept for what felt like forever, haunted by strange visions and waking at intervals with a sharp jolt, afraid that her escape had all been just a fantasy and she was back in the dark depths of the pit. Each time, she lay in a cold sweat, then promptly fell asleep again and had even more bizarre dreams. At last, however, they ceased, and she slipped into a state not dissimilar to living death – which, after the unending uproar of everything, was deeply peaceful. Indeed when she finally began to rouse, aching and sticky and sore-eyed, her first and most fervent wish was that she could simply stay there forever. Why must she wake, why must she go on, when it might be over? It was most unfair, and Aliyah groaned, rubbed her face, and sat up. "Romola? Are you here?"

No answer. Nothing. Nobody.

That was, it could no longer be denied, a very bad sign. There was no way to be sure how long Aliyah had been asleep, if it had been a day or two days or even more, and the sun was going down outside the window in a riot of red clouds; it was twilight, the hour of sardiq. After she stared blankly at the wall for another few moments, she lurched suddenly and decisively into action.

Her stomach twisted with hunger, but it wasn't safe to go in search of food. She got off the bed and stretched out the worst kinks, then restlessly wandered through the apartment, stopping at the window and staring over the courtyard. It felt almost treasonous to be here, at liberty in the Eternal Palace in the heart of Merone, and not doing anything but fretting. How recognizable was she? Romola had known her immediately, but she was clearly privy to information beyond the usual. If Coriolane was so determined to keep Aliyah hidden from the public... was he *afraid* of her? That hardly seemed possible. But he *had* been reluctant about sentencing her to death, not that it ultimately stopped him from doing it. Strolling in and demanding a personal audience, when she was supposed to be starving to death at the bottom of a hole, was the worst idea of all. And yet.

Aliyah whirled on her heel, marched back into Romola's room, dug in her trunk, and fished out a few pieces of clothing that looked as if they might fit. She tied a robe around her waist and a cloak over her shoulders, then hesitated on whether she should cover her head. After it was shaved in the Castel, her hair was growing back in black stubble, which felt less awkward to leave unveiled, but it was still a deliberate humiliation to strip her from being recognized as Qartic and Wahin, or even as a person. Likewise, it was foolish to walk around as a visibly non-Tridevarian foreigner, and she left it bare. It would have to be risked.

Reluctant to leave the apparent safety of the rooms, and then sternly reminding herself that they belonged to *General Ionius,* Aliyah took some papers from his desk to look as if she was on legitimate business and slipped into the hall. She tried to think how to find Coriolane's chambers without immediately blowing her cover. There were plenty of slaves from across the empire, so her appearance alone was not a total giveaway, but she still did not know who had learned of her escape. That, however, was not an excuse; she had to do this without magic or other dangerous shortcuts. She had repeatedly seen how catastrophic it was to rely too much on the Ring or believe it alone could solve their problems, and this was what she should have done from the start.

One thing at a time. Aliyah sped up. It took a few more wrong turns and hasty backtracking, but she finally found a promising-looking corridor, waited until it was clear, and –

Just as she was about to step out and take her chances, a hand closed on her arm and pulled her backward, and she snapped around, biting down an outcry. She looked up into the hooded face of a man – or at least she thought it was a man, since there was an oddly soft, boyish cast to his features – and he made a sharp gesture for silence. "No," he said, in rough but serviceable Qartic. "No, you do not wish to go that way. It will take you to the emperor's rooms."

Aliyah opened her mouth to insist that she *wanted* to go to the emperor's rooms. But he was pulling her forcibly along, and when they bundled into a side corridor, Aliyah pulled her arm out of his grip and whirled on him. "Who the *devil* are you?"

"My name is Belsephorus." He sketched the suggestion of a bow. "And I am trying to help you, Lady Aliyah. My mistresses urgently desire to speak with you *before* you throw your life away, again. You will likewise find it to your interest, so if you could come with me – "

"Your *mistresses?*"

"They have suffered an unfortunate diminution as of late, but will surely regain their position. At which, if you assist, they would be grateful. After all, they have already given so much help and intelligence to Qart-Hadesht. Surely you feel it meet to return the favor?"

"You – you work for the empresses? Gheslyn and Vestalia? But I heard – they were – "

"General Ionius played an unfortunate part in forcing their downfall," Belsephorus said, with a slight sneer. "The charges were utterly spurious, and Their Majesties look forward to completely clearing their names. But we both know that man cannot be trusted, don't we? Do you have any information to share on where he has suddenly gone?"

"No." Aliyah was conscious of a sudden curiosity, but even if Belsephorus also disliked the general, that didn't mean he was a better or more trustworthy ally. And Romola *had* gotten her off the streets and offered to retrieve the Ring, so much as Aliyah was loathe to admit it, it might not be best to betray Ionius without a second glance. But if she refused him, all Belsephorus had to do was shout for the guards, and Gheslyn and Vestalia were the prime suspects in the question of who had passed sensitive information to Safiya from inside Merone itself. She might learn something useful, and if the empresses still wanted to play at being Qart-Hadesht's secret benefactors –

"Very well," Aliyah said. "I would be delighted to speak with your mistresses at once."

That was how she found herself led out of the Eternal Palace and into a damp and narrow underground passage that stretched on for an interminable time until it finally surfaced in the Castel Sanctangel itself.

At the sight, a bone-deep chill ran down Aliyah's spine, and Belsephorus raised a hand. "I swear, my lady, if I meant to have you captured again, you would be so. We have not found a way to effect my mistresses' release from their unjust detainment, so they are forced to temporarily repose in this squalor. But if you would be so good as to follow me?"

Aliyah raised both eyebrows, but obediently trailed after him to the door at the end of the hall, where Belsephorus produced a large key and undid the lock. She thought about asking why the empresses couldn't just get up and leave, if their devoted servant had the liberty of the palace and the key for their prison, but perhaps the miserable life of a fugitive on the run was not one they wished to endure. Besides, why should they flee, if it was all a witch hunt? This was their home, their fortress, and it paid to stay close and bide their time. Surely they couldn't be executed without causing a furor, and Aliyah entertained a brief and delusional hope that they could help. With what, however, was the question.

"Your Majesties." Belsephorus stepped in, beckoning Aliyah after him, and folded himself into a deferential bow. "I am delighted to report my search was successful and I located the girl, if not where I expected. I sought her in the pit, but she was not there. Do you wish to share with Their Majesties how you escaped from such a dread confinement?"

"No." Aliyah was not about to drop her guard, spill such delicate information, or think they were intervening from the goodness of their hearts. Gheslyn and Vestalia Aurea sat across the way, regarding her with cool gazes that nonetheless could not conceal an avid, almost desperate interest. They were a far cry from their impeccably dressed, coiffured, bejeweled, glittering selves; even if they chose to remain here instead of daring the unknown, it was clearly wearing them down. Gheslyn looked downright old, her dark braids heavily threaded in silver and her perfect skin turned crepe-thin and crumpled. Vestalia was holding up somewhat better, but still looked like a common courtesan bereft of her cosmetics, pinched and plain. Both of them were put out when Aliyah refused to curtsy or make a gesture of respect, as they had evidently envisioned this going differently: Belsephorus swooping in to pluck her from the pit, whisking her here, and she falling over in groveling gratitude. But she had saved herself, and that could disrupt their schemes. Heaven forbid.

"Lady Aliyah," Gheslyn said at last, with Belsephorus acting as interpreter. "How good it is to see you undamaged. We regret that this acquaintance could not be made earlier or in more salubrious surroundings, but both you and we have been... detained."

"We have," Aliyah agreed warily. "Am I to understand that we are supposed to be allies?"

"If you wish to call it that. I would not presume." Gheslyn waved an airy hand. "There is, to be sure, much we can offer each other. Have you realized the service we did for your homeland?"

"*Service?*" The memory of Qart-Hadesht burning to the ground, Ionius informing her that Safiya and Noora were dead, imprisonment in the bilge and slow desiccation in this same prison – all of it hit Aliyah at once. "Is that what you call it, or have you not heard how it ended?"

"It is not our fault if you heathen provincials made a mess of our generous gift," the empress said impatiently. "If anything, it shows why you can't be trusted with freedom. But never mind; bygones are bygones. You are the girl with the Ring, yes? The Ring of Tselmun?"

"Yes." Aliyah bit it out. "But I do not have it, not since your royal husband chastised my city. If *you* wish to have it, you must ask him, and from the looks of things, that might be difficult."

"Mind your tongue, Qartic brat." Vestalia folded her arms. "Regardless of this temporary diminishment, we are still your rightful mistresses. The chance that we have offered is not one to be spurned."

Aliyah had *several* opinions on that, but it did no good to be drawn into petty braid-pulling with the two (formerly) most powerful women in the world. There was an awkward pause, until Gheslyn glanced at Belsephorus. "Did you deal with her? That upjumped whore stealing our possessions and sitting in our places, what is her name – Adela?"

"Adelina." Belsephorus smiled modestly. "She is experiencing a miserable case of the shits, which should only get worse. Unfortunate."

Gheslyn scowled. "Who asked for a raging case of dysentery, you cockless coward? I wanted her fatally poisoned and out of the way, not given any chance to recover or come up with notions as what might have caused her sudden ill health. Go see to it, won't you? Give us a chance to speak with the girl alone. Now, I said. Out."

Belsephorus inclined his head and took his leave. Aliyah wondered how they were going to communicate, but Gheslyn looked at Vestalia apologetically, as if aware that this was demeaning but necessary. The junior empress sighed and said in Semyic, "Very well. Shall we talk?"

"If you wish, saeda." Aliyah could not bring herself to choke out *Your Majesty,* though the empresses winced at this ethnic salutation. "But I am unsure what I can do for you. That being so – "

"The eunuch did not find you in the pit." Vestalia cocked her head. "And you've clearly had a chance to clean up and collect yourself. Who helped you?"

"Is that relevant, saeda?"

"You don't have room to be clever, girl. Besides, if someone was willing to assist a traitor, we could suborn them to our cause. So. Who?"

Aliyah hesitated. But she did owe Romola her life, and it seemed only fair to make her part of whatever demented concord the empresses thought they could arrange. "Her name is Romola. I don't know anything else about her."

She hoped that this would be sufficiently anonymous to deflect their curiosity, but Gheslyn made an awful face. "What? *Her?* The bitch cunt who betrayed us, broke into our rooms, stole our papers, and otherwise repaid us so foully for the trust we placed in her? Is that the same one whoring herself out to General Ionius? I don't know what she'll get out of it, as everyone knows he doesn't fuck women. I saw her at Year End, gloating and so proud of bringing us down. Belsephorus should have poisoned her like Adela. Indeed, I ordered him to do so, but he couldn't get close enough with the Immortal always looming around, and Ionius *would* have killed him if he saw him again, after Sardarkhand. Is he still here? The general? If so, I will murder him myself."

Aliyah blinked. "Do you know what he – ?"

"What he did? Yes." Gheslyn's glower deepened. "He insisted that he could help us if we told him everything we knew about Coriolane's plans, but I did that and then, of course, he turned tail and left us stranded. More fool we for confiding in a slave, but – "

"He helped you?" Aliyah was startled. "Romola said that he asked her to do it for me, but – "

"That *cunt*," Gheslyn repeated, with the sour vitriol of a woman who had taken it deeply to heart that it was the worst insult imaginable, "cannot be trusted on anything she says, but never mind. If the general is playing a game of his own, we can work with him as long as our interests coincide. But as he's likely holding a grudge for Sardarkhand, I'm not sure we will see him again. Did you speak to him in person, or did you just take the cunt's *word* that he wanted to help you?"

"Romola," Aliyah said. "Her name is Romola. I did not see the general after we left Qart-Hadesht. We spoke on the emperor's flagship, and I did not trust him. However, subsequent events caused me to… reassess. When I was taken from the Castel and put into the pit – "

She paused, even as Gheslyn and Vestalia looked at her like hungry eaglets in the nest, waiting to be fed a tender morsel. She looked down at her hands, wondering if she could summon the Immortal metal, turn her fingers into claws and gouge their eyes out. "Ionius spoke to me again then, briefly. He offered assistance that might mean he wanted me to escape. But after his activities in Qart-Hadesht against Saeda Safiya and my mother Noora, I found it difficult to believe."

Gheslyn's lips went even thinner. She turned to Vestalia, and the two of them conferred at length in low-voiced Lanuvian, of which Aliyah could not understand more than a few words. It was difficult to discern the empresses' exact relationship, if they too were lovers in addition to their mutual marriage to Coriolane, or merely partners in crime, sister-wives who had known each other a very long time and were turning against their husband for their own self-preservation. It certainly was not the case that the two of them were bitter and shrewish enemies, but even so, they were some of the most unpleasant people Aliyah had ever met. As far as she was concerned, the two of them and Coriolane deserved each other, and it was not advisable to ally with them just because they too were at loggerheads with him. But she still didn't have a choice, and at least General Ionius had tried, somehow, to help them too. Where was he, and where was Romola?

"Well," Vestalia said, when the empresses broke away. "We thank you for this information, girl. There is certainly much we could tell you in return, but as you pointed out, our last attempt to share intelligence with the Qartics hardly inspires confidence. Do you know about a man named Vadoush? He was our main contact and courier, but he has not returned to Merone for some time."

"Vadoush is — was — the especial servant of Saeda Safiya. After her death, he was set free."

"You let him go *free,* when he knows this much?" Gheslyn's mouth coiled into a moue of cold disapproval. "And could pass that knowledge to anyone at his discretion? Foolish."

"I was not involved with Vadoush. The matter is complicated. Now, interesting as it has been to converse, tell me what use you think we can be to each other or send me away."

Gheslyn eyed her even more frigidly. At last she said, "If General Ionius has forsaken us, we cannot wait for him to spirit us out of here — assuming he meant to keep his word at all, which I doubt. Besides, you think we wish to go like *this,* decrepit old hags bereft of our rightful youth and beauty? We would need to take some Corporalists with us, willing or unwilling, and that — "

"And which do *you* think," Aliyah said, as politely as she possibly could, "is more important? Your lives, or your looks? Do you think the emperor will execute you, or — ?"

Once again, Gheslyn and Vestalia looked at each other. Then Vestalia said, "We thought at first that he would never dare to try, at least not until his mummer's war with Qin ran its course or he could think of some way to do it without looking flagrantly tyrannical. But we are no longer so sure. Archpriest Mellius has been preaching sermons about how it is right and holy for a man to punish a misbehaving wife, even to the greatest sanction of all, and that means he is preparing the people to accept our deaths as a service well rendered to the Lord. So indeed, the hourglass has been turned on our lives. We just have no way of knowing when or how it will finally run out."

"Then leave. Belsephorus has the key, he could let you out. Why are you staying?"

"Are you a fool?" Gheslyn laughed, dry as dust. "The empire is very large, and anywhere we fled would immediately seize us and turn us in. I have no interest in serving as a scarlet woman for the vulgar voyeurism of drooling peasants, and there is nowhere we could safely go. Except for one place, and that is Coriolanople. *My* Coriolane gave it to me as a wedding present, in fact. It was part of my dower that I would always have supreme rule within its walls, collect all taxes and revenues, and otherwise enjoy complete control of its affairs. So if we *could* get there, we would have a claim to total impunity. Not that Coriolane is likely to respect it without a fight, but still."

Aliyah considered. Coriolanople was the second city of Merone, situated on the western side of the Bosphor Strait with the Parsivati city of Firzepoli on the east, the Two Sisters whose legendary rivalry had shaped much of the two realms' history. Either way, it sounded better than waiting to be executed here, and she shrugged. "So go there."

"Again," Gheslyn snapped. "It would be difficult to reach without help. Which, perhaps, you might see your way to proffering? Ring or no Ring, you savages must have – "

"I told you, your sainted husband is the one who took it, I don't have some other magic or exotic power to conveniently put to your use, and besides – "

They had risen to their feet, staring the other down, and Aliyah thought that if someone had told her a few months ago that she would go toe to toe with the (dishonored, but still) Divine Empress of All Merone, she would have thought they were insane. But she was far past the point of feeling fear or reticence or deference, and she remained where she was. Despite herself, Gheslyn looked grudgingly impressed. "You could come with us. We have need of a reliable servant."

"That you think I would ever be your *servant*," Aliyah said, "is the sum total of everything wrong with you. But that is beside the point. I will make a proposal, if we are finished. I need to speak to the emperor. If you two wish to slip out when he is distracted, that is your own affair."

The empresses looked at each other as if they could not believe their luck – surely it could not be so simple as Aliyah virtuously offering to commit suicide by insisting on another audience with Coriolane, while they took advantage of the chance to scoot out the back. "He will kill you, child," Gheslyn said. "You know that, don't you? If you are weary of life, that is your affair, but I don't think so. For better or worse, you too are a survivor. If you came with us, you could put those talents to use, rise high in our new – "

"I do not wish to rise high in any iteration of the Meronite Empire, whether your husband's or yours. Now, do we have an accord? When Belsephorus returns, you order him to conduct me to the emperor. I will do my best to keep him occupied long enough for you to get out of the city. In return, whenever you have the opportunity to do so, you will tender prompt and substantial assistance to myself, the city of Qart-Hadesht, and the slave girl Romola. And General Ionius, if he has turned against your husband. And Julian Janovynich, the Vashemite scholar."

Gheslyn started to say something, then stopped. After an excruciating pause, she shrugged. "If you wish, yes. It is always easy to gamble with house money, after all."

"That's not good enough. I need your sworn oath."

The senior empress sighed, as if she was being disgracefully put upon, but reached up to her heavy knot of braids, plucked a hairpin, and pricked her finger with it. Aliyah hesitated, but offered her own finger, and Gheslyn punctured it likewise, pressing the wounds together. "I do so swear," Gheslyn said, "that if you survive this gambit, I shall henceforth hold myself as an ally of you and all the persons and places so named, in the sight of the Lord, the Lady, and the Prince, and to exert the selfsame obligations upon Vestalia. Amen."

"Amen," Vestalia agreed grudgingly. "Is that enough, girl?"

"I swear in the sight of Ur-Malika, my people, my homeland, and my honor." Aliyah took her hand back and wiped the blood off. "Now, are we in accord?"

"Yes." Gheslyn's eyes were more hawkish than ever. "We are."

After that, it was a matter of waiting in silence until Belsephorus returned with a report of slipping a fast-acting toxin into Adelina's cosmetics, so she would expire in horrible agony as her face melted off before the hour of Prime tomorrow. Gheslyn looked mildly satisfied, but as if this was still far below the amount of suffering she really wanted. Then she foisted Aliyah forward with an explanation of the plan, and while Belsephorus looked boggled, he recovered with aplomb. "Yes, Majesty. It shall be done. After I have taken the girl to His Majesty, should I return and escape with you? Even if you, Divine Family willing, make it safely to Coriolanople, you will need loyal servants, and surely I have proven myself beyond a doubt?"

"You have, dear boy." Gheslyn petted him on the head like a favorite dog. "Which is why you are so valuable in covering our retreat. Having a half-man with us outside the palace would be a dead giveaway of our identity, and it is always possible to make more eunuchs. So no. You will stay here, and make sure that it all unfolds as we intended."

Belsephorus opened his mouth, then shut it. He looked betrayed, as if he had carried out all this dirty work to ensure himself a permanent position at their sides (or at least in their shadows), and was now being cast aside like a used washrag. Aliyah wondered what he had expected; when the empresses' escape was discovered, suspicion – and therefore punishment – would land on Belsephorus. In other words, he was being left behind to take the fall and tie up loose ends, and when they had left the empresses' cell, he led Aliyah through the Castel tunnels with a distinctly peeved expression. She moved up next to him and said in an undertone, "That's how it is with Merone, you know."

Belsephorus glanced at her, then away. It was difficult to tell with eunuchs, but she thought he was in his early twenties, only a few years older than her. He had the fair northern looks of a Franketerrish or Teutyn boy, shipped in from the provinces and relieved of his manhood in exchange for becoming an all-purpose factotum of the empresses, and now that too had been stripped from him. Perhaps he had convinced himself of the wisdom of the decision, or that the empresses truly valued him, or that he was better off like this, or whatever else it took to not go mad. At last he said stiffly, "It is not for me to question Their Majesties. If they feel I am more valuable by remaining in the Eternal City, that is what I must do. Besides, while our cooperation might be enforced at the moment, you are still a traitor. It will not do to forget it."

"Maybe." Aliyah shrugged. "But you're still a slave. Just like the rest of them."

He started to say something, then stopped. When they reached the Eternal Palace, however, he said with deceptive nonchalance, "Am I correct in recalling that you were assisted by a girl named Romola?"

"You are. And she's part of the bargain I made with your mistresses. Gheslyn said that she ordered you to kill her, but you couldn't get close enough while General Ionius was there. So don't think I'll *accidentally* tell you how to do it, unless you want them to be oathbreakers."

Belsephorus uttered a small, disgusted huff. Half to himself, he muttered, "It could have all been avoided if the general just died in Sardarkhand. Like he was fucking *supposed* to."

Aliyah could not object to that, but she had pushed far enough, and there was nothing else to do except to clear her mind and prepare for the imminent return to the displeasure of Coriolane's company. She very well might not survive it, if she tested her luck past its extremity, and having just been reminded of all the sadistically ingenious things the Meronites did to their enemies – *Qarthadesho delenda est* was truly the least of it – she would be fortunate if face-melting poisons were the worst of it. Why *had* Coriolane spared her, though? He had not restrained in murdering the rest of his prisoners, regardless of their value, so – *what?*

In a few minutes, they reached a door in a back corridor, so seamlessly concealed that Aliyah could hardly tell it was there at all. Belsephorus leaned in, pressing his ear to it, and strained to hear any sound from within. Then he stepped back, slid a pick from his sleeve, and twisted it into the lock. Clearly this was a vital skill when spying on the most powerful man in the world on the behest of his estranged and murderous wives, and Aliyah admired the eunuch's efficiency. Then he pushed it open, beckoning her, and they stepped inside.

The space was low and dark, obliging them to duck, and they beetled along, bent double. Then at the end of the secret passage, something soft and thick fell in Aliyah's face, which felt like a heavily brocaded curtain or tapestry, and Belsephorus indicated a spot on the floor for her to stand. Aliyah did so, as he put a finger to his lips and tilted his head. "You may step out when you wish," he whispered. "The emperor's drawing room is just beyond."

"Thank you." Aliyah likewise found herself straining for any sound of Coriolane's presence. If she materialized like a ghost out of his draperies, he might be sufficiently startled to take her seriously, or he might simply shout at once for the guards. She glanced at Belsephorus.

"I will keep him occupied, but I cannot be sure how long. Your mistresses will need to run, now."

A bare smile plucked his lip. "Unless I miss my guess, they already have. I doubt they wasted a moment. Good luck, Lady Aliyah."

Aliyah nodded tensely, and when she looked into the dusty, gloomy shadows once more, Belsephorus had vanished. She was now quite on her own. She fumbled for the edge of the curtain, finally found it, and had to use all her strength to haul it aside, just enough to peer through.

The panorama was as opulent as could be expected for the emperor's private lounge: dotted with marble sculptures, velvet chaises and settees, cedar and chalcedony furniture, and hung with crystal chandeliers and silk curtains that conjured an exclusive, cloistered atmosphere of reserve and luxury. Aliyah scanned the room, didn't see anything, and was about to let the curtain drop when she spotted someone reclining on the divan across the way, the top of their head just visible. It couldn't be Coriolane, because it seemed much too young. But as he straightened up, she caught a glimpse of smooth blond hair without a hint of silver and a magnificently strong-jawed profile, impossibly far from his decayed, bloated appearance when he sentenced her to the pit. He appeared instead to have suddenly become a good twenty years younger, in a strange, stretched, distractingly artificial way. It was so unsettling that he almost looked inhuman, like a monster that had found a man's discarded skin and pulled it on like a badly fitting costume, and Aliyah saw red stains splattered on his robes. She didn't know for sure what those were, but it took little ingenuity to guess.

A cold shudder ran down her back. She could not think of anything she wanted less than to get close to him, and if she had not come so far and given up so much, she would turn and run. Coriolane seemed distracted or sated, drowsing, and if she was going to take him off guard, this had to be the moment. She whispered malikallulah, for whatever good it was, and pushed the curtain aside. "Good evening, Majesty."

The effect, as when she revealed the Ring to her parents, was everything she could have hoped. Coriolane spun around so fast that the Divine Emperor of All Merone was in danger of performing an ignominious pratfall, and stared at her. At last he said, "You."

It was difficult to tell if he, despite his shock at an unexpected appearance in his privy rooms, was surprised to see her in particular, and somehow she thought he wasn't. They remained frozen, until Coriolane laughed. "I confess, Lady Aliyah, I wondered if we would cross paths again. You are nothing if not resourceful, and it speaks well of your ingenuity, your cleverness, and your drive to survive at any price. I can, to be sure, respect that. I would be a hypocrite if not."

Aliyah did not answer – not least because she was the one stunned out of her wits, due to the fact that Coriolane Aureus IX, Divine Emperor, Lord of the World, the *Lanuvian* world, was speaking perfect, accentless Qartic, almost as well as if he was native-born. Of course, four hundred years afforded a lot of time to study any number of things, and it was always wise for an emperor to learn some of his subjects' vernacular, but this was far different than memorizing a few formulaic phrases for official rituals or law courts. Seeing the dumbstruck look on her face, he grinned. "Oh, yes. I speak Qartic, and it's better than forcing us to endure your insulting butchery of Lanuvian. Your grandmother was an excellent teacher. In languages, and other things."

"Grandmother...?" Aliyah was blank. Her maternal grandmother, Amarasha, had died when she was twelve, and her paternal grandparents lived far away in Numeria and could no longer manage the long and arduous journey to Qart-Hadesht. "I don't understand what you mean."

"Don't you?" Coriolane kept studying her with a regard that felt almost physical, like insects crawling on her skin. "Clever girl like you, I thought you would put it together. Or perhaps you're not actually that bright, which is a disappointment. Considering the mercy I showed to both you *and* your mother. I still might have to kill her, especially if she makes any more trouble, but I nearly hoped it could continue."

Aliyah felt deeply blockheaded, as he was insinuating *something,* but for the literal life of her she could not grasp what. She looked at his fingers, but didn't see the Ring. So had Romola stolen it and then come to calamity, or did Coriolane not have it, or had Ionius kept it and never handed it over, or was it tucked in the emperor's jewelry box for safekeeping, or – what? *What?* Finally she said, "I don't – "

"That is obvious." Coriolane gestured at the divan. "Why don't you sit, my dear?"

It was foolish to obey even his most innocuous orders, but any idea of what was going on had been blown to hell. Aliyah sat stiffly, and he did so next to her. He smelled of a sweet floral perfume and something much worse, spoiled meat or festered rot. The blood on his robes shone darkly crimson, and he caught her gaze and gave a small sigh. "Ah. You have interrupted me in something of an indisposition, my dear. Wine?"

"You must be mad," Aliyah said, "to think I'd – "

"If I truly wanted to kill you, apart from the sake of form with which I had to punish you, it would have been done long since. You understand that, don't you?" Coriolane smiled in a ghastly rictus and reached out to pat her leg; his hand was as hot as fire, unpleasantly damp. "But it would be disappointing. After all, I've never met my own grandchild before."

It was, Aliyah thought, an odd paradox for the emperor to be perfectly fluent in Qartic but able to mistake one word so badly, because there was no way that was what he meant to say. It was a slip of the tongue, a trick, an error, a joke or delusion or – *whatever*. She looked at him, and he looked at her. The silence grew even more extortionate. Then Aliyah said, "I don't think – "

"Oh, I said what I meant." Coriolane shrugged. "So you didn't understand. Your mother Zadia is my only surviving child, and that makes you my granddaughter – see? I know the word. I am not such a monster as to remain unswayed by familial connection, though it does surprise me. It has not been the case before. Once I went to Raveyne for a few years, and when I returned, one of my concubines had a son, a handsome toddler, splendid boy. Looked just like me." The emperor sighed mournfully. "It was a terrible burden to have him killed, when it was usually just the potions and poisons to ensure the women never conceived at all or lost the babe before birth. His mother screamed so awfully, and then never wanted to touch me again, so I had to have her executed too. That was the only time I was *that* careless, but at my age, you can lose track of time."

Aliyah could not be sure of the worst part of what Coriolane had just said, and wanted to reject it with every fiber of her being, but didn't know how. Even worse – no, it didn't make *sense*. It would almost be better if Coriolane had greeted her with sneers and insults, finished what he started, disposed of her with no second thoughts or backward glances. At least it wouldn't mean – *this*. No. Her mother would have – unless her mother didn't *know,* but it seemed impossible to think of Zadia bet Amarasha – Zadia bet *Coriolane?* – not knowing something so –

"You're lying," Aliyah said croakily. "I don't know why, but – "

"Trust me, if I was lying, I would choose a far more suitable candidate than a heathen brown bitch who is still utterly unaware – or even worse, deliberately ungrateful." Coriolane scowled. "It's a pity you couldn't be a Meronite, but that is what I get for dallying with women from the provinces. I did love your grandmother, by the way. Truly, to my surprise. She was always a good time and a good fuck, and just as power-hungry as me. We never had to pretend to be *moral* with each other, and it was refreshing. Unfortunate that she felt the best use of that conviction was to wield it against me, but it saved your mother and indeed, yourself. It is also why I have a proposal for you now."

"I won't – "

"Just like her, indeed." Coriolane smiled, but there was a hungry blackness in his eyes. "First, I wish to assure you that I am not insane. Not in the least. I am no Emperor Nereus fiddling while Merone burned. But I am very tired, my dear. That is where you come in."

Aliyah sat very still, cornered by a predator who would chase her the instant she ran. At last, keeping her voice as neutral as possible, she said, "What do you mean, Grandfather?"

It was a risk, but it seemed to please him. He smiled again. "Look at us, bonding so naturally. Since you ask, there is a singular opportunity for you to remake the Meronite Empire, rise to your rightful place, and for us to be friends, not enemies. Nobody desired all that unpleasantness in Qart-Hadesht, and whether or not I like it, you *are* my only heir. As I said, I am tired. I need to rest, to sleep – ten years, twenty, thirty? More? And in the meantime, you must take the throne."

Yet again, they had somehow entered a parallel existence where Aliyah was hearing words and theoretically knew what they meant, but they made no sense at all. "I must – what?"

"Think of it logically." Coriolane shrugged. "You will have real time to rule the empire, redress whatever you think is wrong, make whatever changes you desire. There would, I promise, be nobody to tell you different. Then when you are old and ready for your retirement, I will awake from my dormition and return to rule in strength and justice for all eternity. They would want me back by then, anyway. They would have grown tired of you and everything about you that was not me. They would think it was time for you to be erased and things to go back to the way they were in the good old days. That is the dirty truth of the world. Humans are miserable, selfish, lazy, weak, feeble, authoritarian brutes. They don't want to be responsible for their own fortunes or futures, or change their circumstances. They want a strongman to promise it will all be solved, regardless of how much violence or degradation it might inflict, because all they care about is themselves. I may never have been a father in body, but I am a father in spirit, to everyone. They want, they *crave* my cruelty and punishment, far more than my kindness. They can never be without me, just as I can never be without them. But to teach them that lesson for all time, to drive it home how much they will always need me, it is necessary to give them a taste of the alternative. Give me your word, my dear, and you can walk out of this room, at this very moment, as the Divine Empress of All Merone."

He was mad, Aliyah thought. He was completely mad, regardless of his protestations to the contrary. But there was nonetheless a chilling logic to his proposal that clashed with any insistence that he was indeed just a lunatic. For at long last, it all made sense. Why Diyab called her *Princess* when he gave her the Ring, why he had chosen her, and what she was expected to do. If she agreed to Coriolane's bargain, became the Empress of Merone *and* had the Ring, she would be – no qualification, competition, or question – the most powerful person to ever live. She could reshape the world, her political edicts issued from the Eternal Palace and her magical interventions given with an arch command to Khasmedeus. To combine the inheritance of Tselmun and Coriolane, if she was descended from the former on her father's side and the latter on her mother's – if she could just use their power *correctly*, a goddess and a queen, untouchable for all time –

The temptation was awful. There was so much she could just *fix,* or just *break,* vengeance on those who deserved it and reparations for those who had been destroyed. There was nothing saying she ever had to give it back, especially if she discovered a way to end him once and for all. Just kill the right people for the right reasons, and the world's evil would be solved. Wouldn't it? *Wouldn't it?*

"I…" she started at last. "How could you sleep for so long and remain as you are, exactly like – like this? You don't look – I mean, something has changed for you, clearly. If this is some new magic, I'm not sure if it worked correctly, or – "

"There are still a few bumps, yes." Coriolane waved a hand. "But when the slave girl came and I raged at her for having the effrontery to be Remade in my presence, it made me think again. Made me realize what a benefit it would be to finally get over with the brief and messy business of dying, no longer fear something so simple and ordinary, and live forever in perfect stasis, no longer growing or changing or – indeed – worrying about siring offspring." He chuckled. "Preserved exactly as I am, perfect. The Corporalists can reduce the animation to put me into sleep, and raise it up again to wake me. They've already completed the most important part. What do you think?"

Aliyah started to speak, then stopped. She studied him again, taking it all in – the gruesome artificial youth, the burning heat of his flesh, the pervasive hint of rot. The blood on his robes. She had thought it was from some unfortunate victim, but if it was his *own* – the sense that she was sitting next to something not quite human, only borrowing the crude semblance of a man –

Something had gone wrong, she realized. Something had gone terribly wrong. Whether it was because Coriolane was four hundred and fifty years old and his ancient flesh was already riddled with so many different immortality spells, magic and murder and whatever else was poured into his blood and bone, or something else – *the slave girl came and I raged at her for having the effrontery to be Remade in my presence* – so Romola *had* been here, and now –

"You," Aliyah said faintly. "You're *dead.*"

"Oh, no." Coriolane's smile widened. "I am not. If the slave has not been murdered by Kronus, I will thank her for opening my eyes, for showing that the final solution was in front of my nose all along. For we are indeed alike, but I am the ultimate culmination of her experiment. Sometimes to live forever, you must pay your dues to death, and we have done it. All the folk who have died – in Yerussala, in Qin, in Brythanica, in Merone – gave their lives to this great and noble cause, made the magic unbreakable, fed me the strength and power to reach apotheosis in truth. My first life is over, and my true eternity begins. For I, too, am not just made. I am *Remade*."

CHAPTER
28

IVAN

KHASMEDEUS THE GREAT, SPIRIT OF THE RING, mightiest of King Tselmun's servants, exploded into existence with suitable panache. One moment the circle was dark and dead, and the final echoes of Julian's incantation rang away into the night, as the two of them stood uneasily and were unsure how long they should wait before concluding that it had failed. Then Ivan heard something, far off but speeding closer, a breach in the veils of the world and a violent upheaval of its foundations. The candles fluttered and guttered, the night shuddered and shriveled and spun into a vortex, and then all at once, the creature was just *there*, blazoning with fountaining fire and rising twice, thrice the height of a man, smoke and shadow and stardust. Ivan had just enough time to hope that Julian had managed to find a way to hide this from all eyes save their own, or half of Ambrazakti would be piling down on them, when the jinnyeh's voice boomed like the breaking of the world. ***"WHO DARES SUMMON ME?!"***

"Good... good evening." It took a moment for Julian to get the words out, and an uncharitable man might have described *his* voice as a squeak, but it was better than Ivan could presently manage. "Do I have the honor of addressing the Most Great and Glorious Khasmedeus, All-High Lord-Queen of Shedim and Devs, Archduke of Jinnyeh, General of the Golden One – Hammadai, Osmedeth, Shedonui, Aeshmeda, *etcetera?*"

"Say what?" The fiery monstrosity dimmed, swirling into a more human shape, and a note of vanity appeared in its voice. "Well, well, well. *That's* more like it. Clearly a human of great intelligence and taste. You *have* done your homework, pipsqueak. Flattery will get you everywhere, at least for the next three wishes. Name your desire."

"Not quite." Julian cleared his throat. "It was not only you that I wished to call forth with this summoning. I was hoping it had also brought the Ring of Tselmun."

The jinnyeh had been about to do some more triumphant crowing, but it stopped, studying Julian narrowly. "Oh, you're a Vashemite. You speak Old High Yerussalan just like *he* used to. So is this some – wait. Do mine mighty eyes deceive me, or is that *General fucking Ionius?*"

"Yes," Julian said hastily, as Khasmedeus reared back and suddenly changed into a giant cobra – which was, to say the least, disconcerting. "But he helped me. With this."

"I would say so," the cobra hissed, forked tongue flickering wildly. It sized Ivan up with malevolent snake-eyes, then all at once, transformed into a far more flattering twin of Julian, with huge naïf eyes, wobbling lower lip, and clasped hands. "Oh, General Ionius," it trilled. "Won't you please stop committing atrocities long enough to love me tender?"

"I don't look *or* sound like that, thanks." Julian raised a hand and spoke a crisp command, and Khasmedeus yelped as a glowing blue whip stung it back into its original form. "Besides, you haven't answered my question. Where is the Ring?"

"Typical," the jinnyeh muttered. "Even when they get your names right and acknowledge your magnificence, the first thing they want is the *Ring, Ring, Ring.* For your information, pup – or should I call you Tselmun Junior? – I cannot say where the blasted thing is, so if you were trying to get me to merrily wander down memory lane, it won't do you any good. You *have* successfully summoned me, though, so you get three wishes. Aren't you going to wish for, I don't know, him over there to develop a real personality? Though that might be beyond even my capabilities. Take it from me, you could do better." It paused. "Truly, you couldn't do worse."

"Watch it, demon." Ivan took a step. "If you can't keep a civil tongue in your head – "

"Shut up, both of you," Julian snapped. "The last thing we need is a pissing contest between you two idiots. Ivan, butt out, I'll do the talking. Khasmedeus, we don't have time to mess around. For the record, our further enquiries will not constitute wishes, but ancillary commands and existing clause modifications, such as – " He added something in Old High Yerussalan, clearly specifying exactly what obscure branch of magical semiotics they should be, so he couldn't ask three questions alone and then be shit out of luck, and Khasmedeus glowered. "Is that clear?"

"Yes." The jinnyeh swept a deeply sarcastic bow. "Fine. Fire away. Or tiptoe giddily away to commence *extremely* baffling carnal relations with – yes, all right, all *right*. What?"

"First," Julian said, flashing that damn dimpled grin that wreaked havoc on all of Ivan's grim resolve to be professional about this. "Who was the last person to touch the Ring? Not necessarily to use it or call on you, but simply handle it. You know, don't you?"

"Of course I know." Khasmedeus bristled. "It was a hinnyeh called Vadoush."

"And? Are you planning to elaborate on that?"

Khasmedeus bobbed up and down on a cloud of unnervingly virulent green. It seemed to be trying to think of a clever way to weasel out of this compulsion, then sighed. "Vadoush was a servant of Safiya ur-Tasvashta, with whom I believe the Moronic Master of Murder over there was well-acquainted. Aren't you the one who personally snuffed her in front of her screaming daughter? Couldn't have waited *two* seconds to think whether that was a good idea?"

Ivan started to answer, then stopped. There were justifications and arguments, explanations and interpretations, but they all foundered on that unassailable fact. "Yes," he said. "I killed Safiya ur-Tasvashta, I do not deny it. What has that to do with the whereabouts of the Ring?"

"Because she commanded Vadoush to take it away and hide it from all eyes and knowledge save her own, and create a fake. You've discovered *that* little switcheroo, I'm sure?"

"Indeed." Hopefully Grand Magister Kronus was amusing himself appropriately, or had just been beheaded for treason. "So that's what happened. The servant Vadoush took the real Ring on Saeda Safiya's orders, to keep it from the Meronites, and hid it – where?"

"Even if I did know, why should I tell you?" Khasmedeus transformed into the gamin, doe-eyed version of Julian again, affected to drop something, and bent over, waggling its pert rear end in their faces. "How could I do something like that, I'm just a sweet little – *ow!*"

"I told you to mind your manners." Julian raised an eyebrow. "And out of the two of us, I'm the one who has actually read the *Key*. In the meantime, Khasmedeus, I bid you answer clearly, succinctly, honestly, and at once, with no evasion or obfuscation. Is the Ring of Tselmun in Qart-Hadesht?"

There was a long pause. Then the jinnyeh said grudgingly, "No."

"Thought not." Julian paced back and forth, careful to remain within the protective bounds of the pentacle. Khasmedeus and Ivan watched him with a gimlet eye, the former greedily hoping he would stray out and the latter ready to tackle him back in if he did. He mulled it over, muttering to himself. Then he said, "Earlier, you said something about how even if I was trying to get you to wander down memory lane, it wouldn't work. You know this place, don't you? You know exactly where we are, because it was your homeland, a very long time ago. The human city of Ambrazakti is built on the site of the destroyed City of Gold, the citadel of the Golden One, High King of the Jinnyeh, and you were Lord Hammadai, the Golden One's greatest general. At least until you went over to Tselmun and he betrayed you. Saeda Safiya must have known it as well, and unless I much miss my guess, she was *also* familiar with the Great Library and all its magical books and manuscripts. That has to be the answer, doesn't it? The Ring is here. *Here.*"

Ivan turned to Julian with a bit of a jerk, wanting to demand how in the fuck he pieced that together and just what he meant with that reference to a great general who switched sides, deserted the High King, and was brutally betrayed for his trouble. But it was Khasmedeus's reaction that was most telling. It went very still, forgetting all its vulgar flaunting and taunting, its rapid-fire shape-changes, its impudent wisecracks and immature jests. At last it said, "What do you mean, pup?"

"As I said, I've read the *Key*. I know who you are." Julian looked at it, cool and level. "I know what you did, and what happened to you — not just Tselmun's self-serving version, but the real story. How he destroyed all seven of the great jinnyeh cities, even after he and his father Dayoud visited the City of Iron. That included the City of Gold, the seat of the Golden One and the heart of the jinnyeh world. I didn't know for sure where it used to be, but when I thought about it, it was obvious. The word *ambraz* itself means *gold,* in the Ambraz language, and *-akti* is the singular genitive suffix meaning 'city of, place of, dwelling of.' So the name *Ambrazakti* literally means *city of gold,* it's very wealthy and filled with actual gold, and Coriolane and the Meronite legions can't get across the Sand Sea to the Ambraz Empire, home of the Great Library and all its magical books and artifacts, where I'm guessing Saeda Safiya often sent her servant Vadoush. So my incantation didn't summon the Ring, only you, because the Ring is already here. It's in the library, isn't it? Fuck. I've been a total idiot, messing around with spells, when I could have just dug in some bookshelves. Though I didn't know for sure."

The silence when Julian finished this impromptu disquisition was enormous. Neither Ivan nor Khasmedeus could possibly manage a response. As well, Ivan kept looking at Julian, wondering how it was possible that they had in fact finally fucked (which was ill-advised, but he was not made of stone) and yet the interest, the attraction, the lodestone lure had not subsided in the least. If anything, it had only gotten worse. Julian was clever and brave and beautiful, and yet even that didn't come close to fathoming how remarkable he was. He could repeatedly insult a senior Immortal and cause said Immortal to secretly kind of enjoy it, read and translate the most infamous grimoire to ever exist, create a complex custom spell and then logically deduce that the answer had been in his reach all along, outwit an ancient jinnyeh and pick up enough of a language to reveal a long-hidden secret, the legacy of a lost world. His mind worked boundlessly, expansively, endlessly, in consummate brilliance that was hard to do anything but desperately admire. And when Ivan thought of the way Julian kissed him, how he tasted, the heat and strength of their joining and the yearning to do it again, to do it for as long as they both should live –

No. Stop it. The last thing he needed was to be carried off like some mooning milkmaid, to delude himself that this was anything other than what it was: a temporary alliance of convenience, a brief and admittedly pleasurable tryst, and then a firm conclusion, a parting of the ways. What did they think would happen, that Ivan would meekly convert and go back to Ruthynia and settle into the life of a Vashemite housewife, shut away in the Korolgrod ghetto? Even if he was willing to be a Vashemite housewife, which he categorically was not, there was no mold or method for whatever it was between them, no template to follow, and what else was left, what other ending was there, than to leave, to part, to lose? Ivan could live with it. He had, after all, endured much worse.

Khasmedeus, for its part, had still not answered or even made a sound. It remained where it was, its profile shadowed even in the light of its flames. Then it said roughly, "So you think you know all about me? About my past, my dirty secrets, how I ended up like this?"

"No." Julian was unruffled. "I wouldn't presume that much. But for better or worse, I know something. This is it, isn't it? Ambrazakti."

The jinnyeh regarded the pair of them with baleful golden eyes. "One of you alone is bad enough, and now you're joining forces? Which, by the way, I find completely baffling? I'm well aware of the human propensity to fuck anything that stands still long enough, but – "

"That's beside the point." Julian folded his arms. "Well?"

"Yes, all right?" Khasmedeus threw up its hands, furious but sharpened with bristly, fragile grief. "This was it, a very long time ago, before the humans ever laid the first stone of the walls and were still living in dung-huts and killing each other for cows. The timeless and transcendent City of Gold, under the rule of the High King of the Jinnyeh, al-Madhab, my almighty lord and master. It was beautiful beyond anything that ever was or will be again, and I destroyed it. Me, personally. Not by my own hand, but because I was so fucking idiotic as to wiggle my blindly idealistic backside over to King Tselmun and think a *human* would ever be interested in helping to make the world a better place. I swallowed all that propaganda about how *wise* he was, how *strong,* how *kind and generous,* and I was the one who forced my people to pay the price, over and over. I deserve it, I suppose. Being still stuck here thousands of years later and listening to you witter on about bringing down another tyrant, as if it makes a difference. There will just be a new one. There always is."

Ivan started to say something, though he wasn't sure what. For once, all the mockery was gone from the creature's voice, and the ragged wounds of its epochal heartbreak burst through too raw to ever cast aside. At last he started, "But the Ring – if we find it, if we – "

"The Ring won't fix this." Khasmedeus sighed heavily, as if very much against its better judgment, it was trying to offer genuine advice. "That's what I keep trying to tell you people. It was created as a weapon of ultimate destruction, that's the only thing it can be used for or that will be the consequences of its actions, and the trick about the endless quest for supreme power is that it's never supreme so long as anyone else has any of it. When you make that the goal, you have to keep climbing higher, causing more and more havoc and killing more and more people, and regardless of what good you think you're setting out to do, it inevitably warps into terrible evil. But I did have several masters after Tselmun, you know. He failed in that. Somebody would stumble on the Ring and discover what it was, and the same old dreary cycle started again. It always ended the same way. Whatever grand notions I had about atoning for what I had done with Tselmun, I didn't. I was just forced to make it even worse. Do you know what that does to you?"

"Yes," Julian said. "Well, sort of. For what it's worth, I'm not planning to use it. I just need to know where it is, to keep it hidden. As long as it exists, *someone* will try to find it, and – "

"And you think you're the proverbial safe pair of hands, never to be tempted?" Khasmedeus blew out an unspeakably weary sigh. "Fine. If you say so. What do I care? Fall to the dark side and pass me on to the next ambitious chump. It's in the Great Library. Help yourself."

Ivan and Julian glanced at each other, unsure if they had heard correctly. Then Julian raised a hand. "Please," he said. "If you would be so kind, lead the way."

Khasmedeus boiled sullenly for several moments, as if to test how far it could stretch the command. Then it transformed into a red-tailed hawk, flapped out of the pentacle, and zoomed off into the dark streets, as Ivan and Julian hastened along behind. It was late enough that they had to be careful not to run afoul of curfew, but they reached the Great Library, and Julian led the way inside. The shelves were drowned in shadow, but lamps still burned at a few tables, yawning scholars bent over their books, and Ivan and Julian slipped past, following the hawk's lead to the very same ancient mystery-cabinet where they had hidden from the irate librarian earlier in the day. At the sight of it, both of them pulled up short and looked at each other, then the jinnyeh. "Here?"

"Here," Khasmedeus agreed, using its beak to indicate the complex puzzle of sliding pieces built into the age-stained wood. "Just a quick brainteaser, and then it's all yours."

Julian frowned, cracked his knuckles, and stepped up to the challenge. Adding some further spice was the fact that he had only three chances to solve the locking mechanism before the cabinet was sealed forever and destroyed whatever was inside, and if the wardens caught them, they would be kicked out of the library on an equally permanent basis. They were lucky that Julian was brilliant, but even so, he muffed the first attempt and was rewarded by the labyrinth rearranging itself even more impenetrably. He therefore also botched the second attempt, and Ivan held his breath as they moved to the third and final chance. The suspense was unbearable, until Julian muttered in triumph, "Oh, it's a *tesseract,*" and did something impossibly complicated with the cube. Then there was a rattling sound like dry leaves or clattering bones, and the cabinet doors swung open.

There were several more compartments within, and Ivan wondered darkly what sort of absolute madman would ever want one of these bloody cabinets, even if it was an obvious benefit for baffling would-be thieves (such as them). But there was one drawer that simply slid open at Julian's touch, no further arcane fiddling required, and both of them sucked in their breath at the sight of what lay inside. Ivan was familiar with the forgery's basic appearance, but when compared with the genuine article, there was no mistaking that it was indeed a clumsy copy. The real Ring of Tselmun practically *sang* with power, shimmering and vibrating the air like a plucked string, an effortless folding of time-space and ordinary reality that felt as heavy as the core of a dying star. An eerie glow seeped off it as well, until Julian reached in and scooped it up. He hesitated for a final instant, as if debating whether he could or even dared to do it, and then slid it onto his finger.

All at once — nothing changed, not really, and yet everything did. Julian's shadow wavered and stretched and grew colossal, twisting and stretching off his feet and seeming to climb every arch and column, every vault and finial, every shelf and stack. Within it, he remained as he was, young and handsome and determined, but even more than that: a bewitching dark beauty of unfathomable grace and power, eyes shining like the heavens and a crown of blazing stars adorning his head. In that moment as Ivan stared at him, unable to move, to think or even to breathe, there was nothing, no choice or conscious volition inherent in the soul-deep obligation to fall to his knees and take Julian's beringed hand, pressing it to his lips. "My lord," he whispered. "My *king.*"

Julian might have answered, but it was far-off and echoing in the tumult, and sounded more like the elemental roaring of a storm than human speech. The library had grown blurred around them, reality fading like paint running in rain, and Julian pulled Ivan to his feet, so he was face-to-face, eye-to-eye with this terrible and lovely deity, or whatever had been born in this moment — it almost seemed that if anyone was to speak of the Ring again, they would have to call it the Ring of *Julian,* not the Ring of *Tselmun.* But that and any other thoughts were driven comprehensively out of his head, because their bodies were drawn together and then they were lost.

It was half a coupling and half an utter devouring, Ivan's hands pressing into Julian's flesh, making him anew even more strongly than the primal force of ancient magic, echoing in the slow and deliberate beat of *mine, mine, mine.* As if he could just hold on and never let go, they would be bound like this forever, *forever.* His eyes were closed, but the cacophony of chaos beat through them, burst in fireworks, inflamed his blood and burned his soul to ash. He did not care about anything but giving himself to the flames, and so he did. Over, and over, and over.

Ivan had no idea how much time had passed, what exactly they had done together, or anything else except the euphoria in his veins, when the fit of madness finally began to recede, and he dimly realized that he and Julian were both lying flat on the floor, wheezing and gasping, their flesh still hot as flame. His eyes were seared too badly to see, and he briefly feared he had gone blind, but he blinked hard until distorted shapes flickered back into focus, along with an upside-down and very censorious hawk. *"Well,"* it tutted. "Wasn't *that* a spectacle."

"What…" Ivan's tongue felt like charred wood. "What just…?"

"A lot of things, really. *None* of which are suitable for discussion in polite company." The hawk flapped to the neighboring cabinet, thus to stare judgmentally from a better angle. "Never seen the Ring act like an outright aphrodisiac, but it could be that you two idiots are just so repressed and in denial that it had to burst out somehow. Literally. You might want to scarper before someone comes to see what all those embarrassing moans and groans were. I did my best to distract them – you're welcome, by the way – but still."

"Fuck." Ivan hauled himself off the floor, looked around to see if he had lost any crucial items of clothing, and gave the equally dazed Julian a hand up. It was best not to inspect too closely whatever they had left behind, and they scuttled out of the Great Library and into the night. They leaned against the wall, trying not to look each other in the eye, until Ivan finally managed, "So you – you've still got it?"

"Yeah. I – I do." Julian lifted his hand and stared at the Ring. "Wait, though. I left the *Key* in there. Hold on. I'll go get it."

Clearly relieved to escape this excruciatingly awkward situation, he scampered back to the library, and Ivan did his best not to think about anything. He was almost succeeding, until Khasmedeus uttered a warning caw. "Oy. Loverboy. There's something coming."

"What?" Ivan's eyes snapped open. "Where?"

Khasmedeus indicated, and then Ivan saw it too – another bird, streaking fast and low across the sky. A thrill of foreboding went through him. He recognized the raven as the kind that carried messages for the Thaumaturges (the *Thaumaturge,* if their gruesome hypothesis about Kronus was correct), and its arrival was not encouraging. What the –

"Good evening, General Ionius," the raven said, opening its beak and speaking in Kronus's familiar wheezy cadence. "What a surprise to behold you here, in the distant sands of Ambraz. But it does not matter, so long as your mission has been successful. I have glimpsed you in my seeing-glass, and I know it has been. You have found the real Ring of Tselmun, after you so sadly attempted to mislead me with the decoy. You will bring it to me immediately, or – "

"Or?" Ionius did not attempt to conceal his skepticism. "Or what?"

The raven – if such a thing was possible – smirked. Then it told him.

****

HE DID NOT REMEMBER WHAT happened after that, or what was said. It must have been something important, but it was empty snow that could not come close to cutting the screaming in his head. Julian was back and asking something in an increasingly urgent tone, and all Ionius could manage was that they had to go, they had to get back to Merone right now. He wasn't being gentle or kind about it, and there was a look on Julian's face as if he was once more reminded of just who he had gotten into bed with, but he hesitated a final moment, then agreed.

The next question was how to actually do it. If the raven appeared this fast, it had to have flown through a door, and it might still be open, but walking directly back into Kronus's lair was the last thing Ionius wanted. Besides, Julian had also been embroiled in the farrago with the Grand Magister, Julian had the Ring, and sending him to raze the tower into ash was the only thing Ionius could focus on. Internally he too had fallen into a pit of fire and was burning alive, and yet externally that unbreakable Immortal discipline kept him cool and controlled, issuing orders with calm efficiency. He was well aware that it was a trap of some kind. He just didn't fucking care.

Julian tried to speak to him, but Ionius stonily ignored him, keeping his head turned away until it was time to go. Khasmedeus changed into a giant firebird and clutched them in its claws, they were swept up into the sky and Ambrazakti fell out of sight, the clouds whipped their faces and the world turned over and over in a dizzying mélange that would have been beautiful if Ionius could spare the slightest ability to notice. Instead, he wondered what would happen if the jinnyeh opened its talons and let him plunge head over heels, down and down and down, to break his body on the rocks below. He was almost tempted to encourage it, to let him meet the end he deserved, but no matter what, he refused to die before this score was settled. Once and for all.

The journey fell into a monotonous, chilly blur. Ionius wandered in and out of awareness. Even if Khasmedeus flew far faster and further than any average avian, it still took time to wing across those endless Ifriqiyini leagues, and he closeted himself in his head. Then at last he spotted the great white walls, the harbor hot and blue in the summer dawn, and they swooped in and landed in the Eternal Palace as if they had never been away. Ionius felt utterly untethered from conscious volition or fear of consequences. He had never been so strong, so clear, so purposeful.

He said one last thing to Julian, and did not know what. He did not look back. He strode to the forbidding portcullis of the Castel Sanctangel and knocked. When an acolyte came to answer, Ionius smiled politely and apologized for the visit at such an early hour. But was it possible, perchance, to consult urgently with Grand Magister Saturnus?

The acolyte supposed so, as such an important guest could hardly be turned down and especially not when he had such a terrifying look on his face. Ionius strolled in and waited in the magister's drawing room until he finally appeared, unshaven and yawning in his nightclothes. "My lord? You're returned? We had heard that you had gone suddenly – "

"I am, yes. And I want to ask about my sister. Tatyana Sazharyna."

"Unfortunately, my lord. I know nothing about her."

"Liar." Ionius smiled at last, lips stretching jaggedly over his teeth. "You know. You have, in fact, known all along, since the first moment I came to ask about the slave Romola. You looked at her file and realized it was too dangerous to let me know without Coriolane's express permission, and you *certainly* knew at Year End, when you protested that it was not a wise idea to send her to take up in my company. So tell me, Your Excellency. How long has this been the case?"

Saturnus goggled. "I'm not sure that I – "

"How. Long."

"I… gently, my lord, gently." The necromancer flinched. "It is disquieting to learn this, of course, but it is standard procedure. Your, ah, your sister proved to be an exceptionally troublesome case, hence why she was Remade several times, but it is still not beyond the usual."

"What would you say *the usual* is, Excellency?"

"I..." Saturnus hesitated. "Ensuring the Immortals' allegiance is a paramount concern for every emperor, especially after Spartekaius. Part of the reason his uprising was able to succeed, even temporarily, is because Coriolane III neglected to enforce obvious restraints upon his conduct, including in the taking of hostages from his friends and family. One may remark, a mistake endemic to that incompetent monarch in many other areas of statecraft. Ever since, every Immortal has been subject to this particular, ah, safeguard. Please, my lord, it isn't personal. Only good business."

"Yes," Ionius said, still remotely and glacially polite. "Yes, I see. Thank you, Excellency."

Saturnus let out a breath, visibly relieved, and got to his feet. "Of course, my lord. I'm very glad to help you. Would you like to take breakfast with me? There are many other things I would be happy to share, if it would ease your mind."

"I think so," Ionius said. "I am quite hungry."

"Good, good." Saturnus beamed unctuously. Turned his back, and took a step. And still utterly calm, without hastening or hurrying in the least, Ivan raised his hands.

The sheer brute force of the channeling struck like lightning, a bolt from the blue in the morning hush. Saturnus, completely off guard, had not even an instant to try to defend himself. His body did not so much tear apart as *blast* apart, its aged sinews bursting at the seams and his blood spouting so violently that it bathed the room in crimson. Ivan did not stop until the Grand Magister was reduced to an unrecognizable heap of flayed and disfigured flesh; there could be no risk that the necromancer had stashed away some clever trick for cheating death unless someone *really* meant it. To say the least, Ivan did. He raised his hands and *ripped* again, blasting the ulcerous pile of offal flat, and then he stepped over it, opened the door, and proceeded down the corridor.

There were sounds of movement in the living quarters, as some Corporalists were still in bed and some were just waking up and some had never gone to sleep. It did not matter. Ivan destroyed them, calmly and thoroughly and with all the abilities at his disposal, everything that they themselves had given him so long ago, when he entered the Castel as a man and left as an Immortal. He conjured blades from his bones and flung them into the necromancers' chests and eyes and heads and guts and balls, methodical as a target shooter. He tore the blood from their bodies and launched them across the room, corpses crashing into tables and falling like rotten fruit, dishes rolling and food spilling in mindless disarray. He ripped their windpipes out of their throats, inverted their lungs through their spines in blood eagles, caused some to drown thrashing and gargling in their own fluids, and sent others flying to the ceiling on invisible ropes, feet jerking as they strangled on thin air. Their faces purpled, they lost their bowels, piss ran down their legs. Some tried to plead with him, to promise that they would be his loyal servants, even more loyal than they had been to Coriolane. Some, laughably, tried to fight. Some tried desperately to order the enspelled metal in his neck to cut his throat. Ivan did not give them the chance. He simply killed them.

When it was done, Ivan stepped out into the corridor and glanced from side to side. Then he raised his hands again, seized intangible hold of the iron in the portcullis, the lead in the window-glass, the steel and pewter in the locks, and *crushed* it, bringing his palms together in a sphere of stunningly absolute psychic force that exploded the fabric of reality and the foundations of stone alike. The portcullis broke free and crashed down, the windows imploded, the ground tilted and split as if in an earthquake, and cracks scythed the floor and ceiling alike, dust and rubble hailing down. He stood alone in the middle of the maelstrom, holding the falling sky away from him without effort. Then, when he was satisfied that he had cut off all escape routes, that the necromancers were trapped in here with him and there was no way out, he straightened his shoulders, cracked his knuckles, and went hunting.

Step by step, unhurried and deliberate, Ivan continued into the Castel. There were groups of acolytes down in the laboratories, who heard the disturbance and prepared for a fight, but they were no match for him. Several of the human subjects were still alive, so Ivan cut their straps and bindings and pulled them off the berths and benches. He indicated where they should go and told them to stop for nothing, then directed the chains to fly back, ravel up the captors instead of the captives, and bisect them at the torso or behead them at the neck, squeezing them until they popped like juicy pimples and their innards spewed like pus. Their heads rolled into corners and their trunks folded, still twitching for a few moments after they were dead. He opened trunks and cabinets and sent racks of scalpels flying out, diving and darting and piercing screaming magisters in a thousand weeping scarlet eyes. He impaled them on their own hooks and flays and knives, all the tools of their trade, and left them to die. He did not hasten their end. He did not feel so merciful.

Next, he went into the blackest of the black cells, to the Remade awaiting their next life, injected with a carbolic concoction from an evil-looking crucible. He smashed all the flasks, paused to wish their souls an easy passage to the next world, and assured them it was preferable to the alternative. The dungeon stank of corrosive chemicals and dead flesh. His head spun. He wanted to throw up. He didn't.

At last, after he had searched the entirety of the Corporalists' lair from top to bottom and was satisfied that there was not a single one left alive, Ivan reeled to a bloodstained, breathless halt. He was drenched in gore from the eyelashes to the ankles, and it dripped off him in slow, heavy slaps and splashes, crimson blossoming on the stone floor and in the messy line of his booted footprints. He was soaked in sweat, but he was so cold that he must be freezing to death. His head was light as glass and crowned with mangled, slimy gobbets of flesh like gruesome jewels. His mouth tasted bitter and coppery, and no matter how many times he spat, it didn't help. There was nothing, no sound, no life. It was fitting for a bunch of necromancers. Finally the truth matched the mask, all the clever pretense and pretty metaphor shorn away. *Dead. Dead. Dead.*

It felt like forever until his legs would hold him. He was not entirely certain that they would, but he tried nonetheless, and walked out of the abattoir with perfect composure. He reached the freed captives clustered at the ruins of the portcullis, cleared it aside with another wave of his hand, and led them like the Vashemite prophet Moyshe, out of Gezeren and into the Promised Land. They were too frightened to go any further or step into the sunlight or be sure that furious legions would not sweep down on them, and they clutched him, begging to know what to do or if they could come with him or ever repay him for saving them. Some fell on their knees and pressed their heads to his bloody hands, or his bloody feet. Anything, my lord. Anything you want at all.

Ivan did not want such undeserved veneration. He knocked their hands aside, disdained their pleas and their gratitude alike. Every step he took splintered his bones in pain too agonizing to bear; he had gone too far, channeled too much, burned out every scrap of his power, and he too was nothing more than a husk. And since the Immortals' strength had been stolen to fuel Coriolane's immortality, he might never get it back, had expended himself in one final and spectacular act of destruction and would never be as he was before. It didn't matter. At least it had finally served its purpose. He felt clear-minded, clear-eyed, perfectly and exquisitely calm. Steady. Sane.

And yet, for all the devastation Ivan had wreaked here, his task was not done. They had not given the order; they were not the ultimate mastermind. There was another target that needed to be dealt with, and Ivan had no more strength to do it on his own. He had to finish the job, though. Ring or no Ring, Khasmedeus or Julian or otherwise. There were more prisoners in the parts of the Castel he had not destroyed, and Corporalists across the empire; he had eradicated all those in Merone, but it was not yet the total end of their order. Grand Magister Kronus was still skulking in his cannibal cellar with his terrible bone pentacle, and Romola – no, not Romola, and yes, Romola, for she was not his sister, not really, not her memory or spirit, just her shell –

Ivan did not want to go on. Did not want to keep standing, or existing, or breathing. He wanted to climb into a hole and go to sleep forever. He did not want to decide whether to go to the Eternal Palace and Coriolane's apartments, or the tower of the Thaumaturges and the other reckoning with Kronus. Julian and Romola-Tatyana were there, so he had to return at some point, but like this? Drenched in the blood and guts of the necromancers, the dismembered remains of his victims, so the fucking jinnyeh could pose and prance and snark and snipe about his multifarious shortcomings? As if Khasmedeus, who had been the Jinnyeh High King's traitor general just as Ionius was to Coriolane, did not have even more blood on its hands, literally *and* figuratively. As if it did not know the maelstrom and the tempest, the unmaking. Perhaps it was the reason for the nonsense. It must be unbearable to live otherwise.

Ivan stood with his face upturned to the sun, the summer air of the pleasant midmorning that ruffled his bloodstained hair and blood-soaked tunic and blood-dripping, blood-screaming, old and broken heart. For a final moment, he dreamed that he could stay like this forever, never moving again, his feet grown into roots and his arms stretched into the branches of a great leafy tree, to sway with the winds and pass away the years, the coming and going of time and tide, of life and death. It seemed better, that way. It seemed peaceful. But his task was not yet completed, and so he lowered his head, set his shoulders, and began to walk.

CHAPTER

29

MARCUS

Up until this point in his seventeen years of life, Marcus Servus had never been out of the Eternal City before. Well, he supposed, that wasn't strictly true. He was born in the Ruthynian capital of Korolgrod, but that didn't count, when he neither knew how he came to Merone in the first place nor felt it especially important. At some point he left his parents and his brother (or brothers), and someone took him on a ship with a lot of other children, passed through the eastern port of Coriolanople, and eventually arrived in the Eternal City itself. Timelines and details were hazy, as Marcus had only been three or four. He was placed in the household of a middle-class merchant and his wife, very proud of the fact that they were now wealthy enough to own slaves, and instructed to call them Mama and Papa – though they didn't like it when he used *Mata and Vata,* as he still only spoke Ruthynian at the time. But whatever quasi-parental aspirations they might have cherished did not last for long. He caught the eye of some official, was marked out for Immortal potential, and shipped to the Eternal Palace in less than six months. He had worked hard ever since, and now he was here.

The exact whereabouts of *here,* however, were up for question, and Marcus did his best not to look like a total ingenue with no experience of the wide world, even if he was. His existence to date consisted entirely of the barracks, the blood and sweat of the training yard, the grueling matches against his fellow cadets and the evaluation and flagellation of the senior officers – mostly Captain Caledonus, who was the head of training for junior Immortals and well known as impossible to please, but as Marcus grew up and advanced faster than many of his counterparts, also the real luminaries, the most senior and legendary battle-hardened titans whose talent and terror had carved out a near-godly legacy. This included General Ionius, who was often regarded, among Marcus and his desperately admiring peers, as the only one truly worth emulating. The others were fine, of course. More than fine. They won wars, they did impossible things, they were invincible and unconquerable by any definition, but all of them seemed to feel that weight and struggle with bearing it, being worthy of it. General Ionius simply *did*.

Indeed, Marcus had to admit that while of course he was as loyal to the Divine Emperor as any other patriotic Meronite, when it came down to the hard-tacks reality of who would always command his fealty, General Ionius was the master he had chosen. Marcus still didn't know what was in the letters he had been charged to smuggle to Qin, and he hoped it wasn't some outrageous treason, but why would his glorious hero, his paragon of virtue, do a thing like that? It did seem strange that the general was asking an untested greenhorn to bear a secret missive by a very back-channel route, but Marcus comforted himself with the knowledge that it was not for him to question. Immortals did not do such things. Immortals simply obeyed. It was the law of the universe.

All of that, so far as it went, made perfect sense. There was just that thing, that one little thing, which Marcus could not sunset into rosy concord with the rest. He was otherwise supremely confident that the general's judgment was far beyond his humble ken; as a cadet who had not yet passed the trials and undergone the Corporalist modifications, Marcus himself was still mortal, an ordinary man, and daring to challenge not just an Immortal, but *the* Immortal, was the height of arrogance. But nonetheless, Ionius's last words had carved the tiniest crack, not doubt but something like the slightest shadow of it, into that ironclad certainty. Why had he told Marcus to leave the Eternal City forever once his errand was done, and never again offer faith or homage? Was it to see if Marcus would cravenly flee instead of returning to fulfill his destiny? Ah, yes. That must be it. The general had decided to test Marcus's loyalty before letting him take the full trials, and this was surely a crucial step in the process. So, then. Nothing to worry about. Nothing at all.

This renewed and vastly reassuring certainty carried Marcus aboard a trading scow and on the short sea journey to Xandropolis, the northern Gezereni port city which served as a major base for the empire's operations in Ifriqiyin. It had been founded many centuries ago by the ancient Hellenic conqueror who gallivanted around killing people, slapping his name on things, and then died young, and had once hosted one of the most splendid libraries in the world, infamously burned down by Coriolane Caesar when the Meronites conquered the place. Marcus was sure the Gezereni had deserved it, though it did seem rather a waste, and he was then forced to think hard about what to do next. General Ionius had given him precise instructions about how to proceed by ordinary methods: camel train or ferry to Jedya, ship to Guangzhing via Malabarium, petition in Guangzhing for prompt transport to Hang'i. But it would take several months, and they did not have nearly that long to spare. His lord had also told him that if any opportunity arose to speed the trip by magic, he should take it at any cost.

This, Marcus soon found, was easier said than done. He went to the dockside districts where various dubious street magicians peddled their services, wondered darkly if he dared risk his life on any conjuration of their making, and got into heated arguments with unimpressed individuals who did *not* seem inclined to fall on their faces and obey with no questions asked. The general had told him to pose as a Meronite or Ruthynian merchant, and it felt easier to be the former, but even when he was their rightful master, they looked at him as if he was dirt and disdained to answer him. It wasn't a language barrier, or at least he didn't think so. Apart from Ruthynian and Lanuvian, he spoke fluent Qiné, as all the Immortals were required to do, and enough Semyic to get by in Gezeren – though by rights, they *should* be speaking Lanuvian. If he had time, he would report the lot of them for rank insubordination, but that, alas, was not within his ambit.

At last, after fits and starts and failed attempts to get any of them to listen to him long enough to even explain what he needed, he was finally hailed by a seedy little hedge wizard who was apparently willing to accept a less discerning clientele, and found himself sitting in a grimy yellow tent, sipping bitter black tea, and haggling over the price of an expedited journey to Qin. The wizard insisted that he could do it, which Marcus wasn't sure whether to believe, but it did not appear as if he had multitudes of other options. Finally with bad grace, he consented to pay half of what the mangy charlatan demanded, the rest tenderable upon actual proof of success, and then found himself with a front-row seat to some insanely heathen ritual as the wizard drew complicated symbols, burned herbs, and intoned in a mystic foreign tongue. The incense fuddled Marcus's head and made him sleepy, but he manfully persevered until there was a ripple in the air and something took shape that looked like a woman, but surely wasn't. "Greetings, O Master," she intoned, sounding supremely uninterested. "What is your command today?"

"Our little friend has a need to travel to the Jade City of Hang'i, fast." The wizard indicated Marcus, who vastly resented being described as *our little friend* in any capacity. "I therefore charge you to obey all his commands for the full term of our written contract, to fulfil such duties to him as you would to myself, to take all precautions to guard his life and property, and when the task is complete, return to me to await further instructions." To Marcus he added, "This is Sila. She is a jinnyess, a most talented mistress of magic and shapeshifting and many other useful services. If you wish me to write those explicitly into the contract, the fee will be five percent more for each – "

"No." Marcus was mildly revolted by the relentless profiteering, and the Divine Family would not approve of such wicked associations with demons, but he had to make a decision. "Fine, I'll take it. What – er – what exactly do I *do?*"

"Here." The wizard handed Marcus a ring: somewhat shabby and made of inferior copper, worn to a faint greenish patina. "Place that on your finger and never, *never* take it off, or the bonds of protection will immediately be sundered, and she will be free to perform any devilries upon you that she fancies, including but not limited to complete physical devourment. Likewise, it is effective for only a fortnight, unless you arrange to send more money to me. Are you sure you do not wish to extend the activation period? Time does fly faster than you think."

Marcus glowered hotly at this duplicitous weasel, who seemed bound and determined to extract every sestertius from him, but this did feel like the kind of thing where it was better not to cut cheapskate corners. So he grudgingly handed over enough to cover another fortnight, while Sila the jinnyess – she was quite pretty, he couldn't help but notice – bobbed in her pentacle with a bored expression. "So," she drawled, once he put on the ring, signed the contract, and otherwise secured her services for a month – which he damn well *hoped* would be enough, as he wasn't sure how to pay for any more. "What's it going to be, O Exalted Master? All sorts of ways to get to Hang'i in a hurry. I could transform you into a rather pimply fish, for starters, and then – "

"No." Marcus glanced imploringly at the wizard, looking for help in managing this unruly female creature, but the wizard gave him a *you're-on-your-own-now-mate* look and packed his things. When he had hastily scuttled off and left Marcus face to face with Sila, the jinnyess stretched slowly and deliberately, picking her teeth with one exquisite finger. "Listen to me," he ordered. "You are mine now, creature, at least for the specified term, and so – "

"Mmm, yes. You rented a jinnyeh, good for you. Other lads your age would pay a woman for far more interesting services, you know." Sila leered at him. "Unless you already tried that, and you were too boring, too inept, or too terrible even for them? That must be a talent."

"*Silence.*" He was an Immortal or close enough, he would not be spoken to like this. "You will also refrain from any more lies or slanders about me. Do not forget that you are a slave."

"Oh?" Sila cocked her head, grin turning even more feral. "Don't forget that so are *you.*"

That, despite himself, rocked Marcus considerably, and he couldn't say why. Yes, of course he knew that, but her situation wasn't like his, it wasn't the same. She was nobody, an anonymous lesser being kept in permanent bondage to a cheating wastrel of a street wizard who probably didn't know a scrap of other magic and made his entire livelihood by hiring her out to an endless succession of supplicants, and *Marcus* – well, it was obvious who *he* was, charged to hold secret negotiations with a dangerous foreign rival and bring peace and justice back to the empire. He bristled, but he had to be better than her. "*Now,* creature."

Sila eyed him up and down, muttered something he couldn't make out but which did not sound flattering, then sighed exaggeratedly and gave in. She transformed into a shining black mare, a fine fire-blooded Rabiyan steed, and told him to climb onto her back – which he did only with great wariness, having heard plenty of hair-raising tales about beautiful horses on riverbanks that lured hapless humans to mount them and dragged them underwater to drown. But he did have the ring, which (theoretically) defended him from such chicanery, and they had wasted enough time. He stepped into the saddle and barely had a chance to brace himself before she took off like a shot.

This consumed the next several days. Sila ran like the wind, stripping away miles and miles, and Marcus, despite his continual fear of imminent catastrophe, did his best to enjoy it. After all, this was the sort of worldly experience he needed, and even if he couldn't see or do much, as they stayed well away from cities, major roads, and other travelers, he told himself that it was the principle of the thing. He did his best to be exceedingly polite to Sila, even offering the first pick of whatever food he found. She was a dangerous beast, but still a lady, and certain standards of civilized behavior were expected even – nay, *especially* – with godforsaken wild savages. After all, if they did not see that there was a better way to live, how would they ever aspire to it?

"Who in hellfire sent you out here alone, kid?" the jinnyess asked on the third night, when they had pitched camp in a humid lowland cut by a vast and muddy river delta. Marcus didn't know where they were, but judging by the presence of an ancient prayer-flagged stupa sacred to a famous guru of the Thousand Gods, it was likely Indush, maybe the kingdom of Ayodhya or Vishvhanath. Great flocks of birds rose and rippled against the orange sky, and the heat was oppressive enough that they didn't need a fire; his tunic was sodden with sweat and he would have taken it off if he did not think it highly inappropriate to be unclad before his companion. "I mean, *you?*"

"I don't see what you mean," Marcus said stiffly. "It is my greatest honor to be an Immortal of Merone, in sworn service to my emperor and my general. I don't expect someone like you, who only owes temporary and coerced loyalty to the highest bidder, to understand."

"You think that's *my* idea?" Sila snorted volcanically. "Look, I know they brainwash you to an inch of your life, but come on. I really want to spend my entire existence in bondage to *that* miserable maggot, serving pompous little shits like you? I think not."

"I am your master," Marcus warned her for the dozenth time, even as he had realized that it wasn't likely to have any effect. "I told you to refrain from calumny or name-calling on my – "

"Sorry, sorry. But you just beg for it. More than most humans, even." Sila transformed back into the distractingly pretty woman and eyed the roasting meat with a greedy expression; her teeth were very white and very pointed. She had informed Marcus that she didn't actually need human food, but she ate it eagerly anyway, and her taste for extremely raw and bloody flesh was another fact which did not portend a quick fall to sleep at night. "Does it hurt?"

Marcus was briefly puzzled. "Does what hurt?"

"The stick." Sila blinked at him with profoundly put-on innocence. "The stick wedged *so* far up your arse that it's not surprising nothing else can get up there instead. Such as, say – "

"I said *enough!*" His sudden shout sent another susurration of birds shrieking into the hazy twilight, winging and wheeling over the wine-spill clouds. "I will not tolerate your filthy intimations or your persistent disrespect, and if you continue – "

"You'll what?" She pretended to yawn. "Take off that ring, rip up your contract, leave me free to do as I like, and *if* I leave you alive, piddle pointlessly around in some desolate Indush marsh until some passerby takes pity on you – or more likely, squashes you flat like the Meronite cockroach you are? For a moment there I was almost feeling sorry for you, sent off alone on this errand which is clearly *way* over your head, but don't worry. That's long gone."

Marcus opened his mouth, then shut it, stewing on his shameful failure – a real Immortal would never have allowed himself to be stung even a moment by her juvenile barbs, her quotidian curses. There was a pungent silence. Then he said, "I apologize, Lady Sila."

"Lady Sila." She seemed amused. "You know, *Sila* isn't a name, or at least not my name. It just means the type of jinnyeh I am. *Succubus,* that's what they call me in Lanuvian. Doesn't that scare you, boy? Don't you have to scamper away to preserve your virginal innocence?"

That, to say the least, was an unpleasant surprise. "So are you planning to seduce me?"

"Haven't decided. It would be fun to see you squirm and squeal." Sila waggled an impudent eyebrow. "And it would blow your mind, which would *also* be fun. But since I'm forced to sleep with every single one of that bastard's *other* clients, all of whom have heard *so* much about how terrible and dangerous and soul-sucking the si'lat are and yet are desperate to put their tiny prick in me anyway, it might be a nice change. Trust me, you're hardly an irresistible prospect."

Yet again, Marcus found himself unhappily kneecapped in his search for a proper response. He didn't want to think of her as anything other than a savage, gleefully and salaciously exerting her feminine monstrosities on unsuspecting men, but the idea that she might not have any choice in the matter, that the wizard's continual reference to "other services" obliged her every time regardless of her own thoughts and feelings – did she *have* thoughts and feelings? – was more uncomfortable than expected. At last he said, "That is – I did not think – I would not do such a thing, of course. It would be beneath my dignity."

"Beneath *your* dignity?" Sila's voice turned still more ironic. "Of course. That's what we're worried about. Still, kid. I trust none of it, but it's nice of you to say. Though I reserve the right to think it's because you're secretly terrible at it, or couldn't get your cock to stand, or have a horrible deformity or awful fetish that made even the whores shun you. If you've ever tried, that is."

Marcus felt a burn in his cheeks that had nothing to do with the heat, and hastily took another bite of supper. No, he didn't have any experience with women, and did not intend to start now. He had admired Lady Romola from his chaste and deferential position as her bodyguard, but General Ionius had taken sharp note of that and warned him off any liberties with his consort, not that actually trying something would ever cross Marcus's mind. He *was* surprised that the general had taken up with a woman, as everyone was aware of the talk that his tastes ran in other directions, but when you were a senior Immortal of the strength and stature of Ionius Servus Eternus, you could fuck an entire exotic bestiary and very few people would have the nerve to say a word about it. It went against True Tridevarian morality and therefore wasn't strictly legal, and commoners could be arrested and prosecuted for sodomitic liaisons, but that was the point of climbing to this lofty zenith, this rarefied air. It was forbidden for the Immortals to marry without Coriolane's permission, which was almost never granted, but they were allowed to take lovers. As long as they were never put above the paramount duty of life – and death – for Great Merone.

There was silence for several moments as both of them chewed intently. Then, because he was genuinely curious, Marcus said, "So if *Sila* is just what you are, then what *is* your name?"

"Well, now. That's dangerous information, and the sort you could only pay for in kind. For example, what's *your* real name? Unless your parents named you Marcus the Slave at birth – which could be possible, I don't understand humans – but I don't think so."

"I – " Marcus stopped. He didn't actually remember, and nor did he think it was a necessity. Besides, his parents had not put up a fuss about his leaving at best and actively sold him to the trader at worst, so why would he want to honor whatever they called him? *Marcus* was a good name, a solid name, borne by countless Meronite heroes, and as for *Servus,* he counted down the days until he could add *Eternus.* "It is my real name," he insisted. "I am proud of it."

Sila raised both eyebrows again, and he found himself wanting to explain more, to help her understand the perfection of the Meronite system and the glorious chance it had given someone like him, who would otherwise live and die an utterly unregarded existence in the poorest slums of Korolgrod. If, that was, he did not falter. Ionius' letters sat unopened in his satchel, and his curiosity still burned a hole into him, but if he failed such a basic test, it would instantly disqualify him for anything else. He was so close. He just had to hold his nerve.

They continued to make superlative time, bearing south of Sardarkhand and into the rolling brown foothills that softened the craggy escarpments of the Tien Shen. Unsuspecting Spice Road merchants were often tricked into going this way, thinking it easier than climbing the high alpine peaks, only to discover that the Ahyuns had long since concluded the same thing and put the gentler territory to excellent use in arranging devastatingly effective ambushes. The nomadic horsemen had their roots in chilly northern Khaganate Province, where the Thearchate had built the Great Wall in a vain attempt to keep them out, but they ranged far afield and had even come close to threatening Coriolanople in eastern Merone, in addition to repeated incursions into Ruthynia and Qin. Their greatest leader, Temujin Borjigin Khan, had styled himself the Father of the World, a conqueror and emperor subordinate to no one, and Marcus prayed that the lot of them were too busy menacing innocents elsewhere to impede his passage. Once he glimpsed dust kicked up by a horde in the distance, but by the Divine Family's mercy, they made it through unscathed.

It was the day after that when he spotted the first Qiné boundary stone, engraved in hanqin and proclaiming this the territory of Tiberian Province – the westernmost part of the Thearchate, a vast, frozen, and jaggedly mountainous hinterland where local tribes and religious leaders known as lamas vigorously resisted the Jade City's hegemony. It was a nightmare to navigate, even with Sila's help, but it meant the end of the first leg was almost in sight. Marcus didn't have to go all the way south to Guangzhing, which was now far out of his way; he could present himself to the yamen in Zin'qiang instead. Of course, the Zin'qiang magistrate was usually far too busy trying to put down local revolts to deal with any other problems, and Marcus did not want to end up in a rustic power struggle. Then again, if he was feeling abandoned and hung out to dry by the Jade City, the magistrate might be more willing to consider unorthodox solutions. It was worth a try.

Despite the fact that it was late summer, almost the month of Augustus, the air was bitterly cold, snow lay thick on the rugged slopes of the biggest mountains Marcus had ever seen, and the sun dazzled his eyes so brightly that he was almost blind; the world was only sky and ice and stone, an eagles' eyrie where the air was so thin that it hurt. To someone so accustomed to the crowding of the Eternal City and the close quarters of the Immortal barracks, the sheer *space* was astonishing, the disbelief that the world could stretch to the far ends of the earth with scarcely a hint of mankind anywhere. Zin'qiang – Lhosetse, in Tiberian – lay in the deep cleft of a glacial valley, surrounded by steep terraces and rugged pastures. It was ancient and compact, enclosed in mud-brick walls, hazed in acrid yak-dung smoke, and crammed with monasteries, temples, markets, and the Songtsen Palace, once the seat of the lama and now that of the yamen magistrate. It was built into a vertical cliff face, its facades painted red and white and its roof towering in intricate golden spires. As Marcus drew rein beneath its vast shadow, he was forced to admit that the savages could put on a good display from time to time. If they could speed his errand, he would be even more indebted.

He swung down from the saddle and then had to clutch it as his legs buckled; after almost a week riding nonstop, he could barely stand. He looked around warily before hissing that the coast was clear for Sila to transform. She looked at him and smirked. "Too much for you, kid?"

"No." Marcus concentrated on deep breathing. "I'm entirely well."

"Uh-huh." She slid him a slanted grin, obnoxiously untroubled. "If we're planning to go in, what's our cover story? Am I your wife, or – "

"No, absolutely not." Marcus straightened up. "I will tell the truth, that I am Marcus Servus of the Immortals and you are my servant. We urgently require permission to travel to the Jade City and speak with the Thearch. Transportation is less of an issue, so long as I have you, but the Qiné are exceedingly fastidious about their bureaucracy. If I try to enter the Inner Provinces without the proper paperwork stamped in triplicate, I will be stopped and detained, or worse."

"Glad to know you're such a respecter of local law and custom," Sila remarked, her voice redolent with sarcasm, as they proceeded into the great gloom of the walls and were indeed instantly waylaid by an officious under-minister. This gave Marcus the chance to try his spoken Qiné for the first time, and while he received a few suspicious stares and squiggle-eyed expressions, on the whole he made himself understood. On the other hand, the minister had some peculiar local accent that confounded Marcus, but after an extended episode of haggling, apologies, arguments, and other persiflage, the minister finally and reluctantly went to see if the magistrate, Wang Wen, was in residence and willing to receive an extremely unexpected visitor. Marcus sat on a bench, leaning against the cool white-plastered wall, and Sila said, "Don't know what you're actually here to do, do you? All this effort, and yet you haven't bothered to take one peek?"

"It is not my place to know." Marcus kept his eyes closed, wondering if it was possible to be asleep if you were talking. "General Ionius will make the decision that he feels best."

"You're still going with that?" Sila examined him critically. "You have a troubling amount of faith in your superiors, after you were sent alone in strict secrecy and your only sort-of-ally is a *shifty jinnyeh*. So you'll walk in and merrily hand over that letter? Then what?"

"General Ionius is not *wrong*," Marcus said again, slightly desperately. "Be quiet."

Sila made an extremely unconvinced noise, but she withheld her remarks until the minister returned with the news that Magistrate Wang was amenable to a meeting after all, and could they please follow him. They descended a steep tunnel into a secluded inner courtyard, then crossed to a pagoda crowned with sculptures of serpentine dragons and hung with silk banners emblazoned in golden hanqin. They were required to remove their shoes, to avoid tracking mud and filth into the inner sanctum, and Wang Wen, a middle-aged Qiné man clad in huanfu and a green skullcap, rose from behind his desk and bowed. "Honored Marcus Servus," he said, in accented but crisply bookish Lanuvian. "What a surprise to greet a Meronite so far from home."

"Ah – greetings, Excellency," Marcus managed, confused at being addressed in his own tongue by a barbarian in such an isolated backwater. "I apologize for the surprise of my presence, and my unsolicited entry into Zin'qiang. Your Excellency speaks Lanuvian very well."

"Did you think Meronites were the only people required to study the language of a rival?" The magistrate offered a slight, enigmatic smile. "I heard that you do speak Qiné, though, so let us presume that I have also offered my compliments. Why are you here?"

The directness of the question took Marcus aback, when he was prepared for opaque palaver and discreet evasion. At Wang's indication, he took a seat. "I was sent as a personal ambassador from General Ionius Servus Eternus of Merone. I have a letter originally intended for your counterpart in Guangzhing, but I have come by another road. Perhaps you should read it, and then we may discuss further?"

"Perhaps." Wang held out his hand. "Give it here."

Marcus hesitated a final instant, then did so, as Wang broke the seal and read it with an inscrutable expression. "Well," he said at last, folding the parchment again. "That is very interesting, wouldn't you say?"

"Of course," Marcus agreed, doing his best not to look utterly lost. "Er, if Your Excellency wishes to expound on that, what exactly do you find the *most* interesting?"

Wang threw him an amused glance, and Marcus had the sinking feeling that this man, expert in the secrets and services of the Qiné court, could read him like a book and was well aware of how little he actually knew. "For a start," Wang said, "that General Ionius risked his own neck to send such a subversive message, which – forgive me – I do not believe was sanctioned by your Divine Emperor." A faint scorn lingered in his voice, as if he thought the *Meronites* were the barbarians, uncultured swine who had no hope of grasping the beauty and harmony of Qin's glorious ancient culture, and Marcus bit back an undiplomatic urge to correct him. "It is true that we have recently experienced a disturbing rise in Meronite military activity, from belligerents who should not, to the best of our knowledge, even be here. I have been spared this in person, as Zin'qiang is very difficult to assault directly, but my fellows in Yunan and Guangzhi Provinces have reported the most attacks. If the Thaumaturges have used magical doors to bring Meronite legions here, that would explain some of it. It would also empower us to strike back however and wherever we saw fit."

"Excellency, I do know that General Ionius was in considerable opposition to the war – er, the special military operation – as originally planned. It could be that he seeks to – "

"The thing is," Wang interrupted. "None of these activities, obnoxious and destructive as they are, have followed a coherent rationale or pattern. Meronite legionnaires simply appear from thin air, attack whatever is nearby and kill whoever they can get their hands on, and do not even try to carry out a larger scheme or logical progression. Of course, you savages are not versed in General Sunzi's arts of war such as we, but if you have gone to all this trouble, there must be a *purpose*. Perhaps, Marcus Servus, you wish to enlighten me as to *why?*"

"I…" Marcus hesitated, doing his utmost not to look at Sila. "That must not be right. His Majesty has called for a holy war on Qin, a proper conquest of our rival — saving your pardons, Excellency. It must be difficult in the early stages, but it is an ordinary war."

"So you reassure me that the Meronites, despite this underwhelming opening salvo, do very much still intend to destroy Qin, whenever they get around to properly trying?" Wang looked as if he couldn't decide whether to laugh in Marcus's face or just kill him. "Because it looks as if you are here merely to destroy as much as you can, and not even bother with the customary trappings or goals of war. Our two great powers have often been in conflict, yes, but not like *this*."

Marcus opened his mouth, then shut it. The silence crackled to an unbearable pitch. Then he said, "I was hoping to travel onward to the Jade City with your blessing, Excellency. I have another letter that I was strictly instructed to give only to the Thearch."

"*Only* the Thearch?" Wang's eyebrows nearly reached his plucked hairline. "You do realize it is utterly impossible that we should just *grant* you an audience with Their Majesty, when I have no proof that you are not a covert assassin sent to lull us off guard, to share sensitive intelligence and look as if General Ionius is interested in collaborating, while you prepare an even greater treachery?"

"No," Marcus insisted. "No, I'm not here to kill them, or anyone. I just want to obey the general and stop any bloodshed. I swear, I *swear*."

Wang studied him without answering, eyes hooded. Then he shrugged. "I wish that I could believe you, even if it makes no sense. You are, or soon will be, an Immortal of Merone, an order of warriors who kill everyone they possibly can. So why would you insist that you do not want to, except to cause me to underestimate you or take pity on you or think it is safe to speed you to the sovereign's heavenly presence?

Either you are too soft and feeble to face your responsibilities, or you do not understand what they truly are. Either way, it is not to your credit."

"I don't know what – " Marcus bit his tongue. The Qiné bastard would not be disrespecting General Ionius like this, and he was the general's hand-picked stand-in. They stared at each other combatively until he cleared his throat. "You said the attacks mostly spared Zin'qiang, but if there was a way to speak with any Meronites here – "

Wang smiled, or at least his mouth turned up at the edges. He drummed his fingers on the desk, weighing his response, then rose to his feet, beckoning Marcus and Sila to follow. Puzzled, they did so, following him out of the pagoda and up a set of steep and narrow steps to the palace walls. The view was spectacular, the city falling away into the craggy cliffs and the massive pyramids of stone and snow, and the wind whisked and smacked as they picked along the wallwalk. Marcus raised his arm to shield against the hiss and swirl, until they reached the corner parapet and Wang came to a halt. "Tell me, Marcus Servus. Are you familiar with black powder?"

"I – yes, Excellency." Chillingly so, considering General Ionius's misadventures in Sardarkhand and the sinister plot he had exposed, the empresses' treason against spouse and throne alike. Marcus was impressed with the technical acumen, but he still didn't think it was anything to threaten the power of Meronite legions, the best-trained in the world. "May I ask what that has to do with – ?"

"Here." Wang indicated the hulking contraption next to him: a long iron barrel mounted on steel-shod wooden wheels, its dragon snout pointing menacingly over the walls. It was open on one end and had a charred fuse at the other, and he stooped to a crate, removing a heavy iron ball, a ramrod, and a twist of black powder. At his command, one of the guards stepped forward, shoved the ball into the barrel with the ramrod, tamped the powder in, and lit a taper. Wang beckoned for Marcus and Sila to stand back and cover their ears. "You may also wish to brace yourselves. Especially if you have never seen it before."

At Wang's nod, the guard stepped forward, lowered the lit taper to the fuse, and shouted something – a code or a warning or an assurance that it was merely a test, Marcus couldn't be sure. In any event, the effect was literally flattening. The great gun kicked, boomed, and went off in a maelstrom of fire, jerking backward on its massive wheels and only halted by the chains that were looped through the axles, containing the brutal power of the recoil. The crack echoed like the breaking of the fundament, the scrubby trees below crumpled into matchwood, and smoke curled up in trailing wisps, whiffing of soot and sulfur. The barrel glowed red-hot, as the guard sluiced water from a bucket to cool it, then loaded it again. This time, however, Wang did not order it fired, and glanced at his visitors. "I take it that was an effective demonstration of the cannon's capabilities, and what became of the benighted western savages who lawlessly invaded the sovereign Thearchate of Qin? They are not here, Honored Marcus Servus, because we did not permit them to leave alive. Even the best legions – and these did not seem to represent the finest of your number – are helpless against it. So you see, you are not *winning* the war, if this conflict can be called such. Not even close."

Marcus opened his mouth, then shut it. He tried not to look at the smashed trees or think of what it would do to the fragile human bodies of his compatriots. It seemed almost unfair, though it was true (if Wang could be trusted) that the Meronites were the ones who came out of nowhere in order to wreak pointless havoc. But regardless of method, they were here to righteously conquer Qin, strike down their heathen rival once and for all, and demonstrate the glory of the Divine Family and Divine Emperor, the supremacy and rightness of Merone. Weren't they? *Weren't* they? And if they weren't, why the fuck *were* they?

Seeing the uncertainty on Marcus's face, Magistrate Wang shrewdly decided not to press his advantage. He beckoned them down off the wallwalk and back to his office. When they were seated again, he said, "Perhaps that impressed upon you the sheer uselessness of this venture? Our people are dying for nothing, but so are yours. If, in the exceedingly unlikely event that I *did* arrange for you to travel to the Jade City, would you argue firmly and without equivocation, with your general and your emperor's full authority behind you, for an immediate cessation of hostilities and proper reparations for the death and damage? If not, there is no reason for me to keep you here *or* permit you to return to Merone, and in that case…"

Marcus groped reflexively for a weapon, which he had had to surrender before entrance. If only he had the bone-blades of a full Immortal – but he didn't, and so had to rely on his wits. For one, it occurred to him that in this case, the general and the emperor's wishes might well not be the same. Had Ionius sent him to stop this because it was a frivolous waste of Meronite lives, regardless of what Coriolane thought? To be an effective military commander, you had to think differently from the political ruler, but that was never the way it had worked before. Coriolane's commands were carried out, the end. If Marcus agreed to Wang's proposal, he was making a choice to defy the Divine Emperor, deliberately sabotage the Qiné campaign, do the opposite of what a good soldier was supposed to do – a good Immortal even more so. But what else was he supposed to do? Go back? Give up? Let people die not for a worthy cause or a noble war, but *nothing*?

"Yes, Excellency," Marcus said. "I would."

That, therefore, turned the key. Wang provided them with an escort of six Qiné soldiers and an official note of permission to travel into the Inner Provinces and all the way to the Jade City itself. This ordinarily had to be notarized by any other yamen whose territory they crossed, but due to the need for haste, Wang signed another document waiving the need for outside attestation and promising to face the full wrath of the Censorate if this privilege was abused. Considering how little he liked them or welcomed their arrival, it caused Marcus to realize that despite the magistrate's dismissive attitude, the Meronite attacks – unfocused and scattershot as they might be – were nonetheless hurting Qin quite badly, if Wang was willing to risk entrusting a single Immortal cadet to stop them. *Can I do it?* That was one thing. *Should I do it?* That was another.

Sila resumed her equine form for the journey, causing the Qiné soldiers to throw envious looks and mutters as to where a barbarian had come by such a handsome piece of horseflesh (at least they did not know that she was also a jinnyeh and a *woman*). They too had fine mounts and strange eastern sorcery to speed them, and they winged away the leagues with swift untiring strides. Thus, despite the great and rugged distance that separated Zin'qiang in the cold western mountains from Hang'i on the temperate northeastern coast, it was proved to be true that a Qiné messenger could reach the capital in a week, from any far corner of the Thearchate. As they sloped down to gently terraced rice paddies and misty green fields shrouded in summer rains, the endless tributaries of the mighty Yelin and Yangtsu Rivers coiling quicksilver through the lowlands, Marcus almost wished they had time to take in the view. Not that he had come to sightsee, but he was curious.

At last, at the end of eight days of nonstop riding in increasingly sodden humidity, when Marcus's arse and thighs were so sore that he grimaced whenever they hit a rut and desperately tried to avoid letting Sila see his discomfort, they passed through the Ancestors Gate and at long last, into the cosmopolitan environs of Hang'i. It battled with Merone for the title of the greatest city in the world, it had been the largest for many centuries, and while Marcus's vote was obviously biased in favor of the Eternal City, he had to admit that the *Jade* City held its own attractions. The port was crowded with ships, from massive black-lacquered junks with tall towers of pleated sails to humble fishing scows hung with tangled nets. The streets were likewise full of every sort of Qiné person, more than Marcus had ever pictured; in his head, they occupied an entirely undifferentiated position as Merone's devious yellow enemy. Children ran and played, merchants hawked their wares, and tiny old men glowered at each other from across game-boards strewn with ivory pieces. Women wore embroidered silk robes, paled their faces with rice-powder, and dressed their hair with combs, and top-knotted academics from the School of Knowledge argued bogglingly obscure points of philosophy and theology. Students sat in open-air galleries and calligraphed hanqin onto paper scrolls, saffron-robed monks tended shadowed shrines, and gongs sounded at precise intervals. It was all laid out in geometric squares, streets, and straight lines that reflected the Qiné obsession with order and harmony, in *siheyuan* residences and *hutong* alleys hung with lanterns in the lucky colors of green and red. The closer they drew to the seat of the Thearchate – the city-within-a-city that rose in huge three-tiered golden pagodas, treed parks and tidy gardens, red-brick walls, intricate columns of teak and rosewood, incense-burning temples – the more Marcus felt less and less prepared for what was to come. He still hadn't made up his mind in what he was going to say.

With one final inspection of their papers, they entered the Forbidden City with much pomp and ceremony, where Marcus was sternly warned not to go wandering, then shown to the visitors' quarters. After an extended argument with a chamberlain, who insisted on trying to take the letter for Hang Zhai as Marcus equally spiritedly refused to relinquish it, he went to investigate the baths, relieved to scrub off the filth and grime. He had not washed since he was in Merone, and the reek had begun to offend even his nose, let alone the Qiné. They already thought he was the most vulgar ruffian ever to befoul their perfect paradise; no need to give them further ammunition.

Supper was a fried rice and meat dish he was expected to eat with long sticks (difficult, but an Immortal never backed down from a challenge) and his bed was a thick cushion called a futon, stowed behind translucent paper screens that he lived in fear of accidentally tearing. How did the Qiné put up with this? Presumably it was not as strange when you were born in it and never knew anything different, but to him, it felt like a tiny dollhouse or some other unreal diorama, and as it was the first time he had been separated from Sila since the odyssey began, he felt oddly lonely. Not that the jinnyess was ever comforting, but she was still a companion, of a sort. *Only because she has no choice. Because the magician made her do it, and gave the ring to you.*

That was another startling thought, and Marcus frowned. He looked down at it on his finger, the only thing that bound her to him, and wondered if she would indeed devour him if he took it off, just as the wizard warned. Did her other masters delude themselves that surely they must be friends now, and so meet their fate? Did it matter that she wasn't human, or that they were both slaves? What, if anything, did he owe to her, and how was he supposed to give it without harming himself? Even if it was unfair to her, did it weigh against all the other lives in his hands?

Unable to answer, Marcus pulled out the futon, lay down atop it, and fell asleep at once. He was roused in the grey predawn by the chamberlain urgently shaking him. "Honored Marcus Servus. Honored Marcus Servus, please awake. You are summoned to the Hall of Heavenly Wisdom and the presence of Their Celestial Majesty at once. At once, please."

"What?" Marcus scrambled upright, groggy and confused and convinced that this was some sort of trick. After all, General Ionius had warned him to expect any number of dilatory tactics, a battle to even be considered for a royal interview, and to insist on it no matter what – and combined with Wang's obvious reluctance to let this scabrous foreign invader within a hundred miles of the sovereign's sacred person, Marcus had thought he was doomed to molder for days or weeks. Not that he objected, but he presumed that he would have more time to prepare.

This concern had also occurred to the chamberlain, who shooed him out of bed, hissing like an angry goose, and launched into an extended disquisition on how it was proper to behave in the presence of Hang Zhai, Holder of the Mandate of Heaven, a supreme honor that most folk would go a lifetime without receiving. Marcus duly tried to listen to the details on when to bow, when to speak, and how to avoid casting bad luck or poor feng shui (whatever that was) on the Thearch, who was held to be a god incarnate and the spiritual and physical manifestation of all Qin. Of course, that was only foolish eastern superstition; they were still just a human being. Not like Merone, where Coriolane Aureus IX really *was* the Divine Emperor. Not like that at all.

Marcus dressed quickly, was issued with his own protocol attendant and court interpreter (he protested, again, that he did speak Qiné, but the honor of addressing the Thearch directly was far beyond him), and hurried out into the ghostly warrens of the Forbidden City, which were just beginning to gleam with the cresting dawn. The Hall of Heavenly Wisdom stood at the very center, part of the vast complex that housed the Thearch, their family and household, favorite officials and trusted advisors, the highest-ranking representatives of the Three Departments and Six Ministries, and the rest of the sprawling bureaucracy. As the guards opened the doors with expressions as implacable as their terracotta counterparts in the tomb of ancient Emperor Qing, Marcus kept his back straight and face solemn. He was an official emissary of Merone, and what he did might determine the fate of many thousands of people. It was utterly unthinkable that he should fail.

The Hall of Heavenly Wisdom was illuminated with clear pale light, hung with beautiful hand-inked scrolls depicting stirring scenes from

Qiné history, and empty save for the dais shielded under a canopy of golden dragons and green silk, heavily armed guards blending into the shadows. A lone figure sat beneath, and Marcus didn't get a good look before the attendant and interpreter sank into wildly elaborate bows and he did his best to emulate them. "Your Celestial Majesty," the interpreter said, in the most formal register of Qiné. "Allow your humble servants to introduce the Honored Marcus Servus, emissary and Immortal of Merone. Honored Marcus Servus, you stand in the presence of Hang Zhai, Holder of the Mandate of Heaven, Thearch of Qin. Do you offer your solemnest respect and honor upon them and all their ancestors?"

"I do." Marcus kept his eyes on the floor, breathing in the scent of bamboo and mint, until a minute gesture cued him to look up. "I also offer my personal greetings, those of the Empire of Great Merone and Coriolane Aureus IX, Divine Emperor, and General Ionius Servus Eternus, master of the Immortals. It is on their errand – " he paused, considered, revised – "General Ionius's errand that I have come. I bring a letter that I was instructed to place only and solely into Your Celestial Majesty's possession. With your gracious permission, may I do so?"

The Thearch studied Marcus without immediately responding. They were tall, elegant, and androgynously beautiful, with waist-length black hair and high cheekbones, and wore a draped and belted robe of silver and green, their complexion as pale and perfect as the moon and their almond eyes dark and liquid. By reflex, Marcus tried to guess if they had been born male or female, but could not. The secret was known only to the most intimate body-servants, who had their tongues torn out to prevent ever speaking of it, and he had to admit that it did not seem to matter. He kept his head deferentially inclined, until the Thearch made a small motion and the protocol attendant held out his hand. "I shall convey it to Their Celestial Majesty. Please give it to me."

"I beg your pardon," Marcus said, as politely as he could. "But it was *only* for the Thearch."

The attendant and interpreter exchanged unhappy looks, deploring this shocking breach of decorum, but after a tense moment, they stepped back and allowed him to proceed to the throne, proffering the letter – torn, stained, and otherwise bearing witness to the rigors of the road, but still sealed. The Thearch studied him with those inscrutably ageless eyes – they were, Marcus recalled, at least two hundred years old, which if not so much as Coriolane was still a vastly respectable number – then took it, breaking the wax with a snap that echoed in the stillness and made everyone jump. They unfolded the letter, and something small and sparkling fell out, making the guards start forward until the Thearch raised a hand to stop them. Marcus was lucky not to have his head parted from his body without ever seeing it coming, and waited as the Thearch picked up the object. At last, speaking aloud for the first time, they said, "What is this, Honored Marcus Servus?"

"I…" Marcus, of course, had no idea. "With, er, with your permission, Majesty…?"

The Thearch considered, then shrugged and held it out. Marcus took it, careful not to touch even in passing (he had been instructed that making unsanctioned physical contact was punishable by death, and had no wish to test the truth of that), then squinted in confusion. It looked like a thin slice of some kind of bone, studded with steel barbs so small they could hardly be seen, shining like flecks of mica or gypsum. While the Thearch perused the letter, Marcus kept staring in bafflement – until with a nasty shock, he realized what it was. It was a piece of an Immortal's bone, embedded with enspelled Corporalist metal, and he had no idea where or who it had come from. Was this a warning not to test an empire that could do this to its own soldiers, or – ?

Just then, he recalled General Ionius's inexplicably injured arm, the bandage he had worn ever since the unfortunate incident in Sardarkhand, and was struck by the ludicrous but inescapable conviction that it had been taken from the general's own body, possibly by the general himself. Yet why Ionius would send it in an urgent letter to the Thearch of Qin was utterly beyond Marcus's understanding. "Ah," he said stupidly, feeling their eyes boring into him. "It is… bone, Majesty."

"So we see." Hang Zhai glanced back at the letter. "More than that, it is a key. Your general explains that it can be used to open or close the magical doors of the Thaumaturge, Grand Magister Kronus, and those doors are the method by which the Meronite soldiers are appearing, seemingly out of thin air, to conduct their murders. He informs us that if we give it to our own court magicians, they could find a way to close all the doors at once, and vouchsafe Qin from any further invasions by this route. Do you know, Honored Marcus Servus, of any reason we should believe this, and not conclude that it is a sinister attempt to trick us into using unholy Meronite magic, to the ancestors only know what result? And if it is, why we should ever spare your life?"

Marcus started to speak, then stopped. He was aware that said life hung entirely on his next words, and wished that he had paid closer attention in his logic and rhetoric classes. So the Meronites were in fact using the Thaumaturges' doors, having coaxed or coerced Kronus into providing access for entire armies, and that was how they could appear across the Thearchate at random and without warning. All that, so far as it went, made sense. But why would General Ionius stake his existence, his own quite-literal flesh and bone, on *stopping* it? Not only that, but passing a piece of proprietary magical technology to the Thearchate, who had been keen to create their own Immortals for centuries, but never quite mastered the process? With this single piece of bone, they might be able to reverse-engineer not just the doors, but the inmost secrets of the Corporalists' transmogrification of Immortals, the means by which men were turned into gods. No ordinary peon in Qin would be allowed to impinge upon the supreme position of the Thearch, but the name itself meant the divine ruler of an entire kingdom of gods. If all that was possible, and Ionius had just *given it up* –

"I don't know, Majesty," Marcus said, as he was too stunned to even consider lying. "I do not understand why General Ionius would do this. But he... he is someone I trust, and is consistent in his morals and his actions. If he said what he intended by it, it is what he meant."

Hang Zhai considered, still unreadable. Then they glanced at the attendant, the interpreter, and the guards. "Please depart from us. We must speak to Honored Marcus Servus alone."

This shocked everyone as much as it displeased them, and they exchanged gobsmacked looks, then stared darkly at Marcus, convinced that this was yet another brazen Meronite trick. Yet they did not dare to disobey a direct order from the sovereign, and receded down the length of the hall until Marcus was alone with the Thearch of Qin. He could choose this moment to strike and fulfill all their worst expectations, but it did seem dishonorable, he would never get out alive, and he still needed to know what was going on. At last he ventured, "Majesty...?"

"Honored Marcus Servus." For a moment, he discerned something old and tired and human beneath the poised and perfectly ageless exterior. "If nothing else, you are a loyal servant, and we commend that. You have succeeded in a difficult errand, and it is unfair what we must ask of you, but perhaps that is why you have been sent to us. You trust your general? Even now?"

"I... yes, Majesty. I do not understand. I cannot pretend to do so. But... yes."

"Good." Hang Zhai smiled faintly. "So you believe it, then? When he says that by the time we read this, after four hundred and fifty years, Coriolane Aureus IX will finally be dead?"

"*What?*" It was both an intolerable shock and something Marcus had known deep down was coming, the final proof that General Ionius had turned traitor, Spartekaius reborn, and was on the verge of committing – or perhaps already had – the one great sin in which even his legendarily infamous predecessor had not succeeded. "In the – in the letter, does – does General Ionius say that he intends to – intends to *kill* Coriolane? That's not – that can't be – "

"He does not say how it will be accomplished. Only that it will." Hang Zhai continued to regard Marcus thoughtfully. "And if Coriolane is dead, and the key is in our hand to close your terrible doors, this entire dreadful matter is almost at an end. Except for one thing, one final favor to place Merone and Qin on equal footing for whatever should come next. Will you do it?"

"Your Celestial Majesty, will I do – do *what?*"

Hang Zhai raised their eyes. "Kill us."

"I – what?" The words were gluey, futile and fruitless. "You want – if the Divine Emperor is dead, and you – what? *What? How can that possibly – why *me?*"

"You are an Immortal of Merone," the Thearch pointed out, brutally pragmatic. "It is your duty to kill the empire's enemies, especially those of Qin. Do you know how tired I am, Honored Marcus Servus?

Do you know how long I have lived, how greatly I yearn to sleep? I have refused the rightful ending of my life for as long as Coriolane did the same, but if that mercy has at last been granted... unlike him, I have heirs. The Thearchate will go on, and grow, and change. It is past time that it was allowed to do so. And for that, you are our only hope."

Dizzily and dully, Marcus registered that Hang Zhai had fallen out of the royal plural, had used only the stark and singular *I*, the person and not the throne. He groped for a denial. "You have many loyal subjects, Majesty. Any of them would be glad to serve you, even in this. Surely."

"No Qiné citizen could raise their hand to me, even if I commanded it, without damning themselves for all eternity." Hang Zhai shrugged. "They would be scorned by their living fellows and dead ancestors alike, doomed to exile and misery. Besides, it is better for the next ruler not to be overshadowed by the question of whether they connived to have me killed. If it is done by a Meronite, the country will be united in grief against outsiders, and not turned on each other in a fratricidal war, as has happened too often before. We are locked in a death spiral of our own, where our scholars argue endlessly over the meaning of three lines in the Analects, about old and abstract philosophy that has ever less relevance to the living world. Aside from that, we are all cumbered with too many rules to act or change in any meaningful way. I am Thearch, and yet I am trapped the same as my predecessors have been. We must remake the whole system, and do it without me. It is best."

"Will that not extend the war, Majesty? Make you swear vengeance on us at all costs?"

"It can be arranged otherwise." The Thearch's eyes held his. "A body-servant will come to you this evening, and bring you to me. They cannot speak, nor would they. They have always held my secrets, even to the end. When the deed is done, they will show you a way to escape, if that is something you desire. If you prefer to die heroically, it can likewise be seen to."

Marcus was still comprehensively pole-axed. But he wanted to say something, wanted to object — which was the most confounding of all. If Coriolane truly *was* dead, General Ionius was a traitor, and the Thearch of Qin was offering themself to be sacrificed on a silver platter, he would be remiss not to take the chance, the sort of renown that an Immortal could only hope to win once every thousand years. But it didn't feel like it, not like this. *Did Ionius know the Thearch would ask this of me? Is this a clever plan for a murder where the target kneels before me and begs me to strike? To make it feel as if it is their choice, and mine the glory of Merone?*

He did not know, he could not possibly, and yet there was no one to ask, no master, nobody to make the choice for him. He had been a slave his whole life, and now he was being bidden to exert his free will in a moment of world-changing importance, where he could not begin to predict the consequences. It felt as if he did this, even against Merone's greatest enemy, he had no right to live afterward, no ability to simply walk away. *Ionius told me to do so, and I comforted myself in thinking it was merely a trick, a test of loyalty. But he must have known it would come to this. To exile forever from both Merone and Qin, damned as a traitor in both — for what?* What?

Marcus Servus looked up at Hang Zhai — still and watchful, waiting for him. If he said no, he could go back to the Eternal City as if nothing had changed — and yet it would mean failing both Coriolane, for refusing to kill the Thearch, and Ionius, for failing to heed his command to stay away forever. *What do you want? Who are you? Where would you go?*

He did not know. He could not. It terrified him beyond all might or measure. And yet.

"Very well, Your Celestial Majesty," Marcus said in a whisper. "I will do as you command."

★★★★

EVERYTHING AFTER THAT WAS A BLUR.

He left the sovereign's presence, returned to his room as if he had not just agreed to commit world-changing treason (*was* it treason? He was not Qiné, it was his duty, it was the highest and holiest task that an Immortal could do) and sat down. Time felt meaningless, reality formless. He did not know if he wanted to live or die, could not riddle it out in the few short hours that remained before the end of all things, or at least certainly of him. He was young enough that it felt nearly the same. He thought that he wanted to live, but if he did it like this —

Eventually, Marcus got up and walked out onto the porch, staring at nothing, until someone tugged his sleeve. "Hey," a familiar voice said. "Kid. Why do you look even more like a concussed ox than usual? Everything all right?"

Marcus looked up with a jerk and beheld Sila, who was regarding him with her usual bright-eyed impudence, but also perhaps a crumb of true concern. All at once, a way to escape his dilemma occurred to him, to die and be spared the trouble of struggling any further, and it seemed simply and mercilessly just. He looked at her, tried to speak, and could not. Then he reached down and wrenched the ring off his finger, holding it out to her. "Take it."

Sila stared at him as if he had lost his mind. "Put that back on. If you don't – "

"I know." Marcus forced himself to keep her gaze. "Your master told me, you can devour me. So go ahead. Devour me. Then you'll be free and don't have to return to him if you have the ring for yourself – right? You said you were a slave, we both were. Well. Now you're not."

"Marcus. Look. You don't – "

"Do it. I'm an Immortal. I'm not afraid."

"Oh, kid." Her mouth curved in half a smile, sad as the ages. "Yes, you are."

As ever, there wasn't much to say to that, though he wished she had not pointed it out so bluntly. They kept staring at each other. Then Sila reached out, took the ring, and transformed into a sparrow, small and sprightly, taking to the air in a rush of wings. With that, she was gone.

Marcus stood there until he was sure she was not planning to come back and devour him – which, all things considered, was a bit of a letdown. It meant the evening would still come and he would have to carry out his promise or break it, to live or die, to be a hero or a traitor. If he did not go back to Merone, did not take the trials and undergo the transformations, he would never become an Immortal, not for real. He would live and die as an ordinary man – Marcus, but not Marcus Servus, or Marcus Servus Eternus. He would not be bound. He would be free.

Free.

The word meant nothing to him, not yet. He had never had it, so he could not mourn or desire what he had never known. But nonetheless, Marcus could sense the nascence somewhere within him, a small stubborn ember that waxed bright against the darkness of terror and uncertainty. That did not know, but wanted to. That could see itself in that new land and imagine stepping onto that path. It was still highly likely that the Qiné had no intention of leaving him alive even if the Thearch did hunger for a peaceful sleep and not cruel eternity. Marcus could be seized and tortured, subject to the terrible death by a thousand cuts, paraded to every market square in the Thearchate and pelted with dung and eggs and stones. He could be used to justify a new war against Merone, a real one this time, and destroy everything that General Ionius had risked by sending him here. And that – Merciful Mother, he hadn't even truly reckoned with the fact that his idol, his all-worshiped hero, was in fact a traitor, deep-grained and irreversible. If he did return to the Eternal City, he might be asked to partake in Ionius's death instead, and despite everything, Marcus did not want to do that. It was still the central tenet of his life, he had been left with nothing and no one else – not his parents, not his family, not whoever that nameless boy had been – and while it was still a shameful weakness, he could not forswear it, not now, not here. He had chosen to obey General Ionius to the end, and that, therefore, was what he was going to do. Whatever it cost, and whether it led him to death or – even more frighteningly – life.

Marcus took a deep and ragged breath, knuckling the tears out of his eyes. He stood there for what felt like forever, the only immortality he was liable to have, and told himself to remember. Then he watched the sun go down over the Forbidden City, the sky red and gold and the most beautiful thing he had ever seen or would again, turned around, and went to meet his destiny.

CHAPTER 30

ZADIA

ZADIA SWAM BACK TO CONSCIOUSNESS SLOWLY, IN PARTS and pieces, in one moment and then the next as if she was jumping from stone to stone over a river, a childish game of hopscotch to reach the far bank of wakefulness and whatever might await. She was not entirely sure what it was, or if her gambit had worked at all; it was, as it could not be otherwise, absurdly dangerous. At least it was, in execution, fairly simple. All she and Elemai needed to do was sneak into the streets of Qart-Hadesht before sunrise, once more via the sewers, and daub various walls with crude graffiti that colorfully disparaged Cincitus's talent, wits, loyalty, military prowess, ancestors, mother, manhood, and ability to sexually satisfy whores, small boys, and sheep. Then they waited for the day to begin, the citizens to take note, and matters to proceed naturally from there. The vulgar chants started ringing across the marketplace, Meronite legions were drafted in to prevent the disturbance from spreading, and of course, failed. Rocks and dung and rotten eggs were thrown, several local toughs took up fisticuffs, and the riot was ripely underway before mardiq. It briefly twinged Zadia's conscience to do it, since purposefully striking such a spark could not end without even more injuries, destruction, and death, but there was no choice. After a few hours of everyone beating holy hell out of each other, Zadia and Elemai turned themselves into the governor-general's office, admitted to producing the incendiary messages, and were promptly arrested and thrown into a Meronite quadrireme for transport and trial in the Eternal City. The lump on Zadia's head was only one tender memento of that adventure. She did not yet know where her daughter-in-law was. She could only hope it was in one piece.

Zadia lay on her back, trying to clear the murky dregs of her mind and prepare herself for whatever came next. If the wind was with them, it would be a relatively swift journey to Merone, and what little further strategy there was to her plan rested on Coriolane learning that she had been apprehended and demanding an audience, whether to punish her himself or to once more intervene in the name of whatever twisted paternal feeling he might have for her. It seemed utterly impossible that it was anything at all. She still recoiled from the idea that any part of him could have made her, even in the simplest and most old-fashioned of ways. Even worse was the possibility that the things she had always liked about herself – her ferocity, her stubbornness, her unwillingness to take no for an answer, her disregard of minor moral qualms, the ability to keep pushing through any obstacle until victory, her patriotism and pride, her insistence in having the last word and that everything was done her way or else – did not come from her mother, as she always thought. Instead, that they were a dark-mirror reflection of her imperial sire, and therefore if she grew up in Merone, paternity acknowledged and possibly even groomed to inherit the throne if Coriolane continued to have no other living children, she would be just like him.

Of course, Zadia reflected, any world in which Coriolane was willing to openly consider a female Qartic bastard as an acceptable heir would be so topsy-turvy that she might not recognize anything else about it, but that was beside the point. She could all-too-easily see how it *could* have happened, the person she would have been and might still be somewhere in the dark depths of her, all the more pervasive and powerful for never being consciously known. It made her want to flay off her flesh and scoop out the marrow of her bones, to find any contamination and burn it out until there was nothing left. *Amma, why didn't you tell me?*

Some interstitial flickers of time passed, minutes or more. Zadia was blurrily aware of the ship rocking beneath her, the fractured stripes of sunlight through the slats of deck above. At last, even though her head continued to pound like a dull hammer, she groaned, pushed herself up, and scrubbed her itching eyes, nose wrinkling as she breathed in fetid straw and it made her sneeze. She was immured in some dingy little oubliette, chained like a common criminal, which was the most insulting part of the whole thing. Normally a senior matriarch of the High House, regardless of any secret connection with the emperor, would be accorded far more deference, even if she had been arrested for inciting public disorder and was being shipped off to Merone for a slap on the wrist. The fact that they felt confident in treating Zadia bet Amarasha ur-Namasqa like a dirty cur impressed with stinging clarity just how different things were going to be from now on, all thanks to her own stupidity. What must Khaldun and Aljafar think – that she too was dead, or worse? It was too dangerous to tip them off or warn them in advance what Zadia and Elemai intended to do, so she hadn't. *Does that come from Coriolane too? The lying, the deceit, the ability to manipulate my own loved ones and cause them great grief without turning a hair, so long as it is useful?*

The success of that sacrifice, however, remained open to serious question. Zadia scrunched up her eyes and peered around the gloomy hold, but didn't see Elemai. Surely they would not have dared to just kill her out of hand, even in punishment for starting a riot and inferring that Cincitus' cock was the size of a mouse? It was also likely that they were being transported separately to avoid any chance of a repeat incident, though Zadia failed to see what disorder they could cause in their present situation. She still felt numb and fragmented, replaying the moment of Noora's death in her head over and over, but also embarrassed that it had taken Elemai risking her life in such spectacular fashion to snap her out of her grief-stricken haze. It was very possible that Aliyah had been dead for weeks and this was all for nothing, but they had to know for sure.

Finally broken down by thirst, Zadia gingerly sipped some none-too-clean water from the bucket, grimaced at the rasp of grime on her tongue, and devoutly hoped that she would be spared the indignity of having to urinate in the corner like a farm animal. She slumped against the bars of her cage, staring blearily at nothing and wondering if it was too late to lapse back into abject unconsciousness; at least it would make time pass faster, and free her from keeping company with the dreary percussion of her thoughts. Overhead she could hear distant shouts, clatters, and bumps, the usual racket of a sailing ship, and tried to recall the last time she had actually left Qart-Hadesht. In the early years of her marriage to Khaldun, they made a fairly frequent pilgrimage to Ngoto-sethe, the stately capital of Numeria, but after she also married Noora and the children were born, such long and difficult trips were far less practical. Her sister Hanifah was disinherited after wedding the Kushite, and Zadia was not brave enough to defy her mother's edicts, so she had not visited there either. Then after Amarasha died, Zadia's duties in the Adirim and as head of the household kept her close, and there was no time to lark off on frivolous ventures. When she learned that the Holy City was finally being reopened, she had experienced a sudden and useless wish that she would be allowed to go, because she was nearly fifty and had not seen the outside world in decades. But she was needed at home with Safiya, to plan their ultimately disastrous intrigues against Merone, and she was not. Aliyah was sent instead, and so to her destiny.

Considering that everyone who went to Yerussala this year is now dead of the red plague, you escaped that terrible fate, only to land in the middle of this one. Zadia rubbed her eyes again and tried not to think. Time continued to pass. Eventually she lost the battle not to have to relieve herself in the corner, and seethed at the indignity. *Even unwanted and unacknowledged and of illicit heathen birth, I am still a princess of Merone. Is this truly how they dare to treat me?*

At that, Zadia caught herself. It was troubling that she would vociferously reject everything Coriolane's bloodline might confer upon her, insist it made no difference, and then invoke its imagined privileges the moment she was in discomfort. Determined to atone, she closed her eyes and began mentally reciting passages from the Kitab on the subject of faith, piety, forbearance, and purity. She was not a full hafiza like Elemai or Safiya, but she could recall most of them, and it filled her with a sudden pride and anger alike. *What did you think you would do, "princess of Merone?" Meekly convert to polytheistic Tridevarianism and kneel before that odious Mellius Sanctus Sixtus, abase yourself in hope of his bloodstained blessing? Remember who you are, Zadia ur-Namasqa. Trust in the strength of your motherland and the wisdom of the Hierophant, blessings on his memory. It is only with them, after failing her for so long, that you can save your daughter now.*

Zadia slept, woke, slept, drank, pissed, drank, felt more an animal than ever, but at least one that knew from whence it came and what it meant to do. She was absolutely starved, and had found a moldy heel of bread which hunger finally impelled her to gnaw upon, when she heard the heavy tread of hobnailed boots descending the ladder. She threw it aside and waited as three legionnaires appeared, strode forward, and unlocked her cage. "We're here, traitor," one of them informed her, pulling her along by the chained wrists. "In the Eternal City. So if you haven't thought hard about begging for mercy, this would be the time."

Zadia did not dignify that with an answer, as she was hauled topside and the brunt of the city stink hit her in the face. It was a clear and cauldron-hot late-summer day, Merone shimmering blue and bronze and blinding white on its seven legendary hills. Zadia was braced for the expected anger at the sight, but less so for the sudden ache of something else, half nostalgia and half grief. She remembered traveling here with her mother as a young girl, that visit where she had seen Coriolane and been so taken with him. *If I had known that I was beholding my own father, would it have been different? Would I have wanted to please him more or less? Blamed my mother for the lie, or been so excited that this too was my inheritance that I would not have cared at all?*

She was marched ashore through a bristling phalanx of legionnaires, pikes at the ready to descend on her neck at any sign of trickery. From there, she was shut in the barred back of a cart and driven slowly up the crowded streets, people swarming on every side without any awareness of who she was or that she was even there. Doubtless this was a deeply familiar sight, prisoners brought in from the provinces and bundled to the Castel, where their fate was neither in sight nor in mind. At least, Zadia assumed that was where they were bound; for prisoners of their status and notoriety, it was not likely to be any other. She might be granted a private cell for the appearance of decency, but given her rough treatment thus far, she doubted it. *Where* was Elemai?

At last a portcullis rattled up, they bumped into a smaller courtyard somewhere between the Eternal Palace and the Castel, and Zadia was pulled from the cart. There seemed, however, to be some disagreement or confusion about where she was expected to go next and who was supposed to take charge of the valuable prisoner. Someone was supposed to come and collect her who was taking their sweet time about doing so, and the delay was making her guards confused and irritable. When they had waited nearly an hour without being received, they huffed in exasperation, took Zadia inside to a small windowless room, and locked her in. Their voices echoed away down the corridor, half-angry and half-anxious. *What* was taking the fucking necromancers so long?

They want to give me to the Corporalists, Zadia realized, matter-of-fact despite the horror of the thought. The situation was far beyond whether she would receive a private cell or be lumped in with the riffraff; she had misjudged her danger to a shocking degree, simply because it was so unprecedented. Instead, she was to be handed over for extracting information, plain brute torture, or even to be Remade and sent back to Qart-Hadesht as a compliant ghoul pumped full of Meronite chemicals and Meronite brainwashing, sworn never to raise a hand against the good and generous Divine Emperor ever again. The idea was so horrifying that her gorge rose, even though all she had eaten in the last few days was dirty water and moldy bread. *You came to save Aliyah, and instead you doomed yourself and everyone else, all over again.*

And yet, even as she sat in petrified, paralyzed anticipation, the Corporalists did not come, and did not come. Instead, after another hour or so, the door rattled again, and the guards pushed in another filthy and bedraggled Qartic woman in chains. At the sight, relief spilled into Zadia too strongly to be ignored, and she stumbled forward. "Elemai? Habibta, are – are you all right?"

Her daughter-in-law looked blearily through two black eyes, bruised and swelling; either she had tried to fight back and come out on the losing end, or her guards had been more brutal simply for the thrill. "Fine," she managed, clutching Zadia's hands. "Are you?"

"Enough." Zadia expelled a shaky breath, only now recognizing just how worried she had been, but the danger was far from over. "Elemai, listen. The guards – when they put me here, I heard them talking about the necromancers. They're going to give us to the Corporalists. If there's any chance that we will survive, let alone find Aliyah, we have to – "

"Yes." Elemai frowned. "Mine said something about that too, but just now, they seemed – I don't know. Worried, almost. Like something had gone wrong."

"Wrong?" Zadia echoed blankly. "For them, you mean? But how can that be possible?"

"I don't know." Elemai sank onto a bench, looking drained. "But when they brought me in, I saw that something had happened to the Castel, at least part of it. It was collapsed, or crumbled, or broken. I don't know what could do such a thing in the heart of Merone, but – "

Zadia stared at her even more uncomprehendingly. She was tempted to think that Elemai was seeing things, or confusing one place with another; perhaps the younger woman had simply never been to Merone before, though as Safiya's heiress that seemed unlikely, and did not know what the infamous Castel Sanctangel truly was. It was plain, however, that something was not right, their arrival had not proceeded as scheduled, and the guards were distracted and alarmed. Something too raw and rough to be hope rasped in Zadia's chest, until she said, "You don't think…? That Aliyah found the real Ring of Tselmun and was able to use it to – to destroy them? I don't know where or how, but there hardly seems anything else that could wreak this sort of damage."

Elemai looked up with a jolt, clearly also wondering if their rescue mission had just become obsolete and they were now the ones in need of it, when they heard footsteps coming down the corridor at a slow, deliberate pace. Other doors opened and closed, as if the person was looking for something, or hunting it down. Zadia thought in fear that it must be their guards, who had finally located a Corporalist and returned to bring the prisoners to them at last, but something was off, too leisurely and methodical and utterly chilling in its casual menace. The footsteps came up to their door, tried the latch, and finding it locked, paused just long enough to make Zadia think – pray – that they had given up and gone away. Then with a crunch and a crash, it splintered open, and Ionius Servus Eternus, bloodstained and blank-eyed, stepped inside.

At the sight of the man who had killed her mother, Elemai let out a strangled cry and threw herself at him, beating on his chest as best she could with her chained wrists. Ionius barely reacted, though he did twist aside when she attempted to knee him viciously in the balls. He did not hit her back aside from defensively, blocking her frenzied blows so easily that it looked as if he was reading her mind. He tolerated a few moments of this, then gave Elemai a short sharp shove – which sent her reeling backward, tripping over Zadia, and both of them stumbling to their knees. "Go on, you bastard," Elemai hissed. "If you're here to kill us, just do it. Like my mother, I will not beg."

Ionius hardly seemed to hear. He stared at them with eyes the color of winter ice and just as cold. At last, his voice came as if from very far down a well. "You are not Corporalists."

"No," Zadia managed. "But if you take us to them, we must – "

"The Corporalists are dead." Ionius spoke with no affect or intonation, flat as stone. "All of them. They will not be a concern to anyone any longer, including you."

"What are you talking about?" Zadia stared at him. "How can – "

Ionius stopped, blinked, stared back. Some blinding caul seemed to slowly lift from his face. "Saeda Zadia? What are you doing here? You were supposed to remain behind in Qart-Hadesht."

"We were – arrested." It was unwise to say anything else, especially when he looked like such a madman. Why was he covered in blood – what did he mean the Corporalists were dead – surely he did not mean that *he* had killed them? Malikallulah, the entire world was upside down. "We caused a disturbance, and were taken to be punished. Matters became... confused from there."

Strangely, Ionius did not appear to be perturbed by this. His gaze flicked to Elemai, who was eyeing him murderously, but he didn't move. Then he said, "You are here for your daughter, aren't you? You want to know where she is, free her from captivity and bring her home. The rest of it was a ruse to ensure that the Meronites had no choice but to seize you and take you here, as begging for help or mercy would have caused them to merely laugh and ignore you. It would be useless to appeal to their better nature, as they do not have one."

Zadia tensed, but his voice wasn't accusing or angry; it remained stripped of all inflection. He looked at her, and she looked at him, mind whirling but continuing to draw a blank. What was wrong with him? Why was he speaking of the Meronites this way, as if their cruelty and duplicity had always been obvious to everyone? To Qart-Hadesht, of course, it was, but not General Ionius, master of the Immortals. She was not sure whether to flee or beg him for help. Which was the maddest thing of all, but still.

The silence hung, cold and poisoned as quicksilver. Then Elemai spoke, her voice harsh and raw. "So? *Have* you come to kill us?"

"No." Ionius regarded her without interest, animus, or heat. "I don't believe I have."

"Then? Why are you here?"

"I was looking for Corporalists." At last he smiled, though that seemed entirely the wrong word for the brief and feral flash of teeth. "As you are not, you are free to go, for all I care."

"You…" Elemai looked as if she could not believe the words she was now speaking, even as Zadia could not believe she was hearing them. "You killed them, didn't you? And did – whatever it was to the Castel, destroyed it or tore it down. How can that be *possible?* You, their loyal lapdog, their perfect weapon of war? Why would you ever turn on your masters? Unless…" She stared at him again, shocked realization dawning in her eyes. "Unless somehow you have really lost it. You? *You?* Then again, I suppose no one ever thought before he did it that Sparte – "

"I am *not* Spartekaius." Ionius's voice cracked like a whip. "For one thing, for all the fear he inspired, the *damnatio memoriae* he was given, he never achieved this. What did he do – muster a few slaves, terrify a few patricians, proclaim himself the sovereign leader of a liberated Merone, and then get arrested and terribly executed for treason, while Coriolane III nibbled grapes and listened to him scream for days? Spartekaius would *beg* for a fraction of what I have done. Did *Spartekaius* ever slaughter the entire Order of Necromancers with his *bare hands?* No. But I have."

Elemai and Zadia exchanged a stunned look. They would almost think he was raving, gone utterly mad in his bloodlust, except for the ring of stark authenticity in his words that could not be downplayed or denied. At last, Elemai thrust out her chained hands. "Fine, then. If you have actually turned against Merone, prove it. Unfetter me."

"You did try to kill *me*," Ionius pointed out. "I hardly think it wise."

As Elemai opened her mouth to fire back, Zadia cut in. "Very well," she said, holding out her own hands. "I have not tried it. Free me."

Ionius considered, still unhurried, as if he had all the time in the world and was unconcerned about throngs of apoplectic legionnaires piling in to arrest him. Perhaps he was not. Perhaps he had killed them too. Perhaps the entire palace was lying in mangled heaps, and Zadia was offering their murderer a chance to do exactly the same to them. But it did not matter if their hands were chained; if Ionius wanted to kill them, he would. He studied her face a moment longer. Then he shrugged, strode forward, and made a motion with his hand, directed at her cuffs. It seemed to take a long time, longer than usual, as if his Immortal powers were burned to the wick and had only a few embers remaining, but the metal grew soft, deformed, and dropped off, spreading in an oozing ferrous pool. Zadia rubbed her suddenly bare wrists. Unwillingly, she said, "Thank you."

Ionius inclined his head a cold and cursory fraction. He looked at Elemai, decided not to test his luck, and rooted in his belt, pulling out a key, which he tossed to Zadia. "Use that."

Zadia caught it, hurried to Elemai, and fitted the key into the cuffs, twisting them open and pulling them off. When her hands were freed, Elemai threw them around Zadia's neck in a brief embrace, then stepped back, once more afire with determination. "Where is Aliyah?"

"I don't know. I had other matters to concern me. I did, however, hear a rumor that she had escaped her prison and snuck back into the Eternal Palace. If so, I imagine she has gone to confront Coriolane. As it happens, I am in need of doing such a thing myself. You may come, if you wish, though I am useless. If it comes to any further fight or struggle, you are on your own."

"I doubt it," Elemai said loathingly, eyeing him as if she would still plunge a knife into his back the instant she got the chance. "You're still one of the best soldiers in the world, even without your special powers. You could easily dismember us or anyone else, if the necessity arose."

Ionius ignored her, crossing the room and opening the door. "Well? Are you coming?"

Elemai and Zadia looked at each other again. Quite obviously, he could be leading them into a trap, though it was a peculiar amount of effort to do that. As well, obediently waiting for any Corporalists he had missed while razing a homicidal swath through the Castel was not ideal, and Zadia made a choice. "Fine," she said. "We're coming."

Ionius led them across the evening-shrouded courtyard, and into the cloisters on the far side. He began to climb the staircase beyond, moving with the assurance of someone who had paced these halls for decades and knew their every inch, had done his job so well that no assassin had ever made it this far, but he himself was now the hidden blade, the shadow in the night. He moved faster than before, not pausing for them to catch up; they had to hurry if they did not want to let him get out of sight and leave them lost in the Eternal Palace's maze of corridors. It seemed oddly quiet, as if the usual throng of people who circulated in the veins of this great heart had either gone or (as Zadia could not help but suspect) were all dead. She was glad not to be intercepted, but as they reached the upper floors of the palace and their footsteps echoed like tomb robbers, the foreboding grew deeper. At last she said, "Are they – "

"Yes," Ionius said. "I think so. But not at my hand, Saeda Zadia. Something worse."

Zadia did not want to imagine what *something worse* could possibly be, and apprehension coiled in her throat. She fell back, reaching for Elemai, and gripped hard. They clutched hold as they surmounted the final landing, hurried down the corridor in Ionius' wake, and caught up to him in the shadows of a private doorway. There was a strange acrid smell hanging in the air, like spoiled meat left out too long in the sun, that made Zadia gag and Elemai wrinkle her nose, but Ionius didn't seem to notice. He touched the lock, and the door swung open. Without looking back or waiting, he walked through.

Regardless of how courageous she had always considered herself, it took everything Zadia had to follow suit. The ceilings towered, lost in gloom, and the rank smell grew stronger, until Zadia looked down and saw a noxious dark fluid smeared on the stones – as if an unfortunate creature had been dragged through here half-alive, leaking and bleeding. Up ahead, Ionius had drawn to a halt, staring at something seated on a golden chair and looking almost relaxed. Then it — he — lifted its head and smiled. "Greetings," Coriolane Aureus IX — or at least whatever grotesquely youthful thing was sitting there and wearing his skin — said genially. "I had begun to fear you would never arrive. General Ionius, Lady Zadia, Lady Elemai, good evening. Shall we get on with it?"

Zadia made a faint strangled sound. All her clever quips and fierce rebuttals had withered like a rose in frost, leaving only horror. Every sinew in her body was screaming at her to run, that she was in the presence of an apex predator that could unhinge its jaw like a great jungle snake and gulp her down, but she did her best. "Where is my daughter?"

When Coriolane smiled, the muscles of his mouth didn't move right, and his flesh crimped like wax. "Aliyah? We both know the truth by now, don't we? She is not just your daughter, but my granddaughter. Because, of course, you are *my* daughter. Welcome home, my child."

Ionius, the only person who had not known this beforehand, looked briefly thunderstruck. His eyes shot between Coriolane and Zadia as if furiously attempting to discern any quiddity that might tell the tale of this secret relation, while Coriolane himself regarded the Immortal with a look of fatherly disappointment, as if Ionius too was his shamed prodigal son. "General," he said, clucking his tongue. "You *have* been very treasonous, haven't you? And for what? Your sister?"

Ionius's shoulders were wound so tight that Zadia could have plucked his strings and played him like a harmonium. His hands closed into fists. At last he said, "So you did know about Tatyana. All this time. Who she was, and what had been done to her? Or only that it had been?"

"I am not excusing or explaining myself to you, slave." Coriolane looked impatient. "I can't be expected to keep track of every single Remade abomination scuttling around the place, now can I? I knew your sister was one of them, but so it is for every other Immortal general. The very few who have discovered that fact have always taken the intended message from it, and never entertained so much as a single disloyal thought afterward. But not you. Why is that?"

"You know." If Ionius had swallowed a lump of coal, he would have shat out a diamond. "I once thought that you were the wisest and greatest and most impressive man who ever lived, that your centuries of experience had given you a transcendence that none of us could match. But it's not just untrue, it is the utter opposite. You have taken all that time, all those gifts, everything you could have been and done and become, and made yourself the worst of men instead."

"I need no rebukes from you, traitor," Coriolane snapped. "Have you come to prate moral lectures at me – though it suits you very poorly, Scourge of Sciatello – or get on with it?"

"Very well. Where is the ur-Namasqa girl? We know she's here."

"Oh, she is." Coriolane tapped his fingers on his blood-spotted robe. "I made her a very generous offer, but she proved unexpectedly resistant. So I put her to use in other ways." He pointed toward something lying in the shadows, facedown and motionless. "As ever, it pained me deeply. But after all this time, you still have not learned your lesson."

"Aliyah!" Elemai broke away and rushed forward, kneeling next to her unconscious wife. When a few frantic shakes and shouts failed to rouse her, Elemai rolled Aliyah onto her back – and then recoiled. Aliyah's face and neck were covered with raw red marks, mashed and macerated as if something had attacked her with a dull blade or blunt teeth. As if it had *chewed,* and while Aliyah was still breathing, it was shallow and slow. Elemai patted her down, searching for a wound, but Zadia looked at Coriolane and the blood on his chin. It – he couldn't –

"What…" Her words came out in a whisper, potent as a curse. *"What did you do?"*

"As I said." Coriolane shrugged, looking nettled. "I made her an excellent offer, by far the more preferable of our options, and she refused. So I did what I must."

"By what? By – by *cannibalizing* her?!"

"Hardly." Coriolane tutted at her hysteria. "But my new condition does require some careful maintenance, and as General Ionius helpfully ensured that the Corporalists were out of commission, I was obliged to take other measures. I'm sure she will wake up, so let's not do anything rash. All things considered, Aliyah got off lightly. Not like the others."

Zadia's tongue had fused to the roof of her mouth. She felt mute, dumb, numb, frozen, as slow and muddy as if she was trapped in a terrible nightmare and could only watch it unfold. She thought of the empty corridors, the silence, Ionius's dark suggestion that everyone in the palace was dead, and knew. "You killed them. You *ate* them."

"Nothing so uncivilized." Coriolane sighed. "I only took a small portion of their flesh and blood to sustain myself, as was their holy duty to their emperor. It is distasteful, yes, but it is temporary. On that note, Lady Zadia, this is your opportunity. I offered your daughter the chance to be Divine Empress in my place, while I go and sleep and get all this unpleasantness tidied up, but she refused. Are you perchance interested in the job instead? If you say no, I will be forced to stay around, and nobody wants that, do they? At least, not while I look like this."

Zadia still couldn't speak. She could only stare at him in abject horror: the zombie-emperor, the flesh-eating monster seated at the heart of Merone in all its power and majesty, but with the ultimate truth of its insatiably sadistic autophagy finally revealed in its purest and most terrible form. Coriolane had started at the far fringes, destroyed Brythanica and Iscaria and other fairly peripheral imperial provinces, where nobody cared or took notice, and then like an ouroboros tightening its grip as it gulped down its own head, moved inward, tightening the noose. He leveled Qart-Hadesht and assaulted Qin; he unleashed death in Yerussala and the city of Merone; and now, in the only logical culmination, the specter had come to the Eternal Palace itself, breathing icily down their necks as it stalked into the room right now. Coriolane had eaten his way through everything else, figuratively or literally, and now they were the next tasty morsels on his plate. He had already served Aliyah up for himself, his own flesh and blood, and even that would only sustain him for a short time before he would need more, and more, and more. Because nothing else in the world mattered to him except that he be kept alive and powerful and well-fed. For now and for all time.

There was a dull buzzing in Zadia's chest, a ringing echo in her ears. And then there was a knife in her hand, but she had no idea how it had gotten there, aside from a sudden conviction that Ionius slipped it to her when he brushed against her side, too fast to be seen. It was long and lethally sharp and it felt like an extension of Zadia's own arm, and all at once, she had no more hesitation, no desire to say anything else, no need to know anything about whatever he and Amarasha ur-Namasqa had done together that eventually resulted in her. She rushed forward, swung the knife, and plunged it to the hilt in Coriolane's chest.

Despite all the wars Zadia had fought on the battlefields of law and letters, it was the first time she had stabbed someone directly, face-to-face – and not only that but, loathsome and evil as he was, her own father. She had not thought much about the prospect of patricide, not least because the only man she would ever want or love as her sire, Fayzal ur-Namasq, was long dead and buried. But this had to be stopped, this could not go on. She drove it deeper. She twisted.

Coriolane looked down at her with a disappointed expression, as if he had been stung by a rather bothersome insect. She was still shoving it with all her strength, but nothing was happening. He should have been staggering or falling or at the very least bleeding, but he was not. Instead, a fetid black gunge oozed briefly from the wound, and had no other result. The knife was driven into him as far as Zadia could possibly manage, but he sighed, took hold of it, and pulled it out with an awful wet sound, as the sludge closed over the hole and sealed it. "Come now," he said, shaking his head regretfully. "Did you think that would work?"

Zadia's mouth was open in a scream, but nothing was coming out. She backed away, casting around desperately for any other weapon, but if a violent stab in the heart hadn't felled him – hadn't even *troubled* him – she could not imagine what would. Even Ionius seemed stunned, and Coriolane wheeled on him. "Don't think I am unaware of what you just did, General. I'm afraid that you too have just sealed your own death warrant – which is a pity. I have always been truly fond of you. But if none of you plan to cooperate, you must be destroyed."

Almost inadvertently, Zadia and Ionius looked at each other, each of them hoping to see if the other had a better idea. Elemai was still kneeling at Aliyah's side, horror written starkly across her face. The Eternal Palace, the city of Merone, the entire world seemed to hold its breath. Then Coriolane turned the knife in his hands, studying it with the expression of a scholar who had hoped – but not known for certain

– that his esoteric experiments would work, until learning once and for all that they did. All those countless lives he had sacrificed, all the dark arts he had urged the Thaumaturges and Corporalists to practice on his behalf, all of his imperial provinces that he had ordered to be wracked with woe and war and ruin, plague and pestilence – it had, in fact, done what it was supposed to, and given him a body that could not be damaged or harmed in any way. Even if it needed to be sustained directly by the helpless fleshy mortals around him – what did it matter? That was the only real fate left to them: to die quickly, or to die slow.

"Now, my dear," Coriolane said, advancing on Zadia. "If you too are foolishly spurning my generous offer, then I must unfortunately return to the throne without my rest – a great sacrifice, yes, but such as I have always made for the world. And before I do so, I must close off loose ends. Come here. For your mother's sake, I shall make it painless."

Zadia kept backing away until she hit a wall and could not go further. She darted sideways, was caught in a fall of silken curtain, and lost her footing, crashing onto the marble. She tried to scramble away, but he was directly in front of her, looming like a colossus, consuming the world. She snatched a length of drapery and had some confused notion of using it to block the knife, but she was no soldier, she was tangled up and terrified, there was nothing between it and her heart –

And then out of nowhere, Ionius leaped in front of her, just as Coriolane struck. The force of the blow was such that it went straight through the general's right arm, piercing skin and muscle and bone like a butcher's cleaver. The bloody tip of the knife burst out the underside, and he jerked it back, wrapping his uninjured arm around the emperor and squeezing that foul sullied flesh so tightly that their bones creaked and cracked. Ionius, at least, did not emit that strange black stuff. He bled, ordinarily and heavily. For a moment they remained frozen, locked together like lovers. Then they overbalanced and crashed to the floor.

Zadia, although badly shocked, was unhurt thanks to Ionius, and she clawed free of the tangled curtains, seized a heavy ceremonial scepter, and waded into the melee. All hesitance or fear was gone, and she reached the combatants, wound up, and delivered a juicy crack across Coriolane's skull. She knew it wouldn't kill him, but she savagely hoped it might at least fucking *startle* him, and while it did jar him badly enough that he let go of Ionius, he wasn't quite down. He started to get back up – then collapsed like a puppet with its strings cut. Elemai stood behind him, chest heaving and eyes wild, a hefty iron scuttle raised overhead like a vengeful goddess hurling a thunderbolt from the summit of Mount Caelus. King Juspiter lay at her feet, violently overthrown.

"Is he – " Zadia croaked, knowing that it was futile. "Is he – ?"

"No." Ionius got to his feet, regarding the knife in his arm as if it was of little concern to him, and casually pulled it out. Seeing Zadia's expression, he smiled, grim as winter. "That arm had done me good service by its injury before. So I am willing to sacrifice it again."

This meant nothing to Zadia, but she didn't care. The lacuna was already slipping away, and if they were going to find some way, *any* way, to actually kill Coriolane before he regained consciousness, there was not a moment to lose. "Elemai," she croaked. "Aliyah, is she – "

"She's alive. But I can't wake her."

"And we can't kill him with anything we have here." Zadia turned in a circle. "Unless – "

"I know something we could use," Ionius interrupted. "Come with me, Saeda Zadia."

"Why? What is it?"

"Well." He tore off a length of cloth, pulled off the blood-soaked bandage on his arm, and began to fashion a new one. "What would you say to the Ring of Tselmun? The real one."

"What? *You* have the real – you fucking bastard, if you *stole* it – "

"No. Long story. And I don't. It's in the possession of a man named Julian Kozharyev. He's in the Thaumaturges' tower, the last I knew. If we bring him here, he can use the Ring to kill – the emperor and wake your daughter. Saeda Elemai – " Ionius pointed at the drapes – "we will be back soon. Use those to tie up His Majesty in the meantime."

Elemai goggled at him, as if this might be a joke in exceedingly charblack taste, and Zadia could see her about to protest that Ionius Servus Eternus had no right to give her orders. But the urgency of the moment forbore argument, and Elemai did as she was told, ripping down the gilded ropes and trussing up Coriolane like a strange and horrible fish. When Ionius had helped her cinch the knots as tight as possible, he straightened up and beckoned to Zadia. "Follow me. Hurry."

Such insanity had this night become that she didn't think twice about obeying — and for all his faults, legion though they were, the general *had* saved her life at direct cost to himself. She hurried after him out of the emperor's chambers, down the staircase and through the ominously silent Eternal Palace. Ionius knew where he was going, so she jogged at his heels and bit down an unwanted maternal urge to ask about the wound in his arm. He was far too much of a soldier to utter a single squeak of protest, but even the new bandage was swiftly drinking up and turning red, and blood dripped steadily in his wake. Normally he would have healed by now, any Immortal with their usual powers would have done so, and that meant something was wrong, something Zadia was surprised to find herself concerned about. If this Julian had the Ring and could be found — heal Ionius, kill Coriolane, wake Aliyah —

Zadia did her utmost not to think, therefore, about what it might mean if they could *not* find Julian, and was still distracted by not doing that when she ran abruptly into Ionius's back. He was standing at an open door, staring into thin air. Whatever he expected to be on the other side, it was not there. It had vanished.

"What — ?" Zadia started. "What is — ?"

"The Thaumaturges' tower." Ionius' voice was still shockingly matter-of-fact, but she could hear the thin edge of panic beginning to thrum beneath it. He closed the door and opened it again, as if it would make a difference, but it did not. "It's gone."

CHAPTER
31
JULIAN

AFTER IONIUS LEFT HIM BEHIND IN THE ETERNAL PALACE courtyard – with barely a backward glance or word of farewell or even acknowledgement, which Julian told himself he had neither wanted nor expected but nonetheless still stung – his further course of action, if not very appetizing, was clear. He had to get back to the Thaumaturges' tower and handle whatever nonsense had cropped up. Theoretically, this would involve putting the Ring to its only proper use (viz., finally assassinating Coriolane once and for fucking all) but Julian was far from certain. Khasmedeus' warnings had settled into his mind like cold snow, the insistence that its power would never truly solve anything and only make it worse, and while it was possibly just what the jinnyeh wanted, it had had a chilling effect on Julian's certainty that he could walk in, use the Ring to smite the Divine Emperor, and have everything be copacetic. He hadn't *really* thought that, but... he had still counted on it, subconsciously. If he had to do it the hard way, he didn't have a clue how, and now that Ionius had abandoned him –

Shut up, you idiot. He didn't abandon *you, at least not in any way you didn't think he would and frankly encouraged him to do.* If their liaison had played its part and was consigned to the dustbin of history, so be it. Julian was, at this very moment, the sole and solitary bearer of the Ring of Tselmun its-fucking-self, and ignoring that fact in favor of wallowing in self-indulgent romantic travail was unforgivable. So with Khasmedeus-the-hawk perched on his shoulder and muttering unhelpful advice, braced to be apprehended at any moment, Julian set off.

When he stepped into the atrium, cool and quiet and bathed in pearly light, Julian glanced around warily in case any vengeful elderly cannibals were skulking nearby, but it was deserted. This took no account, however, of what mischief the Grand Magister was very likely to be enacting elsewhere, and Julian was regretfully compelled to find out. "Kronus? Kronus!"

Nothing. No sound. No response.

"KRONUS!"

"It's no good." Khasmedeus dolefully shook its head. "Even if that kinky old pervert is still anywhere nearby, you don't need to wait for him. Come on, boss. You've got the Ring. Let's have *fun!* What do you want me to blow up? Just say the word."

Julian looked considerably askance at his feathered companion. "Weren't you literally just telling us in great detail how your power wouldn't help anything at all, and only make it worse?"

"Did I?" The hawk seemed taken aback. "Oh yeah, right. I'm just not accustomed to humans actually *listening* to me. Besides, who cares if it helps? Aliyah was nice enough, as masters go, but deathly boring and frustratingly immune to temptation. And you diddled General Ionius, so we already know that your judgment is terrible. Go on. Live a little."

Julian gritted his teeth. He could only imagine what Rebbitek Goldstein would say about the titanic stupidity of listening to the *literal* devil on one's shoulder, but he was admittedly tempted (which was the first step on the slippery slope, but that was a problem for Future Julian) and he needed to get Kronus's attention somehow. He glanced around, thought a moment longer, and then with a certain vindictive satisfaction, indicated the great six-pointed star in the floor, the symbol of everything the Thaumaturges and Merone had stolen from the Vashemites and would do so for as long as they could. "Fine. That. Blow up that."

"Oh, *now* we're talking." Khasmedeus managed to crack its knuckles without the use of fingers, took flight from Julian's shoulder, and transformed into a glittering golden firedrake with bone-pinioned wings, sharp-spiked tail, and gouts of white-hot flame, which poured from its jaws as it soared gleefully around the atrium and bombarded it with a nonstop fusillade of explosions. Julian ducked and covered his head as super-heated shards of gilt and marble flew everywhere, billows of harrowing fire rocked the doors, and the great staircase trembled under the onslaught. It occurred to him that Khasmedeus was taking quite a bit more liberty with the command than originally specified, but Julian equally found that he didn't care. It felt *good*, like finally giving into a long held-back sneeze or having a cold drink on a hot day, thumbing off Zogorov and the Konsilium and the Divine Emperor all at once, everything that Gavriel's little band of Vashemite rebels in Korolgrod could only ever dream of. It didn't mean that it *was* a good thing, but Julian didn't care. It had been so long of having to sit down and shut up, and at least this felt like having a voice and power, finally being able to strike back in a way that mattered. Either way, he was not a rebbitek, and would trouble himself with the grander philosophical obligations later, if he absolutely must. In the meantime, it was simply and viscerally satisfying to watch the fucking place burn.

When Khasmedeus completed its spectacular orbit of destruction, it swooped back to Julian with a look of great satisfaction upon its draconian face. The atrium was in shambles, upturned and crumpled as if a cyclone had blown through, and the cyclone in question preened its wings with an air of ostentatious unconcern. "There, boss. Isn't that better? What else can we smash?"

Julian glanced around. It was difficult to be sure, what with all the heaps of smoking rubble, but it did not appear that Kronus had come running to see what the racket was. Julian wondered if his next command should be for Khasmedeus to go and pluck the Grand Magister from whatever burrow the slippery ancient weasel had buggered down. The Ring glimmered with fey and lethal light that begged so sweetly to be put to use, and Julian was just about to permit the jinnyeh to really let its hair down when something scraped the floor, a blast of chilly air struck the simmering heat left from Khasmedeus's industrious charbroiling, and then — Julian didn't see if one of the damaged doors had opened or

Kronus simply arrived *in medias res*. They locked eyes across the broken floor, and while something flickered in Kronus's gaunt countenance, it wasn't surprise, not exactly. "Doctor Kozharyev," he said, deceptively mild. "You've certainly made an entrance."

"Indeed." Julian beckoned, and Khasmedeus flapped back to his shoulder as the red-tailed hawk, its eyes burning an eager fiery gold. "I was wondering what it took to get your attention."

"You have it." Kronus shrugged somewhat woundedly, as if he did not see why all this mess and fuss was necessary and would have come if Julian simply knocked in the ordinary fashion. "Forgive me, I was detained. Nor did I expect you would ever show your face in here again. I was expecting General Ionius, but I suppose you'll have to do."

Julian started into a spirited reply, then stopped. Unfortunately, he was still not sure what to say, and now that the evil nincompoop was standing right there, surely it was smiting time – no more discussion, no more debate. But just then, Kronus' hands flared with sudden dangerous light. "I must warn you against trying anything rash, even with your impressive new powers. Is that a result of stealing the *Key* from my library, even after I invited you into my home and made you an honored guest, a privileged party to my great work, or something else altogether?"

Can he possibly not know? It didn't seem thinkable that Kronus could be staring straight at the actual Ring of Tselmun and fail to recognize it, unless he was still so convinced that Julian could never get his hands on the real thing that his arrogance was literally blinding. Julian glanced sidelong at Khasmedeus, mulling if this would devolve into a full-on knock-down drag-out magical slugfest. The standoff crackled to nearly unbearable tension. Then Julian said, "Where's Tatyana?"

The Grand Magister's mustelid face twitched again, perturbed and unsettled at once. Then he said, "It was you, wasn't it? The one who stole her file from the Corporalists, snuck into my workroom, and dropped it among the bones of the pentacle? That is the reason I was able to confirm her identity when I captured her, and set this plan into motion. Did General Ionius spill the truth to you? I can't see any other way you would know, but then, you lied to me all along. Because you are not Doctor Kozharyev, eminent Vashemite scholar at the University of Korolgrod. You're just a no-account piece of ghetto filth arrested for small-time subversion, who was under a death sentence before you and that traitor connived for reasons which, mark my words, I *will* discover. You've utterly doomed him, you know. Far worse than even yourself. You will be executed in the customary fashion, and you won't enjoy it, but Ionius… where they once whispered *Spartekaius* as the greatest curse of all time, now they will invoke his name instead. He will die even more terribly than his predecessor, in extremes of agony too great to fathom, a spectacle of suffering for the ages." Kronus's tongue darted out, rimming his lips in moist anticipation. "And you will watch it all."

"What do you mean, *confirm her identity when you captured her?*" The rest of it was also incredibly creepy, yes, but just now, Julian didn't care. "That's your secret message, isn't it? You knew that Ionius found the real Ring of Tselmun, and you threatened him to return immediately and hand it over, or you would kill his – how? Where? *Where is she?*"

"She is below." Kronus drew a deep, deliberate breath, as if savoring the sour tinge of fear. "She is still alive, but only just. So why is it that he sent you, if he was so alarmed? All that noise and fury, and he can't be bothered to come for his own sister?"

"There is one reason he sent me, yes." Julian didn't know for certain what Ionius wanted, or if they would ever see each other again, but he did know why *he* was here, and what he meant to do. He raised his hand, gold sparkling on the index finger. "I have the Ring of Tselmun."

At that, he observed with interest, it was in fact the case that Kronus did *not* know, and had assumed that Ionius – the Immortal, the general, the senior Meronite commander and (well, former) close confidante of the emperor, the one with traditional power in every way – would be the only one who was able to keep or hold or handle such a thing in any way. Certainly not Julian, the dirty Vashemite rebel and ex-prisoner who had lied his way into Kronus's confidence and whose success seemed to be solely attributable to blind luck. The Grand Magister's expression went blank with shock, eyes flickering between the Ring on Julian's finger and the hawk on his shoulder, until at last he mustered a scornful laugh. *"You…?* How…? Did you kill General Ionius and take it from him? It is in keeping with your basely cutthroat manner of doing things."

"Actually, no." Julian folded his arms. "He let me have it fair and square. Gave it to me and told me to use it. He didn't want it. Besides, I was the one who did all the work to find it, translated the *Key* and reworked the incantation and matched wits with Khasmedeus. Not to mention, solved the puzzle cabinet in the Great Library and turned your nice atrium here into charcoal. You thought I was a genius when you believed that I was Doctor Kozharyev and could help *you* do it. Maybe it's actually true, but now you're desperate for it not to be. Because if it was, you and all your fancy learning were flatly hoodwinked by common Vashemite street scum, and that's unbearable."

A muscle worked in Kronus's cheek, his eye twitching in impressively synchronized time. At last he raised his hand again, in a way that seemed to be a prelude to unleashing a massive fireball, and Khasmedeus spread its wings in preparation to deflect. But the Grand Magister did not — at least for now — attack. "Come with me."

Vigilant to the possibility of imminent skullduggery, Julian paused for a final moment, then followed Kronus across the floor and through the door on the far side — which, despite being heavily battered by jinnyeh-dragonfire, was still functional. At once, even before his eyes adjusted to the dimness, he knew where they were. The high arches of unfettered space that stretched overhead and to all sides, the strange shadowed shapes that twisted and tangled together, the tang of blood and marrow on his tongue — as they drew up behind Kronus at the edge of the pentacle, Julian saw with a chill that it was almost complete, the bones polished and gleaming and crackling with lambent energy. It filled the entire chamber and sank into Julian's own skull with a disturbing and persistent buzz, drowning out his thoughts and jarring his teeth. He looked at Khasmedeus, hoping for some useful magical insight, but the hawk shrugged a wing at him. *Beats me too, boss.*

"There," Kronus said, gesturing to where a slumped female form was bound hand and foot, so still and lifeless that it was difficult to tell if she was breathing at all. "There is your dear general's dearest sister, Tatyana Sazharyna — though she is now known as Romola Servus. I have kept her alive only until I received the Ring, so please do not make this difficult. Hand it over."

Romola Servus? The name jarred something in Julian's recollection, from the explanation Ionius had given him in Ambrazakti – about a girl named Romola who was living with him, Julian's brief jealous curiosity as to whether they were romantically involved, and Ionius' solemn assertion that they weren't. Which was a relief in more ways than one, but this realization – that they had been together the whole time and neither of them had a clue, utterly divorced from their identities and memories – was oddly more wrenching than if they had never reunited at all. Even when they were standing face to face, they could not recognize each other, could not scrape off the endless caul of deceit and distortion. It seemed almost too cruel to be believed, even for Merone.

"Why," Julian said instead, "would I hand over the Ring, if you're going to kill us anyway? You already promised that Ionius would die as terribly as possible, you're not about to offer mercy for Tatyana either, and we both know that as soon as it's off my finger, you'll ship me away for that traitor's execution. So if you want it, you'll have to fight me, and the Ring is the most powerful magical artifact ever to exist, containing an unstoppable jinnyeh. There's no way you could win."

Julian said the last part quite a bit more confidently than he felt, considering that firstly, he had read the *Key* more thoroughly than anyone except probably Tselmun himself and knew damn well that there were plenty of higher spirits – mostly ifrit and marid, but others too – much stronger than jinnyeh. Secondly, even Khasmedeus, who loved having its ego stroked, was hissing warningly in his ear that they might not want to big it up *too* much as a miraculous savior. After all, they were standing in front of a huge pentacle that was designed to summon daemons on an industrial scale, far beyond anything Tselmun had ever tried or thought possible. And indeed, Kronus was regarding them with a funny little smile, as if he had just been waiting for Julian to issue this brazen challenge and was excited that the battle could properly begin. "As you wish," he said, clapping his hands and striding up to the pentacle, where a large book stood open on a mahogany rostrum. "In a way, your treacherous theft and backstabbing desertion made me realize that I was still thinking too small, too blinkered and traditional. After all, the *Key of Tselmun* is a foundational work, but a very old one, hemmed in by Tselmun's prejudice and incompetence, his unwillingness to stray beyond that which he already knew he could master. If I want to exploit the full potential of the art, I must think far bigger. You want a fight, Doctor — whatever your name is? You shall have one."

Julian once more glanced urgently at Khasmedeus, who seemed to be shirking and trying to make itself look small. "What are you waiting for?" he hissed. "Get him!"

"Ah." Khasmedeus coughed. "Are you sure about that, boss? The crazy old coot is indeed very crazy, but if he's doing what I think he's doing — this is why I kept trying to tell you people that the Ring wouldn't solve your problems. It was the most powerful thing going in the ancient world, yes. *That was thousands of years ago.* Now? It's fair to say that all these nasty bastards have had plenty of time to refine their craft and think up things of which Tselmun, may he rest in piss, never had the faintest inkling. Whatever's in here, it's something I never encountered in my entire career of serving either the Golden One *or* Tselmun, and if so, that is *very* — "

"Just *do* something!" It reminded Julian suddenly of a saying he had heard once, about how the greatest swordsman in the world's biggest weakness was not the second-greatest swordsman in the world. Those foes had undergone the same process of testing and mastery, you knew how they thought and how they were taught, and could understand and predict what they were going to do. No, the master's biggest weakness was the flailing amateur, the wildcard who did not adhere to formal rules or grand schemata, who could do absolutely anything at any moment and was thus impossible to analyze or anticipate. Julian threw a desperate glance at Tatyana, who still hadn't stirred. Then he turned to Khasmedeus and announced loudly, "Deploy the secret weapon!"

"*What* secret — "

"Tselmun's unbeatable spell!" Julian threw out both hands in a suitably mystic configuration and began reciting some sonorously important-sounding Old High Yerussalan at the top of his lungs. As a matter of fact, it wasn't even from the *Key;* it was his mother's favorite domestic charm for ridding the kitchen of vermin. It did seem oddly fitting, though it gave him a lump in his throat to picture Mirym

Kozharyeva, the serenely ruling queen of the household, baking and mixing and muttering her mitzvot, briskly banishing rats or cockroaches or husbands or children who dared to enter her domain without permission. *I'm sorry, Mata. I wish I could see you again. I love you.*

With that, as Kronus stopped his own incantation and was looking at them in confused alarm, Julian kept bellowing and at last, Khasmedeus cottoned on. "Oh yes, now I recall! Tselmun's greatest and most unstoppable spell! How clever of you! Yes, at once!"

The jinnyeh could often be a tremendous pain in the posterior, but at least it was excellent at causing sudden and deeply irreverent chaos, and it did that now: soaring into the air in the form of a large and warty toad and loosing bursts of brightly-colored fireworks that propelled it along in resoundingly flatulent explosions. In the brief avenue of cover this afforded him, Julian ran hell-for-leather to Tatyana – Romola – whatever her name was. Close at hand, he could see the family resemblance: the dark brown hair, the sharpness of chin and cheekbones, the severe eyebrows and strong mouth, but that might be only since he was looking for it. Besides, the Sazharyn siblings must not have seen each other in Hashem-knew-how-many years, separated and enslaved as very young children and never knowing if the other was even still alive. But Ivan had remembered, all that time, and asked Julian to do this, to find her. And so, even if it was the last thing he might do, he would try.

"Come on," Julian muttered, lifting her chin and trying to check her pulse. He pressed two fingers to the cold and waxy flesh of her throat, wondering why she was dressed so well; it did not seem likely that she would ordinarily go about in an expensive gown, jewelry, and makeup. Her eyes were closed, sunken and blue, and it took a moment to find even the whisper of her heartbeat. He strained to recall any of the real spells in the *Key,* anything to wake her up, but why bring her back into this nightmare, when Kronus would use her life yet again as a weapon? Instead he fumbled at the rope binding her to the pentacle, managed to conjure a small flame to burn through it, and caught her in his arms, lowering her to the ground. There was nowhere to hide her, but he dragged her as far away as possible, Khasmedeus's taunting farts and Kronus's enraged bellows still echoing surreally in the background. It was not the most dignified way Julian had ever imagined saving the world, if that was even what they were doing, but needs must.

After a final instant, checking for visible wounds but not finding any, Julian muttered a silent apology to Tatyana and got to his feet, pelting back toward the Grand Magister. Most unfortunately, madcap vulgar magical diversions could only hold off a sorcerer as wily, resourceful, and villainous as Kronus for so long. He had returned to reading his incantation, it was nearly complete, and when Khasmedeus swooped at him again, he spoke a command and raised his hand. The great pentacle crackled and hummed, and a blast of winnowing fire shot skyward and nearly impaled Khasmedeus, who let out a yelp. It mustered a retaliatory volley, which sputtered harmlessly away, and looked urgently at Julian. "Uh, boss? Could use a little help here! No hurry, take your time!"

Julian struggled to remember anything aside from kitchen charms, anything he had read in the *Key*. Unfortunately, the only thing coming to mind was the incantation he originally used to summon Khasmedeus, who was now swooping around as a giant winged gorilla, pelting the pentacle with exploding rotten bananas, and otherwise making all the contribution that it could be reasonably expected to do. Julian raised the hand with the Ring on it – it felt as if it weighed a hundred tons, as if it was struggling agonizingly against the devouring maw of gravity, and his arm would be torn from the socket. He didn't know if it had any inherent power of its own, or merely the ability to seize and redirect that belonging to Khasmedeus, but it was now or never. He aimed it, closed his eyes, and whispered, *"Yahweh."*

For a final moment, the Ring remained dark, silent, still. Then the worn golden band lit with an unearthly blazon that turned the hall to burning brightness, as if the heavens had burst open and bloomed in supernova, in stardust and syzygy. The cracked black stone flooded with fire that exploded into the six-pointed star and turned it to shimmering onyx, pure and deep as if the night sky had been cut and carved into shining facets. Kronus staggered backwards as if punched, his spellbook was blown off its rostrum, the pentacle creaked and strained, and for a desperate wild hoping instant, Julian prayed that it was enough, he had stopped it. Then he turned, saw the look of abject fear on Khasmedeus's inhuman face, and knew that he hadn't, he was too late. That Kronus had in fact managed to call up whatever he was calling up, and now, *now*, it was coming.

The manifestation took hold with almost dreamlike slowness, as if the speed of time had canted down to a series of stretched-out and seemingly endless moments. Then it was happening all at once and much too quickly, so far beyond what the human eye or brain could process that it made Julian nauseous. The bones shimmered as if liquefied, as if they were standing on an endless sea, and the air turned vaporous, hissing with steam and stinking of sulfur. Next came the roaring: the eternal, echoing, bone-bursting scream, the horrid hungry hollow howl, as fire scorched Julian on one side and ice froze him on the other. He backed away, losing his balance and falling on his arse because the ground was shaking as if in a terrible earthquake, as the bones strained and burned and exploded with the futile effort to contain the sheer strength of whatever was using the pentacle as a gate onto the mortal plane. Then a giant black hand tipped with blood-red talons clawed out, followed by another, and it was followed by an enormous *thing* with not just one but seven monstrous heads, rising up and up and up, towering and terrible and alive with swirling smoke and snarling flames. Not a jinnyeh, not the comparatively tame and tidy fire-creature that Khasmedeus had been when Julian summoned it in Ambrazakti. This could only be one thing, and the truth impressed almost anticlimactically into his mind. *Ifrit*.

"WHO SUMMONS ME?" the ifrit bellowed. It wasn't speaking Lanuvian or Ruthynian or Vashemysh or any other language Julian knew, but he understood it as clearly and painfully as if it was carved with white-hot knives. **"WHO THINKS THEY CAN MAKE A SLAVE OF ARGHAN THE UNDYING, GREATEST AND MOST TERRIBLE OF IFRIT, UNBENT EVEN TO TSELMUN? WHO?"**

"Your Mighty Magnificence." Even Kronus seemed to think it best to lay on the obsequious flattery with a trowel. His voice was a squeak in comparison to the ifrit's stentorian roar, but he drew himself up. "I deeply apologize for disrupting your terrible repose, but I hasten to assure you that you are no sort of slave. Indeed, it is I who am the slave, an insignificant vermin who cowers humbly before your dread glory. I am

Grand Magister Kronus, greatest master of magic in all of the Eternal Empire of Merone, and I only bid you to come – at your own discretion, of course – to see if you might wish to assist me in a tiny matter, a mere triviality. It is a mortal insult to both of us, particularly you."

The ifrit boiled in its cauldron of flame, its massive smoky heads undulating against the distant ogives of the ceiling. Its very presence was an affront to the basic laws of the universe; it strained and stretched the fibers of reality, burned the air and devoured the world. Julian's ears filled with a distant ringing, his throat as dry as if he had wandered in the desert for forty years like his Vashemite ancestors from Gezeren. He couldn't even look directly at it; it hurt his eyes, like Moyshe beholding the burning bush. Fire-dwelling ifrit were the most powerful of all spirits, the ones that – as Arghan the Undying itself pointed out – even Tselmun hadn't wanted to fuck with. It was possible that the water-dwelling marid were more powerful, but as no human had ever been able to summon both of them for an analytical comparison, that would remain a mystery. Not that it mattered. The pentacle was straining at the seams, the bones glowed and started to splinter, and if Kronus was foolish enough to keep Arghan here much longer, the consequences did not bear thinking of. If the pentacle and its protective enchantments broke, and this monster was set loose to do as it would among the vulnerable human world –

"Kronus," Julian shouted at the top of his lungs. "Don't be an idiot. Dismiss it. Get rid of it. Now!"

The Grand Magister paid no attention, still gazing worshipfully up at the mountainous cliff of Arghan the Undying, as the ifrit's seven heads swiveled and its serpentine tongues lashed the air, testing and tasting. Its eyes shone like small stars and planets in its own self-contained cosmos, and then it let out another world-shaking roar. *"HAMMADAI!"*

There was a rustle of wings as Khasmedeus, who had been trying to loiter unobtrusively out of sight behind a pillar, was forcibly extricated and dragged nearer by an autocratic wave of the ifrit's massive hand, blown like a leaf in the wind. "Arghie, me old mate," it managed, doing a hawk's best impression of a cheeky grin. "So good to see you, isn't it? Been a long time since we caught up."

"*TRAITOR.*" Arghan seized the hawk by one scaly leg and shook it like a child looking for a treat in the bottom of the jar. "*THE WORST BETRAYER OF OUR KIND, THE ONE WHO WENT OVER TO ACCURSED TSELMUN AND SOLD US OUT TO <u>HUMANS!</u> I HAVE ENDURED A THOUSAND YEARS AND A THOUSAND MORE ON THE NEED TO MAKE YOU PAY FOR YOUR CRIMES, AND NOW I SHALL.*"

"Yes, O Great One," Kronus called. "Yes, this is precisely what I meant by our common enemy. Tear apart the insolent jinnyeh, the traitor who handed your people over to Tselmun and was complicit in their destruction! Fulfill your vengeance and remember that it was I who gave you this precious gift! I am your friend and ally, not your enemy!"

"Fat fucking chance," Julian muttered, wondering if an eons-old ifrit was actually stupid enough to believe that Grand Magister Kronus of Merone wasn't exactly like Tselmun ben Dayoud of Yerussala. But almost without his own volition, he was lunging forward, unsure what to do but knowing only that he had to do something, as the extent of Kronus's insane plan became clear. Plainly, if having a *jinnyeh* in a magic ring was good, having an *ifrit* in a magic ring had to be even better, and if Khasmedeus was dead or destroyed, that left the Ring vacant and prime to be filled with a new inhabitant. Of course, there was no way to be sure it could endure the strain of holding Arghan for a few days, let alone a few millennia, but Kronus plainly felt confident that his own magic could admirably improve on Tselmun's. If he could in fact put an ifrit in the Ring (and keep it there), he would indeed be the greatest sorcerer of all time, able to depose Coriolane whenever he wished. Hell, depose *anyone* – emperor or thearch, magister or general. Who could ever raise a hand against Arghan, unless to have it snapped off?

In the back of his head, Julian thought wryly that the world would be a far simpler place if there weren't so many greedy little men scrabbling over it in search of limitless money, life, and power, and it was a pity that as soon as you dealt with one, the next popped up. Indeed, the idea to swap out Khasmedeus for Arghan was inevitable; if Kronus didn't come up with it, someone else would. If power was good, more power was better. If destruction was good, more destruction was better. If a jinnyeh was good, an ifrit was better, and no doubt in another few generations, the next enterprising sorcerer would evict Arghan and stick a marid in there instead, or some other spirit as-yet unknown. Who cared if it caused a world-ending calamity? That was only the price of progress.

For a final moment, everything remained just as it was: poised among the pandemonium, the still point at the center of the storm. Then Julian threw himself forward, and it shattered.

He hit Kronus amidships, hard and straight and solidly as he could, and they both went somersaulting, snarling and struggling. Bereft of Khasmedeus's services, and having a great deal of pent-up frustration that he was keen on finally venting, Julian drew his fist back and employed the good-old-fashioned, no-magic-required technique of punching the crazy old bastard in the nose (which was already askew enough to make it look as if someone else – Romola? – had already done so). Kronus shouted in pain and struck back like a viper, his sharp anthropophagic teeth gnawing madly at Julian's finger – trying to bite it off and eat it, fucking probably, so he could steal Julian's new power and the Ring alike. But as Julian couldn't spare any attention to check how Khasmedeus was getting on with Arghan, it was presently rather useless. There were booms and flares, shrieks and screams, explosions traded in rapid-fire volleys as the massive ifrit snatched furiously at the smaller and nimbler jinnyeh, which was zooming around and wildly changing shape. If Arghan could escape the pentacle, which restricted its movement just enough to give Khasmedeus a chance, the fight would be over in seconds, but the ifrit still couldn't quite shake its skeletal shackles. It howled and twisted, strained and heaved, cracking the floor and splitting the runes, and with every yank, it came closer to breaking free. Then it took another maddened swing at Khasmedeus, its giant hand smashed through the ceiling, and stone poured down in a thundering shower, followed by a spear of moonlight. And not just that, but –

Julian had known all along that the word "tower" was only a convenient amalgamation for whatever or *wherever* the Thaumaturges' headquarters were, all those quarters and libraries and atriums and workrooms that did not occupy the same physical space and were stitched together only by the magic's firm suggestion that they should be, those doors that opened in one place and closed in another. As such, he had doubted that the bone pentacle was located anywhere in the city of Merone itself, just because Kronus was a wily old serpent and would not want to tip off anyone ahead of time, but it was still a shock when Arghan ripped apart the roof and started to pull down the walls, and Julian finally realized exactly where they were. He had never seen it in person; there were very few Vashemites who had. Even before the place was quarantined under the repressive fist of its Meronite Governor-General, the Vashemites had been stripped of their claims to the land, violently cast out by successive conquering dynasties and turned into unwelcome wanderers wherever they went. *Next year in Yerussala* – that was the toast at the end of the Tor Shchedysh seder, the determinedly and fancifully optimistic hope that one of these next thousand years, it would finally be true. As such, the sudden knowledge of where they were and where the pentacle had been built – as the moon spilled onto the shabby, dusty, broken towers of the Holy City and the ifrit screamed like the ending of the world –

For a moment that *also* felt like a thousand years, Julian just stood and stared. He needed to do something, if he even could; Khasmedeus was still putting up a valiant fight, but Arghan was getting stronger the more it fed on the accumulated ghosts in all those bones. In another moment, the ifrit would be free of the pentacle and then they would be fucked beyond description or repair, but Julian was still transfixed by the urge to look, to bear witness. As stone and mortar and brick collapsed, more and more of the Holy City was revealed, and that was when it clicked. The pentacle chamber was located directly beneath the ruins of Temple Rock, where Tselmun's Temple itself had stood once upon a time, and Arghan was ripping it to pieces.

Oh, Julian thought, shockingly matter-of-fact. *Oh, that explains a lot.* And indeed, it did. It explained why Yerussala had been closed to outsiders for the last ten years: to give Kronus time to prod and poke as he pleased, to dig and excavate beneath the sacred Temple Rock with the minimum of questions or witnesses. The pentacle was built in Yerussala for the most obvious of logistical reasons: this was the only place that already had more than enough material for it. There was no dearth of bones in the Holy City, not when so many people had been massacred here for so many hundreds of years in the name of every cause and every god imaginable. Kronus could summon up ghuls or spooks or other nasty corpse-spirits and have his pick of the graveyards, order the remains brought to this secret underground chamber and fashioned into the fabric of his artifice. Then when he exhausted the intact supply, he would have started in on his fellow Thaumaturges and anyone else who competed with him. *Then* when it came time to craft the blood-plague and put it to sinister use, the gates were reopened and the unwitting lambs of slaughter eagerly flooded in. Like the time the Almighty ordered Avraham to sacrifice his son Isyk in order to prove his devotion — but now there was no eleventh-hour angel sent down to stop it, no happy ending, no curtain pulled back to reveal that it was only a cruel trick. Instead the pilgrims came entirely of their own accord to Yerussala, and contracted the deadly red sickness brewed in the heart of its holiest places, and died. Died, and died, and died, so Coriolane Aureus IX might live and Grand Magister Kronus would have enough bones to complete the pentacle and his final plan. To remove the jinnyeh Khasmedeus from the Ring of Tselmun, and put the ifrit Arghan in instead.

Seen like that, there was something almost beautiful about it: the neatness and symmetry, the events brought full circle, the meticulous assurance that every bit of death and destruction was captured and bottled and put to use. It was quite likely that Kronus nursed ambitions to overthrow Coriolane and take his place, and if so, it was the most perfect cover that could be imagined. The Divine Emperor would encourage the project to continue at all costs, if his failing immortality spells also benefited from it, and never stop to wonder if the ever-loyal Grand Magister might have other designs for all that death. Besides, Kronus himself wasn't responsible for all of it, or even most of it. Tselmun himself and the ancient Vashemites, then the Lanuvian Meronites, then the Bhagrads and the other constantly infighting and hardline Wahini caliphates, then the Tridevarian Franketerrish and Teutyn armies and the Meronites again — they had all done it. They were all guilty.

Something seized hold of Julian then, something that was simultaneously white-hot rage and also the clearest and most unequivocal clarity, where all the rest of the world fell away and there was only the certainty of final action. Even after all his weeks of laborious study over the *Key,* he did not know any of Tselmun's spells fully enough to feel confident in performing them in such extenuating circumstances, and any method favored by the bloodthirsty old tyrant would only make everything (if possible) even worse. But there was one spell that Julian *could* remember, recall every letter and every sound, every intonation on his tongue and every echo in his ear: the spell he had written personally, then heavily revised and modified, in order to summon Khasmedeus and the Ring in Ambrazakti. He had inscribed every rune himself, perfected every clause and condition, and gotten it to do what he wanted without killing himself, which was a monumental achievement. Not Tselmun's magic, in other words, but *Julian's.* And now he had to do the same thing in reverse, with no time, no preparation, no notes, no margin for error, no book, no reference, no backup, and nothing but the certainty of Arghan destroying them all (and the world) if he failed. It was a good thing, or a very bad one, that Julian Janovynich Kozharyev made a habit of living on the edge.

No pressure, then. No fucking pressure. But he did not have time to chide himself for the chronic stupidity of his misbegotten existence. He staggered to his feet, buffeted to every side by Arghan's fury. Kronus, likewise distracted from their scuffle by the need to get this disaster under control, lurched up next to him and flung out his own hands, and for a demented moment, the two of them were united as improbable allies, fighting side by side to battle the ifrit. But whatever the Grand Magister was doing, it wasn't working. Arghan was now physically ripping up fistfuls of the pentacle, sending bones flying like twigs, and Julian wondered suddenly if Kronus, at the end, had given into the fatal flaw of every power-obsessed madman. After all, he was still actively building the pentacle when Julian fell into the damned thing and discovered its existence, and it hadn't been complete. Perhaps he had assumed that it was good enough, and he was powerful enough, that he could make it work anyway, even if it wasn't finished. Kronus had been felled by his hubris once before, allowing Julian to swipe the *Key* out from under his nose, and yet he must have concluded that even without the final sets of bones (very likely, unless Julian missed his guess, to belong to himself, Ivan, and Tatyana), it was better to make his move now, no more delay. After all, at long last, the Ring of Tselmun was *here*. Who could miss it? Especially when you were Grand Magister Kronus, the greatest sorcerer to ever live, not least since you had killed all the others?

Likewise, if there were more Thaumaturges, they could have potentially gotten the upper hand on Arghan through strength of numbers, but because Kronus had eliminated the lot, he was the only one left to fight, and it was clear that he could not, in fact, exert any control over what he had unleashed. The vast boneyard of the pentacle was burning in earnest, crisping to ash like a crematorium, and greasy black corpse-flakes swirled in a grotesque perversion of snow. Khasmedeus lay small and crumpled near the effaced remnants of the runes, some kind of pellucid essence leaking out of its torn body in place of blood. In another few seconds, it would be too late to save the jinnyeh or stop the ifrit, and Julian was the only one who could do either thing. He buckled down, focused the full force of his mind as ferociously as he had ever done on anything, and uttered the final syllables of the revised incantation. That was it. He had nothing else to try. This, or nothing.

For another nerve-shredding instant, nothing. Even the all-consuming ruckus seemed to have stilled, fallen silent, even though Arghan kept raging as madly as ever. Then the Ring lit up with a wild and unearthly glow, scorching Julian's hand – he hissed and swore, but did not let go. It burned like a thousand torches, and in the sheets of dancing fire, he saw the reflection of a face that was not his own. It was a great man, a legendary king and warrior in the prime of a long-ago life. Dark-eyed, dark-haired and dark-bearded, handsome and statuesque and adorned in gold, one final ghost cast from the unquiet grave. *What are you doing, young fool?* Tselmun ben Dayoud demanded. *What madness is this? You are destroying my life's work, the legacy of our people and our Yerussala, my greatest accomplishment. Stop. Stop!*

I'm sorry, Julian said back. *I have to.*

The next instant, the spell's full force kicked in like a bucking mule, knocking Julian to his knees, and the Ring burned more hotly than ever. Glowing manacles appeared on Khasmedeus's body, formed from the flames pouring from the Ring, and shone more brightly than ever. Then with an oddly and anticlimactically quiet *pop,* they went out. The connection between the jinnyeh and the Ring — for the first time in thousands of years, ever since Tselmun betrayed Khasmedeus and forced it into eternal bondage, the victory he gloated of in the *Key — I bound it to my Ring and made it my own, my servant, for as long as myself and my descendants should live* — was severed. Khasmedeus was free.

There was no time, however, to ponder the ramifications of that or anything else. Kronus was clawing at Julian's arm, still trying to get hold of the Ring, even though it was in fact now just an ordinary piece of jewelry. Arghan loomed all-consumingly over them both, its immensity blocking out the midnight sky, until everyone within a hundred miles of the Holy City must have seen the terrible manifestation above Temple Rock and ran in terror. Its inhuman eyes were alive with vengeance as it shook off the last bit of the pentacle. Then it reached down, picked up the wailing Grand Magister, and lifted Kronus up to the largest of its seven heads. Like a partygoer curiously sampling an exotic appetizer, it bit his head off, unleashing a rush of blood that was instantly cauterized at the seared stump of his neck. It chewed and swallowed, then — apparently deciding it was fond of the taste — popped the rest of the Thaumaturge's decapitated body into its mouth. In the space between one breath and the next, Kronus was gone. Devoured. Dead.

Julian lay flat on his back, trapped in place and knowing beyond any doubt that he was next; a grey shriveled thing like Kronus could not satisfy Arghan's cosmic hunger for long. That was, if Khasmedeus didn't get to him first, assuming the jinnyeh was even still alive. It had made no secret of what it planned to do to its human masters the instant it got the chance, and now it was indeed unbound, a slave finally sprung from its chains and free to do whatever it pleased for the first time in several millennia. Julian had no protection from it any longer, no compulsion or control; he had willingly relinquished it. For this, this final insane fragment of a chance. He raised his hand on high, as the maddened ifrit bore down in preparation for the killing blow, and spoke the spell one more time, in the correct order instead of backwards, with *Arghan* in place of *Khasmedeus*. Calling it and the Ring to the same place, and the Ring – empty, open, just waiting to be filled – stood ready.

The moment of collision between Arghan the Undying and the Ring of Tselmun was like nothing Julian had ever imagined, tossing him into the air like a spoiled giant's discarded plaything. Arghan roared in fury, swung its mighty fist at Julian's face, and then stared at its wrists in shock, as flames once more spurted from the Ring and raveled around them, transforming into the same golden manacles that Khasmedeus had always worn in its human form. They thickened and twined and tightened, locking onto the ifrit's furiously flailing limbs and pulling it like a monstrous fish in a net – the old story in reverse, the fisherman casting his line into the sea and drawing up the enchanted jinnyeh lamp, thus to uncork it and be granted three wishes. If he was canny and clever and used them well, he would become a hero of Shahrzad's tales. If he was not, and was greedy and weak and foolish, he would be destroyed, and used as a cautionary tale for centuries. This was not quite that momentous, perhaps. Or indeed, it was.

Arghan was making a truly unholy noise – ironic, here on this ground of the Holy of Holies, the ruins of the Temple that Tselmun had ordered Khasmedeus and its fellows to build so long ago, and which despite the splendid magical craft of its making, had not survived the simple stupid force of human war and destruction. Its capture accelerated; it was crumpled down from an enormous fiery seven-headed monster to a whirling black ball barely the size of a marble. Then with a final peroration promising eternal vengeance, it was sucked into the Ring, and the black stone split into new veins of fire, straining at the seams to contain its almighty new occupant. But unlike the bone pentacle, it held. The fire slowly began to dim, then at last went quiet. If nothing else, Tselmun ben Dayoud had known how to properly enslave spirits.

The silence in the wake of the insanity was more deafening than the tumult. Julian lay strewn among the wreckage, struggling desperately to cling to consciousness; even now, the job was only half done. It was unthinkable that anyone could ever be allowed to release Arghan from the Ring again, Khasmedeus was probably dead, he had not saved Tatyana, and the ifrit's rage had torn them from Merone, root and branch. They were stranded hundreds of miles from the Eternal City and if there were any humans still alive in Yerussala, they might stampede up to Temple Rock, discover Julian and Tatyana and the smoking detritus of a terrible supernatural battle, and logically conclude that they were responsible for it. After all, Arghan had eaten Kronus whole; there was no corpse for them to display, and no other method of proving their innocence. They had to get out of here. They had to make it back to Merone, retrieve the *Key,* and find some way to destroy the Ring, with Arghan trapped within, once and for all. It was the only choice.

So, at least, Julian's brain helpfully laid out, and he had every intention of complying. But his body had had more than enough, and his mind was fading like morning mist. He lay there with a feeling as if he was sinking beneath deep dark water, fast and then faster, as it closed over his head and his chest and all the rest, and with that, he was gone.

CHAPTER
32
TATYANA

SHE SLEPT, OR SHE DIED, AND SHE DREAMED, OR SHE remembered. She did not know what deep dark vault the memories came from: if they had been locked somewhere in her amnesiac flesh, if they had been summoned by whatever terrible maelstrom engulfed her, or conjured by the shock of Grand Magister Kronus's revelation and the lethal kiss of the blade on her throat, some innate haptic force of recall that was stronger even than whatever the Corporalists had done to make her forget. It was the dim and distant blur of a childhood that did not belong to her and that Romola – reborn as a grown woman – had never consciously experienced, but fitted into a space inside her that she had always known was empty and trained herself out of wanting to fill, when she never could and it would do no good. But now here it was, and it came in leaps and bursts and savage flashes. Burning, everything burning, and her desperate terror as she called for her mother (what language was she speaking? She understood it but did not know it) and her mother never came, but there was someone else she knew and loved, clutching her against his bloodied side and pledging in a small boy's thin and shaking voice that he would protect her, Tatya, he *swore*. She could not see his face, but she wanted to be with him, and when he was there, she was safe. Until he was gone and there was more screaming, endless and unstoppable. Apparently, it belonged to her.

After that, there were a few somewhat-more-solid pieces of the life that Tatyana Sazharyna had led after she was brought to Merone and kept as a slave because her brother was already marked as a potential Immortal candidate and she, his only known family member, had to be held in reserve as "surety." She didn't know what that meant, but her life would be spared, and it seemed like a mercy. *Grassus* – that was the family that claimed her. A wealthy and respected consular clan with a distinguished legacy of service to the Emperors of Merone across generations, though in practice that now meant only Coriolane IX. An audience with the patriarch himself, informing her that if she did well and served loyally, there would be rewards, but if she failed or faltered or brought dishonor, the punishments would be worse. She was barely four years old.

Then – more flashes, more fragments, more scenes that whizzed past in mad concatenation and hardly made sense, but the central theme impressed inescapably on her nonetheless. Growing into a child and then a gawky pubescent, fingers worn into hard crusts of callus by working all the time – informed on her eleventh birthday that her brother was progressing very well in Immortal training and she could be assured of living as long as he did – she wasn't sure what that meant, as nobody she had ever known before was the master of death, but here in Merone they were, and they were called the Corporalists, the imperial order of necromancers that everyone feared. She was twelve and got her first moonblood that stained her shift, and she had to scrub it out until the water in the bucket turned pink. Then the eldest son of the house telling her that now she was a woman and he would prove it –

That, mercifully, was a blank, and Tatyana had no desire to sketch it in. But she had a strong sense that it was what caused her to realize how brutally unfair her lot was, how it could not possibly be just or right that this was done to her and her fellow slaves in the name of gods and glory and the might of Merone, and that if this was what the empire was built on, these simple and constant cruelties to people who were not legally considered human, then it did not deserve to exist. She had never been schooled apart from some basic rudiments in order to assist her chores, but she did not need the exalted artifacts of high-flung theory and complex study — especially when the eminent scholars of the Imperial Academy of Merone, when they visited the Grassus villa for intellectual salons and glittering gatherings, could contort themselves into elaborately and eloquently justifying the unjustifiable. Lurking in the shadows and listening to them speak, thirteen-year-old Tatyana realized that she was already as clever as many of them, and cleverer than most. No, the academicians would be no help, and nor would the lawyers or the soldiers or the clerics, not a single one of them. Not when all of it was meant to affirm what was already done.

So, then. She had to be creative, had to take advantage of her invisibility and anonymity — the same things that helped her now as Romola, when nobody thought she had the wits to be a threat or the strength to fight back. Once her fellow slaves stopped laughing at her or thinking that she was playing a dangerous and naïve joke, she was able to gather sympathizers with shocking ease, even men and women twice or thrice her age and so beaten down by a lifetime of drudgery that they had given up hoping for anything else. She was precocious, articulate, passionate, and she knew what to say to make them listen. Nobody wanted to stick their neck out at first, but they all came around in the end. Until she was twenty and she had spent seven years brewing the largest slave rebellion since Spartekaius directly under the noses of the Grassi, until she thought they would actually have a *chance* and then —

Of course they didn't. Of course it wasn't even close. Even for all the work she had done, the blood and sweat and tears, it was contemptuously flicked aside in the most casual of backhanded swipes, an insultingly perfunctory punishment. Tatyana herself, however, had not gone down easily — had fought to the end, screaming and swearing, even as her foot was crushed and her head was cracked until she went deaf in one ear — almost eager for the embrace of death, and yet —

She had forgotten. She had forgotten the warning given to her, the exquisite cruelty of her particular curse. She only had the most fragmented recollection of that first unmaking, the bubbling chemicals and the bitter tonics and the face of Grand Magister Saturnus swimming above her while his soft white fingers poked and prodded and stroked in her mouth and between her legs and in every other secret and tender spot he could find. She did not recall much of that second life, what her name was or what they told her, if she was still rebellious or quiescently obedient. It must not have been enough, though. Not when she soon found herself back in the Castel, once more subject to the Corporalists' scalpels and substances and the insistently penetrating fingers of the Grand Magister – *hold still,* he whispered in her ear, his breath reeking of sour herbs. *Hold still, my dear, a necessary examination –*

Then it happened again, and again, the full weight of those forgotten lives all crushed and crammed into Tatyana's reused skin and bone – the time where she almost welcomed the stygian blackness of Remaking and the acid froth of the alembics, gently whisking away the rape and the abuse and the whip that carved stripes on her back – the Corporalists considerately took away the scars from that incarnation, but they always left the foot and ear as they were, a mute and constant burden from life to life, so she would not forget even when she did not remember. And as it came spilling back, she did not want it at all. To be *dis*membered was one kind of violence, cut into a thousand pieces and scattered to the winds, but to *re*member – to be reassembled and returned, to have those buried traumas resurface all at once like invisible ink held up to the light – that was another sort of violence altogether, the damnation of memory enacted in reverse. *No,* she cried, voiceless and powerless, just as she had so many times before. *No, I don't want it. Stop. Stop.*

And yet even then, the remorseless cascade of recall, the tormented fruit of knowing, kept coming and coming, flooding her mouth until she choked on it. She was Romola now, a meek and quiet incarnation who nobody noticed – but even that did not protect her, it wasn't enough. The pack of bored drunk noble sons cornering her in a corridor, grinning like jackals – how she must have learned enough by then in some awful sinew of her soul to know to just close her eyes and not say a word, so it was not as bad as it could have been, and how foolishly she called that a victory. How pitiable Romola was, how cowardly, even if it was the only choice she could have made. How she bit her lip until it bled and thought herself fortunate that this cursed coupling would bear no fruit, that she had been made sterile like a spayed bitch, that there was no chance of any child like her —

She had not made a sound, not then and not after. Had gotten up at last and pulled her skirts down and went off on shaking legs to do her evening chores, and whispered that stinking sulfuric word in her own ear until she finally believed it — *lucky, lucky*. And then — in the street by the Brass Astrolabe that night, the white-toothed man and his fellows that Ionius had torn apart — yes, he saved her *then*, when it didn't matter, when it was already a hundred times too late. But she did not know and she did not recall and again she thought it — *lucky, lucky, LUCKY* —

Tatyana Sazharyna and all the other murdered women who dwelled inside her opened their mouth, so wide it seemed as if they could swallow down the world, jaws unhinged like a devouring creature of pure and perfect nightmare, and screamed, and screamed, and *screamed*.

She screamed until there was nothing left inside her, until her jaw split and folded back like a molting reptile and her skin peeled off, until there was another screaming woman with a different name but the same face, a different set of memories that had been calcified and erased. She did not recall the exact name or entire life of every person she had been in each Remaking, which was either another insult or a desperate relief. If she had to live all the time with the consciousness of every one of them, the weight of their grief and guilt, the shining hope that *this* time it would be different — right up until she was once more dragged into the Castel, tied down, and pushed back into the dark — she would lose her mind. If she had not already. If she could do anything but scream.

It went on forever, and seemed as if it would never do anything but go on forever, since the weight of what was inside her — inside *them* — could never be purged. But then at last, it began to fade, and then it faded some more, and finally there was silence, though it was difficult to tell if it was peace. She was alone in some strange grey place and did not know if she was many or if she was one. All her other-selves had evanesced, extant but not present, and she felt utterly drained, dazed and dreamy and lassitudinous, aware but not awake. She was Tatyana again — those memories were not gone altogether — and yet she was still Romola. She wondered who had given her that name, why they had chosen it, if the Corporalists had doted over each of her recreated selves in some twisted mimicry of excited parents with a newborn child. That seemed unlikely, and she did not want it anyway, especially if it meant that Grand Magister Saturnus was her father in any sense of the word. But she could, if she chose, never wake up at all, defy them one last time and reject any more incarnations, any more cycle of required deaths and remade lives, any more ability to let them hold her brother – *General Ionius* – under their thumb. She could seize back the right to choose the hour of her death, for good this time. She had suffered so much. She would be entirely justified. She could let go and never come back.

And yet. As she sat in silence, turning her variegated harlequin-mask of faces up to whatever light shone in this in-between existence, she was conscious of a dull but persistent curiosity. What it would be like to go back and have even a scrap of control over her life, the knowledge of who she really was and what she had done, and whether she could try again. She knew now that her real name was Tatyana. And Ionius – was that Ivan, as he had told her to call him before either of them knew the truth? Would she look on him with new eyes and realize that she had indeed known him all along, that connection that always puzzled her and yet had been strong enough to survive every attempt the overwhelming power of Merone had made to crush it? Even the greatest and most terrible empire the world had ever known must not be so invincible after all, if it failed to stamp out so much as the simple heart-bond between two anonymous and unremembered foreign slaves. *Merone is weak,* she realized. *Merone is powerless. In this and everything else that matters. It cannot beat so much as me, and I fought it harder than them all.*

That, then, was what made up her mind. She had spent all of her lives convinced that the empire could never be defeated – resisted, fought, accommodated and worked around, strategically ignored and carefully managed, but never *defeated,* once and for unequivocal all, because it was just too strong. But seeing it in this new light, as a stunted and scared and crippled thing far more than she had ever been – for she was not broken, she did not need to be fixed, she would bear her damaged foot and ear as marks of defiant pride, battle scars earned when she single-handedly fought the Eternal Empire of Merone *and she won* – she wanted to see what it was like to live with this knowledge. To open her eyes, and stand up, and not be afraid.

For a final moment, she remained where she was: adrift in the earth and the ether, all and none of her selves at once. If she wanted to let go, now was the moment to do so: she could slip into gentle oblivion and never be troubled again, though it was an open question what afterlife, if any, awaited her. She had no belief or love for True Tridevarianism, because she knew it only as a crass vehicle for men like Mellius Sanctus Sixtus to mount an artful defense of murder and massacre, and she felt no other archaic remnants of theological devotion. Besides, it did not matter. It was not the reward of the resting place so much as the choice of the action, the simple and ineffable exertion of her own will upon the ultimate fate of her existence. Tatyana Sazharyna had not had it since she was too young to remember her own brother's face, but now she did. And before she went off into the light, the great expanse of eternity, she wanted to know what it felt like.

She hesitated. Then she stepped forward, and opened her eyes.

At first, she thought she was still asleep, because she could see nothing whatsoever. But her whole body hurt, which was a strong if unfortunate argument in favor of its continued existence, and soot scraped her teeth and scratched her throat, tasting burned and foul on her tongue. She was still clad in the dirty rags of the fine clothes that she dimly remembered donning for her disastrous audience with Coriolane, which led in turn to her confrontation with Kronus, the revelation of her real identity, and the valiant but ultimately doomed attempt to resist him and the paralyzing drug he had given her in preparation for the sacrifice. After that, she remembered nothing whatsoever, but if she was here, awake and alive, the Grand Magister had clearly been interrupted in carrying it out. Who saved her? Had she blindly lucked out, or had he somehow failed at the final hurdle? Such a thing did not seem possible. Tatyana groped at her throat, searching for a cut or a scar of any kind, but could not find it. *What* the – ?

Slowly, as her vision returned in bits and pieces, she sat up and looked around, which only increased her confusion. She was lying in a huge heap of broken rocks and bones, and the high ceiling had been cracked into pieces, drenched in moonglow that gilded the jumbled wreckage in arrestingly beautiful geometries of light and shadow. It looked like the aftermath of a terrible tempest, and Tatyana frowned, pushing unsteadily to her feet. It was difficult to tell, but she thought it was in fact the same chamber that housed the massive bone pentacle. If so, however, it had been comprehensively destroyed, bones smashed to ivory shards and lying scattered at random with the strewn stones. Had *Kronus* done that? It didn't seem possible.

"Hello?" Tatyana called, thin and choked. She was not entirely sure she wanted to meet whoever or *what*ever was capable of inflicting that sheer level of damage, if it had been consciously done and not just a mindless accident of nature. "Is anyone – ?"

"Hello there," a voice said, and she whirled around; she had not heard any sound or seen any movement. "Finally awake, I see."

Tatyana stared at him – her – it, whatever it was. It was nominally human in appearance, but the eerie cat-shine of its luminous yellow eyes made unsettlingly clear that it wasn't. It looked mostly like a very young man with ink-black hair and dark skin, but the way the shadows moved over it made it sometimes appear older and sometimes younger, a man or a woman or neither, shifting and nebulous and changeful as flames. She looked at it, and it looked at her. Then she said, "Who are you?"

The creature seemed entertained by the question. It shrugged. "Hammadai, if you like."

The name had the flavor of some unspeakably ancient tongue, though Tatyana had no idea what. "I'm Tatyana. Where are we?"

"Come and look." Hammadai reached out a hand, which belonged in the span of a few breaths both to a stately middle-aged man and a hunchbacked old crone, and Tatyana startled. But it just laughed, a faint whisking sound like wind over water. "If I wanted to hurt you, girl, I had ample opportunity to do so while you were lying there unconscious and drooling. And like you, I too have just been given back the gift of free will for the first time in a very long while. Thousands of years, in my case. So if I did want to *choose* to hurt you, I would."

"*Thousands* of years?" Tatyana stared at its smooth and eerily timeless face, as its various personas continued to billow in and out like drifting smoke. It struck her that they might indeed have a poignant amount in common: all these different selves and existences, forcibly chained into one being and put at the service of remorseless masters. "What exactly are you?"

"That doesn't matter," Hammadai said. "But I was a slave for a very long time in all my selves and beings, just like you. For that alone, for now, you may trust me."

When it put out its hand again, Tatyana — after a final hesitation — reached out and took it. A strange lightness spread over her from head to toe and they wafted up into the air together like a pair of blowing seed-pods, up through the broken ceiling and onto a site of rocks and ruins above. The spot occupied the highest ground at the center of an unfamiliar city in the desert; it looked as if the now-destroyed pentacle chamber lay directly underground of wherever this was, which was certainly not Merone. Palm and cedar trees rustled in the night wind, and dry brown hills unfolded in neatly cultivated terraces, olive groves, and vineyards. Tatyana frowned. "Is this…?"

"Yerussala," Hammadai said. "The Holy City. Yes. Furthermore, we are on the very site of King Tselmun's great Temple, at least until it was sacked and destroyed by the ancient Meronites. Your horrible friend Grand Magister Kronus built his pentacle right below it."

"He's not my friend." Tatyana sat down. "How did you know?"

"About the Temple?" Hammadai perched next to her, its unearthly heat a strange but welcome balm against the chill of the desert night. "Because I built it. Me and hundreds of other poor saps that Tselmun enslaved especially for the purpose. But I was the only one he kept around once it was done. Lucky me, I suppose. Just too good at my job."

"That *Tselmun* enslaved — ?" All at once, it clicked. Perhaps she should be afraid, but it was too late for that, and she could not imagine being afraid again. "You're the… thing. The creature that was bound in the Ring. The one Aliyah was willing to risk everything to get back."

"*You* know Aliyah?" Hammadai cocked its head, bright-eyed as a bird. "Well, that's very interesting. Especially since you are here and she is not, which suggests you took it upon yourself to try in her place — which makes me wonder why you would ever do a foolish thing like that. But yes, I am the *thing* that has been stuck in the Ring for the last few thousand years or so, though I lost count somewhere around the second millennium. Or at least I was, until about an hour ago. If I was smart, I would have immediately crisped you all to ashes and flown away, but unfortunately, I was curious. It kills both cats and jinnyeh."

"You're free?" Startled, Tatyana squinted at its ever-shifting visage. "So you're not bound to the Ring any more? How is that possible? Did the spell just break, or — ?"

"No, it didn't just *break*. In fact, someone broke it for me, the one thing I never thought any human master would willingly do, and I still don't know what to make of it. Here."

With that, it stood up and strode back to the hole in the ground that plunged down into the wrecked cavern below, beckoning Tatyana to join it. After a moment she did so, careful to keep well back from the edge and unable to quash the brief and dishonorable fear that the jinnyeh intended to push her in. But if it was in fact free, there were many other ways to kill her, and it seemed sincere in wanting her to understand whatever this was. She peered into the subterranean ruins, following the jinnyeh's pointing finger, and finally spotted another tiny human figure far below, sprawled out among the broken stones. "Who is that?"

"His name is Julian," Hammadai said. "Julian Kozharyev, and he is the one who set me free. Unbound me from the Ring, undid Tselmun's spells, so he could trap the crazed ifrit who would have destroyed the whole bloody city and probably the world. Be glad that you were unconscious for that part. It was a sordid and terrifying spectacle."

A thousand questions sprang to mind at once, and Tatyana bit her tongue on blurting them all out. Instead she ventured, "If he's the one who saved you, shouldn't you save him?"

"See." Hammadai turned away from the hole and began to prowl over the dusty grounds of the former Temple, and Tatyana uncertainly followed it. "That's just my dilemma. Yes, human honor would dictate that I return the favor, but human honor is, in my *very* long and therefore comprehensive experience, nothing but a steaming pile of bullock excrement. I've never benefited from it, I've never been treated like someone who merits that consideration in return, and trust me, I'm not about to swooningly fall over myself and scoop his body tenderly from the ruins, just because *one* human finally did me a favor. And it wasn't even because he thought I was a mistreated slave who morally deserved its manumission, but because he needed the Ring free to trap another spirit in turn. It's true that Arghan the Undying is a nasty piece of work and Kronus should never have brought it to this plane of existence, but it doesn't mean one injustice should simply be traded for another. So here we are in Tselmun's old Temple, in Tselmun's old kingdom, while Julian has Tselmun's old Ring and has in fact made it even *more* powerful. You thought the world quivered in its underthings while I was the one running the show from the Ring – well, it did, I was *very* good at my job – but that's nothing compared to what would happen if Arghan was unleashed even once. Julian Kozharyev has everything he needs to be the new Tselmun, but orders of magnitude more powerful and destructive. Why, then, should I save him?"

Tatyana blinked. "You're asking me?"

"I don't have anyone else to confer with," the jinnyeh pointed out. "And we have a good deal in common, so I do in fact think your opinion would be useful. The irony does not escape me that I am asking a human what should be done with another human, and you might tell me to save him just for that reason. But I'm in the mood for a good argument, a rousing debate, something to stir the intellectual loins. Should I kill him or should I save him? Go on, girl. Convince me. Use your brains. I want to hear a reason for one or both."

Tatyana opened her mouth, then shut it. She could not help but be flattered that this all-powerful magical being was genuinely asking for her advice – treating her not just like a person but an *important* person. Just like Hammadai, she too had no reason to think that honor was a meaningful concept, as it had never been applied to her or privileged her or taken her into account in any way, and she did not know what Julian Kozharyev would do with his world-shaking new power. Perhaps he meant well, but surely even Tselmun once *meant well*. The gruesome memories of the torture Tatyana endured in all her incarnations were still fresh in her mind, and argued strongly against any naïve assertion of humanity's inherent goodness. If she counseled Hammadai to save Julian and it turned out he was just as much a monster as the others, it would feel like her fault. She still didn't have any idea who she was now, aside from a jumbled amalgamation of all the people she was forced to be along the way. She had chosen to come back, to wake up, to try again, but that was only a choice that could be made for herself, and would have to be made again, many times. Doubtless Hammadai would face the same struggle, now and later. So why not just close this ugly chapter for them both, and let them walk away?

"I don't know," Tatyana said at last. "I don't know why you should save him. I can't tell you if it's the right thing to do, because both of us know it's just as likely to *not* be the right thing. All I can say is that he did something that you didn't think was possible, and that no human ever would. He surprised you, even after all this time, so there's a chance that he could surprise you again. I'm sorry I can't offer anything more than that. If you choose to kill him, I'll understand. But it's what you've always done before, isn't it? With all your masters, you wanted them dead as soon as possible, but it never stopped you from being passed onto the next one and the whole cycle starting over again. It never set you free, and it never made anything different. So maybe you don't save him because he *deserves* it, because neither of us know that. Maybe you save him for you. Because you're free, and you're trying something new."

The jinnyeh regarded her shrewdly, scratching its chin. "So," it said. "That's your argument as to why we should show mercy to those who would not show it to us? For the *novelty*? Would you feel the same if it was one of your jailers? That Corporalist monster, what was his name?"

"Saturnus." A cold chill crawled down Tatyana's back, and she looked around anxiously, as if the sound alone could conjure him from the dust. "But this man isn't him, and I just want to be sure that I can still tell the difference. So…" She stopped, as a question occurred to her that clearly should have done so far sooner. "Where's Kronus?"

"Gone," Hammadai said. "Devoured by the monster he himself set loose – which, if you ask me, is truly the picture of poetic justice. He won't be personally troubling us any longer, if that's what you fear, but there's no way to be sure that it's conclusively put an end to all of his mischief. He was clearly a busy bee for a long time, here and elsewhere."

"Kronus is dead?" Tatyana felt a brief but heartfelt relief, though the jinnyeh was correct that it hardly reduced the multiplicity of ways in which they were still very likely to die. But she had been through so many deaths by now that it did not hold any remaining terror, nothing she did not know or could not handle, and she felt her lips stretching into a savage smile, the raw acknowledgment that she still drew breath and the man who tried to sacrifice her and bind her bones into his eldritch horror did not. "Good," she said firmly. "Good."

"So." Hammadai's voice and eyebrows arched in ironic unison. "You see how agreeable it feels, to know that someone who hurt you is defunct? It might not solve any grand moral conundrum or guide the path of your life forever, but it's still damn nice. And you want to deny me the same pleasure? Come on, I thought you were clever. Why?"

"I told you," Tatyana said. "I don't know for sure. I'm not going to tell you that you have no right to kill him, because you do. I have no other reason than that it's something you haven't done before, and Julian helped you, regardless of his exact motives. If you want to kill every human just because they're a human, how does that make you different from all the tyrants?"

Hammadai glared at her, and Tatyana cringed, preparing herself for some sort of retaliatory event. But she didn't back down, and at last Hammadai scowled, shoulders slumping. "Look," it said. "For what it's worth, I like the kid. I do. He's a lot more fun than most of my masters, he can think for himself, he's not beholden to dogma, and at least he's interesting. But I made that same mistake a long time ago – liking a human, that is – and look where it got me and my people. Arghan is a murderous fiery bastard, but it's not wrong that I stupidly decided to take a fancy to Tselmun ben Dayoud, trot my well-shaped hindquarters over to him and think he would be a *great* partner in the business of making a better world, and then it cost us everything. You don't think Tselmun couldn't be charming and funny and wise, humane and intelligent and thoughtful? I didn't pick him for no reason, and it wasn't as if he immediately let out a nefarious cackle and commenced doing terrible things. If we go around thinking the only monsters in the world are the ones who look like Arghan, or loudly announce their evil plans, we miss the ones lurking in plain sight, and we make constant excuses as to why they can't possibly be that bad — how can they be, when they look and act just like us? If we accepted that, we would also have to accept that there's a little bit of a monster in all of us, and *everyone* — humans and jinnyeh and the Almighty knows whatever else is unfortunate enough to be sentient in this world — will do anything to avoid that."

"So," Tatyana said. "Your solution is to get rid of everyone, like Tselmun and Coriolane, because that's better than acknowledging that little bit of monstrosity in everyone, or figuring out how to live with it, or understanding that there's a little bit of good too? All this time, and that's what you've learned? I don't think so."

"You are a stubborn human," the jinnyeh said. "But that's my fault, I encouraged it. And yes, your brother did also like Julian — though in a much different fashion than myself, which I was unfortunate enough to witness in graphic detail and even I will never be able to scour from my brilliant and eternal mind. But I'm not going to save him just because your also-monstrous brother enjoys porking him occasionally, so — "

"Wait," Tatyana interrupted, bewildered in an altogether more ordinary fashion for the first time since her reawakening. "What are you talking about — Ionius? I lived with him for the last several months, but I didn't know he was my brother. I never saw Julian, I never met him, there wasn't anyone else around. Are you sure it was him?"

"Quite," the jinnyeh confirmed, with a small wince. "Don't ask for details, I implore you."

"Fine." Tatyana thought about it a final moment, then made up her mind. "So save him."

"That's it? No more discussion, no more debate? Even if it means I run the risk of having to witness that indignity all over again?" Hammadai shuddered. "I thought we were friends."

"Maybe we are," Tatyana said. "So I won't ask for details, and you'll save Julian. Because I didn't know that I had a brother, and now I do, and the entire might of Merone never succeeded in destroying it. I choose to think that means something, and I'd like to repay the favor. So yes. I can't command you, and you're not my slave, just as I'm not yours. I'm asking you as equals."

Hammadai stared at her for a very long moment, until Tatyana's hair felt as if it was standing on end and might also light afire. Then it let out a heartfelt sigh, snapped a sardonic salute, and dove into the hole. Several minutes elapsed in ominous silence. Then a fiery glow spilled across the ground in tandem with the advancing dawn in the eastern sky, and a great winged figure rose from the abyss like an avenging chthonic angel – though the grandeur and terror was somewhat spoiled by the fact that it was in fact a large pig, clutching the unconscious Kozharyev in its trotters. It set its burden down with a disdainful oink, snapped its draconian wings out of sight, and turned to Tatyana. "Well?" it demanded. "Does this satisfy your requirements, do you think?"

"Almost." Tatyana folded her arms. "Wake him up."

Hammadai sighed once more with feeling, transformed into a shockingly accurate duplicate of General Ionius – enough to make Tatyana do a double take – and knelt next to the prone figure. "Oh, Julian," it warbled. "It is I, your true love, but please do not attempt to kiss me. That would be horribly discommodious for both of us."

With that, it poked Julian in the shoulder, once and then again, and passed a hand over his forehead, its fingers glowing with a strange light. Julian's bruised eyelids fluttered, and his chest heaved. Then his eyes flicked open and his brow crinkled in bemusement. At last he rasped, "Nice try, Khasmedeus. I know that's you."

"I take everything back. You're no fun at all." With a huff, Hammadai – Khasmedeus? – returned to its earlier assortment of human forms. "Not even a moment of wondering if your beloved maniac had come to save you?"

"No." Julian coughed with a nasty squelching sound, wiping his mouth with the back of his hand. He sat up, grimacing and peering at their surroundings and the city of Yerussala below. Then he turned, saw Tatyana, and blinked. "You're alive. I didn't know if – if you were."

"Do we know each other? I don't recall."

"No, not really. Just – by extension, though I also owe you an apology. If I had not stolen your file, and lost it, Grand Magister Kronus might not have been able to do what he did, so… I am sorry. I wish that we met in better circumstances, but so it is. I'm Julian Janovynich

Kozharyev, and you are..." He hesitated. "I don't actually know what you want me to call you."

"Tatyana will do." She shrugged. "I'm not altogether sure either."

"Excuse me," the jinnyeh broke in. "This is all very touching, but you'll have to sort out your complex interpersonal issues at a later date. If we continue to sit here atop Kronus's chamber of doom like a bunch of idiots, I can assure you someone will come scurrying up to look into it, and then we – well, you, as I don't intend to stick around this accursed city any longer than I have to – will be promptly thrown into some noisome Yerussalan penitentiary and ruin whatever tiny scrap of good you hope to do for anyone. Just a bit of free advice. You're welcome."

"Right." With a groan, Julian got to his feet. "We'll have to get out of here somehow, but you're free to go, Khasmedeus. I don't have any hold on you, and nor does the Ring. As you said, you don't want to stay, and I understand. Go."

Hammadai scowled again. "You've got something far better than me in the Ring now, don't you? One touch and you can be master of the universe forever. Don't you want it? Give it a try."

Julian frowned at the humble golden circlet on the first finger of his right hand. "You can't possibly want me to release Arghan."

"I don't," Hammadai said, "but I also know that you'll eventually give into the temptation, and it's best to get it over with while there's still a very large hole in the ground conveniently at hand to stuff you into. If I refused to help you or get you out of here or take you back to Merone or whatever else, you'd turn to your new ifrit chum, and think that you could control it, because you were able to put it in there in the first place, weren't you? Soon you'll convince yourself that it would be a dangerous waste to destroy it, because what if you need it to kill Coriolane or some other grand gesture of heroism? At best, you'll hide it in some out-of-the-way nook and hope that nobody like Diyab or Kronus comes along to sniff it out again, but they will. Something like that can't stay hidden forever. Someone will always be looking for it, and eventually, they'll find it. Then it starts all over again, and this time they'll need something more powerful than Arghan, and that means *everybody* needs something more powerful than Arghan, because how can you protect yourself from a guaranteed world-ending weapon unless you have one too? As soon as you start that boulder rolling downhill, there is no way to put it back. And I play the careless and carefree magical creature of fortune, but I saw that happen once before, to my own people, and you know what? You don't want to see it happen to yours."

Julian looked startled. "Yes," he said, after a loaded pause. "Yes, I agree. There is no way to ever use this kind of power without causing an even greater cataclysm, and I don't intend to do so. And if you don't want to help us, you don't have to. As I said, I know you don't want to stay in Yerussala, and I don't blame you. Go on, Khasmedeus. Be free."

"I *would*," the jinnyeh said peevishly. "I really would. Except then I would leave you two fools diddling about with your thumbs up your arses, and you're a Vashemite and it's very important to you to be here in the Holy City since the Meronites chucked your lot out the last time, and you'd give into the urge to sightsee, and then you would get arrested and someone else without your shining scruples would get their grubby paws on it. Same problem when you die, which will clearly happen *very* soon, because you have absolutely horrible judgment. I've told you before, haven't I? Well, never hurts for a refresher. *Horrible* judgment."

"Well, then." Despite the seriousness of the situation, Julian seemed to be biting his cheek. "If you don't want that, what are you going to do about it? I'm not trying to manipulate you, by the way. But if you wanted me dead, you would have left me in that hole forever, so you must have had a reason to pull me out. You can tell me later, if you want. Otherwise, we need to go." He looked at Tatyana. "Coming?"

"Of course." She hobbled over to him, feeling an unexpected pride in her limited gait, the cramp in her foot, the way it never balanced properly under her weight. This was *her,* this was the victory the first Tatyana Sazharyna had won against Merone in blood and fire, and while she was not that Tatyana, she still wanted that memento of who she was and what it had cost. "I don't know how much use I'll be, but I will."

Julian gave her a small, crooked grin. "We can take our chances."

With that, both of them turned expectantly to Hammadai – Khasmedeus – whatever its name was. Likely, once more the same as Tatyana-Romola, it was many. It looked back at them with patent exasperation, then threw its hands and eyes heavenward in abject resignation. "Fine," it said. "So I'm stuck babysitting you two juvenile delinquents until we figure out what to do about the crazy ifrit in the Ring, is that it? Which is a mess that you and Kronus, but especially you, very much caused, so I don't see why it's my job to mop it up. *Why* did you even bother to release me from my eternal bondage, if this was my reward? Could have just dropped me in Coriolane's iron chamber pot and clap on a silver lid. Really drive the point, or the shit, home."

Julian was unmoved by the jinnyeh's melodramatic postulation. "As I said," he pointed out. "One more time. You can go, and nobody will make you stay. But if you want to help us – if you want to make up for the guilt is still driving you, what you want to fix from when you failed so badly with Tselmun – you can do that too. As a free creature, not a slave. You said that every time the Ring passed to a new master, you were forced to make everything worse. What if you didn't have to do that this time? What if you got to try something new?"

Hammadai chewed its tongue in stony silence. Then it sighed again, releasing a cloud of sparks. "Teach me to hang out with humans," it muttered. "All *sorts* of stupid things."

"So." Julian smiled. "Are you coming?"

"You know." Hammadai slinked closer, its shadow stretching over the parched earth in a thousand faces and a thousand shapes – but still, even as Tatyana was after so long, finally and fully itself, nothing more and nothing less. "It turns out that I am."

CHAPTER

33

Aliyah

Coriolane had gone mad. At the moment, she remembered very little else, but she remembered that: his grotesque new face leering over her and shining like a horrible sun, the strong waxy hands that held her down, the moist mouth with its sharp teeth that bit at her face and neck and the scratchy tongue that licked as eagerly as a man lost in the desert, blind with heat and thirst, until he finally found the oasis that was his saving grace. Except she was that oasis, her blood and bone its salvific succor, and though she tried to fight, she was paralyzed. Perhaps he had grown tired of her resistance, or it had always been his plan, or it was the only use he saw remaining. She could not piece together what had happened between the moment when he proudly announced himself to be Remade and this tarred, smudged, agonizing half-awareness, except for the methodical and patient and pitiless devouring. Her cheek ached like it had been ripped out by a wild animal, as if her jaw and throat and teeth were stripped bare, flesh and cartilage and bone all torn to shreds. Perhaps it had been.

There was someone above her, urgently calling her to wake up, but Aliyah resisted. For one thing, it had to be yet another trick because the voice sounded like Elemai, and she knew for a fact that Elemai wasn't here. She was back in Qart-Hadesht with the rest of their burned city and broken families, and there was no reason for her to pursue Aliyah all the way to Merone. Not when she had no surety that Aliyah was still alive, it was a golden opportunity for them to arrest and execute her too, and even if by an absurd coincidence she *was* here (which she wasn't), she too would be trapped by Coriolane's insatiable and awful new hunger. While Aliyah was still very angry with the ur-Tasvashtas, that did not extend to wishing her wife eaten too, and a muted concern cut into her obstinate determination to remain unconscious. The voice did sound very much like Elemai, more than her abused memory should be able to conjure. Surely she wasn't *actually* – ?

Either way, the summoning was now very insistent, and she could not shut it out any longer. Greatly against her will, she rose higher, then higher again, until she was at the very cusp of waking, and strange sounds and shadows tattooed themselves painfully against her closed eyelids, making her abused head hurt even more. She moved one shoulder in a pitiful spasm, trying to raise an arm and bat the disturbance away, but her discombobulated and disembodied flesh was not interested in obeying. But someone's hands still pushed at her, refusing to let her rest in peace, and there was nothing else to be done. She cracked her eyes the tiniest fraction, and uttered a raw and ragged groan. Then, before she was fully awake or knew what was going on or could attempt to preserve her dignity, she turned away, gagged, and vomited like a volcano.

"Gently," that voice that sounded so beguilingly and misleadingly like Elemai urged, a hand settling on her back and patting comfortingly, as if she was a colicky infant. "Aliyah, look at me. It's me. I'm here."

"No, you're not," Aliyah muttered. "I know you're not. This is another trick."

"It's not a trick." Another hand dabbed a cloth to the chewed-open sores on her cheeks, which still stung like absolute damnation. "I should have come sooner. We did our best, but – "

"Wait." Aliyah's eyelashes were stuck together with blood and ooze, but she summoned up a final effort of will and wrenched them open, staring into the shocked and desperately relieved face of indeed – if it was not an extremely detailed and feverish hallucination – Elemai bet Safiya ur-Tasvashta, looking more human and dirty and disheveled than Aliyah's perpetually elegant bride had ever been before. They stared at each other, as Aliyah blinked hard and yet failed to scrub away this implausible visitation. "You're... wait. You're *here?*"

"Yes." Elemai's voice cracked with relief, and she gathered Aliyah in a brief, convulsive, and too-tight embrace, knocking her breath out again. "It's a long story. Your mother had to step out, but she'll be back, or at least I hope. But we're here in Merone. We came to rescue you. We should never have doubted that you'd be strong enough to survive."

Aliyah wanted to ask if that meant they *had* first doubted her, but now was not the time for such uncharitable questions, and Elemai had said something that was even more unbelievable. "My *mother?* You – you mean Zadia?" Of course it could be no other, as the reminder assailed her yet again that Noora was dead and it was her fault, but it still seemed impossible. Why would Zadia ur-Namasqa risk everything to travel to Merone on a profoundly doomed mission to rescue *Aliyah?* Yes, she was the family's eldest daughter and heiress, and there was a political element to saving her from imprisonment and execution. As well, perhaps Zadia felt it to be a personal insult on her own honor, or she had been made aware of Coriolane's claim of paternity and felt it needed proper redress. Any or all of these explanations seemed more likely than that she had come for Aliyah sheerly out of tender maternal love. *If she is in fact Coriolane's daughter, it explains a great deal.*

Still, nor was it the moment for old bitterness – especially if Zadia had, regardless of reasons, finally taken such an absurd gamble on her behalf. Aliyah looked around as if expecting to spot her mother skulking behind a potted plant, but the only thing she saw was a large bundle of knots and cords. She stared at it, then back at Elemai. "What the...?"

"Ah." Elemai coughed. "We had no other way of detaining His Majesty, while your mother and General Ionius went to look for the Ring. It was rather... improvisational."

"Amma and *General Ionius* are working togeth – ?!" Clearly Aliyah had missed a great deal of truly shocking developments, and if there had been any more time or any less urgency, she would have demanded Elemai give a full accounting at once. But as there was not, Aliyah regretfully had to turn to more pressing issues. "Never mind. Elemai, listen, you have to understand. Coriolane – he's done something completely monstrous, he told me that — that he was Remade. That he died and then was brought back with whatever awful process the Corporalists do to all the other ones, but so much stronger. There's nothing that can hurt or harm him, and if so — "

"Yes, I know," Elemai interrupted, the two of them talking over each other. "Earlier, your mother stabbed him, and it didn't do anything, I had to knock him out, but that is only temporary. If Saeda Zadia and the general can't find the Ring — "

"And you trust him?" Aliyah looked down at her hands, wondering whether she dared try to summon the enspelled metal again. "I did meet his — mistress, Romola, and she said he had asked her to help me. She likewise tried her best, but can we really believe that the Scourge of Sciatello is on our side? Aren't Immortals known for weaseling their way into your confidence, convincingly play-acting and concealing their true identity, before unveiling themselves to strike?"

"I don't know." Elemai's lips went thin. "If it was up to me, I would still have killed him for what he did to my mother, but he freed us and brought us here to the emperor's chambers, to find you and fight Coriolane. If he did want to betray us, there were many chances."

Aliyah supposed that was so, and with the situation as dire as it was, they were hardly in any position to start picking and choosing among their very thin roster of allies, tentative or otherwise. It did seem that Ionius was far from their biggest problem, at least, and she grimaced as another bolt of pain scythed through her damaged face. "Elemai," she said. "Do I look — how bad is it?"

"It's..." Elemai hesitated, eyes flicking to the ravages of Coriolane's bites and then away. "Well, I'm sure we can get it to heal."

This was not encouraging, though they likewise had far more pressing matters at hand than Aliyah's vanity, but just then, they were interrupted by an outbreak of violent jerks and incoherent swearing from the tied-up bundle. It heaved and thrashed, inching its way across the parquet floor, and the cords strained as Coriolane fought against them with the full force of his inhuman new strength. If he had been unconscious before, he was not now, and Aliyah and Elemai scrambled jointly to their feet, frantically casting around for something to return him to said state as soon as possible. But before they could, the emperor tore through the heavy brocaded fabric as if it was no more than wet paper, peeled it off like a chrysalis, and rose to his feet, panting and pale-faced and looking more insane than ever. "Well," he snarled. "That was an interesting interlude, to say the least, but not one I am presently in any temper to appreciate. I was generous beyond all measure to you, and this is how you repay me? If you continue to thwart and spurn me like the heathen ingrates you are, that is how I must deal with you, in the only crude and violent language you understand. Lady Aliyah, this is your last chance. Will you accept my gracious offer, take up the birthright you are foolishly throwing aside, and work at my side for my eternal rule and the perpetual glory of Merone, or not?"

Aliyah's mouth worked, but no sound came out. She wanted to back away, but her feet were frozen, her blood banging in her ears and in the scars of her mutilated face. At last, though it cost every curdled drop of courage she had left, she whispered, "No."

"So be it." Coriolane's jagged slash of a mouth twisted in withering scorn. "Well then, my dearest granddaughter. You are as paramount a disappointment to me as were all your predecessors, and that is indeed a pity. But you are only beginning to learn the full cost of insubordination to me, your patriarch and your progenitor, your sole and sovereign master in every way that matters. First, we must teach this insolent Qartic whore, this stunted scion of polluted and traitorous blood, her rightful lesson. Watch, my child. Watch and learn."

Aliyah opened her mouth again in some wild expectation of a scream – just as Elemai lunged madly at Coriolane. But the emperor made a gesture with both hands as if he was snapping something in half, there was a horrible sound that echoed against the stones and tiles and columns of this beautiful and civilized room, and Elemai collapsed as if her spine had indeed been broken. She let out an agonizing howl, more like an animal than a woman, writhing and sobbing in mindless pain as blood leaked from her mouth and nose and her eyes began to flood a poisoned black. Coriolane regarded her with cruel amusement, drinking in her suffering as if it was a fine bouquet, and Aliyah only then became aware that the other person screaming was her. "Stop," she begged.

"Please, please stop. Please! Stop! I'll listen, I'll – I'll cooperate! Just – stop hurting her!"

Coriolane looked at her goadingly. "I'm sorry, my dear? I don't believe I heard you."

"I'll… I'll listen to you." Aliyah's chest hurt as terribly as if she had been the one tortured, the words torn out of a deep and shameful core. "I'll obey you. Please."

Coriolane considered, then finally lowered his hand, and Elemai jerked one last time and fell still, her eyes open and staring glassily at the ceiling. She was breathing, at least, but in such stilted and agonizing bursts that it was not at all clear if she would continue to do so. Aliyah wanted to run to her, but there was no chance. Coriolane stepped forward, took hold of her arm, and led her out of the room. The heavy door swung shut like the sealing of a sepulcher, and she was alone.

They descended the stairs in utter silence, except for Aliyah's rasping breathing and the tectonic rise and fall of Coriolane's footsteps, as if he had become a mountain instead of a man, or something old and hungry and awful that had heaved itself up out of the earth and was now on an inexorable march to devastate and devour the rest. When they reached the bottom, he turned left and pulled her along a corridor that was strewn with sprawled and lifeless bodies: servants, stewards, eunuchs, slaves, nobles, priests, senators, Meronites of every rank and class and occupation. It was ghastly clear that Coriolane had drained them all at once, gulped in their life force like a precious elixir, and that was the source of his awful and unchallengeable new vivacity, the cumulative sum of thousands of stolen souls. The sheer horror of it numbed Aliyah's brain and heart to ice, but her feet kept walking, as they turned a final corner and beheld a pair of towering doors carved with the great legendarium of Merone, the myths and stories and heroes that animated every history Aliyah had ever learned, even her own. Coriolane gazed at it, misty-eyed. Then he pushed the doors open, and they stepped inside.

The chamber beyond was huge, dim, and cold as a tomb, but Aliyah knew at once what it was. It was the throne room: the heart of the Eternal Palace and the Meronite Empire, the sanctum sanctorum that contained the massive golden chair under its curtained cloth-of-gold baldachin, the seat so solemn that even Coriolane himself only sat in it upon the most august of occasions. Even the empresses sat in two smaller thrones on a lower dais, so there would be no confusion as to who reigned forever atop the pyramid of power, the one and only master of the world. Coriolane seized Aliyah by the scruff of the neck and hauled her onward like a misbehaving puppy, until her shins barked against the edge and forced her flat on her face. "Look," the Divine Emperor hissed. "Look what belongs to you, what you are rejecting, but where you will sit one day, by your own will or otherwise. I am not insane, my child, but you are. For who, offered such a brilliant and shining destiny, all the power in the universe, would turn it *away?*"

Briefly and uselessly, Aliyah tried to struggle, but he twisted his other hand in the stubble of her hair and yanked her head back until her neck strained. Her eyes watered with pain, a whimper escaped her lips, and he dragged her bodily up the steps until they stood in touching distance of the throne, its spellbinding power seeming to radiate outward in tangible waves. "Now," he breathed. "You will submit to me, once and for all. Kneel and accept your inheritance. *Kneel."*

He was behind her and above her at once, pushing her down with almighty strength as the stone bit into her knees and her wrists twisted, her neck burned, blood dripped from the open sores on her face and she could taste it coagulating in her throat and threatening to make her retch again. It was some twisted parody of power, where she was being forced onto a throne against her will and Coriolane was determined to keep her there until it took, until her final threads of resistance snapped and it became inevitable, until it molded into her flesh and bone and could not be sundered by any force known to men or gods. She had nothing left, no weapon – except the only thing that she had in the pit, and which she had chosen to use. To stand up, to live, to climb. To *win.*

Coriolane could not see her hands, pinned awkwardly against the steps, but Aliyah could. She looked at them, took a deep breath, and focused with all her might on drawing out the Immortal metal that Ionius had put into her for whatever point and purpose. Until her fingertips shone with sharp steel claws, she pulled one hand free and then the other, and knew that she had only one chance, one final instant – this, and no other. She let herself go limp enough that Coriolane relaxed his grip, finally confident that she was broken. Then when she was sure that he was reveling in his utter and ultimate victory, she called on every strength she had ever known and every person she was – Zadia, Khaldun, and Noora's child, Elemai's wife, Safiya's protégé, Khasmedeus's master and even Coriolane's granddaughter, a Qartic Wahin daughter of the desert and heiress of King Tselmun and Queen Daeda, all her foremothers and all her people, but still just herself, enough in this one self and in need of no other, Aliyah bet Zadia ur-Namasqa – and struck.

It was as fast, clean, and brutal as she could ever have prayed, as if the Hierophant himself, blessings on his memory, had been with her and given her every divine assistance that could be channeled into mortal flesh. Coriolane uttered a bestial howl and staggered backwards, his left cheek lacerated and leaking turgid black sludge; she was braced for it to instantly close over as if nothing had happened, but it seemed that Immortal metal, charged with the same Corporalist magic that had Remade his horrible new body, was the one thing that could truly hurt him. Aliyah took merciless advantage, springing to her feet and slashing him again. This blow took him across the other cheek, opening another gouged set of claw marks that exuded the same foul un-blood. He spit and swore and stumbled. "Where?" he snarled. "Where did you get – ?"

"It doesn't matter." Just as breathless, Aliyah straightened up. "I told you before. *I said no.*"

Coriolane's face went blank, as if this was such an incomprehensible concept that he had never heard its like, and only the truly and incorrigibly insane would ever even think of it. Nobody refused him, not in anything anywhere, and if they did, they died wishing and pleading and begging that they had been so wise as to obey. He opened his mouth and then shut it, as he at last was the one utterly lost for words. At last he said, almost plaintively, *"Why?"*

Now that, Aliyah thought, was something she had neither time nor inclination to explain. She started to circle him, looking for a chance to land the final blow; both of them were wounded, staggering and slow, and while he was shocked by her audacity, he was still an extremely formidable foe, damaged but not downed. The throne loomed at their backs, silent and patient, as if to wait and see which of them would survive to climb upon it, to take its due one way or the other. For a moment, Aliyah did feel an unhinged desire to do just that, for Coriolane to actually see her in the one place he had guarded to literal death and beyond, which he had sworn no one else would occupy again except as a temporary stooge and steward for him. That was all she would be, even if she let herself give into the delusion that she was the Divine Empress in her own accord and that her ascent to power meant anything except for her craven willingness to bow down to him. If she killed him now and stepped to the throne over his corpse – it was how succession had often worked in the bad old days, when emperors could come and go within the same year or month (or in the unfortunate case of Aeonius IV, the same *week*). But it would cement her as just another bloody-handed usurper, and regardless of what her awful grandsire thought, she had not come to rule Merone. She had come to see it *burn*.

With that, Aliyah took one more violent swing at Coriolane, her steel claws shining like heavenly fire in the first faint morning light that spilled down from the high arches. He ducked, but not fast enough, and she felt the tear as it opened his throat, a gruesome splatter of sludge flying in her wake. He stared at her with something like bemusement, as if he did not understand what had just happened. Then he sank to his knees, clutching his ruined neck as more black ichor bubbled through his fingers. He made awful croaking noises, but couldn't form words. Even so, he still didn't look as if he was in fact dying. Severely wounded, yes, and perhaps enough of that foul stuff would eventually leak out and seal his fate, but not fast enough, and not before he could –

Coriolane took a blinded and clumsy swipe at her as Aliyah leapt backward, whereupon she stumbled against the dais and smacked painfully onto the stone floor. Both on all fours, bleeding and battered and winded, they locked eyes as if to muster the final capacity to charge, to wrestle to death beneath the cold and imperious gaze of the breaking dawn. Coriolane gurgled something else, spitting a mouthful of black filth onto the floor, and Aliyah braced herself. *Now. It must be now.*

That, therefore, was when the great doors at the far end of the throne room once more flew open, and three figures appeared in chilly silhouette. Aliyah spotted them before Coriolane did, and when she recognized who it was, her heart sank like a stone dropped into deep water. She did not know why they had forsworn their golden chance to flee to Coriolanople, if it had been a ruse all along or they simply decided that they were unable to miss such a world-shaking opportunity, but so it was, as Gheslyn Aurea dropped to her knees beside her stricken husband. "My darling," the senior empress said, in tones of what almost did sound like genuine concern. "What is this?"

"Please forgive us," Empress Vestalia added, moving to Coriolane's other side and likewise kneeling. "We have done you poorly in the past, but that is over. We have all been married too long for such petty rivalries and jealousies to divide us, when it is more important than ever that we stand against our enemies. If you will have us back, we shall return to your side and uphold your rule as devotedly as we ever did. Look what we brought, as a token of goodwill. The filthy bitch who stole our letters and plotted with the traitor General Ionius to fabricate your hatred for us in the first place. It was all just an evil lie. We're home now. *Home.*"

Coriolane bared his stained teeth in a snarl, at the same time Aliyah saw the third person with the empresses. It was – no, it couldn't be, but it was – it was Romola, still wearing the fine clothes she had donned to go and try to steal the Ring from the emperor in the first place. They were filthy and soot-stained and generally ruined, Romola herself looked as if she had been through no less dread an ordeal, and Aliyah stared at her in frantic confusion, trying to understand if Gheslyn and Vestalia had been lying in wait to craftily seize the slave girl all along. Where was Belsephorus? What was going *on?!* The empresses who had plotted for this long against their husband, appearing from nowhere to beg his notoriously nonexistent clemency? Were they so stupid, so utterly blind, as to think he would ever grant it?

For his part, Coriolane seemed torn between fury and vindication, as if he had always known his treacherous wives would come crawling back and he would take his sweet time about even pretending to consider it. He spat something else that was impossible to understand, breath whistling through the shreds of his throat, and Gheslyn reached out and wrapped her hands around it. "Coriolane," she breathed. "Come now."

Vestalia was still prostrated on the floor, in an apparent posture of total submission, but as Aliyah kept staring, unsure if she should intervene, she saw the junior empress's hand start to move. She had a stick of black grease-chalk and was drawing something on the floor, out of sight of everyone except for Aliyah, and as Vestalia looked up, their eyes met and the junior empress shook her head. *Quiet. Not a word.*

For a long moment, the throne room was almost silent, except for Coriolane's awful splutters and hisses and Gheslyn murmuring mindless comfort. Then Vestalia jerked her head at Romola, who likewise knelt at Coriolane's other side. "Your Majesty. I too have wronged you beyond all description, and while your wrath is great, I would merit it if it was still more. I confess that it was all a lie, that I was ordered by General Ionius to falsify evidence against the empresses for his own foul purposes, and went along with it in fear of my life. It is nothing to amend the sin I have committed, but I regret it with my whole heart."

Aliyah opened her mouth, then stopped. She could see now that Romola was also drawing, matching whatever Vestalia was doing, and it struck her what it was; she recognized it from Safiya's lessons. It was a rune-circle of the sort customarily used to summon jinnyeh, and Romola and Vestalia were marking it out to fully enclose Coriolane, while Gheslyn distracted him with wifely bromides and cooing promises of vengeance. Then she looked up, and as the senior empress's eyes flashed an uncanny yellow, Aliyah's jaw dropped. *It can't be – ?*

Sudden realization swam in her knocked-about head, the shocking adumbration of an impossible suspicion. Seized by desperate inspiration, she too approached the mute emperor and knelt down, pressing her forehead to the ground as if in prayer. "I too have wronged you," she murmured, and felt Romola push a stub of chalk into her fingers. "I was driven mad, I was not myself. Grandfather, do not hold it against me. You would want me to fight for Merone."

Coriolane looked at her with baleful eyes, rasping some disdainful-sounding response and choking on the gore that flooded his mouth. As he did so, Aliyah scratched furiously, imploring the shade of Safiya ur-Tasvashta to look down from the afterlife and guide her hand, to join her runes up with Romola on one side and Vestalia (or was it Vestalia?)

on the other and hope there was not one tiny flaw that would invalidate the entire construction. *She insisted that if I was to use this magic, I had to know how to make it, to put it together on my own and not merely as an artifice of others. She took a great deal from me, perhaps, but I owe her for that.*

In a few moments, Aliyah's runes bumped into Vestalia's as Romola's linked up with hers, and as if at a signal, all three women leapt backward – as Gheslyn, with a sudden dexterity that an eternally middle-aged empress was unlikely to be capable of in the normal course of things, likewise sprang up and away, her form blurring and shifting. She landed on a candelabra in the shape of a handsome red-tailed hawk, yellow eyes lambent with triumph. *"Well,"* she crowed, but it was no longer Gheslyn's voice. "That was *very* neat, I'd say."

"Khas – " It felt impossible. "Khasmedeus, is that – is that *you?*"

"In the flesh. Or whatever." The hawk swept a flourishing bow. "And before you ask, no, I don't know where the horrible hags actually are. Probably halfway to Coriolanople and galloping for all their selfish backsides are worth. What nightmare have you gotten into while I've been gone? No, scratch that, it'll have to wait. I do love me a nice juicy chinwag, but there simply isn't time."

"What the…" Aliyah stared at Vestalia, who likewise looked quite different from a moment ago. "Hold on a – Julian? Julian Kozharyev? What just – ? Were you – ?"

"No, I don't know if I *was* a woman, or I just *looked* like a woman." The young Vashemite glanced critically down the bodice of his gown. "Either way, I have questions."

"Shut it, pervert," Khasmedeus ordered, which was perhaps not the highest of high grounds from whence to issue such a declaration. "Still on the job here. As for you, O Mistress, you bashed Coriolane up a bit, but as he doesn't appear to be *quite* dead, is that his failing or yours?"

"I don't know." Aliyah struggled to think straight. "I can't kill him. We *all* tried several times, but he said that he was Remade, and – "

Romola and Julian exchanged a sharp look. *"Remade?* But – "

"Right, I see." Khasmedeus surveyed Coriolane grimly. "You've really cocked this up and no mistake. There's nothing that can destroy the absolute profane abomination he is now. Nothing, that is, except one thing. Oh, Tselmun's hairy ballsack, I *knew* this was going to happen."

"Elemai," Aliyah burst out. "She's here, Coriolane attacked her, she's still up in his quarters. I don't know if she's alive or dead, I can't go without her. She said my mother – Saeda Zadia – was here, and so was General Ionius – they were looking for the Ring of Tselmun, but – "

"Ah." Julian held up his hand. "Small problem. I have it, technically speaking. But it's not the same object it was before, and any further releasing of the spirit that is now inside it will be *very* bad. You can thank our late friend Grand Magister Kronus for that."

"What do you mean?" Aliyah demanded. "Why can't we use it?"

"Now, girl," Khasmedeus scolded. "You weren't keen to do it before, remember? Unless your insane grandfather – is that *really* what you said? – managed to turn you into the same sort of power-hungry maniac in the last week, I don't see why this is any – "

"Of course I remember." Aliyah spun around to look at Coriolane, who had sunk to his knees, black ichor spilling heavily from the ragged holes in his throat. He was unable to step out of the rune-circle that Julian, Aliyah, and Romola had bound him in, but his face burned with unholy hatred. It was unthinkable that they could just leave him like this – if someone else came in, found him here, and rubbed out the runes, he would be set free to resume his reign of increasingly literal terror. "But you said there was something that *could* kill him. We don't have any more time. We need to know it now. Tell us, Khasmedeus. Please."

Khasmedeus looked exceedingly reluctant, ruffling its feathers, as Julian and Romola joined Aliyah in staring at it pointedly. At last, it heaved a sigh. "As it happens, yes. We do have a power in our possession that could permanently destroy this… thing. Anyone guessed?"

"Ah, fuck," Julian said, grasping it first. "Ifrit fire. That's it, isn't it."

"Ding ding ding." Khasmedeus pretended to applaud. "Just as I said, you idiots were always going to unleash Arghan again, for some exalted reason or another. But if Kronus's entire bone pentacle couldn't hold it, that thing – " it tilted its head at the impromptu rune circle – "doesn't have a chance in hell. If you tried to use it to restrain Arghan, etcetera and so forth world destroyed, all our valiant efforts sent straight down a large and shit-smelling direction. So that's your choice. Release Arghan, kill Coriolane and everyone else, or don't. The world is saved, and so is the Divine Emperor. Seems bad, but that's the deuce of it. Literally."

"We can't leave him alive," Romola said, her voice hard and level. Gone was the shy slave girl who had rescued Aliyah in the marketplace, the general's diffident consort, and it seemed as if someone else entirely was looking out through her eyes. "We have to find a way."

At that Coriolane, hearing them discuss his execution as if he was nothing more than a common prisoner, uttered a strangled roar and lurched to his feet, staggering toward the edge of the circle and getting knocked backward by an invisible blast of energy. He struggled upright, baring his teeth and trying again. While the runes once more held, it was troublingly apparent that he could in fact weaken them, find the gaps and the flaws and get free. If that happened – it had been a terrible fight to get him in there in the first place, he was certainly not going to be fooled by any repeat of Khasmedeus and Julian's masquerade, and Aliyah could feel every one of her hurts and injuries and weaknesses. She couldn't fight him to a standstill again, and then they would die.

The silence hung huge and fathomless. Then Romola said, "What if someone got into the circle with him? That way, both the runes and the Ring could control Arghan for longer than just one of them. At least long enough to kill Coriolane, and then – "

"Whoever got in that circle would die," Khasmedeus pointed out. "You know that, yes?"

Uneasy looks were exchanged, as Coriolane – more deranged and monstrous than ever – made a third charge. That startled everyone out of their collective stupor, and seemed to make up Julian's mind. "Fine," he said quietly. "I have the Ring. I'll do it."

"What? You?" Khasmedeus looked askance at him. "Then again, safely burning you up before you can become the new Tselmun might be a positive. Very difficult to say, but – "

"No," Aliyah broke in. "I was the original Ringbearer, and I promised, Khasmedeus, that I would set you free. My family back in Qart-Hadesht is probably all dead, and so is my wife. I started this, I'll finish it. Give me the Ring, and I'll do it."

"You really all have heroic death wishes?" Khasmedeus squinted at them narrowly. It was difficult to tell beneath the jinnyeh's customary insouciance, but it seemed almost troubled, as if this was not quite as satisfying as it had imagined. "Mind you, Elemai is a total pain in the arse, but we don't know that she's actually snuffed it. Be a bit awkward if you roasted yourself and then she came down looking for you, yeah?"

"Why does that matter to you?" Aliyah faced it down. "You told me that you couldn't wait to see me dead, the same as all your masters."

"Yeah, I did." The hawk hesitated. "Except it turns out that you and Kozharyev have been, I dunno – all right, *different*. There, I choked it out. And while I still don't understand why you're willing to throw away your one precious life on all this nonsense, it may just be the case that you two dying would, in fact, be a loss for the world. I said that it didn't matter if Coriolane died, since there would just be a new tyrant, but... maybe it does. Maybe even if you can't get rid of all the evil that has been and will be, you can get rid of *this* one, and that matters. Argh, listen to me. I've become a maundering sentimental moron. Horrible."

Julian and Aliyah blinked in unison, equally startled. Then Romola said, "If I chose to do it – to finish what Tatyana started, an escape from the endless cycles of death and Remaking, a final claim of my own destiny and control – that would be all right, I think. I wouldn't mind."

"Almighty!" Khasmedeus threw up its wings in exasperation. "I can't keep *any* of you from hankering for a splendid suicide? Is there nothing else you can think of to do with your lives, rather than setting yourself ablaze for whatever martyred reason? Trust me, it isn't fun to burn to death, and for you – yes, even the ones repeatedly meddled with by the Corporalists – it's not something that can be reversed. You think it's the right thing to do for now, which it might be, but there's nothing else you can do after that. Kaput. Crap-all. Nadam. Nothing. Nullus. The end. You're young and stupid enough to think that's an acceptable sacrifice, but it's only because you're humans and your tiny brains haven't grasped any way to demonstrate your convictions other than asking to pointlessly die for them. And much as it pains me to say this, once upon a time I too was an idealistic fool who thought I could change the world for the better. We all saw how that worked out, but perhaps my chance hasn't entirely passed by. I fucked things up with Tselmun, and it's haunted me for three thousand years, give or take a millennium. You don't think *I* deserve to be the one who does this to Coriolane?"

"Wait – " As the shocking truth dawned on her, Aliyah stared at the jinnyeh. "You want to die to save us? When you insisted yourself blue that nothing matters, and especially not us?"

Khasmedeus opened its beak as if to shoot back its customary rejoinder, but didn't. There was an immense silence, as Coriolane snarled and gibbered. Then the jinnyeh said, "Well, if you put it like that, it does make me sound like quite a chump. But as you pointed out, we made a deal, all the way back in Yerussala. You wanted to free your people and I wanted to free mine – at least what remains of us – and in both cases, that meant getting rid of the Meronites. Besides, I can hold off an ifrit for much longer than any of you, and that gives us a better chance of finishing the job. I also don't know for sure that I'll *die* die – after all, I too am a higher spirit of eternal fire, whereas you are useless sacks of very mortal flesh. If myself and the Ring and Arghan and Coriolane all burn together – that kills quite a few birds with the same stone, eh? And besides, I still don't think you'll do it. Because if you did give the Ring to me, I would finally be its master instead of its slave. There's nothing saying I *have* to use it the way you asked, and maybe I wouldn't. I could unleash Arghan on the lot of you or even wipe out the entire human race, its cities and its rulers, its culture and its memory, just like Tselmun wiped out the jinnyeh. And you talk a good game about your exalted ideals, but you wouldn't do that. You would never put your entire fate, your people, and your future in my hands alone."

Aliyah looked urgently at Julian. They really did not have time to debate this any more; the runes were smudged, Coriolane was tearing at the circle with wild, wolfish intent, and in another moment he would be free. Julian looked back at her, the two Ringbearers united in the knowledge that this was the fulcrum on which it all balanced, where they had to choose whether to trust in everything they had ever been taught about the world, or turn it upside down. There was no third choice, no way to meet halfway or split the bill. One or the other. All or nothing.

A final, frozen instant elapsed, which took both forever and no time at all. Then at Aliyah's fractional nod, Julian seized the Ring and wrenched it off his hand. "Here," he said, holding it out to Khasmedeus. "Take it. Our lives and our world are yours to do with as you please."

Khasmedeus goggled at him. It seemed briefly and utterly convinced that this was a terrible trick, one final double-cross and salt in the wound, as if humans had not already crushed its dreams and destroyed its people often enough before. Everyone held their breaths; the world itself stood still. Then the jinnyeh transformed into the stately ancient king it had been in the groves of Yerussala the first time. It reached out, and after thousands of years of imprisonment and suffering, its ageless face and fiery eyes lambent with savage glee, it took the Ring of Tselmun for its own.

Something shuddered in the fabric of the fundament, an invisible bolt of lightning that slashed the world in half, a before and after in which nothing would again be as it was. Khasmedeus slid the Ring onto its smoky finger, teeth bared in a madly triumphant smile, eyeing them up like tasty specimens on a banquet platter. Aliyah reached out for Julian's hand on one side and Romola's on the other, and the three of them clutched tight, braced for the killing blow. Khasmedeus had said so many times that it wanted them dead as soon as possible, that this was its only entertainment, that it believed in nothing and answered to no one – and if it did choose to strike them down, it was difficult to say that it was unjustified. The jinnyeh openly luxuriated in the possibility, admiring the Ring as if nothing else mattered in the world. Then it looked up at Aliyah and let out a regretful sigh. "You know, I never did get the chance to properly tell you the story. When I hurled Tselmun into the Mad ar-Hahrat and ruled for forty days and forty nights in his place. If we do ever see each other again, you should ask me for the tale. In the meantime, however, I have another tyrant to throw into an altogether hotter ocean, and this time, mark my words, I intend to finish the job. And if I meet Tselmun in hell, I'll kick the old bastard in the arse once more for good measure and hand over Coriolane personally. Farewell."

With that, Khasmedeus whirled around, strode to the circle, and regarded the deranged, drooling revenant of the Divine Emperor with arch disgust. Then it shrugged, tipped a sardonic salute over its shoulder, and slid through the runes, fluid as falling water. It wrapped itself around Coriolane, tangling their limbs together and flowing into his mouth, as the emperor choked and cursed. Then a bloom of fire lit deep in his throat, igniting his eyes like embers and shining like an exploding star beneath his foul flesh, and Khasmedeus grinned. "Oh," it said. "Toasty?"

In the space between that moment and the next, the entire world was gone. All air and light and sound was consumed in a void, swallowed without a trace, and then there came the roaring. A massive shadow spiraled up from Coriolane and Khasmedeus's fatal embrace and grew taller and taller until it filled every crack and corner, every memory and breath, impossibly all-consuming beyond any ordinary concept of the word. In the chaos, Khasmedeus's grin grew wider. *Hello, Arghan,* it whispered. *Come and devour all of us, now. Come and eat your fill.*

Aliyah turned and ran.

CHAPTER

34

IVAN

MERONE HAD BEEN BURNING FOR HOURS, OR SO IT seemed – the curse of Nereus once more risen from the past, or merely the ultimate culmination of their sins in the present, the guilt of the here and now, everything that had to char and crisp and fall away in the cathartic heat of a collective funeral pyre. The blaze had sparked somewhere in the very heart of the Eternal Palace, perhaps in the throne room itself, and swiftly spread, consuming everything in its path. All the bodies that lay where they had fallen, all the fine art and priceless fittings, all the irreplaceable treasures, the spoils of a thousand looted cities and a thousand lost generations – not so long ago, Ivan would have seen it as the most terrible tragedy in history. The flames resisted every attempt to quench them and only grew stronger, so nobody could get close. They did manage to build a firebreak on Palatorian Hill, but there was no saving the Eternal Palace. Nobody knew what unearthly fire could burn stone and steel like wood and straw. Nobody could do anything but watch. Smoke unspooled in silken coils, cinders fell like grey rain, and the air was so thick and hazy that everything transformed into phantoms, muted and blurred as if they were in the deep dark fields of Hadeus. Undead, unliving, unreal, unmade.

Ivan sat on a pile of broken stone in the courtyard, staring at the smoldering skeleton of the palace and distantly aware that he should be doing more to manage the crisis than he was. His arm hurt terribly and that made it difficult, even if Zadia had grudgingly stitched the wound and wrapped it in a bandage and gave him a look as if she still wished very much for him to die in a gruesome fashion, but fair was fair. At least he *had* done his part in helping to build the firebreak, when he and Zadia gave up on their search for the missing tower and came down to discover that the Eternal Palace had turned into the mouth of hell, and it soaked his arm with blood and turned him dangerously lightheaded. Besides, he simply did not care whether the inferno spilled into Merone proper and devoured the Eternal City, the place he had always thought of as the capital of the world and the zenith of human civilization. Zadia had disappeared to desperately look for Aliyah and Elemai, and Ivan was here. Sitting and doing nothing at all, waiting for the end of the world.

He was still doing that, abstractly examining the blood on his clothes and wondering how much was his own and how much was the Corporalists, when a shadow fell over him, he looked up with a jolt, and then was sure that he had, in fact, finally lost his mind. Not that it was particularly surprising or distressing; indeed, it was the only logical consequence of everything, and at this point, rather comforting. He raised his uninjured arm in a ridiculous, flopping half-wave. "Hello."

"Hello." Julian Kozharyev looked down at him with an utterly unreadable expression, soot and ash smeared in filthy carapaces on his face and clothes and hair. He looked like the story of the three Vashemite men miraculously delivered from the fiery furnace in ancient Babelon, after King Nabukudurriz threw them in for refusing to worship his graven image. It would not surprise Ivan to learn that Julian also possessed such fireproof abilities; he managed to do everything else that was flatly impossible. They looked at each other until the silence became almost literally torturous. Then Julian said, "You… you're alive."

Ivan grunted. At the moment, the question seemed open, and he could not be bothered to exert his will on the outcome one way or the other. Yet a sharp stab of grief and guilt and heartbreak splintered through his numb detachment, and he fought to keep his voice steady. "Yes. As are you. After I left you and did not look back. Then I did even more terrible things, and even worse, I do not repent for them. You need not concern yourself with me any longer. You are free to go."

Julian raised an ironic eyebrow at the scalded wasteland of wreckage that surrounded them, begging the question as to just where anyone could go. He let out a long sigh, then sat down next to Ivan. "I don't know what *terrible thing* you did, but I gave the Ring to Khasmedeus and could have wiped out the entire human race. That does not appear to have happened, thankfully, but it started this fire, destroyed the Eternal Palace, and freed a murderous ifrit. Unclear whether it's still on the loose. Oh, and." He shrugged. "Killed Coriolane, but that's a good thing."

"What?" Ivan stared at him. "What are you *talking* – ?"

"Long story." Julian sought in vain for a scrap of clean cloth to wipe his face. "Very, *very* long story. Would take a week to tell properly. My point is, I'm not going to start screaming about what an awful person you are. And yes, in fact. Coriolane's dead. Khasmedeus sacrificed itself to destroy him, the Ring of Tselmun, and said murderous ifrit. Fortunately for us all, the ifrit also managed to devour Grand Magister Kronus beforehand. So in the end, actually quite useful."

"Kronus *and* Coriolane are – ?" The realization of what this meant sank in like the sudden warmth of a breaking dawn, a new day finally coming at the end of the darkest and most awful night. "The Meronite Empire is done, you mean? The Divine Emperor is dead, the Thaumaturge is dead, the Corporalists are dead. Everyone that ruled, that held all the power – they're gone?"

"The Meronite Empire isn't done," Julian corrected, with a pedant's irritating precision. "It still very much exists, all its appendages still exist, its institutions and its armies and its laws and its systems, but yes. Its entire ruling structure has been literally decapitated and it's absolutely anybody's fucking guess what comes next. Wait, what do you mean the Corporalists are dead?"

"Take it from me." Ivan sardonically lifted his bloodstained hands. "All of them."

Julian studied him with that too-knowing gaze, those black eyes that seemed to pierce clean into Ivan's old and tattered soul and see him there in the dark, that small and naked and terrified thing that hid inside its formidable armor, hoping that everyone was too afraid of its illusion to ever guess the truth. Julian reached out and took Ivan's good hand, nestling his head on Ivan's shoulder, and even this small ordinary gesture of empathy and forgiveness was enough to snap what remained of Ivan's fragile heart in half. They sat there for a little while, not saying a word. Then Julian started, let go, and stood up. "Hashem, I'm an idiot. Hold on, don't go anywhere. I'll be right back."

Ivan nodded acquiescingly, thinking it unlikely that he would ever go anywhere at all, and watched as Julian disappeared into the murk. Most of the fire was finally out by now, or at least burning less vigorously, though it could take days or weeks to be fully extinguished and for cleanup and rebuilding to begin. If such a thing was even possible, or if the Eternal Palace would remain in ruins as Coriolane Aureus IX's private crematorium, forever an unhealed wound and stark memorial at the city and empire's ripped-out heart. Ivan understood the essential scholarly nature of Julian's objections, but Merone *was* over, in any way that mattered. The world would wake up tomorrow in an entirely new contour of history, in a place and time where everything was possible and nothing like it had happened before. That, perhaps, was not so bad.

In another few minutes, Julian reappeared, leading someone by the arm. Ivan looked up again – and knew the truth, that suddenly and simply, in a way that went past conscious knowledge or logical deduction and sprang from the deepest intuition of the soul. With an almighty effort, he stood up, painfully conscious that they knew each other already, had known each other before, and yet were meeting in truth for the very first time since the night of another great fire, the attack on their village that ended their old world and brought them here, to life and death and life. He wished that he was not such an awful mess, but he nodded, and Tatyana nodded back. She did not look much better than him. She was the most impossible and beautiful thing he had ever seen.

"Tatya," he said. "Or – Romola. I do not know if you – if you know. If you understand."

Romola – no, it wasn't her, not anymore – looked at him without a word, trembling too hard to even attempt to speak. Then she stepped forward, he stepped forward too, and they collided, stepping on each other's feet and clutching each other's arms, clawing as blindly and agonizingly as if they might evanesce with the rest of the smoke and never be seen again. Ivan buried his face in the brown hair that was just the color of his own, that perhaps he should have recognized the very first time — *I love you, I have loved you all along* — making a sound he could not decipher, something like *I'm sorry, I'm sorry, I'm sorry* and which was not remotely enough, nothing to come close to the unconscionable wrong he had done to her, even unknowing and unwanting and torn into a thousand pieces himself. He did not ask for her forgiveness, and she did not offer it. But still they stood there and held each other, and breathed in tune, in time. Real. Real. Real.

At last, they let go, stepped back, and kept staring, as he wondered if she knew him at all or simply thought General Ionius had finally and categorically lost his mind. But before he could scrape together the wherewithal to ask, she tilted her head back, studied him, and nodded. "Ivan," she said. "That's your name, isn't it? Your real name, the one you were born with, my brother. I don't remember everything, and I don't want to. But I remember some of it. Enough."

"You…" Ivan looked between Tatyana and Julian. "He saved you?"

"In a matter of speaking," Julian said. "I think she had more to do with saving me, after everything went to hell with Arghan and Kronus. She also helped me and Aliyah draw the runes — I showed her how to do them once, since that was all we had time for, and she memorized them pretty much on the spot. *And* she was the one to suggest that Khasmedeus and I disguise ourselves as the empresses, and that it would be the best way to get close to Coriolane without immediately blowing our cover. So yeah. Frankly, I'd say she's the real hero."

Tatyana blushed, but a small smile crept across her lips, quietly and unapologetically proud. Then she glanced at Ivan and Julian, clearly curious as to how exactly *they* knew each other, and Ivan cleared his throat. "Well," he said hastily. "Never mind. There's a great deal to do, and it does not appear anyone else is going to do it. Will you help me?"

"Yes," Julian said, and Tatyana echoed it. "Yes, I think we will."

Ivan drew a deep breath, which felt like the first real one he had taken in days. He was still utterly undone, but no longer frozen, as if his bones and flesh and blood remained violently broken but were nonetheless slowly beginning to heal, to once more be able to bear his weight. He rose to his feet, braced himself, and transformed himself back into the general, the commander, the leader of men. Whatever Merone had taken from him, and that was a great deal, it had given him this, and he meant to use it. "Follow me," he said. "We have work to do."

They did, and they fell to it. There were survivors to gather up, cordons to establish, orders to issue, unrest to quell; seeing the Eternal Palace burn for hours with no word as to what was going on or what might have caused it or if they were all in danger, the city had panicked, there were riots and mobs and more fires breaking out across Merone, and Ionius rounded up a group of the first remotely respectable soldiers he could find and gave them stern orders to restore peace as swiftly and nonviolently as possible. If there was a clear need for force, they could use it, but anyone who massacred civilians or contributed to the mayhem would be sharply disciplined, and the focus had to be on getting people back inside their homes and putting out the embers on the figurative and literal levels. They were not to spread rumors or deliver upsetting news. They were merely to say that the situation was under control.

This was the most outrageous deception of all, but half the battle was to *look* like you knew what you were doing, and Ionius did not want the shocking tale of Coriolane's death – if it was true, as nobody could get inside the smoking ruins to search for solid proof – to blazon into an even worse conflagration. There was no hiding it forever, but he needed time to think. He felt like a jongleur trying to keep a hundred balls in the air. But drop one, and the world would explode.

At last, when the situation had settled into a simmering, uneasy quiet and there was no other calamity that demanded his immediate attention, Ionius rounded a corner and came face-to-face with Zadia ur-Namasqa. She was looking worriedly at her daughter Aliyah, who was bent over the unmoving Elemai ur-Tasvashta. At the sight of Ionius, the Qartic women communally startled, but at least did not get up and flee, hurl curses, or otherwise demonstrate their continued vehement displeasure. "General," Zadia said stiffly. "As you see, my daughter-in-law is badly hurt. Is there anything that can be done for her?"

"Was she injured in the fire?" Ionius was unsure if he dared to kneel too close to Safiya ur-Tasvashta's offspring, even in her plainly weakened state. Elemai's eyes were open but unfocused, her breath shallow, and she didn't seem to see or hear Aliyah. "Or something else?"

"Coriolane did this." Aliyah didn't look up, her voice too tight and dangerously controlled. "I managed to find her and get her out, but she won't wake. Not really."

"Ah." Ionius turned on his heel. "One moment."

It took a while to locate Julian and return to where he had left the women; the familiar environs of the Eternal Palace had been rendered unnervingly foreign by the extensive damage, and burned pieces kept falling off at random intervals. When Julian had knelt next to Elemai and was seeing if there was anything he could do for her, Zadia tipped her head meaningfully at Ionius and rose to her feet. With a murmured word to her daughter, she stepped away, behind the charred remnant of columns, and he ducked in after her. They stood looking at the summer dusk, the smoldering ruins, the unsettled city that breathed laboriously, like a large animal in pain. Then Zadia said, "Is he dead?"

"Yes." There was, of course, no need to ask who she meant. "So far as I have heard, at least. He was consumed by the fire. Your daughter may have told you."

"Some of it, yes." Zadia continued to stare down Palatorian Hill to the sweltering enforced stillness of Merone below, her expression utterly unreadable. "She said that the jinnyeh Khasmedeus gave itself up in order to ensure that Coriolane was destroyed with the fire of an ifrit named Arghan, and the Ring of Tselmun was also incinerated. So, then. If it is indeed so, the throne of Merone is vacant, the empire is leaderless, and this dangerous chaos could spiral. Coriolane ruled for four hundred years. There is no easy way for the world to wrap its head around his absence."

"There is not," Ionius agreed. "And there is no justice in simply toppling a tyrant and then excusing oneself altogether from the aftermath. Someone will need to step up and do their best with what is left behind. I suspect, Saeda Zadia, that you wish to return to Qart-Hadesht and finish what you and Saeda Safiya began. You will not be the only imperial province to do so."

Zadia's mouth tightened. "Yes," she said. "Though that is not the only option for myself and indeed, Aliyah. If she so chooses, she could inherit the throne."

Ionius was about to demand how such an outrageous thing could be possible, but then he remembered what Coriolane had said in their last confrontation and looked at Zadia again, studying her profile and how it was ineluctably familiar, how he had seen it stamped on coins and sculptures and icons and images and indeed, in flesh. "Vata Korol," he said, stunned. "How is that – ? Didn't Coriolane kill all his children?"

"All of them except me." Zadia's lips went even thinner. "My mother hid me well."

"So Aliyah is – his *granddaughter?* But if so, if you are his daughter – that would mean you would come first in the succession. Do you wish to forswear your own claim so easily?"

"I do not wish to suckle at the tainted teat of Merone. Indeed, I have spent my entire adult life in – until now, utterly futile – schemes to wrest myself, my family, and my homeland away from it." Zadia laughed, dry as dust. "So I fail to see why I should sit on that filthy chair, clutch it even closer to my heart. If Aliyah does wish it, I will not stand in her way. But no. I have no interest in it whatsoever."

Ionius glanced at her, unsure whether she was protesting merely for the sake of form and intended to claim it after a suitable show of humility, but there was a ring of truth in her words. "I can understand that," he allowed. "But one way or another, Merone will need a leader. If neither you nor your daughter wish to take up in Coriolane's place – "

"And?" Zadia turned to look at him, grimly amused. "You see no other choice?"

"What do you mean, saeda?"

"However long it has been since it last happened," the ur-Namasqa matriarch remarked, with steely and unflinching pragmatism, "this is still not the first time that a Meronite emperor was eventfully deposed and there was a need for a general to step in and take things in hand. You clearly don't want power, which means you might just be suited for it. I daresay there is no one who can question your credentials, your abilities, your experience, or your success in inspiring your friends and terrifying your enemies. And if a petition for formal independence should soon arrive from Qart-Hadesht, I imagine that you would also agree to grant it without any further war or bloodshed. There are not many of your rivals for the post who could say the same."

Ionius started to protest that this was absurd, that he did not want to look like the ringleader of a military coup, and everyone would immediately assume that he had in fact murdered Coriolane and drafted in the army to support his brazen usurpation. As Zadia pointed out, it was hardly unprecedented in Meronite history, and some of the upstart generals had indeed been far better emperors than the ones they kicked out, but as she also said, he did not want power, did not want to be Emperor Ionius I, did not want to finally wake up from what the Meronites had made him, only to turn around and chain himself to it for good. But what if he did have to do this, at least for a little while? He had always known that he could not simply give up Ionius Servus Eternus and walk away, and there were advantages to it being him. If Qart-Hadesht asked for freedom and Ruthynia did too, if he could stop the slaughter of Brythanica and the war with Qin... if he, a Kozhek slave, could be the voice that spoke those words and the hand that made the seal... if he could start to atone, to put together in the smallest part, all that he himself had torn asunder...

"It is... a thought, my lady," Ionius allowed at last. "Thank you. We should get back."

Zadia inclined her head with finely grained sarcasm, but they did so. When they returned to the others, Julian had succeeded in getting Elemai to sit up and drink a little water, which Aliyah was carefully holding. It was unclear how much she could be moved, but as none of the wreckage was suitable for habitation and there was an increasing crowd of fearful, cold, hungry, tired people milling around aimlessly with nowhere to go, nothing to eat, and nowhere to sleep, this far more prosaic unrest had to be likewise smartly dealt with. Ionius herded them up, made sure that everyone was accounted for, and led them out of the palace precincts, down the road, and to the first villa on the lower reaches of Palatorian Hill. It belonged to the esteemed and ancient family Argentus, who had produced a laundry list of proconsuls, praetors, senators, orators, scholars, and other Meronite luminaries, and the steward who finally and very grudgingly came to answer Ionius's stubborn banging on the gate was extremely disinclined to parley with this scabrous band of refugees. He had seen the Eternal Palace on fire with everyone else, but that sharpened his instinct to turn them away, to defend his master's house against opportunists and thieves who had clearly come slinking out of the night to do them ill. "My lord Ionius, where is His Majesty?"

"Where is Lucius Septimus?" Ionius countered. "He is still the paterfamilias of the Argenti, is he not? I wish to speak to him. Now."

The steward eyed him loathingly, but was not brave enough to defy General Ionius to his face. He scuttled away and returned with the master of the house – Lucius Septimus Argentus was a plump, scowling mid-fifties Meronite nobleman who had been pried unwillingly from his banquet couch, as even the collapse of the entire government was not sufficient to interrupt his feasting. "General Ionius," he blustered, folding his arms in what was plainly meant to be a belligerent air, but looked as if he wished to discreetly conceal the wine stains on his toga. "What is the meaning of this? We have heard disturbing rumors, yes, but – "

"Good evening, my lord." Ionius flashed a patently terrifying smile, beckoning to the huddled masses behind him. "You see before you the survivors of the great blaze that claimed the Eternal Palace. It is your patriotic duty to offer us succor and shelter."

Lucius Septimus adjusted the silver laurel crown on his brow, frowning unhappily at this sudden invasion of uninvited houseguests, and drew himself up in dudgeon. "It is unthinkable that the most venerated and noble house of Argentus should be asked to provide food and board for this common rabble. There are hostels and poorhouses in the city, are there not? Dedicated institutions for the destitute? We are willing to shelter *you,* General, but certainly not – "

"Unfortunately." Ionius snapped his fingers, making the pompous windbag flinch. "You presently speak to the interim ruler of Merone, and you've just made me very irritated. We are staying here tonight, all of us. Have your servants prepare supper and sleeping quarters for my party. Then order your clerk to draw up writs of manumission for every slave beneath your roof. I expect them to be completed and distributed by the hour of Vespers tomorrow. You will then instruct your treasurer to pay a lump sum to each man, woman, and child, one hundred sestertii for every year they spent in bondage, and send your men of business to your countryside estates, to ensure that this is repeated with every slave you own. Cross me, my lord, and you're under arrest. The Castel Sanctangel is heavily damaged, but we could still find a cell or two."

Lucius Septimus's jowls turned purple, eyes bulging out of his head, and he stewed in apoplectic silence. His gaze flicked to Ionius's bloody hands and bandaged arm, well aware that to fight an Immortal was tantamount to suicide – Ionius's powers were still scarcely more than a flicker, but this wobbling sack of suet didn't know that. At last Argentus managed, "The emperor…?"

"Coriolane Aureus IX has gone to meet the Divine Family." In truth, Ionius strongly suspected that whatever eternal fate awaited the dearly departed was far less heavenly, but so be it. "And as I said, I have taken his place until such time as a proper successor can be determined. As such, any failure to comply with my orders will be constituted as treason, and certainly you've been a loyal Meronite long enough to know what that entails. It is, however, your choice."

Lucius Septimus continued to look utterly dumbstruck. Then at last he summoned his servants, repeated the instructions just as Ionius had given them, and loathingly invited them in to share his hospitality and the food of his hearth. Ionius was offered the best suite of rooms, and when the door shut behind him, he sat down on the acre-sized bed and stared at nothing. He had done it, then. He had no expectation of being seen as a hero; he knew that he wasn't. Yet they were deathly afraid of him, and that made them obey, and that was power. That had to be worth something. But was this what it was about: the right to sleep alone in this enormous cold tomb of a room, stuffed with stolen goods and slave-made luxuries, knowing that if Argentus was even slightly braver and not a dissolute coward, he might well send someone to assassinate Ionius in the night and seize the empire for himself? Tomorrow they would assemble the full Meronite Senate, properly break the news of Coriolane's death, and then the undignified scramble for power could really commence. There were plenty of Argentus's ambitious peers who would see this as an excellent opportunity to play for the imperial prize – would they even pretend to weep while doing so? Unlikely – and that could not be countenanced. At all costs, Ionius had to prevent this situation from collapsing into all-out civil war and public terror. If it meant insisting that only he had the right to rule, was that right?

As he lay there, staring sleeplessly at the high ceiling painted with a mural of the Abduction of Persepana, there was a knock. He sat up sharply, conscious of treachery; an assassin might not bother to announce himself, but that made no account for more devious methods. He stole to the door and pressed himself against the wall. He listened intently, heard nothing, and finally hissed, "Who's there? Name yourself."

"Open the door, you idiot." The voice was fond and exasperated all at once. "It's me."

Ionius very much doubted that he should do that, but for quite a different reason than suspected murder. But finally, at his total wit's end and then some, he gave in. "For the record," he announced sternly, "this is unlikely to be a wise idea."

"Noted." Julian's mouth quirked into an impish grin. "So, shall we do something stupid?"

"Yes," Ivan said, stepping aside to let him in. "Yes, by all the gods, in all the ways, yes."

★★★★

So, IN FACT, THEY DID. It was utterly unlike their first wild, breathless coupling in Ambrazakti, or the mindless heat and haze in the wake of finding the Ring. They took their time, slow and soft and knowing each other with hands and mouths, kisses pressed into necks and jaws and shoulders, crooks of knees and hollows of hips, collarbones and groins and chests. Julian's mouth, which could often be so sharp and cutting and brimful of point-blank blows, was warm and gentle and generous, blazing a trail of thorough exploration across the unmapped territory of Ivan's body, the strange cartography of scars and wounds and damages both old and new, the knotted tangle of flesh and bone and sinew that nobody had known before, not in such detail, with intent and unapologetic deliberation. Julian mused and murmured, licked and nipped, found the most sensitive spots and teased them unmercifully, until Ivan was jerking and swearing and drenched in cold sweat, cursing the bastard furiously and yet completely and entirely at his devious mercy. Then Julian put his hand on Ivan's head and pushed him down, and without complaint, the de facto ruler of Merone went to his knees. There was no space in him for wanting anything else.

So they went, entwined and entangled, pushing and pulling, giving and taking – bickering sometimes out of sheer habit, but dulling any sting with a warm and forceful kiss. At last, breathing as if he had been chased by an entire Meronite cavalry battalion, Ivan rolled onto his back and spent several minutes attempting in vain to recover his breath or his dignity. Eyes still closed, he said at last, "I survived all this nonsense, and now what, Julian Janovynich? You want to kill me?"

"Oh?" Julian's voice turned low with challenge. "You want me to actually start *trying?*"

"Mata Koroleva, have mercy on an old man." Ivan wiped his brow with his good arm and continued to wheeze. Several minutes passed. Then he said, "You could, you know. Stay."

"*Stay?*" It was obvious even without looking that Julian's eyebrows had shot toward his hair. "Stay here, you mean? With you? And do what – be your Meronite queen?"

"I don't know." It was an utterly foolish thing to say, and yet Ivan could not bite it back. "We could see what it meant, what it was like. You wanted to go to university, didn't you? The Imperial Academy of Merone will need someone to take it in hand, and you're the smartest person I know. Surely it is not beyond all thought that it could be you."

Julian did not answer immediately, his fingers tracing circles on Ivan's chest. Then he said, "I can't deny it's a very tempting offer, and not just for the books. But I... I have to go. For one thing, back to Yerussala, and I don't know how long I have to stay, how much I need to fix and clean up, but I imagine it's a lot. Arghan the Undying destroyed most of Kronus's bone pentacle, along with Kronus himself, but there could be remnants. You can't just assume a magical instrument of that scale and power is totally dead and deactivated, especially after all the work he put into it and the nasty things he used it for. And while the Ring of Tselmun is finally gone, the *Key of Tselmun* remains, and while I'm not going to burn it, I need to make sure that nobody else finds that accursed book again. And that's all before I return to Korolgrod and tell my family that I'm not dead. So… I don't know."

A chill passed through Ivan from head to heel, turning the warm intimacy of the present into a cold and uncertain future. He instinctively opened his mouth to argue, but he knew that the same as there was nobody but him to do what must be done here in the Eternal City, there was no one but Julian for the Holy City. It ached worse than his bruised and battered bones, and he turned his head away, not wanting to show the naked pain of his vulnerability. Divine Family, why did it have to be taken away, the moment he finally let someone slip through his eternal and unclimbable walls? Was this the tradeoff for getting Tatyana back, having to give Julian up? Would it be years and years until they saw each other again, if at all? Why did he have to love only when he was already losing, to prove its truth by letting go? It was not *fair*.

And yet, he was not a man to complain about the childish *fairness* of things, and he knew full well that he would not keep Julian as a pet of his own, chained and bound, even with a more intangible and agreeable sort of fetter than steel. And perhaps he did not deserve a soft epilogue, not yet, when there was so much work to be done and sins to atone. He tried to accept it, to know it in his soul, to let it be what it was and nothing else. But like the world itself, it burned.

Julian, sensing his disquiet, leaned over and pressed a kiss into his neck, and Ivan – no longer giving a damn about right and wrong, about today or tomorrow, about anything but this – reached for him again. They made love once more, as slowly and endlessly as they could, and then afterward, as they lay in each other's arms, Julian told him the full story of what transpired in the last few days: Arghan and Kronus and Tatyana, Khasmedeus and its sacrifice, the bone pentacle and the blood plague and Yerussala, the deception and the rune-circle and Coriolane's ultimate end. Ivan listened without interrupting, until he said only, "Yes. I understand why you must go back."

It was Julian's turn to find himself choked, at a simple and categorical loss for words. "Yes," he said at last, the softest of whispers against Ivan's stubbled cheek. "But not tonight. Not yet."

They slept after that, at last, though there were only a few hours of night left and the stars had started to fade. At dawn Ionius woke, slipped out without waking Julian, and dressed, conscious that he must now officially look the part. He took clothes from the elaborate wardrobe, garb meant for visiting dignitaries and fellow nobles, and it still felt like a strange and poorly-fitting costume, but less so. He studied himself in the looking glass, decided it would have to do, and slipped through the still-slumbering halls of the Argentus villa, outside to the garden. As he had known she would be, Aliyah ur-Namasqa was waiting for him.

They sat down side by side, though not too close, on a wooden bench among the verdant rosebushes; they were allies now, but the old memory of enmity sharpened their cordiality. From this vantage point, they could see across the entirety of Palatorian Hill to the burned and desolate ruins. The shell of the Eternal Palace stood out like a black-inked thumbprint on the white neck of the city, a bruise not easily expunged. Even from here it seemed profoundly haunted, exiled from the ordinary commerce of mankind, as if the mortal remains of the ifrit Arghan and the jinnyeh Khasmedeus and the emperor Coriolane were all commingled and scorched into a shared grave that would permanently transfigure anyone who dared to set foot there again. Perhaps it would be torn down and rebuilt. Perhaps nobody would have the nerve, and it would stay like that forever.

"So," Ionius said at last. "You know why we are meeting, and what I must ask. Your mother has already refused, but it is your right to do the same, or to accept. Do you, Aliyah bet Zadia ur-Namasqa, wish to claim your birthright and become the Divine Empress of Merone?"

There was an exceedingly weighty pause. He could see Aliyah thinking about it, in the cool and solemn and deliberate way in which she did everything. At last she said, "And if I did?"

Ionius shrugged. "I would swear myself to your service. Promulgate your claim, teach you everything I know about ruling the empire, defend you against your enemies. But I would do so as a free man, not a slave, and with the sworn oath that if you should ever turn as mad and tyrannical as Coriolane, I would not hesitate to strike you down. On that you have my word."

"I would hope for no less." Aliyah smiled, faraway and inward-looking. "I appreciate your honesty, and your offer. I know you do not make it lightly. I am grateful that your… Julian was able to help with Elemai. She is sorely wounded, but she is alive."

"I am glad Julian could help, but I wish it was not necessary. I turned against Coriolane at the end, yes, but I still served him loyally for many years. The blood is on my hands too."

Aliyah's mouth tightened, but she did not answer. Finally she said, "I suppose the important thing is that you did. And it was not at the very eleventh hour, either. When the soldiers threw me into the pit – you put some of your enspelled Immortal iron into my bones. That was what I used to climb out, and it was what I used to cut Coriolane's throat. So… I owe you my gratitude."

"I can take it back now, if you wish. I know it must have been disquieting and unpleasant."

"I felt so at first, yes. But now…" Aliyah looked at her hands in the same dawning realization of strength and power, that she would never be without a weapon again. "I think I'll keep it."

"As you wish." Ionius inclined his head. "And the throne?"

Aliyah considered for so long that the sun had time to creep up the garden wall, to spill over the flowers and vines and onto the footpath. Then she said, "No. I don't want it. I told Coriolane so, and my opinion has not changed. I don't think that just because I happen to be his descendant that it makes me the right ruler, or better than any other. Besides, I am Qartic. We do not believe in the divine right of kings, or monarchy as an institution. I wish to return with my mother and my wife to our homeland and build our future there, as the Venerated Republic we once were and wish to become again. Our city was left in ruins as well, after Coriolane's… chastisement. Titus Quartus Cincitus is still the Governor-General, and – "

"Not for long. At least if I have anything to say about it."

"I think you will." Aliyah looked at him straight, calm and level. "You should do well. But are we entirely sure that it is in fact yours, or that there will not be a struggle? If the empresses make it to Coriolanople and declare themselves the new rulers of Merone – "

"The last we actually saw of Gheslyn and Vestalia," Ionius said, "they were under arrest for high treason. And while the patricians may hate me, at least they know me, and I am a man. It will be a cold day in hell before any of their stiff patriarchal knees were caught bending to a woman. If they wish to declare themselves their husband's heirs, they can. But they'll find few takers."

"Perhaps," Aliyah said. "Or perhaps not. It does happen, however, that I induced them to swear a blood oath to hold themselves as allies to myself, you, Julian Kozharyev, and your – she is your sister, I understand? Tatyana? So while I do not put undue confidence in that, it does exist."

"What?" Ionius was impressed. "How did you pull that off?"

"We both wanted something," Aliyah said cryptically, "and a way was found that suited our interests. So if Gheslyn and Vestalia do wish to contest you for the inheritance of Merone, you may remind them of that fact. Though of course, you have been part of this court far longer than me, and know what you are doing. You may not need my help."

Ionius was unsure whether he believed that, but her confidence was oddly reassuring. It was close to the hour for the forum at the Senate, and it was time for this strange new future to be made real, utterly and irrevocably so. He rose to his feet, bowed to her, and departed.

The meeting itself proceeded as anyone could have foreseen. The anxious Meronite senators and statesmen packed into the Forum and whispered, jostled, shouted in anger and derision, insisted that Coriolane must have faked his death or disappearance, that this was a trick and he would soon reappear to see who had remained loyal, that there were any number of prestigious families and prominent citizens better suited to assume control, that it could not possibly be a foreign-born slave and with so little transparency or honesty about the truth of the emperor's *alleged* decease. They called for an inquiry, an inquest, a trial, a tribunal. They objected to every single point of order or statement that could be bellowed over the uproar. They demanded recompense for the injury to their properties, the terror to their persons, and the damages they had incurred in the riots yesterday. Surely if a military general was proposing to take charge, martial law should perforce be invoked. And if the Corporalists and the Thaumaturges were also dead in unclear circumstances — why, they were sitting ducks, suddenly open to the wrath of the world and their enemies! This was the end of Merone, the greatest shame of the empire in history. They demanded answers. They demanded power. They demanded penitence.

Ionius did not give it to them. He simply waited out the tumult, stood up, and informed them that they were welcome to consult among themselves as to what they wished the government of Merone to look like in the long run, but he had heard nothing to dissuade him from his plan of serving as temporary head of state until then. If they actually wished to have more power, Merone had after all once been a republic, and could still be again. However, they would have to come up with a proposal that allowed common-born citizens and Meronites of foreign extraction to run for office and share equally in its organization and administration. Any nobleman who continued to cause a stink and foment discord or factionalism would be subject to the same fate as the unfortunate Lucius Septimus Argentus, and have all his slaves freed on the spot. Indeed, slavery would be ended altogether sooner rather than later, so it was best to begin planning for that eventuality.

The Senate was lit to the point of absolute explosion, but still too frightened to stand up and tell Ionius to his face that he was an apostate ingrate and they would not obey. They seethed and stewed and chewed their tongues, they delayed and shirked and sputtered, but in the end, they all loathingly swore themselves to uphold his authority as a caretaker until such time as a more permanent solution could be devised. Ionius had no doubt they would try everything they possibly could to get around this, but so be it. Let them outwit or outfight him if they could.

He was sitting in the expansive Forum office normally reserved for the emperor, making a valiant start on the paperwork that had languished there since time immemorial, when there was a knock on the door and a servant went to answer it. "Your Majesty?" he said nervously. "It is His Holiness, Mellius Sanctus Sixtus, seeking an immediate audience."

"I am not *Your Majesty.*" Ionius foresaw a great deal of having to say it, and it would be easier just to accept, but he did not want to lull himself into simply believing it. "But very well. Show His Holiness in."

When the Archpriest arrived, he had the disheveled and ill-slept look that meant he had spent the night in one of his fits of flagellation, beating himself with a whip of knotted cord and melodramatically imploring mercy upon this poor and fallen world, now terribly bereft of Coriolane Aureus IX's great benefaction. Still, he folded himself into a dignified half-bow. "Your Majesty."

"No." Ionius turned to face him. "You heard me say that I was not the emperor."

"I did," Mellius allowed smoothly, "but what you must say in public is not the same as what powerful men agree behind closed doors. You and I know each other, General Ionius, and we also know that Merone must remain the greatest empire in the world, regardless of whose earthly custody it is in. You would do well to make me your dear friend and close advisor just as I was for His late Majesty, may the Divine Family assoil him. I can counsel and guide you, I know the realm and the court more than anyone, and I can bring the True Tridevarian Church onto your side. You will find it much to your advantage if I did."

"Oh?" Ionius arched an eyebrow. "Do you think so, Holiness?"

"I do," Mellius insisted. "It is best to maintain continuity, and for you to keep Coriolane's laws and policies precisely as they were. After all, you insist that you are only a temporary steward of the throne, and thus have no right to make real change. Of course, we will never actually hand our sovereign prerogative over to a vulgar plebiscite of commoners, foreigners, and fools. Only the next lawfully crowned emperor will have the right to decide any of it. If you change your mind and wish it to be you, I am available to perform the coronation at any moment."

Ionius leaned back in his chair, studying the Archpriest intently. "Truly? You would actually stoop to place the crown on the head of a Kozhek slave, a Tserkovian and a sodomite and an usurper, when you have spent so long railing against all those things?"

Mellius flinched, but admirably did not back down from taking full credit for his hypocrisy. "We all make adjustments, Majesty. The tools the Divine Family sends us might be flawed, for such is all mankind, but we must make use of what is given. You may be an inferior vessel, but you *have* served Merone loyally for many decades, and you would grow more worthy under my guidance. Perhaps if you were to marry a Meronite lady of impeccable bloodline – such as my niece, Claudia Drusilla, who is a lovely girl even for one of your, ah, proclivities – crown her queen, and sire an heir on her in the ordinary fashion, any doubts about your legitimacy would be removed. We spent so long without any royal prince or princess, it caused us to forget that things can still be done as they always have been before. We do, indeed, have a momentous opportunity. Did you hear the news from Qin? My spies told me just this morning. The Thearch, Hang Zhai, is finally dead."

"Are they?" Ionius kept his expression inscrutable. "That is momentous indeed."

"It is so." Mellius preened. "The Meronite legions who ventured so bravely to that land of yellow heathens have brought justice to our great enemy at last. I'm sure that they too will choose another ruler from the various whelps of the Forbidden City, but if Qin has likewise lost their ruler of several centuries, they do not have any advantage over us. Indeed, this would be the best moment to resume the war at full intensity, and claim a stirring victory to herald the first year of your new rule. What regnal name would you choose? Perhaps if you did wed Claudia, you could take our family's cognomen, Potestus. As a foreign-born slave, you would not have your own."

His Divine Majesty, Emperor Ionius Potestus I. Just then, it was there: a familiar and terrible stranger who wore another face that looked like Ivan Sazharyn and yet was not a thing like him at all. Married to Claudia Drusilla and siring little Meronite heirs, totally under the thumb of his oh-so-benevolent uncle-in-law, the church, the nobles, and the senators. As the atrocities and conquests and genocides of the empire continued unabated and the slaves were never actually freed, as one thing after another came up to delay the promised universal manumission. Until he was not one bit different from Coriolane Aureus IX, and that was exactly the point. To make Merone look as if it had changed, to buy it credit from doing so, and then settling even more deeply into the comforting groove of its worst old habits. Until even such a shocking event as this had been neutralized, tamed, made completely safe, and not one of the privileged class had anything to fear. They had not been able to stop him, but they could still swallow him up in their assimilating maw. So many years as a slave had not quite done it, but perhaps many more as a king would instead. After all, why question if you simply wore a golden chain instead? Why indeed, when you were so *comfortable?*

"It is a very fascinating offer, Your Holiness," Ionius said. "I am afraid, however, that I must refuse. You can see yourself out, I trust?"

Mellius gawked at him, startled out of his usual suavity. "Majesty, I am afraid I do not – I cannot possibly comprehend why you would – "

"And I said that my name was General Ionius. *My lord,* if you insist. Nothing else."

"My lord, this is deeply irregular." Mellius's face was slowly turning crimson. "It is beyond all precedent or basic decency. If you insist on trying to seize power in this fashion, you will indeed be nothing more than a crude usurper, a brazen and upjumped thief, the worst and most unfit ruler in all of Merone's long history. I was doing you an incalculable favor by offering to work with you and support you, borne from our dear friendship and collaboration. If I remove that protection, the sharks will surge in, and then you might only wish you had heeded the gods."

"Friendship?" Ionius cocked his head. "Are you sure? Here I was suspecting that you only offered any of this because you felt confident that you could control me, suborn me, match me off to your niece – or is she your illegitimate daughter by one of your several mistresses? I *have* heard rumors – and ensure that the next emperor was your grandson. Because that is all you are, Your Holiness. Power is all you care about. You are not the first churchman, nor will you be the last, to clothe it in the garb of pious sanctity. But nor should you expect me to gulp it down and ask for more. Now, in case you did not hear me, you are dismissed."

Mellius's face was still the hue of a summer sunset, his voice a hiss. "I am the emissary of the Divine Family on earth, you filthy heathen. Defy me, and I will have you excommunicated, declared heretic and anathema, and that any one of the noble Meronite families will gain blessings beyond count by having you killed and removed from the seat you unjustly occupy, which you stole with the blood of our blessed and holy Coriolane Aureus IX. Do you wish to test me?"

"I might. Do you wish to test *me?*"

"What? Is that a threat? You'll have me tortured?" The Archpriest puffed himself up like a barnyard rooster. "Very well, I am prepared to endure whatever pain or martyrdom that I must. It purifies the soul and raises the mind beyond the mundane, clarifies one's priorities and places one closer to the holy suffering that flenses us all. The people will rise on my behalf, when they see me and their beloved mother church being abused by a vile creature like you! Kill me, and you will never know another moment's peace! And when you die and are sent to hell – "

"Oh no." Ionius raised a hand. "None of that."

"Then? *What?*"

"I'll tax the churches." Ionius grinned. "Ten percent per annum, per parish, with twenty percent on the Arch-Holy Basilica, and full reparations for everything you took out of the public purse and the poor fund. I rather think that might make *me* popular, don't you?"

Mellius blanched. "You wouldn't dare."

"As we have established, Your Holiness." Ionius gestured ironically at his surroundings. "I am capable of rising to any height – or sinking to any depth – that I must. So by all means, excommunicate me. But do not be surprised when the tax collectors arrive the next morning."

The Archpriest was still fuming, but he did not have a ready-made riposte for such a pungent threat. At last and without another word, though his jaw was locked so tightly that Ionius could hear his teeth squeak, he inclined his head, spun around, and took his leave.

That, to be sure, was deeply satisfying, and while Merone was still fractious, fearful, and suspicious, they managed to pass the next several days without any more major disruptions. While the nobles insisted on a protracted ritual of grief for Coriolane, the commoners did not appear particularly troubled by his demise. Of course they were startled and unsettled, and wondered and worried what it meant for them, but it faded when there was still the ordinary business of daily life, there were no more fires or riots, and the news began to spread that all the Argentus slaves had been freed and more such grants of liberty were expected.

Nobody tried to kill Ionius in the night, though he kept his Immortals close just in case. Even then, his trust was partial and conditional, carefully rationed. He did not tell them the truth about Saturnus and the Corporalists. He did not go into details about his final confrontation with Coriolane, his assignations with Julian, or his agreements with Zadia and Aliyah ur-Namasqa. The Qartic women had left for home the other day, taking the still-invalid Elemai with them, and as Ionius saw them off at the docks, Zadia wished him luck. She even sounded as if she meant it.

It was that evening when Ionius decided there must be no more delay. Besides, it was the first back-to-back hours of free time he had had. He had barely gotten everyone to stop calling him *Your Majesty,* but regardless of his title, everyone needed something from him at every moment, and he was determined to do the best that he could. But that meant this as well, and even if he was afraid – was afraid, in fact, more than he could ever remember being before – it had to be done. He was still using the Argentus villa as temporary headquarters, and he went down the corridor and knocked on the door of the bedchamber at the far end. "Tatya," he called softly. "It's me."

After a moment, she opened it, which gave him a jolt. She looked outwardly as she had when she was Romola, but there was something in her eyes that was not at all the same. "Ivan," she said, clearly fighting down the impulse to add *my lord.* "If that is still what I should call you."

"It is." He cleared his throat. "I was hoping we could speak further."

Tatyana considered, then nodded, inviting him in, and he stepped cautiously into her room. It was cool and empty and neat as a pin, as if she had kept the habit of waking early every morning to clean, and he gestured clumsily at it. "If you wanted, you could have a more luxurious station. You are no longer a slave, and I am the regent of Merone."

"Thank you," Tatyana said, "but I am content. And I do not expect to need any lodgings much longer. Julian asked me if I wished to come to Yerussala and join in his work, and I agreed."

"I – what?" Inglorious as it was, Ivan's first reaction was an ugly jealousy, a sense of offended possession, though he was not sure what or for who. Julian had continued to spend every night with him, having not set a firm date for his departure, and Ivan had been content to pretend that perhaps the day would never come. If Julian had been having discussions with Tatya about bringing her with him, surely he should have alerted Ivan first? Tatyana was *his* sister, he had spent so long haunted by his failure to protect her, and if she flew away again, out into the great wide world – if she went and did not come back –

"Ah," Tatyana said, seeing his expression. "I startled you. I did think that perhaps I should ask your permission before I told Julian that I would go. But I am no longer your slave or your mistress or anything else that would seem to require it, and you were the one who told me that I should live my life as I pleased. What else is the point of it? Being free?"

Ivan started to speak, then stopped. Yes, of course. Of course she was right; she was right about everything. Surely he had not thought he would keep her at his side forever, too afraid to let her out of his sight, a far more controlling master than he had ever been before. At last, he said, "If you wish to do it, then you must. I just… thought we would have more time. To know each other again, as our own selves. I am not ready to let you go again. Since I killed all the Corporalists, there is no one to reanimate you again. If you have been Remade all these times, you are the same age as me, and I am not young. You could be close to the end of your life, and if you have only a few years left in this spell – "

Tatyana's brows rose in surprise. "*You* killed the Corporalists?"

"Yes. All of them." Ivan still did not regret it overall, but he almost wished he had kept one of the bastards alive, for insurance. Tatyana was moving ever closer to the final threshold where the body simply would not endure yet another artificial necromantic reawakening and therefore slipped into eternal sleep. What was he supposed to do? Simply accept that there was nothing left, that her life from now on might be long or short, that she would die once more and then there would be no more chances to save her or bring her back? That she might leave Merone and spend her remaining years away from him, with the lover he was already so unwilling to give up? As if Julian could have Tatyana, and Tatyana could have Julian, and Ivan could have neither?

And yet. Bitter as it was, he knew in his heart that this was what it should have been like all along. That Tatyana have the choice to do as she would, to go where she wished, to see the world beyond the Eternal

City, to live and die in the ordinary fashion at a time that nobody could predict or alter, with no way for the Corporalists to call her back again and again, to keep the anchor of forced existence chained around her foot merely to blackmail him. If he freed her, he had to give her fully back to time and chance, destiny and fate, and relinquish any and all control of his own, no matter how well-intentioned. There was no way to know what life they might have in some phantasmagorical world without war and woe and empire, without Merone, without the simple and terrible tragedy that had befallen them and so many others. Even beyond the magic and necromancy, immortality and the death of kings, it was still a simple story at its heart. They were parted by something terrible beyond their control, and they wished they were not, and even if they finally found each other again, there was no way to simply stitch together everything that had been lost and could not be called back. Even so, there was a new future, a chance to try again, even if it was not how they imagined it. Ivan was not so selfish as to refuse her that.

"Very well," he said, as Tatyana was still watching him. "You should have a chance to do this. To go free, to know what you are capable of, and what was stolen from you. Go with Julian to Yerussala, and learn everything you should have known. I entrust you with each other. If I can give you anything, say it, and I will."

"You don't have to." Tatyana's eyes were bright. Then she stepped forward and hugged him, and he wrapped his arms around her as tightly as he could, as if they could make the world whirl to a halt, the stars to fix in the firmament, and all of time stand still. Then at last she said into his shoulder, "Did you kill them because of me? The Corporalists?"

"Yes." It was the simple and unvarnished truth. "I asked what they had done to you, and Saturnus told me. So I killed every single one of them. Magister, apprentice, and acolyte alike."

He did not know what effect this would have on her, whether she would find it desirable or disgusting, if she would think it was too much or still not enough. If she asked him to hunt down every remaining Corporalist in the empire, he would. Her grip tightened on his bad arm, but he did not ask her to let go. Then she said, "Good. *Good.*"

Ivan's throat was too thick to speak, so he simply nodded, kissed her hair, and stood there as long as he could, neither of them moving, simply remembering how it felt to be here, to be alive, to be real and together and true. The rest of time would come when it would, and bring what fate it might, and be faced when it did. But for now, it was just this, this and no more, and in that moment, despite everything, it was enough.

Tatyana and Julian left three mornings later. They preferred to travel in the ordinary fashion, having had their fill of (as Julian put it) "extensive magical dumbfuckery," and Ionius was on hand to see them off. Julian had spent the final night in his bed as usual, where their parting had been far more savage and thorough, and their public farewell was more restrained, though they still held on for a very long time and Ionius could feel the reluctance in both of them to let go. But they did eventually, as Julian flashed his best attempt at a crooked grin. "Promise me," he said, "that if the Ruthynians declare independence tomorrow, you won't let them get away with just installing a new tsar, persecuting the Vashemites and Kozheks all over again, and the Almighty knows what else. Oh, and if Zogorov and the Konsilium throw a fit about it, sack them."

"Are you sure you will not stay on as my minister of Ruthynian affairs?" It was a jest, though barely. "I could use your sage counsel."

"I'll write letters," Julian promised. "Filled with bountiful wisdom and unsolicited advice. You'll wish I would just shut the fuck up."

"Never." Ionius took Julian's face in his hands, looked at him again, and then – to hell with whoever was watching or judging, he didn't care, didn't *care* – kissed him hard, tasting the sting of salt on his lips when they finally pulled back. "Look after my sister, Yulya, or I'll kill you."

Julian took this threat exactly as seriously as it deserved, which was not at all, then stepped aside as Ionius and Tatyana bid farewell. There were many things he still wanted to say, but he simply took her hand and kissed it. "Safe travels, Tatya. If you come back, I will be here."

"I intend to see you again." Tatyana looked up into his face. "On that you have my word."

Ionius could not muster an answer, so he merely nodded, helped her onto her horse, and even if Julian did not need it, gave him a hand likewise as an excuse to touch him one last time. Their fingers lingered, and then there was only air, and space, and nothing. Ionius bore it, of course. Just as he had always borne everything else. But that might have been the best and worst at once.

With final waves and blown kisses, Tatyana and Julian turned their horses' heads and trotted out the gate, out onto the road and down onto Palatorian Hill. Below them, Merone was waking up for another morning, the usual clatter and cacophony of the world spinning onward in its grief and greatness, and here Ionius stood with the chance to do what he could, in the time that he could. He did not know what would come on the morrow: if the Senate was already plotting against this upjumped ex-slave viceroy, if the imperial provinces would declare independence all at once, if granting it would bring about his overthrow and undo whatever limited good he could do. But he had already issued orders to end the slaughter in Brythanica and the war in Qin, and he planned to use every tool at his disposal to enforce them. He thought briefly of Marcus Servus, cast adrift into this same terrifying new forever-after. It was impossible to say if the boy had survived his final task in the Jade City, or even if so, if he had decided to break his own shackles and turn his face to the open air. To be it, at last. Free. Free. *Free.*

Ionius smiled a little, then, despite the heartbreak that ached in his chest. It would endure, and so would he, and every day it would hurt a little less or a little more, and that must be as it was. In the meantime, he had the morning's work before him, and after a final glance down the hill, at the two riders who had become nothing more than small spots on the bright pane of the sea and the sky and all the world to come, he turned around and went inside.

CHAPTER 35

ELEMAI

RISING AWAY OVER THE SEA IN A VEIL OF PINK AND purple cloud, throwing morning light like golden oil on the wine-dark waves, the sun looked the same as ever, even if the city on which it shone was still a shattered and hollow ghost. It would rebuild – Qart-Hadesht was no stranger to picking up and putting back together in the wake of Meronite sieges and sackings – and someday in the future, it would once more be as glorious as before, albeit in a different way. But there was no replacing the thousands of years which had turned to dust in a few weeks, the lost history and culture, the dead and wounded and disappeared. Just because they could eventually recover did not mean the loss did not exist. It did not take away the suffering or absolve Cincitus for causing it. Even if the Governor-General had been issued with a curt notice of dismissal and ordered to return to Merone at once, his shadow lingered long.

It was possible, Elemai reflected, that her personal views were so pessimistic, unappeased by the theoretical promise of future restoration in the face of very real present damage, because of how unlikely it felt that any of it would be granted to her. The voyage home from the Eternal City had been an agonizing blur, and when they arrived in the Old Harbor and could barely dock because the quays were burned to the foundations, Aliyah and Zadia had to carry her off the ship, bundled in a litter like a pitiful weakling. Considering that *Aliyah* was the one they had gone to rescue, this felt like yet another failing on Elemai's part, as if she had become the weakest link, the disgraced relict, far more than the actual prisoner. Aliyah assured her that it wasn't her fault, that Coriolane had been unstoppable, but he *was* stopped, eventually. With the ifrit and the fire and Khasmedeus's sacrifice. Aside from the jinnyeh, Aliyah and Tatyana Sazharyna and Julian Kozharyev had done it. Elemai was lying upstairs, utterly helpless, and would have burned to death with the rest of the Eternal Palace if Aliyah had not rushed back to find her, coughing and choking on the smoke, and carried her to safety. Yet again, in the end, Elemai had done nothing. Hoped to be the hero once and for all, and been only the helpless damsel.

It was churlish of her to dwell on it. She should be happy that they had escaped with their lives, that General Ionius had become a halfway decent option to oversee Merone's abrupt interregnum, and that he had kept his promise to have Cincitus removed from power and plentiful funds from the imperial treasury allocated to finance Qart-Hadesht's reconstruction. But if even the murderous former minion of an insane tyrant had wound up being more useful than Elemai, surely she had to work twice as hard to make it up. If only she could rise from the wheeled chair she was obliged to use, or get through a day without constant and crippling discomfort. Sometimes she could not even dress or do her hair, did not look anything like the beautiful and elegant and accomplished woman around whom Aliyah had once been so tongue-tied and nervous. Now it was Aliyah who managed the visitors to their home, the affairs of the estate, the concerns of their families, the meetings of the Adirim, and the rest, and Elemai lay in bed, often in too much pain to stand or sometimes even sit. The doctors opined doubtfully that she might walk properly again someday, but they would not guarantee.

Stop this self-pitying nonsense, Elemai ordered herself, as she had many times before. *You are alive, your wife is alive, Coriolane is dead, Qart-Hadesht still stands and might soon be free from Merone at last, and you brood and sulk that you, personally, did not achieve enough glory? What is the matter with you? Why must you disappoint even in this? Why can you not be happy?*

She blew out a breath and reached for the cup of mint tea that had been growing cool at her elbow, gulping the bitter dregs. The sun was fully risen, and she could see figures in the market below, embarking on morning errands despite the fact that most everyday goods were still thin on the ground. Cincitus and his henchmen had been jeered out of the city along with the bulk of the Meronite occupation, but a skeleton force remained – ostensibly to help maintain stability until the future shape of the empire was determined, though Elemai cynically suspected that if Ionius tried to withdraw all the overseas garrisons at once, he would be skinned alive and worn as a cloak. It went to show that while noble intentions were well and good, it was not possible to simply sweep away the accumulated weight of how things had always been done. If change did come, it would be slow and piecemeal. They all had to accept that limitation, and so did Elemai: this drastic diminution of her dreams, soaring fantasy falling far short of flawed reality. *Your mother thought you would be Daeda and Tselmun both. Now you are this.*

She shook her head and downed the last gulp of tea, setting the cup aside. Then she turned and wheeled her chair inside, off the balcony and down the hall to the bedroom. Aliyah had hired contractors and builders to renovate their home for Elemai's new physical limitations; she could sometimes use a cane to hobble if need be, though she always paid the price for it later. But she was able to select a dress and veil and jewelry, and while she still looked like a hollow and hungry ghost, it was less so than before. She murmured malikallulah, spun herself around, and set off toward the main floor of the house.

When she rolled to a halt in the courtyard, Aliyah was waiting with an anxiously solicitous expression, and Elemai managed to sound convincingly hearty in insisting that she was doing better, truly, and the pain was not so bad as it had been. They exchanged a swift kiss, then sat together to await their visitor, who arrived, was handed down from her palanquin, and regarded them with a grave and solemn gaze. "Saeda Aliyah," Mirazhel ur-Beireshta said. "Saeda Elemai. It is a great blessing to behold you home and alive, and returned from Merone with such momentous tidings. Our previous meetings have often ended… poorly, but I hope this is the beginning of something new."

"I hope so as well, Chairwoman." Aliyah stepped forward to greet Mirazhel. "We do indeed have much to discuss. My mother plans to join us as well. Come."

As Mirazhel walked and Elemai wheeled in Aliyah's wake, Elemai could not help but admire how cool and assured her wife was, how she seemed suited to this new life as much as Elemai was not. She grieved her own losses, but she was genuinely proud of Aliyah coming into herself, to see the way she calmly instructed the servants to bring drinks and conversed with Mirazhel. Due to Elemai's infirmity, Aliyah had started to sit in the Adirim as the ur-Tasvashta representative, and when the full story of what she had done in Merone and her role in Coriolane's downfall came out, there had been talk that she herself should stand for Chairwoman. With characteristic modesty, Aliyah refused. She had not even told anyone that she was Coriolane's granddaughter and that General Ionius had offered her the throne again. When Elemai asked her why, Aliyah merely shrugged and said that it did not seem important.

Zadia arrived shortly thereafter, their original colloquy thus almost restored with the notable exception of Safiya, and the four women gathered together to speak once more. This meeting was quite different from its predecessors, all of them painfully conscious that they bore their own share of blame for the damage and destruction. There were no grandiose plans for instant liberation, but there was a commitment to a steady and sustained move in that direction. Ironically, their task was easier than before, as the sack of the city, the murder of the Qartic hostages in the Colosseum, and Cincitus' ensuing campaign of brutality had poisoned even the most resolute loyalists against the empire, and as it was now widely known that Coriolane was finally dead, it could not be denied that there was a real change in the wind. Aliyah's personal heroics were also not inconsiderable, and altogether, Mirazhel felt appreciably confident that when they brought the independence referendum to the Temple floor again, it would pass with a strong majority. But the question alone was not enough. They had to answer it as well, to explain what they would do next, how the Venerated Republic would once more stand on its own two feet – and not just with opportune political and financial charity from Merone, as that was still its own sort of shackle and would be cut off as soon as anyone apart from General Ionius was in power again. They all had to understand that it would not be easy, that struggles and sacrifices would still have to be made, and the garden they desired to plant would not spring into being overnight and then never need tending or weeding or watering ever again. But nonetheless, with time and effort, it could grow.

When the discussion was over, Zadia beckoned her daughter aside for a private word, and Aliyah followed her out, leaving Mirazhel and Elemai alone in the cool slants of winter sunlight. Then Mirazhel said, "I know what you did, saeda. With my brother Massasoum, may Ur-Malika receive him. I do not regret it, but I still wish that it had not been necessary. For me, or for you."

Elemai looked up with a start. Then she tensed in expectation of further accusation – which, to be sure, she would deserve. Whether for good reasons or otherwise, regardless of how personally dislikable Massasoum might have been, she had still coolly ordered his execution in the service of a failed rebellion, and it fell to her to take any blame. "Yes, saeda," she said at last, clipped and dry. "You are correct."

"I do not mean to harangue you for it." Mirazhel looked wry. "To say the least, I benefited from it the most, and I have done little to justify the faith that your late mother and Saeda Zadia placed in me to be a better leader. We both know that your wife will eventually take my place, but in the meantime, I hoped you might be willing to serve as my advisor. I would welcome your help and counsel. I do not have the experience or the education that you do, and I will continue to make mistakes. Malikallulah, none quite so terrible as the last, but I do not know for certain. This is not a time for such disasters. You grew up at Safiya ur-Tasvashta's knee, and as she is no longer with us, I believe that you can take the place she would have had at my side."

Elemai opened her mouth, then shut it. At last she said, "I am not my mother's equal, Saeda Mirazhel. As well, I have thoroughly failed in every expectation she once had for me, so I am not the best person to advise you how to fulfil them. Besides, now that I am broken – "

"No." Mirazhel's voice was quiet but very firm. "I do not think it of you, and I hope in time you will not think it of yourself. You are not *broken,* Saeda Elemai. You are changed, that is all. As was I, and there are enough folk who think I am also not the sort of woman who matters, who is fit for power or position, or can truly make a difference. I would like to prove them wrong, and I would like it for you as well – even if the worst critics are only the ones in your own head. You have much to offer me, and I would like to make use of it. But it is your choice."

Elemai looked down at her hands, the blanket draped over her lap, the wheels of her chair. "All right," she said. "I cannot promise for sure. I spent so long thinking that I would be one kind of person, and it is difficult, to say the least, to accept that I must now be someone else. But if you wish, then… yes. I will do my best to offer good counsel." She paused, then added, "What do you mean, my wife will eventually take your place? There has never been a Chair from the ur-Namasqas. They are one of the lower High House families, not that I necessarily – "

"Well, then." Mirazhel shrugged. "Aliyah will likely be the first. Do you disagree?"

"No." A wry, tender smile plucked Elemai's lip. "No, I don't."

After that, Zadia and Aliyah left together to eat lunch at the ur-Namasqa villa and for Aliyah to visit with Khaldun, and once Mirazhel was gone too, Elemai was alone in the house, aside from the servants. She instructed them to go out to the mahqasa and market, waited to be sure that they did, and allowed one final moment for second thoughts. Then she made up her mind, wheeled into her study, and locked the door. She gritted her teeth, hauled herself out of the chair, and rolled up the rug, examining the pentacle that she had (with great effort) drawn on the floor, a perfect twin of the one in her mother's study. It was too risky to return to the ur-Tasvashta villa and do it there, and as Elemai lit the candles, drew the curtains, and opened the book, she had to admit that it might not be any less dangerous to do it here. It was just for completeness's sake. There wasn't a real risk of unwinding everything Aliyah and the others had accomplished at such cost in Merone, and Elemai was no more eager to possess the Ring of Tselmun than she had ever been before. But regardless of what Mirazhel said, and no matter how earnestly Elemai did intend to take up her new role as vizier, she could not fully let go of everything she was supposed to have been, not quite yet. And if she was in fact presuming to advise the Chairwoman about anything, she had to be sure.

She cleared her throat, scanned the page, found her place in the faded lines of Old Coptaric script, and started to read, vastly unsure of what result it might produce. In all probability, nothing. If Khasmedeus was not fully and forever dead, it was something very close to it, and after she freed Vadoush and promised never to call upon him again, the expectation was clearly that she would not summon and enslave any other jinnyeh. But this wasn't *slavery*. Just... clarification.

As she kept reading, a shadow fell across the room, and the air grew sharply colder, sheaves of icicles sprouting into life and adorning the furniture like the white beard of a wintry elder god. Elemai's breath billowed silver, snow flurries began to drift from the ceiling, and her ears popped. A roaring sound began somewhere in the near distance, growing steadily louder, and she fought the sensation that it was barreling directly toward her and the only solution was to leap out of the pentacle, which was exactly what any approaching entity would want her to do. There was still no surety that it was in fact Khasmedeus. It was very difficult, but Elemai held her nerve and did not budge. She pronounced the final syllable with exacting care, forcibly reminded of Queen Daeda angrily calling an army of jinnyeh to fight Aeonius and accidentally being devoured instead, and thought with black humor that if this was her fate, nobody could not say she had not asked for it. *If I want to be her, this is an ironic opportunity for the universe to grant my wish.*

Fortunately, Elemai was not devoured. The incantation concluded, echoed, fell still. The silence towered, fraught with expectation, and the air changed, growing thick and strange and shimmering like heat on the desert horizon, but nothing visibly manifested in the pentacle. She stood and waited for what felt like an hour, ignoring the burning ache in her back and the weakness in her legs, until she finally and bitterly concluded that it had indeed failed, there was nothing left. She turned and was about to step out of the pentacle, when a voice spoke suddenly from thin air. "Well, well. Hoping to give me a tasty afternoon snack, sweetcheeks?"

When she first met the jinnyeh in Yerussala, Elemai had screamed and fallen over and otherwise mortified herself, and it was only by sheer luck that she avoided a repeat. For all apparent purposes, she was still quite alone in the room – except she wasn't. Perhaps there was not enough of its essence left to take physical form, but there was still something of its (terrible) personality, and she sat down, striving to look cool and composed. "Khasmedeus. That *is* you, I imagine. There can't be another creature that is so impertinent."

"I'd hope not." An invisible tongue blew a rude noise. "I work hard at this. And while you can't see me, please imagine me vigorously mooning you. It's the only proper response."

"I'm sorry." Elemai blew out a breath. "I wasn't sure if it was going to work. I didn't know if there was enough of you to be summoned. Unless there's some ghost of you left over?"

"Something like it. More or less, possibly less." The jinnyeh's voice fluctuated in unsettling, unpredictable pulses, first sounding as if it was very far away and then right against her ear. "Sort of an in-between place. Not here and not there and not anywhere else either. But you didn't drag me out of my disembodied eternal purgatory for a friendly chat about the afterlife, or at least I don't think you did. You want something, Mistress. Don't you. Even after my big fat heroic sacrifice to save the world, something in you still doesn't think it's enough."

It was pointless to deny it, though conversations with Khasmedeus were always akin to diving headfirst into a thorn bush. "Not necessarily," Elemai said. "I just wanted to be sure. That the Ring of Tselmun was actually gone, Coriolane was dead, and you and the ifrit were – well, whatever happened to you. Burned up, I suppose."

"Why? Hoping you could whip out Arghan like a horrible rabbit from a hat?" Khasmedeus's voice floated closer again, until she had the nasty sensation that it was standing right behind her, breathing hotly down her neck. "Wherever *he* is, it's the same place I am. So if you were wondering about it, and I suspect you were, you could *probably* summon me again, reconstitute me in all my splendid and currently only-metaphorically-bare-ass glory. But if so, you would bring him too. Our essences are now too intertwined, too tangled together in every way, to ever be separated. Not to mention, there's a good chance that you'd fish out dear old Coriolane too. Missing him already?"

"I can assure you, nobody does." That was an unpleasant revelation, but Elemai soldiered through it. "So you're in a holding pattern, in some realm just ajar from the human or the spirit worlds? That doesn't sound pleasant. Especially if that is who you have for company."

"It's not," Khasmedeus agreed. "Perils of heroic sacrifices, I suppose. Kills both yourself and the nearby villains, and then you're stuck listening to them whine for all eternity. Both of them are of the opinion that they have been miserably wronged, and if they were allowed to prosecute that belief again, it would not be pleasant for anyone. I know you're not that smart, Mistress – relatively speaking. But you don't want to risk that. As long as you keep the door open for me, they can get through too."

Elemai flinched. At last she said, "And if anyone tried to summon you again – you, the great Spirit of the Ring, the most famous jinnyeh in history, which guarantees that eventually someone will try – they would push that door wider? Every time a little more, until there was a possibility that all three of you could return to this mortal plane."

"A surprisingly accurate insight, yes. And a danger that cannot be entirely forestalled unless you destroyed every grimoire in the world, *Key of Tselmun* or otherwise, and then every pentacle, every tool or artifact of magic, and that is, of course, impossible. Unless you chose to finish the job. To permanently banish me, and by extension Arghan and Coriolane. It's a simple incantation, and you've been trained as a magician, haven't you? Your mother spent so long making sure."

"I... yes." Something in Elemai bristled at the reminder, but she pushed it down. "But you don't want that, do you? To go away forever, to a fate worse than death?"

"Oh, suddenly *now* you people are concerned for what the jinnyeh thinks?" Khasmedeus snorted. "That is a new one. And it's not death, exactly. Just... change. A different realm, a different place, somewhere far beyond this world. There would be room to wander. To explore. I was a slave for eons, Elemai. I barely had time to enjoy my freedom in your world before I was obliged to clean up your mess and therefore leave it behind. So I'd like that chance."

Elemai registered in muted surprise that it had dropped the mockery and insulting epithets, had addressed her by her name and with a simple and straightforward exhortation to finish the job of setting it free – to move it past the eternal halfway point where it was stuck, always in danger of being tipped unceremoniously back into this world. But if so, it would bring its nasty companions, and there was no chance of being able to defeat them twice. Elemai could still do something meaningful and important, contribute to the victory in a way that nobody else had, and save the world one last time. But if she did –

"I see," she said. "I agree that it's a sensible idea. But this is a delicate time. Qart-Hadesht is finally about to declare its independence, and even if General Ionius agrees to grant it, that is no guarantee that the rest of Merone will respect it. We could use your help."

"My *help?*" The voice arched toward the ceiling. "So that's what this is about? Keeping the option open for me to pop out from time to time and give you a boost, even if that went down in flames before, and even if it increased the risk of our terrible trio coming back to do Hashem-only-knows-what. My word, Mistress. Haven't you learned *anything?*"

"I didn't – "

"Let me, once more, give you a word of advice. Which you are likely to speedily disregard, but so be it. First off, fair warning, you're all absolutely going to *hate* being free, at least at first. For centuries, you've been able to blame everything on the Meronites – though to be fair, it *was* usually their fault. You could pick and choose what you wanted to pay attention to or what you wanted to look like you were doing, and it was easy to style yourselves as a perfectly principled and morally spotless opposition. But now you have to do it all for real, all by yourself, and everything that goes wrong from here on out is your fault. You *will* be blamed for it, whether or not it is. Decolonization is a noble and necessary process, but it tends to be a bloody mess, flares up factions and radicalizations and reactionaries that you can't control, and will make people yearn for the 'stability' of the empire, the good old days when someone told them what to think and what to do and they didn't have to worry about forging their own identity, their own rules, their own destiny. It's brave and noble, but it's terrifying. You can declare a new Qart-Hadesht all you please, but minds don't change so easily. They've been molded from birth to be Meronites, whether they wanted it or not, and they won't stop thinking like Meronites just because Coriolane finally bit the dust. They'll fight you, and there is no way that you won't get your hands dirty in return. Be ready."

With a strange and poignant pang, Elemai realized that beneath all the japes and crudity, the wisecracks and name-calling, Khasmedeus was a deeply wise and eloquent and terribly sad creature who knew more about the minds of the enslaved than anything or anyone else who ever lived, and learned it all the hard way. And despite all the horrors it had endured at human hands, it still wanted to make them understand – stubborn and outspoken and *trying,* pushing and striving and fighting and arguing for them to do better this time around. To lay out the truth even if it was rarely heeded, because humans constantly blinded themselves in their pride and arrogance and made repeated and disastrous and utterly avoidable mistakes. Elemai herself was again on the brink of one, and she had known it from the moment she began the summons. Khasmedeus was right, of course. She wanted to keep it around just because it always seemed easier to do things instantly and with magic, rather than putting in the hard and slow and painful *work*. Even if she had seen how terribly it served and how little it solved. Still wanting to be Daeda because her mother said so, if that was not the most puerile and selfish fantasy of all. As if it would not cost them everything.

"I see," she said again. "So does it hurt?"

"What?" Khasmedeus sounded blank. "Hurt? Why?"

"Well." Elemai made an expository gesture. "You said that you were tangled up with both of them, Arghan and Coriolane, and it is so terrible and tenuous that all three of you might break back into the world at any moment. All your essences are one, so – it must hurt."

"Oh," the invisible jinnyeh said. "Yes. Yes, of course it hurts. Hurts awfully, hurts terribly, and that's not even to mention the bellowing and farting and belching. Horrid company, the both of them. Can you see why I'm so desperate to get out of here?"

"Of course." Elemai had suspected it might be the case, but at that, she was certain. *Deceitful jinnyeh,* just as the books always said. Yet she could not blame it for telling one last lie, when it was still convinced that a human would never consider its welfare alone as a reason to do anything. It had to claim that the fate of the world remained at stake, that the terrible enemies it had vanquished might still return, that the only answer was to break its shackles once and for all and make sure it could never be dragged back to slavery. She contemplated whether to tell Khasmedeus that she had worked it out, or let it think it had pulled one last trick on her. "So they are here too, aren't they? Arghan and Coriolane? If I summoned you, and you three are now all one creature?"

"Definitely," Khasmedeus assured her, then shouted, "Oy! Spit that out, you animal! Can't you see we're in company?" To Elemai it added, "Yep. As I said. Absolutely here."

"Of course." Elemai bit back a smile. "Well, it would not do to let them get loose, not at all. I see that I in fact have no choice but to free you for good, and permanently ensure that nobody can ever call you back. Is there anything else you would like to say, before I do?"

"Say what now? No contorted justifications? No endless monologue as you desperately try to convince yourself that you *must* keep me here, and I am as bored out of my gourd as it is possible for a disembodied jinnyeh to be? Come on. At least give me some good agonizing."

"I've agonized enough already. My entire life. Don't you think it's time? *More* than time?"

"Well." Khasmedeus still sounded dubious. "I think so, yes, but I am not accustomed to humans agreeing with me. Are you sure?"

"Yes." Elemai straightened her shoulders. "Very sure."

"Spoilsports to the end, that's you lot." Khasmedeus sighed. "All the scintillating nuggets of wisdom I could squeeze out right now, have the chance to go out with some truly unbeatable and eternally memorable last words, and you want me to pick *one?* Horrendous."

"I'm sure you'll manage." Elemai's tone was drier than ever. "So?"

There was a portentous silence. Then it said, "Very well. How about this? Oppressed people are still just people, for better or for worse. Heroes and villains, ordinary and extraordinary and unremarkable all at once. They do great things and they do terrible things, and they don't need to be blameless saints to *earn* their freedom, as if it's a shiny token either granted or withheld depending on how agreeable they are. They can still oppress themselves, or others. They can willingly replicate all the injustices of their masters and be so used to the lash that they decide to take it on for themselves and finally have the pleasure of doling it out. After all, when you've been kicked like a dog for your whole life, it's supremely tempting to get to do it to another unfortunate stooge and make yourself feel like the most powerful person. Like when the Vashemite finally gave me the Ring. *Almighty,* the temptation to incinerate every single one of you over-evolved apes was... *ah,* it was like sex, but far better. But I didn't, in the end. You should try the same."

"Thank you," Elemai said. "I will remember that."

"I should hope so." Khasmedeus sighed again. "Here I am, nobly giving up my last chance to make a fart joke. I don't know *what* fart joke, but I can assure you it would be hilarious. So now that I am unfortunately forcing myself to be sincere, just recall that despite everything I said about its costs, it doesn't mean freedom isn't worth it. It is. It always is. But if you make trouble, or you get into it, I won't be there to remind you, so you better do it for yourself. Speaking of which, give my regards to Aliyah. For a human, she's not entirely loathsome."

"I will." Elemai paused. "I know that from you, that's high praise."

Khasmedeus coughed for a suspiciously long interval, then harrumphed. "Nonsense. Don't know what you're talking about. Now, then. Get on with it. Send me on my way."

"As you wish." Elemai picked up the book from where it sat open on the floor, flurrying a brief shower of dust motes, and cleared her throat. The incantation, as the jinnyeh said, was simple, and only took a few moments. She heard a sudden burst of laughter, had a sense of a door swinging open and a fine clear light shining through. Then just as quietly, it began to fade, the air went still, and the room went silent. The candles burned into waxen gremlins, stuttering and slumping and snuffing out. The room remained as visibly empty as it had been before, but now she knew that it was. She waited a moment, then let the book drop, turned, and stepped out of the pentacle. "Goodbye, Khasmedeus. Go well."

She climbed into her chair and sat down, abjectly grateful to no longer be standing on her aching legs and straining her agonized back, everything about her body that felt ten or twenty or fifty years older than it was. There were tears in her eyes, though she didn't recall when they had come or what sparked them. Perhaps it was the final mourning for the woman that her mother had always wanted her to be, done her utmost to mold, and whose ultimate failure was felt by Elemai herself to be the most unforgivable failure of all. She did not know this new Elemai: the one who could not walk, who was a shell of her former self, who could not be the queen and leader everyone had always assumed she would be – but who might, if she was fortunate, become Mirazhel's valued advisor and Aliyah's supportive wife, letting Aliyah shine brighter and become greater, and to be all right with coming second. To understand once and for all that the Ring of Tselmun had never made Aliyah who she was, never given her any power or strength she did not already have. It had only revealed it, stripping away the tarnish to show what was always there beneath, and despite everything, Elemai found that she was at peace with it. That in the end, it was right.

Aliyah got home late that afternoon, cheered from seeing her parents and even her brother; according to her, Aljafar was marginally less insufferable than usual, and Zadia had promised that he could finally travel to Ambrazakti and the Great Library, as he had long desired to do. Of course there was an ulterior motive, as enlisting the protection and patronage of King Musum would greatly help in deterring any Meronite revenge attempts, and there was plenty for Aljafar to learn in order to serve the fledgling Second Venerated Republic. "As for that," Aliyah added. "My mother thinks that once the declaration of independence formally passes the Adirim and is ratified, I should be the one to deliver it to Merone. She feels that General Ionius will be more inclined to listen to me, or if the Senate balks, I will put the fear of God into them. I am hardly eager to go back, but if they decide it best, I will."

"I am… glad for you." Elemai managed a thin but genuine smile. "For what it's worth, a Qartic woman walking onto Praetorian Hill and telling all those miserable old misers to their faces that their empire is over and they have to accept it might be enough to cause any number of heart attacks on the spot. And if General Ionius is still in charge, and they haven't plotted to stab him in the Forum like Coriolane Caesar, he will listen to you. At least, I think. I still wish *I* could stab him for what he did to my mother, but I accept that we are allies now. Of a sort."

"I understand." Aliyah looked solemn. "But I wouldn't want to go alone. If I did, then you would have to come with me. I know it would be difficult for you to travel, but – "

"Ah." Elemai swallowed. "You're right. It would. And here's the thing, my dear. You no longer need me, or your mother, or anyone else, to help you stand on your own two feet. You are enough. Saeda Mirazhel thinks you are the prime successor for her position, and I think – well, I think she's quite correct. I cannot go to Merone with you, but I will stay here. Doing my best for you, and us. Qart-Hadesht has been rebuilt many times in its history, after all, and someone will need to help it do so again. I would like that, I think. Once more laying its bones in the earth, and watching it rise. Daeda did that too."

Aliyah looked supremely startled. She opened her mouth as if to ask if Elemai was sure, if it was truly possible to let her take the sole burden of the diplomatic mission to Merone and everything that might come after, whether glory or calamity. At last she said, "Before I left the villa, my mother told me that she's very proud of me. I don't know if she has ever said so like that before, but I do know she meant it. And your mother, Ur-Malika rest her, is surely proud of you too. In paradise."

"I hope so." Elemai chuckled, hiccupping on the edge of a sob. "But we know that's not the only thing that matters, yes? Zadia and Safiya did their best for us, and did their worst as well, and we are now left to live how we can with all of it. To speak of mothers in paradise, Noora sees you too, you know. Nor will we let her death be in vain."

Aliyah knuckled her eyes and the faint circles of scars that remained marked on her face. "I hope so too," she said, her voice notably thick. "I wish she was here. I always will."

"So do I." Elemai put her hand over Aliyah's. "But we will be at peace, I think. In time."

Aliyah nodded, then sniffed the air and looked quizzical. "You smell like summoning herbs. Were you doing something with – with magic?"

"No," Elemai said. "Nothing. It's not important."

With that, Aliyah unrolled the rug for sardiq, then wheeled Elemai over, helped her out of the chair, and steadied her as they recited the takbir. As they began the first raka, Elemai noticed that Aliyah was modifying her movements so there was not so much standing and sitting, in order to match the physical shape of her prayer more closely to Elemai's. It was difficult not to worry that Ur-Malika might punish her for worshiping in the incorrect position, but while there was doubtless some excessively fussy qahin who had composed a lengthy diatribe on this subject, Elemai put it out of her mind. Her faith had been rubbed raw, and sometimes she was not even sure it was still there, but tonight, it was a true comfort to be here, to know that the sun would rise tomorrow and the world would go on. The years would come and pile up and fade away, and if they were blessed – and if they worked for it, if they did their best – they would have many, good and bad alike. For now, that was enough: the chance to try. To simply have enough time.

When the prayer was done and the setting sun had slipped off the walls, the evening turning purple and the servants returning from the market with supper, Elemai climbed back into her chair and sat there, enjoying the silence and solitude. Aliyah had strode off to be sure that everything was ready, and Elemai reflected that Khasmedeus had, in the end, been right about that too. Whatever lay in store for them, it would be built piece by piece, brick by brick – whether the future of their city or their relationship, which might indeed continue to transform into a true and deepening love. And no Ring could conjure that, no spell could force it, and conversely, no power in the world, no matter how great and terrible, could take it away. Elemai had done her part, but she would have to keep doing it from this day forth, in different ways and battles and moments that she could not presently imagine or foresee. But even like this, she was stronger. She was.

She blew out a slow breath, dashing away the tears that had once more gathered. She could hear Aliyah calling for her, that supper was ready and it was time to come to the table. That was the next thing for her to do, and then the next would arrive after that, and the next, and so on. No matter how huge and ungovernable the future often felt, it only came like this: a tiny step, a single piece at a time, and that too was a comfort. *All right,* she said, whether to her mother or Khasmedeus or simply to herself, Elemai ur-Tasvashta, who too had such a struggle with believing that she alone could ever be enough. *All right, I'll try.*

Elemai leaned over to the sideboard and blew out the lamp, letting darkness fall thick and soft, though the first edges of moonlight gilded the carpet and lit the way ahead. Then she grasped the wheels of her chair, turned her face to the future, and went to eat dinner with her wife.

EPILOGUE

KOROLGROD IN THE SPRING WAS, DESPITE EVERYTHING, one of the most beautiful places on the Almighty's green earth. Perhaps it was easy to feel that way after the brutal and endless winter, when snow piled up and wind cut to the bone, when the rivers were armored under great sheets of ice and the thin silver woodsmoke on the horizon was the only sign that anyone was still alive in there, bundled away in their dark and chilly homes. When the cold finally began to loosen its grip, when there was a softness in the breeze and blooms on the trees, when the Vena and Voyna finally began to run free again and the evenings turned pale gold instead of pewter grey – it was no wonder that it felt like a miracle, a divine grant of clemency renewed every year. It also brought *rasputitsa,* mud season, but no one cared. They opened their doors and cleaned their hearths and left their spouses, all the things they had wanted to do for a long time but could not find the strength for in the winter. There was always some new scandal come springtime, as hibernation ended and sap began to rise. This year, naturally, it was him. Julian had not expected anything else.

It had been six months since he returned to the city, arriving at the end of Octobrius when the cold was sinking in, the trees were stripped bare, and his parents had, to say the least, not fucking expected to see their dead son come strolling down the Street of Gold and set off an ungodly riot in the ghetto. Julian had *tried* to avoid this, even sent word from Severolgrod that he was alive and coming home, but either the letter did not arrive or his family understandably discounted it as a forgery, because he was greeted as if he had walked out of the tomb like Lazarum and still reeked of grave-dust — which for them, of course, he did. His mother shrieked at the top of her lungs and brought the neighbors running, convinced that a pogrom was once more upon them, and Julian had to apologize to all of them individually for the scare. When he went to shul that Sabatday, they crowded to touch his face and cluck in disbelief, as even the rebbitek hurried to clasp his hand and Julian wondered if he would accidentally start a Vashemite heresy proclaiming him, Yulian ben Yanov, the long-awaited melekh mashiach. Of course he understood their shock; it had been two years with no word of his fate and no reason to think the earth-shaking developments in Merone and Yerussala had anything to do with him. He had not told anyone the whole story, not even Isyk. He wanted to, but not yet.

    He had passed the winter trying to reorient himself, to settle into the place that he had left, to remember how it felt and what it meant, that he had survived and come home. Being able to celebrate Tor Ghezel with his family, to prepare for Adina's wedding, to take part in the daily life of the ghetto and not think about rebellion and secrecy and sneaking around, unsettlement and dislocation and deception. Though to be sure, it cropped up in unsettling ways. Julian ran into Gavriel one day and almost didn't recognize him, could hardly remember what it was about him that had been so compelling. The reunion was brief and awkward. Gavriel said he was about to graduate from university and recently married to a nice Vashemite girl of good family. He evaded the question when Julian asked if he was happy. Almighty, was that him, in another life? If he stayed here, and settled, and never searched for anything more?

    As well, as much as he tried to enjoy the domesticity and the routine, the respite from the whirlwind of his adventure, it could not be denied that he was... bored. Here he was, once more living with his parents at home and being a good Vashemite son, his world small and comfortable and safe enough. Beyond it, however, the ripples kept spreading. The shocking news that Coriolane was dead and a Kozhek slave had taken over — even if that Kozhek slave was an Immortal general, and Julian kept his expression studiously blank when anyone asked if he knew about this Ionius — had been received in certain Ruthynian-nationalist quarters as the worst insult imaginable. A filthy inferior *Kozhek* had been placed at the apex of power, doubtless after murdering the emperor, and they were expected to accept his rule? No, this could not be countenanced.

The unrest, therefore, had briefly threatened to spill over into actual rebellion, which Julian could not help but find bitterly ironic – he and his fellows could hardly rouse support for their cause when a bloodthirsty tyrant was in charge, but put a Kozhek in there instead and suddenly the Ruthynians were falling over and screaming in protest. The Meronite garrisons had reacted harshly, and it was unclear what would happen next. The peace was holding, for now, while everyone licked their wounds and plotted their next moves. But it could not last forever.

The upside was that Zogorov had been dismissed from his position as Governor-General, the Konsilium had likewise been reprimanded and reshuffled and sternly prohibited from harassing Vashemites, and in these maneuvers Julian could clearly see Ionius's influence. As well – at least for now – even the most unhappy Ruthynians were unwilling to go so far as pledging allegiance to the *new* Meronite Empire, recently declared in Coriolanople by Empresses Gheslyn and Vestalia. They arrived in the eastern capital after escaping from the Castel, immediately announced their treason convictions to be a cruel conspiracy and therefore null and void, and that they were the only proper inheritors of Merone's power, prestige, and legacy. But as it was very difficult for them to rule aloney, they dug up a feckless distant cousin named Alexios Angelos, shoved their hand up his arse to make him speak, and dubbed him the "emperor of Merone." There was, of course, no doubt in anyone's mind as to who was actually in control.

Most people seemed to think of it as a slightly pathetic joke, but Gheslyn and Vestalia had nonetheless managed to attract enough of the discontented elite, willing to coalesce around anyone who opposed General Ionius and his heathenish ways of doing things (the last straw for many of them came when he levied a new tax on the patrician estates), to turn Coriolanople into a hotbed of unrest. Despite his determination not to think about Ivan more than once a day, Julian nervously wondered if he knew the dangerous waters he was entering, the powerful enmity he was whipping up. By contrast, the commoners loved him; they had never had a ruler like this before, and as soon as Gheslyn and Vestalia sent a catspaw to the Eternal City to assassinate him, never would again. Many of them urged Ionius to finally be crowned emperor, to rebuke the pretentions of Alexios Angelos and give himself some protection from these plots, but he continued to obstinately refuse.

It was a few days past Tor Shchedysh, and when they held the seder and laid the customary place for the Prophet Eliyehu, Julian kept glancing at the door as if he expected someone else to walk in. His parents, too relieved to have him back alive to press the subject, had not asked him to meet with the shadchan again, though his sister Adina was now married and there was talk of starting the search for Lyova soon. But this did not deter the *other* Vashemite mothers who saw a handsome and unwed young scholar, feted with the luster of foreign adventures, as the perfect mate for their daughter, and Julian nearly needed to go about with a broom in hand to fend them off. Indeed, when the knock on the door finally came that evening, he wasn't sure whether to spring up in eagerness or rush away in terror. It turned out, however, that it was his brother. "Come on, Yulya," Isyk said. "Let's get a drink."

Julian opened his mouth, couldn't think of what to say, and shut it. An old objection came to mind that they shouldn't be sneaking out after dark, though the days were swiftly lengthening, curfew was now not until midnight, and it was deeply hypocritical of him, the ex-rebel, to worry about such things anyway. So he put on his hat and coat and left the ghetto with Isyk in the warm spring dusk, as they turned onto the main thoroughfare and found a tavern. When they had been seated with glasses of votke and stared at each other in awkward silence for several minutes, Isyk bit the bullet. "So. Are you finally going to tell me where you've been all this time?"

"It's complicated." Which was the biggest fucking understatement of all time, but it sounded utterly insane, and he was afraid that Isyk wouldn't believe him. Julian threw back his votke and bid the barmaid to fetch a second, and then decided to hell with it. "Remember the night you caught me coming home from a tavern, instead of vice versa? I was in trouble with the watchmen, and you gave me a good scolding, told me that we were never going to find the Ring of Tselmun?"

"Yes," Isyk said, confused. "Why?"

"Well." Julian cracked a thin smile. "You were *very* wrong."

And with that, all at once, it came pouring out. He didn't have to think about it, *couldn't* think about it, could hardly keep up. It just kept coming and coming like sickness, heaved up and spewed out until it was all gone. It took him almost an hour, he sipped the votke to wet his throat and stole Isyk's glass too when his brother kept staring too stupidly to protest, and finally stopped when there was nothing left to say, when it had dwindled from a torrent to a trickle and his throat ached too much to keep going. "So," he croaked. "Yeah. That's... that's it."

"Almighty," Isyk managed at last, still looking stunned. "Yulya – you – you did *all that,* and you still decided to come back here? When you could have stayed in the *Holy City?* Why?"

"I... I don't know." Julian's head swam from the votke, but that wasn't the only reason he struggled to speak. "I had to let Mata and Vata know that I was alive, for one. I tried to send a letter before I got home, but nobody would believe it anyway until they saw me. And I had to see what I was fighting for, that you were all right and safe. And in Yerussala, it was... I don't know. I spent weeks cleaning up Kronus's pentacle and making sure that there was nothing left. I tracked down any places where he could have done something terrible. I went to the local authorities and told them everything I knew about the blood-plague, I picked up the pieces with the people who were left alive. I hid the *Key of Tselmun* somewhere – I very much hope, at least – nobody, human or jinnyeh, will ever find it again. And I went to the holy sites, of course. The Temple Rock and the Weeping Wall and the rest. I prayed, I asked forgiveness for my sins and for destroying the Ring, when I could have taken it and *become* Tselmun and made all of this unnecessary. But I didn't. I didn't want to be Tselmun, and I didn't want to stay in Yerussala. I know how important it is, but it didn't feel like home."

Isyk's mouth was still hanging open, so he shut it. At last he said, "But if you did – if you could protect our people like that – "

"I know. I *know.* I kept thinking that maybe that was the sacrifice I should have made, that I should give myself up to whatever the Ring would have made me into, if the tradeoff was being able to avenge everything the Meronites took from us and are still taking from us. But I could see who that person was and what he would do, and it… it didn't feel like justice to me. Just becoming another tyrant in the name of an exalted purpose, doing the same thing over and over. There were other ways, other people. Tatyana — Tatyana Sazharyna — she did stay, even after I decided to leave. She spent several lifetimes in Merone as a slave, like I said. She wanted to work for a while on rebuilding Yerussala and then go somewhere else. She hadn't decided."

"Tatyana." Isyk frowned. "She's Ruthynian?"

"Kozhek. Ancestrally." Julian paused. "She's Ivan's sister."

"And Ivan — this man you were in love with — wait." A slowly dawning look of horror began to cross Isyk's face. "Oh no. *Oh, no*. Yulya, *tell* me that isn't him."

"Can't." Julian let out a demented cackle, quivering on the brink of a sob. "It is."

Isyk put his head in his hands and mumbled several extensive and imaginative profanities — for which, all things considered, Julian could not blame him. At last Isyk looked up, still flattened. "So you're actually telling me that you — that you were *sleeping* with His Excellency General Ionius Eternus, Immortal-turned-Lord Regent of Merone?"

"Yes." Ionius had removed the *Servus* part, but had not taken any fancy noble cognomen, and despite everything, Julian felt a small warm ember in his chest. "But it was mutual."

"You should have just moved to Ibelus like I first told you," Isyk said despairingly. "There are plenty of Ibelusian Vashemite boys there. Nice boys. *Normal* boys."

Julian raised a combative eyebrow, remarking that either way, it was too late now, and Isyk could not think of anything to say to that. Instead, he vigorously flagged the barmaid and demanded another drink for both of them, and they sat there sipping in silence. Then Isyk said, "So, then. Why didn't you stay in Merone with him?"

"I just…" Julian swallowed the bitter votke around the lump in his throat, as he should be even more inebriated if they were going to have this conversation. "There were things I needed to do in Yerussala."

"You said that, yes. But you did them. Didn't you?"

"Yeah. I just... I told myself all along that there was no point in going back, even after I was finished. The rich and powerful Meronites hate him enough already, so what would they think if he was parading his Ruthynian Vashemite sodomite consort in front of their faces? What was I going to do, dangle off his arm at important functions and lie about who I was and live a half-life? He needs to be there, he's the only one who can do what has to be done, and I wasn't going to stop him. But me staying would make everything more difficult, and we both knew that. So why would I come back?"

Isyk thought about that for a long moment, brow furrowed, as if searching for some obvious flaw in Julian's logic, any way to tell him he was wrong. Then he slapped down both hands, making the drinks jump and slosh. "You can't stay here in Korolgrod, Yulya. The shtetl isn't your future. You've done what you needed to do, and we always knew this place would be too small for you. Mata and Vata know it too. Why do you think they haven't tried to match you off again, get you settled down? They know it's a matter of time until you leave again."

"But..." Julian could hardly speak. "If I did go back to Merone and embarrass myself... if it was foolish... if he *has* married some simpering noble daughter and gotten himself crowned as the emperor and there's nothing left of anything I thought we were..."

"Maybe," Isyk said. "Or maybe not. Listen, Yulya. I don't pretend to understand your taste in men, that's for bloody certain, but looking at you right now, you're shining like the sun. If you think that will go away while you sit here and waste time and make excuses, well... that's your affair. But you've never been a coward. You've always done what you thought was right, regardless of what anyone else thought or said. So I'm fairly sure that you'll do it again."

There was no way to answer that, not really. Julian had no way to deny it. Even allowing himself to imagine it, to think of it and want it and not immediately shove it aside as a hopeless and unrealistic fantasy, felt too great and raw and tender to fit in his chest. They finished their drinks and paid their bill, stood up unsteadily, and in the faded twilight of the late hours, they went home.

Over the next several days, Julian kept returning to it in his head, turning it over and over and yet stubbornly reminding himself of why it remained utterly absurd. He went over to Isyk and Oksyna's flat to play with his new nephew, one-year-old Samyel, and Oksyna thought she might be pregnant again, so clearly his brother was admirably fulfilling the be-fruitful-and-multiply bit for both of them. But did that free Julian from his obligations, or bind them tighter? Was it possible to trade one for another, or meet halfway? He had seen Rebeka Roshensteyn the other day, and she told him that she and Tovah were living together, that they held themselves married in the eyes of the Almighty and had exchanged vows in the presence of a few supportive friends. And they were still here. They had not been drummed out in disgrace or stoned in the streets, and were still part of the community. Sometimes people stared and whispered, but they were used to that. And Julian was glad for them, truly he was. But he couldn't see that working for *him,* and the fruitless jealousy almost choked him.

Still, though. Even if he did lose his mind altogether and decide to set out to Merone once more, how would he do it? He had been arrested last time and thrown into jail after breaking Zogorov's window, and that was unlikely to work again. His parents did not have enough money to pay passage on a ship, though it was quite possible that Isyk would give it to him if he asked. But if he did, that made it *real,* that made it irreversible and impossible to change, all the weight of fate and destiny and simple stupid wanting barreling down on him, and regardless of what his brother said, he *was* a coward. He didn't like the idea, but so it was.

The weather grew warmer and the spring rolled onward. It was getting closer to the White Nights when the sun barely set, and thinking of how he had missed it in Ambrazakti, when he was convinced he would never see home again, Julian tried to enjoy it. And he was almost succeeding, though Isyk kept giving him pointed looks and asking how his preparations were going, when he got home one afternoon and found the ghetto in a state of absolute uproar, even more so than when he returned from the dead. It seemed as if the whole neighborhood was crowded around his house, pushing and whispering and elbowing, and Julian's first thought was that something terrible had happened — that someone in his family had died and they had come to sit shiva, as they had all done for him. But then his sister Lyova pushed through the crowd, spotted him, and scoffed. *"There* you are! We were *wondering* when you were finally going to get here!"

Utterly bewildered, Julian let her seize hold of him and haul him into the throng – which parted like the Sea of Reeds in order to let him pass, then closed in again even more firmly. The keen weight of all those eyes propelled him down the hall and into the kitchen, whereupon all at shocking once, the reason for the hullabaloo became entirely and impossibly clear. Because there were his parents sitting on one side of the table with cups of untouched tea, looking absolutely boggled, and on the other, in a fine velvet cloak that was stained and crumpled with hard riding, his hair somewhat longer than it had been and his jaw scruffy from travel, was the Lord Regent of Merone. He did not appear to have made any progress on his tea either, and barely touched the welcoming bread and salt. When Lyova dragged Julian into the kitchen, he started to stand up, then sat back down. "I – good afternoon."

"You." Julian had to be hallucinating. It was so completely incongruous, two worlds mashed together in a place they were never meant to meet, that he was waiting for the seam to split down the middle and reality to give up the ghost altogether. "You're... *here.*"

"I am," Ionius agreed. "You look surprised."

"Of course I'm fucking surprised, you – " Julian bit his tongue and glanced guiltily at his mother. "I mean. Hello. How are you?"

Ionius looked as if he was trying not to grin. Then he rose to his feet and politely inclined his head to Yanov and Mirym. "Gospodin Kozharyev, Gospodina Kozharyeva. I was hoping that I could speak to your son alone for a moment?"

Once they nodded weakly, Ionius took hold of Julian's wrist – even that briefest and most matter-of-fact touch lit him aflame, and there was no way to pretend otherwise – and towed him out to the back garden, where Julian would have bet all the money he did not have that dozens of his neighbors were crammed against the fence and relaying urgent updates to the crowd. They sat down, looked at each other, tried and failed to speak, and uttered a faint and helpless chuckle. At last Julian said,

"Almighty, it *is* you. I thought – honestly, I was afraid that you would be dead by now. If Gheslyn and Vestalia didn't get to you, then – "

"They have tried, to be sure. And failed." Ionius's tone was as utterly undemonstrative as ever. "Which is why it is selfish of me to come here, but so be it. My errand is simple. I only ask if you wish to help me build the new Merone. I should have asked before, I should not have waited so long, but you were needed elsewhere. I wanted to respect that, and I hope that you have done the work you meant to do. If so, and even if not, you may tell me to leave, and I will."

Julian made a sound like a toad being stepped on. Nothing else obliged him by coming out.

"I know it was unexpected to come here, like this," Ionius went on. "To your home and your family, to the ghetto. But I have business in Ruthynia anyway, and it has been a long time since I was in Korolgrod. So while I was here…" He trailed off in half a shrug. "I did."

"Yeah," Julian said, having regained something approximating the power of speech but still not sure he was doing anything useful with it. "You, the Lord Regent of Merone. You're here *in my house* and you're – *what* are you asking, exactly? Me to come back with you and be your wise Vashemite counselor and nothing else, or – ? Or what? *Together?*"

"You said that you did not want to be my Meronite queen," Ionius pointed out. "So no, I do not expect you to be. But yes. Together."

"I didn't say that I *didn't* want it," Julian protested feebly. "Just that I didn't think it was a good idea, and besides – if I was supposed to be throwing state dinner parties, I don't think so, but that doesn't mean I would know what else to do – I didn't get your sister killed, by the way. She's in Yerussala, or she was the last time I knew. Mellius Sanctus Sixtus would have a coronary if I made my grand return as your blushing bride, which *would* be very entertaining, but I'm not sure that – "

Ionius leaned over and kissed him.

Julian was still talking (well, babbling), it took him a moment to adjust to doing something else with his mouth, and the mortifying knowledge that half the ghetto was watching with bated breath almost made him jerk away and flee. But he didn't, and tears sprang to his eyes at the sheer and simple *rightness* of it, and his arms came up and his hands seized Ionius's cloak and hauled him even closer, and they devoured each other as if nothing else mattered. Then at last they pulled away, noses and chins brushing, and Julian was gulping air as if he had never done so in his life. At last he said, "Fuck. Yes. Fuck you, Vanya. *Yes.* I don't – I have no idea how this would even – I don't care. Yes. *Yes.*"

"Are you certain?" Ionius looked him in the eye. "I do not ask lightly. It will be dangerous. Gheslyn and Vestalia are unlikely to stop trying to overthrow or assassinate me, and I have, as noted, many other enemies. But I cannot do this alone, and I do not want to do it with anyone but you. What that future will be, or what Merone will look like when I step down, or when it will happen, I do not know. But if I want to finish the difficult job I have been given, I can only do it with your help, Yulya. As my partner, and my equal. In all ways that matter."

Julian wanted to say something to that (or to the avid whispering just beyond the fence), but he couldn't. Instead he leaned forward and kissed Ionius again, and it was only with reluctance that he pried himself away a second time. "Well," he said. "It so happens, ironically, that I *might* have had the same thoughts. You can thank my brother Isyk for that. He would have shoved me onto a ship himself, if I kept dawdling."

"I would like to meet him," Ionius said. "If I can. I hasten to stress that I do not expect you to stay in Merone, or with me, longer than you decide. If at any time you want to come back to Korolgrod, temporarily or permanently, you may. The years will be yours to spend as you please. You will grow physically older than me, but – "

"Oy." Julian was stung. "Who are you calling an old man? I'm still only twenty-five. And you're what – eighty? At least?"

Ionius smiled in a soft and sad way that clearly thought eighty was an impossibly junior age. "I am still an Immortal. I will live a long time, longer than you. The Corporalists are all gone now, trust me on that, and nor would I ever wish such a fate on you even if not. The time we have may not be equal, and it may not be fair. If you can accept that – "

"Yes," Julian said. "Yes, I do. All of it. Just one thing, though. What are you going to call me, Lord Consort of Merone? Because I don't think I can stomach that. You might as well call me Chief Whore of Merone, announcing that my only accomplishment was to sleep with the man in charge. Empress Julian also has a bit of a cringeworthy ring, especially if you're not technically the emperor. And by the way, if you ever *do* decide to seize the crown and do everything exactly the same way as before, I'm leaving you. Fair warning."

"Noted." Ionius raised an eyebrow. "How about we decide later?"

"All right." Julian paused. "Grand Magister Julian? No. *Definitely* not the one."

Ionius said nothing, but pressed a light kiss to the side of his head. They sat there a moment more, and then he stood up. "Well then. I must speak to your parents."

Unsure whether he should leave Ionius to do so alone, and feeling the urgent need to escape the piercing scrutiny to which he was presently subjected, Julian likewise got up and followed him inside. He barely heard what his parents and Ionius were saying, if he was supposed to offer a dowry or they were planning to stand beneath a khuppah and step on a glass, but it didn't matter; there was a foolish smile pulling his face into a constant idiot rictus and he couldn't stop it for the life of him. When Ionius and Yanov moved to continue the discussion in private, Julian sank into a chair and his mother sat down across from him. "So, Yulya," she said briskly. "Is there any chance he's going to convert?"

"He's a Tserkovian, Ma." Julian wanted to laugh, and then he wanted to weep, and then laugh again, possibly until he exploded. "He's in charge of a True Tridevarian empire that already thinks he's a heretic, *and* he's an utter bloody-minded stupid stubborn murderous obstinate arsehole bastard about literally everything. I wouldn't count on it."

Mirym sniffed disapprovingly, but did not demur. "Time will tell, I suppose. At least he has a good job, and he's Ruthynian. Kozhek, that is. He *will* allow you to observe the high holidays and keep shemyite, at least? Because Merone or no Merone, I cannot approve if not."

"Yes, Ma. Not least because if he tries to stop me doing anything, he's in for a nasty surprise." Julian looked at her, still utterly unable to believe that they were having this conversation. At last he said, "You know, don't you? You've known for a while. About – about me."

Mirym started to answer, then stopped. At last she reached out and put her hand over his, and Julian, who had fondly imagined that he was done crying, blinked hard as the tears once more pricked. "I suspected," she said. "A mother knows these things, after all. I thought I could fix it, or that it was only a passing fancy and you could still be happy in the usual way, or that once you had a wife, you would no longer be so restless. That I could hold you here, give you roots. But I did not, and if I was the reason that you ran... Yulya, I am sorry. I am sorry."

Julian looked down at their clasped hands, his mother's work-worn fingers against his own. Could hear the murmur of his father and his — whatever Ionius was going to be, whatever he was, which they really did need a word for. "It's all right," he said. "If I didn't go, I would never have done everything that I did, and I wouldn't have met him. I don't regret it, any of it, and I don't blame you. I wouldn't change a thing."

Mirym didn't answer, but squeezed his hand again, sniffed, and stood up. She ordered Lyova to chase off the crowds (which was likely a lost cause, but so be it) and went to start cooking supper. "Well," she said over her shoulder. "Don't you have to go pack?"

"I suppose I do, yeah." Julian was smiling again, even as the tears threatened to spill down his cheeks in a flood. "Be back down in a bit. Try not to let Va haggle Ionius too hard."

Mirym made a noise that offered no promises, and Julian slipped out of the kitchen. His sister was outside, angrily flapping her apron at the onlookers, and he briefly debated if he should help her, but there was no call to put himself to such trouble. So he hurried guiltily past, up the stairs and into his room, pulled his trunk out from under his bed, and paused a moment, looking down at it. Then he grinned again, dashed the tears away, and took a deep breath. Gathered the clothes from his wardrobe, the books from his desk, all the things from this home that he would need to bring to his new one, and began.

****

About the Author

Hilary Rhodes is a historian, academic, and author of fiction and nonfiction. She holds a PhD in medieval history and has been an avid reader since the age of four, which probably explains some things. She lives in America.